JEFFREY ARCHER

JEFFREY ARCHER

A MATTER OF HONOUR

SHALL WE TELL THE PRESIDENT?

FIRST AMONG EQUALS

A Matter of Honour first published in Great Britain in 1986 by
Hodder and Stoughton Limited
Shall We Tell the President? first published in Great Britain in 1977 by
Jonathan Cape Limited
First Among Equals first published in Great Britain in 1984 by
Hodder and Stoughton Limited

This edition first published in Great Britain in 1988 by

The Octopus Group Limited
Michelin House
81 Fulham Road
London SW3 6RB

ISBN: 0 86273 516 5

Printed and bound in the United Kingdom by William Clowes Limited, Beccles

CONTENTS

A MATTER OF HONOUR

PART ONE

THE KREMLIN MOSCOW

May 19, 1966

CHAPTER ONE

The Kremlin, Moscow, May 19, 1966

"It's a fake," said the Russian leader, staring down at the small exquisite painting he held in his hands.

"That isn't possible," replied his Politburo colleague. "The Tsar's icon of St George and the Dragon has been in the Winter Palace at Leningrad under heavy guard for over fifty years."

"True, Comrade Zaborski," said the old man, "but for fifty years we've been guarding a fake. The Tsar must have removed the original some time before the Red Army entered St Petersburg and overran the Winter Palace."

The head of State Security moved restlessly in his chair as the cat and mouse game continued. Zaborski knew, after years of running the KGB, who had been cast as the mouse the moment his phone had rung at four that morning to say that the General Secretary required him to report to the Kremlin – immediately.

"How can you be so sure it's a fake, Leonid Ilyich?" the diminutive figure inquired.

"Because, my dear Zaborski, during the past eighteen months, the age of all the treasures in the Winter Palace has been tested by carbon-dating, the modern scientific process that does not call for a second opinion," said Brezhnev, displaying his new-found knowledge. "And what we have always thought to be one of the nation's masterpieces," he continued, "turns out to have been painted five hundred years after Rublev's original."

"But by whom and for what purpose?" asked the Chairman of State Security, incredulous.

"The experts tell me it was probably a court painter," replied the Russian leader, "who must have been commissioned to execute the copy only months before the Revolution took place. It has always worried the curator at the Winter Palace that the Tsar's traditional silver crown was not attached to the back of the frame, as it was to all his other masterpieces," added Brezhnev.

"But I always thought that the silver crown had been removed by a souvenir hunter even before we had entered St Petersburg."

"No," said the General Secretary drily, his bushy eyebrows rising every time he had completed a statement. "It wasn't the Tsar's silver crown that had been removed, but the painting itself."

"Then what can the Tsar have done with the original?" the Chairman said, almost as if he were asking himself the question.

"That is exactly what I want to know, Comrade," said Brezhnev, resting his hands each side of the little painting that remained in front of him. "And you are the one who has been chosen to come up with the answer," he added.

For the first time the Chairman of the KGB looked unsure of himself.

"But do you have anything for me to go on?"

"Very little," admitted the General Secretary, flicking open a file that he removed from the top drawer of his desk. He stared down at the closely typed notes headed 'The Significance of the Icon in Russian History'. Someone had been up all through the night preparing a ten-page report that the leader had only found time to scan. Brezhnev's real interest began on page four. He quickly turned over the first three pages before reading aloud: " 'At the time of the Revolution, Tsar Nicholas II obviously saw Rublev's masterpiece as his passport to freedom in the West. He must have had a copy made which he then left on his study wall where the original had previously hung.' " The Russian leader looked up. "Beyond that we have little to go on."

The head of the KGB looked perplexed. He remained puzzled as to why Brezhnev should want State Security involved in the theft of a minor masterpiece. "And how important is it that we find the original?" he asked, trying to pick up a further clue.

Leonid Brezhnev stared down at his Kremlin colleague.

"Nothing could be more important, Comrade," came back the unexpected reply. "And I shall grant you any resources you may consider necessary in terms of people and finance to discover the whereabouts of the Tsar's icon."

"But if I were to take you at your word, Comrade General Secretary," said the head of the KGB, trying to disguise his disbelief, "I could so easily end up spending far more than the painting is worth."

"That would not be possible," said Brezhnev, pausing for effect, "because it's not the icon itself that I'm after." He turned his back on the Chairman of State Security and stared out of the window. He had always disliked not being able to see over the Kremlin wall and into Red Square. He waited for some moments before he proclaimed, "The money the Tsar might have raised from selling such a masterpiece would only have kept Nicholas in his accustomed lifestyle for a matter of months, perhaps a year at the most. No, it's what we believe the Tsar had secreted *inside* the icon that would have guaranteed security for himself and his family for the rest of their days."

A little circle of condensation formed on the window pane in front of the General Secretary.

"What could possibly be that valuable?" asked the Chairman.

"Do you remember, Comrade, what the Tsar promised Lenin in exchange for his life?"

"Yes, but it turned out to be a bluff because no such document was hidden . . ." He stopped himself just before saying "in the icon".

Zaborski stood silently, unable to witness Brezhnev's triumphant smile.

"You have caught up with me at last, Comrade. You see, the document was hidden in the icon all the time. We just had the wrong icon."

The Russian leader waited for some time before he turned back and passed over to his colleague a single sheet of paper. "This is the Tsar's testimony indicating what we would find hidden in the icon of St George and the Dragon. At the time, nothing was discovered in the icon which only convinced Lenin that it had been a pathetic bluff by the Tsar to save his family from execution."

Zaborski slowly read the hand written testimony that had been signed by the Tsar hours before his execution. Zaborski's hands began to tremble and a bead of sweat appeared on his forehead long before he had reached the last paragraph. He looked across at the tiny painting, no larger than a book, that remained in the centre of the Chairman's desk.

"Not since the death of Lenin," continued Brezhnev, "has anyone believed the Tsar's claim. But now, there can be little doubt that if we are able to locate the genuine masterpiece, we will undoubtedly also be in possession of the promised document."

"And with the authority of those who signed that document, no one could question our legal claim," said Zaborski.

"That would undoubtedly prove to be the case, Comrade Chairman," replied the Russian leader. "And I also feel confident that we would receive the backing of the United Nations and the World Court if the Americans tried to deny us our right. But I fear time is now against us."

"Why?" asked the Chairman of State Security.

"Look at the completion date in the Tsar's testimony and you will see how much time we have left to honour our part of the agreement," said Brezhnev.

Zaborski stared down at the date scrawled in the hand of the Tsar – June 20, 1966. He handed back the testimony as he considered the enormity of the task with which his leader had entrusted him. Leonid Ilyich Brezhnev continued his monologue.

"So, as you can see, Comrade Zaborski, we have only one month left before the deadline, but if you can discover the whereabouts of the original icon, President Johnson's defence strategy would be rendered virtually useless, and the United States would then become a pawn on the Russian chessboard."

CHAPTER TWO

Appleshaw, England, June 1966

"And to my dearly beloved and only son, Captain Adam Scott, MC, I bequeath the sum of five hundred pounds."

Although Adam had anticipated the amount would be pitiful, he nevertheless remained bolt upright in his chair as the solicitor glanced over his half-moon spectacles.

The old lawyer who was seated behind the large partners' desk raised his head and blinked at the handsome young man before him. Adam put a hand nervously through his thick black hair, suddenly conscious of the lawyer's stare. Then Mr Holbrooke's eyes returned to the papers in front of him.

"And to my dearly beloved daughter, Margaret Scott, I bequeath the sum of four hundred pounds." Adam was unable to prevent a small grin spreading across his face. Even in the minutiae of his final act, father had remained a chauvinist.

"To the Hampshire County Cricket Club," droned on Mr Holbrooke unperturbed by Miss Scott's relative misfortunes, "twenty-five pounds, life membership." Finally paid up, thought Adam. "To the Old Contemptibles, fifteen pounds. And to the Appleshaw Parish Church, ten pounds." Death membership, Adam mused. "To Will Proudfoot, our loyal gardener part time, ten pounds, and to Mrs Mavis Cox, our daily help, five pounds."

"And finally, to my dearly beloved wife Susan, our marital home, and the remainder of my estate."

This pronouncement made Adam want to laugh out loud because he doubted if the remainder of Pa's estate, even if they sold his premium bonds and the pre-war golf clubs, amounted to more than another thousand pounds.

But mother was a daughter of the Regiment and wouldn't complain, she never did. If God ever announced the saints, as opposed to some Pope in Rome, Saint Susan of Appleshaw would be up there with Mary and Elizabeth. All through his life 'Pa', as Adam always thought of him, had set such high standards for the family to live up to. Perhaps that was why Adam continued to admire him above all men. Sometimes the very thought made him feel strangely out of place in the swinging sixties.

Adam began to move restlessly in his chair, assuming that the proceedings were now drawing to a close. The sooner they were all out of this cold, drab little office the better, he felt.

Mr Holbrooke looked up once more and cleared his throat, as if he were about to announce who was to be left the Goya or the Hapsburg diamonds. He pushed his half-moon spectacles further up the bridge of his nose and stared back down at the last paragraphs of his late client's testament. The three surviving members of the Scott family sat in silence. What could he have to add? thought Adam.

Whatever it was, the solicitor had obviously pondered the final bequest several times, because he delivered the words like a well-versed actor, his eyes returning to the script only once.

"And I also leave to my son," Mr Holbrooke paused, "the enclosed envelope," he said, holding it up, "which I can only hope will bring him greater happiness than it did me. Should he decide to open the envelope it must be on the condition that he will never divulge its contents to any other living person." Adam caught his sister's eye but she only shook her head slightly, obviously as puzzled as he was. He glanced towards his mother who looked shocked. Was it fear or was it distress? Adam couldn't decide. Without another word, Mr Holbrooke passed the yellow envelope over to the Colonel's only son.

Everyone in the room remained seated, not quite sure what to do next. Mr Holbrooke finally closed the thin file marked Colonel Gerald Scott, DSO, OBE, MC, pushed back his chair and walked slowly over to the widow. They shook hands and she said, "Thank you," a faintly ridiculous courtesy, Adam felt, as the only person in the room who had made any sort of profit on this particular transaction had been Mr Holbrooke, and that on behalf of Holbrooke, Holbrooke and Gascoigne.

He rose and went quickly to his mother's side.

"You'll join us for tea, Mr Holbrooke?" she was asking.

"I fear not, dear lady," the lawyer began, but Adam didn't bother to listen further. Obviously the fee hadn't been large enough to cover Holbrooke taking time off for tea.

Once they had left the office and Adam had ensured his mother and sister were seated comfortably in the back of the family Morris Minor, he took his place behind the steering wheel. He had parked outside Mr Holbrooke's office in the middle of the High Street. No yellow lines in the streets of Appleshaw – yet, he thought. Even before he had switched on the ignition his mother had offered matter-of-factly, "We'll have to get rid of this, you know. I can't afford to run it now, not with petrol at six shillings a gallon."

"Don't let's worry about that today," said Margaret consolingly, but in a voice that accepted that her mother was right. "I wonder what can be in that envelope, Adam," she added, wanting to change the subject.

"Detailed instructions on how to invest my five hundred pounds, no doubt," said her brother, attempting to lighten their mood.

"Don't be disrespectful of the dead," said his mother, the same look of fear returning to her face. "I begged your father to destroy that envelope," she added, in a voice that was barely a whisper.

Adam's lips pursed when he realised this must be *the* envelope his father had referred to all those years ago when he had witnessed the one row between his parents that he had ever experienced. Adam still remembered his father's raised voice and angry words just a few days after he had returned from Germany.

"I have to open it, don't you understand?" Pa had insisted.

"Never," his mother had replied. "After all the sacrifices I have made, you at least owe me that."

Over twenty years had passed since that confrontation and he had never heard the subject referred to again. The only time Adam ever mentioned it to his sister she could throw no light on what the dispute might have been over.

Adam put his foot on the brake as they reached a T-junction at the end of the High Street.

He turned right and continued to drive out of the village for a mile or so down a winding country lane before bringing the old Morris Minor to a halt. Adam leapt out and opened the trellised gate whose path led through a neat lawn to a little thatched cottage.

"I'm sure you ought to be getting back to London," were his mother's first words as she entered the drawing room.

"I'm in no hurry, mother. There's nothing that can't wait until tomorrow."

"Just as you wish, my dear, but you don't have to worry yourself over me," his mother continued. She stared up at the tall young man who reminded her so much of Gerald. He would have been as good-looking as her husband if it wasn't for the slight break in his nose. The same dark hair and deep brown eyes, the same open, honest face, even the same gentle approach to everyone he came across. But most of all the same high standards of morality that had brought them to their present sad state. "And in any case I've always got Margaret to take care of me," she added. Adam looked across at his sister and wondered how she would now cope with Saint Susan of Appleshaw.

Margaret had recently become engaged to a City stockbroker, and although the marriage had been postponed, she would soon be wanting to start a life of her own. Thank God her fiancé had already put a down-payment on a little house only fourteen miles away.

After tea and a sad uninterrupted monologue from his mother on the virtues and misfortunes of their father, Margaret cleared away and left the two of them alone. They had both loved him in such different ways although Adam felt that he had never let Pa really know how much he respected him.

"Now that you're no longer in the army, my dear, I do hope you'll be able to find a worthwhile job," his mother said uneasily, as she recalled how difficult that had proved to be for his father.

"I'm sure everything will be just fine, mother," he replied. "The Foreign Office have asked to see me again," he added, hoping to reassure her.

"Still, now that you've got five hundred pounds of your own," she said, "that should make things a little easier for you." Adam smiled fondly at his mother, wondering when she had last spent a day in London. His share of the Chelsea flat alone was four pounds a week and he still had to eat occasionally. She raised her eyes and, looking up at the clock on the mantelpiece, said, "You'd better be getting along, my dear, I don't like the thought of you on that motorbike after dark."

Adam bent down to kiss her on the cheek. "I'll give you a call tomorrow," he said. On his way out he stuck his head around the kitchen door and shouted to his sister, "I'm off and Ill be sending you a cheque for fifty pounds."

"Why?" asked Margaret, looking up from the sink.

"Just let's say it's my blow for women's rights." He shut the kitchen door smartly to avoid the dish cloth that was hurled in his direction. Adam revved up his BSA and drove down the A303 through Andover and on towards London. As most of the traffic was coming west out of the city, he was able to make good time on his way back to the flat in Ifield Road.

Adam had decided to wait until he reached the privacy of his own room before he opened the envelope. Lately the excitement in his life had not been such that he felt he could be blasé about the little ceremony. After all, in a way, he had waited most of his life to discover what could possibly be in the envelope he had now inherited.

Adam had been told the story of the family tragedy by his father a thousand times – "It's all a matter of honour, old chap," his father would repeat, lifting his chin and squaring his shoulders. Adam's father had not realised that he had spent a lifetime overhearing the snide comments of lesser men and suffering the side-long glances from those officers who had made sure they were not seen too regularly in his company. Petty men with petty minds. Adam knew his father far too well to believe, even for a moment, that he could have been involved in such treachery as was whispered. Adam took one hand off the handle bars and fingered the envelope in his inside pocket like a schoolboy the day before his birthday feeling the shape of a present in the hope of discovering some clue as to its contents. He felt certain that whatever it contained would not be to anyone's advantage now his father was dead, but it did not lessen his curiosity.

He tried to piece together the few facts he had been told over the

years. In 1946, within a year of his fiftieth birthday, his father had
resigned his commission from the army. *The Times* had described Pa as
a brilliant tactical officer with a courageous war record. His resignation
had been a decision that had surprised *The Times* correspondent,
astonished his immediate family and shocked his regiment, as it had
been assumed by all who knew him that it was only a matter of months
before crossed swords and a baton would have been sewn on to his
epaulette.

Because of the colonel's sudden and unexplained departure from the
regiment, fact was augmented by fiction. When asked, all the colonel
would offer was that he had had enough of war, and felt the time had
come to make a little money on which Susan and he could retire before
it was too late. Even at the time, few people found his story credible,
and that credibility was not helped when the only job the colonel
managed to secure for himself was as secretary of the local golf club.

It was only through the generosity of Adam's late grandfather,
General Sir Pelham Westlake, that he had been able to remain at
Wellington College, and thereby be given the opportunity to continue
the family tradition and pursue a military career.

After leaving school, Adam was offered a place at the Royal Military
Academy, Sandhurst. During his days at the RMA, Adam was to be
found diligently studying military history, tactics, and battle procedure
while at weekends he concentrated on rugby and squash, although his
greatest success came whenever he completed the different cross-
country courses he encountered. For two years, panting cadets from
Cranwell and Dartmouth only saw his mud-spattered back as Adam
went on to become the Inter-Services champion. He also became the
middleweight boxing champion despite a Nigerian cadet breaking his
nose in the first round of the final. The Nigerian made the mistake of
assuming the fight was already over.

When Adam passed out of Sandhurst in August 1956, he managed
ninth place in the academic order of merit, but his leadership and
example outside the classroom was such that no one was surprised
when he was awarded the Sword of Honour. Adam never doubted from
that moment he would now follow his father and command the
regiment.

The Royal Wessex Regiment accepted the colonel's son soon after he
had been awarded his regular commission. Adam quickly gained the
respect of the soldiers and popularity with those officers whose currency was not to deal in rumour. As a tactical officer in the field he had
no equal, and when it came to combat duty it was clear he had inherited
his father's courage. Yet, when six years later the War Office published
in the *London Gazette* the names of those subalterns who had been made
up to Captain, Lieutenant Adam Scott was not to be found on the list.
His contemporaries were genuinely surprised, while senior officers of

the regiment remained tight-lipped. To Adam it was becoming abundantly clear that he was not to be allowed to atone for whatever it was his father was thought to have done.

Eventually Adam was made up to captain, but not before he had distinguished himself in the Malayan jungle in hand-to-hand fighting against the never-ending waves of Chinese soldiers. Having been captured and held prisoner by the Communists, he endured solitude and torture of the kind that no amount of training could have prepared him for. He escaped eight months after his incarceration only to discover on returning to the front line that he had been awarded a posthumous Military Cross. When, at the age of twenty-nine, Captain Scott passed his staff exam but still failed to be offered a regimental place at the staff college, he finally accepted he could never hope to command the regiment. He resigned his commission a few weeks later; there was no need to suggest that the reason he had done so was because he needed to earn more money.

While he was serving out his last few months with the regiment, Adam learned from his mother that Pa only had weeks to live. Adam made the decision not to inform his father of his resignation. He knew Pa would only blame himself and he was at least thankful that he had died without being aware of the stigma that had become part of his son's daily life.

When Adam reached the outskirts of London his mind returned, as it had so often lately, to the pressing problem of finding himself gainful employment. In the seven weeks he had been out of work Adam had already had more interviews with his bank manager than with prospective employers. It was true that he had another meeting lined up with the Foreign Office, but he had been impressed by the standard of the other candidates he had encountered on the way, and was only too aware of his lack of a university qualification. However, he felt the first interview had gone well and he had been quickly made aware of how many ex-officers had joined the service. When he discovered that the chairman of the selection board had a Military Cross, Adam assumed he wasn't being considered for desk work.

As he swung the motorbike into the King's Road Adam once again fingered the envelope in his inside jacket pocket hoping, uncharitably, that Lawrence would not yet have returned from the bank. Not that he could complain: his old school friend had been extremely generous in offering him such a pleasant room in his spacious flat for only four pounds a week.

"You can start paying more when they make you an ambassador," Lawrence had told him.

"You're beginning to sound like Rachmann," Adam had retorted, grinning at the man he had so admired during their days at Wellington. For Lawrence – in direct contrast to Adam – everything seemed to come so easily – exams, jobs, sport and women, especially women. When he had won his place at Balliol and gone on to take a first in PPE, no one was surprised. But when Lawrence chose banking as a profession, his contemporaries were unable to hide their disbelief. It seemed to be the first time he had embarked on anything that might be described as mundane.

Adam parked his motorbike just off Ifield Road, aware that, like his mother's old Morris Minor, it would have to be sold if the Foreign Office job didn't materialise. As he strolled towards the flat a girl who passed gave him a second look: he didn't notice. He took the stairs in threes and had reached the fifth floor, and was pushing his Yale key into the lock when a voice from inside shouted, "It's on the latch."

"Damn," said Adam under his breath.

"How did it go?" were Lawrence's first words as he entered the drawing room.

"Very well, considering," Adam replied, not quite sure what else he could say as he smiled at his flatmate. Lawrence had already changed from his City clothes into a blazer and grey flannels. He was slightly shorter and stockier than Adam with a head of wiry fair hair, a massive forehead and grey thoughtful eyes that always seemed to be inquiring.

"I admired your father so much," he added. "He always assumed one had the same standards as he did." Adam could still remember nervously introducing Lawrence to his father one Speech Day. They had become friends immediately. But then Lawrence was not a man who dealt in rumours.

"Able to retire on the family fortune, are we?" asked Lawrence in a lighter vein.

"Only if that dubious bank you work for has found a way of converting five hundred pounds into five thousand in a matter of days."

"Can't manage it at the present time, old chum – not now Harold Wilson has announced a standstill in wages and prices."

Adam smiled as he looked across at his friend. Although taller than him now, he could still recall those days when Lawrence seemed to him like a giant.

"Late again, Scott," he would say, as Adam scampered past him in the corridor. Adam had looked forward to the day when he could do everything in the same relaxed, superior style. Or was it just that Lawrence was superior? His suits always seemed to be well-pressed, his shoes always shone and he never had a hair out of place. Adam still hadn't fathomed out how he did it all so effortlessly.

Adam heard the bathroom door open. He glanced interrogatively towards Lawrence.

"It's Carolyn," whispered Larence. "She'll be staying the night . . . I think."

When Carolyn entered the room Adam smiled shyly at the tall, beautiful woman. Her long, blonde hair bounced on her shoulders as she walked towards them, but it was the faultless figure that most men couldn't take their eyes off. How did Lawrence manage it?

"Care to join us for a meal?" asked Lawrence, putting his arm round Carolyn's shoulder, his voice suddenly sounding a little *too* enthusiastic. "I've discovered this Italian restaurant that's just opened in the Fulham Road."

"I might join you later,' said Adam, "but I still have one or two papers left over from this afternoon that I ought to check through."

"Forget the finer details of your inheritance, my boy. Why not join us and spend the entire windfall in one wild spaghetti fling?"

"Oh, have you been left lots of lovely lolly?" asked Carolyn, in a voice so shrill and high-pitched nobody would have been surprised to learn that she had recently been Deb of the Year.

"Not," said Adam, "when considered against my present overdraft."

Lawrence laughed. "Well, come along later if you discover there's enough over for a plate of pasta." He winked at Adam – his customary sign for "Be sure you're out of the flat by the time we get back. Or at least stay in your room and pretend to be asleep."

"Yes, do come," cooed Carolyn, sounding as if she meant it – her hazel eyes remained fixed on Adam as Lawrence guided her firmly towards the door.

Adam didn't move until he was sure he could no longer hear her penetrating voice echoing on the staircase. Satisfied, he retreated to his bedroom and locked himself in. Adam sat down on the one comfortable chair he possessed and pulled his father's envelope out of his inside pocket. It was the heavy, expensive type of stationery Pa had always used, purchasing it at Smythson of Bond Street at almost twice the price he could have obtained them at the local W.H. Smith's. 'Captain Adam Scott, MC' was written in his father's neat copperplate hand.

Adam opened the envelope carefully, his hand shaking slightly, and extracted the contents: a letter in his father's unmistakable hand and a smaller envelope which was clearly old as it was faded with time. Written on the old envelope in an unfamiliar hand were the words 'Colonel Gerald Scott' in faded ink of indeterminate colour. Adam placed the old envelope on the little table by his side and, unfolding his father's letter, began to read. It was undated.

MY DEAR ADAM,

Over the years, you will have heard many explanations for my sudden departure from the regiment. Most of them will have been farcical, and a few of them slanderous, but I always considered it better for all concerned to keep my own counsel. I feel, however, that I owe you a fuller explanation, and that is what this letter will set out to do.

As you know, my last posting before I resigned my commission was at Nuremberg from February 1945 to October 1946. After four years of almost continuous action in the field, I was given the task of commanding the British section which had responsibility for those senior ranking Nazis who were awaiting trial for war crimes. Although the Americans had overall responsibility, I came to know the imprisoned officers quite well and after a year or so I had even grown to tolerate some of them – Hess, Doenitz and Speer in particular – and I often wondered how the Germans would have treated us had the situation been reversed. Such views were considered unacceptable at the time. 'Fraternisation' was often on the lips of those men who are never given to second thoughts.

Among the senior Nazis with whom I came into daily contact was Reichsmarshal Hermann Goering, but unlike the three other officers I have previously mentioned, here was a man I detested from the first moment I came across him. I found him arrogant, overbearing and totally without shame about the barbaric acts he had carried out in the name of war. And I never once found any reason to change my opinion of him. In fact, I sometimes wondered how I controlled my temper when I was in his presence.

The night before Goering was due to be executed, he requested a private meeting with me. It was a Monday, and I can still recall every detail of that encounter as if it were only yesterday. I received the request when I took over the Russian watch from Major Vladimir Kosky. In fact Kosky personally handed me the written request. As soon as I had inspected the guard and dealt with the usual paperwork, I went along with the duty corporal to see the Reichsmarshal in his cell. Goering stood to attention by his small low bed and saluted as I entered the room. The sparse, grey-painted, brick cell always made me shudder.

"You asked to see me?" I said. I never could get myself to address him by his name or rank.

"Yes," he replied. "It was kind of you to come in person, Colonel. I simply wish to make the last request of a man condemned to death. Would it be possible for the corporal to leave us?"

Imagining it was something highly personal I asked the corporal to wait outside. I confess I had no idea what could be so private when the man only had hours to live but as the door closed he saluted again and then passed over the envelope you now have in your possession. As I took it, all he said was, "Would you be good enough not to open this until after my execution tomorrow." He then added, "I can only hope it will compensate for any blame that might later be placed on your shoulders." I had no idea what he could be alluding to at the time and presumed some form of mental instability had overtaken him. Many of the prisoners confided in me during their last few days, and towards the end, some of them were undoubtedly on the verge of madness.

Adam stopped to consider what he would have done in the same circumstances, and decided to read on to discover if father and son would have taken the same course.

However, Goering's final words to me as I left his cell seemed hardly those of a madman. He said quite simply: "Be assured. It is a masterpiece; do not underestimate its value." Then he lit up a cigar as if he was relaxing at his club after a rather good dinner. We all had different theories as to who smuggled the cigars in for him, and equally wondered what might also have been smuggled out from time to time.

I placed the envelope in my jacket pocket and left him to join the corporal in the corridor. We then checked the other cells to see that all the prisoners were locked up for the night. The inspection completed, I returned to my office. As I was satisfied that there were no more immediate duties I settled down to make out my report. I left the envelope in the jacket pocket of my uniform with every intention of opening it immediately after Goering's execution had been carried out the following morning. I was checking over the orders of the day when the corporal rushed into my office without knocking. "It's Goering, sir, it's Goering," he said, frantically. From the panic on the man's face, I didn't need to ask for any details. We both ran all the way back to the Reichsmarshal's cell.

I found Goering lying face downwards on his bunk. I turned him over to find he was already dead. In the commotion that immediately followed I quite forgot Goering's letter. An autopsy a few days later showed that he had died from poisoning, the court came to the conclusion that the cyanide capsule that had been found in his body must have been implanted in one of his cigars.

As I had been the last to see him alone and privately, it took only a few whispers before my name was linked with his death. There was, of course, no truth in the accusation. Indeed I never doubted for one moment that the court had delivered the correct verdict in his case and that he justly deserved to be hanged for the part he had played in the war.

So stung was I by the continual behind-the-back accusations

that I might have helped Goering to an easy death by smuggling in the cigars that I felt the only honourable thing to do in the circumstances was to resign my commission immediately for fear of bringing further dishonour to the regiment. When I returned to England later that year, and finally decided to throw out my old uniform, I came across the envelope again. When I explained to your mother the details of the incident she begged me to destroy the envelope as she considered it had brought enough dishonour to our family already, and even if it did point to whoever had been responsible for helping Goering to his suicide, in her opinion such knowledge could no longer do anyone any good. I agreed to comply with her wishes and although I never opened the envelope I could never get myself to destroy it, remembering the last sentence Goering had uttered about it being a masterpiece. And so finally I hid it among my personal papers.

However, since the imagined sins of the father are inevitably visited upon the next generation, I feel no such qualms should influence you. If there is therefore anything to be gained from the contents of this envelope I make only one request, namely that your mother should be the first to benefit from it without ever being allowed to know how such good fortune came about.

Over the years, I have watched your progress with considerable pride and feel confident that I can leave you to make the correct decision.

If you are left in any doubt about opening the envelope yourself, destroy it without further consideration. But if you open it only to discover its purpose is to involve you in some dishonourable enterprise, be rid of it without a second thought.

MAY GOD BE WITH YOU.

YOUR LOVING FATHER,

GERALD SCOTT

Adam read the letter over once again, realising how much trust his father had placed in him. His heart thumped in his chest as he considered how Pa's life had been wasted by the murmurings and innuendoes of lesser men – the same men who had also succeeded in bringing his own career to a premature halt. When he had finished reading the missive for a third time he folded it up neatly and slipped it back into its envelope.

He then picked up the second envelope from the side table. The words 'Colonel Gerald Scott' were written in a faded bold script across it.

Adam removed a comb from his inside pocket and wedged it into the corner of the envelope. Slowly he began to slit it open. He hesitated for a moment before extracting two pieces of paper, both yellowed with age. One appeared to be a letter while the other seemed to be a document of some sort. The crest of the Third Reich was embossed at the head of the letterpaper above the printed name of Reichsmarshal Hermann Goering. Adam's hands began to tremble as he read the first line.

It began, *Sehr geehrter Herr Oberst Scott:*

CHAPTER THREE

As the black Chaika limousine drove out under the Spasskaya Bashnya and on to Red Square, two Kremlin guards in khaki uniforms sprang to attention and presented arms. A shrill whistle sounded which ensured that Yuri Efimovich Zaborski would experience no delays on his route back to Dzerzhinsky Square.

Zaborski touched the corner of his black felt hat in automatic acknowledgment of the salute although his thoughts were elsewhere. As the car rumbled over the cobbled stones, he didn't even glance at the long snake-like queue that stretched from Lenin's Tomb to the edge of Red Square. The first decision he had to make would undoubtedly be the most important: which of his senior operatives should be charged with the task of heading the team to find the Tsar's icon? He continued to ponder the problem as his driver took him across Red Square, passing the grey façade of the GUM department store away to his left before driving along Neitsa Kuibysheva.

Within moments of leaving his leader, the Chairman of State Security had formed in his own mind a shortlist of two. Which of those two, Valchek or Romanov, should be given the nod still taxed him. In normal circumstances he would have spent at least a week making such a decision but the General Secretary's deadline of June 20 left him with no such freedom. He knew he would have to make the choice even before he reached his office. The driver cruised through another green light past the Ministry of Culture and into Cherkasskiy Bolshoy Pereulok lined with its imposing block-like, grey buildings. The car remained in the special inside lane that could be used only by senior Party officials. In England, he was amused to learn that they had plans for such a traffic lane – but it would only be for the use of buses.

The car came to an abrupt halt outside KGB headquarters. It hadn't helped that they had been able to cover the three kilometre journey in less than four minutes. The driver ran round and opened the back door to allow his master to step out but Zaborski didn't move. The man who rarely changed his mind had already done so twice on the route back to Dzerzhinsky Square. He knew he could call on any number of bureaucrats and academics to do the spade work but someone with flair was going to have to lead them and be responsible for reporting back to him.

His professional intuition told him to select Yuri Valchek, who had proved over the years to be a trusty and reliable servant of the State. He was also one of the Chairman's longest serving heads of department. Slow, methodical and reliable, he had completed a full ten years as an agent in the field before confining himself to a desk job.

In contrast, Alex Romanov, who had only recently become head of his own section, had shown flashes of brilliance in the field but they had been so often outweighed by a lack of personal judgment. At twenty-nine, he was the youngest and, without question, the most ambitious of the Chairman's select team.

Zaborski stepped out on to the pavement and walked towards another door held open for him. He strode across the marble floor and stopped only when he reached the lift gates. Several silent men and women had also been waiting for the lift but when it returned to the ground floor and the Chairman stepped in to the little cage, none of them made any attempt to join him. Zaborski travelled slowly up towards his office, never failing to compare it unfavourably with the speed of the one American elevator he had experienced. They could launch their rockets before you could get to your office, his predecessor had warned him. By the time Zaborski had reached the top floor and the gates had been pulled back for him, he had made up his mind. It would be Valchek.

A secretary helped him off with his long black coat and took his hat. Zaborski walked quickly to his desk. The two files he had asked for were awaiting him. He sat down and began to pore over Valchek's file. When he had completed it, he barked out an order to his hovering secretary: "Find Romanov."

Comrade Romanov lay flat on his back, his left arm behind his head and his opponent's right over his throat preparing for a double knee-thrust. The coach executed it perfectly and Romanov groaned as he hit the floor with a thud.

An attendant came rushing over to them and bent down to whisper in the coach's ear. The coach reluctantly released his pupil who rose slowly as if in a daze, bowed to the coach and then in one movement of right arm and left leg took the legs from under him and left him flat on the gymnasium floor before making his way quickly to the off-the-hook phone in the office.

Romanov didn't notice the girl who handed him the phone. "I'll be with him as soon as I have had a shower," was all she heard him say. The girl who had taken the call had often wondered what Romanov looked like in the shower. She, like all the other girls in the office, had seen him in the gymnasium a hundred times. Six foot tall with that long, flowing blond hair – he resembled a Western film star. And those eyes, 'piercing blue' the friend who shared her desk described them.

"He's got a scar on his . . ." the friend confided.

"How do you know that?" she had asked, but her friend had only giggled in reply.

The Chairman meanwhile had opened Romanov's personal file for a second time, and was still perusing the details. He began to read the different entries that made up a candid character assessment which Romanov would never see unless he became Chairman:

Alexander Petrovich Romanov, Born Leningrad, March 12, 1937. Elected full Party member 1958.
Father: Peter Nicholevich Romanov, served on the Eastern Front in 1942. On returning to Russia in 1945 refused to join Communist Party. After several reports of anti-State activities supplied by his son he was sentenced to ten years in prison. Died in jail October 20, 1948.

Zaborski looked up and smiled – a child of the State.

Grandfather: Nicholai Alexandrovich Romanov, merchant, and one of the wealthiest landowners in Petrograd. Shot and killed on May 11, 1918, while attempting to escape from the forces of the Red Army.

The Revolution had taken place between the princely grandfather and the reluctant comrade father.

Alex, as he preferred to be known, had nevertheless inherited the Romanov ambition so he enrolled for the Party's Pioneer organisation at the age of nine. By the age of eleven, he had been offered a place at a special school at Smolensk – to the disgust of some of the lesser Party workers who considered such privileges should be reserved for the sons of loyal Party officials, not the sons of those in jail. Romanov immediately excelled in the classroom, much to the dismay of the Director who had been hoping to disprove any Darwinian theories. And at fourteen he was selected as one of the Party's élite and made a member of the Komsomol.

By the age of sixteen, Romanov had won the Lenin language medal and the junior gymnastics prize and despite the Director's attempts to

undermine young Alex's achievements, most members of the school
board recognised Romanov's potential and ensured that he was still
allowed to take up a place at university. As an undergraduate he
continued to excel in languages, specialising in English, French and
German. Natural flair and hard work kept him near the top of every
subject he specialised in.

Zaborski picked up the phone by his side. "I asked to see Romanov,"
he said curtly.

"He was completing his morning work-out at the gymnasium,
Chairman," replied his secretary. "But he left to change the moment he
heard you wanted to see him."

The Chairman replaced the phone and his eyes returned to the file in
front of him. That Romanov could be found in the gymnasium at all
hours came as no surprise: the man's athletic prowess had been
acknowledged far beyond the service.

During his first year as a student, Romanov had continued diligently
with his gymnastics and even gone on to represent the State side until
the university coach had written in bold letters across one of his reports,
"This student is too tall to be considered for serious Olympic competition." Romanov heeded the coach's advice and took up judo. Within
two years, he had been selected for the 1958 Eastern Bloc games in
Budapest and within a further two years found other competitors
preferred not to be drawn against him on his inevitable route to the
final. After his victory at the Soviet games in Moscow the Western press
crudely described him as 'The Axe'. Those who were already planning
his long term future felt it prudent not to enter him for the Olympics.

Once Romanov had completed his fifth year at the university and
obtained his diploma (with distinction), he remained in Moscow and
joined the diplomatic service.

Zaborski had now reached the point in the file at which he had first
come across the self-confident young man. Each year the KGB were
able to second from the diplomatic service any person they considered
to be of exceptional talent. Romanov was an obvious candidate.
Zaborski's rule, however, was not to enlist anyone who didn't consider
the KGB to be the élite. Unwilling candidates never made good
operatives and sometimes even ended up working for the other side.
Romanov showed no such doubt. He had always wanted to be an officer
of the KGB. During the next six years he carried out tours at their
embassies in Paris, London, Prague and Lagos. By the time he had
returned to Moscow to join the headquarters staff he was a sophisticated operative who was as relaxed at an ambassadorial cocktail party
as he was in the gymnasium.

Zaborski began to read some of the comments he himself had added
to the report during the last four years – in particular how much
Romanov had changed during his time on the Chairman's personal

staff. As an operative, he had reached the rank of major, having served successfully in the field before being appointed head of a department. Two red dots were placed by his name indicating successful missions. A defecting violinist attempting to leave Prague and a general who had thought he was going to be the next head of a small African state. What impressed Zaborski most about his protégé's efforts was that the Western press thought the Czechs were responsible for the first and the Americans for the second. Romanov's most significant achievement, however, had been the recruitment of an agent from the British Foreign Office whose parallel rise had only assisted Romanov's career. Romanov's appointment as head of a department had surprised no one, himself included, although it soon became clear to Zaborski that he missed the raw excitement of field work.

The Chairman turned to the last page, a character assessment, in which the majority of contributors were in accord: ambitious, sophisticated, ruthless, arrogant but not always reliable were the words that appeared with regularity in almost every summation.

There was an assertive rap on the door. Zaborski closed the file and pressed a button under his desk. The doors clicked open to allow Alexander Petrovich Romanov to enter the room.

"Good morning, Comrade Chairman," said the elegant young man who now stood to attention in front of him. Zaborski looked up at the man he had selected and felt a little envy that the gods had bestowed so much on one so young. Still, it was he who understood how to use such a man to the State's best advantage.

He continued to stare into those clear blue eyes and considered that if Romanov had been born in Hollywood he would not have found it hard to make a living. His suit looked as if it had been tailored in Savile Row – and probably had been. Zaborski chose to ignore such irregularities although he was tempted to ask the young man where he had his shirts made.

"You called for me," said Romanov.

The Chairman nodded. "I have just returned from the Kremlin," he said. "The General Secretary has entrusted us with a particularly sensitive project of great importance to the State." Zaborski paused. "So sensitive in fact that you will report only to me. You can hand-select your own team and no resources will be denied you."

"I am honoured," said Romanov, sounding unusually sincere.

"You will be," replied the Chairman, "if you succeed in discovering the whereabouts of the Tsar's icon."

"But I thought . . ." began Romanov.

CHAPTER FOUR

Adam walked over to the side of his bed and removed from the bookshelf the Bible his mother had given him as a Confirmation present. As he opened it a layer of dust rose from the top of the gold-leaf-edged pages. He placed the envelope in Revelation and returned the Bible to the shelf.

Adam strolled through to the kitchen, fried himself an egg and warmed up the other half of the previous day's tinned beans. He placed the unwholesome meal on the kitchen table, unable to put out of his mind the slap-up meal Lawrence and Carolyn must now be enjoying at the new Italian restaurant. After Adam had finished and cleared his plate away, he returned to his room and lay on the bed thinking. Would the contents of the faded envelope finally prove his father's innocence? A plan began to form in his mind.

When the grandfather clock in the hall chimed ten times, Adam lifted his long legs over the end of the bed and pulled the Bible back out of the bookshelf. With some apprehension Adam removed the envelope. Next, he switched on the reading light by the side of the small writing desk, unfolded the two pieces of paper and placed them in front of him.

One appeared to be a personal letter from Goering to Adam's father, while the other had the look of an older, more official document. Adam placed this second document to one side and began to go over the letter line by line. It didn't help.

He tore a blank piece of paper from a notepad that he found on Lawrence's desk and started to copy down the text of Goering's letter. He left out only the greeting and what he assumed to be a valediction –'*hochachtungsvoll*' – followed by the Reichsmarshal's large, bold signature. He checked over the copy carefully before replacing the original in its faded envelope. He had just begun the same process with the official document, using a separate sheet of paper, when he heard a key turning, followed by voices at the front door. Both Lawrence and Carolyn sounded as if they had drunk more than the promised bottle of wine, and Carolyn's voice in particular had ascended into little more than a series of high-pitched giggles.

Adam sighed and switched off the light by the side of the desk so they wouldn't know he was still awake. In the darkness he became more sensitive to their every sound. One of them headed towards the kitchen, because he heard the fridge door squelch close and, a few seconds later, the sound of a cork being extracted – he presumed from his last bottle of white wine, as they were unlikely to be so drunk that they had started on the vinegar.

Reluctantly he rose from his chair, and circling his arms in front of him, he made his way back to the bed. He touched the corner of the bedstead and quietly lowered himself on to the mattress, then waited impatiently for Lawrence's bedroom door to close.

He must have fallen asleep because the next thing he remembered was the tick of the hall clock. Adam licked his fingers and rubbed them over his eyes as he tried to get accustomed to the dark. He checked the little luminous dial on his alarm clock: ten past three. He eased himself off the bed gingerly, feeling more than a little crumpled and weary. Slowly he groped his way back towards the desk, banging his knee on the corner of a chest of drawers during his travels. He couldn't stop himself cursing. He fumbled for the light switch, and when the bulb first glowed it made him blink several times. The faded envelope looked so insignificant – and perhaps it was. The official document was still laid out on the centre of the table alongside the first few lines of his handwritten duplicate.

Adam yawned as he began to study the words once more. The document was not as simple to copy out as the letter had been, because this time the hand was spidery and cramped, as if the writer had considered paper an expensive commodity. Adam left out the address on the top right hand corner and reversed the eight digit number underlined at the head of the text, otherwise what he ended up with was a faithful transcript of the original.

The work was painstaking, and took a surprisingly long time. He wrote out each word in block capitals, and when he wasn't certain of the spelling he put down the possible alternative letters below; he wanted to be sure of any translation the first time.

"My, you do work late," whispered a voice from behind him.

Adam spun round, feeling like a burglar who had been caught with his hands on the family silver.

"You needn't look so nervous. It's only me," said Carolyn, standing by the bedroom door.

Adam stared up at the tall blonde who was even more attractive clad only in Lawrence's large unbuttoned pyjamas and floppy slippers than she had been when he had seen her fully dressed. Her long, fair hair now dropped untidily over her shoulders and he began to understand what Lawrence had meant when he had once described her as someone who could turn a match stick into a Cuban cigar.

"The bathroom is at the end of the corridor," said Adam, a little feebly.

"It wasn't the bathroom I was looking for, silly," she giggled. "I don't seem able to wake Lawrence. After all that wine he's passed out like a defeated heavyweight boxer." She sighed, "And long before round fifteen. I don't think anything will rouse him again until morning." She took a step towards him.

Adam stammered something about feeling rather whacked himself. He made sure his back shielded her from any sight of the papers on the desk.

"Oh, God," said Carolyn, "you're not queer, are you?"

"Certainly not," said Adam, a little pompously.

"Just don't fancy me?" she asked.

"Not that exactly," said Adam.

"But Lawrence is your chum," she said. Adam didn't reply.

"My God this is the sixties, Adam. Share and share alike."

"It's just that . . ." began Adam.

"What a waste," said Carolyn, "perhaps another time." She tiptoed to the door, and slipped back out into the corridor, unaware of her German rival.

The first action Romanov took on leaving the Chairman's office that morning was to return to his *alma mater* and hand-pick a team of twelve researchers. From the moment they had been briefed they proceeded to study in pairs on four-hour shifts, so that the work could continue night and day.

The early information had come in almost by the hour and the researchers had quickly been able to establish that the Tsar's icon had remained in his private quarters at the Winter Palace at Petrograd until as late as December 1914. Romanov studied religiously a photo of the small delicate painting of St George and the Dragon. St George in tiny mosaics patterns of blue and gold while the dragon was in fiery red and yellow. Although he had never shown any interest in art, Romanov could well understand why people could be moved by the little masterpiece. He continued to read details of the icon's history, but still couldn't work out why it was so important to the State. He wondered if even Zaborski knew the reason.

A royal servant who had testified before the People's Court a year after the Revolution claimed that the Tsar's icon had disappeared for a few days in 1915 after the visit of Ludwig Ernst, Grand Duke of Hesse. At the time, the inquisitors had taken scant interest in the misplaced icon because it was still on the wall of the Tsar's study when they had stormed the Winter Palace. What concerned the court more was why, in the middle of a fierce war with the Kaiser's Germany, the Grand Duke of Hesse should want to visit the Tsar at all.

The Professor of History at the university had immediately been asked for his opinion. The great academic was puzzled by the request, as the KGB had never shown any interest in the nation's past history before. Nevertheless, he briefed Romanov on everything that was known of the incident. Romanov pored over his report once again. The Grand Duke, it was thought, had been on a secret visit to his sister Alexandra, the Tsarina. Historians now believed that it had been his intention to secure a cease-fire between Germany and Russia, in the hope that Germany could then concentrate her war efforts on the British and the French.

There was no proof that the Tsar made any promises on behalf of his people but the Grand Duke, it seemed, did not return to Germany empty-handed. As the reports of the proceedings of the People's Court showed, another palace servant had been instructed to wrap up the Tsar's icon and pack it with the Grand Duke's belongings. However, no one on the palace staff could properly explain to the court how a few days later the icon reappeared in its rightful place on the wall of the Tsar's private study.

Romanov's chief researcher, Professor Oleg Konstantinov, having studied the professor's notes and the other researchers' contributions, had underlined his own conclusion in red ink.

"The Tsar must have replaced the original painting with a brilliant copy having handed over the real icon for safe-keeping to his brother-in-law, the Grand Duke."

"But why," asked Romanov, "when the Tsar had a palace full of Goyas, El Grecos, Titians and Rubens did he bother to smuggle out one icon and why does Brezhnev want it back so badly?"

Romanov instructed the professor and his twenty-four researchers to turn their talents to the Royal House of Hesse in the hope of tracing what had then happened to the Tsar's icon. Within ten days, they possessed between them more information about the Grand Duke and his family than any professor at any university had managed to gather in a lifetime. As each file appeared on his desk Romanov laboured through the night, checking every scrap of information that might give him a lead to the whereabouts of the original painting. He came to a dead end when, after the Grand Duke's death, the painting had been left to his brother who was tragically killed in a plane crash. Nothing had been seen or heard of the icon after that day.

By the beginning of the third week, Romanov had reached the reluctant conclusion that there was nothing new on the whereabouts of the icon to be discovered. He was preparing his final report for the Chairman of the KGB when one researcher, Comrade Petrova, whose mind did not work in parallel lines, stumbled across an article in the London *Times* of Wednesday, November 17, 1937. Petrova bypassed the research leader and handed the relevant photocopy to Romanov personally, who, over the next few hours read the news item so often that he came to know it off by heart.

In keeping with the Thunderer's tradition, the foreign correspondent remained anonymous. The article carried the date-line 'Ostend, November 16, 1937'.

It read:

Grand Duke George of Hesse and four members of his family were tragically killed this morning when a Sabena aircraft carrying them from Darmstadt to London crashed in thick fog over the Belgian countryside.

The Grand Duke had been on his way to England to attend the wedding of his younger brother, Prince Louis, to the Hon. Joanna Geddes. The young prince had been waiting at Croydon Airport to greet his family when the news was broken to him. He immediately cancelled his original wedding plans and announced they would be rescheduled with a small private service in the Chapel at Windsor.

The Times went on:

Prince Louis, who succeeds his brother as the Grand Duke of Hesse, will leave for Ostend with his bride later today in order that they can accompany the five coffins on their journey back to Germany. The funerals will all take place in Darmstadt on November 23.

It was the next paragraph that the researcher had circled boldly.

Some of the late Grand Duke's personal belongings, including several wedding presents for Prince Louis and his bride, were scattered for miles in the vicinity of the crashed aircraft. The German Government announced this morning that a senior German general has been appointed to lead a team of salvage experts to ensure the recovery of any family possessions that still belong to the Grand Duke's successor.

Romanov immediately called for the young researcher. When Anna Petrova arrived a few minutes later she gave no impression of being overawed by her head of department. She accepted that it would be hard to make any impression on him with the clothes she could afford. However, she had put on the prettiest outfit she possessed and cut her hair in the style of an American actress called Mia Farrow whom she had seen in one of the few films not banned by the authorities. She hoped Romanov would notice.

"I want you to scour _The Times_ every day from November 17, 1937 for six months, and also check the German and Belgian press during the same period in case you come across anything that would show what the salvage experts had discovered." He dismissed her with a smile.

Within twenty-four hours Comrade Petrova barged back into Romanov's office without even bothering to knock. Romanov merely raised his eyebrows at the discourtesy before devouring an article she had discovered in the Berlin *Autslung* of Saturday, January 19, 1938.

"The investigation into the crash last November of the Sabena aircraft that was carrying the Hesse royal family to London has now been concluded. All personal possessions belonging to the family that were discovered in the vicinity of the wreckage have been returned to the Grand Duke, Prince Louis, who, it is understood, was particularly saddened by the loss of a family heirloom that was to have been a wedding gift from his brother, the late Grand Duke. The gift, a painting known as the 'Tsar's Icon', had once belonged to his uncle, Tsar Nicholas II. The icon of St George and the Dragon, although only a copy of Rublev's masterpiece, was considered to be one of the finest examples of early twentieth-century craftsmanship to come out of Russia since the Revolution."

Romanov looked up at the researcher. "Twentieth-century copy be damned," he said. "It was the fifteenth-century original and none of them realised it at the time – perhaps not even the old Grand Duke himself. No doubt the Tsar had other plans for the icon had he managed to escape."

Romanov dreaded having to tell Zaborski that he could now prove conclusively that the original Tsar's icon had been destroyed in a plane crash some thirty years before. Such news would not ensure promotion for its messenger, as he remained convinced that there was something far more important than the icon at stake for Zaborski to be so involved.

He stared down at the photograph above the *Zeitung* report. The young Grand Duke was shaking hands with the general in charge of the salvage team which had been successful in returning so many of the Prince's family possessions. "But did he return them all?" Romanov said out loud.

"What do you mean?" asked the young researcher. Romanov waved his hand as he continued to stare at the pre-war, faded photograph of the two men. Although the general was unnamed, every schoolboy in Germany would have recognised the large, impassive, heavy-jowled face with the chilling eyes which had become infamous to the Allied powers.

Romanov looked up at the researcher. "You can forget the Grand Duke from now on, Comrade Petrova. Concentrate your efforts on Reichsmarshal Hermann Goering."

When Adam woke his first thoughts were of Carolyn. His yawn turned into a grin as he considered her invitation of the night before. Then he remembered. He jumped out of bed and walked over to his desk: everything was in place exactly as he had left it. He yawned for a second time.

It was ten to seven. Although he felt as fit as he had been the day he left the army some seven weeks before, he still completed a punishing routine of exercise every morning. He intended to be at his peak when the Foreign Office put him through a physical. In moments he was kitted out in a singlet and a pair of running shorts. He pulled on an old army tracksuit and finally tied up his gym shoes.

Adam tiptoed out of the flat, not wanting to wake Lawrence or Carolyn – although he suspected she was wide awake, waiting impatiently. For the next thirty-four minutes he pounded the pavement down to the Embankment, across Albert Bridge, through Battersea Park to return by way of Chelsea Bridge. Only one thought was going through his mind. After twenty years of gossip and innuendo was this going to be the one chance to clear his father's name? The moment he arrived back at the flat, Adam checked his pulse: 150 beats a minute. Sixty seconds later it was down to 100, another minute 70, and before the fourth minute was up it was back to a steady 58. It's the recovery that proves fitness, not your speed, his old Physical Training Instructor at Aldershot had drummed into him.

As Adam walked back through to his room there was still no sign of Carolyn. Lawrence, smart in a grey pinstripe suit, was preparing breakfast in the kitchen while glancing at the sports pages of the *Daily Telegraph*.

"The West Indies made 526," he informed Adam forlornly.

"Have we begun our innings?" shouted Adam from the bathroom.

"No, bad light stopped play."

Adam groaned as he stripped for the shower. He was ready for his morning game of finding out how long he could last under the freezing jets. The forty-eight needles of ice cold water beat down on his back and chest, which made him take several deep intakes of breath. Once you survive the first thirty seconds you could stay under for ever, the instructor had assured them. Adam emerged three minutes later, satisfied but still damning the PTI from whose influence he felt he would never escape.

Once he had towelled himself down Adam walked back to his bedroom. A moment later he had thrown on his dressing-gown and joined his friend in the kitchen for breakfast. Lawrence was now seated at the kitchen table concentrating hard on a bowl of cornflakes, while running a finger down the Foreign Exchange rates in the *Financial Times*.

Adam checked his watch: already ten past eight. "Won't you be late for the office?" he asked.

"Dear boy," said Lawrence, "I am not a lackey who works at the kind of bank where the customers keep shop hours."

Adam laughed. "But I will, however, have to be shackled to my desk in the City by nine thirty," Lawrence admitted. "They don't send a driver for me nowadays," he explained. "In this traffic, I told them, it's so much quicker by tube."

Adam started to make himself breakfast.

"I could give you a lift on my motorbike."

"Can you imagine a man in my position arriving at the headquarters of Barclays Bank on a motorbike? The Chairman would have a fit," he added, as he folded the *Financial Times*.

Adam cracked a second egg into the frying pan.

"See you tonight then, glorious, unwashed and unemployed," jeered Lawrence as he collected his rolled umbrella from the hat stand.

Adam cleared away and washed up, happy to act as housewife while he was still unemployed. Despite years of being taken care of by a batman he knew exactly what was expected of him. All he had planned before his interview with the Foreign Office that afternoon was a long bath and a slow shave. Then he remembered that Reichsmarshal Goering was still resting on the table in the bedroom.

"Have you come up with anything that would indicate Goering might have kept the icon for himself?" asked Romanov, turning hopefully to the researcher.

"Only the obvious," Anna Petrova replied in an offhand manner.

Romanov considered reprimanding the young girl for such insolence, but said nothing on this occasion. After all, Comrade Petrova had proved to be far the most innovative of his team of researchers.

"And what was so obvious?" inquired Romanov.

"It's common knowledge that Hitler put Goering in charge of all the art treasures captured on behalf of the Third Reich. But as the Führer had such fixed personal opinions as to what constituted quality, many of the world's masterpieces were judged as 'depraved' and therefore unworthy to be put on public view for the delectation of the master race."

"So what happened to them?"

"Hitler ordered them to be destroyed. Among those works condemned to death by burning were such masters as Van Gogh, Manet, Monet – and especially the young Picasso who was considered unworthy of the blue-blooded Aryan race Hitler was grooming to rule the world."

"You are not suggesting Goering could have stolen the Tsar's icon," asked Romanov staring up at the ceiling, "only then to burn it?"

"No, no. Goering was not that stupid. As we now know, he didn't always obey the Führer's every word."

"Goering failed to carry out Hitler's orders?" said Romanov in disbelief.

"Depends from which standpoint you view it," Petrova replied. "Was he to behave as his lunatic master demanded or turn a blind eye and use his common sense?"

"Stick to the facts," said Romanov, his voice suddenly sharp.

"Yes, Comrade Major," said the young researcher in a tone that suggested she believed herself to be indispensable, at least for the time being.

"When it came to it," Petrova continued, "Goering did not destroy any of the denounced masterpieces. He held some public burnings in Berlin and Dusseldorf of lesser known German artists, who would never have fetched more than a few hundred marks on the open market in the first place. But the masterpieces, the real works of genius, were moved discreetly over the border and deposited in the vaults of Swiss banks."

"So there's still an outside chance that having found the icon . . ."

"He then had it placed in a Swiss bank," added Petrova. "I wish it were that simple, Comrade Major," said the researcher, "but unfortunately Goering wasn't quite as naïve as the newspaper cartoonists of the time made him out to be. I think he deposited the paintings and antiques in several Swiss banks and to date no one has ever been able to discover which banks or the aliases he used."

"Then *we* shall have to do so," said Romanov. "Where do you suggest we start?"

"Well, since the end of the war many of the paintings have been found and restored to their rightful owners, including the galleries of the German Democratic Republic. Others, however, have appeared on walls as far-flung as the Getty Museum in California and the Gotoh in Tokyo, sometimes without a fully satisfactory explanation. In fact, one of Renoir's major works can currently be seen hanging on the walls of the Metropolitan Museum in New York. It undoubtedly passed through Goering's hands although the curator of the museum has never been willing to explain how the gallery came into possession of it."

"Have all the missing pictures now been found?" asked Romanov anxiously.

"Over seventy per cent, but there are still many more to be accounted for. Some may even have been lost or destroyed, but my guess is that there are still a large number that remain lodged in Swiss banks."

"How can you be so certain?" demanded Romanov, fearful that his last avenue might be closing.

"Because the Swiss banks always return valuables when they can be certain of a nation's or individual's right of possession. In the case of the Grand Duke of Hesse and the Tsar's icon there was no proof of ownership, as the last official owner was Tsar Nicholas II and he, as every good Russian knows, Comrade, had no successors."

"Then I must do exactly what Goering did and retrace his steps by going direct to the banks. What has been their policy to date?" asked Romanov.

"That differs from establishment to establishment," said Petrova. "Some banks wait for twenty years or more and then try either by extensive research or advertising to contact the owner or their next of kin. In the case of the Jews who lost their lives under the Nazi regime, it has often proved impossible to trace a legitimate owner. Although I have been unable to prove it, I suspect they kept the rewards and split the proceeds among themselves," said Petrova. "Typical capitalists."

"That is neither fair nor accurate, Comrade," said Romanov, glad to show that he had also been doing some research. "Because that is another of the great myths perpetrated by the poor. In fact, when the banks have been unable to discover the rightful owner of any treasure left with them they have handed it over to the Swiss Red Cross to auction."

"But if the Tsar's icon had ever been auctioned we would have heard about it by now through one of our agents?"

"Precisely," said Romanov. "And I've already checked through the inventory of the Red Cross: four icons have been disposed of during the last twenty years and none of them was St George and the Dragon."

"Then that can only mean some unscrupulous bankers have disposed of the icon privately once they felt sure no one was going to make a claim."

"Another false premise, I suspect, Comrade Petrova."

"How can you be so certain?" the young researcher asked.

"For one simple reason, Comrade. The Swiss banking families all know each other intimately and have never in the past shown any propensity for breaking the law. Swiss justice, in our experience, is as tough on corrupt bankers as it is on murderers, which is precisely why the Mafia was never happy about laundering its money through the established banks. The truth is that Swiss bankers make so much money dealing with honest people that it has never been in their best interests to become involved with crooks. There are remarkably few exceptions to this rule, which is the reason so many people are willing to do business with the Swiss."

"So, if Goering stole the Tsar's icon and deposited it in a Swiss bank vault, it could be anywhere in the world by now?" said Petrova.

"I doubt it."

"Why?" sighed Petrova, a little peeved that her deductions were now proving wide of the mark.

"Because for the past three weeks I have had heaven knows how many operatives combing Europe for the Tsar's icon. They have spoken to nearly every major curator, keeper, dealer and crook in the art world and yet they still haven't come up with a single lead. And why not? Because the only people who have seen the icon since 1917 were the Hesses and Goering, which leaves me with only one hope if it was not destroyed when the Grand Duke's plane crashed," said Romanov.

"Namely?" asked Petrova.

"That while the rest of the world is under the illusion that the original still hangs in the Winter Palace, it has, for the past twenty years, been lodged in a Swiss bank waiting for someone to claim it."

"A long shot," said the researcher.

"I am aware of that," said Romanov sharply, "but don't forget that many Swiss banks have a twenty-five-year rule before disclosure, some even thirty. One or two even have no deadline at all as long as enough money has been deposited to cover the housing of the treasure."

"Heaven knows how many banks there might be who fall into that category," sighed Petrova.

"Heaven knows," agreed Romanov, "and so might you by nine o'clock tomorrow morning. And then it will be necessary for me to pay a visit to the one man in this country who knows everything about banking."

"Am I expected to start straight away, Comrade Major?" the researcher asked coyly.

Romanov smiled and looked down into the girl's green eyes. Dressed in the dull grey uniform of her trade, no one would have given her a second look. But in the nude she was quite magnificent. He leaned over until their lips nearly met.

"You'll have to rise very early Anna, but for now just turn out the light."

CHAPTER FIVE

It took Adam only a few more minutes before he had checked over both documents again. He put the original back in the faded envelope and replaced it in the Bible on his bookshelf. Finally he folded his duplicated copy of Goering's letter into three horizontal pieces and cut it carefully along the folds into strips which he placed in a clean envelope and left on his bedside table. Adam's next problem was how to obtain a translation of the document and Goering's letter without arousing unnecessary curiosity. Years of army training had taught him to be cautious when faced with an unknown situation. He quickly dismissed the German Embassy, the German Tourist Board and the German Press Agency as all three were too official, and therefore likely to ask unwanted questions. Once he was dressed he went to the hall and began to flick through the pages in the London E–K Directory until his finger reached the column he had been searching for.

German Broadcasting
German Cultural Institute
German Federal Railway
German Hospital
German Old People's Home

His eye passed over 'German Technical Translations' and stopped at a more promising entry. The address was given as Bayswater House, 35 Craven Terrace, W2. He checked his watch.

Adam left the flat a few minutes before ten, the three pieces of the letter now safely lodged in the inside pocket of his blazer. He strolled down Edith Grove and into the King's Road, enjoying the morning sun. The street had been transformed from the one he had known as a young subaltern. Boutiques had taken the place of antiquarian book-shops. Record shops had replaced the local cobbler, and Dolcis had given way to Mary Quant. Take a fortnight's holiday, and you couldn't be sure anything would still be there when you returned, he reflected ruefully

Crowds of people spilled out from the pavement on to the road, staring or hoping to be stared at, according to their age. As Adam passed the first of the record shops he had no choice but to listen to 'I Want to Hold Your Hand' as it blared into the ears of everyone within shouting distance.

By the time Adam reached Sloane Square the world had almost returned to normal – Peter Jones, W. H. Smith's and the London Underground. The words his mother sung so often over the kitchen sink came back to him every time he walked into the square.

And you're giving a treat (penny ice and cold meat)
To a party of friends and relations,
They're a ravenous horde, and they all came aboard
At Sloane Square and South Kensington stations.

He paid a shilling for a ticket to Paddington and, installed in a half-empty carriage, once again went over his plan. When he emerged into the open air at Paddington he checked the street name and, once he was sure of his bearings, walked out on to Craven Road until he came to the first available newsagent and then asked the directions for Craven Terrace.

"Fourth road on the left, mate," said the shopkeeper, not bothering to look up from a pile of *Radio Times* on which he was pencilling names. Adam thanked him and a few minutes later found himself standing at the end of a short drive, looking up at the bold green and yellow sign: The German Young Men's Christian Association.

He opened the gate, walked up the drive and strode confidently through the front door. He was stopped by a porter standing in the hallway.

"Can I help you, guv'nor?"

Adam put on an exaggerated military accent and explained that he was looking for a young man called Hans Kramer.

"Never 'eard of 'im, sir," said the porter, almost standing to attention when he recognised the regimental tie. He turned to a book that lay open on the desks. "'E isn't registered," he added, a Woodbine-stained thumb running down the list of names in front of him. "Why don't you try the lounge or the games room?" he suggested, gesturing with the thumb to a door on the right.

"Thank you," said Adam, not dropping the plummy tones. He walked smartly across the hall and through the swing doors – which judging from the lack of paint on the base looked as if they had been kicked open more often than they had been pushed. He glanced around the room. Several students were lounging about reading German papers and magazines. He wasn't sure where to start, until he spotted a studious-looking girl on her own in a corner, poring over a copy of *Time* magazine. Brezhnev's face stared out from the cover. Adam strolled over and took the empty seat beside her. She glanced sideways at him and couldn't hide her surprise at his formal dress. He waited for her to put the paper down before asking, "I wonder if you could assist me?"

"How?" enquired the girl, sounding a little apprehensive.

"I just need something translated."

She looked relieved. "I will see if I can help. Have you brought something with you?" "Yes I have, I hope it isn't too difficult," he said. Adam took the envelope from his inside pocket and extracted the first paragraph of Goering's letter.

Then he put the envelope back in his pocket, took out a little notebook and waited expectantly. He felt like a cub reporter.

She read the paragraph over two or three times, then seemed to hesitate.

"Is anything wrong?"

"Not exactly," she replied, still concentrating on the words in front of her. "It's just that it's a little bit old-fashioned so that I might not be able to give you the exact sense."

Adam breathed a sigh of relief.

She repeated each sentence slowly, first in German and then in English as if wanting to feel the meaning as well as just translating the words.

"Over the last . . . past year we have come to know . . . each other somewhat . . . no, no," she said, "quite well." Adam wrote each word down as the girl translated them.

"You have never disguised – perhaps a better meaning is 'hidden' –" she added, "your distaste for the National Socialist Party."

She raised her head and stared at Adam. "It's only out of a book," he assured her. She didn't look convinced but nevertheless continued. "But you have at every time . . . no, at all times, behaved with the courtesy of an officer and a gentleman."

The girl looked up, even more puzzled, as she had now reached the last word.

"Is that all?" she asked. "It doesn't make sense. There has to be more."

"No, that's it," said Adam, quickly taking back the sheet of paper. "Thank you," he added. "It was most kind of you to help."

He left the girl and was relieved to see her shrug resignedly and return to her copy of *Time*. Adam went in search of the games room.

When he swung the door open he found a young man in a World Cup T-shirt and brown suede shorts. He was tapping a table tennis ball up and down listlessly.

"Care for a game?" said the boy, not looking at all hopeful.

"Sure," said Adam, removing his jacket and picking up the table tennis bat at his end of the table. For twenty minutes Adam had to play flat out to make sure he lost 18–21, 21–12, 17–21. As he replaced his jacket and congratulated his opponent he felt sure he had gained the young man's confidence.

"You put up good fight," said the German. "Give me good game."

Adam joined him at his end of the table. "I wonder if you could help me with something?" he said.

"Your backhand?" said the young man.

"No, thank you," said Adam, "I just need a paragraph of German translated." He handed over the middle paragraph of the letter. Once again, the would-be translator looked puzzled.

"It's from a book, so it may seem a little out of context," Adam said, unconvincingly.

'Okay, I try." As the boy began to study the paragraph, the girl who had already translated the first section came into the games room. She made her way towards them.

"This hard to make out, I am not good translation for," the young man said. "My girlfriend better, I think. I ask her. *Liebling, kannst Du dies für den Herrn ins Englische?*" Without looking at Adam he passed the second paragraph over to the girl who immediately said, "I knew there was more."

'No, no, don't bother," said Adam, and grabbed the piece of paper away from the girl. He turned back to the boy and said, "Thank you for the game. Sorry to have bothered you," and walked hurriedly out into the corridor, heading for the front door.

"Did you find 'im, sir?"

"Find him?" said Adam.

"Hans Kramer," said the porter.

"Oh, yes, thank you," said Adam. As he turned to leave he saw the young boy and his girlfriend were following close behind.

Adam ran down the drive and hailed a passing taxi.

"Where to?" said the cabbie.

"The Royal Lancaster Hotel."

"But that's only just round the corner."

"I know," said Adam, "but I'm already late."

"Suit yourself, guv," said the cabbie, "it's your money."

As the cab moved off Adam peered out of the back window to see his table-tennis opponent in conversation with the porter. The girl stood alongside them, pointing to the taxi.

Adam only relaxed when the cab turned the corner and they were out of sight.

In less than a minute the taxi had drawn up outside the Royal Lancaster. Adam handed the cabbie half a crown and waited for the change. Then he pushed through the revolving doors of the hotel and hung around in the foyer for a few moments before returning to the pavement again. He checked his watch: twelve thirty. Easily enough time for lunch, he thought, before going on to his interview with the Foreign Office. He headed across the Bayswater Road into the park at a brisk pace, knowing he couldn't hope to find a pub until he reached Knightsbridge.

Adam recalled the table tennis match. Damn, he thought. I should have thrashed him. At least that would have given him something else to think about.

Romanov's eye ran down the list of the fourteen banks. There was still an outside chance that one of them might be in possession of the Tsar's icon, but the names meant nothing to him. It was another world, and he knew he would now have to seek advice from an expert.

He unlocked the top drawer of his desk and flicked through the red book held only by the most senior ranking officers in the KGB. Many names had been scratched out or over-written as regimes came and went but Aleksei Andreovich Poskonov had remained in his present position as Chairman of the National Bank for nearly a decade, and only Gromyko the Foreign Secretary had served in any office longer. Romanov dialled a number on his private line and asked to be put through to the Chairman of Gosbank. It was some considerable time before another voice came on the line.

"Comrade Romanov, what can I do for you?"

"I urgently need to see you," said Romanov.

"Really." The gravelly tones that came from the other end of the line sounded distinctly unimpressed. Romanov could hear pages being flicked over. "I could manage Tuesday, say eleven thirty?"

"I said it was urgent," repeated Romanov. "It concerns a State matter that can't wait."

"We are the nation's bankers and do have one or two problems of our own, you might be surprised to hear," came back the unrepentant voice. Romanov checked himself and waited. There was more flicking of pages. "Well, I suppose I could fit you in at three forty-five today, for fifteen minutes," said the banker. "But I must warn you that I have a long-standing engagement at four."

"Three forty-five it is then," said Romanov.

"In my office," said Poskonov. The phone went dead.

Romanov cursed out loud. Why did everyone feel obliged to prove their manhood with the KGB? He began to write down the questions he needed answered in order to put his plan into operation. He couldn't afford to waste even a minute of his allocated fifteen. An hour later he asked to see the Chairman of the KGB. This time he was not kept waiting.

"Trying to play the capitalists at their own game, are we?" said Zaborski, once Romanov had outlined his intentions. "Be careful. They've been at it a lot longer than we have."

"I realise that," said Romanov. "But if the icon is in the West I'm left with little choice but to use their methods to get my hands on it."

"Perhaps," said the Chairman. "But with your name such an approach could be misunderstood."

Romanov knew better than to interrupt the brief silence that ensued. "Don't worry, I'll give you all the backing you need – although I've never had a request quite like this one before."

"Am I allowed to know why the icon is so important?" Romanov enquired.

The Chairman of the KGB frowned. "I do not have the authority to answer that question, but as Comrade Brezhnev's enthusiasm for the arts is well known you must have been able to work out that it is not the painting itself that we are after."

What secret can the painting hold? thought Romanov, and decided to press on. "I wondered if . . ."

The Chairman of the KGB shook his head firmly.

Bugs don't have eyes, thought Romanov, but you know what that something is, don't you?

The Chairman rose from his desk and walked over to the wall and

tore another page from the calendar. "Only ten days left to find the
damn thing," he said. "The General Secretary has taken to phoning me
at one o'clock every morning."

"One o'clock in the morning?" said Romanov joining in the game.

"Yes, the poor man can't sleep, they tell me," said the Chairman,
returning to his desk. "It comes to all of us in time – perhaps even you,
Romanov, and maybe earlier than you expect if you don't stop asking
questions." He gave his young colleague a wry smile.

Romanov left the Chairman a few minutes later and returned to his
office to go over the questions that did need to be answered by the
Chairman of Gosbank. He couldn't help becoming distracted by
thoughts of what could possibly be the significance of such a small
painting, but accepted that he must concentrate his efforts on finding it
and then perhaps the secret it contained would become obvious.

Romanov reached the steps of Neglinnaya 12 at three thirty because he
knew he needed more than the fifteen minutes he had been allocated if
he was to get all his questions answered. He only hoped Poskonov
would agree to see him immediately.

After announcing himself at the reception desk he was accompanied
by a uniformed guard up the wide marble staircase to the first floor,
where Poskonov's secretary was waiting to greet him. Romanov was led
to an anteroom. "I will inform the Chairman of the bank that you have
arrived, Comrade Romanov," the secretary said, and then disappeared
back into his own office. Romanov paced up and down the small
anteroom impatiently, but the secretary did not return until the hands
on the clock were in a straight line. At three fifty, Romanov was ushered
into the Chairman's room.

The young major was momentarily taken aback by the sheer
opulence of the room. The long red velvet curtains, the marble floor and
the delicate French furniture wouldn't, he imagined, have been out of
place in the Governor's rooms at the Bank of England. Romanov was
reminded not for the first time that money still remained the most
important commodity in the world – even in the Communist world. He
stared at the old stooped man with the thinning grey hair and bushy
walrus moustache who controlled the nation's money. The man of
whom it was said that he knew of one skeleton in everyone's cupboard.
Everyone's except mine, thought Romanov. His check suit might have
been made before the Revolution and would once again be considered
'with it' in London's King's Road.

"What can I do for you, Comrade Romanov?" inquired the banker
with a sigh, as if addressing a tiresome customer who was seeking a
small loan.

"I require one hundred million American dollars worth of gold
bullion immediately," he announced evenly.

The chairman's bored expression suddenly changed. He went scarlet and fell back into his chair. He took several short, sharp breaths before pulling open a drawer, taking out a square box and extracting a large white pill from it. It took fully a minute before he seemed calm again.

"Have you gone out of your mind, Comrade?" the old man inquired. "You ask for an appointment without giving a reason, you then charge into my office and demand that I hand over one hundred million American dollars in gold without any explanation. For what reason do you make such a preposterous suggestion?"

"That is the business of the State," said Romanov. "But, since you have inquired, I intend to deposit equal amounts in a series of numbered accounts across Switzerland."

"And on whose authority do you make such a request?" the banker asked in a level tone.

"The General Secretary of the Party."

"Strange," said Poskonov. "I see Leonid Ilyich at least once a week and he has not mentioned this to me," the Chairman looked down at the pad in the middle of his desk, "that a Major Romanov, a middle-ranking" – he stressed the words –"officer from the KGB would be making such an exorbitant demand."

Romanov stepped forward, picked up the phone by Poskonov's side and held it out to him. "Why don't you ask Leonid Ilyich yourself and save us all a lot of time?" He pushed the phone defiantly towards the banker. Poskonov stared back at him, took the phone and placed it to his ear. Romanov sensed the sort of tension he only felt in the field.

A voice came on the line. "You called, Comrade Chairman?"

"Yes," replied the old man. "Cancel my four o'clock appointment, and see that I am not disturbed until Major Romanov leaves."

"Yes, Comrade Chairman."

Poskonov replaced the phone and, without another word, rose from behind his desk and walked around to Romanov's side. He ushered the young man into a comfortable chair on the far side of the room below a bay window and took the seat opposite him.

"I knew your grandfather," he said in a calm, matter-of-fact tone. "I was a junior commodity clerk when I first met him. I had just left school and he was very kind to me but he was just as impatient as you are. Which was why he was the best fur trader in Russia and thought to be the worst poker player."

Romanov laughed. He had never known his grandfather and the few books that referred to him had long ago been destroyed. His father talked openly of his wealth and position which had only given the authorities ammunition finally to destroy him.

"You'll forgive my curiosity, Major, but if I am to hand over one hundred million dollars in gold I should like to know what it is to be spent on. I thought only the CIA put in chits for those sort of expenses without explanation."

Romanov laughed again and explained to the Chairman how they had discovered the Tsar's icon was a fake and he had been set the task of recovering the original. When he had completed his story he handed over the names of the fourteen banks. The banker studied the list closely while Romanov outlined the course of action he proposed to take, showing how the money would be returned intact as soon as he had located the missing icon.

"But how can one small icon possibly be that important to the State?" Poskonov asked out loud, almost as if Romanov were no longer in the room.

"I have no idea," replied Romanov truthfully and then briefed him on the results of his research.

There was an exasperated grunt from the other chair when Romanov had finished. "May I be permitted to suggest an alternative to your plan?"

"Please do," said Romanov, relieved to be gaining the older man's cooperation.

"Do you smoke?" asked the banker, taking a packet of Dunhill cigarettes from his coat pocket.

"No," said Romanov, his eyebrows lifting slightly at the sight of the red box.

The old man paused as he lit a cigarette. "That suit was not tailored in Moscow either, Major," the banker said, pointing at Romanov with his cigarette. "Now, to business – and do not hesitate to correct me if I have misunderstood any of your requirements. You suspect that lodged in one of these fourteen Swiss banks" – the Chairman tapped the list with his index finger – "is the original Tsar's icon. You therefore want me to deposit large amounts of gold with each bank in the hope that it will give you immediate access to the head of the family, or chairman. You will then offer the chairman the chance to control the entire hundred million if they promise to cooperate with you?"

"Yes," said Romanov. "Bribery is surely something the West has always understood."

"I would have said 'naïve' if I hadn't known your grandfather, though to be fair it was he who ended up making millions of roubles, not me. Nevertheless, how much do you imagine is a lot of money to a major Swiss bank?"

Romanov considered the question. "Ten million, twenty million?"

"To the Moscow Narodny Bank perhaps," said Poskonov. "But every one of the banks you hope to deal with will have several customers with deposits of over a hundred million each."

Romanov was unable to hide his disbelief.

"I confess," continued the chairman, "that our revered General Secretary showed no less incredulity when I informed him of these facts some years ago."

"Then I will need a thousand million?" asked Romanov.

'No, no, no. We must approach the problem from a different standpoint. You do not catch a poacher by offering him rabbit stew."

"But if the Swiss are not moved by the offer of vast amounts of money, what *will* move them?"

"The simple suggestion that their bank has been used for criminal activity," said the chairman.

"But how . . ." began Romanov.

"Let me explain. You say that the Tsar's icon hanging in the Winter Palace is not the original but a copy. A good copy, painted by a twentieth-century court painter, but nevertheless a copy. Therefore why not explain to each of the fourteen banks privately that, after extensive research, we have reason to believe that one of the nation's most valuable treasures has been substituted with a copy and the original is thought to have been deposited in their bank? And rather than cause a diplomatic incident – the one thing every Swiss banker wishes to avoid at any cost – perhaps they would, in the interests of good relationships, consider checking in their vaults items that have not been claimed for over twenty years."

Romanov looked straight at the old man, realising why he had survived several purges. "I owe you an apology, Comrade Poskonov."

"No, no, we each have our own little skills. I am sure I would be as lost in your world as you appear to be in mine. Now, if you will allow me to contact each of the chairmen on this list and tell them no more than the truth – a commodity I am always obliged to trade in although I imagine your counterparts are not so familiar with – namely that I suspect the Tsar's icon is in *their* bank, most of them will be disinclined to hold on to the masterpiece if they believe in so doing a crime has been perpetrated against a sovereign state."

"I cannot overstress the urgency," said Romanov.

"Just like your grandfather," Poskonov repeated. "So be it. If they can be tracked down, I shall speak to every one of them today. At least that's one of the advantages of the rest of the world waking up after us. Be assured I shall be in touch with you the moment I have any news."

"Thank you," said Romanov, rising to leave. "You have been most helpful." He was about to add, as he normally did in such circumstances, I shall so inform my Chairman, but he checked himself, realising the old man wouldn't have given a damn.

The chairman of Gosbank closed the door behind him and walked over to the bay window and watched Romanov run down the steps of the bank to a waiting car. I couldn't have supplied you with the one hundred million in gold bullion at this particular time, even if the General Secretary had ordered me to, he thought to himself. I doubt if I have ten million dollars worth of gold left in the vaults at this moment.

The General Secretary has already ordered me to fly every available ounce to the Bank of New York – so cleverly was his ploy disguised that the CIA had been informed about the deposit within an hour of its arrival. It's hard to hide over 700 million dollars in gold, even in America. I tried to tell him. The chairman watched Romanov's car drive away. Of course if, like your grandfather, you read the *Washington Post* as well as *Pravda*, you would already have known this. He returned to his desk and checked the names of the fourteen banks.

He knew instantly which of the fourteen had to be phoned.

Adam stepped out of Tattersalls Tavern on the corner of Knightsbridge Green and headed past the Hyde Park Hotel towards the Royal Thames Yacht Club. It seemed a strange place for the Foreign Office to hold an interview, but so far everything connected with the application had been somewhat mysterious.

He arrived a few minutes early and asked the ex-Royal Marines sergeant on the door where the interviews were taking place.

"Sixth floor, sir. Take the lift in the corner," he pointed ahead of him, "and announce yourself at reception."

Adam pressed a button and waited for the lift. The doors opened immediately and he stepped in. A rather overweight, bespectacled man of roughly his own age who looked as if he never turned down the third course of any meal followed him at a more leisurely pace. Adam touched the sixth button, but neither man spoke on their journey up to the sixth floor. The large man stepped out of the lift in front of Adam.

"Wainwright's the name," he informed the girl on the reception desk.

"Yes, sir," said the girl, "you're a little early, but do have a seat over there." She gestured towards a chair in the corner, then her eyes moved on to Adam and she smiled.

"Scott," he informed her.

"Yes, sir," she repeated. "Could you join the other gentleman? They will be seeing you next." Adam went over and picked up a copy of *Punch* before settling down next to Wainwright, who was already filling in the *Telegraph* crossword.

Adam soon became bored with flicking through endless issues of *Punch* and took a more careful look at Wainwright. "Do you by any chance speak German?" Adam asked suddenly, turning to face the other interviewee.

"German, French, Italian and Spanish," Wainwright replied, looking up. "I assumed that was how I managed to get this far," he added somewhat smugly.

"Then perhaps you could translate a paragraph from a German letter for me?"

"Delighted, old fellow," said Adam's companion, who proceeded to remove the pair of thick-lensed glasses from his nose, and waited for Adam to extract the middle paragraph of the letter from his envelope.

"Now, let me see," Wainwright said, taking the little slip of paper and replacing the glasses. "Quite a challenge. I say, old fellow, you're not part of the interviewing team by any chance?"

"No, no," said Adam, smiling. "I'm in exactly the same position as you – except I don't speak German, French, Italian or Spanish."

Wainwright seemed to relax. "Now let me see," he repeated, as Adam took out the small notebook from his inside pocket.

" 'During the past year you cannot have failed to . . . notice that I have been receiving from one of the guards a regular, regular . . . regular supply'," he said suddenly, "yes, 'supply of Havana cigars. One of the few pleasures I have been allocated' – no, 'allowed', better still 'permitted' – despite my . . . incarceration'. That's the nearest I can get," Wainwright added. " 'The cigars themselves have also served another purpose'," Wainwright continued, obviously enjoying himself, " 'as they contained tiny capsules . . .' "

"Mr Scott."

"Yes," said Adam, jumping up obediently.

"The Board will see you now," said the receptionist.

"Do you want me to finish it off while they're finishing you off, old chap?" said Wainwright.

"Thank you," Adam replied, "if it's not too much trouble."

"Far easier than the crossword," Wainwright added, leaving on one side the little unfilled half-matrix of squares.

Alex Romanov was not a patient man at the best of times, and with the General Secretary now ringing up his chief twice a day, these were not the best of times.

While he waited for results of the chairman of Gosbank's inquiries he re-read the research papers that had been left on his desk, and checked any new intelligence that had been sent back by his agents in the field. Romanov resented the scraps of information the chairman of Gosbank must have been receiving by the hour, but he made no attempt to pester the old man despite his time problem.

Then the chairman of the bank called.

On this occasion Romanov was driven straight over to the State Bank at Neglinnaya 12 and ushered up to the finely furnished room without a moment's delay. Poskonov, dressed in another of those suits with an even larger check, was standing to greet him at the door.

"You must have wondered if I had forgotten you," were Poskonov's opening words as he ushered Romanov to the comfortable chair. "But I wanted to have some positive news to give you rather than waste your time. You don't smoke, if I remember correctly," he added, taking out his packet of Dunhill cigarettes.

"No, thank you," Romanov said, wondering if the chairman's doctor realised how much the old man smoked.

The chairman's secretary entered the room and placed two empty glasses, a frosted flask and a plate of caviar in front of them.

Romanov waited in silence.

"I have, over the past two days, managed to talk to the chairmen of twelve of the banks on your original list," Poskonov began, as he poured two vodkas, "but I have avoided making contact with the remaining two."

"Avoided?" repeated Romanov.

"Patience, Comrade," said Poskonov, sounding like a benevolent uncle. "You have longer to live than I so if there is any time to be wasted it must be yours."

Romanov lowered his eyes.

"I avoided one of the chairmen," Poskonov continued, "because he is in Mexico showing President Ordaz how not to repay their loan to Chase Manhattan while at the same time borrowing even more dollars from the Bank of America. If he pulls that off I shall have to recommend to the General Secretary of the Party that he is offered my job when I retire. The second gentleman I have avoided because he is officially in Chicago, closing a major Eurobond deal with Continental Illinois, while in fact he is booked in at the St Francis Hotel in San Francisco with his mistress. I feel certain you would agree, Comrade Major, that it would not advance our cause to disturb either of these gentlemen at this precise moment. The first has enough problems to be going on with for the rest of the week, while the second may well have his phone tapped – and we wouldn't want the Americans to discover what we are searching for, would we?"

"Agreed, Comrade," said Romanov.

"Good. Anyway as they both return to Switzerland early next week we have quite enough to be going on with for now."

"Yes, but what –" Romanov began.

"It will please you to know," continued Poskonov, "that of the twelve remaining chairmen all have agreed to cooperate with us and five have already phoned back. Four to say they have run a thorough check on the possessions of customers who have been out of contact with the bank for over twenty years, but have come up with nothing that remotely resembles an icon. In fact, one of them opened a deposit box in the presence of three other directors that had not been touched since 1931 only to discover it contained nothing but a cork from a 1929 bottle of Taylor's port."

"Only a cork?" said Romanov.

"Well, 1929 was a vintage year," admitted the chairman.

"And the fifth?" inquired Romanov.

"Now that, I suspect, may be our first breakthrough," continued

Poskonov, referring to the file in front of him. He adjusted his spectacles with the forefinger of his right hand before continuing. "Herr Dieter Bischoff of Bischoff et Cie" – he looked up at his guest, as if Romanov might have recognised the name – "an honourable man with whom I have dealt many times in the past – honourable, that is, by Western standards of course, Comrade," added the chairman, obviously enjoying himself. "Bischoff has come up with something that was left with the bank in 1938. It is unquestionably an icon, but he has no way of knowing if it is the one we are looking for."

Romanov leapt up from his seat in excitement. "Then I had better go and see for myself," said Romanov. "I could fly out today," he added. The chairman waved him back into his chair.

"The plane you require does not leave Sheremtyevo airport until four thirty-five. In any case, I have already booked two seats on it for you."

"Two?" inquired Romanov.

"You will obviously need an expert to accompany you, unless you know considerably more about icons than you do about banking," Poskonov added. "I also took the liberty of booking you on the Swissair flight. One should never fly Aeroflot if it can be avoided. It has managed only one aviation record consistently every year since its inception, namely that of losing the most passengers per miles flown, and a banker never believes in going against known odds. I have fixed an appointment for you to see Herr Bischoff at ten o'clock tomorrow morning – unless, of course, you have something more pressing to keep you in Moscow, Comrade?"

Romanov smiled.

"I note from your file that you have never served in Switzerland," said the old man, showing off. "So may I also recommend that you stay at the St Gothard while you are in Zurich. Jacques Pontin will take excellent care of you. Nationality has never been a problem for the Swiss, only currency. And so that brings my little investigation up to date, and I shall be in touch again as soon as the two itinerant chairmen return to Switzerland next Monday. All I can do for the moment however, is wish you luck in Zurich."

"Thank you," said Romanov. "May I be permitted to add how much I appreciate your thoroughness."

"My pleasure, Comrade, let's just say that I still owe your grandfather a favour, and perhaps one day you will find you owe me one, and leave it at that."

Romanov tried to fathom the meaning of the old man's words. There was no clue to be found in Poskonov's expression and so he left without another word. But as Romanov walked down the wide marble staircase, he considered the banker's sentiment again and again because throw-away lines were never delivered to an officer of the KGB.

By the time Romanov had returned to Dzerzhinsky Square, his secretary informed him that Herr Bischoff's assistant had telephoned from Zurich to confirm his appointment with the chairman at ten o'clock the following morning. Romanov asked him to call the manager at the St Gothard Hotel and book two rooms. "Oh, and confirm my flight with Swissair," he added before walking up two floors to see the Chairman and brief him on his meeting he had had with the head of the National Bank.

"Thank God for that," were Zaborski's first words. "With only nine days left at least you've given me something to discuss with the General Secretary when he calls at one tomorrow morning."

Romanov smiled.

"Good luck, Comrade. Our Embassy will be alerted to your every need. Let us fervently hope that you will be able to return the masterpiece to the walls of the Winter Palace."

"If it is in that bank, it will be in your hands by tomorrow night," said Romanov, and left the Chairman smiling.

When he walked into his own office he found Petrova waiting for him.

"You called for me, Comrade?"

"Yes, we're going to Zurich." Romanov looked at his watch. "In three hours' time. The flight and the rooms are already booked."

"In the names of Herr and Frau Schmidt, no doubt," said his lover.

CHAPTER SIX

When Adam emerged from the interview he felt quietly confident. The chairman's final words had been to ask him if he would be available for a thorough medical in a week's time. Adam had told them he could think of nothing that would stop him attending. He looked forward to the opportunity of serving in the British Foreign Service.

Back in the waiting room Wainwright looked up and handed him back his piece of paper.

"Thank you very much," said Adam, trying to look casual by slipping it into his inside pocket without looking at the results.

"What was it like, old chap?" his companion asked cautiously.

"No trouble for a man who has German, French, Spanish and Italian as part of his armoury," Adam assured him. "Best of luck, anyway."

"Mr Wainwright," said the secretary, "the Board will see you now."

Adam took the lift to the ground floor and decided to walk home, stopping on the corner of Wilton Place to buy a bag of apples from a barrow boy who seemed to spend most of his time on the lookout for the police. Adam moved on, going over in his mind the Board's questions and his answers – a pointless exercise he decided, although he still felt confident the interview had gone well. He came to such a sudden halt that the pedestrian behind only just stopped himself bumping into Adam. What had attracted his attention was a sign which read: 'The German Food Centre'. An attractive girl with a cheerful smile and laughing eyes was sitting at the cash register by the doorway. Adam strode into the shop and went straight over to her without attempting to purchase a single item.

"You have not bought anything?" she inquired with a slight accent.

"No, I'm just about to," Adam assured her, "but I wondered, do you speak German?"

"Most girls from Mainz do," she replied, grinning.

"Yes, I suppose they would," said Adam, looking at the girl more carefully. She must have been in her early twenties, Adam decided, and he was immediately attracted by her friendly smile and manner. Her shiny, dark hair was done up in a pony tail with a big red bow. Her white sweater and neat pleated skirt would have made any man take a second look. Her slim legs were tucked under the chair. "I wonder if you would be kind enough to translate a short paragraph for me?"

"I try," she said, still smiling.

Adam took the envelope containing the final section of the letter out of his pocket and handed it over to her.

"The style is a bit old-fashioned," she said, looking serious. "It may take a little time."

"I'll go and do some shopping," he told her, and started walking slowly round the long stacked shelves. He selected a little salami, frankfurters, bacon, and some German mustard, looking up now and then to see how the girl was progressing. From what he could make out, she was only able to translate a few words at a time, as she was continually interrupted by customers. Nearly twenty minutes passed before he saw her put the piece of paper on one side. Adam immediately went over to the cash register and placed his purchases on the counter.

"One pound two shillings and sixpence," she said. Adam handed over two pounds and she returned his change and the little piece of paper.

"This I consider a rough translation, but I think the meaning is clear."

"I don't know how to thank you," said Adam, as an elderly woman joined him in the queue.

"You could invite me to share with you your frankfurters," she laughed.

"What a nice idea," said Adam. "Why don't you join me for dinner tonight?"

"I was not serious," she said.

"I was," smiled Adam. Another person joined the queue and the old lady immediately behind him began to look restive.

Adam grabbed a leaflet from the counter, retreated towards the back of the store, and began to scribble down his name, address and phone number. He waited for the two customers in front of him to pay, then handed over to her a 'once in a lifetime' Persil offer.

"What's this?" the girl asked innocently.

"I've put my name and address on the centre page," Adam said. "I will expect you for dinner at about eight this evening. At least you know what's on the menu."

She looked uncertain. "I really was only joking."

"I won't eat you," said Adam. "Only the sausages."

She looked at the leaflet in her hand and laughed. "I'll think about it."

Adam strolled out on to the road whistling. A bad morning, a good afternoon and – perhaps – an even better evening.

He was back at the flat in time to watch the five forty-five news. Mrs Gandhi, the new Prime Minister of India, was facing open revolt in her cabinet and Adam wondered if Britain could ever have a woman Prime Minister. England were 117 for seven in their first innings, with the West Indies still well on top. He groaned and turned off the television. Once he had put the food in the fridge he went into his bedroom to assemble the full text of the Goering letter. After he had read through all the little slips of paper he took out his notepad and began to copy out the translations in order: first, the paragraph supplied by the girl from the YMCA, then Wainwright's handwritten words from the notepad, and finally the section of the letter translated by the lovely girl from Mainz. He read the completed draft through slowly a second time.

NUREMBERG
OCTOBER 15, 1946

DEAR COLONEL,

Over the past year, we have come to know each other quite well. You have never disguised your distaste for the National Socialist party, but you have at all times behaved with the courtesy of an officer and a gentleman.

During the year you cannot have failed to notice that I have been receiving from one of the guards a regular supply of Havana cigars – one of the few pleasures I have been permitted, despite my incarceration. The cigars themselves have also served another purpose, as each one contained a capsule with a small amount of poison. Enough to allow me to survive my trial, while ensuring that I shall cheat the executioner.

My only regret is that you, as the officer in charge of the watch during the period when I am most likely to die, may be held responsible for something to which you were never a party. To make amends for this I enclose a document in the name of one Emmanuel Rosenbaum which should help with any financial difficulties you face in the near future.

All that will be required of you –

"Anyone at home?" shouted Lawrence. Adam folded up the pieces of paper, walked quickly over to the bookcase and inserted them alongside the original letter in the Bible seconds before Lawrence put his head round the door.

"Bloody traffic," said Lawrence cheerfully. "I can't wait to be appointed chairman of the bank and be given that luxury flat on the top floor, not to mention the chauffeur and the company car."

Adam laughed. "Had another hard day at the office, darling?" he mimicked, before joining him in the kitchen. Adam started removing food from the fridge.

"Guess who's coming to dinner," said Lawrence as each new delicacy appeared.

"A rather attractive German girl, I hope," said Adam.

"What do you mean, 'hope'?"

"Well, it could hardly have been described as a formal invitation so I'm not even certain she'll turn up."

"If that's the situation I may as well hang around in case she gives you the elbow and you need someone to help you eat that lot."

"Thanks for the vote of confidence, but I think you'll find it's your turn to be missing, presumed dead. Anyway, what about Carolyn?" said Adam.

"Carolyn was yesterday's girl, to quote the esteemed Harold Wilson. How did you come across your *gnädiges fräulein?*"

"She was serving at a food store in Knightsbridge."

"I see. We're down to shop assistants now."

"I have no idea what she is or even what her name is, come to that," said Adam. "But I am hoping to find out tonight. As I said, your turn to disappear."

"*Natürlich.* As you see, you can rely on me to provide a helping hand if you need anything translated."

"Just put the wine in the fridge and lay the table."

"Are there no serious jobs for a man of my accomplishments to be entrusted with?" chuckled Lawrence.

When eight o'clock chimed, the table was set and Adam had everything ready on the boil. By eight thirty both of them stopped pretending and Adam served up two plates of frankfurters, salami and lettuce with a baked potato and sauerkraut sauce. He then hung up his Goons apron behind the kitchen door and took the chair opposite Lawrence, who had begun pouring the wine.

"Oh, *mein liebes Mädchen*, you look ravishing in that Harris tweed jacket," said Lawrence, raising his glass.

Adam was just about to retaliate with the vegetable spoon when there was a loud knock on the front door. The two men stared at each other before Adam leaped to open it. Standing in the doorway was a man well over six foot with shoulders like a professional bouncer. By his side, dwarfed by him, was the girl that Adam had invited to dinner.

"This is my brother, Jochen," she explained. Adam was immediately struck by how beautiful she looked in a dark blue patterned blouse and pleated blue skirt that fell just below the knee. Her long dark hair, now hanging loose looked as if it had just been washed and shone even under the forty watt light bulb that hung in the hall.

"Welcome," said Adam, more than a little taken aback.

"Jochen is just dropping me off."

"Yes, of course," said Adam. "Do come in and have a drink, Jochen."

"No, I thank you. I have a date as well, but I will pick up Heidi at eleven o'clock, if all right by you?"

"Fine by me," said Adam at last learning her name.

The giant bent down and kissed his sister on both cheeks. He then shook hands with Adam before leaving them both on the doorstep.

"I am sorry to be late," said Heidi. "My brother did not get back from work until after seven."

"It was no problem," said Adam, leading her into the flat. "If you had come any earlier I wouldn't have been ready for you. By the way, this is my flatmate, Lawrence Pemberton."

"In England the men also need a chaperone?" said Heidi.

Both men laughed. "No, no," said Lawrence. "I was just on my way out. Like your brother, I already have a date. As you can see the table is only laid for two. I'll be back around eleven, Adam, just to make sure you're safe." He smiled at Heidi, put on his coat and closed the door behind him before either could object.

"I hope I don't drive him away," said Heidi.

"No, no," said Adam, as she took Lawrence's place at the table. "He's already late for his girlfriend. Charming girl called Carolyn, a social worker." He quickly topped up her wine, pretending it hadn't already been poured.

"So I am going to eat my own sausages, after all," she said, laughing. And the laughter didn't stop for the rest of the evening, as Adam learned about Heidi's life in Germany, her family and the holiday job she had taken while on vacation from Mainz University.

"My parents only allow me to come to England because my brother is already in London; it is to help my languages course. But now, Adam, I would like to know what you are doing when you are not picking up girls in food stores."

"I was in the army for nine years and I'm now hoping to join the Foreign Office."

"In what capacity, if that is the right expression?" Heidi asked.

"It's the right expression, but I'm not sure I know the right answer," said Adam.

"When someone says that about the Foreign Service it usually means they are a spy."

"I don't know what it means, to be honest, but they're going to tell me next week. In any case, I don't think I'd make a very good spy. But what are you going to do when you return to Germany?"

"Complete my final year at Mainz and then I hope to find a job as a television researcher."

"What about Jochen?" asked Adam.

"He will join my father's law practice as soon as he is arriving home."

"So how long will you be in London?" he found himself asking.

"Another two months," she said. "If I can stand the job."

"Why do you carry on with it if it's that bad?"

"There is no better way to test your English than impatient shoppers who speak all different accents."

"I hope you stay the full two months," said Adam.

"So do I," she replied, smiling.

When Jochen arrived back punctually at eleven o'clock, he found Adam and Heidi washing the dishes.

"Thank you for a most interesting evening," she said, wiping her hands.

"Not a good word," reprimanded Jochen. "Not interesting, I think. Lovely, happy, delightful, enjoyable perhaps, but not interesting."

"It was all those things," said Adam, "but it was also interesting." She smiled.

"May I come and buy some more sausages tomorrow?"

"I would like that," said Heidi, "but don't hold up any sour old women this time with translation demands. By the way you never tell me why you needed the strange paragraph translated. I have been wondering who is this Rosenbaum and what it is he left to someone."

"Next time perhaps," said Adam, looking a little embarrassed.

"And next time you can bring my sister home yourself," said Jochen, as he shook Adam's hand firmly.

After Heidi had left, Adam sat down and finished off the last glass of wine, aware that he hadn't spent such a lovely, happy, delightful, enjoyable and interesting evening for a long time.

A black limousine with dark windows and unlit number plates remained parked in the VIP area of Zurich Kloten. Fastidious Swiss policemen had twice gone up to the car and checked the driver's credentials before Major Romanov and Anna Petrova, emerged from the customs hall and took their places in the back of the car.

It was already dark as the driver moved off towards the neon glow of the city. When the car drew up outside the St Gothard Hotel the only words that passed between Romanov and the driver were, "I shall return to Moscow on the Tuesday morning flight."

Jacques Pontin, the manager of the hotel, was stationed at the door waiting to greet the new arrivals; he introduced himself immediately, and as soon as he had checked them both in he banged a little bell with the palm of his hand to summon a porter to assist the guests with their bags. A moment later a young man in his early twenties, dressed in green livery, appeared.

"Suite seventy-three and room seventy-four," Jacques instructed before turning back to Romanov. "I do hope your stay will prove to be worthwhile, Herr Romanov," he said. "Please do not hesitate to call upon me if there is anything you need."

"Thank you," said Romanov as he turned to join the porter who stood sentinel-like by the door of an open lift. Romanov stood to one side to allow Anna to go in first. The lift stopped at the seventh floor and the porter led the way down a long corridor to a corner suite. He turned the key in the lock and invited the two guests to go in ahead of him. The suite was as Romanov had expected, in a different league from the finest hotels he ever experienced in either Moscow or Leningrad. When he saw the array of gadgets in the marble bathroom he reflected that even prosperous travellers to Russia, if seasoned visitors, brought their own bath plugs with them.

"Your room is through there, madam," the porter informed the researcher, and unlocked an adjoining door. Although smaller in size, the room maintained the same unassuming elegance. The porter returned to Romanov, handed him his key and asked if there would be anything else he would require. Romanov assured him there was nothing and passed over a five-franc note.

Once again the porter gave a slight bow, and closing the door behind him, left Romanov to unpack while Anna Petrova went to her own room.

Romanov started to undress and then disappeared into the bath-room. He studied himself in the mirror. Although he was vain about his looks, he was even more vain about the state of his physique. At twenty-nine, despite being six feet, he still only weighed 165 pounds on Western scales, and his muscles remained hard and taut.

By the time Romanov had returned to the bedroom, he could hear the shower beating down in the adjoining bathroom. He crept over to the door and edged it open. He could see quite clearly the outline of Anna standing in the steaming shower. He smiled and noiselessly moved back across the thick carpet, slipped under the sheets and into the researcher's bed. He waited for her to turn off the steaming shower.

Adam stepped out of the freezing shower. Within minutes he was dressed and joined Lawrence in the kitchen for breakfast.

"Still unable to charge you for hot water, am I?" Lawrence said as Adam peered over his flatmate's shoulder, trying to take in the latest Test score.

"Why can't we produce any really fast fast bowlers?" he asked rhetorically.

"Can't stay and chatter to the unemployed," said Lawrence, picking up his briefcase. "Shah of Iran wants to discuss his financial problems with me. Sorry to rush off before you've had your cornflakes but I can't afford to keep His Imperial Majesty waiting."

Left on his own, Adam boiled himself an egg and burned some toast before he turned to the newspaper to learn of the latest casualties in Vietnam and President Johnson's proposed tour of the Far East. At this rate he decided he wasn't going to win the *Daily Mail*'s 'Housewife of the Year' competition. He eventually cleared away in the kitchen, made his bed and tidied up behind Lawrence – nine years of self-discipline wasn't going to change old habits that quickly – then he settled down to plan another day.

He realised he could no longer avoid making a decision. He sat once again at his desk and began to consider how to get the official document translated without arousing further suspicion.

Almost absent-mindedly he removed the Bible from the bookshelf and extracted the letter he had read the night before. The final paragraph still puzzled him. He considered Heidi's translation once again:

All that will be required of you is to present yourself at the address printed on the top right-hand corner of the enclosed document, with some proof that you are Colonel Gerald Scott. A passport should prove sufficient. You will then be given a bequest that I have left to you in the name of Emmanuel Rosenbaum.

I hope it will bring you good fortune.

Adam turned his attention to the document. He was still quite unable to discern what the bequest could possibly be, let alone whether it was of any value. Adam mused over the fact that such an evil man could involve himself in an act of kindness hours before he knew he was going to die – an act that now left him with no choice about his own involvement.

Romanov gathered the blankets together and in one movement hurled them on to the floor to expose Anna curled up like a child, knees almost touching her exposed breasts. Anna's hand groped for a corner of the sheet to cover her naked body.

"Breakfast in bed?" she murmured hopefully.

"Dressed in ten minutes, or no breakfast at all," came back the reply. Anna lowered her feet gingerly on to the thick carpet and waited for the room to stop going round in circles before heading off towards the bathroom. Romanov heard the shower burst forth its jets. "Ahhh," came the pitiful cry. Romanov smiled when he remembered that he had left the indicator locked on dark blue.

During breakfast in the dining room they mulled over the approach he intended to take with the bank if Petrova were able to confirm that the icon was in fact Rublev's original masterpiece. He kept looking up from the table and then suddenly, without warning, said, "Let's go."

"Why?" Anna asked, as she bit into another slice of toast. Romanov rose from the table and without bothering to offer an explanation strode out of the room and headed straight for the lift. Petrova caught up with her master only moments before the lift gate closed. "Why?" she asked again, but Romanov did not speak until they were both back in his suite. He then threw open the large window that overlooked the railway station.

"Ah, it's outside your room," he said, looking to his right, and quickly walked through to the adjoining bedroom. He marched past the dishevelled double bed, jerked open the nearest window, and climbed outside. Petrova stared down from the seventh floor and felt giddy. Once Romanov had reached the bottom rung of the fire escape, he ran to a passing tram. Petrova would never have made it if she hadn't been lifted bodily on to the tram by Romanov's sheer strength.

"What's going on?" she asked, still puzzled.

"I can't be sure," said Romanov, looking out of the back of the tram. "All I do know for certain is what the local CIA agent looks like."

The researcher looked back in the direction of the hotel, but all she could see was a mass of anonymous people walking up and down the pavement.

Romanov remained on the tram for about a mile before he jumped off and hailed a passing taxi going in the opposite direction.

"Bischoff et Cie," he said as he waited for his puffing assistant to join him.

The cab headed back in the direction of the hotel, winding in and out of the morning traffic, until it came to a halt in front of a large brown granite building that filled the entire block. Romanov paid off the driver and stood in front of imposing doors made of thick glass and covered in wrought iron welded to look like the branches of a tree. By the side of the doors, carved inconspicuously into the stone and inlaid with gilt, were the words 'Bischoff et Cie'. There was no other clue as to what kind of establishment lay within.

Romanov turned the heavy wrought-iron knob and the two Russians stepped into a spacious hall. On the left-hand side of the hall stood a solitary desk behind which a smartly dressed young man was seated.

"*Guten morgen, mein Herr,*" he said.

"Good morning," said Romanov. "We have an appointment with Herr Dieter Bischoff."

"Yes, Herr Romanov," said the receptionist checking the list of names in front of him. "Will you please take the lift to the fifth floor where you will be met by Herr Bischoff's secretary." When the two of them stepped out of the lift they were greeted by a lady in a neat plain suit. "Will you please follow me," she said, without any trace of accent. The two Russians were escorted along a picture-lined corridor to a comfortable room which more resembled the reception room of a country house than a bank.

"Herr Bischoff will be with you in a moment," the lady said, withdrawing. Romanov remained standing while he took in the room. Three black-and-white framed photographs of sombre old men in grey suits, trying to look like sombre old men in grey suits, took up most of the far wall, while on the other walls were discreet but pleasant oils of town and country scenes of nineteenth-century Switzerland. A magnificent oval Louis XIV table with eight carved mahogany chairs surrounding it dominated the centre of the room. Romanov felt a twinge of envy at the thought that he could never hope to live in such style.

The door opened and a man in his mid-sixties, followed by three other men in dark grey suits, entered the room. One look at Herr Bischoff and Romanov knew whose photograph would eventually join that of the other three grey, sombre men.

"What an honour for our little bank, Mr Romanov," were Bischoff's first words as he bowed and shook the Russian by the hand. Romanov nodded and introduced his assistant, who received the same courteous bow and handshake. "May I in turn present my son and two of my partners, Herr Muller and Herr Weizkopf." The three men bowed in unison, but remained standing while Bischoff took his seat at the head of the table.

At his gesture both Romanov and Anna sat down beside him.

"I wonder if I might be permitted to check your passport?" asked Bischoff, as if to show that the formal business had begun. Romanov took out the little blue passport with a soft cover from his inside pocket and handed it over. Bischoff studied it closely, as a philatelist might check an old stamp, and decided it was mint. "Thank you," he said, as he returned it to its owner.

Bischoff then raised his hand and one of the partners immediately left them. "It will only take a moment for my son to fetch the icon we have in safe-keeping," he confided "Meanwhile perhaps a little coffee – Russian," he added.

Coffee appeared within moments borne by yet another smartly dressed lady.

"Thank you," said Petrova, clearly a little overawed, but Romanov didn't speak again until Herr Bischoff's son reappeard with a small box and handed it over to his father.

"You will understand that I have to treat this matter with the utmost delicacy," the old man confided. "The icon may not turn out to be the one your Government is searching for."

"I understand," said Romanov.

"This magnificent example of Russian art has been in our possession since 1938, and was deposited with the bank on behalf of a Mr Emmanuel Rosenbaum."

Both visitors looked shocked.

"*Nevozmozhno*," said Anna, turning to her master. "He would never . . ."

"I suspect that's exactly why the name was chosen in the first place," Romanov said curtly to Anna, annoyed at her indiscretion. "Can't you see? It makes perfect sense. May I see the icon now?" said Romanov, turning back to the bank's Chairman.

Herr Bischoff placed the box in the centre of the table. The three men in grey suits each took a pace forward. Romanov looked up. "Under Swiss law we must have three witnesses when opening a box in someone else's name," explained the old man.

Romanov nodded curtly.

Herr Bischoff proceeded to unlock the metal box with a key he produced from his pocket, while his son leaned over and undid a second lock with a different key. The little ceremony completed, Herr Bischoff pushed up the lid of the box and turned it round to face his guests. Romanov placed his hands into the box like an expectant child does with a Christmas stocking, and drew out the icon. He stared at the beautiful painting. A small wooden rectangle that was covered in tiny pieces of red, gold and blue making up the mosaic of a man who looked as if he had all the worries of the world on his shoulders. The face although sad, still evoked a feeling of serenity. The painting Romanov held in his hand was quite magnificent, as fine as any he had seen at the Winter Palace. No one in the room was quite sure what would happen next as Romanov offered no opinion.

It was Anna who finally spoke.

"A masterpiece it is," she said, "and undoubtedly fifteenth century but as you can see it's not St George and the Dragon."

Romanov nodded his agreement, still unable to let go of the little painting. "But do you know the origin of this particular icon?" Romanov asked.

"Yes," Anna replied, glad to be appreciated for the first time. "It is the Icon of St Peter, you see he holds the keys . . . painted by Dionisiy in 1471, and although it is undoubtedly one of the finest examples of his work, it is not the Tsar's icon."

"But does it belong to the Russian people?" asked Romanov, still hopeful of some reward for all his trouble.

"No, Comrade Major," said the researcher emphatically. "It belongs to the Munich Gallery, from where it has been missing since the day Hitler was appointed Reichs Chancellor."

Herr Bischoff scribbled a note on a piece of paper in front of him. At least one bank in Munich was going to be happy to do business with him in the future.

Romanov reluctantly handed back the icon to Herr Bischoff, only just managing to say, "Thank you."

"Not at all," said Herr Bischoff imperturbably, replacing the icon in the box and turning his key in his lock. His son completed the same routine with his own key and then departed with the unclaimed treasure. Romanov rose, as he considered nothing more could be gained from the meeting – although he believed he had discovered Goering's alias, or one of them.

"I wonder if I might be permitted to have a word with you in private, Herr Romanov," asked the elderly banker.

"Of course."

"It is rather a delicate matter I wish to put to you," said Herr Bischoff, "so I thought you might prefer your associate to leave us."

"That won't be necessary," said Romanov, unable to think of anything Bischoff might have to say that he wouldn't later need to discuss with Petrova.

"As you wish," said Bischoff. "I am curious to discover if there was any other reason behind your request to see me."

"I don't understand what you mean," said Romanov.

"I felt perhaps I knew the real reason you had selected this bank in particular to start your inquiry."

"I didn't select you," said Romanov. "You were only one of –" he stopped himself.

"I see," said Bischoff, himself now looking somewhat bemused. "Then may I be permitted to ask you a few questions?"

"Yes, if you must," said Romanov, now impatient to get away.

"You are Alexander Petrovich Romanov?"

"You must already believe that or we would not have proceeded this far."

"The only son of Peter Nicholevich Romanov?"

"Yes."

"And grandson of Count Nicholai Alexandrovich Romanov?"

"Is this to be a history lesson on my family tree?" asked Romanov, visibly irritated.

"No, I just wanted to be sure of my facts as I am even more convinced it would be wise for your associate to leave us for a moment," the old man suggested diffidently.

"Certainly not," said Romanov. "In the Soviet Union we are all equal," he added pompously.

"Yes, of course," said Bischoff, glancing quickly at Anna before continuing. "Did your father die in 1946?"

"Yes. He did," said Romanov, beginning to feel distinctly uncomfortable.

"And you are the only surviving child?"

"I am," confirmed Romanov proudly.

"In which case this bank is in possession . . ." Bischoff hesitated as a file was put in front of him by one of the men in grey. He placed a pair of gold, half-moon spectacles on his nose, taking as long as he could over the little exercise.

"Don't say anything more," said Romanov quietly.

Bischoff looked up. "I'm sorry, but I was given every reason to believe your visit had been planned."

Petrova was now sitting on the edge of her seat, enjoying every moment of the unfolding drama. She had already anticipated exactly what was going to happen and was disappointed when Romanov turned to speak to her.

"You will wait outside," was all he said. Petrova pouted and rose reluctantly to leave them, closing the door behind her.

Bischoff waited until he was certain the door was closed, then slid the file across the table. Romanov opened it gingerly. On the top of the first page was his grandfather's name underlined three times. Below the name were printed row upon row of incomprehensible figures.

"I think you will find that we have carried out your grandfather's instructions in maintaining a conservative portfolio of investments with his funds." Bischoff leaned across and pointed to a figure showing that the bank had achieved an average increase of 6·7 per cent per annum over the previous forty-nine years.

"What does this figure at the foot of the page represent?" asked Romanov.

"The total value of your stocks, bonds and cash at nine o'clock this morning. It has been updated every Monday since your grandfather opened an account with this bank in 1916." The old man looked up proudly at the three pictures on the wall.

"*Bozhe Moi*," said Romanov, as he took in the final figure. "But what currency is it in?"

"Your grandfather only showed faith in the English pound," said

Herr Bischoff.

"*Bozhe Moi*," Romanov repeated.

"May I presume from your comment that you are not displeased with our stewardship?"

Romanov was speechless.

"It may also interest you to know that we are in possession of several boxes, the contents of which we have no knowledge. Your father also visited us on one occasion soon after the war. He appeared satisfied and assured me that he would return, but we never heard from him again. We were saddened to learn of his death. You might also prefer in the circumstances to return and investigate the boxes at another time," the banker continued.

"Yes," said Romanov quietly. "Perhaps I could come back this afternoon?"

"The bank will always be at your service, Your Excellency," replied Herr Bischoff.

No one had addressed a Romanov by his title since the Revolution. He sat in silence for some time.

Eventually he rose and shook hands with Herr Bischoff. "I will return this afternoon," he repeated before joining his companion in the corridor.

Neither uttered a word until they were back on the street outside the bank. Romanov was still so overcome by what he had learned that he failed to notice that the man he had so deftly avoided at the hotel was now standing in a tram queue on the far side of the road.

CHAPTER SEVEN

The pastor sat at the table studying the document but didn't offer an opinion for some considerable time. When he had heard Adam's request he had invited the young man into the privacy of his little office at the back of the German Lutheran Church.

It turned out to be a stark room dominated by a wooden table and several wooden chairs that didn't match. A small black crucifix was the only ornament on the blank whitewashed walls. Two of the unmatching chairs were now occupied by Adam and the pastor. Adam sat bolt upright while the man of God, clad from head to toe in a black cassock, elbows on the table and head in hands, stared down at the copy of the document.

After some considerable time, without raising his eyes he offered, "This is a receipt, if I am not mistaken. Although I have little knowledge of such things, I am fairly confident that Roget et Cie, who must be Swiss bankers based in Geneva, have in their possession an object described herein as 'The Tsar's Icon'. If I remember my history correctly, the original can be viewed somewhere in Moscow. It appears," he continued, his eyes still fixed on the document, "that if the holder of this receipt presents himself in Geneva he will be able to claim the aforementioned icon of St George and the Dragon, deposited there by a Mr Emmanuel Rosenbaum. I confess," said the pastor, looking up for the first time, "that I've never seen anything like it before." He folded up the copy of the document and handed it back to Adam.

"Thank you," said Adam. "That has been most helpful."

"I am only sorry that my superior the Bishop is away on his annual retreat because I feel sure he would have been able to throw more light on the matter than I have."

"You have told me everything I need to know," said Adam, but couldn't resist asking, "Are icons at all valuable?"

"Once again, I must confess that I am not the best man from whom to seek such an opinion. All I can tell you is that, as with all art, the value of any object can vary from one extreme to the other without any satisfactory explanation to us normal mortals."

"Then there is no way of knowing the value of this particular icon?" asked Adam.

"I wouldn't venture an opinion, but no doubt the art auctioneers Sotheby's or Christie's might be willing to do so. After all, they claim in their advertisements that they have an expert in every field waiting to advise you."

"Then I shall put their claim to the test," said Adam, "and pay them a visit." Adam rose from his chair, shook hands with the pastor and said, "You have been most kind."

"Not at all," said the pastor. "I was only too pleased to assist you. It makes a change from Frau Gerber's marital problems and the size of the churchwarden's marrows."

Adam took a bus up to Hyde Park Corner and jumped off as it turned left into Knightsbridge. He walked through the subway and continued briskly down Piccadilly towards the Ritz. He had read somewhere that Sotheby's was in Bond Street, although he couldn't remember having ever seen it.

He walked another hundred yards before turning left, where he shortened his stride to check all the signs on both sides of the road. He passed Gucci's, Cartier's, Asprey's and was beginning to wonder if his memory had failed him and whether he should check in the telephone directory. He continued on past the Irish Tourist Board and Celines before he finally spotted the gold lettering above a little newspaper kiosk on the far side of the road.

He crossed the one-way street and entered the front door by the side of the kiosk. He felt like a boy on his first day at a new school, unsure of his surroundings and not certain to whom he should turn for advice. Most of the people who passed him went straight up the stairs and he was just about to follow them when he heard a voice say, "Up the stairs and straight through, madam. The auction is due to start in a few minutes."

Adam turned and saw a man in a long, green coat. The name 'Sotheby' was embroidered over his left-hand pocket.

"Where do I go if I want something valued?" Adam asked.

"Straight along the passage, sir, as far as you can go and you'll see a girl on the left-hand side in reception," barked his informant. Adam thanked him presuming that the guide's former place of work could only have been on an Aldershot drill square . . . He walked along to the reception area. An old lady was explaining to one of the girls behind the counter that her grandmother had left the vase to her several years before and she wondered what it might be worth.

The girl only glanced at the heirloom before asking, "Can you come back in about fifteen minutes? By then our Mr Makepeace will have had time to look at it and will be able to give you an estimate."

"Thank you, my dear," said the old lady expectantly. The girl picked up the large ornate vase and carried it to a room in the back. She returned a few moments later to be faced with Adam.

"May I help you, sir?"

"I'm not sure," began Adam. "I need some advice concerning an icon."

"Have you brought the piece with you, sir?"

"No, it's still abroad at the moment."

"Do you have any details?"

"Details?"

"Artist's name, date, size. Or better still do you have a photograph of the piece?"

"No," said Adam sheepishly. "I only know its title but I do have some documentation," he added, handing over the receipt he had shown the pastor.

"Not a lot to go on," said the girl, studying the German transcript. "But I'll ask Mr Sedgwick, the head of our Russian and Greek Icon department, if he can help you."

"Thank you," said Adam, as the girl picked up the phone.

"Is Mr Sedgwick able to advise a customer?" the girl inquired. She listened for a moment then replaced the phone.

"Mr Sedgwick will be down in a few moments, if you would care to wait."

"Certainly," said Adam, feeling somewhat of a fraud. While the girl attended to the next customer Adam waited for Mr Sedgwick and studied the pictures on the wall. There were several photos of items that had come under the auctioneer's hammer in recent sales. A large painting by Picasso called 'Trois Baigneuses' had been sold for fourteen thousand pounds. As far as Adam could make out the brightly coloured oil was of three women on a beach dancing. He felt confident they were women because they had breasts even if they weren't in the middle of their chests. Next to the Picasso was a Degas of a girl at a ballet lesson; this time there was no doubt it was a girl. But the painting that most caught Adam's eye was a large oil by an artist he had never heard of called Jackson Pollock that had come under the hammer for eleven thousand pounds. Adam wondered what sort of people could afford to spend such sums on works of art.

"Wonderful example of the artist's brushwork," said a voice behind him. Adam turned to face a tall, cadaverous figure with a ginger moustache and thinning red hair. His suit hung on him as if from a coathanger. "My name is Sedgwick," he announced in a donnish voice.

"Scott," said Adam, offering his hand.

"Well, Mr Scott, why don't we sit over here and then you can let me know how I can help you."

"I'm not sure you can," admitted Adam, taking the seat opposite him. "It's just that I have been left an icon in a will and I was hoping it might turn out to be valuable."

"A good start," said Sedgwick, unfolding a pair of spectacles which he had removed from his top pocket.

"It may not be," said Adam, "because I know nothing about paintings and I wouldn't want to waste your time."

"You won't be wasting my time," Sedgwick assured Adam. "We sell many items for less than ten pounds, you know." Adam hadn't known and Sedgwick's gentle voice made him feel less apprehensive. "Now am I to understand you do not have a photograph of this particular icon?"

"That's right," said Adam. "The icon is still abroad, and to be honest I've never laid eyes on it."

"I see," said Sedgwick, folding up his glasses. "But can you tell me anything of its provenance?"

"A little. It is known as 'The Tsar's Icon' and the subject is St George and the Dragon."

"How strange," said Sedgwick. "Someone else was inquiring after that particular painting only last week but he wouldn't leave his name."

"Someone else wanted to know about the Tsar's Icon?" said Adam.

"Yes, a Russian gentleman, if I wasn't mistaken." Sedgwick tapped his glasses on his knee. "I checked on it extensively for him but found little that wasn't already well documented. The man wondered if it had ever passed through our hands, or even if we had heard of it. I was able to explain to him that the great work by Rublev remains in the Winter Palace for all to see. One can always be certain that it's an original from the Winter Palace because the Tsar's silver crown will be embedded in the back of the frame. Since the fourteenth century many copies of Rublev's masterpiece have been made and they vary greatly in quality and value; but the one he seemed interested in was a copy made for Tsar Nicholas by a court painter circa 1914. I was unable to find any trace of such an icon in any of the standard works on the subject. Do you have any documentation on your icon?" Sedgwick inquired.

"Not a lot," said Adam. "Although I do have a copy of the receipt that was left to me in the will," he added, and handed it over.

Mr Sedgwick once again unfolded his glasses before studying the paper for several moments. "Excellent, quite excellent," he said eventually. "It seems to me that, as long as Roget et Cie will release it, a copy of the Tsar's icon painted by the court painter of the time, belongs to you. But you will have to go and pick it up yourself, that's for certain."

"But is it worth all that trouble?" asked Adam. "Can you give me any idea of its value?"

"Hard to be precise without actually seeing it," Sedgwick said returning the document.

"So what is the lowest figure I might expect to get for it?"

The older man frowned. "Ten," he said, after considerable thought. "Perhaps fifteen, but with an absolute top of twenty."

"Twenty pounds," said Adam, unable to hide his disappointment. "I'm sorry to have wasted your time, Mr Sedgwick."

"No, no, no, Mr Scott, you misunderstand me. I meant twenty *thousand* pounds."

CHAPTER EIGHT

"A little more caviar, Comrade?" inquired Petrova across the lunch table.

Romanov frowned. His pretence at 'strictly confidential information' only to be passed on at the highest level had merely elicited a knowing smile from his companion who was also not inclined to believe that her boss had a pressing appointment at the Consulate that afternoon, an appointment that he had forgotten to mention to her before.

Anna held out a spoon brimming with caviar and pushed it towards Romanov as if she was trying to feed a reluctant baby.

"Thank you – *no*," said Romanov firmly.

"Suit yourself," said the young woman before it disappeared down her own throat. Romanov called for the bill. When he was presented with the slip of paper he couldn't help thinking that for that price he could have fed a Russian family for a month. He paid without comment.

"I'll see you back in the hotel later," he said curtly.

"Of course," said Petrova, still lingering over her coffee. "What time shall I expect you?"

Romanov frowned again. "Not before seven," he replied.

"And do you have any plans for me this afternoon, Comrade Major?"

"You may do as you please," said Romanov, and left the table without further word. Once on the street, he set off in the opposite direction to the bank, but he doubted if he had fooled the researcher, who was still eyeing him suspiciously through the restaurant window; or the agent, who had waited patiently on the far side of the road for nearly two hours.

By three o'clock Romanov was once again seated in the private room on the fifth floor looked down on by the three photographs of the Herr Bischoffs, and with the fourth Herr Bischoff sitting opposite him and the fifth Herr Bischoff standing behind him.

"We are in possession of . . ." began Herr Bischoff, in the same deliberate, formal way that had dictated the pace of the morning session, ". . . five boxes which have remained unopened since your father visited us in 1945." Romanov was unable to hide his surprise at the mention of his father but decided not to ask the banker for any details of his visit. "Should it be your desire to inspect the contents . . ."

"Why else would I have returned?" asked Romanov, already made impatient by the measured voice and studied ritual.

"Indeed," said Herr Bischoff, seemingly unaware of any discourtesy. "Then all we now require is that you sign a disclaimer in order to legalise the situation under Swiss law." Romanov looked apprehensive. "It is only a formality." The Russian still didn't speak. "You can rest assured, Your Excellency, that you are not the only one of your countrymen who from time to time sits in that chair."

Herr Bischoff slid a sheet of paper across the table. There were over twenty clauses of German, all in small print. Romanov scrawled his signature between the two X's with the proffered gold pen. He made no attempt to discover what he was signing. If they hadn't stolen his grandfather's heritage already, why should they be bothering to try now, he considered.

"Perhaps you will be kind enough to accompany me," said Herr Bischoff, quickly passing the sheet of paper to his son who left immediately. He rose and led Romanov silently back to the corridor. But on this occasion they travelled down in the chairman's private lift all the way to the basement.

When the doors opened Romanov might have thought they had entered a jail had the bars not been made of highly polished steel. A man who was seated behind a desk on the far side of the bars jumped up the moment he saw the chairman and turned the lock on the steel door with a long-shafted key. Romanov followed Herr Bischoff through the open door then waited until they were both locked inside. The guard preceded them down a corridor, not unlike that of a wine cellar with temperature and humidity gauges every few yards. The light was barely bright enough to ensure that they did not lose their footing. At the end of the corridor, they found Herr Bischoff's son waiting in front of a vast circular steel door. The old man nodded and the younger Herr Bischoff placed a key in a lock and turned it. Then the chairman stepped forward and undid a second lock. Father and son pushed open the nine inch thick door but neither made any attempt to enter the vault.

"You are in possession of five boxes. Numbers 1721, 1722, 1723, 1724 . . ."

"And 1725, no doubt," interrupted Romanov.

"Precisely," said Herr Bischoff, as he removed a small package from his pocket and added, "This is your envelope and the key inside it will open all five boxes." Romanov took the envelope and turned towards the open cavern. "But we must open the bank's lock first before you proceed," said Herr Bischoff. "Will you be kind enough to follow us?" Romanov nodded and both Herr Bischoffs proceeded into the vault. Romanov ducked his head and stepped in after them. Young Mr Bischoff opened the upper lock of the five boxes, three small ones above two large ones, making a perfect cube. "Once we have left, Your Excellency," said the old man, "we shall pull the door closed, and when you require it to be opened you have only to press the red button on the side wall to alert us. But I must warn you that at six o'clock the vault locks itself automatically and it cannot be reopened until nine the following morning. However, a warning alarm will sound at five forty-five." Romanov checked the clock on the wall: three seventeen. He couldn't believe he would need over two hours to find out what was in the five boxes. The two Herr Bischoffs bowed and left.

Romanov waited impatiently for the vast door to close behind him. Once alone in the Aladdin's cave he looked around the room and estimated there must have been two or three thousand boxes filling the four walls, giving them the appearance of a library of safes. He suspected there was more private wealth in that one vault than most countries on earth could call on. He checked the numbers of his own boxes and stood waiting like an orphan who has been told there will be second helpings.

He decided to start with one of the small boxes. He turned the key and heard the lock click before pulling out the stiff drawer to discover it was full of papers. He flicked through them to find they were title deeds to many large tracts of land in Bohemia and Bulgaria – once worth millions, now controlled by the Socialist State. As he checked each document, the old saying 'not worth the paper they were written on' sprang to mind. Romanov moved to the second box which he discovered contained the bond certificates of companies once managed by His Excellency Count Nicholai Alexandrovich Romanov. The last time they had declared a profit was in 1914. He cursed the system he had been born under as he moved on to the third box which contained only one document, his grandfather's will. It took only moments to discover that it had all been left to his father and therefore he was the lawful owner of everything – and nothing.

Dismayed, Romanov knelt down to study the two larger boxes, both of which looked big enough to hold a cello. He hesitated before placing his key in the lock, turning it and pulling out the vast container.

He stared down in anticipation.

It was empty. He could only presume that it had been that way for over fifty years unless his father had removed everything and there was no reason to believe that. He quickly unlocked the fifth box and in desperation pulled it open.

The box was split into twelve equal compartments. He raised the lid of the first compartment and stared down in disbelief. Before him lay precious stones of such size, variety and colour that would have made anyone who was not royal gasp. Gingerly he lifted the lid off the second compartment, to find it contained pearls of such quality that one single string of them would have transformed a plain girl into a society beauty. As he opened the third box his amazement did not lessen and he understood for the first time why his grandfather had been considered one of the most enterprising merchants of the century. And now it all belonged to Alex Romanov, an impecunious Government official who was already wondering how he could possibly enjoy such riches.

It took Romanov a further hour to go through the contents of the remaining nine compartments. When he reached the last one – almost an anti-climax, in that it contained nothing but gold coins – he felt thoroughly exhausted. He checked the clock on the wall: five thirty. He began to replace the lids on each of the compartments, but during the treasure hunt he had come across one object of such magnificence that he could not resist removing it. He paused as he held up the long heavy gold chain weighted by a medallion, also made of solid gold, that hung from it. On one side was an engraved picture of his grandfather – Count Nicholai Alexandrovich Romanov, a proud, handsome man – while on the other was a profile of his grandmother, so beautiful that she surely could have worn any of the jewellery in that treasure trove with distinction.

For some time, Romanov held the chain in his hand before finally placing it over his head and letting the medallion fall from his neck. He gave the piece one last look before tucking it under his shirt. When he had replaced the lid on the last compartment he slid the box back into place and locked it.

For the second time that day Romanov's thoughts returned to his father and the decision he must have made when faced with such a fortune. He had gone back to Russia with his secret. Had he planned to rescue Alex from the life of drudgery that was all he could look forward to? His father had always assured him that he had an exciting future but there were secrets he was too young to share and he, in turn, had passed that information on to the authorities. His reward a place at the Komsomol. But his father must have taken that secret to the grave because Alex would never have learned of the fortune if it had not been for Poskonov.

His mind turned to the old banker. Had he known all along or was it just a coincidence that he had been sent by Poskonov to this bank first? Members of his chosen profession didn't survive if they believed in coincidence.

A false move and the State would not hesitate to send him to the same grave as his father and grandfather. He would have to be at his most skilful when he next came into contact with the old banker, otherwise he might not live to choose between power in his homeland or wealth in the West.

"After I have found the Tsar's icon I will make my decision," he said, quite audibly. He turned suddenly as the alarm bell's piercing sound rang out. He checked the clock and was surprised by how much time he had spent in the locked room. He walked towards the vault door and on reaching it pressed the red button without looking back. The great door swung open to reveal two anxious-looking Herr Bischoffs. The son stepped quickly into the vault, walked over to the five boxes and made safe the bank's locks.

"We were beginning to get quite worried about the time," said the old man. "I do hope you found everything to your satisfaction."

"Entirely," said Romanov. "But what happens if I am unable to return for some considerable time?"

"It's of no importance," Herr Bischoff replied. "The boxes will not be touched again until you come back, and as they are all hermetically sealed your possessions will remain in perfect condition."

"What temperature are the boxes kept at?"

"Fifty degrees fahrenheit," said Herr Bischoff, somewhat puzzled by the question.

"Are they airtight?"

"Certainly," replied the banker. "And watertight, not that the basement has ever been flooded," he added quite seriously.

"So anything left in them is totally safe from any investigation?"

"You are only the third person to look inside those boxes in fifty years," came back the firm response.

"Excellent," said Romanov, looking down at Herr Bischoff. "Because there is just a possibility that I shall want to return tomorrow morning, with a package of my own to deposit."

"Can you put me through to Mr Pemberton, please?" said Adam.

There was a long pause. "We don't have a Mr Pemberton working here, sir."

"That is Barclays International in the City, isn't it?"

"Yes, sir."

"Mr Lawrence Pemberton. I feel certain I've got the right branch."

The silence was even longer this time. "Ah, yes," came back the eventual reply. "Now I see which department he works in. I'll find out if he's in." Adam heard the phone ringing in the background.

"He doesn't seem to be at his desk at the moment, sir, would you like to leave a message?"

"No thank you," said Adam, and replaced the receiver. He sat alone thinking, not bothering to switch on the light as it grew darker. If he was to carry through the idea he still needed some information which Lawrence as a banker should find easy to supply.

A key turned in the door and Adam watched Lawrence enter and switch the light on. He looked startled when he saw Adam seated in front of him.

"How does one open a Swiss bank account?" were Adam's first words.

"I can't imagine one would find it that easy if all you have to offer is next week's unemployment cheque," said Lawrence. "Mind you, they usually keep a code name for English customers," he added, as he put his copy of the *Evening News* on the table. "Yours could be 'pauper'."

"It may surprise you to learn that it was a serious question," said Adam.

"Well," said Lawrence, taking the question seriously, "in truth, anyone can open a Swiss bank account as long as they have a worthwhile sum to deposit. And by worthwhile I mean at least ten thousand pounds."

"Yes, but how would you go about getting the money out?"

"That can be done over the phone or in person, and in that way Swiss banks don't differ greatly from any bank in England. Few customers, however, would risk the phone, unless they're resident in a country where there are no tax laws to break. In which case why would they need the gnomes of Zurich in the first place?"

"What happens when a customer dies and the bank can't be sure who the rightful owner of the assets is?"

"They would do nothing but a claimant would have to prove that they were the person entitled to inherit any deposits the bank held. That's not a problem if you're in possession of the correct documentation such as a will and proof of identity. We deal with such matters every day."

"But you just admitted that it's illegal!"

"Not for those clients resident overseas, or when it becomes necessary to balance our gold deposits, not to mention the bank's books. But the Bank of England keeps a strict watch over every penny that goes in and out of the country."

"So, if I were entitled to a million pounds worth of gold left to me by an Argentinian uncle deposited in a Swiss bank, and I was in possession of the right legal documents to prove I was the beneficiary, all I would have to do is go and claim it?"

"Nothing to stop you," said Lawrence. "Although under the law as it currently stands, you would have to bring it back to this country, and sell the gold to the Bank of England for the sum they deemed correct, and then pay death duty on that sum." Adam remained silent. "If you do have an Argentinian uncle who has left you all that gold in Switzerland, your best bet would be to leave it where it is. Under this Government, if you fulfilled the letter of the law, you would end up with about seven and a half per cent of its true value."

"Pity I haven't got an Argentinian uncle," said Adam.

"He doesn't have to be Argentinian," said Lawrence, watching his friend's every reaction closely.

"Thanks for the information," said Adam and disappeared into the bedroom.

The last pieces of the jigsaw were beginning to fit into place. He was in possession of Roget's receipt of the icon originally meant for his father; all he needed now was a copy of the will to show that the document had been left to him. He could then prove that he was the owner of a worthless or priceless – he still had no way of being sure which – copy of the Tsar's icon. He lay awake that night recalling the word in his father's letter. "If there is anything to be gained from the contents of this envelope I make only one request of you, namely that your mother should be the first to benefit from it without ever being told how such good fortune came about."

When Romanov returned to the hotel, via the Russian Consulate, he found Petrova in her room dressed in jeans and a bright pink jersey, sitting in a corner reading, her legs dangling over the side of the chair.

"I hope you had a fruitful afternoon?" he inquired, politely.

"I certainly did," Anna replied. "The galleries in Zurich are well worthy of a visit. But tell me about *your* afternoon. Did it also turn out to be fruitful?"

"It was a revelation, my little one, nothing less. Why don't we have a quiet supper in my room so I can tell you all about it while we celebrate in style?"

"What a magnificent idea," said the researcher. "And may I be responsible for ordering dinner?"

"Certainly," said Romanov.

Petrova dropped her book on the floor and began to concentrate on the extensive *à la carte* menu that had been left by Romanov's bedside table. She spent a considerable time selecting each dish for their banquet and even Romanov was impressed when it finally appeared.

Anna had chosen as an entrée gravad laks edged with dill sauce. Accompanying it was a half-bottle of Premier Cru Chablis 1958. Between mouthfuls Romanov told her of the contents of his family inheritance and as he described each new treasure the researcher's eyes grew larger and larger.

Romanov's monologue was only once interrupted, by a waiter who wheeled in a trolley on which sat a silver salver. The waiter lifted the salver to reveal a rack of lamb surrounded by courgettes and tiny new potatoes. To accompany this particular dish, the hotel had provided a Gevrey Chambertin.

The final course, a fluffy raspberry soufflé, required in the researcher's view only the finest Chateau Yquem. She had selected the 'fortynine, which only made her lapse into singing Russian folk songs which Romanov felt, given the circumstances, was somewhat inappropriate.

As she drained the last drop of wine in her glass Petrova rose and, slightly unsteady, said "To Alex, the man I love."

Romanov nodded his acknowledgment and suggested it might be time for them to go to bed, as they had to catch the first flight back to Moscow the following morning. He wheeled the trolley out into the corridor and placed a 'Do not disturb' sign over the door knob.

"A memorable evening," smiled the researcher, as she flicked off her shoes. Romanov stopped to admire her as she began to remove her clothes, but when he unbuttoned his shirt, the researcher stopped undressing and let out a gasp of surprise.

"It's magnificent," she said in awe. Romanov held up the gold medallion. "A bauble compared with the treasures I left behind," he assured her.

"Comrade lover," Anna said in a childlike voice, pulling him towards the bed, "you realise how much I adore, admire and respect you?"

"Um," said Romanov.

"And you also know," she continued, "that I have never asked you for any favour in the past."

"But I have a feeling you are about to now," said Romanov as she lifted back the sheet.

"Only that if the gold chain is nothing more than a mere bauble, perhaps you might allow me to wear it occasionally?"

"Occasionally?" said Romanov, staring into Anna's eyes. "Why occasionally? Why not permanently, my darling?" and without another word he removed the gold chain from around his neck and placed it over the young girl's head. Anna sighed as she fingered the thick gold rings that made up the chain that Romanov didn't let go of.

"You're hurting me, Alex," she said with a little laugh. "Please let go." But Romanov only pulled the chain a little tighter. Tears began to run down her cheeks as the metal began to bite into her skin.

"I can't breathe properly," gasped the researcher. "Please stop teasing." But Romanov only continued to tighten the chain around her throat until Anna's face began to turn red as it filled with blood.

"You wouldn't tell anyone about my windfall, would you, my little one?"

"No, never, Alex. No one. You can rely on me," she choked out desperately.

"Can I feel absolutely certain?" he asked with an edge of menace now in his voice.

"Yes, yes of course, but please stop now," she piped, her delicate hands clutching desperately at her master's blond hair, but Romanov only continued to squeeze and squeeze the heavy gold chain around her neck like a rack and pinion, tighter and tighter. Romanov was not aware of the girl's hands clinging desperately to his hair, as he twisted the chain a final time. "I'm sure you understand that I must feel absolutely certain that you wouldn't share our secret – with anyone," he explained to her. But she did not hear his plea because the vertebrae in her neck had already snapped.

On his morning run along the Embankment, Adam mulled over the tasks that still needed to be carried out next.

If he took the morning flight out of Heathrow on Wednesday, he could be back in London by the same evening, or Thursday at the latest. But there were still several things that had to be organised before he could leave for Geneva.

He came to a halt on the pavement outside his block and checked his pulse, before climbing the stairs to the flat.

"Three letters for you," said Lawrence. "None for me. Mind you," he added as his flatmate joined him in the kitchen, "two of them are in buff envelopes." Adam picked up the letters and left them on the end of his bed en route to the shower. He survived five minutes of ice-cold water before towelling down. Once he was dressed he opened the letters. He began with the white one, which turned out to be a note from Heidi thanking him for dinner, and hoping she would be seeing him again some time. He smiled and tore open the first of the buff envelopes, which was yet another missive from the Foreign Office Coordination Staff.

Captain Scott – the rank already seemed out of place – was requested to attend a medical at 122 Harley Street at three o'clock on the following Monday, to be conducted by Dr John Vance.

Finally he opened the other brown envelope and pulled out a letter from Lloyds, Cox and King's branch in Pall Mall, informing Dear Sir/Madam that they had been in receipt of a cheque for five hundred pounds from Holbrooke, Holbrooke and Gascoigne, and that his current account at the close of business the previous day was in credit to the sum of £272.18.4d. When Adam checked through the account it showed that at one point he had, for the first time in his life, run up an overdraft – a situation that he knew would have been frowned upon had he still been in the army, for as little as twenty years before it was in some regiments a court-martial offence for an officer to be overdrawn.

What would his brother officers have said if he told them he was about to remove two hundred pounds from the account with no real guarantee of a return?

Once Adam had finished dressing, he rejoined Lawrence in the kitchen.

"How was the Shah of Iran?" he asked.

"Oh, very reasonable really," said Lawrence, turning a page of the *Daily Telegraph*, "considering the circumstances. Promised he would do what he could about his current financial embarrassment, but he was a bit pushed until the West allowed him to raise the price of oil."

"Where did you eventually take him to lunch?" asked Adam enjoying the game.

"I offered him a shepherd's pie at the Green Man, but the bloody fellow became quite snotty. It seems he and the Empress had to pop along to Harrods to be measured up for a new throne. Would have gone along with him of course, but my boss wanted his wastepaper basket emptied, so I missed out on the Harrods deal as well."

"So what are you up to today?"

"I shouldn't let you in on this," said Lawrence, peering at the photograph of Ted Dexter the defeated English cricket captain, "but the Governor of the Bank of England wants my views on whether we should devalue the pound from $2.80 to $2.40."

"And what are your views?"

"I've already explained to the fellow that the only 240 I know is the bus that runs between Golders Green and Edgware, and if I don't get a move on I'll miss my beloved 14," said Lawrence, checking his watch. Adam laughed as he watched his friend slam his briefcase shut and disappear out of the door.

Lawrence had changed considerably over the years since he had left Wellington. Perhaps it was that Adam could only remember him as school captain and then leaving with the top classics scholarship to Balliol. He had seemed so serious in those days and certainly destined for greater things. No one would have thought it possible that he would end up as an investment analyst at Barclays DCO. At Oxford contemporaries half joked about him being a cabinet minister. Was it possible that one always expected too much of those idols who were only a couple of years older than oneself? On leaving school their friendship had grown. And when Adam was posted to Malaya, Lawrence never accepted the army report that posted his friend as missing presumed dead. And when Adam announced that he was leaving the army, Lawrence asked for no explanation and couldn't have been kinder about his unemployment problem. Adam hoped that he would be given the chance to repay such friendship.

Adam fried himself an egg and a couple of rashers of bacon. There wasn't much more he could do before nine thirty, although he did find time to scribble a note to his sister, enclosing a cheque for fifty pounds.

At nine thirty he made a phone call. Mr Holbrooke – Adam wondered if he actually had a christian name – couldn't hide his surprise at receiving a call from young Mr Scott. Now that my father is dead, *I* must be old Mr Scott, Adam wanted to tell him. And Holbrooke sounded even more surprised by his request. "No doubt connected in some way with that envelope," he muttered, but agreed to put a copy of his father's will in the post that afternoon.

Adam's other requirements could not be carried out over the phone, so he locked up the flat and jumped on a bus heading up the King's Road. He left the double-decker at Hyde Park Corner and made his way to Lloyds Bank in Pall Mall, where he joined a queue at the Foreign Exchange counter.

"May I help you?" asked a polite assistant when he finally reached the front.

"Yes," said Adam. "I would like fifty pounds in Swiss francs, fifty pounds in cash and a hundred pounds in traveller's cheques."

"What is your name?" she enquired.

"Adam Scott."

The girl entered some calculations on a large desk-top machine before cranking the handle round several times. She looked at the result, then disappeared for a few moments to return with a copy of the bank statement Adam had received in the morning post.

"The total cost, including our charges, will be £202.1.8d. That would leave your account in credit with £70.16s.4d.," she informed him.

"Yes," said Adam, but didn't add that in truth it would only be £20.16s.4d. the moment his sister presented her cheque. He began to hope that the Foreign Office paid by the week, otherwise it would have to be another frugal month. Unless of course . . .

Adam signed the tops of the ten traveller's cheques in the cashier's presence and she then handed over five hundred and ninety-four Swiss francs and fifty pounds in cash. It was the largest sum of money Adam had ever taken out at one time.

Another bus journey took him to the British European Airways terminal in Cromwell Road where he asked the girl to book him on a return flight to Geneva.

"First class or economy?" she asked.

"Economy," said Adam, amused by the thought that anyone might think he would want to go first class.

"That will be thirty-one pounds please, sir." Adam paid in cash and placed the ticket in his inside pocket, before returning to the flat for a light lunch. During the afternoon he called Heidi who agreed to join him for dinner at the Chelsea Kitchen at eight o'clock. There was one more thing Adam needed to be certain about before he joined Heidi for dinner.

Romanov was woken by the ringing of the phone.

"Yes," he said.

"Good morning, Comrade Romanov, it's Melinac, the Second Secretary at the Embassy."

"Good morning, Comrade, what can I do for you?"

"It's about Comrade Petrova," Romanov smiled at the thought of her now lying in the bath. "Have you come across the girl since you reported her missing?"

"No," replied Romanov. "And she didn't sleep in her bed last night."

"I see," said the Second Secretary. "Then your suspicions that she might have defected are beginning to look a serious possibility."

"I fear so," said Romanov, "and I shall have to make a full report of the situation to my superiors the moment I get back to Moscow."

"Yes, of course, Comrade Major."

"I shall also point out that you have done everything possible to assist me with this problem, Comrade Second Secretary."

"Thank you, Comrade Major."

"And brief me the moment you come up with any information that might lead us to where she is."

"Of course, Comrade Major." Romanov replaced the phone and walked across to the bathroom in the adjoining room. He stared down at the body hunched up in the bath. Anna's eyes were bulging in their sockets, her face contorted and the skin already grey. After throwing a towel over the dead researcher's head and locking the door, he went into his own bathroom for an unusually long shower.

He returned and sat on his side of the bed, only a towel around his waist, and picked up the phone. He ordered breakfast which arrived fifteen minutes later, by which time he had dressed. Once he had finished orange juice and croissants he returned to the phone trying to recall the name of the hotel's manager. It came back to him just as the receptionist said, "*Guten morgen, mein Herr.*"

"Jacques, please," was all Romanov said. A moment later he heard the manager's voice, "Good morning, Herr Romanov."

"I have a delicate problem that I was hoping you might be able to help me with."

"I shall certainly try, sir," came back the reply.

"I am in possessiosn of a rather valuable object that I wish to deposit with my bank and I wouldn't want . . ."

"I understand your dilemma entirely," said the manager. "And how can I be of assistance?"

"I require a large container in which to place the object."

"Would a laundry basket be large enough?"

"Ideal, but does it have a secure lid?"

"Oh, yes," replied Jacques. "We often have to drop them off down lift shafts."

"Perfect," said Romanov.

"Then it will be with you in a matter of moments," said Jacques. "I shall send a porter to assist you. May I also suggest that it is taken down in the freight elevator at the rear of the hotel, thus ensuring that no one will see you leaving?"

"Very considerate," said Romanov.

"Will a car be calling to collect you?"

"No," said Romanov. "I –"

"Then I shall arrange for a taxi to be waiting. When will you require it?"

"In no more than half an hour."

"You will find it parked outside the freight entrance in twenty minutes time."

"You have been most helpful," said Romanov, before adding, "the Chairman of the State Bank did not exaggerate his praise of you."

"You are too kind, Herr Romanov," said Jacques. "Will there be anything else?"

"Perhaps you would be good enough to have my account prepared so that there will be no delay."

"Certainly."

Romanov put the phone down wishing he could export such service to Moscow. He only waited a moment before he dialled the first of two local numbers. On both occasions his wishes were immediately gran-

ted. As he replaced the phone for the third time there was a gentle tap
on the door. Romanov went quickly over to answer it. A young porter
stood in the corridor, a large laundry basket by his side. He smiled
politely. Romanov merely nodded and pulled in the basket. "Please
return as soon as the taxi has arrived," said Romanov. The porter
bowed slightly, but said nothing.

As soon as the porter had left, Romanov locked the door and put the
chain in place before wheeling the laundry basket into the main
bedroom and leaving it by the side of the bed. He undid the tough
leather straps and threw open the lid.

Next, he unlocked the bathroom door and lifted Petrova's stiff body
in his arms before trying to cram it into the basket. Rigor mortis had
already gripped the body; the legs refused to bend and the researcher
didn't quite fit in. Romanov placed the naked Petrova on the floor. He
held his fingers out straight and suddenly brought them down with
such force on the right leg that it broke like a branch in a storm. He
repeated the action on her left leg. Like the guillotine, it didn't require a
second attempt. He then tucked the legs under her body. It amused
Romanov to consider that, had it been he who had been murdered,
Anna Petrova would never have been able to get him in the basket
whatever she had tried to break. Romanov then wheeled the trolley into
the researcher's bedroom and, after emptying all her drawers, including Anna's clothes, clean and dirty, her shoes, her toilet bag, toothbrush and even an old photograph of himself he hadn't realised she
possessed he threw them in the basket on top of her. Once he had
removed the gold medallion from around her neck and was certain that
there was nothing of the researcher's personal belongings left, he
covered up the body with a hotel bath towel, and sprayed it with a
liberal amount of Chanel No. 5 that had been left courtesy of the hotel.

Finally he strapped the lid down securely and wheeled the creaking
basket out and left it by the outer door.

Romanov began to pack his own case but there was a knock on the
door before he had finished.

"Wait," he said firmly. There was a muffled reply of "*Ja, mein Herr.*"
A few moments later Romanov opened the door. The porter entered,
nodded to him and began to tug at the laundry basket, but it took a firm
shove from Romanov's foot before it got moving. The porter sweated
his way down the corridor as Romanov walked by the side of the basket,
carrying his suitcase. When they reached the rear of the hotel Romanov
watched as the basket was wheeled safely into the freight elevator
before he stepped in himself.

When the ground floor doors opened Romanov was relieved to be
greeted by Jacques who was standing by a large Mercedes waiting for
him with the boot already open. The taxi driver and the porter lifted up
the laundry basket and wedged it into the boot, but Romanov's suitcase

could not be fitted in as well so it had to be put in the front of the car alongside the driver's seat.

"Shall we forward your bill to the Consulate, *mein Herr?*" asked Jacques.

"Yes, that would be helpful . . ."

"I do hope everything has worked out to your satisfaction," said Jacques, as he held open the back door of the Mercedes for his departing guest.

"Entirely," said Romanov.

"Good, good. And will your young colleague be joining you?" asked the manager, looking back over his shoulder towards the hotel.

"No, she won't," said Romanov. "She has already gone on to the airport ahead of me."

"Of course," said Jacques, "but I am sorry to have missed her. Do please pass on my best wishes."

"I certainly will," said Romanov, "and I look forward to returning to your hotel in the near future." "Thank you sir," the manager said as Romanov slipped into the back seat leaving Jacques to close the door behind him.

When Romanov arrived at the Swissair office his suitcase was checked in and he waited only moments before continuing on to the bank. Herr Bischoff's son, accompanied by another man, also clad in a grey suit, was waiting in the hall to greet him.

"How pleasant to see you again so soon," volunteered the young Herr Bischoff. His deep voice took Romanov by surprise. The taxi driver waited by the open boot while Herr Bischoff's companion, a man of at least six foot four and heavily built, lifted out the laundry basket as if it were a sponge cake. Romanov paid the fare and followed Herr Bischoff into the far lift.

"We are fully prepared for your deposition following your phone call," said Herr Bischoff. "My father was only sorry not to be present personally. He had a long-standing engagement with another customer and only hopes that you will understand." Romanov waved his hand.

The lift travelled straight to the ground floor where the guard, on seeing young Herr Bischoff, unlocked the great steel cage. Romanov and the two bankers proceeded at a leisurely pace down the corridor, while the giant carried the basket in their wake.

Standing with folded arms by the vault door was another of the partners Romanov recognised from the previous day. Herr Bischoff nodded and the partner placed his key in the top lock of the vault door without a word. Herr Bischoff then turned the second lock and together they pushed open the massive steel door. Herr Bischoff and his partner walked in ahead of Romanov and opened the top lock of all five of his boxes, while the guard placed the laundry basket on the floor beside them.

"Will you require any assistance?" asked Herr Bischoff as he handed his Russian client a personal sealed envelope.

"No thank you," Romanov assured him, but did not relax until he had seen the vast door close behind him and all four of his Swiss helpers left invisibly on the other side.

Once he felt certain he was alone, he stared down at the one large box he knew to be empty: it was smaller than he had recalled. Beads of sweat appeared on his forehead as he unlocked it, pulled it out and raised the airtight lid. It was going to be a tight fit. Romanov unstrapped the laundry basket and removed everything except the body. He stared down at the contorted face, the deep marks in the skin around the neck had turned to a dark blue. He bent over and lifted the researcher up by her waist, but as no part of the body moved other than her broken legs he had to drop her into the box head first. Even then he had to adjust her various limbs in order that the box could be shut: had Anna been even an inch taller the exercise would have proved pointless. He then stuffed the girl's belongings down at the sides of her body, leaving only the Chanel-covered towel behind in the laundry basket.

Romanov proceeded to replace the lid on the airtight box, before pushing it back securely in place and locking it. He then double-checked it could not be opened without his own personal key. He was relieved to find he could not budge it. He hesitated for a moment glancing at the second large box, but accepted that this was not the time to indulge himself: that would have to wait for another occasion. Satisfied that everything was back in place he closed and strapped down the lid of the laundry basket and wheeled it back to the entrance of the vault. He pressed the little red button.

"I do hope you found everything in order," said the young Herr Bischoff once he had returned from locking the five boxes.

"Yes, thank you," said Romanov. "But would it be possible for someone to return the laundry basket to the St Gothard Hotel?"

"Of course," said the banker, who nodded towards the large man.

"And I can be assured that the boxes will not be touched in my absence?" he asked as they walked down the corridor.

"Naturally, Your Excellency," said Herr Bischoff, looking somewhat aggrieved at such a suggestion. "When you return," he continued, "you will find everything exactly as you left it."

Well, not exactly, Romanov thought to himself.

When they stepped out of the lift on the ground floor, Romanov spotted Herr Bischoff's father with another customer.

A Rolls-Royce accompanied by a police motorcycle whisked the Shah of Iran quickly away, and the chairman discreetly waved his farewell.

When they reached the entrance to the bank, the young Herr Bischoff bowed. "We shall look forward to seeing you again when you are next in Zurich, Your Excellency," he said.

"Thank you," said Romanov, who shook hands with the young man and walked out on to the pavement to find the anonymous black car waiting to take him to the airport.

He cursed. This time he *did* spot the agent he had seen earlier in the hotel.

CHAPTER NINE

"Kill him, sir," the corporal whispered in Adam's ear.

"Not much hope of that," muttered Adam as he bounced into the centre of the ring.

The lean, muscle-bound instructor stood waiting for him. "Let's have a few rounds and see how you make out, sir." Adam bobbed and weaved around the Physical Training Instructor looking for an opening.

Adam led with a left and received a tap on the nose for his trouble. "Keep your guard up," said the sergeant major. Adam led again, catching the instructor a full blow on the chest, but was punished with a sharp left jab into the side of his head. He wobbled and his ear tingled but this time he managed to keep his guard up when a right and left followed. "You're feeble, sir, that's your problem. You couldn't knock the skin off a rice pudding." Adam feinted with his right and then swung a left with such force that when it caught the sergeant major full on the chin he staggered and fell.

The corporal standing by the side of the ring smirked as the instructor remained on the floor. Eventually he managed to get back on his feet.

"I'm sorry," said Adam, his guard up and ready.

"Don't be sorry, you bloody fool . . . sir. You landed a bloody good punch. A technical knockout, to be accurate, so I'll have to wait for a day or two to seek my revenge." Adam breathed a sigh of relief and lowered his guard. "But that doesn't mean you're off the hook. It's weight training for you now, sir. Beam work and floor exercises."

For the next hour the sergeant major chased, kicked, harried and badgered Adam until he finally collapsed in a heap on the floor, incapable of lifting an evening paper.

"Not bad, sir. I feel sure the Foreign Office will be able to find some niche for you. Mind you," he added, "as most of that lot are about as wet as a dish cloth even *you*'ll have a chance to shine."

"You are most flattering, Sergeant Major," said Adam from a supine position.

"Up, sir," the instructor bellowed. Adam unwillingly got to his feet as quickly as his tired body would allow.

"Don't tell me, Sergeant Major."

"It's the recovery that proves fitness, not the speed," they said in unison.

"Sad day when you left the army," said the instructor to Adam once they were back in the Queen's Club changing room. "Can't name a lot of officers who have put me on the floor." The instructor touched his chin tenderly. "That will teach me to underestimate a man who survived nine months of Chink food. So let's hope the Foreign Office doesn't underestimate you as well."

The sergeant major rose from the bench by his locker. "Same time Wednesday?"

"Can't make it Wednesday, Sergeant Major. I may not be back from a trip to Geneva."

"Swanning around Europe nowadays, are we?"

"I could manage Thursday morning if that suits you,' Adam said, ignoring the jibe.

"Your check-up with the quack is next Monday, if I remember correctly."

"Right."

"Thursday at ten then, it will give you a little longer to think about my right-hook."

The Chairman of the KGB studied the report on the desk in front of him: something didn't ring true. He looked up at Romanov. "Your reason for visiting Bischoff et Cie was because they claimed to be in possession of a fifteenth-century icon that might have fitted the description of the one we are searching for?"

"That is correct, Comrade, and the chairman of Gosbank will confirm that he personally arranged the meeting."

"But the icon turned out to be of St Peter and not of St George and the Dragon."

"Also confirmed by Comrade Petrova in her report."

"Ah, yes, Comrade Petrova," said Zaborski, his eyes returning to the sheet of paper in front of him.

"Yes, Comrade."

"And later that evening Comrade Petrova mysteriously failed to keep an appointment with you?"

"Inexplicably," said Romanov.

"But which you reported to Comrade Melinski at the Embassy." He paused: "You were responsible for selecting Petrova yourself, were you not?"

"That is correct, Comrade Chairman."

"Does that not reveal a certain lack of judgment on your part?"

Romanov made no attempt to reply.

The Chairman's eyes returned to the file. "When you awoke the next morning, there was still no sign of the girl?"

"She also failed to turn up to breakfast as arranged," said Romanov, "and when I went to her room all her personal belongings had gone."

"Which convinced you she had defected."

"Yes, sir," said Romanov.

"But the Swiss police," said Zaborski, "can find no trace of her. So I keep asking myself why would she want to defect? Her husband and her immediate family live in Moscow. They are all employed by the State, and it is not as if this was her first visit to the West."

Romanov didn't offer an opinion.

"Perhaps Petrova disappeared because she might have been able to tell us something you didn't want us to hear."

Still Romanov said nothing.

The Chairman's gaze once again returned to the file. "I wonder what it was that young Petrova wanted to tell us? Who else you were sleeping with that night, perhaps?" Romanov felt a shiver of fear as he wondered how much Zaborski really knew. Zaborski paused and pretended to be checking something else in the report. "Perhaps she could tell us why you felt it necessary to return to Bischoff et Cie a second time." Once again, Zaborski paused. "I think I may have to open an inquiry into the disappearance of Comrade Petrova. Because, Comrade Romanov, by the time you returned to the bank a third time," said the Chairman, his voice rising with each word, "every second-rate spy from here to Istanbul knew that we were searching for something." The Chairman paused. Romanov was still desperate to find out if Zaborski had any real evidence. Neither man spoke for some time. "You have always been a loner, Major Romanov, and I do not deny that at times your results have allowed me to overlook certain indiscretions. But I am not a loner, Comrade. I am a desk man, no longer allowed your freedom of action." He fiddled with the paperweight of Luna 9 on the desk in front of him.

"I am a file man, a paper man. I make reports in triplicate, I answer queries in quadruplicate, explain decisions in quintuplicate. Now I will have to explain the circumstances of Petrova's strange disappearance to the Politburo in multiplicate."

Romanov remained silent, something the KGB had taken several years to instil into him. He began to feel confident that Zaborski was only guessing. If he had suspected the truth the interview would have taken place in the basement where a less intellectual approach to questioning was carried out.

"In the USSR," continued Zaborski, now rising from his chair, "despite our image in the Western world, we investigate a suspicious death," he paused, "or defection more scrupulously than any other nation on earth. You, Comrade Romanov, would have found your chosen profession easier to follow had you been born in Africa, South America or even Los Angeles."

Still Romanov did not venture an opinion.

"The General Secretary informed me at one o'clock this morning that he is not impressed by your latest efforts, distinctly unimpressed were the exact words he used, especially after your excellent start. All he is interested in, however, is finding the Tsar's icon, and so, for the time being, Comrade, he has decided there will be no investigation. But if you ever act in such an irresponsible way again it will not be an inquiry you are facing, but a tribunal, and we all know what happened to the last Romanov that faced a tribunal."

He closed the file. "Against my better judgment and because we are left with less than a week, the General Secretary has allowed you a second chance in the belief that you will indeed come up with the Tsar's icon. Do I make myself clear, Comrade?" he barked.

"Very clear, Comrade Chairman," said Romanov, and turning smartly on his heel quickly left the room.

The Chairman of the KGB waited for the door to close before his eyes settled back on the file. What was Romanov up to, Zaborski needed to know suddenly realising that his own career might now be on the line. He flicked down a switch on the little console by his side. "Find Major Valchek," he ordered.

"I've never actually had champagne and caviar," admitted Adam, as he looked up at the beautiful girl who sat opposite him across the table. He loved the way she tied her hair, and the way she dressed, the way she laughed, but most of all the way she smiled.

"Well, don't get frightened, because I can't imagine caviar will ever find its place on this particular menu," teased Heidi. "But perhaps soon when you are the proud owner of the Tsar's icon, that is if Mr Rosenbau . . ."

Adam put a finger to his lips. "No one else knows about that, not even Lawrence."

"That may be wise," Heidi whispered. "He will only expect you to invest all the money you make from the sale in his boring bank."

"What makes you think I'd sell it?" asked Adam, trying to discover how much she had worked out.

"If you own a Rolls-Royce and you are out of work you do not then go and hire a chauffeur."

"But I've only got a motorbike."

"And you'll have to sell that as well if the icon turns out to be worthless," she said, laughing.

"Would you like a coffee to follow?" asked the waiter, who was already clearing their table in the hope of fitting in two more customers before the night was out.

"Yes, please. Two cappuccinos," said Adam. He turned his gaze back to Heidi. "Funnily enough," he continued as the waiter retreated, "the only time I've ever rung Lawrence at the bank the telephonist couldn't immediately locate him."

"What's so surprising about that?" asked Heidi.

"It was as if they had never heard of him," said Adam, "but perhaps I was imagining it."

"A bank that size must have over a thousand employees. You could go years without knowing everyone who worked there."

"I suppose you're right," Adam said, as two coffees were placed in front of them.

"When do you plan on going to Geneva?" Heidi asked, after she had tried a sip of the coffee and found it too hot.

"First thing Wednesday morning. I hope to be back the same evening."

"Considerate."

"What do you mean?" asked Adam.

"To choose my one day off to fly away," she said. "Not very romantic."

"Then why not come with me?" he asked, leaning across the table to take her hand.

"That might turn out to be more significant than sharing your sausages."

"I would hope so and in any case, you could be most useful."

"You do have a way with words," said Heidi.

"You know I didn't mean it that way. It's simply that I don't speak German or French and I've never been to Switzerland other than on a school skiing trip – and then I kept falling over." Heidi tried her coffee again.

"Well?" said Adam, not letting go of her hand.

"The Swiss speak perfect English," she said eventually, "and should you have any problem with the bank, you can always get in touch with Lawrence."

"It would only be for the day," said Adam.

"And a waste of your money."

"Not very romantic," said Adam.

"Touché."

"Think about it," said Adam. "After the cost of your return flight I will be left with only £19,969. I don't know how I'll get by."

"You really mean it, don't you?" said Heidi, sounding serious for the first time. "But women are not impulsive creatures."

"You could always bring Jochen along with you."

Heidi laughed. "He wouldn't fit on the plane."

"Do say you'll come," said Adam.

"On one condition," said Heidi thoughtfully.

"Separate planes?" said Adam grinning.

"No, but if the icon turns out to be worthless you will let me refund the price of my ticket."

"It couldn't be worth less than thirty-one pounds, so I agree to your terms," said Adam. He leaned over and kissed Heidi on the lips. "Perhaps it will take more than one day," he said. "Then what would you say?"

"I would demand separate hotels," replied Heidi, "if it wasn't for the high cost of the Swiss franc," she added.

"You are always so reliable, Comrade Romanov. You fulfil the primary qualification for a successful banker." Romanov studied the old man carefully looking for some sign that he knew exactly what had been awaiting him at the bank.

"And you are always so efficient, Comrade Poskonov," he paused, "the only qualification necessary in my chosen profession."

"Good heavens, we are beginning to sound like a couple of ageing commissars at an annual reunion. How was Zurich?" he asked, as he lit a cigarette.

"Like a Polish tractor. The bits that worked were fine."

"From that I assume the bits that didn't work failed to produce the Tsar's icon," the chairman said.

"Correct, but Bischoff turned out to be most helpful, as was Jacques. My every need was catered for."

"Your every need?"

"Yes," replied Romanov.

"Good man, Bischoff," said the banker. "That's why I sent you to him first." The old man slumped down into his chair.

"Was there any other reason you sent me to him first?" asked Romanov.

"Five other reasons," said Poskonov, "but we'll not bother with any of them until you have found your icon."

"Perhaps I'd like to bother now," said Romanov firmly.

"I've outlived two generations of Romanovs," said the old man raising his eyes. "I wouldn't want to outlive a third. Let's leave it at that for now, I'm sure we can come to an understanding when the spotlight is no longer on you."

Romanov nodded.

"Well, you will be pleased to learn that I have not been idle in your absence. But I fear my results also resemble a Polish tractor."

The banker waved Romanov to a seat before he reopened his file which had grown in size since he had last seen it. "Originally," the chairman began, "you presented me with a list of fourteen banks, eleven of which have now confirmed that they are not in possession of the Tsar's icon."

"I have been wondering about that – is their word to be taken at face value?" asked Romanov.

"Not necessarily," said the banker. "But on balance the Swiss prefer not to become involved rather than tell a deliberate lie. In time the liar is always found out, and I still, from this office, control the cash flow of eight nations. I may not wield what they would call financial clout but I can still put the odd spanner in the works of the capitalist monetary system."

"That still leaves us with three banks?" said Romanov.

'Correct, Comrade. The first is Bischoff et Cie, whom you have already visited. But the other two have refused to cooperate in any way."

"Why is it your influence does not extend to them?"

"The most obvious of reasons," replied Poskonov. "Other interests exert a stronger influence. If, for example, your major source of income emanates from the leading Jewish families, or alternatively the Americans, no amount of pressure will ever allow you to deal with the Soviet Union." Romanov nodded his understanding. "That being the case," continued Poskonov, "there still has to be an outside chance that one of these two banks is in possession of the Tsar's icon, and as they are never going to admit as much to Mother Russia I am not sure what I can recommend you do next."

The banker sat back and waited for Romanov to take in his news.

"You are unusually silent," Poskonov ventured, after he had lit another cigarette.

"You have given me an idea," said Romanov. "I think the Americans would describe it as a 'long shot'. But if I'm right, it will be the Russians who will get the home run."

"Baseball is a game that I've never understood but I am, however, glad to have been of some use today. Although I suspect you will still need this, whatever your long shot." Poskonov removed a single piece of paper from his file and handed it over to Romanov. On it were the words: Simon et Cie, Zurich (refused), Roget et Cie, Geneva (refused).

"No doubt you will be returning to Switzerland very soon."

Romanov stared directly at the banker.

"I wouldn't recommend you visit Bischoff et Cie on this trip, Alex. There will be time enough for that in the future."

Romanov straightened his fingers.

The old man returned his stare. "You won't find me as easy to get rid of as Anna Petrova," he added.

CHAPTER TEN

The elderly-looking man took his place at the back of the taxi queue. It was hard to estimate his height because he looked so bent and frail. A large overcoat that might have been even older than its wearer reached almost to the ground and the fingers that could only just be seen peeping through the sleeves were covered in grey woollen mittens. One hand clung on to a little leather suitcase, with the initials E.R. in black looking so worn that it might have belonged to his grandfather.

One would have had to bend down or be very short to see the old man's face – a face that was dominated by a nose that would have flattered Cyrano de Bergerac. He shuffled forward slowly until it was his turn to climb into a taxi. The operation was a slow one, and the driver was already drumming his fingers against the wheel when his passenger told him in guttural tones that he wanted to be taken to the bankers, Daumier et Cie. The driver moved off without asking for further directions. Swiss taxi-drivers know the way to the banks in the same way as London cabbies can always find a theatre and New York's yellow cabs a westside bar.

When the old man arrived at his destination he took some time sorting out which coins to pay with. He then pushed himself slowly out on to the pavement and stood gazing at the marble building. Its solidity made him feel safe. He was about to touch the door when a man in a smart blue uniform opened it.

"I have come to see –" he began in stilted German, but the doorman only pointed to the girl behind the reception desk. He shuffled over to her and then repeated, "I have come to see Herr Daumier. My name is Emmanuel Rosenbaum."

"Do you have an appointment?" she asked.

"I fear not."

"Herr Daumier is in conference at the moment," said the girl, "but I will find out if there is another partner available to see you." After a phone conversation in German she said, "Can you take the lift to the third floor?" Mr Rosenbaum nodded with obvious signs of reluctance, but did as he was bid. When he stepped out of the lift, only just before the door closed on him, another young woman was standing there ready to greet him. She asked him if he would be kind enough to wait in what he would have described as a cloakroom with two chairs. Some time passed before anyone came to see him, and the old man was unable to hide his surprise at the age of the boy who eventually appeared.

"I am Welfherd Praeger," said the young man, "a partner of the bank."

"Sit down, sit down," said Mr Rosenbaum. "I cannot stare up at you for so long." The young partner complied.

"My name is Emmanuel Rosenbaum. I left a package with you in 1938, and I have returned to collect it."

"Yes, of course," said the junior partner, the tone of his voice changing. "Do you have any proof of your identity, or any documentation from the bank?"

"Oh, yes," came back the reply, and the old man handed over his passport and a receipt that had been folded and unfolded so many times it was now almost in pieces.

The young man studied both documents carefully. He recognised the Israeli passport immediately. Everything seemed to be in order. The bank's receipt, too, although issued in the year of his birth, appeared authentic.

"May I leave you for a moment, sir?"

"Of course," said the old man, "after twenty-eight years I think I can wait for a few more minutes."

Shortly after the young man had left the woman returned and invited Mr Rosenbaum to move to another room. This time it was larger and comfortably furnished. Within minutes the junior partner returned with another man, whom he introduced as Herr Daumier.

"I don't think we have ever met, Herr Rosenbaum," said the chairman courteously. "You must have dealt with my father."

"No, no," said Mr Rosenbaum. "I dealt with your grandfather, Helmut."

A look of respect came into Herr Daumier's eyes.

"I saw your father only on one occasion, and was sad to learn of his premature death," added Rosenbaum. "He was always so considerate. You do not wear a rose in your lapel as he did."

"No, sir, a tiny rebellion."

Rosenbaum tried to laugh but only coughed.

"I wonder if you have any further proof of identity other than your passport?" Herr Daumier asked politely.

Emmanuel Rosenbaum raised his head and, giving Herr Daumier a tired look, turned his wrist so that it faced upwards. The number 712910 was tattooed along the inside.

"I apologise," said Daumier, visibly embarrassed. "It will take me only a few minutes to bring your box up, if you will be kind enough to wait."

Mr Rosenbaum's eyes blinked as if he were too tired even to nod his agreement. The two men left him alone. They returned a few minutes later with a flat box about two feet square and placed it on the table in the centre of the room. Herr Daumier unlocked the top lock while the other partner acted as a witness. He then handed over a key to Rosenbaum saying, "We will now leave you, sir. Just press the button underneath the table when you wish us to return."

"Thank you," said Rosenbaum, and waited for the door to close behind them. He turned the key in the lock and pushed up the lid. Inside the box was a package in the shape of a picture, about eighteen by twelve inches, covered in muslin and tied securely. Rosenbaum placed the package carefully in his old suitcase. He then shut the box and locked it. He pressed the button under the table and within seconds Herr Daumier and the junior partner returned.

"I do hope everything was as you left it, Herr Rosenbaum," said the chairman, "it has been some considerable time."

"Yes, thank you." This time the old gentleman did manage a nod.

"May I mention a matter of no great consequence?" asked Herr Daumier.

"Pray do so," said the old man.

"Is it your intention to continue with the use of the box? The funds you left to cover the cost have recently run out."

"No, I have no need for it any longer."

"It's just that there was a small charge outstanding. But in the circumstances we are happy to waive it."

"You are most kind." Herr Daumier bowed and the junior partner accompanied their client to the front door, helped him into a taxi and instructed the driver to take Mr Rosenbaum to Zurich airport.

At the airport, the old man took his time reaching the check-in desk, because he appeared to be frightened of the escalator, and with the suitcase now quite heavy the flight of steps was difficult to negotiate.

At the desk he produced his ticket for the girl to check and was pleased to find that the passenger lounge was almost empty. He shuffled over towards the corner and collapsed on to a comfortable sofa. He checked to be sure he was out of sight of the other passengers in the lounge.

He flicked back the little knobs on the old suitcase and the springs rose reluctantly. He pushed up the lid, pulled out the parcel and held it to his chest. His fingers wrestled with the knots for some time before they became loose. He then removed the muslin to check his prize. Mr Rosenbaum stared down at the masterpiece. 'The Cornfields' by Van Gogh – which he had no way of knowing had been missing from the Vienna National Gallery since 1938.

Emmanuel Rosenbaum swore, which was out of character. He packed the picture safely up and returned it to his case. He then shuffled over to the girl at the Swissair sales desk and asked her to book him on the first available flight to Geneva. With luck he could still reach Roget et Cie before they closed.

The BEA Viscount landed at Geneva airport at eleven twenty-five local time that morning, a few minutes later than scheduled. The stewardess advised passengers to put their watches forward one hour to Central European Time.

"Perfect," said Adam. "We shall be in Geneva well in time for lunch, a visit to the bank and then back to the airport for the five past five flight home."

"You're treating the whole thing like a military exercise," said Heidi, laughing.

"All except the last part," said Adam.

"The last part?" she queried.

"Our celebration dinner."

"At the Chelsea Kitchen again, no doubt."

"Wrong," said Adam. "I've booked a table for two at eight o'clock at the Coq d'Or just off Piccadilly."

"Counting your chickens before they're hatched, aren't we?" said Heidi.

"Oh, very droll," said Adam.

"Droll? I do not understand."

"I'll explain it to you when we have that dinner tonight."

"I was hoping we wouldn't make it," said Heidi.

"Why?" asked Adam.

"All I have to look forward to tomorrow is the check-out counter at the German Food Centre."

"That's not as bad as a work-out with the sergeant major at ten," groaned Adam. "And by ten past I shall be flat on my back regretting I ever left Geneva."

"That will teach you to knock him out," said Heidi. "So perhaps we ought to stay put after all," she added, taking him by the arm. Adam leant down and kissed her gently on the cheek as they stood in the gangway waiting to be let off the plane. A light drizzle was falling out on the aircraft steps. Adam unbuttoned his raincoat and attempted to shelter Heidi beneath it as they ran across the tarmac to the Immigration Hall.

"Good thing I remembered this," he said.

"Not so much a raincoat, more a tent," said Heidi.

"It's my old army trenchcoat," he assured her, opening it up again. "It can hold maps, compasses, even an overnight kit."

"Adam, we're just going to be strolling around Geneva in the middle of summer, not lost in the Black Forest in the middle of winter."

He laughed. "I'll remember your sarcasm whenever it pours."

The airport bus that travelled to and from the city took only twenty minutes to reach the centre of Geneva.

The short journey took them through the outskirts of the city until they reached the magnificent still lake nestled in the hills. The bus continued alongside the lake until it came to a halt opposite the massive single-spouting fountain that shot over four hundred feet into the air.

"I'm beginning to feel like a day tripper," said Heidi, as they stepped out of the bus, pleased to find the light rain had stopped.

Both of them were immediately struck by how clean the city was as they walked along the wide litter-free pavement that ran alongside the lake. On the other side of the road neat hotels, shops and banks seemed in equal preponderance.

"First we must find out where our bank is so that we can have lunch nearby before going to pick up the booty."

"How does a military man go about such a demanding exercise?" asked Heidi.

"Simple. We drop in at the first bank we see and ask them to direct us to Roget et Cie."

"I'll bet your little arm must have been covered in initiative badges when you were a Boy Scout."

Adam burst out laughing. "Am I that bad?"

"Worse," said Heidi. "But you personify every German's image of the perfect English gentleman." Adam turned, touched her hair gently and leaning down, kissed her on the lips.

Heidi was suddenly conscious of the stares from passing strangers. "I don't think the Swiss approve of that sort of thing in public," she said. "In fact, I'm told some of them don't approve of it in private."

"Shall I go and kiss that old prune over there who is still glaring at us?" said Adam.

"Don't do that, Adam, you might turn into a frog. No, let's put your plan of campaign into action," she said, pointing to the Banque Populaire on the far side of the avenue.

When they had crossed the road Heidi inquired of the doorman the way to Roget et Cie. They followed his directions, once again admiring the great single-spouted fountain as they continued on towards the centre of the city.

Roget et Cie was not that easy to pinpoint, and they walked past it twice before Heidi spotted the discreet sign chiselled in stone by the side of a high wrought-iron and plate-glass door.

"Looks impressive," said Adam, "even when it's closed for lunch."

"What were you expecting – a small branch in the country? I know you English don't like to admit it but this is the centre of the banking world."

"Let's find that restaurant before our entente cordiale breaks down," said Adam. They retraced their steps towards the fountain and, as the sun was trying to find gaps between the clouds, they chose a pavement café overlooking the lake. Both selected a cheese salad and shared a half bottle of white wine. Adam was enjoying Heidi's company so much that he began to tell her stories of his army days. She had to stop him and point out that it was nearly two. He reluctantly called for the bill. "The time has now come to discover if the Tsar's icon really exists," he said.

When they had returned to the entrance of the bank Adam pushed open the heavy door, took a step inside and stared around the gloomy hall.

"Over there," said Heidi, pointing to a woman who was seated behind a desk.

"Good morning. My name is Adam Scott. I have come to collect something that has been left to me in a will."

The woman smiled. "Have you made an appointment with anyone in particular?" she asked, with only the slightest trace of accent.

"No," said Adam. "I didn't realise that I had to."

"I'm sure it will be all right," said the lady. She picked up a phone, dialled a single number and held a short conversation in French. Replacing the phone she asked them both to go to the fourth floor.

As Adam walked out of the lift, he was surprised to be met by someone of his own age.

"Good afternoon, my name is Pierre Neffe and I am a partner of the bank," said the young man in perfect English.

"I did warn you that I would be redundant," whispered Heidi.

"Don't speak too soon," replied Adam. "We haven't even begun to explain our problem yet."

M. Neffe led them to a small, exquisitely furnished room.

"I could settle down here," said Adam, taking off his coat, "without any trouble."

"We do like to make our customers feel at home," said M. Neffe condescendingly.

"You obviously haven't seen my home," said Adam. M. Neffe did not laugh.

"How can I help you?" was all the young partner offered by way of reply.

"My father," began Adam, "died last month and left me in his will a receipt for something I think you have had in your safe-keeping since 1938. It was a gift given to him by one of your customers." Adam hesitated. "A Mr Emmanuel Rosenbaum."

"Do you have any documentation relating to this gift?" inquired M. Neffe.

"Oh, yes," said Adam, digging into the map pocket of his trenchcoat. He passed over the Roget et Cie receipt to the young banker. M. Neffe studied it and nodded. "May I be permitted to see your passport, Mr Scott?"

"Certainly," said Adam, delving back into his trenchcoat and passing it to M. Neffe.

"If you will excuse me for one moment." M. Neffe rose, and left them on their own.

"What do you imagine they are up to now?" said Heidi.

"Checking first if they still have the icon, and second if my receipt is authentic. 1938 was rather a long time ago."

As the minutes ticked by, Adam started to feel disappointed, then depressed, and finally began to believe it was all going to turn out to be a complete waste of time.

"You could always take one of the pictures off the wall and put it in your trenchcoat," teased Heidi. "I'm sure it would fetch a good price in London. Perhaps even more than your beloved icon."

"Too late," said Adam as M. Neffe reappeared with another banker whom he introduced as M. Roget.

"Good morning," said M. Roget. "I am sorry that my father is not here to meet you, Mr Scott, but he has been held up in Chicago on business." He shook hands with both Adam and Heidi. "We have on file a letter from Mr Rosenbaum giving clear instructions to the bank that the box is not to be opened by any other than" – he looked at the piece of paper he had brought with him – "Colonel Gerald Scott, DSO, OBE, MC."

"My father," said Adam. "But as I explained to M. Neffe, he died last month and left me the gift in his will."

"I would be happy to accept what you say," said M Roget, "if I might be allowed sight of a copy of the death certificate and of the will itself."

Adam smiled at his own foresight and once more searched in his trenchcoat before removing a large brown envelope with the words 'Holbrooke, Holbrooke and Gascoigne' printed in heavy black letters across the top. He took out copies of his father's death certificate, the will and a letter marked 'To Whom It May Concern' and passed them to M. Roget, who read all three documents slowly, then handed them to his senior partner, who after he had read them whispered in his chairman's ear.

"Would you object to us phoning Mr Holbrooke in your presence?" asked M. Roget.

"No," said Adam simply. "But I must warn you that he is rather curmudgeonly."

"Curmudgeonly?" said the banker. "A word I am not familiar with, but I think I can sense its meaning." He turned and spoke to M. Neffe, who swiftly left the room, only to return a minute later with a copy of the English Law Society Register, 1966.

Adam was impressed by the bank's thoroughness as M. Roget checked that the number and address on the letterhead corresponded with the number and address in the Year Book. "I don't think it will be necessary to call Mr Holbrooke," said M. Roget, "but we have encountered one small problem, Mr Scott."

"And what is that?" asked Adam, nervously.

"Mr Rosenbaum's position is somewhat overdrawn, and the bank's rule is that an account must be cleared before any box can be opened."

Adam's pulse raced as he assumed that he hadn't brought enough money to cover this eventuality.

"The account is only 120 francs in debit," continued M. Roget, "which is the charge for housing the box over the past two years since Mr Rosenbaum's deposit ran out."

Adam breathed a sigh of relief. He took out his wallet and signed a traveller's cheque and handed it over.

"And finally," said M. Roget, "we will need you to sign a form of indemnity for the bank."

M. Roget passed over a long form containing clause after clause in tightly printed French at which Adam only glanced before passing it over to Heidi. She studied each clause carefully. M. Roget used the time to explain to Adam that it was a standard disclaimer clearing the bank of any liability concerning what might be in the box and Adam's legal claim to it.

Heidi looked up and nodded her agreement.

Adam signed on the dotted line with a flourish.

"Excellent," said the banker. "All we have to do now is go and retrieve your box."

"I suppose it could be empty," said Adam once the two of them were left alone again.

"And it could be jam-packed with gold doubloons, you old pessimist," said Heidi.

When both men returned a few minutes later, M. Neffe was carrying a flat metal box about twelve by nine inches, and some three inches deep.

Adam was disappointed by its modest size, but didn't show his feelings. M. Roget proceeded to undo the top lock with the bank's key and then handed Adam a small faded envelope with signatures scrawled across the waxed seal. "Whatever is in the box belongs to you, Mr Scott. When you have finished, perhaps you would be kind enough to let us know. Until then we shall remain outside in the corridor."

Both men left the room.

"Come on," said Heidi, "I can't wait." Adam opened the envelope and a key fell out. He fumbled with the lock which clicked and then he pushed up the lid. Inside the box was a small flat package wrapped in muslin and tied tightly with string. The knots took some undoing and then finally an impatient Adam tore off the string before slowly removing the muslin. They both stared at the masterpiece in disbelief.

The simple beauty of the golds, reds and blues left them both speechless. Neither of them had expected the icon to be so breathtaking. St George towering over the dragon, a massive sword in hand on the point of plunging it into the heart of the beast. The fire that belched from the dragon's jaw was a deep red and made a startling contrast to the gold cloak that seemed to envelop the saint.

"It's magnificent," said Heidi, eventually finding her voice.

Adam continued to hold the tiny painting in his hand.

"Say something," said Heidi.

"I wish my father had seen it, perhaps it would have changed his whole life."

"Don't forget he wanted it to change yours," said Heidi.

Adam finally turned the icon over and found on the back a small silver crown inlaid in the wood. He stared at it, trying to recall what Mr Sedgwick of Sotheby's had said that proved.

"I wish my father had opened the letter," said Adam, turning the icon back over and once again admiring St George's triumph. "Because it was his by right."

Heidi checked there was nothing else left inside the box. She then flicked down the lid and Adam locked it again with his key. He tucked the muslin round the masterpiece, tied it up firmly and zipped the little painting into the map pocket of his trenchcoat.

Heidi smiled. "I knew you'd be able to prove that you needed that coat even if it didn't rain."

Adam walked over to the door and opened it. The two bankers immediately returned.

"I hope you found what you had been promised," said M. Roget.

"Yes, indeed," said Adam. "But I shall have no further need of the box," he added, returning the key.

"As you wish," said M. Roget, bowing, "and here is the change from your traveller's cheque, sir," he said, passing over some Swiss notes to Adam. "If you will excuse me I will now take my leave of you. Monsieur Neffe will show you out." He shook hands with Adam, bowed slightly to Heidi and added with a faint smile, "I do hope you didn't find us too cur – mud – geonly." They both laughed.

"I also hope that you will enjoy a pleasant stay in our city," said M. Neffe as the lift took its leisurely pace down.

"It will have to be very quick," said Adam. "We have to be back at the airport in just over an hour."

The lift stopped at the ground floor and M. Neffe accompanied Adam and Heidi across the hall. The door was held open for them but they both stood aside to allow an old man to shuffle past. Although most people would have stared at his nose Adam was more struck by his penetrating eyes.

When the old man eventually reached the woman at the reception desk, he announced, "I have come to see Monsieur Roget."

"I'm afraid he's in Chicago at the moment, sir, but I'll see if his son is available. What name shall I tell him?"

"Emmanuel Rosenbaum." The woman picked up the phone and held another conversation in French. When she had replaced it she asked, "Would you go to the fourth floor, Mr Rosenbaum?"

Once again he had to take the fearsome lift, and once again he only just got out before its great teeth sprang back on him. Another middle-aged woman accompanied him to the waiting room. He politely declined her offer of coffee, thumping his heart with his right hand.

"Monsieur Roget will be with you shortly," she reassured the old gentleman.

He did not have to wait long before a smiling M. Roget appeared.

"How nice to make your acquaintance, Monsieur Rosenbaum, but I'm afraid you have just missed Mr Scott."

"Mr Scott?" the old man uttered in surprise.

"Yes. He left only a few minutes ago, but we carried out the instructions as per your letter."

"My letter?" said Mr Rosenbaum.

"Yes," said the banker, opening for the second time that morning a file which had remained untouched for over twenty years.

He handed a letter to the old man.

Emmanuel Rosenbaum removed a pair of glasses from his inside pocket, unfolded them slowly and proceeded to read a hand that he recognised. It was a bold script written in thick black ink.

FORSTHAUS HAARHOT
AMSBERG 14
VOSSWINNEL
SACHSEN
GERMANY
SEPTEMBER 12, 1945

DEAR M. ROGET,

I have left in your safe-keeping a small icon of St George and the Dragon in my box 718. I am transferring the ownership of that painting to a British army officer, Colonel Gerald Scott, DSO, OBE, MC. If Colonel Scott should come to claim the icon at any time please ensure that he receives my key without delay.

My thanks to you for your help in this matter, and I am only sorry we have never met in person.

YOURS SINCERELY,

EMMANUEL ROSENBAUM

"And you say that Colonel Scott came to collect the contents of the box earlier today?"

"No, no, Monsieur Rosenbaum. The colonel died quite recently and left the contents of the box to his son, Adam Scott. Monsieur Neffe and I checked all the documents including the death certificate and the will, and we were left in no doubt that they were both authentic and that everything was in order. He was also in possession of your receipt." The young banker hesitated. "I do hope we did the right thing, Monsieur Rosenbaum?"

"You certainly did," said the old man. "I came only to check that my wishes had been carried out."

M. Roget smiled in relief. "I feel I ought also to mention that your account had run into a small deficit."

"How much do I owe you?" asked the old man, fumbling in his breast pocket.

"Nothing," said M. Roget. "Nothing at all. Monsieur Scott dealt with it."

"I am in debt to Mr Scott. Are you able to tell me the amount?"

"One hundred and twenty francs," said M. Roget.

"Then I must repay the sum immediately," said the old man. "Do you by any chance have an address at which I can contact him?"

"No, I'm sorry I am unable to help you there," said M. Roget. "I have no idea where he is staying in Geneva." A hand touched M. Roget's elbow, and M. Neffe bent down and whispered in his ear.

"It appears," said M. Roget, "that Mr Scott was planning to return to England shortly because he had to check in at Geneva airport by five."

The old man lifted himself up. "You have been most helpful, gentlemen, and I will not take up any more of your time."

"It's flight BE 171 and your seats are 14A and B," the man behind the check-in counter told them. "The plane's on time so you should be boarding at gate Number Nine in about twenty minutes."

"Thank you," said Adam.

"Do you have any luggage that needs checking in?"

"No," said Adam. "We only spent the day in Geneva."

"Then have a good flight, sir," said the man, handing over their boarding passes. Adam and Heidi started walking towards the escalator that would take them to the departure lounge.

"I have seven hundred and seventy Swiss francs left," said Adam, thumbing through some notes, "and while we're here I must get my mother a box of decent liqueur chocolates. When I was a boy I used to give her a minute box every Christmas. I swore when I grew up if I ever got to Switzerland I would find her the finest box available." Heidi pointed to a counter that displayed row upon row of ornate boxes. Adam walked over and selected a large, gold-wrapped box of Lindt chocolates which the girl behind the counter gift-wrapped and placed in a carrier bag.

"Why are you frowning?" asked Adam after collecting his change.

"She's just reminded me that I have to be back behind a till tomorrow morning," said Heidi.

"Well, at least we've got the Coq d'Or to look forward to tonight," said Adam. He checked his watch. "Not much else we can do now except perhaps pick up some wine in the duty free."

"I'd like to find a copy of *Der Speigel* before we go through customs."

"Fine," said Adam. "Why don't we try the paper shop over in the corner."

"A call for Mr Adam Scott. Will Adam Scott please return to the BEA desk on the ground floor," came booming out over the public address system.

Adam and Heidi stared at each other. "Must have given us the wrong seat allocation, I suppose," said Adam, shrugging. "Let's go back and find out."

They returned downstairs and walked over to the man who had handed them their boarding passes. "I think you put a call out for me," said Adam. "My name is Scott."

"Oh, yes," said the man. "There's an urgent message for you," he said, reading from a pad in front of him. "Please call Monsieur Roget at Roget et Cie on Geneva 271279." He ripped off the piece of paper and handed it over. "The phones are over there in the far corner behind the KLM desk, and you'll need twenty centimes."

"Thank you," said Adam, studying the message, but it gave no clue as to why M. Roget should need to speak to him.

"I wonder what he can want," said Heidi. "It's a bit late to ask for the icon back."

"Well, there's only one way I'm going to find out," said Adam, passing over the bag to her. "Hang on to that and I'll be back in a moment."

"I'll try and pick up my magazine at the same time, if I can find a newspaper shop on this floor," said Heidi as she gripped the brightly coloured bag which contained the chocolates.

"Right," said Adam. "Meet you here in a couple of minutes."

"*Roget et Cie. Est-ce-que je peux vous aider?*"

"I am returning Monsieur Roget's call," said Adam, making no attempt to answer in French.

"Yes, sir. Whom shall I say is calling?" asked the telephonist, immediately switching to English.

"Adam Scott."

"I'll find out if he's available, sir."

Adam swung round to see if Heidi had returned to the BEA counter, but as there was no sign of her he assumed she must still be looking for a newspaper. Then he noticed an old man shuffling across the hall. He could have sworn he had seen him somewhere before.

"Mr Scott?" Adam leaned back into the box.

"Yes, Monsieur Roget, I am returning your call."

"Returning my call?" said the banker, sounding puzzled. "I don't understand."

"There was a message left at the BEA counter asking me to phone you. Urgent."

"There must be some mistake, I didn't leave any message. But now that you have rung, it might interest you to know that just as you were leaving Mr Emmanuel Rosenbaum paid us a visit."

"Emmanuel Rosenbaum?" said Adam, "but I assumed he was . . ."

"Could you assist me, please, young lady?" Heidi looked up at the old man who had addressed her in English, but with such a strong mid-European accent. She wondered why he had taken for granted that she spoke English but decided it must be the only language he felt confident conversing in.

"I am trying to find a taxi and I am already late, but I fear my eyesight is not what it used to be."

Heidi replaced the copy of *Der Speigel* on the shelf and said, "They're just through the double doors in the centre. Let me show you."

"How kind," he said. "But I do hope I am not putting you to too much trouble."

"Not at all," said Heidi, taking the old man by the arm and guiding him back towards the door marked 'Taxi et Autobus'.

"Are you sure it was Rosenbaum?" said Adam anxiously.

"I'm certain," replied the banker.

"And he seemed happy about me keeping the icon?"

"Oh, yes. That was not the problem. His only concern was to return your 120 francs. I think he may try and get in touch with you."

"BEA announce the departure of their flight BE 171 to London Heathrow from gate Number Nine."

"I must leave," said Adam. "My plane takes off in a few minutes."

"Have a good flight," said the banker.

"Thank you, Monsieur Roget," said Adam and replaced the receiver. He turned towards the BEA counter and was surprised to find that Heidi had not yet returned. His eyes began to search the ground floor for a paper shop as he feared she might well not have heard the departure announcement. Then he spotted her walking out through the double door, helping the old man he had noticed earlier.

Adam called out and quickened his pace. Something didn't feel quite right. When he reached the automatic door he had to check his stride to allow it to slide back. He could now see Heidi standing on the pavement in front of him, opening a taxi door for the old man.

"Heidi," he shouted. The old gentleman suddenly turned and once again Adam found himself staring at the man he could have sworn he had seen at the bank. "Mr Rosenbaum?" he questioned. Then with a movement of his arm that was so fast and powerful it took Adam by surprise, the old man threw Heidi into the back of the taxi, jumped in beside her, and pulling the taxi door closed, hollered at the top of his voice, "*Allez vite.*"

For a moment Adam was stunned but then he dashed to the side of the taxi and only just managed to touch the handle as it accelerated away from the kerb. The car's sudden momentum knocked Adam backwards on the pavement, but not before he saw the petrified look on Heidi's face. He stared at the number plate of the departing car: B-7-1-2 – was all he could catch, but at least he recognised it was a blue Mercedes. Desperately he looked around for another taxi but the only one in sight was already being filled up with luggage.

A Volkswagen Beetle drew up on the far side of the concourse. A woman stepped out of the driver's seat and walked to the front to open the boot. A man joined her from the passenger's side and lifted out a suitcase, before she slammed the boot lid back into place.

On the kerb, the two of them embraced. As they did so, Adam sprinted across the road and opening the passenger door of the Volkswagen, leapt inside and slid into the driver's seat. The key was still in the ignition. He turned it on, threw the car into gear, slammed his foot on the accelerator and shot backwards. The embracing couple stared at him in disbelief. Adam jerked the gear lever out of reverse into what he hoped was first. The engine turned over slowly, but just fast enough for him to escape the pursuing man. It must be third, he thought, and changed down as he began to follow the signs to the centre of Geneva.

By the time he reached the first roundabout he had mastered the gears, but had to concentrate hard on remaining on the right-hand side of the road. "B712 . . . B712," he repeated to himself again and again, to be sure it was fixed in his memory. He checked the number plate and the passengers of every blue taxi he passed. After a dozen or so, he began to wonder if Heidi's taxi might have left the motorway for a minor road. He pressed the accelerator even harder – 90, 100, 110, 120 kilometres an hour. He passed three more taxis but there was still no sign of Heidi.

Then he saw a Mercedes in the outside lane some considerable distance ahead of him, its lights full on and travelling well above the speed limit. He felt confident that the Volkswagen was powerful enough to catch the Mercedes especially if it had a diesel engine. Metre by metre he began to narrow the gap as he tried to fathom out why the old man would want to kidnap Heidi in the first place. Could it be Rosenbaum? But he had wanted him to keep the icon, or so the banker had assured him. None of it made sense, and he drove on wondering if at any moment he was going to wake up.

When they reached the outskirts of the city Adam hadn't woken up as he followed carefully the taxi's chosen route. By the next roundabout only three cars divided them. "A red light, I need a red light," Adam shouted, but the first three traffic lights into the city remained stubbornly green. And when one finally turned red, a van suddenly pulled in front of him, lengthening the gap between them. Adam cursed as he leaped out of the car and started running towards the taxi, but the light changed back to green just before he could reach it and the Mercedes sped away. Adam sprinted back to the Volkswagen and only just managed to drive the car across the junction as the light turned red. His decision to get out of the car had lost him several crucial seconds and when he looked anxiously ahead he could only just spot the taxi in the distance.

When they reached the Avenue de France, running parallel with the west side of the lake, both cars weaved in and out of the traffic, until the Mercedes suddenly turned left and climbed up a slight hill. Adam threw his steering wheel over to follow it, and for several yards careered up the wrong side of the road, narrowly missing a post van meandering down towards him. He watched carefully as the taxi turned left again, and in order to keep in contact he veered in front of a bus so sharply that it was forced to slam on its brakes. Several passengers, thrown from their seats, waved their fists at him as the bus's horn blared.

The taxi was now only a couple of hundred yards ahead. Once again Adam began to pick up some ground when suddenly it swerved into the kerbside and screeched to a halt. Nothing seemed to happen for the next few seconds as Adam weaved his way towards the stationary taxi, skidding to a halt directly behind the Mercedes. He then leaped out of the car and ran towards the parked vehicle. But, without warning, the old man jumped out of the taxi on the far side of the car and sprinted off up a side-street carrying with him Heidi's airport shopping bag and a small suitcase.

Adam pulled the back door open and stared at the beautiful girl who sat motionless. "Are you all right, are you all right?" he shouted, suddenly realising how much she meant to him. Heidi did not move a muscle and made no reply. Adam put his arms on her shoulders and looked into her eyes but they showed no response. He began to stroke her hair and then without warning her head fell limply on to his shoulder like a rag doll and a small trickle of blood started to run from the corner of her mouth. Adam felt cold and sick and began to tremble uncontrollably. He looked up at the taxi-driver. His arms were loose by his side and his body slumped over the wheel. There was no sign of life in the middle-aged man.

He refused to accept that they were dead.

Adam kept holding on to Heidi as he stared beyond her: the old man had reached the top of the hill.

Why did he still think of him as an old man? He was obviously not old at all, but young and very fit. Suddenly Adam's fear turned to anger. He had a split second to make a decision. He let go of Heidi, jumped out of the car and started to sprint up the hill after her killer. Two or three onlookers had already gathered on the kerbside and were now staring at Adam and the two cars. He had to catch the man who was still running. Adam moved as fast as he could but the trenchcoat he was wearing slowed him down, and by the time he too had reached the top of the hill the killer was a clear hundred yards ahead of him, weaving his way through the main thoroughfare. Adam tried to lengthen his stride as he watched the man leap on to a passing tram, but he was too far behind to make any impression on him and could only watch the tram moving inexorably into the distance.

The man stood on the tram steps and stared back at Adam. He held up the shopping bag defiantly with one hand. The back was no longer hunched, the figure no longer frail, and even at that distance, Adam could sense the triumph in the man's stance. Adam stood for several seconds in the middle of the road helplessly watching the tram as it disappeared out of sight.

He tried to gather his thoughts. He realised that there was little hope of picking up a taxi during the rush hour. Behind him he could hear sirens of what he presumed were ambulances trying to rush to the scene of the accident. "Accident," said Adam. "They will soon discover it was murder." He tried to start sorting out in his mind the madness of the last half hour. None of it made sense. He would surely find it was all a mistake . . . Then he touched the side of his coat, touched the package that held the Tsar's icon. The killer hadn't gone to all that trouble for £20,000 – murdering two innocent people who happened to have got in his way – why, why, *why*, was the icon that important? What had the Sotheby's expert said? "A Russian gentlemen had inquired after the piece." Adam's mind began to whirl. If it was Emmanuel Rosenbaum and that was what he had killed for, all he had ended up with was a large box of Swiss liqueur chocolates.

When Adam heard the whistle behind him he felt relieved that help was at hand but as he turned he saw two officers with guns out of their holsters pointing towards him. He instinctively turned his jog into a run, and looking over his shoulder he saw that several police were now giving chase. He lengthened his stride again and, despite the trench-coat, doubted if there were a member of the Swiss force who could hope

to keep up the pace he set for more than a quarter of a mile. He turned
into the first alley he came to and speeded up. It was narrow – not wide
enough for even two bicycles to pass. Once he was beyond the alley he
selected a one-way street. It was crammed with cars, and he was able
swiftly and safely to move in and out of the slow-moving oncoming
traffic.

   In a matter of minutes he had lost the pursuing police, but he still ran
on, continually switching direction until he felt he had covered at least
two miles. He finally turned into a quiet street and halfway down saw a
fluorescent sign advertising the Hotel Monarche. It didn't look much
more than a guest house, and certainly wouldn't have qualified under
the description of an hotel. He stopped in the shadows and waited,
taking in great gulps of air. After about three minutes his breathing was
back to normal and he marched straight into the hotel.

CHAPTER ELEVEN

He stood naked, staring at the image of Emmanuel Rosenbaum in the
hotel mirror. He didn't like what he saw. First he removed the teeth,
then began to click his own up and down: he had been warned that the
gums would ache for days. Then painstakingly he shed each layer of his
bulbous nose, admiring the skill and artistry that had gone into
creating such a monstrosity. It will be too conspicuous, he had told
them. They will remember nothing else, had come back the experts'
reply.

   When the last layer had been removed, the aristocratic one that took
its place looked ridiculous in the centre of such a face. Next he began on
the lined forehead that even moved when he frowned. As the lines
disappeared, so the years receded. Next the flaccid red cheeks, and
finally the two chins. The Swiss bankers would have been amazed at
how easily the sharp rubbing of a pumice stone removed the indelible
number on the inside of his arm. Once more he studied himself in the
mirror. The hair, short and greying, would take nature longer. When
they had cut his hair and smeared that thick, mud-like concoction all
over his scalp he realised how an Irishman must feel to be tarred and
feathered. Moments later he stood under a warm shower, his fingers
massaging deep into the roots of his hair. Black treacly water started to
run down his face and body before finally disappearing down the plug

hole. It took half a bottle of shampoo before his hair had returned to its normal colour, but he realised that it would take considerably longer before he stopped looking like a staff sergeant in the United States Marines.

In a corner of the room lay the long baggy coat, the shiny shapeless suit, the black tie, the off-white shirt, woollen mittens and the Israeli passport. Hours of preparation discarded in a matter of minutes. He longed to burn them all, but instead left them in a heap. He returned to the main room and stretched himself out on the bed like a yawning cat. His back still ached from all the bending and crouching. He stood up, then touched his toes and threw his arms high above his head fifty times. He rested for one minute before completing fifty press-ups.

He returned to the bathroom and had a second shower – cold. He was beginning to feel like a human being again. He then changed into a freshly ironed cream silk shirt and a new double-breasted suit.

Before making one phone call to London and two more to Moscow he ordered dinner in his room so that no one would see him – he had no desire to explain how the man who checked in was thirty years younger than the man eating alone in his room. Like a hungry animal he tore at the steak and gulped the wine.

He stared at the colourful carrier bag but felt no desire to finish off the meal with one of Scott's liqueur chocolates. Once again he felt anger at the thought of the Englishman getting the better of him.

His eyes then rested on the little leather suitcase that lay on the floor by the side of his bed. He opened it and took out the copy of the icon that Zaborski had ordered he should always have with him so that there could be no doubt when he came across the original of St George and the Dragon.

At a little after eleven he switched on the late-night news. They had no photograph of the suspect, only one of that stupid taxi-driver who had driven so slowly it had cost the fool his life, and the pretty German girl who had tried to fight back. It had been pathetic, one firm clean strike and her neck was broken. The television announcer said the police were searching for an unnamed Englishman. Romanov smiled at the thought of police searching for Scott while he was eating steak in a luxury hotel. Although the Swiss police had no photograph of the murderer, Romanov didn't need one. It was a face he would never forget. In any case, his contact in England had already told him a lot more about Captain Scott in one phone call than the Swiss police could hope to discover for another week.

When Romanov was told the details of Scott's military career and decorations for bravery he considered it would be a pleasure to kill such a man.

Lying motionless on a mean little bed, Adam tried to make sense of all

the pieces that made up a black jigsaw. If Goering had left the icon to
his father, and his alias had been Emmanuel Rosenbaum, then a real-
life Emmanuel Rosenbaum didn't exist. But he *did* exist: he had even
killed twice in his attempt to get his hands on the Tsar's icon. Adam
leaned over, switched on the bedside light, then pulled the small
package out of the pocket of his trenchcoat. He unwrapped it carefully
before holding the icon under the light. St George stared back at him –
no longer looking magnificent, it seemed to Adam, more accusing.
Adam would have handed the icon over to Rosenbaum without a
second thought if it would have stopped Heidi from sacrificing her life.

By midnight Adam had decided what had to be done, but he didn't
stir from that tiny room until a few minutes after three. He lifted himself
quietly off the bed, opened the door, checked the corridor, and then
locked the door noiselessly behind him before creeping down the stairs.
When he reached the bottom step he waited and listened. The night
porter had nodded off in front of a television that now let out a dim,
monotonous hum. A silver dot remained in the centre of the screen.
Adam took nearly two minutes to reach the front door, stepping on a
noisy floorboard just once: but the porter's snores had been enough to
cover that. Once outside, Adam checked up and down the street but
there was no sign of any movement. He didn't want to go far, so he
stayed in the shadows by the side of the road, moving at a pace
unfamiliar to him. When he reached the corner he saw what he was
searching for and it was still about a hundred yards away.

There was still no one to be seen, so he quickly made his way to the
phone box. He pressed a twenty centime coin into the box and waited.
A voice said, "*Est-ce-que je peux vous aider?*" Adam uttered only one word,
"International." A moment later another voice asked the same
question.

"I want to make a reverse charge call to London," said Adam firmly.
He had no desire to repeat himself.

"Yes," said the voice. "And what is your name?"

"George Cromer," replied Adam.

"And the number you are speaking from?"

"Geneva 271982." He reversed the last three digits: he felt the police
could well be listening in on all calls to England that night. He then told
the girl the number in London he required.

"Can you wait for a moment, please?"

"Yes," said Adam as his eyes checked up and down the street once
again, still looking for any unfamiliar movement. Only the occasional
early morning car sped by. He remained absolutely motionless in the
corner of the box.

He could hear the connection being put through. "Please wake up,"
his lips mouthed. At last the ringing stopped and Adam recognised the
familiar voice which answered.

"Who is this?" Lawrence asked, sounding irritated but perfectly awake.

"Will you accept a reverse charge call from a Mr George Cromer in Geneva?"

"George Cromer, Lord Cromer, the Governor of the Bank of Eng –? Yes, I will," he said.

"It's me, Lawrence," said Adam.

"Thank God. Where are you?"

"I'm still in Geneva but I'm not sure you're going to believe what I'm about to tell you. While we were waiting to board our plane home a man pulled Heidi into a taxi and later murdered her before I could catch up with them. And the trouble is that the Swiss police think I'm the killer."

"Now just relax, Adam. I know that much. It's been on the evening news and the police have already been around to interview me. It seems Heidi's brother identified you."

"What do you mean *identified* me? I didn't do it. You know I couldn't do it. It was a man called Rosenbaum, not me, Lawrence."

"Rosenbaum? Adam, who is Rosenbaum?"

Adam tried to sound calm. "Heidi and I came to Geneva this morning to pick up a gift from a Swiss bank that Pa had left me in his will. It turned out to be a painting. Then when we returned to the airport, this Rosenbaum grabbed Heidi thinking she had got the painting which didn't make any sense because the damned icon's only worth £20,000."

"Icon?" said Lawrence.

"Yes, an icon of St George and the Dragon," said Adam. "That's not important. What's important is that . . ."

"Now listen and listen carefully," interrupted Lawrence, "because I'm not going to repeat myself. Keep out of sight until the morning and then give yourself up at our Consulate. Just see you get there in one piece and I'll make sure that the Consul will be expecting you. Don't arrive until eleven because London is an hour behind Geneva and I'll need every minute to arrange matters and see that the consul staff is properly organised."

Adam found himself smiling for the first time in twelve hours.

"Did the killer get what he was after?" Lawrence asked.

"No, he didn't get the icon," said Adam, "he only got my mother's chocolates . . ."

"Thank God for that and keep out of sight of the Swiss police because they are convinced it was you who killed Heidi."

"But . . ." began Adam.

"No explanations. Just be at the Consulate at eleven. Now you'd better get off the line," said Lawrence. "Eleven, and don't be late."

"Right," said Adam, "and . . ." but the phone was only giving out a long burr. Thank God for Lawrence, he thought: the Lawrence of old who didn't need to ask any questions because he already knew the answers. Christ, what had he got himself involved in? Adam checked the street once again. Still no one in sight. He quickly stole the two hundred yards back to the hotel. The front door remained unlocked, the porter asleep, the television screen still faintly humming, the silver dot in place. Adam was back on his bed by five minutes past four. He didn't sleep. Rosenbaum, Heidi, the taxi driver, the Russian gentleman at Sotheby's. So many pieces of a jigsaw, none of them fitting into place.

But the one thing that worried him most was the conversation with Lawrence – the Lawrence of old?

The two policemen arrived at the Hotel Monarche at twenty past seven that Thursday morning. They were tired, discontent and hungry. Since midnight they had visited forty-three hotels on the west side of the city, on each occasion with no success. They had checked over a thousand registration cards and woken seven innocent Englishmen who had not come anywhere near fitting the description of Adam Scott.

At eight they would be off duty and could go home to their wives and breakfasts; but they still had three more hotels to check before then. When the landlady saw them coming into the hall she waddled as quickly as possible from the inner office towards them. She loathed the police and was willing to believe anyone who told her that the Swiss pigs were even worse than the Germans. Twice in the last year she had been fined and once even threatened with jail over her failure to register every guest. If they caught her once more she knew they would take her licence away and with it her living. Her slow mind tried to recall who had booked in the previous evening. Eight people had registered but only two had paid cash – the Englishman who hardly opened his mouth, Mr Pemberton was the name he had filled in on the missing card, and Maurice who always turned up with a different girl whenever he was in Geneva. She had destroyed both their cards and pocketed the money. Maurice and the girl had left by seven and she had already made up their bed, but the Englishman was still asleep in his room.

"We need to check your registration cards for last night, madame."

"Certainly, monsieur," she replied with a warm smile, and gathered together the six remaining cards: two Frenchmen, one Italian, two nationals from Zurich and one from Basle.

"Did an Englishman stay here last night?"

"No," said the landlady firmly. "I haven't had an Englishman," she added helpfully, "for at least a month. Would you like to see the cards for last week?"

"No, that won't be necessary," said the policeman. The landlady grunted with satisfaction. "But we will still need to check your unoccupied rooms. I see from the certificate that there are twelve guest bedrooms in the hotel," the policeman continued. "So there must be six that should be empty."

"There's no one in them," said the landlady. "I've already checked them once this morning."

"We still need to see for ourselves," the other officer insisted.

The landlady picked up her pass key and waddled towards the stairs, which she proceeded to climb as if they were the final summit of Everest. She opened bedrooms five, seven, nine, ten, eleven. Maurice's room had been remade within minutes of his leaving but the old lady knew she would lose her licence the moment they entered twelve. She just stopped herself from knocking on the door before she turned the key in the lock. The two policemen walked in ahead of her while she remained in the corridor, just in case there was any trouble. Not for the first time that day she cursed the efficiency of Swiss police.

"Thank you, madame," said the first policeman as he stepped back into the corridor. "We are sorry to have troubled you," he added. He put a tick on his list next to the Hotel Monarche.

As the two policemen made their way downstairs the landlady walked into room number twelve, mystified. The bed was undisturbed, as if it had not been slept in, and there was no sign of anyone having spent the night there. She called on her tired memory. She hadn't drunk that much the previous night – she touched the fifty francs in her pocket as if to prove the point. "I wonder where he is," she muttered.

For the past hour Adam had been crouching behind a derelict coach in a railway goods yard less than half a mile from the hotel. He had a clear view for a hundred yards in every direction. He had watched the early morning commuters flooding in on every train. By twenty past eight Adam judged they were at their peak. He checked that the icon was in place and left his hideout to join the flood as they headed to work. He stopped at the kiosk to purchase a newspaper. The only English paper on sale at that time in the morning was the *Herald–Tribune*: the London papers didn't arrive until the first plane could land, but Adam had seen the *Herald–Tribune* come in on the train from Paris. He made two other purchases at the station kiosk before rejoining the scurrying crowds: a city map of Geneva and a large bar of Nestlé's chocolate.

There were still over two hours to kill before he could present himself at the Consulate. Although it was some way in the distance, he could already see the building he had marked out as his next place of sanctuary. He steered a route towards it that allowed him to stay in contact with the largest number of people. When he arrived in the square he continued under the shop awnings round the longest route, clinging to the wall, always avoiding the open spaces. It took a considerable time but his judgment was perfect. He reached the front door as hundreds of worshippers were leaving from the early morning Communion service.

Once inside, he felt safe. St Peter's was set out like most of the great cathedrals of the world and Adam found his bearings in a matter of moments. He made his way slowly down the side aisle towards the Lady Chapel, dropped some coins in one of the collection boxes, lit a candle and placed it in a vacant holder below a statue of the Virgin Mother. He then fell on his knees, but his eyes never closed. A lapsed Catholic, he found he no longer believed in God – except when he was ill, frightened or in an aeroplane. After about twenty minutes had passed Adam was distressed to see that there were now only a handful of people left in the cathedral. Some old ladies dressed in black filled a front pew, moving their rosary beads methodically and chanting, "*Ave Maria, gratia plena, Domine teum, Benedicta . . .*" A few tourists were craning their necks to admire the King beam roof, their eyes only looking upwards.

Adam rose slowly, his eyes darting from side to side. He stretched his legs and walked over to a confessional box partly hidden behind a pillar. A small sign on the wooden support showed that the box was not in use. Adam slipped in, sat down and pulled the curtain closed.

First he took out the *Herald–Tribune* from his trenchcoat pocket, and then the bar of chocolate. He tore the silver paper from the chocolate and began to munch greedily. Next he searched for the story. Only one or two items of English news were on the front page, as most of the articles were devoted to what was happening in America. "The pound still too high at $2.80?" one headline suggested. Adam's eye passed over the smaller headlines until he saw the paragraph he was looking for. It was in the bottom left-hand corner: "Englishman sought after German girl and Swiss taxi-driver murdered." Adam read the story, and only began to tremble when he discovered they knew his name:

"Captain Adam Scott, who recently resigned his commission from the Royal Wessex Regiment, is wanted . . . please turn to page fifteen." Adam began to turn the large pages. It was not easy in the restricted space of a confessional box. ". . . for questioning by the Geneva police in connection with . . ."

"*Au nom du Père, du Fils et du Saint Esprit.*"

Adam looked up from the paper startled and considered making a dash for it. But he allowed his long-ago training to take hold as he found himself saying automatically, "Father, bless me, for I have sinned and wish to confess."

"Good, my son, and what form has this sin taken?" asked the priest in accented but clear English.

Adam thought quickly, I must give him no clue as to who I am. He looked out through the gap in the curtain and was alarmed to see two policemen questioning another priest by the west door. He drew the curtains tight and turned to the only accent he could ever imitate with any conviction.

"I'm over from Dublin, Father, and last night I picked up this local girl in a bar and took her back to my hotel."

"Yes, my son."

"Well, one thing led to another, Father."

"Another what, my son?"

"Well, I took her up to my room."

"Yes, my son?"

"And she started to undress."

"And then what happened?"

"She started to undress me."

"Did you try to resist, my son?"

"Yes, Father, but it got harder."

"And did intercourse take place?" asked the priest.

"I'm afraid so, Father. I couldn't stop myself. She was very beautiful," Adam added.

"And is it your intention to marry this girl, my son?"

"Oh, no, Father. I'm already married and have two lovely children, Seamus and Maureen."

"It is a night you must for ever put behind you."

"I'd like to, Father."

"Has this happened before?"

"No, Father, it's the first time I've been abroad on my own. I swear to it."

"Then let it be a lesson to you, my son, and may the Lord find it in his mercy to forgive you this abominable sin and now you must make your act of contrition."

"Oh my God . . ."

When Adam had completed the act of contrition the priest pronounced absolution and told him he must as penance say three decades of the Rosary.

"And one more thing."

"Yes, Father?"

"You will tell your wife everything the moment you return to Ireland or you cannot hope for atonement. You must promise me that, my son."

"When I see my wife, I will tell her everything that happened last night, Father," Adam promised, as he once again checked through the curtains. The police were no longer anywhere to be seen.

"Good, and continue to pray to our Blessed Lady to keep you from the evils of temptation."

Adam folded up his paper, pushed it in the trenchcoat and bolted from the little box and took a seat on the end of a pew. He lowered his head and began to whisper the Lord's Prayer as he opened the map of Geneva and began to study the road plan. He had located the British Consulate on the far side of a large garden square by the time he reached 'Deliver us from evil.' He estimated that it was just over a mile away from the cathedral, but seven streets and a bridge had to be negotiated before he would be safe. He returned to the Lady Chapel and his knees. Adam checked his watch. It was too early to leave St Peter's so he remained head in hands for another thirty minutes, going over the route again and again. He watched a party of tourists as they were conducted through the cathedral. His eyes never left them as they began to move nearer and nearer to the great door at the west end of the aisle. He needed to time it to perfection.

Suddenly Adam rose and walked quickly down the side aisle reaching the porch only a yard behind the party of tourists. They shielded him out on to the square. Adam ducked under a shop awning at the side of the road, then walked round three sides of the square to avoid the one policeman on duty by the north corner. He crossed the first road as the light turned red and headed up a one-way street. He kept on the inside of the pavement, knowing he had to turn left at the end of the road. Two uniformed policemen came round the corner and walked straight towards him. He jumped into the first shop without looking and turned his back on the pavement.

"*Bonjour, monsieur,*" said a young lady to Adam. "*Vous désirez quelque chose?*" Adam looked around him. Lissome mannequins in knickers and bras with suspenders and long black nylon stockings stood all around him.

"I'm looking for a present for my wife."

The girl smiled. "Perhaps a slip?" she suggested.

"Yes," said Adam, "definitely a slip. Do you have one in burgundy?" he asked, as he half turned to watch the policemen stroll past.

"Yes, I think so, but I'll have to check in the stockroom."

Adam had reached the next street corner long before she had returned with 'just the thing'.

He managed the next three crossings without incident and with only two hundred yards to go could already feel his heart thumping as if it was trying to escape from his body. On the final corner there was only one policeman in sight, and he seemed intent on directing traffic. Adam kept his back to the officer as he could now see the garden square that had only shown up on the map as a tiny green blob. On the far side of the road he spotted a Union Jack hanging above a blue door.

Never run the last few yards, especially when it's open ground, his sergeant had told him many times when on patrol in the Malayan jungle. He crossed the road and stood on the edge of the small park, only fifty yards away from safety. A policeman was patrolling aimlessly up the road but Adam suspected that was only because there were several consulates standing adjacent to one another. He watched the officer carefully. It took the man two minutes to reach the French Consulate before he turned and continued his leisurely walk back.

Adam ducked behind a tree in the corner of the little park and selected another tree on the far side of the road only yards from the Consulate front door that would shield him from the oncoming policeman. He estimated that by walking at a speed that wouldn't attract attention he could cover the last thirty yards in under ten seconds. He waited for the policeman to reach his farthest point.

He checked the Consulate door again, relieved to see a girl go in and a man carrying a briefcase come out on to the street. There seemed to be no guard in sight as the door remained half open. He looked up at the bay window on the first floor. He could see two men staring out at the park as if waiting expectantly for someone to arrive. Lawrence had succeeded. In moments he would be safe. Adam pulled up the collar of his trenchcoat and set off as the cathedral clock behind him struck eleven. The policeman was now a few paces from reaching his farthest point but still walking in the opposite direction. Adam crossed the road at a measured stride. When he reached the tramlines in the centre he had to stop suddenly to let a car pass by. The policeman turned to start his journey back.

For several seconds Adam remained motionless between the tramlines as he stared at the tree he had selected to shield him if the policeman turned before he could reach the front door. He took a confident pace towards the British Consulate. A tall man of athletic build, his head covered in a stubble of short fair hair, stepped out to greet him.

Adam would not have recognised him but for the eyes.

PART TWO

10 DOWNING STREET
LONDON SW1

June 17, 1966

CHAPTER TWELVE

10 Downing Street, London SW1, June 17, 1966

When Sir Morris Youngfield left the Prime Minister he still was unable to work out why the possession of any icon could be that important.

Leaving Number 10 behind him, Sir Morris marched quickly into the Foreign Office courtyard and within moments was stepping out of the lift on the seventh floor. When he walked into his office, Tessa, his secretary, was laying out some papers for him.

"I want a D4 assembled immediately," he said to the woman who had served him so loyally for fourteen years. "And ask Commander Busch to join the team."

Tessa raised her eyebrows but Sir Morris ignored her silent comment as he knew he couldn't hope to get to the bottom of this one without the cooperation of the Americans. Once more Sir Morris considered the Prime Minister's instructions. Harold Wilson hadn't needed to explain that he didn't get that many transatlantic calls from Lyndon Johnson seeking his help.

But why a Russian icon of an English saint?

As Romanov moved towards him, Adam took a pace backwards from the tramlines to allow the tramcar to pass between them. When the tram had passed Adam was no longer to be seen. Romanov snarled at such an amateur trick, sprinted the twenty yards necessary to catch up with the tram and to the astonishment of the passengers, leapt on. He began checking over the faces row by row.

Adam waited for the tramcar to travel another twenty yards before he emerged from behind a tree on the far side of the road. He felt confident he could reach the safety of the Consulate door long before Heidi's killer could hope to return. He checked the other side of the road and swore under his breath. The policeman patrolling was now only a few paces from the Consulate and heading relentlessly towards it. Adam looked back at the tram which had just been passed by another heading towards him. To his dismay, he saw his adversary leap from one platform to the other with the agility of a top-class gymnast. With the policeman now only yards from the Consulate door Adam was left with no choice but to retreat and sprint back up the one-way street. After fifty yards he glanced over his shoulder. The man he knew only as

Rosenbaum couldn't have looked less like a helpless old man as he started running towards him.

Adam jumped between the cars and buses and dodged around the milling pedestrians as he tried to lengthen the fifty yards distance between them. At the first crossroad he saw a plump lady coming out of a phone box a few yards away. He changed direction quickly and leapt into the empty box, crouching into the far corner. The door slowly squelched shut. Rosenbaum came hurtling round the corner and was twenty yards past the box before he realised that Adam had shot back out and down the road in the opposite direction. Adam knew he had at least five seconds before Rosenbaum could hope to see which direction he had chosen. One and two and three and four and five, he counted as he ran along the road. He then checked right, before mounting three steps and pushing through some swing doors. He found himself in front of a small counter, behind which sat a young woman holding a small wad of tickets.

"*Deux francs, monsieur,*" said the girl. Adam looked at the little box, quickly took out two francs and made his way down the long dark passage and through another set of swing doors. He stood at the back waiting for his eyes to become accustomed to the dark. It was the first performance of the day and the cinema was nearly empty. Adam chose a seat on the end of a row that was an equal distance from both exits.

He stared at the screen, thankful that the movie had just begun, because he needed some time to formulate a plan. Whenever the screen was bright enough he checked the little red road on the map, and then using the top of his thumb as a one-inch ruler, he was able to estimate that the nearest border into France was only eight miles away at Ferney-Voltaire. From there he could travel to Paris via Dijon and be back home almost as quickly as it would take him to sit through *Exodus* a second time. Having decided on his route, the next problem for Adam was how to travel. He dismissed all forms of public transport and settled on hiring a car. He remained in his seat during the interval to double-check the routes. The moment Paul Newman reappeared on the screen, he folded up the map and left the cinema by the exit which had been least used during the past four hours.

When Sir Morris entered the room for the meeting of the 'Northern Department', he found the rest of the D4 were already assembled, and familiarising themselves with the files that had been presented to them only an hour before.

He glanced round the table at the specially selected D4, all hand-picked men but only one of them did he consider his equal. And it wasn't the old war-horse Alec Snell who had served at the Foreign Office longer than any of them and was touching his moustache nervously as he waited for Sir Morris to take his seat. Next to him sat

Brian Matthews, known in the Department as the 'well-balanced man': a grammar school boy with a double first and a chip on both shoulders. Opposite him was Commander Ralph Busch, the CIA representative with a short fuse, who after five years attached to the Embassy in Grosvenor Square considered himself more British than the British, and even imitated the Foreign Office style of dress to prove it. At the far end of the table, Sir Morris's second in command, who some said was a little too young, although everyone except Tessa had forgotten that Sir Morris had held his job at the same age.

The four members of the committee stopped talking once Sir Morris had settled in his seat at the head of the table.

"Gentlemen," he began – the only lady present being Tessa, whose existence he rarely acknowledged – "the Prime Minister has given this D4 his full blessing. And he requires detailed reports to be sent to him every twelve hours, wherever he is, and at any time of the night or day if there should be any unexpected development. So, as you can see, there is no time to waste. This particular D4 has coopted as part of its team a liaison officer from the CIA, Commander Ralph Busch. I have worked with Commander Busch several times over the past five years and I am delighted that the American Embassy has chosen him to represent them."

The man seated on Sir Morris's right bowed slightly. At five feet nine inches, with broad, muscular shoulders and a neat black beard, he looked every inch the sailor whom Player's cigarettes were always trying to please. Indeed, a sailor wouldn't have been a bad guess because Busch had been a commander in PT boats during the Second World War.

"From the latest reports I have received," Sir Morris continued, opening the file in front of him, "it appears that Scott never reached the Consulate this morning, despite our request for the police to have no more than a token force on duty within two hundred yards of the park.

"Since our sketchy information yesterday, BEA have confirmed," said Sir Morris consulting a note in front of him, "that Scott received a call from Roget et Cie while he was at the airport. After considerable pressure from our Ambassador and Interpol we have learned from Mr Roget that the purpose of Scott's visit to the bank was to pick up an unknown bequest from a Mr Emmanuel Rosenbaum. Further checking shows that a Mr Rosenbaum arrived in Zurich yesterday morning and travelled on to Geneva in the afternoon. He left his hotel first thing this morning and has subsequently vanished from the face of the earth. None of this would be of any great significance if Mr Rosenbaum had not boarded the aeroplane to Zurich from –" Sir Morris couldn't resist a short dramatic pause "– Moscow. I think it is not unreasonable therefore to assume that Mr Rosenbaum, whoever he is, works directly or indirectly for the KGB.

"The KGB, as we know to our cost, is well serviced in Geneva, by a large number of East Europeans working under the guise of the United Nations for ILO and WHO, all with the necessary diplomatic status they need to carry out undercover work. What still remains a mystery to me is why Mr Rosenbaum should be willing to kill two innocent people for a relatively obscure icon. That brings my report up to date. But perhaps you have come up with something new," said Sir Morris turning to his Number Two.

Lawrence Pemberton looked up from his end of the table. "Since our meeting this morning, Sir Morris," he began, "I have spoken to Scott's sister, his mother and a firm of solicitors in Appleshaw who administered his father's will. It transpires that Scott was left with nothing of any real importance in the will apart from an envelope which his mother says contained a letter from Reichsmarshal Hermann Goering." There was an immediate buzz around the table until Sir Morris tapped his knuckle on the desk.

"Do we have any idea of the contents of Goering's letter?" asked Sir Morris.

"The whole letter, no, sir. But one of our examination entrants, a Mr Nicholas Wainwright, was asked by Scott to translate what we now believe was a paragraph from the letter because later Wainwright asked the examination board if it was part of his test." Lawrence extracted a piece of paper from the file in front of him and read out the paragraph:

During the year you cannot have failed to notice that I have been receiving from one of the guards a regular supply of Havana cigars – one of the few pleasures I have been permitted, despite my incarceration. The cigars themselves have also served another purpose, as each one contained a capsule with a small amount of poison. Enough to allow me to survive my trial, while ensuring that I shall cheat the executioner.

"That's all?" said Sir Morris.

"I'm afraid so," said Lawrence, "although I believe it confirms what Scott told me last night was his reason for travelling to Geneva. There is no doubt in my mind that the package he went to pick up contained the icon of St George and the Dragon left to his father by Goering."

"St George and the Dragon," said Matthews interrupting, "but that's the icon that half of the KGB have been searching for during the past two weeks and my Department has been trying to find out why."

"And what have you come up with?" asked Sir Morris.

"Very little," admitted Matthews. "But we began to assume that it must be a decoy because the Tsar's icon of St George and the Dragon hangs in the Winter Palace at Leningrad and has done so for three hundred years."

"Anything else?" asked Sir Morris.

"Only that the section leader in search of the icon is Alex Romanov," said Matthews.

Snell gave out a low whistle. "Well, at least we know we're dealing with the First Division," he said.

There was a long silence before Sir Morris offered, "One thing is clear. We have to get to Scott first and must assume that it's Romanov we're up against. So what are we doing about it?"

"As much as we can get away with," said Lawrence. "Along with the Americans we have seventeen men operatives in Geneva, all of them trying to find Scott."

"The Swiss police have a thousand doing the same job, though heaven knows whose side they imagine they're on," added Snell.

Lawrence chipped back in. "And it's been almost impossible to convince them that Scott is not in any way responsible for the two murders. So we may have to get him out without relying on their cooperation."

"But what do you imagine would be the outcome if Romanov or this Rosenbaum, who must also be part of the KGB, manages to get to Scott before we do?" asked Matthews.

"A civilian up against one of the Russians' most ruthless agents. That's all we need," said Commander Busch.

Lawrence inclined his head towards the American. "I've known Adam for most of my life. The irony of his particular predicament is that it was I who, without his knowledge, recommended that he should be interviewed for a place in the Northern Department. It was my intention that he should join us as soon as he had completed his course as a trainee. If Romanov or any of his cohorts come face to face with Scott they'd better remember that he was awarded a Military Cross when faced with a thousand Chinese."

"But if it turned out to be Romanov," asked Snell, "would Scott be able to kill him?"

"I would have said no before Rosenbaum murdered his girlfriend," said Lawrence.

"I wouldn't be confident of his chances even then," said Busch.

"Neither would I," added Matthews.

"That's because you don't know Adam Scott," said Lawrence.

Matthews lowered his eyes in order to avoid a clash with his boss. His boss. Ten years his junior. A shortlist of two and they had chosen another Oxbridge man to be Under-Secretary. Matthews knew that as far as the Foreign Office was concerned, he had gone to the wrong school and the wrong university. He should have taken his father's advice and joined the police force. There were no class barriers there, and he would probably have been a chief superintendent by now.

Sir Morris ignored the little outburst which had become fairly common since he had selected Pemberton to leapfrog the older man.

"Are we allowed to know," interrupted Snell, looking straight at Busch, "why a relatively obscure icon is of such disproportionate importance to both Russia and the United States?"

"We are as mystified as you," said the American. "All we can add to your current information, is that two weeks ago the Russians deposited gold bullion in New York to the value of over seven hundred million dollars without any explanation. We are, of course, not certain at the moment there is any connection."

"Seven hundred million dollars?" said Sir Morris. "You could buy half the countries in the United Nations for that."

"And every icon that has ever been painted," said Matthews.

"Let's get down to what we actually know, and stop guessing at what might be," said Sir Morris turning back to his Number Two. "What's the exact IA position?"

Lawrence undid a folder with a red band around it, the words 'Immediate Action' printed across the top in black. He did not need to refer to it, but still glanced down from time to time to check he had not forgotten anything. "As I have already briefed you, we have seventeen agents in the field and the Americans are flying a further twelve into Geneva today. With the Russians and the Swiss roaming the city like knights of the round table in search of the Holy Grail, I can only believe that someone will come across Scott fairly soon. One of our biggest problems, as I explained, is that the Swiss are unwilling to cooperate. As far as they are concerned, Scott is a common criminal on the run and should they get to him first they have made it clear they will not allow him diplomatic immunity.

"We, as well as the Swiss police, and undoubtedly the Russians," continued Lawrence, "have started checking out all the obvious places: hotels, guest houses, restaurants, airports, car hire companies, even lavatories, and we remain in constant touch with every one of our agents on the ground. So if Scott suddenly appears out of nowhere we should be able to go to his aid at a moment's notice." Lawrence looked up to observe that one of the team was taking down all the details. "Added to that, the Post Office are intercepting every call made to Barclays DCO from Geneva. If Scott does try to get in contact with me again at the bank or at my flat it will be put through to this office automatically," he said.

"Is he aware that you work for the Service?" asked Snell, putting a hand through his dark hair.

"No. He, like my dear mother, still thinks I'm a bank official in the International Department of Barclays DCO. But it won't be long before he works out that that's only a front. Unlike my mother, he doesn't always believe everything I tell him and after our conversation last night he is bound to have become suspicious."

"Do we have anything else to go on?" Sir Morris asked, looking up at Lawrence.

"Not a lot more at the moment, sir. We are doing everything possible, remembering this is not a home match; but I still anticipate that the exercise will be over one way or another within twenty-four hours. Because of that I have requested overnight facilities to be set up in the building should you feel we need them. When you return after dinner you will find beds already made up in your offices."

"No one will be going out to dinner tonight," said Sir Morris.

The cinema opened on to the busy pavement and Adam slipped into the main stream of commuters who were now returning home for dinner. As he kept walking he made certain of as little head movement as possible but his eyes never stayed still, checking everything within 180 degrees. After he had covered three blocks, he spotted a red Avis sign swinging in the afternoon breeze on the far side of the road. He safely reconnoitred the crowded crossing, but once his foot touched the far pavement he froze on the spot. Just ahead of him in a fast, jostling crowd stood a man in a raincoat. He was continually looking around, while making no attempt to walk in either direction. Was he one of Rosenbaum's men, the police, or even British? There was no way of telling whose side he was on. Adam's eyes didn't leave the man as he took out an intercom and, putting it to his mouth, whispered into it. "Nothing to report, sir. Still no sign of our man, and I haven't seen any of the KGB either."

Adam, unable to hear the words, switched into a side road and almost knocked over a boy selling papers. '*Le soldat anglais toujours à Genève*' the headline blared. Quickly he crossed another road, where he came to a stop again, this time behind a marble statue in the centre of a small patch of grass. He stared at the building in front of him but he knew there would be no point in his trying to hide there. He started to move away as a large, empty touring coach drew up and parked in front of the block. Smart blue lettering along the side of the coach proclaimed 'The Royal Philharmonic Orchestra'. Adam watched as some musicians walked out of the front door and climbed on to the coach carrying their instrument cases of assorted lengths and widths. One was even lugging a large kettle drum which he deposited in the boot of the coach. As the musicians continued to stream out of the hotel Adam decided he wouldn't get a better opportunity. When the next group came through the double doors he walked quickly forward and stepped into the middle of them before anyone could have spotted him. He then continued on past them through the open hotel door. The first thing he spotted in the crowded lobby was a double bass leaning against the wall. He glanced at the label around the neck of the unwieldy case.

'Robin Beresford.'

Adam walked over to the counter and gestured to the clerk. "I need my room key quickly – I've left my bow upstairs and now I'm holding everyone up."

"Yes, sir. What room number?" asked the clerk.

"I think it's 312, or was that yesterday?" said Adam.

"What name, sir?"

"Beresford – Robin Beresford."

The clerk handed him key 612. His only comment was: "You were three floors out."

"Thank you," said Adam. As he left the counter, he turned to check that the receptionist was already dealing with another customer. He walked smartly over to the lift which was disgorging still more musicians. Once it had emptied he stepped in, pressed the button for the sixth floor, and waited. He felt exhilarated as the lift doors eventually slid across and he was alone for the first time in several hours. When the doors opened again he was relieved to find there was no one standing in the corridor. He made his way quickly along the passage to room 612.

As he turned the key and opened the door he said firmly in as good a French accent as he could manage, "Room service", but as no one responded, he stepped in and locked the door behind him. An unopened suitcase had been left in one corner. Adam checked the label. Obviously Mr Beresford hadn't even had time to unpack. Adam checked the room, but there was no other sign of the hotel guest apart from a piece of paper on the side table. It was a typed itinerary:

'European Tour: Geneva, Frankfurt, Berlin, Amsterdam, London.

'Geneva, Bus 5.00 to Concert Hall rehearsal 6.00, Concert perform-ance 7.30, encores 10.00.

'Programme: Mozart's Horn Concerto, First Movement, Brahms's Second Symphony, Schubert's Unfinished Symphony.'

Adam looked at his watch: by the time Robin Beresford had completed the 'Unfinished Symphony' he would be over the border; but he still felt safe to remain in Room 612 until it was dark.

He picked up the phone by the bed and dialled room service. "Beresford, 612," he announced, and ordered himself some dinner before going into the bathroom. On the side of the basin was propped a little plastic bag with the words 'Compliments of the Management' printed across it. Inside Adam found soap, a tiny toothbrush, tooth-paste and a plastic razor.

He had just finished shaving when he heard a knock on the door and someone calling "Room service". Adam quickly covered his face with lather again and put on a hotel dressing gown before he opened the door. The waiter set up a table without giving Adam a second look. When he had finished his task he inquired, "Will you sign the bill, please, sir?"

He handed Adam a slip of paper. He signed it 'Robin Beresford' and added a fifteen per cent tip.

"Thank you," said the waiter and left. As soon as the door closed behind him, Adam's eyes settled on the feast of onion soup, rump steak with green beans and potatoes, and finally a raspberry sorbet. A bottle of house wine had been uncorked and needed only to be poured. He suddenly didn't feel that hungry.

He still couldn't accept what he had gone through. If only he hadn't pressed Heidi into joining him on this unnecessary journey. A week before she hadn't even known him and now he was responsible for her death. He would have to explain to her parents what had happened to their only daughter. But before Adam could face them he still had to come up with some explanation for the things he hadn't yet begun to understand. Not least the unimportant icon. Unimportant?

After he had half finished the meal he wheeled the trolley out into the corridor and placed the 'Do not disturb' sign on the door. Once back in the bedroom he stared out of the window over the city. The sun looked as if it had another hour allocated for Geneva. Adam lay down on the bed and began to consider what had happened in the last twenty-four hours of his life.

"Antarctic is in possession of an icon of St George and the Dragon. But we know from our files of that period that that particular icon was destroyed when the Grand Duke of Hesse's plane crashed over Belgium in 1937."

"That may well be what is written in your files," said the man on the other end of the phone. "But what if your information at Langley turns out to be wrong and the icon was found by Goering but not returned to the Grand Duke?"

"But Stalin confirmed at Yalta that the icon and its contents had been destroyed in the plane crash. He agreed to make no protest while he was not in possession of the original document. After all, that was the reason Roosevelt appeared to be gaining so little at the time while Stalin was getting so much in return. Can't you remember the fuss Churchill made?"

"I certainly can because he had worked out that it wasn't Britain who was going to benefit from such a decision."

"But if the Russians have now discovered the existence of the original icon?"

"You are suggesting they might also get their hands on the original document?"

"Precisely. So you must be sure to get to Antarctic before the Russians do, or for that matter, the Foreign Office."

"But I'm part of the Foreign Office team."

"And that's precisely what we want the Foreign Office to go on believing."

"And who's been sleeping in my bed, said Mother Bear."

Adam woke with a start. Looking down at him was a girl who held a double bass firmly by the neck with one hand and a bow in the other. She was nearly six foot and certainly weighed considerably more than Adam. She had long, gleaming red hair that was in such contrast to the rest of her that it was as if the Maker had started at the top and quickly lost interest. She wore a white blouse and a black flowing skirt that stopped an inch above the ground.

"Who are you?" asked Adam, startled.

"I'm not Goldilocks, that's for sure," parried the girl. "More to the point, who are you?"

Adam hesitated. "If I told you, you wouldn't believe me."

"I can't imagine why not," she said. "You don't look like Prince Charles or Elvis Presley to me, so go on, try me."

"I'm Adam Scott."

"Am I meant to swoon and run to your side, or scream and run away?" she inquired.

Adam suddenly realised that the girl couldn't have watched television or read a paper for at least two days. He switched tactics. "I thought my friend Robin Beresford was meant to be booked into this room," he said confidently.

"And so did I until I saw you on my bed."

"You're Robin Beresford?"

"You're quite sharp for someone who has just woken up."

"But Robin?"

"It's not my fault my father wanted a boy," she said. "And you still haven't explained what you're doing on my bed."

"Is there any hope of you listening to me for five minutes without continually interrupting?" asked Adam.

"Yes, but don't bother with any more fairy stories," said Robin. "My father was a born liar, and by the time I was twelve I could see through him like a pane of glass."

"I should have a seat if I were you," said Adam. "This may take longer than the average double bass accompaniment."

"I'll remain on my feet, if you don't mind," said Robin. "At least until the first lie."

"Suit yourself. What would you like first? The good news or the bad news?"

"Try me on the bad news," said Robin.

"The Swiss police want to arrest me and. . . ."

"What for?" interrupted Robin.

"Murder," said Scott.

"What's the good news?" she asked.

"I'm innocent."

Romanov stood in the Ambassador's office and rested his fingers on the table. "I blame myself," he said very quietly, "even more than I blame any of you. I underestimated the Englishman. He's good, and if any of you are hoping to kill him before I get to him you'll have to be *very* good." No one assembled in the Ambassador's office that night was disposed to disagree with the Comrade Major. Romanov paused to study the group of men who had been flown in from several Eastern satellites at short notice. All with long records of service to the State but only one of them, Valchek, was known to Romanov personally and he worked too closely with Zaborski to be trusted. Romanov had already faced the fact that only a few of them were acquainted with Geneva. He could only pray that the British and Americans were suffering from the same problem.

His eyes swept around the room. The Swiss police had the best chance of finding Scott and they weren't being at all helpful, he thought ruefully. However, Romanov had been pleased to learn from their head man stationed in Geneva that the Swiss had also refused to cooperate with the British or the Americans.

"Comrades," he said, the moment they had all settled, "there is no need to remind you that we have been entrusted with a vital assignment for the Motherland." He paused to check if any of the faces registered the slightest suggestion of cynicism. Satisfied, he continued, "We will therefore maintain a tight surveillance over Geneva in case Scott is still holed up somewhere in the city. My own guess is that, like all amateurs, he is, and will wait until it's dark, perhaps even first light, before he makes a run for the nearest border. The French border will be his most obvious choice. Despite going to war against the Germans twice in the past fifty years, the English have never bothered to master the German language, although a few of them can manage to speak passable French. So he's more likely to feel safe in that country. It also offers him the opportunity to cross only one border before reaching the coast.

"If he's stupid enough to try and leave by plane he will find we have the airport covered; if by train, we have the stations manned. But my guess is still that he will try to escape by motor vehicle.

"I shall therefore take five men to the French border with me while Major Valchek will take another five to Basle to cover the German crossing point. The rest of you will remain on surveillance in Geneva. Those of you who have just arrived will relieve those agents who are in the field already. And don't expect Scott to be roaming around looking like a tourist on holiday. Study your picture of the Englishman carefully and even be prepared for him to try and get away with some amateur disguise."

Romanov paused for effect. "The man who brings me the Tsar's icon need have no fear for his future prosperity when we return home." Hopeful expressions appeared on their faces for the first time as Romanov pulled out the duplicate icon from his pocket and held it high above his head for all to see.

"When you find the original of this your task will be completed. Study it carefully, Comrades, because no photographs are being issued. And remember," Romanov added, "the only difference between this and Scott's icon is that his has a small silver crown embedded in the back of the frame. Once you see the crown you will know that you have found the missing masterpiece."

Romanov put the icon back in his pocket and looked down at the silent men.

"Remember that Scott is good but he's not that good."

CHAPTER THIRTEEN

"You're not bad, Scott, not bad at all," said Robin, who had remained standing by the double bass throughout Adam's story. "Either you're one hell of a liar, or I've lost my touch." Adam smiled up at the massive girl, who made the bow she was holding in her right hand look like a toothpick.

"Am I permitted to see this icon, or am I just supposed to take your word for it?"

Adam jumped off the bed and pulled out the package containing the Tsar's icon from the map pocket of his trenchcoat. Robin put her double bass up against the wall and leaving the bow propped against it, lowered herself into the only chair in the room.

Adam handed the icon over to her. For some time, she stared at the face of St George without making any comment. "It's magnificent," she said at last. "And I can understand anyone wanting to possess it. But no painting could be worth the tragedy and trouble you've had to go through."

"I agree it's inexplicable," said Adam. "But Rosenbaum or whatever his real name is has been willing to kill twice to get his hands on the piece, and he's already convinced me that as long as I am in possession of the icon then I'll be the next in line."

Robin continued to stare at the tiny pieces of gold, red, blue and yellow that made up St George and the Dragon.

"No other clues?" she asked, looking up.

"Only the letter given to my father by Goering."

Robin turned the painting over. "What does that mean?" she asked, pointing to the tiny silver crown embedded in the wood.

"That proves it was once owned by a Tsar, according to the man from Sotheby's. And greatly enhances its value, he assured me."

"Still couldn't be worth killing for," said Robin. She handed the icon back to Adam. "So what other secret is St George keeping to himself?"

Adam shrugged and frowned, having asked himself the same question again and again since Heidi's death. He returned the silent saint to his trenchcoat.

"What was to have been your plan if you had stayed awake?" asked Robin. "Other than making the bed?"

Adam smiled. "I hoped to call Lawrence again once I could be sure he had returned home and check if he had any more news for me. If he wasn't back, or couldn't help, I was going to hire a car and try to get across the Swiss border to France and then on to England. I felt sure that between Rosenbaum and his men and the Swiss Police they would between them have had all the airports and stations fully covered."

"No doubt Rosenbaum will have also thought that much out as well, if he's half as good as you claim," said Robin. "So we'd better try and get in touch with your friend Lawrence and see if he's come up with any bright ideas." She pushed herself up out of the chair and walked across to the phone.

"You don't have to get yourself involved," said Adam hesitantly.

"I am involved," said Robin. "And I can tell you it's far more exciting than Schubert's Unfinished. Once I've got your friend on the line I'll pass him over to you and then no one will realise who's phoning." Adam told her the number of the flat and she asked the girl on the switchboard to connect her.

Adam checked his watch: eleven forty. Surely Lawrence would be home by now? The phone didn't complete its first two rings before Robin heard a man's voice on the line. She immediately handed the receiver over.

"Hello, who is that?" asked the voice. Adam was reminded how strange he always found it that Lawrence never announced his name.

"Lawrence, it's me."

"Where are you?"

"I'm still in Geneva."

"My clients were waiting for you at eleven o'clock this morning."

"So was Rosenbaum."

"Who is Rosenbaum?"

"A six-foot, fair-haired, blue-eyed monster, who seems determined to kill me."

Lawrence did not speak for some time. "And are you still in possession of our patron saint?"

"Yes, I am," said Adam. "But what can be so important about . . ."

"Put the phone down and ring me back again in three minutes."

The line went dead. Adam couldn't fathom the sudden change in his old friend's manner. What had he missed during those months he had lodged with him? He tried to recall details that he had previously considered unimportant and that Lawrence had so skilfully disguised.

"Is everything all right?" asked Robin, breaking into his thoughts.

"I think so," said Adam, a little mystified. "He wants me to ring back in three minutes. Will that be all right with you?"

"This tour's already lost eight thousand pounds of the taxpayers' money, so what difference can a few international calls make?" she said.

Three minutes later, Robin picked up the receiver and repeated the number. In one ring Lawrence was back on the line.

"Only answer my questions," said Lawrence.

"No, I will not answer your questions," said Adam, becoming increasingly annoyed with Lawrence's manner. "I want one or two of my own answered before you get anything more out of me. Do I make myself clear?"

"Yes," said a more gentle sounding Lawrence.

"Who is Rosenbaum?"

Lawrence didn't immediately reply.

"You'll get nothing further from me until you start telling the truth," said Adam.

"From your description I have every reason to believe Rosenbaum is a Russian agent whose real name is Alex Romanov."

"A Russian agent? But why should a Russian agent want to get his hands on my icon?"

"I don't know," said Lawrence. "We were rather hoping you might be able to tell us."

"Who's we?"

Another long silence.

"Who's we?" repeated Adam. "You can't really expect me to go on believing you work for Barclays DCO."

"I work at the Foreign Office," said Lawrence.

"In what capacity?"

"I am not at liberty . . ."

"Stop being so pompous, Lawrence. In what capacity?"

"I'm the Number Two in a small section that deals in . . ." Lawrence hesitated.

"Espionage I think is the current jargon we laymen are using," said Adam, "and if you want my icon that badly you had better get me out of this mess alive because Romanov is willing to kill for it as I am sure you are aware.''

"Where are you?"

"The Richmond Hotel."

"In a public phone box?" asked Lawrence, sounding incredulous.

"No, in a private room."

"But not registered in your name?"

"No, in the name of a friend. A girlfriend."

"Is she with you now?" asked Lawrence.

"Yes," said Adam.

"Damn," said Lawrence. "Right. Don't leave that room until seven a.m., then phone on this number again. That will give me enough time to get everything in place."

"Is that the best you can do?" said Adam, but the phone had already gone dead. "It looks as if I'm stuck with you for the night," he told Robin as he replaced the phone.

"On the contrary, it is I who am stuck with you," said Robin, and disappeared into the bathroom. Adam paced around the room several times before he tested the sofa. Either he had to rest his head on a cushion, balanced on the thin wooden arm, or he had to let his legs dangle over the far end. By the time Robin had come back out clad in a pair of sky-blue pyjamas he had selected the floor as his resting place.

"Not much of a chair, is it?" said Robin. "But then British Intelligence didn't warn me to book a double room." She climbed into the bed and turned out the light. "Very comfortable," were the last words she uttered.

Adam lay down flat on the bedroom floor, using the cushion from the chair as a pillow and a hotel dressing gown as a blanket. He slept intermittently, his mind switching between why the icon could be that important, how Lawrence knew so much about it, and, most immediate, how the hell were they going to get him out of the hotel alive?

Romanov waited patiently for the phone to be picked up.

"Yes," said a voice that he recognised immediately.

"Where is he?" were the only words Romanov uttered. Four words were all he received from Mentor in reply before the phone went dead.

Adam woke with a start an hour before he was due to phone Lawrence back. For nearly forty minutes he lay on the floor with only Robin's steady breathing to remind him he was not alone. Suddenly he became aware of a strange sound coming from the corridor outside – two or three steps, a pause, then whoosh, two or three steps, a pause, another whoosh. Adam raised himself up silently from the floor and crept to the door. The rhythm of Robin's breathing never faltered. Whoosh: it now sounded closer. He picked up a heavy wooden coathanger from the table by the door. He gripped it firmly in his right hand, raised it above

his head and waited. Whoosh – and a newspaper shot under the door
and the steps moved on. He didn't have to bend down to see that it was
his photograph that dominated the front page of the international
edition of the *Herald–Tribune*.

Adam took the paper into the bathroom, closed the door silently,
switched on the light and read the lead article. It was yesterday's story
with guarded comments from his old commanding officer and embarrassed silence from his mother. He felt helpless.

He crept up to Robin hoping she wouldn't wake. He silently picked
up the phone and dragged it to the bathroom. He could only just
manage to close the door behind him. He dialled the operator and
repeated the number.

When the ringing stopped, he immediately said, "Is that you,
Lawrence?"

"Yes," came back the reply.

"Things have become much worse now. I'm still holed up in the
hotel but my picture is on the front page of every paper."

"I know," said Lawrence. "We tried to prevent it, but yet again the
Swiss wouldn't cooperate."

"Then I may as well give myself up to the Swiss," said Adam.
"Damn it all, I am innocent."

"No, Adam, in Switzerland you're guilty until proven innocent and
you must have worked out by now that you're involved in something far
more important than a double murder."

"What could be more important than a double murder when the rest
of the world thinks you're the murderer?" asked Adam angrily.

"I can understand exactly how you feel, but your only chance now is
to carry out my instructions to the letter and treat with suspicion every
other person with whom you come into contact."

"I'm listening," said Adam.

"Just remember everything I say because I am only going to tell you
once. The Royal Philharmonic Orchestra are staying in the same hotel
as you. They are going on to Frankfurt at ten o'clock this morning.
Leave your room at five to ten, join the orchestra in the lobby and then
make your way to the front door where you'll find their coach parked.
We will have a car waiting for you on the far side of the road. The car is
a black Mercedes and you will see a man in grey chauffeur's uniform
holding the door open for you. We have already arranged that no other
car will be able to park on that side of the road between nine thirty and
ten thirty, so you can't mistake it. Just get into the back and wait. There
will be another man in the back with you and you will then be driven to
the safety of our Consulate. Do you need me to repeat any of that?"

"No," said Adam, "but . . ."

"Good luck," said Lawrence, and the phone went dead.

By seven he had showered and shaved, while Robin remained

unrepentant in a deep sleep. Adam envied her; only a twig had to break outside and he was wide awake. Two years of living in the Malayan jungle, never knowing when the Chinese would strike, never being able to sleep for more than two or three hours at a time if one wanted to stay alive, still kept its hold on him.

Robin did not stir for another thirty minutes, during which time Adam sat on the sofa and went over Lawrence's plan in his mind. At ten to eight she finally woke, even then taking several minutes before she was fully conscious. Robin blinked at Adam and a large grin appeared on her face.

"So you didn't murder me while I slept,"she said.

"I don't think you'd have noticed if I had," said Adam.

"When your father is an habitual drunk and comes home at all hours of the night, you learn to sleep through anything," she explained, placing both feet firmly on the carpet. "Aren't you meant to have phoned London by now?"

"I already have."

"And what is the master plan to be?" she asked, rubbing her eyes on her way to the bathroom.

"I will be leaving with you," said Adam.

"Most of my one-night stands don't bother to stay that long," she remarked as she closed the bathroom door behind her. He tried to read the paper while the bath was filling up.

"Does that mean we're sharing a room in Frankfurt as well?" she asked a few minutes later when the bathroom door reopened, as if the conversation had never been interrupted.

"No, as soon as we're clear of the hotel I leave you at the coach and make my own way to a car on the far side of the road."

"That sounds more like the men in my life," she said. "But at least we can have a farewell breakfast," she added, picking up the phone. "I'm nuts about kippers. How about you?"

Adam didn't answer. He had begun looking at his watch every few moments. The waiter arrived with breakfast about fifteen minutes later: Adam waited in the bathroom. When he reappeared he showed no interest in the food, so Robin ate four kippers and most of the toast. Nine o'clock passed; a porter took away the breakfast trolley and Robin began to pack. The phone rang and Adam jumped nervously as Robin picked it up.

"Yes, Stephen," she said. "No, I won't need any help with my luggage. Not this time." She put the phone down. "We depart for Frankfurt at ten."

"I know," said Adam.

"We ought to make Lawrence the orchestra manager. He seems to know everything even before it's been decided." Adam had been thinking the same thing. "Well, at least I've found someone to help with my luggage for a change," added Robin.

"I'll carry the double bass for you if you like," offered Adam.

"I'd like to see you try," said Robin. Adam walked over to the large instrument that was propped up in its case against the wall. He tried the double bass from all angles but couldn't manage to do better than hold it off the floor for a few moments. Robin joined him and with one flick she had the stem on her shoulder and the instrument balanced perfectly. She walked up and down the bedroom demonstrating her prowess.

"It's a matter of skill, my puny friend," she said. "And to think I believed all those stories last night about your outrunning half the Swiss police force to spend a night with me."

Adam tried to laugh. He picked up his trenchcoat, checking the icon was zipped up. But he couldn't stop himself shaking from a combination of fear and anticipation.

Robin looked at him. "Don't worry," she said gently. "It will all be over in a few minutes' time." Then she saw the paper on the floor. "I should sue them if I were you."

"Why?" asked Adam.

"You're a lot better looking than that." Adam smiled and walked across, and just managed to get his arms round her to give her a hug.

"Thanks for everything," he said. "But now we have to go."

"You're sounding more like one of my lovers all the time," said Robin, mournfully.

Adam picked up her suitcase while Robin jerked up the stem of the double bass on to her shoulder. She opened the door and checked the corridor: two of her colleagues from the RPO were waiting by the lift, otherwise there was nobody else in sight. Robin and Adam joined the two musicians and after "Good mornings" no one spoke until the lift doors slid open. Once the doors were closed Robin's colleagues couldn't resist taking a closer look at Adam. At first Adam was anxious they had recognised him from the newspaper. Then he realised that it was who Robin had spent the night with that fascinated them. Robin gave him a lewd wink, as if she fully intended to live off this one for a long time. For his part Adam ducked behind the double bass and remained in the corner breathing deeply in and out as the lift trundled down towards the ground floor. The doors sprang open and Robin waited for her two colleagues to leave before she shielded Adam as best she could all the way across the foyer. His eyes were now fixed on the front door. He could see the bus taking up most of the road and several members of the orchestra were already clambering on. One more minute and he should be safely away. He watched as the drums were packed carefully in the large boot.

"Oh, God, I forgot," said Robin. "I'm meant to put this in the boot at the back of the bus."

"Do it later," said Adam sharply. "Just keep going until you reach the coach door." Then he saw the car on the far side of the road. He felt light with relief, almost dizzy. The car door was being held open for him. Another man was seated in the back just as Lawrence had promised. Ten o'clock struck somewhere in the distance. The man dressed in chauffeur's uniform, hat pulled down over his forehead, stood by the open door. He turned towards the hotel in anticipation. Adam stared towards him as the man's eyes scanned the hotel entrance. The uniform wasn't a good fit.

"Into the bus," hissed Adam.

"With this thing? They'll kill me," said Robin.

"If you don't, he'll kill me."

Robin obeyed, despite the adverse comments as she lumbered down the aisle with her double bass screening Adam from the gaze of anyone on the far side of the road. He wanted to be sick.

Adam slumped into a seat next to Robin with the double bass between them.

"Which one?" she whispered.

"In the chauffeur's uniform."

Robin glanced out of the window. "He may be evil, but he's damned good looking," she said, inconsequentially.

Adam looked disbelieving. Robin smiled apologetically.

"Everybody's in," called a man from the front of the bus, "and I've double-checked and we seem to have one extra."

Oh, my God, thought Adam, he's going to throw me off the bus.

"My brother," shouted Robin from the back. "He's only travelling with us for part of the journey."

"Oh, that's okay then," said the manager. "Well, let's be on our way." He turned to the driver.

"He's started looking at the bus," said Robin. "But I don't think he can see you. No, you're all right, he's now turned his gaze back to the hotel entrance."

"I didn't realise you had a brother," said the manager, who was suddenly standing beside them. The coach moved slowly out of the square.

"Neither did I until this morning," mumbled Robin, still looking out of the window. She turned and faced her boss. "Yes, I forgot to mention to you that he might be in Switzerland at the same time as the orchestra. I do hope it's not going to cause a problem."

"Not at all," said the manager.

"Adam, this is Stephen Grieg who, as you will already have gathered, is the orchestra's manager."

"Are you a musician as well?" asked Stephen as he shook Adam's hand.

"No, I can truthfully say that I have never been able to master any instrument," said Adam.

"He's tone deaf," butted in Robin. "Takes after my father. He's in tyres, actually," she continued, enjoying herself.

"Oh, really. Which company are you with?" enquired Stephen.

"I'm with Pirelli," said Adam, mentioning the first tyre company that came into his head.

"Pirelli, the company that produces those fabulous calendars?"

"What's so special about their calendars?" asked Robin innocently. "If you want one I'm sure Adam can get you one."

"Oh, that would be great," said Stephen. "I hope it won't put you to too much trouble."

"No trouble at all," said Robin, leaning over Adam conspiratorially. "Actually, to let you in on a little family secret there is a rumour at HQ that Adam will soon be joining the main board. The youngest member in the company's history, you know."

"How impressive," said the manager, taking a closer look at the orchestra's latest recruit.

"Where shall I send the calendar?" bleated out Adam.

"Oh, direct to the RPO. No need to tell you the address, is there?"

"In a brown envelope, no doubt," said Robin. "And don't worry about the year. It's not the dates that he gets worked up about."

"What time are we expecting to reach Frankfurt, Stephen?" shouted a voice from the front. "Must leave you now," said the manager. "Thanks for the promise of a calendar. Robin's right, of course – any year will do."

"Who taught you to spin a yarn like that?" asked Adam, as soon as he was out of earshot.

"My father," said Robin. "You should have heard him at his best. In a class of his own. The problem was my mother still believed every word."

"He would have been proud of you today."

"Now we've found out what you do for a living," said Robin, "may we learn what's next on the agenda for the youngest director of Pirelli?"

Adam smiled. "I've started to reason like Rosenbaum, and I think he'll stay in Geneva for at least an hour, two at the most, so with luck I'll get a fifty-mile start on him." He unfolded the map across the two seats.

His finger ran along the road the bus was travelling on, and it was Robin who spoke first.

"That means you could make Zurich airport before he has any chance of catching up with you."

"Perhaps," said Adam, "but that would be too much of a risk. Whoever Rosenbaum is," he went on, abiding by Lawrence's request to be cautious by not letting Robin into his secret, "we now know for certain that he has a professional organization behind him so I must expect the airports to be the first place he will have covered. And don't forget the Swiss police are still on the lookout for me as well."

"So why don't you come on to Frankfurt with us?" asked Robin. "I can't believe you'll have any trouble from Stephen."

"I've thought about that already but discounted it also as too great a risk," said Adam.

"Why?"

"Because, when Rosenbaum has had time to think about it," said Adam, "the one thing he'll remember is this bus. Once he's found out the direction we're heading in he's sure to come after us."

Robin's eyes returned to the map. "So you'll need to decide where and when to get off."

"Exactly," whispered Adam. "I can risk sixty to seventy miles, but not a lot further."

Robin's finger ran along the little road. "About here," she said, her finger stopping on a little town called Solothurn.

"Looks about the right distance."

"But once you're off the bus what will you do for transport?"

"I've little choice but to walk or thumb lifts – unless I pinch another car."

"With your luck, Rosenbaum will be the one person who stops to pick you up."

"Yes, I've thought about that as well," said Adam. "I would have to find a long stretch of road where I can see without being seen for about one hundred yards, and then thumb lifts only from British cars or cars with British number plates."

"They taught you a trick or two in the army, didn't they?" said Robin. "But how do you intend to cross the frontier with your passport?"

"That's one of the many problems I haven't yet come up with a solution for."

"If you decide to stay with us," said Robin, "it wouldn't be a problem."

"Why?" asked Adam.

"Because whenever we cross a border they only count the number of people on the bus and the number of passports, and as long as they tally the customs officials don't bother to check everyone individually. After all, why should they? The RPO is not exactly an unknown quantity. All I would have to do is add your passport to the bundle and mention it to the manager."

"It's a clever idea but it's not on. If Rosenbaum caught up with me while I'm still on this bus then I would be left with no escape route."

Robin was silent for a moment. "Once you're on your own will you contact Lawrence again?"

"Yes. I've got to let him know what happened this morning, because whoever he's dealing with must have a direct line to Rosenbaum."

"Could it be Lawrence himself?"

"Never," said Adam.

"Your loyalty is touching," said Robin, turning to look at him, "but what you actually mean is you don't want to believe it could be Lawrence."

"What are you getting at?"

"Like my mother didn't want to believe that my father was a liar and a drunk. So she turned a blind eye to his little foibles. You know even when he dropped dead of cirrhosis of the liver, her only words were, 'strange for a man who never drank'."

Adam thought about his relationship with Lawrence and wondered if you could know someone for twenty years and really not know them at all.

"Just be wary how much you let him know," advised Robin.

They sat in silence as Adam checked the map and went over all the different routes he could take once he had left the bus. He decided to aim for the German border and take the long route back to England, from Hamburg or Bremerhaven, rather than the shorter, more obvious route via Calais or Ostend.

"Got it," said Robin suddenly.

"Got what?" said Adam, looking up from the map.

"How we solve your passport problem," she murmured.

Adam glanced at her hopefully. "If you let me have your passport," she explained, "I'll substitute it for the member of the orchestra who most resembles you. No one will notice anything strange at our end until we're back home in Britain on Sunday night."

"Not a bad idea, if there is anyone who remotely resembles me."

"We'll have to see what we can do," said Robin. She sat bolt upright, her eyes moving slowly from person to person. By the time she had scanned all those in the bus from front to back, a small smile appeared on her face. "There are two of our lot who bear a passable resemblance to you. One is about five years older and the other is four inches shorter, but you go on working out the safest way of escape while I carry out some research. Let me have your passport," she said. Adam handed it over and then watched Robin walk up to the front and sit next to the manager. He was chatting to the driver about the most convenient place to stop for lunch.

"I need to check something in my passport," Robin broke in. "Sorry to bother you."

"No bother. You'll find them all under my seat in a plastic bag," he said, and continued his conversation with the driver.

Robin bent down and started to shuffle through the passports as if searching for her own. She picked out the two she had considered as possible substitutes and compared the photographs. The shorter man's photo looked nothing like Adam. The older man's was at least five years out of date but could have passed for Adam as long as the officials didn't study the date of birth too carefully. She bundled up the passports, placing Adam's in the middle. She then put them back in the plastic bag and returned the bag under the manager's seat.

Robin made her way back to her seat. "Take a look at yourself," she said, slipping the passport over to Adam. He studied the photo.

"Other than the moustache, not a bad likeness, and it's certainly my best chance in the circumstances. But what will happen when you return to London and they find out my passport has been substituted?"

"You'll be back in England long before us," said Robin. "So put this one in an envelope with the calendar and send it direct to the RPO in Wigmore Street, W1, and I'll see that they return yours." Adam vowed to himself that if he ever got back to London, he would become a life subscriber to the Friends of the Royal Philharmonic.

"That seems to have solved one of your problems."

"For the moment at least," said Adam. "I only wish I could take you with me for the rest of the trip."

Robin smiled. "Frankfurt, Berlin, Amsterdam – just in case you get bored. I wouldn't mind meeting up with Rosenbaum. But this time face to face."

"He might just have met his match," said Adam.

"Can I have a last look at the icon?" Robin asked, ignoring the comment.

Adam bent down to retrieve his trenchcoat and slipped the painting out of his map pocket, careful to shield it from anyone else's view. Robin stared into the eyes of St George before she spoke again. "When I lay awake last night waiting for you to ravish me, I passed the time trying to fathom out what secret the icon held."

"I thought you were asleep," said Adam smiling. "When all along we were both doing the same thing. Anyway, did you come up with any worthwhile conclusions?"

"First, I decided your taste was for male double bass players," said Robin, "or how else could you have resisted me?"

"But what about St George and the Dragon?" asked Adam, grinning.

"To begin with I wondered if the little pieces of mosaic made up a code. But the picture is so magnificently executed that the code would have to have been worked out afterwards. And that didn't seem credible."

"Good thinking, Batman."

"No, you're Batman. So I wondered if there was another painting underneath. I remembered from my schooldays that Rembrandt and Constable often painted on the top of their paintings, either because they didn't care for their original effort or because, in the case of

Rembrandt, he couldn't afford another canvas."

"If that were the answer only an expert could have carried out the task of removing every piece of paint."

"Agreed," said Robin. "So I dismissed that as well. My third idea was that the crown on the back" – she turned the icon over and stared at the little piece of silver embedded in the wood – "indicates as your expert suggested that this is the original by Rublev and not a copy as you have been led to believe."

"I had already considered that," said Adam, "during my sleepless night and although it would place a far higher value on the work, it is still not enough to explain why Rosenbaum would kill indiscriminately for it."

"Perhaps someone else needs St George every bit as much as Rosenbaum does," said Robin.

"But who and why?"

"Because it's not the icon they're after, but something else. Something hidden in or behind the painting."

"That was the first thing I checked," said Adam smugly. "And I'm convinced that it's a solid piece of wood."

"I don't agree with you," said Robin as she began tapping the wood all over like a doctor examining someone's chest. "I've worked with instruments all my life, watched them being made, played with them, even slept with them, and this icon is not solid right through, though God knows how I can prove it. If something is hidden inside it was never intended to be discovered by laymen like ourselves."

"Quite an imaginative little thing, aren't you?" said Adam.

"Comes naturally," she said as she handed the icon back to Adam. "Do let me know if you ever discover what is inside," she added.

"When I get five minutes to myself I might even spend some time on one or two of my own theories," said Adam, returning the icon to his trenchcoat pocket.

"Two more kilometres to Solothurn," said Robin, pointing out of the window at a signpost.

Adam buttoned up his coat. "I'll see you off," she said, and they both made their way up the aisle. When Adam reached the front of the coach he asked the driver if he could drop him off just before they reached the next village.

"Sure thing," said the driver without looking back.

"Leaving us so soon?" said Stephen.

"Afraid so," said Adam. "But thanks for the lift. And I won't forget the calendar." The driver pulled into a lay-by, pressed a knob and the hydraulic doors swung back.

"Bye, Robin," said Adam, giving her a brotherly kiss on the cheek.

"Goodbye, baby brother," said Robin. "Give my love to mother if you see her before I do." She smiled and waved at him as the door swung closed and the coach returned to the highway to continue its journey on to Frankfurt.

Adam was on his own again.

CHAPTER FOURTEEN

Professor Brunweld was rarely treated with any respect. It was the fate of academics, he had long ago concluded. The 'President' was all they had said and he had wondered if he should believe it. Certainly they had got him out of bed in the middle of the night and escorted him silently to the Pentagon. They wanted Brunweld's expert opinion, they had assured him. Could it be possible? After Cuba and Dallas he'd begun to believe anything was possible.

He had read that the Pentagon had as many floors below the ground as there were above it. He could now confirm that as an established fact.

Once they had handed him the document they left him alone. They only wanted one question answered. He studied the clauses for over an hour and then called them back. It was, he told them, in his opinion, authentic and if the Russians were still in possession of their copy, also signed in 1867, then his adopted country was – what was that awful American expression? Ah, yes – in all sorts of trouble.

He began to realise how serious it was when they told him that he would not be allowed to leave the Pentagon until Monday. That didn't surprise him once he'd seen the date on the bottom of the treaty. So it was to be three days of solitude away from his demanding students and chattering wife. He would never have a better opportunity to settle down and read the collected works of Proust.

Romanov knew he couldn't risk standing by the side of the car for much longer. He was too conspicuously dressed not to be noticed by everyone who came out of the hotel. Three minutes later he threw his grey cap on the back seat and instructed Valchek to get rid of the car and then return to the Consulate.

Valchek nodded. He had already carried out Romanov's orders to kill the two British agents as if he had been asked to fix a burst water pipe. The only thing that hadn't run to plan was when Valchek tried to button up the dead chauffeur's uniform. Romanov thought he detected the suggestion of a smirk on Valchek's face when he realised who would have to be the chauffeur.

Romanov slipped into the shadows and waited for another half hour, by which time he was sure the plan must have been aborted from the London end. He hailed a taxi and asked the driver to take him to the Soviet Consulate. He didn't notice the taxi-driver's look of disbelief at his passenger's chauffeur-clad vision.

Could he really have lost Scott twice? Had he also underestimated him? Once more and Zaborski was going to require a very convincing explanation.

On his way back to the Consulate an image kept flashing across Romanov's mind, but he couldn't make any sense of it. Something had happened outside the hotel that didn't quite fit. If he could only think clearly for a moment he felt certain it would become clear to him. He kept playing the last thirty minutes over in his mind, as if rewinding the reel of an old film; but some of the frames still remained blurred.

Once Romanov was back in the Consulate Valchek handed him a large envelope which he was informed had just arrived in the diplomatic pouch from Moscow.

Romanov read over the decoded telex a second time, still unable to fathom its possible significance.

"Information has come to light concerning the late Colonel Gerald Scott, DSO, OBE, MC, that may prove useful when you make contact with your quarry. Full documentation will be with you by morning, latest, A1."

Romanov wondered what headquarters had discovered about Scott's father that could possibly prove of interest to him. It was still his avowed intention that the son would be despatched to join the father long before any further missive from Moscow had arrived.

Romanov thought of his own father and the escape route he had made possible by leaving such a fortune, and how for the sake of advancement he had betrayed him to the State. Now, for the sake of further advancement he had to kill Scott and bring home the icon. If he failed . . . He dismissed both fathers.

"Either he's very clever or he's living on an amateur's luck," Romanov said, moving into the small office that had been made available for his use. Valchek who followed him did not comment other than to ask what he should do next.

"Tell me what you saw when we were at the hotel."

"What do you mean?" asked Valchek.

"Don't ask questions," said Romanov, changing back into his own clothes, "answer them. Tell me everything you remember seeing, from the moment we drew up outside the hotel."

"We arrived at the Richmond a few minutes before ten," began

Valchek, "parked the Mercedes on the far side of the road, and waited for Scott to show up. We stayed put for a few minutes after ten but Scott never materialised."

"No, no, no. Be more specific. Don't just generalise. For instance, do you remember anything unusual taking place while we were waiting?"

"Nothing in particular," said Valchek. "People continually entering and leaving the hotel – but I'm sure Scott wasn't among them."

"You are fortunate to be so certain. What happened next?" asked Romanov.

"Next? You instructed me to go back to the Consulate and wait for you to return."

"What time was that?"

"It must have been about seven minutes past ten. I remember because I checked my watch when that coach left."

"The coach?" said Romanov.

"Yes, the one that was being loaded up with musical instruments. It left about . . ."

"Instruments, that's it," said Romanov. "Now I remember what was worrying me. Cellos, violins, and a double bass that didn't go into the boot." Valchek looked puzzled but said nothing. "Ring the hotel immediately and find out who was on that bus and where they are heading." Valchek scurried away.

Romanov checked his watch: ten fifty-five. We are going to have to move, and move quickly. He pressed the intercom by the side of the phone. "I want a fast car, and more important, a superb driver." Valchek returned as Romanov replaced the receiver. "The bus was hired by the Royal Philharmonic Orchestra, who are on a European tour . . ."

"Where are they heading next?" asked Romanov.

"Frankfurt."

He strolled away from the village, having checked everything with a professional soldier's eye. The main street was deserted but for a little boy who relentlessly kicked a plastic football into a gap in the hillside which he was using as a goal. The boy turned when he saw Adam and kicked the ball towards him. Adam kicked it back and the boy took it in his arms, a wide smile appearing on his face. The smile disappeared as he watched Adam continue quickly up the hill. There were only a few old houses on the main road. On one side was a dangerous ravine with tree-covered hills rising in the distance, while on the other side stretched green fields in which cows, bells round their necks, munched happily away. It made Adam feel hungry.

He went further up the road until he came to a sharp bend in the hill. Standing on the corner he could see down the hill for about half a mile without being seen. He tested the feasibility of his plan for several minutes and soon became expert at picking out British cars or cars with British number plates as far as two or three hundred yards away. It didn't take long to work out how few foreigners bought British.

During the next twenty minutes he thumbed optimistically at seven cars with English number plates heading towards Lausanne, but they all ignored him. He had forgotten just how easy it had been for him when he was a cadet in uniform. In those days almost everyone would stop. He checked his watch: he could only risk it for a few more minutes. Three more cars refused to pull up and when a fourth slowed down it only sped away again as Adam ran towards it.

By eleven twenty Adam decided he could no longer chance being seen on the road. He stared down the ravine, realising there was no alternative left open to him now but to travel by foot. He shrugged and began to climb down one of the steep trails that led into the valley, in the hope of meeting up with the other road that was marked clearly on the map.

He cursed when he looked at the open ground between him and safety. If only he'd started an hour earlier.

"I fear Antarctic has become expendable."

"Why?"

"Because we now know his father was involved in helping Goering to an easy death."

"I don't understand."

"No reason why you should although it's quite simple. That patriotic stiff-upper-lipped Englishman of yours is the son of the bastard who smuggled a cyanide capsule into Goering's cell at Nuremberg. His reward for services rendered turns out to be the Tsar's icon."

"But all the members of D4 are convinced that he's our only hope."

"I don't give a damn what your D4 thinks. If the father would side with the Germans during a war, why shouldn't the son side with the Russians in peace?"

"Like father, like son."

"Precisely."

"So what am I expected to do?"

"Just keep us briefed as to what the Foreign Office is up to. Our agents in Switzerland will do the rest."

"Faster!" said Romanov, aware that it was not possible as the Ambassador's driver was proving to be a consummate professional. Not once did Romanov feel that he had missed a gap, a light, a chance to overtake. In fact another five kilometres an hour on the speedometer might well have seen them over the precipice. The moment they were on the highway, with full lights blazing and the driver's hand almost lodged on the horn, the speedometer rarely fell below 130 kilometres an hour. "We must beat them to the border," he kept repeating as he thumped his fist on the leather dashboard. After they had covered one hundred kilometres in fifty-five minutes, the three men began watching ahead of them for the coach, but it was another thirty kilometres before Valchek was able to point ahead and shout, "That must be them, about a kilometre up the hill."

"Force them off the road," said Romanov, his eyes never leaving the bus. The Embassy driver swung out to overtake and once he was in front immediately cut across, forcing the coach driver to throw on his brakes and swerve into the side. Valchek waved dictatorially at the coach driver to slow down and the man stopped the vehicle just off the road on the edge of the mountain.

"Don't either of you speak. Just leave everything to me," said Romanov, "and remain near the driver in case there's trouble." Romanov jumped out of the car and ran towards the coach, his eyes already searching for anyone who might be attempting to leave it. He banged on the door impatiently until the driver pressed a knob and the big doors swung open. Romanov leapt on, with the other two following only paces behind. He took out his passport from an inside pocket, flashed it in the frightened driver's face and shouted, "Who's in charge here?"

Stephen Grieg stood up. "I am the manager of the company, and I can . . ."

"Swiss police," said Romanov. Grieg was about to ask a question when Romanov said, "When you left your hotel in Geneva this morning, did you take on any extra passengers?"

"No," said Grieg. Romanov scowled. "Unless you count Robin Beresford's brother."

"Robin Beresford's brother?" inquired Romanov, his eyebrows raising interrogatively.

"Yes," said the manager. "Adam Beresford. But he only travelled with us as far as Solothurn. Then he got off."

"Which one of you is Robin?" said Romanov, staring around a sea of men's faces.

"I am," piped up a voice from the back. Romanov marched down the bus and saw the double bass case and then everything fitted into place. It always worried him when something was out of context. Yes, that was what hadn't rung true. Why hadn't she put the double bass in the boot with all the other large instruments? He stared down at the heavy-framed woman who now sat behind the monstrous instrument.

"Your brother is the one called Adam?"

"Yes," said Robin.

"Quite a coincidence."

"I don't understand what you mean," she said, trying not to sound nervous.

"The man I am looking for just happens to be called Adam as well."

"Common enough name," said Robin. "Perhaps you've never read the first chapter of the Bible?"

"Six foot one inch, perhaps two inches, dark hair, dark eyes, slim and fit. Not a convincing brother for you," added Romanov studying her frame.

Robin pushed back her red hair but didn't rise. Romanov could sense from the nervous expressions on the faces around him that it was Scott who had been on the bus.

"Where was your *brother*," he emphasised the word, "intending to go once he had left the coach?" Romanov asked, tapping his passport against his other hand, like a baton.

"I have no idea," said Robin, still not changing her expression from one of uninterested politeness.

"I will give you one more chance to cooperate with me. Where was your brother heading?"

"And I'll tell you once more, I don't know."

"If you refuse to answer my questions," said Romanov, "I shall have to arrest you."

"On whose authority?" asked Robin calmly.

Romanov considered showing her his passport but realised that this girl was sharper than either the driver or the manager.

"With the authority of the Swiss police," Romanov said confidently.

"Then no doubt you'll be happy to show me proof of your identity."

"Don't be insolent," Romanov said sharply. He towered over her.

"It is you who are insolent," said Robin, standing up. "You drive in front of our coach like a lunatic, nearly sending us down the mountain, then the three of you burst in like a bunch of Chicago mobsters, claiming to be Swiss police. I have no idea who you are or what you are, but I'll let you into two secrets. You touch me and there are forty men on this coach who will beat you and your two cronies to pulp. And even if you managed to get off this bus alive, we are members of the Royal Philharmonic Orchestra of Great Britain, and as such are guests of the Swiss Government. In a few moments when we cross the border, we will become guests of the West German Government, so you're about to get yourself on to every front page in the world. Single-handedly, you will bring a totally new meaning to the words 'diplomatic incident'." She leaned forward and pointing a finger at him said, "So I'm telling you, whoever you are, in as ladylike fashion as I can, 'piss off'."

Romanov stood staring at her for some moments and then backed away as Robin's eyes remained glued on him. When he reached the front he waved at Valchek and the chauffeur, indicating that they should leave the coach. Reluctantly they obeyed him. The coach driver closed the door the moment Romanov's foot touched the ground and he quickly moved into first gear and drove back on to the highway.

The entire orchestra turned round and gave Robin the kind of ovation normally reserved for the entrance of the leader of the orchestra.

It went unappreciated. Robin had collapsed back into her seat, shaking uncontrollably, only too aware that not one of the forty men on that coach would have lifted a finger against Rosenbaum.

Sir Morris Youngfield glanced round the table: everyone was in place despite the few minutes' notice the head of D4 had given them.

"Let's hear the latest report," said Sir Morris, looking up at his Number Two, who was once again seated at the far end of the table.

"Not clever, sir, I'm afraid," began Lawrence. "Two of our most experienced agents were selected to pick up Scott at the Richmond Hotel as planned and then take him to the safety of the British Consulate."

"So what happened?" asked Sir Morris.

"No one at our Geneva office can be certain. Our men certainly never turned up at the hotel and they haven't been seen since."

"What are the Swiss police saying?" asked Busch.

"They are not being very helpful," said Lawrence, turning to the American. "They are aware that we are not the only foreign power involved and as is their custom in such circumstances, they have no intention of being seen to favour either side."

"Bloody Swiss," said Snell with feeling.

"And where do we imagine Scott is now?" asked Matthews.

"We've also drawn a blank on that," said Lawrence. Matthews smiled at Lawrence's embarrassment. "We feel certain he must have got on the coach with the girl—" he looked down at the sheet of paper on the table in front of him "— Robin Beresford. But he wasn't on it when we were waiting for them at the border. The orchestra is due at their Frankfurt hotel in about one hour so we will be able to find out more then. The German police are being far more cooperative," Lawrence added.

"Meanwhile what else are *we* doing?" asked Sir Morris.

"Checking all the usual places as well as keeping a close eye on Romanov who, incidentally, turned up on the French border last night. One of our old hands recognised him despite the fact that he's cut his hair very short; doesn't suit him, apparently."

"So Scott could be anywhere by now?" said Matthews. "Do you think he's still in Switzerland, or managed to cross one of the borders?"

Lawrence hesitated. "I have no idea," he said without expression.

Sir Morris stared at him from the far end of the table but didn't comment.

"Do you think he'll contact you again?" asked Snell.

"Almost certainly if he's still alive."

"If Romanov is still in Geneva, Scott *must* still be alive," said Busch. "Because the moment he gets his hands on the icon he will head east."

"Agreed," said Lawrence, "and we have men stationed at the airport checking every flight out to the East. I therefore suggest we follow up any further leads and assemble again tomorrow at seven a.m. unless Scott contacts me before then."

Sir Morris nodded and rose to leave. Everyone stood.

"Thank you, gentlemen," he said, and walked towards the far end of the room. As he passed Lawrence, he murmured, "Perhaps you could come to my office when you have a moment."

Adam slipped and stumbled the last few yards down the ravine before finally landing with a bump on his backside. His hands were cut and bleeding in several places, his trousers torn and smeared with clay and earth. He sat still for about two minutes trying to get his breath back as he looked back up towards the road. He had taken just under an hour to cover what a stone could have managed in three seconds. Still, there had been one advantage: no one could have seen him from the road. He gazed across the valley ahead. Anyone would be able to see him now, but he had left himself with no alternative.

Judge by eye, check by map. The map wasn't much help but he estimated the distance to the far ridge to be about two more miles. At least the map had promised him there was a road, hidden from sight on the other side of the ridge. He studied the terrain – rolling green fields, no hedgerows to shield him, and then one wide, shallow river. He reckoned he could cover the ground to the road in about twenty minutes. He checked that the icon was securely in place and then set off at an even pace.

Romanov had hardly uttered a word since the three men had been unceremoniously removed from the coach, and Valchek and the driver certainly hadn't ventured any opinions. Romanov knew the girl had called his bluff, and he couldn't afford a further diplomatic incident which would undoubtedly be reported back to his Chairman in Moscow. But Romanov would never forget the girl with the man's name.

Solothurn was about forty kilometres back in the direction they had already travelled, and the driver could have completed the journey in about twenty minutes had Romanov not insisted on slowing down as they passed every vehicle that travelled towards them. They checked the occupants of each vehicle on the other side of the road, just in case Scott had managed to thumb a lift. It was a necessary precaution in Romanov's judgment, but it meant a total time of thirty-one minutes before they arrived back in Solothurn. At least Romanov felt confident Scott wasn't heading for the German border – unless he had been very well disguised or travelled in the boot of a car.

As soon as they reached Solothurn Romanov instructed the driver to leave the car in the middle of the village while they split up to see if they could discover any clues as to the route Scott might have taken. None of the locals whom they questioned had seen anyone resembling Scott that morning, and Romanov was beginning to wonder which border he should now head for when he saw the driver kicking a football back to a little boy. Romanov ran down the hill and was about to remonstrate with him when the boy turned and kicked the ball hard at the Russian. Romanov trapped the ball automatically and kicked it firmly past the boy and into the goal. Romanov turned towards the driver and was about to shout at him when the ball reappeared at his feet. He picked it up in anger and was going to throw it back at the boy when he saw his hopeful smile. Romanov held the ball high above his head. The boy ran up and jumped towards the ball but however hard he tried he couldn't reach it.

"Have you seen any strangers this morning?" he asked in slow deliberate French.

"Yes, yes," said the boy. "But he didn't score a goal."

"Where did he go?" asked Romanov.

"Up the hill," said the boy. To the child's dismay, Romanov dropped the ball and began to run. Valchek and the driver followed after him.

"*Non, non,*" cried the little boy who followed after them. Romanov looked back to see the boy was standing on the spot where Adam had been thumbing lifts, pointing out over the ravine.

Romanov quickly turned to the driver. "Get the car, I need the glasses and the map." The driver ran back down the hill once again followed by the boy. A few minutes later the Mercedes drew up by Romanov's side. The driver jumped out and handed the glasses over to Romanov, while Valchek spread a map out on the car bonnet.

Romanov focused the binoculars and began to sweep the hills in the distance. It was several minutes before the glasses stopped and settled upon a brown speck climbing up the farthest hill.

"The rifle," were Romanov's only words.

Valchek ran to the boot of the car and took out a Dragunov sniper's rifle with telescopic sights. He assembled the long, slim weapon with its distinctive wooden skeleton stock and checked that it was loaded. He then raised it, moved it around until it felt comfortable nestled in his shoulder and swept the ground in front of him until he too focused on Scott. Romanov followed Adam's relentless stride with the binoculars. Valchek's arm moved with him, keeping the same pace. "Kill him," said Romanov. Valchek was grateful for the clear windless day as he kept the rifle sight in the middle of the Englishman's back, waited for three more strides, then slowly squeezed the trigger. Adam had almost reached the top of the ridge when the bullet tore through him. He fell to the ground with a thud. Romanov smiled and lowered the glasses.

Adam knew exactly what had ripped through his shoulder and where the shot must have come from. He instinctively rolled over until he reached the nearest tree. And then the pain began. Although the bullet had lost a lot of its power at such a distance, it still stung like an adder's bite, and blood was already beginning to seep through his trenchcoat from the torn muscle. He turned his head and gazed back behind him. He could see no one but he knew Romanov must be standing there waiting to take a second shot.

Turning with difficulty, he looked back up towards the edge of the hill. Only thirty yards to the safety of the ridge, but he would have to run over the top, remaining exposed for several vital seconds. Even if he made it Romanov would still be able to reach him by car within thirty minutes.

Nevertheless, that was his one chance. Slowly, very slowly, he crawled inch by inch up the ridge, thankful for the tree that he could still use as protection. One arm followed one leg, like a beached crab. Once he had covered ten yards he knew the angle would be against him and Romanov would have a flat, slow-moving target to aim at. He moved four more lengths of his body and stopped.

You can't hold a rifle up on your shoulder for ever, Adam thought. He counted to two hundred slowly.

"I suspect he's going to make a run for it," Romanov told Valchek as he raised the glasses, "which will give you about three seconds. I'll shout the moment he moves." Romanov kept the glasses trained on the tree. Suddenly Adam jumped up and sprinted as though it were the last twenty metres of an Olympic final. Romanov shouted "Now" and Valchek pulled the rifle up into his shoulder, focused on the moving man and squeezed the trigger as Adam threw himself over the ridge. The second bullet whistled by the side of Adam's head.

Romanov cursed, as he stared through the binoculars, knowing that Valchek had missed. He turned to the open map. The others joined him around the car as he began to consider the alternatives. "He should reach that road in about ten minutes," he said, putting his finger in the middle of a small red line that ran between Neuchâtel and the French border. "Unless the first bullet hit him, in which case it could take him longer. So how long will it take you to get to that border?" Romanov asked the driver.

The chauffeur studied the map. "About twenty-five, at most thirty minutes, Comrade Major," came back the reply.

Romanov turned and looked back towards the hills. "Thirty minutes, Scott, that's how long you've got to live."

When the car sped away, the little boy ran home as fast as he could. He quickly told his mother everything he had seen. She smiled understandingly. Only children always had such vivid imaginations.

When Adam looked up, he was relieved to see the road was only about a mile away. He jogged towards it at a steady pace, but found that the running caused him even more discomfort. He was anxious to stop and check the wound but waited till he reached the road. The bullet had torn through the outer flesh of his shoulder muscle leaving him in considerable pain. An inch lower and he would have been unable to move. He was relieved to see that the blood had only made a small stain on his trenchcoat. He folded a handkerchief in four and placed it between his shirt and the wound. He knew he daren't risk a hospital. As long as he could get to a pharmacy by nightfall, he felt he could take care of the problem himself.

Adam checked the map. He was now only a few kilometres from the French border, and decided, because of the wound, to cross into France as quickly as possible rather than keep to his original plan of going up through Basle and on to Bremerhaven.

Desperately he began to thumb at any car that passed, no longer bothering with the nationality of the number plates. He felt he was safe for about twenty minutes but after that he would have to disappear back into the hills. Unfortunately there were far fewer cars driving towards the French border than there had been on the Basle road, and they all ignored his plea. He feared that the time was fast approaching for him to return to the hills when a yellow Citroën drew into the side of the road a few yards ahead of him.

By the time Adam had reached the car the woman in the passenger seat had already wound down the window.

"Where – are – you – going?" asked Adam, pronouncing each word slowly and carefully.

The driver leant across, took a lengthy look at Adam and said in a broad Yorkshire accent, "We're on our way to Dijon. Any use to you, lad?"

"Yes, please," said Adam, relieved that his scruffy appearance had not put them off.

"Then jump in the back with my daughter."

Adam obeyed. The Citroën moved off, as Adam checked out of the back window; he was relieved to see an empty road stretching out behind him.

"Jim Hardcastle's the name," said the man, as he moved the car into third gear. Jim appeared to have a large, warm smile perpetually imprinted on his chubby red face. His dark ginger hair went straight back and was plastered down with Brylcreem. He wore a Harris tweed jacket and an open-necked shirt that revealed a little red triangle of hair. It looked to Adam as if he had given up attempts to do anything about his waistline. "And this is the wife, Betty," he said, gesturing with his elbow towards the woman in the front seat. She turned towards Adam, revealing the same ruddy cheeks and warm smile. Her hair was dyed blonde but the roots remained an obstinate black. "And sitting next to you is our Linda," Jim Hardcastle added, almost as an afterthought. "Just left school and going to work for the local council, aren't you, Linda?" Linda nodded sulkily. Adam stared at the young girl whose first experiment with make-up hadn't worked that well. The dark over-lined eye shadow and the pink lipstick did not help what Adam considered was an attractive girl probably in her late teens. "And what's your name, lad?"

"Dudley Hulme," said Adam, recalling the name on his new passport. "And are you on holiday?" he asked, trying to keep his mind off the throbbing shoulder.

"Mixing business with pleasure," said Jim. "But this part of the trip is rather special for Betty and myself. We flew to Genoa on Saturday and hired the car to tour Italy. First we travelled up through the Simplon Pass. It's a bit breathtaking after our home town of Hull."

Adam would have asked for details, but Jim didn't reckon on any interruptions. "I'm in mustard, you see. Export director for Colman's, and we're on our way to the annual conference of the IMF. You may have heard of us." Adam nodded knowingly. "International Mustard Federation," Jim added. Adam wanted to laugh, but because of the pain in his shoulder, managed to keep a straight face.

"This year they've elected me President of the IMF, the high point of my career in mustard, you might say. And, if I may be so bold as to suggest, an honour for Colman's as well, the finest mustard in the world," he added, as if he said it at least a hundred times a day. "As President I have to preside over the conference meetings and chair the annual dinner. Tonight I shall be making a speech of welcome to delegates from all over the world."

"How fascinating," winced Adam, as the car went over a pothole.

"It certainly is," said Jim. "People have no idea how many makes of mustards there are." He paused for a second and then said, "One hundred and forty-three. There's no doubt the Frogs make one or two good attempts and even the Krauts don't do too badly, but there's still nothing to beat Colman's. British is best after all, I always say. Probably the same in your line of country," said Jim. "By the way, what is your line of country?"

"I'm in the army," said Adam.

"What's a soldier doing thumbing a lift on the borders of Switzerland?"

"Can I speak to you in confidence?" asked Adam.

"Mum's the word," said Jim. "We Hardcastles know how to keep our traps shut."

In the case of Jim's wife and daughter, Adam had no proof to the contrary.

"I'm a captain in the Royal Wessex, at present on a NATO exercise," began Adam. "I was dumped off the coast at Brindisi in Italy last Sunday with a false passport and ten English pounds. I have to be back in barracks at Aldershot by midnight Saturday." When he saw the look of approbation appear on Jim's face, he felt even Robin would have been proud of him. Mrs Hardcastle turned around to take a more careful look at him.

"I knew you were an officer the moment you opened your mouth," said Jim. "You couldn't have fooled me. I was a sergeant in the Royal Army Service Corps in the last war myself. Doesn't sound much, but I did my bit for the old country." The acronym for the Corps – "Rob All Serving Comrades' – flashed through Adam's mind. "Have you seen any action yourself, Dudley?" Jim was asking.

"A little in Malaya," said Adam.

"I missed that one," said Jim. "After the big one was over, I went back into mustard. So where's the problem in getting you back to England?"

"There are about eight of us trying to reach Aldershot, and a thousand Americans trying to stop us."

"Yanks," said Jim with disdain. "They only join wars just as we're about to win them. All medals and glory, that lot. No, I mean is there any real problem?"

"Yes, the border officials have been briefed that eight British officers are attempting to get over into France and the Swiss love to be the ones to pull us in. Only two officers out of twelve made it back to barracks last year," said Adam, warming to his own theme. "Both were promoted within weeks."

"The Swiss," said Jim. "They're even worse than the Americans. They don't even join in a war – happy to fleece both sides at the same time. They won't pick you up, lad, believe me. I'll see to that."

"If you can get me across the border, Mr Hardcastle, I'm confident I will be able to make it all the way back to Aldershot."

"Consider it done, lad."

The fuel indicator was flashing red. "How many kilometres left when that happens?" demanded Romanov.

"About twenty, Comrade Major," said the driver.

"Then we should still make the French border?"

"Perhaps it might be safer to stop and fill up," suggested the driver.

"There is no time for safety," said Romanov. "Go faster."

"Yes, Comrade Major," said the driver, who decided it was not the occasion to point out they would run out of petrol even more quickly if he was made to push the car to its limits.

"Why didn't you fill the tank up this morning, you fool?" said

Romanov.

"I thought I was only taking the Consul to lunch at the town hall today, and I had intended to fill the tank up during my lunch hour."

"Just pray for your sake that we reach the border," said Romanov. "Faster."

The Mercedes touched 140 kilometres per hour and Romanov relaxed only when he saw a sign saying, '*Rappelle Douanes dix kilomètres*'. A few minutes later a smile grew on his face as they passed the five-kilometre sign, and then suddenly the engine spluttered as it tried helplessly to continue turning over at the speed the pressed-down accelerator was demanding. The indicator on the speedometer started to drop steadily as the engine continued to chug. The driver turned off the ignition and threw the gear lever into neutral. The sheer momentum of the heavy Mercedes took them another kilometre before the car slowed to a complete stop.

Romanov did not even look at the driver as he jumped out of the car and began running the last three kilometres towards the border.

"I've come up with an idea," said Jim, as they passed a signpost warning drivers that the border was only two kilometres away.

"What's that, sir?" asked Adam, who could now feel his shoulder beating like a steady tune hammered out by a child on a tin drum. "When it comes to the time for us to present our passports, you put your arm round Linda and start cuddling her. Leave the rest to me."

Mrs Hardcastle turned round and gave Adam a much closer look as Linda went scarlet. Adam looked across at the mini-skirted pink-lipped Linda and felt embarrassed by the predicament her father had placed his daughter in. "Don't argue with me, Dudley," continued Jim confidently. "I promise you what I have in mind will work." Adam made no comment and neither did Linda. When they reached the Swiss border a few moments later, Adam could see that there were two checkpoints about one hundred yards apart. Drivers were avoiding one line of traffic in which a row was going on between a customs official and an irate lorry driver. Jim drove up straight behind the gesticulating Frenchman. "Give me your passport, Dudley," he said. Adam handed over the violinist's passport.

Why did you choose this line? Adam wanted to ask.

"I chose this line," continued Jim, "because by the time it comes for our passports to be inspected I reckon the customs officer will be only too happy to allow us through without much fuss." As if in reaction to his logic, a long queue started to form behind Jim, but still the argument raged in front of them. Adam remained alert, continually looking out of the back window, waiting for the moment when Romanov would appear. When he turned back, he was relieved to find that the lorry in front of them was being told to pull over into the side and wait.

Jim drove quickly up to the customs post. "Get necking, you two," he said.

Up until that point Adam had kept his hands hidden in his trenchcoat pocket because they were so scratched and bruised. But he obeyed Jim and took Linda in his arms and kissed her perfunctorily, one eye still open watching for Romanov. To his surprise she parted his lips and began exploring inside his mouth with her tongue. Adam thought about protesting but realised there was no way he could make it sound gallant or credible.

"The wife, the daughter and the future son-in-law," said Jim, handing over the four passports.

The policeman started to check.

"What was all the trouble about, officer?"

"Nothing for you to worry about," said the policeman, flicking through the passports. "I hope it hasn't inconvenienced you."

"No, no," said Jim. "They didn't even notice," he said, pointing over his shoulder and laughing.

The policeman shrugged and, handing the passports back, he said, "*Allez,*" waving them on.

"Sharp as mustard Jim, that's what they call me back in Hull." He looked over his shoulder towards Adam. "You can stop that now, Dudley, thank you." Adam felt Linda release him with some reluctance.

She glanced at him shyly, then turned towards her father. "But we still have to go over the French border, don't we?"

"We have already been alerted to look out for him and I can assure you he hasn't been through this post," said the senior customs officer. "Otherwise one of my men would have spotted him. But if you want to double-check, be my guest."

Romanov went quickly from officer to officer showing them the blown-up photograph of Adam, but none of them could recall anyone resembling him. Valchek joined him a few minutes later and confirmed that Scott was not in any of the cars still waiting to be allowed over the border and that the Mercedes was being pushed into the border garage.

"Is it back to the hills, Comrade Major?" asked Valchek.

"Not yet. I want to be absolutely certain he hasn't managed to cross the border."

The senior official emerged from his post in the centre of the road. "Any luck?" he asked.

"No," said Romanov grimly. "You seem to be right."

"I thought as much. If any of my men had let the Englishman through they would have been looking for a new job by now."

Romanov nodded in acknowledgment. "Could I have missed any of your staff?''

"Doubt it – unless there's a couple of them taking a break. If so you'll find them in the bar about a hundred metres up towards the French border point.''

Four customs officers and a French waitress were the only people to be found in the bar. Two of the officers were playing pool while the other two sat at a corner table, drinking coffee. Romanov took the photo out once more and showed it to the two men at the pool table. They both shook their heads in an uninterested fashion and returned to potting the multi-coloured balls.

The two Russians made their way to the bar. Valchek passed Romanov a cup of coffee and a sandwich, which he took over to the table where the other two border guards sat. One of them was telling his colleague the trouble he had had with a French lorry driver who was trying to smuggle Swiss watches over the border. Romanov pushed the photograph of Scott across the table.

"Have you seen this man today?''

Neither showed any sign of recognition and the younger one quickly returned to his story. Romanov sipped his coffee, and began to consider whether he should make a run for Basle or call for reinforcements to sweep the hills. Then he noticed that the young man's eyes kept returning to the photo. He asked once again if he had seen Scott.

"No, no,'' said the young officer, a little too quickly. In Moscow Romanov would have had a 'yes' out of him within minutes, but he would have to follow a more gentle approach here.

"How long ago?'' Romanov asked quietly.

"What do you mean?'' asked the policeman.

"How long ago?'' repeated Romanov in a firmer voice.

"It wasn't him,'' said the officer, sweat now appearing on his forehead.

"If it wasn't him, how long ago wasn't it him?''

The officer hesitated. "Twenty minutes, maybe thirty.''

"What make of vehicle?''

The young officer hesitated. "A Citroën, I think.''

"Colour?''

"Yellow.''

"Other passengers?''

"Three. Looked like a family. Mother, father, daughter. He was in the back with the daughter. The father said they were engaged.''

Romanov had no more questions.

Jim Hardcastle managed to keep a one-sided conversation going for over an hour.

"Naturally,'' he said, "the IMF holds its annual conference in a different city every year. Last year it was in Denver in Colorado, and next year it'll be at Perth in Australia, so I manage to get around a bit. But as the export man you have to get used to a lot of travel."

"I'm sure you do," said Adam, trying to concentrate on his benefactor's words while his shoulder throbbed on.

"I'm only President for a year, of course," continued Jim. "But I have plans to ensure that my fellow delegates won't forget 1966 in a hurry."

"I'm sure they won't," said Adam.

"I shall point out to them that Colman's has had another record year on the export side."

"How impressive."

"Yes, but I must admit that most of our profits are left on the side of the plate," he said, laughing.

Adam laughed as well but sensed that Mrs Hardcastle and Linda might have heard the line before.

"I've been thinking, Dudley, and I'm sure the wife would agree with me, that it would be most acceptable to us if you felt able to join the presidential table for dinner tonight – as my guest, of course." Mrs Hardcastle nodded, as did Linda with enthusiasm.

"I can think of nothing that would give me greater pleasure," said Adam. "But I fear my commanding officer might not be quite as delighted to hear I had stopped on the way back to England to take in a party. I do hope you'll understand."

"If he is anything like my old CO I certainly do," said Jim. "Still, if you should ever be Hull way, look us up." He took a card out of his top pocket and passed it over his shoulder.

Adam studied the embossed letters and wondered what 'MIFT' stood for. He didn't ask.

"Where in Dijon would you like to be dropped off?" asked Jim as he drove into the outskirts of the town.

"Anywhere near the centre that's convenient for you," replied Adam.

"Just holler when it suits you then," said Jim. "Of course, I always maintain that a meal without mustard . . ."

"Can you drop me on the next corner?" said Adam suddenly.

"Oh," said Jim, sad to be losing such a good listener. And he reluctantly drew the car up alongside the kerb.

Adam kissed Linda on the cheek before getting out of the back. He then shook hands with Mr and Mrs Hardcastle.

"Nice to have made your acquaintance," said Jim. "If you change your mind you'll find us at the hotel . . . Is that blood on your shoulder, lad?"

"Just a graze from a fall – nothing to worry about. Wouldn't want the Americans to think they'd got the better of me."

"No, no, of course not," said Jim. "Well, good luck."

As the car moved off Adam stood on the pavement watching them disappear. He smiled and tried to wave, then turning, he walked quickly down a side street looking for a shopping precinct. Within moments he was in the centre of town, relieved to find that all the shops were still open. He began to search up and down the street for a green cross above a door. Adam had to walk only fifty yards before he spotted one. He entered the shop tentatively and checked the shelves.

A tall man with short fair hair, wearing a long leather coat, stood in the corner with his back to the entrance. Adam froze. Then the man turned round, frowning at the packet of tablets he wanted to purchase, while at the same time rubbing his thick Gallic moustache.

Adam walked up to the counter.

"Do you speak English, by any chance?" he asked the dispenser, trying to sound confident.

"Passable, I hope," came back the reply.

"I need some iodine, cotton wool, a bandage and heavy Elastoplast. I fell and bruised my shoulder on a rock," Adam explained.

The dispenser quickly put the order together without showing much interest.

"This is what you require but you will find that the trade names are different," explained the dispenser. "That will be twenty-three francs," he added.

"Will Swiss do?"

"Certainly."

"Is there a hotel anywhere nearby?" asked Adam.

"Around the next corner, on the other side of the square."

Adam thanked him, handed over the Swiss notes, and then left the pharmacy in search of the hotel. The Hotel Frantel was, as promised, only a short distance away. He walked across the square and up the steps into the hotel to find several people were waiting at reception to be booked in. Adam swung his trenchcoat over his blood-stained shoulder and walked past them as he checked the signs on the wall. He then strode across the entrance hall as though he were a guest of several days' standing. He followed the sign he had been looking for which took him down a flight of stairs, to come head on with three further signs. The first had the silhouette of a man on the door, the second a woman, the third a wheelchair.

He opened the third tentatively and was surprised to find behind it nothing more than a sizeable square room with a high-seated lavatory against the wall. Adam locked himself in and let his trenchcoat fall to the ground.

He rested for a few minutes before slowly stripping to the waist. He then ran a basinful of warm water.

Adam was thankful for the endless first-aid seminars every officer had to go through, never believing they would serve any purpose.

Twenty minutes later the pain had subsided and he even felt comfortable.

He picked up his coat with his right hand and tried to throw it back over his shoulder. The very movement caused the icon to fall out of the map pocket and on to the tiled floor. As it hit the ground, the sound made Adam fear that it might have broken in half. He stared down anxiously and then fell to his knees.

The icon had split open like a book.

CHAPTER FIFTEEN

When Adam returned to the Hotel Frantel an hour later few guests would have recognised the man who had crept in earlier that afternoon.

He wore a new shirt, trousers, tie and a double-breasted blazer that wouldn't be fashionable in Britain for at least another year. Even the raincoat had been ditched because the icon fitted snugly into the blazer pocket. He considered the shop had probably given him a poor exchange rate for his traveller's cheques but that was not what had been occupying his mind for the past hour.

He booked himself into a single room in the name of Dudley Hulme and a few minutes later took the lift to the third floor.

Lawrence picked the phone up even before Adam heard the second ring.

"It's me," said Adam.

"Where are you?" were Lawrence's first words.

"I'll ask the questions," said Adam.

"I can understand how you feel," said Lawrence, "but . . ."

"No buts. You must be aware by now that someone on your so called team has a direct line to the Russians because it was Romanov and his friends who were waiting for me outside the hotel in Geneva, not your lot."

"We realise that now," said Lawrence.

"We?" said Adam. "Who are we? Because I'm finding it rather hard to work out who's on my side."

"You don't believe that . . ."

"When you get your girlfriend murdered, chased across Europe by professional killers, shot at and . . ."

'Shot at?" said Lawrence.

"Yes, your friend Romanov took a shot at me today, hit me in the shoulder. Next time we meet I intend it to be the other way round and it won't be the shoulder."

"There won't be a next time," said Lawrence, "because we'll get you out safely if you'll only let me know where you are."

The memory of Robin's words, "Just be wary of how much you let him know," stopped Adam from telling Lawrence his exact location.

"Adam, for God's sake, you're on your own; if you don't trust me who can you trust? I admit it looks as if we let you down. But it won't happen again."

There was another long silence before Adam said, "I'm in Dijon."

"Why Dijon?"

"Because the only person who would give me a lift was going to a mustard conference in Dijon."

Lawrence couldn't stop himself smiling. "Give me your number and I'll phone you back within the hour."

"No," said Adam, "I'll phone *you* back in one hour."

"Adam, you've got to show some trust in me."

"Not now that I know what it is you're all after, I can't afford to trust anybody."

Adam replaced the phone and stared down at the icon which lay open on the bed. It wasn't the signature of Stoeckle or Seward that worried him. It was the date – June 20, 1966 – that read like a death warrant.

"Good night, sir," said the doorkeeper as the senior civil servant left Century House that evening. "Another late night for you," he added sympathetically. He acknowledged the doorman by raising his rolled umbrella a few inches. It *had* been another late night, but at least they had caught up with Scott again. He was beginning to develop quite a respect for the man. But how they failed to pick him up in Geneva still required a fuller explanation than the one Lawrence Pemberton had supplied the D4 with that afternoon.

He set off at a brisk pace towards the Old Kent Road, conspicuous in his black coat and pin-striped trousers. He tapped his umbrella nervously before hailing a passing taxi.

"Dillon's bookshop, Malet Street," he told the driver, before getting in the back. Already seven thirty, but he still wouldn't be too late and a few minutes either way wasn't going to make that much difference. Pemberton had agreed to remain at his desk until all the loose ends were tied up and he was sure that nothing could go wrong this time. He allowed himself a wry smile as he thought how they had all accepted his plan. It had the double advantage of ensuring enough time for them to get their best men into position, while keeping Scott well out of sight in a deserted hideaway. He hoped that this was the last time they would expect him to come up with an original proposal.

"Eight shillings, guv'nor," said the taxi-driver, as he drew up outside Dillon's. He handed over the money and added a sixpenny tip. He stood staring at the window of the university bookshop, watching the reflection of the taxi as it moved off. The moment the taxi had turned the corner into Gower Street he began walking away. In moments he had reached a side road into which he turned. Ridgmount Gardens was one of those streets which even London cabbies had to think about for a few moments. He had walked only a matter of yards before he disappeared down some stone steps to a basement flat. He inserted a Yale key in the front door lock, turned it quickly, stepped inside and closed the door behind him.

During the next twenty minutes he made two telephone calls – one international, one local – and then had a bath. He emerged back on Ridgmount Gardens less than an hour later dressed in a casual brown suit, pink floral open shirt and brown brogue shoes. The parting in his hair had changed sides. He returned to Dillon's on foot and hailed another taxi.

"The British Museum," he instructed the driver, as he stepped into the back. He checked his watch: nearly ten past eight. Scott would be fully briefed by now, he thought, although his associates would be already on the way back to Dijon, as his plan had allowed for a two-hour delay.

The taxi drew up outside the British Museum. He paid and walked up the twelve steps in front of the museum, admiring the Byzantine architecture as he regularly did each week, before walking back down again to hail another taxi.

"Middlesex Hospital, please," was all he said. The taxi executed a U-turn and headed west.

Poor bastard. If Scott hadn't opened that envelope in the first place the icon would have ended up with its rightful owner.

"Shall I drive up to the entrance?" asked the cabbie.

"Yes, please."

A moment later he strolled into the hospital, checked the board on the wall as if he were looking for a certain ward, then walked back out on to the street. From the Middlesex Hospital it always took him about three minutes at a steady pace to reach Charlotte Street, where he stopped outside a house and pressed a buzzer attached to a little intercom.

"Are you a member?" inquired a voice suspiciously.

"Yes."

On the hour Adam phoned and listened carefully to all Lawrence had to say.

"I'll take one more risk," said Adam, "but if Romanov turns up this time I'll hand over the icon to him personally and with it a piece of property so valuable that no amount of money the Americans could offer would be sufficient to purchase it back."

When Adam put the phone down Lawrence and Sir Morris played the conversation back over again and again.

"I think *property*'s the key word," said Sir Morris.

"Agreed," said Lawrence, "But what piece of property could be that valuable to both the Russians and the Americans?"

Sir Morris began slowly rotating the globe that stood by the side of his desk.

"What does that buzz mean?" asked Romanov. "We are not running out of petrol again, are we?"

"No, sir," said the chauffeur. "It's the new calling device now fixed to all ambassadorial cars. It means they expect me to check in."

"Turn round and go back to that petrol station we passed a couple of miles ago," Romanov said quietly.

Romanov started tapping the dashboard impatiently as he waited for the petrol station to reappear on the horizon. The sun was going down quickly and he feared it would be dark within the hour. They had travelled about ninety kilometres beyond Dijon and neither he nor Valchek had even seen a yellow Citroën going either way.

"Fill up again while I phone Geneva," Romanov said the moment he saw the petrol station. He ran to the phone box while Valchek still kept a watchful eye on the passing traffic.

"I am answering your signal," said Romanov when he was put through to the euphemistically titled Second Secretary.

"We've had another call from Mentor," said the Second Secretary. "How far are you from Dijon?"

The member stumbled about the dimly lit room until he came across an unoccupied table wedged up against a pillar in one corner. He sat down on a little leather stool by its side. He swivelled around nervously, as he always did when waiting for someone to bring him his usual malt whisky on the rocks. When the drink was placed on the table in front of him he sipped at it, in between trying to discover if there were any new faces spread around the dark room. Not an easy task, as he refused to put on his glasses. His eyes eventually became accustomed to the dim light thrown out by the long red fluorescent bulb that stretched above the bar. All he could make out were the same old faces staring at him hopefully; but he wanted something new.

The proprietor, noticing that a regular customer had remained on his own, came out and sat opposite him on the other little stool. The member never could get himself to look the man in the eyes.

"I've got someone who's very keen to meet you," whispered the proprietor.

"Which one?" he asked, looking up once more to check the faces at the bar.

"Leaning on the juke box in the corner. The tall, slim one. And he's young," added the proprietor. He looked towards the blaring machine. A pleasing new face smiled at him. He smiled nervously back.

"Was I right?" asked the proprietor.

"Is he safe?" was all he asked.

"No trouble with this one. Upper-class lad, right out of a top-drawer public school. Just wants to earn a bit of pocket money on the side."

"Fine." The member took a sip of whisky.

The proprietor walked over to the juke box. The member watched him talking to the young man. The boy downed his drink, hesitated for a moment, then strolled across the crowded floor to take the empty stool.

"My name is Piers," the young man said.

"Mine's Jeremy," the member said.

"A gentle name," said Piers. "I've always liked the name Jeremy."

"Would you care for a drink?"

"A dry Martini, please," said Piers.

The member ordered a dry Martini and another malt whisky. The waiter hurried away. "I haven't seen you here before."

"No, it's only my second time," said Piers. "I used to work in Soho, but it's got to be so rough lately, you never know who you might end up with."

The drinks arrived and the member took a quick gulp.

"Would you like to dance?" asked Piers.

"It's an emergency," the voice said. "Is the tape on?"

"I'm listening."

"Antarctic is in Dijon and he's discovered what's in the icon."

"And did he give them any clue?"

"No, all he told Pemberton was that he was in possession of a piece of property so valuable that no amount of money we could offer would be sufficient to purchase it back."

"Indeed," said the voice.

"The British think the important word is property," said the caller.

"They're wrong," said the voice on the other end of the line. "It's purchase."

"How can you be so sure?"

"Because the Russian Ambassador in Washington has requested a meeting with the Secretary of State on June 20 and he's bringing with him a bullion order to the value of 720 million dollars in gold."

"So where does that leave us?"

"On our way to Dijon so that we can be sure to lay our hands on that icon before the British or the Russians. The Russians obviously feel confident that it will soon be in their possession, so my bet is that they must already be on the way."

"But I've already agreed to go along with the British plan."

"Try not to forget which side you're on, Commander."

"Yes, sir. But what are we going to do about Antarctic if we get our hands on the icon?"

"It's only the icon we're after. Once that's in our possession, Antarctic is expendable."

Adam checked his watch: a few minutes after seven.

It was time for him to leave because he had decided not to carry out Lawrence's instructions to the letter. *He* intended to be waiting for *them*, and not as Lawrence had planned. He locked the bedroom door and returned to reception where he paid for the use of the room and the telephone calls he had made.

"Thank you," he said to the receptionist, and turned to leave.

"Dudley." Adam froze on the spot.

"Dudley," the voice boomed again. "I almost didn't recognise you. Did you change your mind?" A hand thumped him on the shoulder – at least it wasn't the left shoulder, he thought – as he stared down at Jim Hardcastle.

"No," said Adam, wishing he possessed the guile of Robin's father. "I think I was spotted in town so I had to get a change of clothes and keep out of sight for a few hours."

"Then why don't you come to the mustard dinner?" said Jim. "No one will see you there."

"Wish I were able to," said Adam, "but I can't afford to lose any more time."

"Anything I can do to help?" said Jim conspiratorially.

"No, I've got to get to . . . I have a rendezvous just outside the town in less than an hour."

"Wish I could take you there myself," said Jim. "Do anything to help an old soldier, but I'm a bit stuck tonight – of all nights."

"Don't give it a second thought, Jim, I'll be all right."

"I could always take him, Dad," said Linda, who had slipped up by her father's side and was listening intently.

They both turned towards Linda who was wearing a tight-fitting black crêpe dress that started as low and ended as high as it dared while her freshly washed hair now fell to her shoulders. She looked up hopefully.

"You've only just got your licence, lass. Don't be daft."

"You always treat me like a child when there's something worthwhile to do," came back her immediate response.

Jim hesitated. "How far is this rendezvous?" he asked apprehensively.

"About five, maybe six miles," said Adam, "but I'll be fine. I can get a taxi easily."

"The lass is right," said Jim, and taking his car keys out of his pocket, he turned to her and added, "but if you ever let on to your mother I'll kill you." Jim took Adam by the hand and shook it furiously.

"But I'll be just fine . . ."

"I won't hear of it, lad. Never forget, that in the end we're both on the same side, and good luck."

"Thank you, sir," said Adam reluctantly.

Jim beamed. "You'd better be getting along, lass, before your mother shows up."

Linda happily took Adam by the hand and led him away to the car park.

"Which direction?" she asked, once they were seated in the car.

"The Auxerre road," said Adam, looking down at the piece of paper on which he had written the directions Lawrence had read over the phone to him.

Linda set off at a slow pace, seeming at first to be unsure of the car, but once they had reached the outskirts of the town Adam suggested that she might go a little faster.

"I'm very nervous," she said, as she put her hand on Adam's knee.

"Yes, I can tell you are," said Adam, crossing his legs quickly. "Don't miss the turning," he added when he noticed a signpost pointing to the left.

Linda swung down off the main road on to a country lane while Adam kept his eyes peeled for the building Lawrence had described. It was another two miles before it came into sight.

"Draw into the side," said Adam, "and turn the lights off."

"At last," said Linda, sounding more hopeful, as she brought the car to a halt.

"Thank you very much," said Adam, as he touched the door handle.

"Is that all I get for risking life and limb?" asked Linda.

"I wouldn't want you to be late for the dinner."

"That dinner will be about as exciting as a dance at the Barnsley Young Conservatives."

"But your mother will be worried about you."

"Dudley, you're so up-tight."

"I wouldn't be in normal circumstances but if you stay much longer your life could be in danger," Adam said quietly.

Linda turned ashen. "You're not joking, are you?"

"I wish I was," said Adam. "Now, when I get out of this car you must turn round and go back to the hotel and never mention this conversation to anyone, especially your mother."

"I will," Linda said, sounding nervous for the first time.

"You're a fantastic girl," said Adam, and took her in his arms and gave her the longest, warmest kiss she had ever experienced. Adam then got out of the car and watched her do a five-point turn before she headed off back in the direction of Dijon.

He checked his watch: an hour and a half still to go before they were due, and by then it would be pitch dark. He jogged over to the airfield and studied the burnt-out buildings that ran alongside the road. It was exactly as Lawrence had described it. It was like a ghost town and Adam was confident that no one else could be there yet as they still wouldn't have had enough time to carry out Lawrence's plan.

Looking across the runway, Adam spotted the ideal place to hide while he waited to see which of the two plans he had prepared would prove necessary.

Flight Lieutenant Alan Banks was thankful that the moon shone so brightly that night. He had landed the little Beaver full of combat men in far worse conditions when a runway had been lit up like the Blackpool seafront.

Banks circled the perimeter of the airfield once and studied the two runways carefully. The airport had been out of action for such a long time that none of the aircraft manuals included a detailed ground plan.

The flight lieutenant was breaking every rule in the book, including piloting an unmarked aircraft informing the French that they would be landing in Paris; not easy to explain overshooting an airport by over a hundred miles.

"I can make a landing on the north–south runway more easily," Banks said, turning to the SAS captain, who sat crouched in the back with his five men. "How near to that hangar do you want me to go?" he said, pointing out of the window.

"Stay well clear, at least a couple of hundred yards," came back the reply. "We still don't know what to expect."

The six SAS men continued to stare cautiously out of the side windows. They had been briefed to pick up a lone Englishman called Scott who would be waiting for them, and then get out fast. It sounded easy enough but it couldn't be that easy otherwise they wouldn't have been called in.

The pilot swung the Beaver round to the south and put the nose down. He smiled when he spotted the burnt-out Spitfire that had been left derelict on the corner of the runway. Just like the ones his father used to fly during the Second World War. But this one had obviously never made it home. He descended confidently and as the little plane touched down it bounced along not because the pilot lacked experience but because the surface of the runway was so badly pitted.

Flight Lieutenant Banks brought the plane to a halt about two hundred yards from the hangar and swung the fuselage round a full circle ready for that quick getaway the captain seemed so keen to execute. He pressed the button that cut the propellers' engines and turned the lights out. The whirring slowed to an eerie whisper. They were forty-three minutes early.

Adam watched the new arrivals suspiciously from the cockpit of the Spitfire some four hundred yards away. He wasn't going to make a run for it across that open ground while the moon shone so brightly. His eyes never left the little unmarked plane as he waited for some clue as to who the occupants might be. He estimated it would be another fifteen minutes before the moon would be shielded by clouds. A few minutes more passed before Adam watched six men drop out of the blind side of the aircraft and lie flat on the tarmac on their stomachs. They were correctly dressed in SAS battle kit but Adam remained unconvinced while he still recalled Romanov's chauffeur's uniform. The six soldiers made no attempt to move. Neither did Adam as he was still uncertain which side they were on.

All six men on the ground hated the moon and even more the open space. The captain checked his watch: thirty-six minutes to go. He raised his hand and they began to crawl towards the hangar where Pemberton had said Scott would be waiting, a journey which took them nearly twenty minutes, and with each movement they made they became more confident that Pemberton's warning of an enemy waiting for them was unjustified.

At last a mass of clouds reached the moon and a shadow was thrown across the whole airfield. The SAS captain quickly checked his watch. Five minutes to go before the rendezvous was due. He was the first to reach the door of the hangar and he pushed it open with the palm of his hand. He wriggled in through the gap. The bullet hit him in the forehead even before he had found time to raise his gun.

"Move, laddies," shouted the second in command, and the other four were up in a flash, firing in an arc in front of them and running for the protection of the building.

As soon as Adam heard the Scottish brogue, he jumped out of the cockpit and sprinted across the tarmac towards the little plane whose propellers were already beginning to turn. He jumped on the wing and climbed in by the side of the surprised pilot.

"I'm Adam Scott, the man you've come to pick up," he shouted.

"I'm Flight Lieutenant Alan Banks, old chap," said the pilot, thrusting out his hand. Only a British officer could shake hands in such a situation, thought Adam, relieved if still terrified.

They both turned and watched the battle.

"We ought to get going," said the pilot. "My orders are to see you are brought back to England in one piece."

"Not before we are certain none of your men can make it back to the plane."

"Sorry, mate. My instructions are to get you out. Their orders are to take care of themselves."

"Let's at least give them another minute," Adam said.

They waited until the propellers were rotating at full speed. Suddenly the firing stopped and Adam could hear his heart thumping in his body.

"We ought to get moving," said the pilot.

"I know," replied Adam, "but keep your eyes skinned. There's something I still need to know."

Years of night marches made it possible for Adam to see him long before the pilot.

"Get going," said Adam.

"What?" said the pilot.

"Get going."

The pilot moved the joystick forward and the plane started moving slowly down the crumbling runway.

Suddenly a dark figure was running towards them firing long bursts straight at them. The pilot looked back to see a tall man whose fair hair shone in the moonlight.

"Faster, man, faster," said Adam.

"The throttle's full out," said the pilot, as the firing began again, but this time the bullets were ripping into the fuselage. A third burst came but by then the plane was going faster than the man and Adam let out a scream of delight when it left the ground.

He looked back to see that Romanov had turned around and was now firing at someone who was not wearing an SAS uniform.

"They couldn't hope to hit us now unless they've got a bazooka," said Flight Lieutenant Banks.

"Well done, well done," said Adam turning back to the pilot.

"And to think my wife had wanted me to go to the cinema tonight," said the pilot laughing.

"And what were you hoping to see?" asked Adam.

"*My Fair Lady*."

"Isn't it time for us to be going home?" asked Piers, removing his hand from the member's leg.

"Good idea," he said. "Just let me settle the bill."

"And I'll pick up my coat and scarf," said Piers. "Join you upstairs in a few moments?"

"Fine," he said. Catching the eye of the proprietor the member scribbled his signature in the air. When the 'account' appeared – a bare figure written out on a slip of paper without explanation – it was, as always, extortionate. As always, the member paid without comment. He thanked the proprietor as he left and walked up the dusty, creaky stairs to find his companion already waiting for him on the pavement.

He hailed a taxi and while Piers climbed in the back he directed the cabbie to Dillon's bookshop.

"Not in the cab," he said, as his new friend's hand began to creep up his leg.

"I can't wait," said Piers. "It's way past my bedtime."

"Way past my bedtime," his companion repeated involuntarily, and checked his watch. The die must have been cast. They would have moved in by now: surely they had caught Scott this time and, more important, the . . . ?

"Four bob," said the cabbie, flicking back the glass. He handed over five shillings and didn't wait for any change.

"Just around the corner," he said, guiding Piers past the bookshop and into the little side street. They crept down the stone steps and Piers waited as he unlocked the door, switched on the lights, and led the young man in.

"Oh, very cosy," said Piers. "Very cosy indeed."

Flight Lieutenant Alan Banks stared out of his tiny window as the plane climbed steadily.

"Where to now?" said Adam, relief flooding through his body.

"I had hoped England but I'm afraid the answer is as far as I can manage."

"What do you mean?" said Adam anxiously.

"Look at the fuel gauge," said Alan Banks, putting his forefinger on a little white indicator that was pointing half way between a quarter full and empty. "We had enough to get us back to Northolt in Middlesex until those bullets ripped into my fuel tank."

The little white stick kept moving towards the red patch even as Adam watched it and within moments the propellers on the left side of the aircraft spun to a halt.

"I am going to have to put her down in a field. I can't risk going on as there are no other airports anywhere nearby. Just be thankful it's a clear moonlit night."

Without warning the plane began to descend sharply. "I shall try for that field over there," said the flight lieutenant, sounding remarkably blasé as he pointed to a large expanse of land to the west of the aircraft. "Hold on tight," he said as the plane spiralled inevitably down. The large expanse of land suddenly looked very small as the plane began to approach it.

Adam found himself gripping the side of his seat and gritting his teeth.

"Relax," said the pilot. "These Beavers have landed on far worse places than this," he went on, as the wheels touched the brown earth. "Damn mud. I hadn't anticipated that," he cursed as the wheels lost their grip in the soft earth and the plane suddenly nosedived forward. A few seconds passed before Adam realised he was still alive but upside down swinging from his seat belt.

"What do I do next?" he asked the pilot but there was no reply.

Adam tried to get his bearings and began to rock his body backwards and forwards until he could touch the side of the plane with one hand while gripping the joystick with his feet. Once he was able to grab the side of the fuselage he undid the belt and collapsed on to the roof of the plane.

He picked himself up, relieved to find nothing was broken. He quickly looked around but there was still no sign of the pilot. Adam clambered out of the plane, glad to feel the safety of the ground. He scrambled around for a considerable time before he found Alan Banks some thirty yards in front of the aircraft motionless on his back.

"Are you all right?" asked the pilot before Adam could ask the same question.

"I'm fine, but how about you, Alan?"

"I'm OK. I must have been thrown clear of the aircraft. Just sorry about the landing, old chap, have to admit it wasn't up to scratch. We must try it again some time."

Adam burst out laughing as the pilot slowly sat up.

"What next?" Banks asked.

"Can you walk?"

"Yes, I think so," said Alan, gingerly lifting himself up. "Damn," he said, "it's only my ankle but it's sure going to slow me down. You'd better get going without me. That bunch back there with the arsenal can only be about thirty minutes behind us."

"But what will you do?"

"My father landed in one of these bloody fields during the Second World War and still managed to get himself back to England without being caught by the Germans. I owe you a great debt of gratitude, Adam, because if I can get back I'll be able to shut him up once and for all. Which lot are chasing us this time, by the way?"

"The Russians," said Adam who was beginning to wonder if perhaps there was a second enemy.

"The Russians – couldn't be better. Anything less and Dad wouldn't have accepted it as a fair comparison."

Adam smiled as he thought of his own father and how much he would have liked Alan Banks. He touched the icon instinctively and was relieved to find it was still in place. The pilot's words had only made him more determined to get back to England.

"Which way?" asked Adam.

The pilot looked up at the Great Bear. "I'll head east, seems appropriate, so you'd better go west, old fellow. Nice to have made your acquaintance," and with that he limped off.

"I'm not sure how much longer I can last, Comrade Major."

"You must try to hold on, Valchek. It's imperative that you try. We cannot afford to stop now," said Romanov. "I know that plane isn't far. I saw it falling out of the sky."

"I believe you, Comrade, but at least let me die a peaceful death on the side of the road, rather than endure the agony of this car."

Romanov glanced across at his colleague who had been shot in the abdomen. Valchek's hands were covered in blood, and his shirt and trousers were already drenched as he tried helplessly to hold himself in. He continued to clutch on to his stomach like a child who is about to be sick. The driver had also been shot, but in the back while attempting to run away. If he hadn't died instantly, Romanov would have put the next bullet into the coward himself. But Valchek was a different matter. No one could have questioned his courage. He had first taken on the British flat on their stomachs and then the Americans charging in like the seventh cavalry. Romanov had Mentor to thank for ensuring that they had been there first. But he must now quickly warn him that someone else was also briefing the Americans. Romanov, however, felt some satisfaction in having tricked the Americans into turning their fire on the British while he and Valchek waited to pick off the survivors. The last survivor was an American who fired at Valchek continually as they were making their getaway.

Romanov reckoned he had a clear hour before the French, British and Americans would be explaining away several bodies on a disused airfield. Romanov's thoughts returned to Valchek when he heard his comrade groan.

"Let's turn off into this forest," he begged. "I cannot hope to last much longer now."

"Hold on, Comrade, hold on," repeated Romanov. "We can't be far away from Scott. Think of the Motherland."

"To hell with the Motherland," said Valchek. "Just let me die in peace." Romanov looked across again and realised that he could be stuck with a dead body within a few minutes. Despite Valchek's efforts the blood was now seeping on to the floor like a tap that wouldn't stop dripping.

Romanov noticed a gap in the trees ahead of him. He switched his lights on to full beam and swung off the road on to a dirt track and drove as far as he could until the thicket became too dense. He switched off the headlights and ran round the car to open the door.

Valchek could only manage two or three steps before he slumped to the ground, still holding on to his intestines. Romanov bent down and helped him ease himself up against the trunk of a large tree.

"Leave me to die, Comrade Major. Do not waste any more of your time on me."

Romanov frowned.

"How do you wish to die, Comrade?" he asked. "Slowly and in agony, or quickly and peacefully?"

"Leave me, Comrade. Let me die slowly, but you should go while you still have Scott in your sights."

"But if the Americans were to find you, they might force you to talk."

"You know better than that, Comrade." Romanov accepted the rebuke, then rose and after a moment's thought, ran back to the car.

Valchek began to pray that once the bastard had left someone might find him. He'd never wanted this assignment in the first place, but Zaborski needed two extra eyes on Romanov and Zaborski was not a man to cross. Valchek wouldn't talk, but he still wanted to live.

The bullet from the 9mm Makarov went straight through the back of Valchek's temple and blew away one side of his head. Valchek slumped to the ground and for several seconds his body trembled and spasmed, subsiding into twitches as he emptied his bowels and bladder on to the brown earth.

Romanov stood over him until he was certain he was dead. Valchek would probably not have talked, but this was not a time for taking unnecessary risks.

When he woke the next morning he felt the same familiar guilt. Once again he swore it would be the last time. It was never as good as he had anticipated, and the regret always lingered on for several hours.

The expense of keeping up an extra flat, the taxi fares and the club bills nearly made it prohibitive. But he always returned, like a salmon to its breeding ground. "A queer fish," he murmured out loud, and then groaned at his own pun.

Piers began to wake, and for the next twenty minutes he made his companion forget those regrets. After a moment of lying in exhausted silence the older man slipped out of bed, took ten pounds out of his wallet and left it on the dresser before going to run himself a bath. He anticipated that by the time he returned the boy and the money would have gone.

He soaked himself in the bath wondering about Scott. He knew he should feel guilty about his death. A death that, like so many others before him, had been caused by his picking up a young Pole who he had thought was safe. It was now so many years ago that he couldn't even remember his name.

But Mentor had never been allowed to forget the name of the young aristocratic KGB officer he had found sitting on the end of their bed when he woke the next morning, or the look of disgust he showed for them both.

CHAPTER SIXTEEN

Adam lay flat on his stomach in the bottom of the empty barge. His head propped on one side, he remained alert to the slightest unfamiliar sound.

The bargee stood behind the wheel counting the three hundred Swiss francs for a second time. It was more than he could normally hope to earn in a month. A woman standing on tiptoes was eyeing the notes happily over his shoulder.

The barge progressed at a stately pace down the canal and Adam could no longer see the crashed plane.

Suddenly, far off in the distance, he heard distinctly the report of what sounded like a gunshot. Even as he listened the woman turned and scuttled down the hatch like a frightened rat. The barge ploughed its course on slowly through the night while Adam listened anxiously for any other unnatural noises, but all he could hear was the gentle splash of the water against the barge's hull. The clouds had moved on and full moon once again lit up the bank on both sides of the river. It became abundantly clear to Adam as he watched the towpath that they were not moving very fast. He could have run quicker. But even if it had cost him the remainder of his money, he was grateful to be escaping. He lowered himself again and curled up in the bow of the boat. He touched the icon, something he found himself doing every few minutes since he had discovered its secret. He did not move for another half hour, although he doubted that the barge had covered more than five miles.

Although everything appeared absolutely serene, he still remained alert. The river was far wider now than when he had first leapt on the barge.

The bargee's eyes never left him for long. He stood gripping the wheel, his oil-covered face not much cleaner than the old dungarees he wore – which looked as if they were never taken off. Occasionally he took a hand from the wheel, but only to remove the smokeless pipe from his mouth, cough, spit and put it back again.

The man smiled, took both hands off the wheel and placed them by the side of his head to indicate that Adam should sleep. But Adam shook his head. He checked his watch. Midnight had passed and he wanted to be off the barge and away long before first light.

He stood up, stretched, and wobbled a little. His shoulder, although healing slowly, still ached relentlessly. He walked up the centre of the barge and took his place next to the wheel.

"La Seine?" he asked, pointing at the water.

The bargee shook his head, no. "Canal de Bourgogne," he grunted.

Adam then pointed in the direction they were moving. "*Quelle ville?*"

The bargee removed his pipe. "*Ville? Ce n'est pas une ville, c'est Sombernon,*" he said, and put the stem back between his teeth.

Adam returned to his place in the bow. He tried to find a more comfortable position to relax and, curling up against the side of the boat, rested his head on some old rope and allowed his eyes to close.

"You know Scott better than any of us," said Sir Morris, "and you still have no feel as to where he might be now, or what he might do next, do you?"

"No, sir," admitted Lawrence. "The only thing we know for certain is that he has an appointment for a medical on Monday afternoon, but somehow I don't think he'll make it."

Sir Morris ignored the comment. "But someone was able to get to Scott, even though we didn't call D4," he continued. "That icon must hold a secret that we haven't begun to appreciate."

"And if Scott is still alive," said Lawrence, "nothing is going to convince him now that we're not to blame."

"And if we're not, who is?" asked Sir Morris. "Because someone was so desperate to discover our next move that they must have taken one hell of a risk during the last twenty-four hours. Unless, of course, it was you," said Sir Morris. The Permanent Secretary rose from his desk and turned around to look out of his window on to Horse Guards Parade.

"Even if it was me," said Lawrence, his eye resting on a picture of the young Queen which stood on the corner of his master's desk, "it doesn't explain how the Americans got there as well."

"Oh, that's simple," said Sir Morris. "Busch has been briefing them direct. I never doubted he would from the moment he joined us. What I hadn't anticipated was how far the Americans would go without keeping us informed."

"So it was you who told Busch," said Lawrence.

"No," said Sir Morris. "You don't end up sitting behind this desk risking your own skin. I told the Prime Minister, and politicians can always be relied on to pass on your information if they consider it will score them a point. To be fair, I knew the Prime Minister would tell the President. Otherwise I wouldn't have told him in the first place. More important: do you think Scott can still be alive?"

"Yes, I do," said Lawrence. "I have every reason to believe that the man who ran across the tarmac to our waiting plane was Scott. The French police, who incidentally have been far more cooperative than the Swiss, have informed us that our plane crashed in the field twelve miles north of Dijon but neither Scott nor the pilot were to be found at the scene of the crash.''

''And if the French reports on what took place at the airport are accurate,'' said Sir Morris, ''Romanov escaped and they must have had a couple of hours' start on us.''

''Possibly,'' said Lawrence.

''And do you think it equally possible,'' asked Sir Morris, ''that they have caught up with Scott and are now in possession of the icon?''

''Yes, sir, I fear that is quite possible,'' Lawrence said. ''But I can't pretend it's conclusive. However, the BBC monitoring service at Caversham Park picked up extra signals traffic to all Soviet embassies during the night.''

''That could mean anything,'' said Sir Morris, removing his spectacles.

''I agree, sir. But NATO reports that Russian strategic forces have been placed at a state of readiness and several Soviet Ambassadors across Europe have requested formal audiences with their Foreign Secretaries, ours included.''

''That *is* more worrying,'' said Sir Morris. ''They don't do that unless they are hoping for our support.''

''Agreed, sir. But most revealing of all is that the Active Measures section of the KGB, First Chief Directorate, has booked pages of advertising space in newspapers right across Europe and, I suspect, America.''

''Next you'll be telling me they hired J. Walter Thompson to write the copy,'' growled Sir Morris.

''They won't need them,'' said Lawrence. ''I suspect it's a story that will make every front page.''

If it hadn't been for the ceaseless throbbing in his shoulder, Adam might not have woken so quickly. The barge had suddenly swung at 90° and started heading east when Adam woke up with a start. He looked at the bargee and indicated that as the river was far wider now could he ease them nearer to the bank so he could jump off. The old man shrugged his shoulders pretending not to understand as the barge drifted aimlessly on.

Adam looked over the side and despite the lateness of the hour could see the bed of the river quite clearly. He tossed a stone over the side and watched it drop quickly to the bottom. It looked almost as if he could reach down and touch it. He looked up helplessly at the bargee who continued to stare over his head into the distance.

''Damn,'' said Adam, and taking the icon out of his blazer pocket held it high above his head. He stood on the edge of the barge feeling like a football manager asking the referee for permission to subsitute a player. Permission was granted and Adam leaped into the water. His feet hit the canal bed with a thud and knocked the breath out of his body despite the fact that the water only came up to his waist.

Adam stood in the canal, the icon still held high above his head as the barge sailed past him. He waded to the nearest bank and clambered up on to the towpath, turning slowly round as he tried to get some feel for direction. He was soon able to distinguish the Plough again and plot a course due west. After an hour of soggy jogging he began to make out a light in the distance which he estimated to be under a mile away. His legs were soaking and cold as he started to squelch his way across a field towards the first rays of the morning sun.

Whenever he came to a hedge or gate he climbed over or under like a Roman centurion determined to hold a straight line with his final destination. He could now see the outline of a house, which as he got nearer he realised was no more than a large cottage. He remembered the expression 'peasant farmer' from his school geography lessons. A little cobbled path led up to a half-open wooden door that looked as if it didn't need a lock. Adam tapped gently on the knocker and stood directly below the light above the doorway so that whoever answered would see him immediately.

The door was pulled back by a woman of perhaps thirty, who wore a plain black dress and a spotless white apron. Her rosy cheeks and ample waist confirmed her husband's profession.

When she saw Adam standing under the light she couldn't mask her surprise – she had been expecting the postman, but he didn't often appear in a neat navy blue blazer and soaking grey trousers.

Adam smiled. "*Anglais,*" he told her, and added, "I fell in the canal."

The lady burst out laughing and beckoned Adam into her kitchen. He walked in to find a man evidently dressed for milking. The farmer looked up and when he saw Adam he joined in the laughter – a warm, friendly laugh more with Adam than against him. When the woman saw that Adam was dripping all over her spotless floor she quickly pulled down a towel from the rack above the fire and said, "*Enlevez-moi ça,*" pointing to Adam's trousers.

Adam turned towards the farmer for guidance but his host only nodded his agreement and added with a mime of pulling down his own trousers.

"*Enlevez-les, enlevez-les,*" the woman repeated, pointing at him, and handed him the towel.

Adam removed his shoes and socks but the farmer's wife went on pointing until he took off his trousers, and she didn't budge before he had finally removed his shirt and underclothes and wrapped the towel around his waist. She stared at the large bandage on his shoulder but then quickly picked up everything except his blazer and took them over to the sink while he stood by the fire and dried himself.

Adam hitched up the towel around his waist, as the farmer beckoned him to join him at the table, pouring a large glass of milk for his guest and another for himself. Adam sat down next to the farmer, hanging his fashionable new blazer over the back of the chair near the fire. A delicious aroma arose from the pan where the farmer's wife was frying a thick slice of bacon which she had cut from the joint hanging in the smoky recess of the chimney.

The farmer raised his glass of milk high in the air.

"Winston Churchill," he toasted. Adam took a long gulp from his own glass and then raised it dramatically.

"Charles de Gaulle," he said, and finished off the warm milk as if it had been his first pint at the local pub.

The farmer picked up the jug once more and refilled their glasses. "*Merci*," said Adam, turning to the farmer's wife as she placed in front of him a large plate sizzling with eggs and bacon. She nodded and handed Adam a knife and fork before saying, "*Mangez*."

"*Merci, merci*," Adam repeated, as she cut him a thick oval slice from the huge loaf in front of him.

Adam began to devour the freshly cooked food which was the first meal he'd managed since the dinner he'd ordered at Robin's expense.

Without warning the farmer suddenly rose from his place and thrust out his hand. Adam also got up and shook it gratefully, only to be reminded how sore his shoulder still was.

"*Je dois travailler à la laiterie*," he explained.

Adam nodded, and remained standing as his host left the room, but the farmer waved him down with a further, "*Mangez*."

When Adam had finished the last scrap of food – he did everything except lick the plate – he took it over to the farmer's wife who was busy removing a pot from the stove in order to pour him a large, steaming cup of hot coffee. He sat back down and began to sip at it.

Adam tapped the jacket pocket almost automatically to make sure the icon was still safely in place. He pulled it out and studied St George and the Dragon. He turned it over, hesitated and then pressed the silver crown hard. The icon split in half like a book revealing two tiny hinges on the inside.

He glanced up at the farmer's wife, who was now wringing out his socks. Adam noticed his pants had already joined the trousers on the rack above the fire. She removed an ironing board from a little alcove by the side of the stove and began to set it up, showing no interest in Adam's discovery.

Once again he stared down at the inside of the open icon which was now laid flat on the table in front of him. The true irony was that the woman pressing his trousers was able to understand every word on the parchment while at the same time unable to explain the full significance to him. The complete surface of the inside of the icon was covered by a parchment which was glued to the wood and fell only a centimetre short of the four edges. Adam swivelled it round so that he could study it more clearly. The scrawled signatures in black ink at the bottom and the seals gave it the look of a legal document. On each reading he learned something new. Adam had been surprised originally to discover it was written in French until he came to the date on the bottom – June 20, 1867 – and then he remembered from his military history lectures at Sandhurst that long after Napoleonic times most international agreements remained conducted in French. Adam began to reread the script again slowly.

His French was not good enough to translate more than a few odd words from the finely handwritten scroll. Under *Etas Unis* William Seward's bold hand was scrawled across a crest of a two-headed eagle. Next to it was the signature of Edward de Stoeckle below a crown that mirrored the silver ornament embedded in the back of the icon. Adam double-checked. It had to be some form of agreement executed between the Russians and the Americans in 1867.

He then searched for other words that would help to explain the significance of the document. On one line he identified: '*Sept million deux cent mille dollars d'or (7.2 mille)*' and on another '*Sept cent dix huit million deux cent mille dollars d'or (718.2m) le 20 Juin, 1966.*'

His eyes rested on a calendar hanging by a nail from the wall. It was Friday, June 17, 1966. If the date in the agreement were to be believed, then in only three days the document would no longer have any legal validity. No wonder the two most powerful nations on earth seemed desperate to get their hands on it, thought Adam.

Adam read through the document line by line searching for any further clues, pondering over each word slowly.

His eyes came to a halt on the one word that would remain the same in both languages.

The one word he had not told Lawrence.

Adam wondered how the icon had ever fallen into the hands of Goering in the first place. He must have bequeathed it to his father unknowingly – for had he realised the true importance of what was hidden inside it, he would surely have been able to bargain for his own freedom with either side.

"*Voilà, voilà,*" said the farmer's wife, waving her hands as she placed warm socks, pants and trousers in front of Adam. How long had he spent engrossed in his fateful discovery? She looked down at the upside down parchment and smiled. Adam quickly snapped the icon closed and then studied the masterpiece carefully. So skilfully had the wood been cut that he could no longer see the join. He thought of the words of the letter left to him in his father's will: "But if you open it only to discover its purpose is to involve you in some dishonorable enterprise, be rid of it without a second thought." He did not need to give a second thought to how his father would have reacted in the same circumstances. The farmer's wife was now standing hands on hips, staring at him with a puzzled look.

Adam quickly replaced the icon in his jacket pocket and pulled back on his trousers.

He could think of no adequate way of thanking the farmer's wife for her hospitality, her lack of suspicion or inquisitiveness, so he simply walked over to her, took her gently by the shoulders, and kissed her on the cheek. She blushed and handed him a small plastic bag. He looked inside to find three apples, some bread and a large piece of cheese. She removed a crumb from his lip with the edge of her apron and led him to the open door.

Adam thanked her and then walked outside into his other world.

PART THREE

THE WHITE HOUSE
WASHINGTON DC

June 17, 1966

CHAPTER SEVENTEEN

The White House, Washington DC, June 17, 1966

"I don't want to be the first god-damn President in the history of the United States to hand back an American state rather than be founding one."

"I appreciate that, Mr President," said the Secretary of State. "But . . ."

"Where do we stand on this legally, Dean?"

"We don't, Mr President. Abraham Brunweld, the leading authority on documents of this period, confirms that the terms of the ninety-nine-year lease are binding on both sides. The lease was signed on behalf of Russia by Edward de Stoeckle, and for the US by the then Secretary of State, William Seward."

"Can this agreement still be valid today?" asked the President, turning to his chief legal officer, Nicholas Katzenbach.

"It certainly can, sir," said the Attorney General. "But only if they can produce their original. If they do, the UN and the international court at The Hague would have no choice but to support the Russian claim. Otherwise no international agreement signed by us in the past or in the future would carry any credibility."

"What you're asking me to do is lie down and wag my tail like a prize labrador while the Russians shit all over us," said the President.

"I understand how you feel, Mr President," said the Attorney General, "but it remains my responsibility to make you aware of the legal position."

"God dammit, is there a precedent for this kind of stupidity by a Head of State?"

"The British," chipped in Dean Rusk, "will be facing a similar problem with the Chinese in 1999 over the New Territories of Hong Kong. They have already accepted the reality of the situation and indeed have made it clear to the Chinese Government that they are willing to come to an agreement with them."

"That's just one example," said the President, "and we all know about the British and their 'fair play' diplomacy."

"Also, in 1898," continued Rusk, "the Russians obtained a ninety-nine-year lease on Port Arthur in Northern China. The port was vital to them because, unlike Vladivostok, it is ice-free all year round."

"I had no idea the Russians *had* a port in China."

"They don't any longer, Mr President. They returned it to Mao in 1955, as an act of goodwill between fellow Communists."

"You can be damn sure the Russians won't return this piece of land to *us* as an act of goodwill," said the President. "Am I left with any alternative?"

"Short of military action to prevent the Soviets claiming what they will rightfully see as theirs, no sir," replied the Secretary of State.

"So one Johnson buys the land from the Russians in 1867 and another has to sell it back in 1966. Why did Seward and the President ever agree to such a damn cockamaney idea in the first place?"

"At the time," said the Attorney General, removing his spectacles, "the purchase price of the land in question was seven point two million dollars and inflation was then virtually unheard of. Andrew Johnson could never have imagined the Russians wanting to purchase it back at ninety-nine times its original value, or in real terms, seven hundred and twelve point eight million dollars in gold bullion. In reality, years of inflation have made the asking price cheap. And the Russians have already lodged the full amount in a New York bank to prove it."

"So we can't even hope that they won't stump up in time," said the President.

"It would seem not, sir."

"But why did Tsar Alexander want to lease the damn land in the first place? That's what beats me."

"He was having trouble with some of his senior ministers at the time over the selling off of land belonging to Russia in Eastern Asia. The Tsar thought this transaction would be more palatable to his inner circle if he presented it as nothing more than a long lease, with a buy-back clause, rather than an outright sale."

"Why didn't Congress object?"

"After Congress ratified the main treaty, the amendment was not strictly subject to approval by the House, because no further expenditure by the United States government was involved," Rusk explained. "Ironically, Seward was proud of the fact he had demanded such a high premium in the repayment clause. At the time he had every reason to believe it would be impossible to repay."

"Now it's worth that in annual oil revenue alone," said the President, looking out of the Oval Office window towards the Washington Monument. "Not to mention the military chaos it's going to create in this country if they've got their hands on their copy of the treaty. Don't ever forget that I was the President who asked Congress to spend billions of dollars putting the early warning system right across that border so the American people could sleep easy."

Neither adviser felt able to contradict their elected leader.

"So what are the British doing about all this?"

"Playing it close to the chest, as usual, Mr President. It's an English national who is thought to be in possession of the treaty at the moment and they still seem quietly confident that they will get their hands on him and the icon before the Russians, so they may yet turn out to be our saviours."

"Nice to have the British coming to *our* rescue for a change," said the President. "But have we meanwhile been sitting on our asses while they try to solve our problems for us?"

"No, sir. The CIA have been on it for over a month."

"Then it's only surprising that the Russians haven't got their hands on the icon already."

Nobody laughed.

"So what am I expected to do next? Sit and wait for the Soviets to move 712 million dollars of gold from their New York bank to the US Treasury before midnight on Monday?"

"They must also deliver their original copy of the agreement to me at the same time," said Rusk. "And they have only sixty hours left to do that."

"Where's our copy, at this moment?" asked the President.

"Somewhere deep in the vaults of the Pentagon. Only two people know the exact location. Since the Yalta conference, our copy of the treaty has never seen the light of day."

"Why have I never been told about it before today?" asked the President. "At least I could have put a stop to so much expenditure."

"For over fifty years, we've believed the Russians' copy was destroyed at the time of the Revolution. As the years passed it became clear that the Soviets accepted this as a *fait accompli* with the final acknowledgment of this fact coming from Stalin at Yalta. Brezhnev must have come across something within the last month that convinced him that their copy had only been mislaid."

"Christ, another month and we would have had a home run."

"That is correct, sir," said the Secretary of State.

"Do you realise, Dean, that if the Russians turn up at your office before midnight on Monday with their copy, all I'll be able to do will be so much piss in a thunderstorm?"

CHAPTER EIGHTEEN

When the cottage door closed behind Adam, all he could make out was the outskirts of a small town. While it was still so early he felt safe to jog towards the '*centre ville*', but as soon as the early-morning workers began to appear on the streets, he slowed to a walk. Adam opted not to go straight into the centre of the town but to look for somewhere to hide while he considered his next move. He came to a halt outside a multi-storey car park and decided he was unlikely to find a better place to formulate a plan.

Adam walked through an exit door at ground level and came to a lift that indicated that the car park was on four floors. He ran down the steps to the lowest level, tentatively pulled back the door to the basement, and found it was badly lit and almost empty. Adam had chosen the basement as he assumed that it would be the last floor to fill up with customers. He walked around the perimeter of the floor and studied the layout. Two cars were parked in the far corner, and a thick layer of dust suggested that they had been there for some time. He crouched down behind one of them and found that he was safely out of sight to all but the most inquisitive.

He began to fantasise that someone might park a car on that floor and leave the keys in the ignition. He checked the doors of the two cars already parked but both were securely locked. He settled back to work out a more serious plan of how he could reach the coast by nightfall.

He was deep in thought when he heard a scraping noise that made him jump. He peered round the gloomy basement, and out of the darkness a man appeared pulling behind him a plastic dustbin half full of rubbish. Adam could barely see the old man dressed in a dirty brown coat that stretched nearly to the ground and left little doubt about the height of the previous employee. He wasn't sure what he would do if the man continued to walk towards him. But as he came nearer Adam could see that he was stooped and old; the stub of a cigarette protruded from his lips. The cleaner stopped in front of him, spotted a cigarette packet, picked it up and checked to be sure it was empty before dropping it in the dustbin. After that, a sweet paper, a Pepsi-Cola can and an old copy of *Le Figaro* all found their way into the dustbin. His eyes searched slowly round the room for more rubbish, but still he didn't notice Adam tucked away behind the farthest car. Satisfied that his task was completed, he dragged the dustbin across the floor and pushed it outside the door. Adam began to relax again but after about two minutes, the old man returned, walked over to a wall and pulled open a door that Adam hadn't previously noticed. He took off the long brown coat and replaced it with a grey one that didn't look in a much better state but at least it made a more convincing fit. He then disappeared through the exit. Moments later Adam heard a door close with a bang.

The cleaner had ended his day.

Adam waited for some time before he stood up and stretched. He crept around the edge of the wall until he reached the little door. He pulled it open quietly and removed the long brown coat from its nail, then headed back to his place in the corner. He ducked down as the first of the morning cars arrived. The driver swung into the far corner in such a fluent circle that Adam felt sure it must have been a daily routine. A short dapper man with a pencil moustache, dressed in a smart pin-stripe suit, jumped out of the car carrying a briefcase. Once he had locked the car door he proceeded with fast mincing strides towards the exit. Adam waited until the heavy door swung back into place before he stood up and tried on the brown coat over his blazer. It was tight on the shoulders and a little short in the arm, but at least it made him look as if he might have worked there.

For the next hour he watched the cars as they continued to arrive at irregular intervals. Tiresomely, all the owners carefully locked their doors and checked them before disappearing through the exit with their keys.

When he heard ten o'clock strike in the distance Adam decided that there was nothing to be gained by hanging around any longer. He had crept out from behind the car that was shielding him and began to make his way across the floor towards the exit when a Rover with English registration plates swung round the corner and nearly blinded him. He jumped to one side to let the car pass but it screeched to a halt beside and the driver wound down his window.

"All – right – park – here?" the driver asked, emphasizing each word in an English accent.

"*Oui, monsieur,*" said Adam.

"Other – floors – marked – *privé,*" the man continued, as if addressing a complete moron. "Anywhere?" His arm swept round the floor.

"*Oui,*" repeated Adam, "bert ay merst paak you," he added, fearing he sounded too much like Peter Sellers.

Balls, was what Adam expected to hear him reply. "Fine," was what the man actually said. He got out of the car, and handed Adam his keys and a ten franc note.

"*Merci,*" said Adam, pocketing the note and touching his forehead with his hand. "*Quelle – heure – vous – retournez?*" he asked playing the man at his own game.

"One hour at most," said the man as he reached the door. Adam waited by the car for a few minutes but the man did not come back. He opened the passenger door and dropped the food bag on the front seat. He then walked round to the other side and climbed in the driver's seat, switched on the ignition and checked the fuel gauge: a little over half full. He revved the engine and drove the car up the ramp until he reached the first floor, where he came to a halt unable to escape. He needed a two-franc piece to make the arm swing up and let him out. The lady in the car behind him reluctantly changed his ten-franc note once she realised there was no other way of getting out.

Adam drove quickly out on to the road looking for the sign 'Toutes Directions'. Once he had found one, it was only minutes before he was clear of the town and travelling up the N6 to Paris.

Adam estimated that he had two hours at best. By then the police would surely have been informed of the theft of the car. He felt confident he had enough petrol to reach Paris; but he certainly couldn't hope to make Calais.

He remained in the centre lane of the N6 for most of the journey, always keeping the speedometer five kilometres below the limit. By the end of the first hour Adam had covered nearly ninety kilometres. He opened the bag the farmer's wife had given him and took out an apple and a piece of cheese. His mind began to drift to Heidi, as it had so often in the past two days.

If only he had never opened the letter.

Another hour passed before he spotted him limping up a hill only a few hundred yards from the main road. A broad smile came over Romanov's face when he realised he could get to Scott long before he could hope to reach the road. When Romanov was within a few yards of him the flight lieutenant turned round and smiled at the stranger.

When Romanov left Banks thirty minutes later hidden behind a tree with a broken neck he reluctantly admitted that the young pilot officer had been as brave as Valchek – but he couldn't waste any more time trying to discover in which direction Scott was heading.

Romanov headed west.

The moment Adam heard the siren he came out of his reverie. He checked the little clock on the dashboard. He had only been driving for about an hour and a half. Could the French police be that efficient? The police car was now approaching him fast on his left but Adam maintained the same speed – except for his heartbeat, which climbed well above the approved limit – until the police car shot past him.

As the kilometres sped by, he began to wonder if it might be wiser to turn off on to a quieter road, but decided, on balance, to risk pushing on to Paris as quickly as possible.

He remained alert for further sirens as he continued to follow the signs to Paris. When he finally reached the outskirts of the city, he proceeded to the Boulevard de l'Hôpital and even felt relaxed enough to bite into another apple. In normal circumstances he would have appreciated the magnificent architecture along the banks of the Seine, but today his eyes kept returning to the rear view mirror.

Adam decided he would abandon the vehicle in a large public car park: with any luck it could be days before anyone came across it.

He turned down the Rue de Rivoli and took in at once the long colourful banners looming up in front of him. He could hardly have picked a better place, as he felt sure it would be packed with foreign cars.

Adam backed the Rover in the farthest corner of the square. He then wolfed down the last piece of cheese, and locked the car. He started walking towards the exit, but had only gone a few yards when he realised that the strolling holidaymakers were amused by his ill-fitting brown jacket which he had completely forgotten. He decided to turn back and throw the coat in the boot. He quickly took it off and folded it in a small square.

He was only a few yards away from the car when he saw the young policeman. He was checking the Rover's number plate and repeating the letters and numbers into an intercom. Adam inched slowly back, never taking his eyes from the officer. He only needed to manage another six or seven paces before he would be lost in the throng of the crowd.

Five, four, three, two, he backed, as the man continued speaking into the intercom. Just one more pace . . . "*Alors!*" hollered the lady on whose foot Adam stepped.

"I'm so sorry," said Adam, instinctively in his native language. The policeman immediately looked up and stared at Adam, then shouted something into the intercom and began running towards him.

Adam dropped the brown coat and swung round quickly, nearly knocking the stooping lady over before sprinting off towards the exit. The car park was full of tourists who had come to enjoy the pleasures of the Louvre, and Adam found it hard to pick up any real speed through the dense crowd. By the time he reached the entrance to the car park he could hear the policeman's whistle a few paces behind him. He ran across the Rue de Rivoli, through an archway and into a large square.

By then another policeman was coming from his right, leaving him with no choice but to run up the steps in front of him. When he reached the top he turned to see at least three other policemen in close pursuit. He threw himself through the swing door and past a group of Japanese tourists who were surrounding the Rodin statue that stood in the hallway. He charged on past a startled ticket collector, and on up the long marble staircase. "*Monsieur, monsieur, votre billet?*" he heard shouted in his wake.

At the top of the staircase he turned right and ran through *The Special '66' Centuries Exhibition*, Modern – Pollock, Bacon, Hockney – into the Impressionist room – Monet, Manet, Courbet – desperately looking for any way out. On into Eighteenth Century – Fragonard, Goya, Watteau – but still no sign of an exit. Through the great arch into Seventeenth Century – Murillo, Van Dyck, Poussin – as people stopped looking at the pictures and turned their attention to what was causing such a commotion. Adam ran on into Sixteenth Century – Raphael, Caravaggio, Michelangelo – suddenly aware that there were ony two centuries of paintings to go.

Right or left? He chose right, and entered a huge square room. There were three exits. He slowed momentarily to decide which would be his best bet when he became aware that the room was full of Russian icons. He came to a halt at an empty display case. '*Nous regrettons que ce tableau soit soumis à la restauration.*'

The first policeman had already entered the large room and was only a few paces behind as Adam dashed on towards the farthest exit. There were now only two exits left open for him from which to choose. He swung right, only to see another policeman bearing straight down on him. Left: two more. Ahead, yet another.

Adam came to a halt in the middle of the Icon Room at the Louvre, his hands raised above his head. He was surrounded by policemen, their guns drawn.

CHAPTER NINETEEN

Sir Morris picked up the phone on his desk.

"An urgent call from Paris, sir," said his secretary.

"Thank you, Tessa." He listened carefully as his brain quickly translated the exciting news.

"*Merci, merci*," said Sir Morris to his opposite number at the French Foreign Ministry. "We will be back in touch with you as soon as we have made all the necessary arrangements to collect him. But for now, please don't let him out of your sight." Sir Morris listened for a few moments before he said: "And if he has any possessions on him, please keep them guarded under lock and key. Thank you once again." His secretary took down every word of the conversation in shorthand – as she had done for the past seventeen years.

Once the police had snapped the handcuffs on Adam and marched him off to a waiting car, he was surprised how relaxed, almost friendly, they became. He was yanked into the back of the car by the policeman to whom he was attached. He noticed that there was a police car in front of him and yet another behind. Two motorcycle outriders led the little motorcade away. Adam felt more like visiting royalty than a criminal who was wanted for questioning for two murders, two car thefts and travelling under false identification. Was it possible at last that someone had worked out he was innocent?

When Adam arrived at the Sûreté on the Ile de la Cité, he was immediately ordered to empty all his pockets. One wrist watch, one apple, one hundred pounds in traveller's cheques, eight francs, and one British passport in the name of Dudley Hulme. The station inspector asked him politely to strip to his vest and pants. It was the second time that day. Once Adam had done so, the inspector carefully checked every pocket of the blazer, even the lining. His expression left Adam in no doubt he hadn't found what he was looking for.

"Do you have anything else in your possession?" the officer asked in slow, precise English.

Damn silly question, thought Adam. You can see for yourself. "No," was all he replied. The inspector checked the blazer once again but came across nothing new. "You must be dressed," he said abruptly.

Adam put back on his shirt, jacket and trousers but the inspector kept his tie and shoelaces.

"All your things will be returned to you when you leave," the inspector explained. Adam nodded as he slipped on his shoes, which flapped uncomfortably when he walked. He was then accompanied to a small cell on the same floor, locked in and left alone. He looked around the sparsely furnished room. A small wooden table was placed in its centre, with two wooden chairs on either side. His eyes checked over a single bed in the corner which had on it an ancient horse-hair mattress. He could not have described the room properly as a cell because there were no bars, even across the one small window. He took off his jacket, hung it over the chair and lay down on the bed. At least it was an improvement over anything he had slept on for the past two nights, he reflected. Could it have only been two nights since he had slept on the floor of Robin's hotel room in Geneva?

As the minutes ticked by, he made only one decision. That when the inspector returned, he would demand to see a lawyer. "What the hell's the French for lawyer?" he asked out loud.

When an officer eventually appeared, in what Adam estimated must have been about half an hour, he was carrying a tray laden with hot soup, a roll, and what looked to Adam like a steak with all the trimmings and a plastic cup filled to the brim with red wine. He wondered if they had got the wrong man, or if this was simply his last meal before the guillotine. He followed the officer to the door.

"I demand to speak to a lawyer," he said emphatically, but the policeman only shrugged.

"*Je ne comprends pas l'Anglais*," he said, and slammed the door behind him.

Adam settled down to eat the meal that had been set before him, thankful that the French assumed good food should be served whatever the circumstances.

Sir Morris told them his news an hour later and then studied each of them round the table carefully. He would never have called the D4 if he hadn't felt sure that Adam was at last secure. Matthews continued to show no emotion. Busch was unusually silent while Snell looked almost relaxed for a change. Lawrence was the only one who seemed genuinely pleased.

"Scott is locked up in the Ministry of the Interior off the Place Beauvais," continued Sir Morris, "and I have already contacted our military attaché at the Embassy . . ."

"Colonel Pollard," interrupted Lawrence.

"Colonel Pollard," said Sir Morris, "who has been sent over in the Ambassador's car and will bring Scott back to be debriefed at our Embassy in Faubourg St Honoré. Sûreté rang a few moments ago to confirm that Colonel Pollard had arrived." Sir Morris turned towards his Number Two. "You will fly over to Paris tonight and conduct the debriefing yourself."

"Yes, sir," said Lawrence, looking up at his boss, a smile appearing on his face.

Sir Morris nodded. A cool lot, he considered, as he stared round that table, but the next half hour would surely find out which one of them it was who served two masters.

"Good. I don't think I shall need any of you again today," said Sir Morris as he rose from his chair.

Mentor smiled as Sir Morris left the room; his task had already been completed. So simple when you can read upside-down shorthand.

A black Jaguar bearing CD plates had arrived at police headquarters a few minutes earlier than expected. The traffic had not been as heavy as the colonel had anticipated. The inspector was standing on the steps as Pollard jumped out of the car. The policeman looked at the flapping Union Jack on the bonnet and considered the whole exercise was becoming rather melodramatic.

Pollard, a short, thickset man, dressed in a dark suit, regimental tie and carrying a rolled umbrella, looked like so many of those Englishmen who refuse to acknowledge that they could possibly be abroad.

The inspector took Pollard directly through to the little room where Adam had been incarcerated.

"Pollard's the name, Colonel Pollard. British Military Attaché stationed here in Paris. Sorry you've been put through this ordeal, old fellow, but a lot of paperwork had to be completed to get you out. Bloody red tape."

"I understand," said Adam, jumping off the bed and shaking the colonel by the hand. "I was in the army myself."

"I know. Royal Wessex, wasn't it?"

Adam nodded, feeling a little more confident.

"Still, the problem's been sorted out now," continued the colonel. "The French police have been most cooperative and have agreed to let you accompany me to our Embassy."

Adam looked at the colonel's tie. "Duke of York's?"

"What? Certainly not," said Pollard, his hand fingering his shirt front. "Green Jackets."

"Yes, of course," said Adam, pleased to have his mistake picked up.

"Now I think we ought to be cutting along, old fellow, I know you'll be relieved to hear that they won't be laying any charges."

The colonel didn't know just how relieved Adam did feel.

The inspector led them both back out into the hall where Adam had only to identify and sign for his personal belongings. He put them all in his pocket, except for the watch, which he slipped over his wrist, and his shoelaces, which he quickly inserted and tied. He wasn't surprised they didn't return Dudley Hulme's passport.

"Don't let's hang around too long, old fellow," said the colonel, beginning to sound a little anxious.

"I won't be a moment," said Adam. "I'm just as keen to get out of this place as you are." He checked his laces before following Colonel Pollard and the inspector out to the waiting Jaguar. He noticed for the first time that the colonel had a slight limp. A chauffeur held the door open for him; Adam laughed.

"Something funny, old fellow?" asked the colonel.

"No. It's just that the last chauffeur who offered to do that for me didn't look quite as friendly."

Adam climbed into the back of the Jaguar and the colonel slipped in beside him.

"Back to the Embassy," said Pollard, and the car moved off briskly.

Adam stared in horror at the flapping Union Jack.

CHAPTER TWENTY

When Adam awoke he was naked.

He looked around the sparse room but this time unlike the French jail he was unable to see what was behind him: his arms, legs and body were bound tightly by a nylon cord to a chair that had been placed in the middle of the room, and which made him all but immobile.

When he looked up from the chair all he could see was Colonel Pollard standing over him. The moment the colonel was satisfied that Adam had regained consciousness he quickly left the room

Adam turned his head to see all his clothes laid out neatly on a bed at the far side of the cell. He tried to manoeuvre the chair, but he could barely manage to make it wobble from side to side, and after several minutes had advanced only a few inches towards the door. He switched his energies to trying to loosen the cords around his wrists, rubbing them up and down against the wood of the slats, but his arms were bound so tightly that he could only manage the slightest friction.

After struggling ineffectively for several minutes he was interrupted by the sound of the door swinging open. Adam looked up as Romanov strode through. He decided he was no less terrifying at close quarters. He was followed by another man whom Adam didn't recognise. The second man was clutching what looked like a cigar box as he took his place somewhere behind Adam. Pollard followed him, carrying a large plastic sheet.

Romanov looked at Adam's naked body and smiled; enjoying his humiliation he came to a halt directly in front of the chair.

"My name is Alexander Petrovich Romanov," he announced with only a slight accent.

"Or Emmanuel Rosenbaum," said Adam, staring at his adversary closely.

"I am only sorry that we are unable to shake hands," he added, as he began circling the chair. "But I felt in the circumstances certain precautions were necessary. First I should like to congratulate you on having eluded me for so long, but as you will now realise my source in London can place a call every bit as quickly as yours."

"Your source?" said Adam.

"Don't be naïve, Captain. You must be painfully aware by now that you're in no position to be asking questions, only answering them."

Adam fixed his gaze on a brick in the wall in front of him, making no attempt to follow Romanov's circumnavigations.

"Pollard," said Romanov sharply, "put Captain Scott back in the centre of the room. He seems to have managed to move at least a foot in his getaway attempt."

Pollard did as he was bid, first spreading the plastic sheet on the floor, then manoeuvring Adam till the chair was on the centre of the sheet.

"Thank you," said Romanov. "I think you have already met our Colonel Pollard," he continued. "That's not his real name, of course, and indeed he's not a real colonel either, but that's what he always wanted to be in life, so when the opportunity arose, we happily obliged.

"In fact the good colonel did serve in the British Army, but I fear he entered the service of King and country as a private soldier and eighteen years later left, still as a private soldier. And despite an injury to his leg – unfortunately not received from any known enemy of the Crown – he was unable to claim a disability pension. Which left him fairly destitute. But, as I explained, he always wanted to be a colonel," continued Romanov. "It was a good attempt of yours 'The Duke of York's?' but as the colonel had genuinely served with the Green Jackets it was the one tie he felt safe wearing."

Adam's eyes remained fixed on the wall. "Now I confess, our mistake over the Union Jack was lax but as it is impossible to fly the Russian flag upside down without everyone noticing, it was perhaps understandable. Although, in truth, Pollard should have spotted it immediately, we must be thankful that you did not until the car doors were safely locked."

Romanov stopped his endless circling and stared down at the nude body.

"Now I think the time has come for you to be introduced to our Dr Stavinsky who has so been looking forward to making your acquaintance because he hasn't had a lot of work to do lately and he fears he might be becoming a little rusty."

Romanov took a pace backward allowing Stavinsky to come and take his place immediately in front of Adam. The cigar box was still tucked under his arm. Adam stared at the diminutive figure who seemed to be sizing him up. Stavinsky must have been no taller than five feet and wore an open-necked grey shirt and a badly creased grey suit that made him resemble a junior clerk in a not very successful solicitor's office. A one-day bristle covered his face, leaving the impression that he hadn't expected to be working that day. His thin lips suddenly parted in a grin as if he had come to some conclusion.

"It is a pleasure to make your acquaintance, Captain Scott," began Stavinsky. "Although you are an unexpected guest of the Embassy you are most welcome. You could of course make our association very short by simply letting me have one piece of information. In truth" – he let out a small sigh – "I only require to know the whereabouts of the Tsar's icon." He paused. "Although I have a feeling it's not going to be that easy. Am I correct?"

Adam didn't reply.

"It doesn't come as a great surprise. I warned Comrade Romanov that after his laudatory description of you a simple series of questions and answers would be unlikely to suffice. However, I must follow the normal procedure in such circumstances. As you will find, the Russians go by the book every bit as much as the British. Now you may have wondered," added Stavinsky as if it were an afterthought, "why a man who never smokes should be seen carrying a Cuban cigar box."

Stavinsky waited for Adam's reply but none was forthcoming.

"Ah, no attempt at conversation. I see you have been through such an experience before. Well, then I must continue talking to myself for the moment. When I was a student at the University of Moscow my subject was chemistry, but I specialised in one particular aspect of the science."

Adam feigned no interest as he tried not to recall his worst days in the hands of the Chinese.

"What few people in the West realise is that we Russians were the first to pioneer, at university level, a Department of Scientific Interrogation with a full professorial chair and several research assistants. They are still without one at either Oxford or Cambridge I am told. But then the West continues to preserve a quixotic view of the value of life and the right of the individual. Now, as you can imagine, only certain members of the university were aware of the existence of such a department, let alone able to enrol as a student – especially as it was not on the curriculum. But as I had already been a member of the Perviyotdel it was common sense that I should add the craft of torture to my trade. Now I am basically a simple man," continued Stavinsky, "who had previously shown little interest in research but once I had been introduced to the 'cigar box' I became, overnight, an enthralled and retentive pupil. I could not wait to be let loose to experiment." He paused to see what effect he was having on Scott, and was disappointed to be met by the same impassive stare.

"Torture, of course, is an old and honourable profession," continued Stavinsky. "The Chinese have been at it for nearly three thousand years as I think you have already experienced, Captain Scott, and even you British have come a long way since the rack. But that particular instrument has proved to be rather cumbersome for carrying around in a modern world. With this in mind, my tutor at Moscow, Professor Metz, has developed something small and simple that even a man of average intelligence can master after a few lessons."

Adam was desperate to know what was in the box but his look remained impassive.

"With torture, as with making love, Captain Scott, foreplay is the all-important factor. Are you following me, Captain?" asked Stavinsky.

Adam tried to remain relaxed and calm.

"Still no response, Captain Scott, but as I explained I am in no hurry. Especially, as I suspect in your case, the whole operation may take a little longer than usual, which I confess will only add to my enjoyment. And although we are not yet in possession of the Tsar's icon I *am* at least in control of the one person who knows where it is."

Adam still made no comment.

"So I will ask you once and once only before I open the box. Where is the Tsar's icon?"

Adam spat at Stavinsky.

"Not only ill-mannered," remarked Stavinsky, "but also stupid. Because in a very short time you will be desperate for any liquid we might be kind enough to allow you. But, to be fair, you had no way of knowing that."

Stavinsky placed the box on the floor and opened it slowly.

"First, I offer you," he said, like a conjurer in front of a child, "a six-volt nickel-cadmium battery, made by EverReady." He paused. "I thought you would appreciate that touch. Second," he continued, putting his hand back in the box, "a small pulse generator." He placed the rectangular metal box next to the battery. "Third, two lengths of wire with electrodes attached to their ends. Fourth, two syringes, fifth, a tube of collodion glue and finally, a phial, of which more later. When I say 'finally', there are still two items left in the box which I shall not require unless it becomes necessary for us to progress to Stage Two in our little experiment, or even Stage Three."

Stavinsky placed everything in a straight line on the floor in front of Adam.

"Doesn't look a lot, I confess," said Stavinsky. "But with a little imagination I'm sure you will be able to work out its potential. Now. In order that Comrade Romanov and the colonel can enjoy the spectacle I am about to offer it is necessary to add a few details about the nervous system itself. I do hope you are following my every word, Captain Scott, because it is the victim's knowledge which allows him to appreciate the true genius of what is about to follow."

It didn't please Adam that Stavinsky spoke English so well. He could still vividly remember how the Chinese had told Adam what they were going to do to him in a language that he couldn't understand. With them, he had found it easier to allow his mind to drift during their diatribe but he still ended up in a fridge for four hours.

"Now to the practical," continued the grey figure. "By sending a small electrical impulse to the end of the synapse, it is possible to pass

on a large electric message to thousands of other nerves within a
fraction of a second. This causes a nasty sensation not unlike touching a
live wire when the electrical power has been left on in one's home, more
commonly known as an electric shock. Not deadly, but distinctly
unpleasant. In the Moscow school this is known as Stage One and there
is no necessity for you to experience this if you are now willing to tell me
where I can find the Tsar's icon.''

Adam remained impassive.

"I see you have not paid attention during my little lecture so I fear we
will have to move from the theoretical to the practical."

Adam began reciting to himself the thirty-seven plays of
Shakespeare. How his old English master would have been delighted
to know that after all those years of drumming the complete
Shakespearean canon into a reluctant student, Adam could still recall
them at a moment's notice.

Henry VI part one, Henry VI part two, Henry VI part three, Richard II . . .

Stavinsky picked up the tube of collodion glue, removed the cap and
smeared two lumps of it on Adam's chest.

. . . *Comedy of Errors, Titus Andronicus, The Taming of the Shrew* . . .

The Russian attached the two electrodes to the glue, taking the wires
back and screwing them to the six-volt battery, which in turn was
connected to the tiny pulse generator.

. . . *Two Gentlemen of Verona, Love's Labour's Lost, Romeo and Juliet* . . .

Without warning, Stavinsky pressed down the handle of the generator for two seconds during which time Adam received a two-hundred-
volt shock. For those seconds Adam screamed as he experienced
excruciating pain as the volts forced their way to every part of his body.
But the sensation was over in a moment.

"Do feel free to let us know how exactly you feel. You are in a
soundproof room, and therefore you won't be disturbing anyone else in
the building."

Adam ignored the comment and gripping the side of the chair,
mumbled . . . *Richard III, Midsummer Night's Dream, King John* . . .

Stavinsky pressed the plunger down for another two seconds. Adam
felt the pain instantly the second time. The moment it was over he felt
violently nauseated, but he managed to remain conscious.

Stavinsky waited for some time before he volunteered an opinion.
"Impressive. You have definitely qualified to enter Stage Two, from
which you can be released immediately by answering one simple
question. Where is the Tsar's icon?''

Adam's mouth had become so dry that he couldn't speak, let alone
spit.

"I did try to warn you, Captain Scott.'' Stavinsky turned towards the
door. "Do go and fetch the captain some water, Colonel.

. . . *The Merchant of Venice, Henry IV part one, Henry IV part two* . . .

A moment later Pollard was back, and a bottle was thrust into Adam's mouth. He gulped half the contents down until it was pulled away.

"Mustn't overdo it. You might need some more later. But that won't be necessary if you let me know where the icon is."

Adam spat what was left of the water towards where his adversary was standing.

Stavinsky leapt forward and slapped Adam hard across the face with the back of his hand. Adam's head slumped.

"You give me no choice but to advance to Stage Two," said Stavinsky. He looked towards Romanov who nodded. Stavinsky's thin lips parted in another smile. "You may have wondered," he continued, "how much more harm I can do with a simple six-volt battery, and indeed having seen in numerous American gangster movies an execution by the electric chair you will know a large generator is needed to kill a man. But first it is important to remember that I don't want to kill you. Second, my science lessons didn't end at Stage One. Professor Metz's mind was also exercised by the feebleness of this stage and after a lifetime of dedicated research he came up with an ingenious solution known as 'M', which the Academy of Science named after him in his honour. If you inject 'M' into the nervous system, messages can be transmitted to all your nerves many times more efficiently, thus allowing the pain to multiply without actually proving fatal.

"I only need to multiply a few milli-amps by a suitable factor to create a far more interesting effect – so I must ask you once again, where is the Tsar's icon?"

. . . *Much Ado About Nothing, Henry V, Julius Caesar* . . .

"I see you are determined that I should proceed," said Stavinsky, removing a syringe from the floor and jabbing the long thin needle into a phial before withdrawing the plunger until the barrel of the syringe was half full. Stavinsky held the needle in the air, pressed the knob and watched a little spray flow out like a tiny fountain. He moved behind Adam.

"I am now going to give you a lumbar puncture which if you attempt to move will paralyse you from the neck down for life. By nature I am not an honest man but on this occasion I must recommend you to trust me. I assure you that the injection will not kill you because, as you already know, that is not in our best interest."

Adam didn't move a muscle as he felt the syringe go into his back. *As You Like* . . . he began. Then excruciating pain swept his body, and suddenly, blessedly, he felt nothing.

When he came round there was no way of telling how much time had passed. His eyes slowly focused on his tormentor pacing up and down the room impatiently. Seeing Adam's eyes open, the unshaven man stopped pacing, smiled, walked over to the chair and ran his fingers slowly over the large piece of sticking plaster that covered Adam's two-day-old shoulder wound. The touch appeared gentle, but to Adam it felt like a hot iron being forced across his shoulder.

"As I promised," said Stavinsky. "A far more interesting sensation is awaiting you. And now I think I'll rip the plaster off." He waited for a moment while Adam pursed his lips. Then, in one movement, he tore the plaster back. Adam screamed as if the bullet had hit him again. Romanov came forward, leaned over and studied the wound.

"I'm relieved to see my colleague didn't miss you completely," Romanov said before adding, "can you imagine what it will be like when I allow Mr Stavinsky to wire you up again and then press the little generator?"

". . . *Twelfth Night, Hamlet, The Merry Wives of Windsor . . .*" Adam said aloud for the first time.

"I see you wish to leave nothing to the imagination," said Romanov and disappeared behind him. Stavinsky checked that the wires were attached to the collodion glue on Adam's chest and then he returned to the generator. "I shall press down the handle in three seconds' time. You know what you have to do to stop me."

". . . *Troilus and Cressida, All's Well That Ends Well . . .*"

As the handle plunged down the volts seemed to find their way to every nerve ending in his body. Adam let out such a scream that if they had not been in a soundproofed room anyone within a mile would have heard him. When the initial effect was over he was left shaking and retching uncontrollably. Stavinsky and Pollard rushed forward to the chair and quickly undid the nylon cords. Adam fell on his hands and knees, still vomiting.

"Couldn't afford to let you choke to death, could we?" said Stavinsky. "We lost one or two that way in the early days but we know better now."

As soon as the sickness subsided, Stavinsky threw Adam back up on to the chair and Pollard tied him up again.

"Where is the Tsar's icon?" shouted Stavinsky.

". . . *Measure for Measure, Othello, King Lear . . .*" Adam said, his voice now trembling.

Pollard picked up another bottle of water and thrust it at Adam's lips. Adam gulped it down but it was as a tiny oasis in a vast desert. Romanov came forward and Stavinsky took his place beside the plunger.

"You are a brave man, Scott," said Romanov, "with nothing left to prove, but this is madness. Just tell me where the icon is and I will send Stavinsky away and order the colonel to leave you on the steps of the British Embassy."

". . . *Macbeth, Antony and Cleopatra . . .*"

Romanov let out a sigh and nodded. Stavinsky pushed the plunger down once again. Even the colonel turned white as he watched Adam's reaction. The pitch of the scream was even higher and the muscles contorted visibly as Adam felt the volts reach the millions of little nerve ends in his body. When once more he had been released, Adam lay on the floor on his hands and knees. Was there anything left in his stomach that could still possibly come up? He raised his head, only to be hurled back on to the chair and bound up again. Stavinsky stared down at him.

"Most impressive, Captain Scott, you have qualified for Stage Three."

When Lawrence arrived at Orly Airport that evening he was looking forward to a quiet dinner with his old friend at the Ambassador's residence. He was met at the barrier by Colonel Pollard.

"How is he?" were Lawrence's first words.

"I hoped you were going to tell us," said Pollard, as he took Lawrence's overnight suitcase. Lawrence stopped in his tracks and stared at the tall, thin soldier who was in the full dress uniform of the Royal Dragoon Guards.

"What do you mean?" said Lawrence.

"Simply that," said Pollard. "I followed your instructions to the letter and went to pick up Scott at the Ile de la Cité but when I arrived I was informed that he had been taken away twenty minutes earlier by someone else using my name. We contacted your office immediately but as you were already en route the Ambassador ordered me straight to the airport while he phoned Sir Morris."

Lawrence staggered and nearly fell. The colonel came quickly to his side. He didn't understand what Lawrence meant when he said, "He's bound to believe it's me."

When Adam regained consciousness, Romanov stood alone.

"Sometimes," said the Russian, continuing as if Adam had never passed out, "a man is too proud to show lack of resolution in front of the torturer or indeed one of his own countrymen, especially a traitor. That is why I have removed Stavinsky and the colonel from our presence. Now I have no desire to see Stavinsky continue his experiment to Stage Three, but I can stop him only if you will tell me where you have put the icon."

"Why should I?" said Adam belligerently. "It's legally mine."

"Not so, Captain Scott. What you picked up from the bank in Geneva is the priceless original painted by Rublev which belongs to the Union of Soviet Socialist Republics. And if that icon were to appear in any auction house or gallery in the world, we would immediately claim it as a national treasure stolen by the seller."

"But how could that be . . . ?" began Adam.

"Because," said Romanov, "it is you who are now in possession of the original that the Tsar left in the safe-keeping of the Grand Duke of Hesse and for over fifty years the Soviet Union has only had a copy." Adam's eyes opened wide in disbelief as Romanov removed from the inside pocket of his overcoat an icon of St George and the Dragon. Romanov paused and then turned it over; a smile of satisfaction crossed his face as Adam's eyes registered the significance of the missing crown.

"Like you," continued Romanov, "I only have this one on loan – but you tell me where the original is and I will release you and exchange the copy for the original. No one will be any the wiser and you'll still be able to make yourself a worthwhile profit."

"Old lamps for new," said Adam with a sneer.

Romanov's eyes narrowed menacingly. "Surely you realise, Scott, that you are in possession of a priceless masterpiece that belongs to the Soviet Union. Unless you return the icon you are going to cause considerable embarrassment for your country and you will probably end up in jail. All you have to do is tell me where the icon is and you can go free."

Adam didn't even bother to shake his head.

"Then the time has obviously come to let you into some information you will be more interested in," Romanov said, extracting a single sheet of paper from an envelope he removed from his inside pocket. Adam was genuinely puzzled, quite unable to think what it could be. Romanov opened it slowly and held it up so that Adam could only see the back.

"This single sheet of paper reveals a sentence carried out in Moscow in 1946 by Judge I. T. Nikitchenko – the death sentence," continued Romanov, "pronounced on a certain Major Vladimir Koski, the Russian guard in charge of the Soviet watch the night Reichsmarshal Hermann Goering died." He turned the paper round so Adam could see it. "As you can see, Major Koski was found guilty of collaboration with the enemy for financial gain. It was proved he was directly responsible for smuggling cyanide into the Reichsmarshal's cell on the night he died." Adam's eyes widened. "Ah, I see I have dealt the ace of spades," said Romanov. "Now I think you will finally tell me where the icon actually is because you have an expression in England, if I recall correctly: fair exchange is no robbery. Your icon for my icon, plus the legal judgment that will finally vindicate your father's honour."

Adam closed his eyes, painfully aware for the first time that Romanov had no idea what was inside the icon.

Romanov was unable to hide his anger. He walked to the door and flung it open. "He's yours," he said.

Dr Stavinsky re-entered the room and, smiling, continued as if nothing had interrupted him. "Professor Metz was never really satisfied with Stage Two because he found the recovery time even for an extremely brave and fit man like yourself could sometimes hold him up for hours, even days. So during his final years at the university he devoted his time to finding how he could possibly speed the whole process up. As for all geniuses the final solution was staggering in its simplicity. All he had to produce was a chemical formula that when injected into the nervous system caused an immediate recovery – a rapid analgesic. It took him twelve years and several deaths before he came up with the final solution," said Stavinsky, removing another phial from the cigar box and plunging the needle of a second syringe into the seal on the top of the phial.

"This," Stavinsky said, holding up the little phial in triumph, "when injected into your blood stream, will aid recovery so quickly that you may even wonder if you ever went through any pain in the first place. For this piece of genius Metz should have been awarded the Nobel Prize, but it was not something we felt he could share with the rest of the scientific world. But because of him I can repeat the process you have just experienced again and again, never permitting you to die. You see, I can keep this generator pumping up and down every thirty minutes for the next week if that is your desire," said Stavinsky, as he stared down at Adam's white, disbelieving face flecked with yellow specks of his vomit.

"Or I can stop immediately after I have administered the antidote the moment you let me know where the Tsar's icon is."

Stavinsky stood in front of Adam and half filled the syringe. Adam felt intensely cold, yet the shock of his torture had caused him to sweat profusely. "Sit still, Captain Scott, I have no desire to do you any permanent injury." Adam felt the needle go deep in and moments later the fluid entered his blood stream.

He could not believe how quickly he felt himself recovering. Within minutes he no longer felt sick or disorientated. The sensation in his arms and legs returned to normal while the wish never to experience Stage Two again became acute.

"Brilliant man, Professor Metz, on that I'm sure we can both agree," said Stavinsky, "and if he were still alive I feel certain he would have written a paper on your case." Slowly and carefully Stavinsky began to smear more lumps of jelly on Adam's chest. When he was satisfied with his handiwork he once again attached the electrodes to the jelly.

"*Coriolanus, Timon of Athens, Pericles.*" Stavinsky thrust his palm down and Adam hoped that he would die. He found a new level to scream at, as his body shook and shook. Seconds later he felt ice cold and, shivering uncontrollably, he started to retch.

Stavinsky was quicky by his side to release him. Adam fell to the ground and coughed up what was left in his body. When he was only spitting, Pollard placed him back in the chair.

"You must understand I can't let you die, Captain. Now where is the icon?" Stavinsky shouted.

In the Louvre, Adam wanted to scream, but his words barely came out as a whisper, the inside of his mouth feeling like sandpaper. Stavinsky proceeded to fill the second syringe again and injected Adam with the fluid. Once again it was only moments before the agony subsided and he felt completely recovered.

"Ten seconds, we go again. Nine, eight, seven . . ."

"*Cymbeline.*"

". . . six, five, four . . ."

"*The Winter's Tale.*"

". . . three, two, one."

"*The Tempest.* Aahhhh," he screamed and immediately fainted. The next thing Adam remembered was the cold water being poured over him by the colonel before he began to retch again. Once tied back in the chair Stavinsky thrust the syringe into him once more, but Adam couldn't believe he would ever recover again. He must surely die, because he wanted to die. He felt the syringe jab into his flesh again.

Romanov stepped forward and looking straight at Adam, said, "I feel Dr Stavinsky and I have earned a little supper. We did consider inviting you but felt your stomach wouldn't be up to it, but when we return fully refreshed Dr Stavinsky will repeat the entire exercise again and again until you let me know where you have hidden the icon."

Romanov and Stavinsky left as Colonel Pollard came back in. Romanov and the colonel exchanged a few sentences which Adam could not make out. Then Romanov left the room, closing the door quietly behind him.

Pollard came over to Adam and offered him the water bottle. Adam gulped it down and was genuinely surprised how quickly he was recovering. Yet although his senses were returning to normal Adam still doubted he could survive one more time.

"I'm going to throw up again," said Adam and suddenly thrust his head forward. Pollard quickly undid the knots and watched Adam slump to his hands and knees. He threw up some spit and rested before the colonel helped him gently back into the chair. As he sat down Adam gripped both sides of the chair firmly, then with all the strength he could muster jack-knifed forward, swung the chair over his head, and brought it crashing down on top of the unsuspecting colonel. Pollard collapsed in a heap, unconscious, on the floor in front of Adam and never heard him utter the words, "*Henry VIII* and *Two Noble Kinsmen* – I'll bet that's one you've never heard of, Colonel. Mind you, to be fair, not everyone thinks Shakespeare wrote it."

Adam remained on his knees over the colonel's body, wondering what his next move should be. He was grateful that the soundproofed room was now working in his favour. He waited for a few more seconds as he tried to measure what was left of his strength. He picked up the water bottle that had been knocked over and drained it of its last drops.

He then crawled across to the bed and pulled on his pants and socks, shoes, and his not so white shirt, followed by his trousers. He was about to put on the blazer, but found the lining had been ripped to shreds. He changed his mind and stumbled like an old man back towards the colonel, removed his Harris tweed coat and slipped it on. It was large round the shoulders but short at the hips.

Adam made his way to the door, feeling almost exhilarated. He turned the handle and pulled. The door came open an inch – nothing happened – two inches – still nothing. He stared through the crack but all he could see was a dark corridor. As he pulled the door wide open the hinges sounded to Adam like racing tyres screeching. Once he was certain that no one was going to return, he ventured into the corridor.

Standing against the wall he stared up and down the thin windowless passage, waiting for his eyes to adjust to the dark. He could make out a light shining through a pebbled pane in a door at the far end of the corridor, and began to take short steps towards it. He continued on, as if he were a blind man, creeping slowly forward until he saw another beam of light coming from under a door to his right about ten yards away from the one he needed to reach. He edged cautiously on and was only a pace away from the first door when it opened abruptly and out stepped a small man in a white tunic and blue kitchen overalls. Adam froze against the wall as the kitchen hand removed a packet of cigarettes and a box of matches from his pocket and headed away in the opposite direction. When the man reached the glazed door he opened it and walked out. Adam watched the silhouette outlined against the pebbled window, a match being struck, a cigarette being lit, the first puff of smoke; he even heard a sigh.

Adam crept past what he now assumed was a kitchen and on towards the outer door. He turned the knob slowly, waiting for the silhouette to move. The outer door also possessed hinges which no one had bothered to oil for months. The smoker turned round and smiled as Adam's left hand landed firmly in his stomach. As the smoker bent over, Adam's right fist came up to the man's chin with all the force he could muster. The smoker sank in a heap on the ground, and Adam stood over him thankful that he didn't move.

He dragged the limp body across the grass, dumped it behind a bush and remained kneeling by it while he tried to work out his bearings. Adam could just make out a high wall ahead of him with a gravelled courtyard in front of it. The wall threw out a long shadow from the moon across the tiny stones. About twenty yards . . . Summoning up every ounce of energy, he ran to the wall and then clung to it like a limpet, remaining motionless in its shadow. Slowly and silently he moved round the wall, yard by yard, until he reached the front of what he now felt sure was the Russian Embassy. The great green wooden gates at the front entrance were open, and every few seconds limousines

swept past him. Adam looked back up towards the front door of the
Embassy and at the top of the steps he saw a massive man, medals
stretching across his formal dress jacket, shaking hands with each of his
departing guests. Adam assumed he was the Ambassador.

One or two of the guests were leaving by foot. There were two armed
gendarmes on the gate who stood rigidly to attention and saluted as
each car or guest passed by.

Adam waited until a vast BMW, the West German flag fluttering on
its bonnet, slowed as it passed through the gates. Using the car to shield
him, Adam walked out into the centre of the drive, then, following
closely behind, walked straight between the guards towards the road.

"*Bonsoir*," he said lightly to the guards as the car moved forward: he
was only a yard from the road. "Walk," he told himself, "don't run.
Walk, walk until you are out of their sight." They saluted deferentially.
"Don't look back." Another car followed him out, but he kept his eyes
firmly to the front.

"*Tu cherches une femme?*" a voice repeated from the shadows of a recessed
doorway. Adam had ended up in a badly lit one-way street. Several
men of indeterminate age seemed to be walking aimlessly up and down
the kerbside. He eyed them with suspicion as he moved on through the
darkness.

"Wha –?" said Adam, stepping sharply into the road, his senses
heightened by the unexpected sound.

"From Britain, eh? Do you search for a girl?" The voice held an
unmistakable French accent.

"You speak English," said Adam, still unable to see the woman
clearly.

"You have to know a lot of languages in my profession, *chéri*, or you'd
starve."

Adam tried to think coherently. "How much for the night?"

"*Eh bien*, but it's not yet midnight," said the girl. "So I would have to
charge two hundred francs."

Although he had no money Adam hoped the girl might at least lead
him to safety.

"Two hundred is fine."

"*D'accord*," said the girl, at last stepping out of the shadows. Adam
was surprised by how attractive she turned out to be. "Take my arm
and if you pass a gendarme say only, '*Ma femme*'."

Adam stumbled forward.

"Ah, I think you drink too much, *chéri*. Never mind, you can lean on
me, yes."

"No, I'm just tired," said Adam, trying hard to keep up with her
pace.

"You have been to a party at Embassy, *n'est-ce pas?*"

Adam was startled.

"Don't be surprised, *chéri*. I find most of my regulars from the Embassies. They can't risk to be involved in casual affairs, *tu comprends?*"

"I believe you," said Adam.

"My apartment is just round the corner," she assured him. Adam was confident he would get that far but he took a deep breath when they arrived at a block of flats and first saw the steps. He just managed to reach the front door.

"I live on the top of the house, *chéri*. Very nice view," she said matter-of-factly, "but I'm afraid – how you say – no lift."

Adam said nothing, but leaned against the outside wall, breathing deeply.

"You are *fatigué*," she said. By the time they had reached the second floor she almost had to drag Adam up the last few steps.

"I don't see you getting it up tonight, *chéri*," she said, opening her front door and turning on the light. "Still, it's your party." She strode in, turning on other lights as she went.

Adam staggered across the floor towards the only chair in sight and collapsed into it. The girl had by this time disappeared into another room and he had to make a supreme effort not to fall asleep before she returned.

As she stood in the light of the doorway Adam was able to see her properly for the first time. Her blonde hair was short and curly and she wore a red blouse and a knee-length skin-tight black skirt. A wide white plastic belt emphasised her small waist. She wore black mesh stockings and what he could see of her legs would have normally aroused him had he been in any other condition.

She walked over to Adam with a slight swing of the hips, and knelt down in front of him. Her eyes were a surprisingly luminous green.

"Would you please give me the two hundred now?" she asked, without harshness. She ran her hand along his thigh.

"I don't have any money," said Adam quite simply.

"What?" she said, sounding angry for the first time. Placing her hand in his inside pocket she removed a wallet and asked, "Then what's this? I don't play the games," handing the thick wallet over to Adam. He opened the flap to find it was jammed full of French francs and a few English notes. Adam concluded that the colonel was obviously paid in cash for his services.

Adam extracted two one-hundred francs and dutifully handed them over.

"That's better," she said, and disappeared into the other room.

Adam checked quickly through the wallet to discover a driving licence and a couple of credit cards in the colonel's real name of Albert Tomkins. He quickly looked around: a double bed that was wedged up against the far wall took up most of the floor space. Apart from the chair he was settled in the only other pieces of furniture were a dressing table and a tiny stool with a red velvet cushion on it. A stained blue carpet covered most of the wooden floor.

To his left was a small fireplace with logs stacked neatly in one corner. All Adam wished to do was fall asleep but with what strength was left in his body, he pushed himself up, wobbled over to the fireplace and hid the wallet between the logs. He lurched back towards the chair and fell into it as the door reopened.

Again the girl stood in the light of the doorway but this time she wore only a pink negligée, which even in his present state Adam could see right through whenever she made the slightest movement. She walked slowly across the room and once more knelt down beside him.

"How you like it, *mon cher*? Straight or the French way?"

"I need to rest," said Adam.

"For two hundred francs you sleep in any 'otel," she said in disbelief.

"I only want to be allowed to rest a few minutes," he assured her.

"*L'Anglais*," she said, and began to try to lift Adam out of the chair and towards the bed. He stumbled and fell, landing half on and half off the corner of the mattress. She undressed him as deftly as any nurse could have done before lifting his legs up on to the bed. Adam made no effort to help or hinder her. She hesitated for a moment when she saw the shoulder wound, bewildered as to what kind of accident could have caused such a gash. She rolled him over to the far side and pulled back the top sheet and blanket. Then she walked around to the other side of the bed and rolled him back again. Finally she pushed him flat on his back and covered him with the sheet and blankets.

"I could give you French if you like," she said. But Adam was already asleep.

CHAPTER TWENTY-ONE

When Adam eventually awoke the sun was already shining through the small window of the bedroom. He blinked as he took in his surroundings and tried to recall what had happened the night before. Then it all came back to him and suddenly he felt sick again at the memory. He sat on the edge of the bed but the moment he tried to stand he felt giddy and weak, and fell back down. At least he had escaped. He looked around the room but the girl was nowhere to be seen or heard. Then he remembered the wallet.

He sat bolt upright, gathering himself for a few moments before standing up again and trying to walk. Although he was still unsteady it was better than he had expected. It's only the recovery that counts, not the speed, he thought ironically. When he reached the fireplace he fell on his knees and searched among the logs, but the colonel's wallet was no longer there. As quickly as he could he went to the jacket hanging over the back of the chair. He checked in the inside pocket: a pen, a half-toothless comb, a passport, a driving licence, some other papers, but no wallet. He searched the outside pockets: a bunch of keys, a penknife, a few assorted coins, English and French, but that was all that was left. With a string of oaths he collapsed on the floor. He sat there for some time and didn't move until he heard a key in the lock.

The front door of the flat swung open and the girl sauntered in carrying a shopping basket. She was dressed in a pretty floral skirt and white blouse that would have been suitable for any churchgoer on a Sunday morning. The basket was crammed with food.

"Woken up, 'ave we, *chéri? Est-ce-que tu prends le petit déjeuner?*"

Adam looked a little taken aback.

She returned his stare. "Even working girls need their breakfast, *n'est-ce pas*? Sometimes is the only meal I manage all day."

"Where's my wallet?" asked Adam coldly.

"On the table," said the girl, pointing.

Adam glanced across the room, to see that she had left the wallet in the most obvious place.

"It is not necessary of you to 'ide it," she reprimanded him. "Because I'm a whore don't think I'm a thief." With this she strode off into the kitchen, leaving the door open.

Adam suddenly knew how big Tom Thumb felt.

"Coffee and croissants?" she shouted.

"Fantastic," said Adam. He paused. "I'm sorry. I was stupid."

"Not to think about it," she said. "*Ça n'est rien.*"

"I still don't know your name," said Adam.

"My working name is Brigitte, but as you 'ave not use my services last night or this morning you can call me by my real name – Jeanne."

"Can I have a bath, Jeanne?"

"The door in the corner, but don't take too long, unless you like croissants cold." Adam made his way to the bathroom and found Jeanne had provided for everything a man might need: a razor, shaving cream, soap, flannel, clean towels – and a gross box of Durex.

After a warm bath and a shave – delights Adam had nearly forgotten – he felt almost back to normal again, if still somewhat fragile. He tucked a pink towel around his waist before joining Jeanne in the kitchen. The table was already laid and she was removing a warm croissant from the oven.

"Good body," she said, turning round and scrutinising him carefully. "Much better than I usually 'ave." She put the plate down in front of him.

"You're not so bad yourself," said Adam grinning, taking the seat opposite her.

"I am 'appy you notice," said Jeanne. "I was beginning to think about you." Adam spread the roll liberally with jam and didn't speak again for several seconds.

"When 'ave you last eat?" asked Jeanne as he devoured the final scrap left on the plate.

"Yesterday lunch. But I emptied my stomach in between."

"Sick, eh? You mustn't drink so much."

"I think 'drained' might be a better word. Tell me, Jeanne," said Adam, looking up at her, "are you still available for work?"

She checked her watch. "One of my regulars is at two this afternoon, and I must be back on the streets by five. So it would 'ave to be this morning," she said matter-of-factly.

"No, no, that's not what I meant," said Adam.

"You could quickly give a girl, how do you say in England? – a complex," said Jeanne. "You not one of those weird ones, are you?"

"No, nothing like that," said Adam, laughing. "But I would be willing to pay you another two hundred francs for your services."

"Is it legal?"

"Absolutely."

"*Alors*, that makes a change. 'Ow long you need me?"

"An hour, two at the most."

"It's better than the rate for my present job. What am I expected to do?"

"For one hour I want every man in Paris to fancy you. Only this time you won't be available – at any price."

"Scott has just contacted me a few minutes ago," said Lawrence to the assembled D4.

"What did he have to say?" asked the anxious Sir Morris.

"Only that he was turning back the clock."

"What do you think he meant by that?" asked Snell.

"Geneva would be my guess," said Lawrence.

"Why Geneva?" said Matthews.

"I'm not certain," said Lawrence, "but he said it had something to do with the German girl, or the bank, but I can't be sure which."

No one spoke for some time.

"Did you trace the call?" asked Busch.

"Only the area," said Lawrence, "Neuchâtel on the German Swiss border."

"Good. Then we're in business again," said Sir Morris. "Have you informed Interpol?"

"Yes sir, and I've personally briefed the German, French and Swiss police," added Lawrence, which was the only true word he had spoken since the meeting had begun.

Jeanne took forty minutes to get herself ready and when Adam saw the result he let out a long whistle.

"No one is going to give me a second look, even if I were to empty the till in front of them," he told her.

"That is the idea, *n'est ce pas?*" Jeanne said, grinning.

"Now, are you sure you know exactly what you have to do?"

"I know well." Jeanne checked herself once more in the long mirror. "We 'ave rehearse like military exercise four times already."

"Good," said Adam. "You sound as if you're ready to face the enemy. So let's begin with what in the army they call 'advance to contact'."

Jeanne took out a plastic bag from a drawer in the kitchen. The single word 'Céline' was printed across it. She handed it over to Adam. He folded the bag in four, and stuffed it into his jacket pocket before walking into the corridor. She then locked the flat door behind them, and they walked down the stairs together and out on to the pavement.

Adam hailed a taxi and Jeanne told the driver "Tuileries gardens". Once they had arrived, Adam paid the fare and joined Jeanne on the pavement.

"*Bonne chance,*" said Adam as he remained on the corner, allowing Jeanne to walk twenty yards ahead of him. Although he still felt unsteady he was able to keep up at her pace. The sun beat down on his face as he watched her walk in and out of the ornate flower beds. Her pink leather skirt and tight white sweater made almost every man she passed turn and take a second look. Some even stopped in their tracks and continued watching until she was out of sight.

The comments she could hear and Adam, twenty yards behind, couldn't, ranged from "*Je payerais n'importe quoi*", which she reluctantly had to pass up, to just plain '*putain*', which Adam had told her to ignore. Her part had to be acted out, and for two hundred francs she would just have to suffer the odd insult.

Jeanne reached the far side of the gardens and did not look back: she had been instructed not to turn around in any circumstances. Keep going forward, Adam had told her. He was still twenty yards behind her when she reached the Quai des Tuileries. She waited for the lights to turn green before she crossed the wide road, keeping in the centre of a throng of people.

At the end of the quai she turned sharp right, and for the first time could see the Louvre straight in front of her. She had been too

embarrassed to admit to him that she had never been inside the
building before.

Jeanne climbed the steps to the entrance hall. By the time she had
reached the swing doors, Adam was approaching the bottom step. She
continued on up the marble staircase with Adam still following
discreetly behind.

When Jeanne reached the top of the stairs she passed the statue of the
Winged Victory of Samothrace. She proceeded into the first of the large
crowded rooms and began counting to herself, noting as she passed
through each gallery that there was at least one attendant on duty in
each, usually standing around aimlessly near one of the exits. A group
of schoolchildren were studying 'The Last Supper' by Giovanni but
Jeanne ignored the masterpiece and marched straight on. After passing
six attendants she arrived in the room Adam had described to her so
vividly. She strode purposefully into the centre and paused for a few
seconds. Some of the men began to lose interest in the paintings.
Satisfied by the impact she was making, she flounced over to the guard,
who straightened up his jacket and smiled at her.

"*Dans quelle direction se trouve la peinture du seizième siècle?*" Jeanne asked
innocently. The guard turned to point in the direction of the relevant
room. The moment he turned back, Jeanne slapped him hard across
the face and shouted at him at the top of her voice: "*Quelle horreur! Pour
qui est-ce que vous me prenez?*"

Only one person in the Icon Room didn't stop to stare at the
spectacle. "*Je vais parler à la Direction,*" she screamed, and flounced off
towards the main exit. The entire charade was over in less than thirty
seconds. The bemused guard remained transfixed, staring after his
assailant in bewilderment.

Jeanne continued on through the three centuries more quickly than
H.G. Wells. She took a left turn into the sixteenth-century room as
instructed and then another left brought her back into the long
corridor. A few moments later, she joined Adam at the top of the marble
staircase leading down to the front entrance.

As they walked back down the steps together, Adam handed her the
Céline bag and was about to set off again, when two attendants waiting
on the bottom step threw out their arms indicating they should halt.

"Do you wish a run for it?" she whispered.

"Certainly not," said Adam very firmly. "Just don't say anything."

"*Madame, excusez moi, mais je dois fouiller votre sac.*"

"*Allez-y pour tout ce que vous y trouvez!*" said Jeanne.

"Certainly you can search her bag," said Adam, returning to her side
before Jeanne could say anything more. "It's an icon, quite a good one,
I think. I purchased it in a shop near the Champs-Elysées only this
morning."

"*Vous me permettez, monsieur?*" the senior attendant asked suspiciously.

"Why not?" said Adam. He removed the Tsar's icon from the bag and handed it over to the attendant, who seemed surprised by the way things were turning out. Two more attendants rushed over and stood on each side of Adam.

The senior attendant asked in broken English if Adam would mind if one of the gallery's experts were to look at the painting.

"Only too delighted," said Adam. "It would be fascinating to have a second opinion."

The senior attendant was beginning to look unsure of himself. "*Je dois vous demander de me suivre*," he suggested in a tone that was suddenly less hostile. He ushered them quickly through to a little room at the side of the gallery. The attendant put the Tsar's icon in the middle of a table that dominated the room. Adam sat down and Jeanne, still bemused, took the seat beside him.

"I'll only be a moment, sir." The senior attendant almost ran out while the two other attendants remained stationed near the door. Adam still did not attempt to speak to Jeanne although he could see that she was becoming more and more apprehensive. He shot her a little smile as they sat waiting.

When the door eventually opened, an elderly man with a scholarly face preceded the senior attendant.

"*Bonjour, monsieur*," the man began, looking at Adam, the first man who did not show an overt interest in Jeanne. "I understand that you are English," and without giving either of them more than a glance, he picked up the icon.

He studied the painting carefully for some time before he spoke. Adam felt just a moment's apprehension. "Most interesting. Yes, yes." One of the attendants put a hand on his truncheon.

"Interesting," he repeated. "I would be so bold as to suggest," he hesitated, "late nineteenth century, eighteen seventy, possibly eighty. Fascinating. Not that we have ever had anything quite like it at the Louvre," he added. "You do realise it's an inferior copy," he said as he handed the icon back to Adam. "The original Tsar's icon of St George and the Dragon hangs in the Winter Palace in Leningrad. I've seen it, you know," he added, sounding rather pleased with himself.

"You certainly have," said Adam under his breath as he placed the icon back in its plastic bag. The old man bowed low to Jeanne and said as he shuffled away, "Funnily enough, someone else was making inquiries about the Tsar's icon only a few weeks ago." Adam was the only person who didn't seem surprised.

"I was only –" began the senior attendant.

"Doing your duty," completed Adam. "A natural precaution, if I may say so," he added a little pompously. "I can only admire the way you carried out the entire exercise."

Jeanne stared at them both, quite unable to comprehend what was happening.

"You are kind, *monsieur*," said the attendant, sounding relieved. "Hope you come again," he added, smiling at Jeanne.

The attendant accompanied the two of them to the entrance of the Louvre, and when they pushed through the door he stood smartly to attention and saluted.

Adam and Jeanne walked down the steps and into the Paris sun.

"Well, now can I know what that's all about?" asked Jeanne.

"You were *magnifique*," said Adam, not attempting to explain.

"I know, I know," said Jeanne. "But why you need Oscar-winning show by me when the picture was always yours?"

"True," agreed Adam. "But I had left it in their safe-keeping overnight. And without your bravura performance it might have taken considerably longer to convince the authorities that it belonged to me in the first place."

Adam realised from the look on her face that Jeanne had no idea what he was talking about.

"You know, that my first time in the Louvre?" said Jeanne linking her arm in Adam's.

"You're priceless," said Adam, laughing.

"That I'm not," she said, turning to face him. "Two hundred francs was our bargain even if it belongs to you or not."

"Correct," said Adam, taking out the colonel's wallet and extracting two hundred francs, to which he added another hundred. "A well-earned bonus," said Adam.

She pocketed the money gratefully. "I think I'll take an evening off," she said.

Adam held her in his arms and kissed her on both cheeks as if she was a French general.

She kissed him on the lips and smiled. "When you next in Paris, *chéri*, look me up. I owe you one – on the house."

"How can you be so sure?"

"Because Antarctic was willing to give Pemberton too many facts?"

"What do you mean?"

"You told me that Pemberton said he would never phone back if you let him down again. Not only did he phone back but he peppered you with facts. Which way did he say he was going?"

"Back to Geneva. Something to do with the German girl and the bank."

"The girl's dead and the bank's closed for the weekend. He must be on his way to England."

"I would like to rent a car which I will be dropping off at the coast. I haven't decided which port yet," he told the girl behind the counter.

"*Bien sûr, monsieur,*" said the girl. "Would you be kind enough to fill in the form, and we will also need your driving licence." Adam removed all the papers from his inside pocket and passed over the colonel's driving licence. He filled in the forms slowly, copying the signature off the back of the colonel's Playboy Club card. He handed over the full amount required in cash hoping it would speed up the transaction.

The girl picked up the cash and counted the notes carefully before checking the back of the licence against the signature on the form. Adam was relieved that she hadn't spotted the disparity in the dates of birth. He replaced all Albert Tomkins's documents and wallet in his inside jacket pocket, as the girl turned round and removed an ignition key from a hook on a board behind her.

"It's a red Citroën, parked on the first floor," she told him. "The registration number is stamped on the key ring."

Adam thanked her and walked quickly up to the first floor where he handed the key over to an attendant, who drove the car out of its parking space for him.

When the attendant returned the key, Adam handed him a ten-franc note. Exactly the same sum as the other man had given him to let him know if an Englishman who fitted Adam's description tried to hire a car. What had he promised? Another hundred francs if he phoned within five minutes of seeing him.

PART FOUR

THE KREMLIN, MOSCOW

June 19, 1966

CHAPTER TWENTY-TWO

The Kremlin, Moscow, June 19, 1966

Leonid Ilyich Brezhnev entered the room, hardly allowing the other four members of the inner quorum of the Defence Council enough time to stand. Their faces were firm, resolute, no different from their public image – unlike Western politicians.

The General Secretary took his place at the head of the table and nodded to his colleagues to sit.

The last time the inner quorum of the Defence Council had been summoned to a meeting at an hour's notice had been at the request of Khrushchev, who was hoping to enlist support for his Cuban adventure. Brezhnev would never forget the moment when his predecessor had uncontrollably burst into tears because they forced him to order the Soviet ships to return home. From that moment, Brezhnev knew it could only be a matter of time before he would succeed Khrushchev as the leader of the Communist world. On this occasion he had no intention of bursting into tears.

On his right sat Marshal Malinovsky, Minister of Defence: on his left Andrei Gromyko, the young Foreign Minister. Beside him sat the Chief of the General Staff, Marshall Zakharov, and, on his left, Zaborski. Even the seating plan confirmed Brezhnev's obvious displeasure with the Chairman of the KGB.

He raised his eyes and stared up at the massive oil painting of Lenin reviewing an early military parade in Red Square: a picture no one other than members of the Politburo had seen since it disappeared from the Tretyakov in 1950.

If only Lenin had realised the icon was a fake in the first place, Brezhnev reflected . . . Yet, despite the traditional Russian pastime of blaming the dead for everything that goes wrong, he knew that Vladimir Ilyich Lenin was beyond criticism. He would have to find a living scapegoat.

His eyes rested on Zaborski. "Your report, Comrade Chairman."

Zaborski fingered a file in front of him although he knew the contents almost off by heart. "The plan to locate the Tsar's icon was carried out in an exemplary fashion," he began. "When the Englishman, Adam Scott, was caught and later . . . questioned" – they all accepted the euphemism – "by Comrade Dr Stavinsky in the privacy of our Embassy in Paris, the Englishman gave no clue as to where we would find the icon. It becme obvious he was a professional agent of the West. After three hours, interrogation was momentarily suspended. It was during this period that the prisoner managed to escape."

"Managed," interjected Brezhnev.

Just as he had taught his subordinates over the years, the Chairman of the KGB made no attempt to reply.

"Don't you realise," continued the General Secretary, "that we had within our grasp the opportunity to turn the very land the Americans use for their early warning system into a base for our short range missiles? If it had proved possible to retrieve our icon it would also have been possible to site those very missiles along a border less than a thousand eight hundred kilometres from Seattle – two thousand kilometres from Chicago. Not only could we have made the Americans' early warning system redundant, we could have greatly improved our ability to detect any enemy missiles while they were still thousands of kilometres from our nearest border."

The General Secretary paused to see if the Chairman of the KGB had any further explanation to offer but Zaborski kept his eyes fixed on the table in front of him. When Brezhnev began again it was almost in a whisper:

"And for such a prize we would not have had to sacrifice one life, one rocket, one tank or even one bullet – because all this was ours by right. But if we fail to locate the Tsar's icon in the next thirty-six hours we will never be given such a chance again. We will have lost our one opportunity to remove a star from the American flag."

Foreign Secretary Gromyko waited until he was certain Brezhnev had completed his statement before he inquired:

"If I may ask, Comrade Chairman, why was Major Romanov allowed to continue being involved in such a sensitive operation after it was suspected he had killed" – with this he glanced down at the papers in front of him – "Researcher Petrova?"

"Because when that situation was drawn to my attention," replied Zaborski, at last looking up, "I had only seven days left to tomorrow's deadline, and in my judgment there was *no one* who could have taken over Romanov's place at such short notice –"

There was a timid knock on the door. All the faces round the table showed surprise. The Minister of Defence had given specific orders that no one was to interrupt them.

"Come," shouted Brezhnev.

The great door inched open and a secretary appeared in the gap; the thin piece of paper in his hand shook, betraying his nervousness. The Minister of Defence waved him in as Brezhnev had no intention of turning around to see who it was. The secretary walked quickly towards them. As soon as he had deposited the telex on the table he turned, and almost ran from the room.

Brezhnev slowly unfolded his tortoise-shell glasses before picking up the missive. Once he had read through the cable, he looked up at the expectant faces in front of him. "It seems an Englishman left an icon in the Louvre and picked it back up this morning."

The blood quickly drained from Zaborski's face.

The four ministers round the table all began talking together, until Brezhnev raised the vast palm of his right hand. There was immediate silence. "I intend to continue my plans on the assumption that it will still be us who gets to the Englishman first."

Brezhnev turned towards his Foreign Minister. "Alert all our Western Ambassadors to be prepared to brief the Foreign Ministers of the country in which they reside on the full implications of honouring the amendment to the treaty. Then instruct Anatoly Dobrynin in Washington to demand an official meeting with the Secretary of State to be fixed for late Monday. At the same time I want a further meeting arranged between our Ambassador at the United Nations and U Thant."

Gromyko nodded as Brezhnev turned his attention to the Chief of the General Staff. "See that our strategic forces in all zones are put at a state of readiness to coincide with the timing of the announcement of our diplomatic initiative." Malinovsky smiled. The General Secretary finally turned to the Chairman of the KGB. "Do we still have advertising space booked in every major newspaper in the West?"

"Yes, Comrade General Secretary," replied Zaborski. "But I cannot be certain they will be willing to print the statement as you have prepared it."

"Then pay every one of them in advance," said Brezhnev. "Few Western editors will withdraw a full page advertisement when they already have the money in the bank."

"But if we then don't find the icon . . ." began the Chairman of the KGB.

"Then your last duty as Chairman of State Security will be to withdraw all the advertisements," said the General Secretary of the Communist Party.

CHAPTER TWENTY-THREE

Adam wound down the car window and immediately the warm summer air flooded in. He had decided to avoid the main road to Calais in favour of the N1 to Boulogne. He still considered it possible that Romanov would have men watching at every port on the Channel coast although he doubted if Lawrence or the Americans were aware he had escaped.

Once he had cleared the outskirts of the French capital, he was confident that he could average seventy kilometres an hour the rest of the way. But what he hadn't anticipated was running into a hundred or more cyclists, daubed in their various stripes of reds, greens, blues, blacks and golds, bobbing along ahead of him. As he drifted past them Adam was able to accurately check that they were averaging 40 miles an hour.

Having followed the build up for the forthcoming World Cup in Britain, he was also able to make out the national colours of France, Germany, Italy and even Portugal. He honked his horn loudly as he passed a group of four men quite near the front, clad in red, white and blue T-shirts with the British team van driving just head of them. A few moments later he had overtaken the leaders, and was able to put the car back into fourth gear.

He switched on the car radio and fiddled around for some time before he tuned in to the Home Service of the BBC. He settled back to listen to the news in English for the first time in days. The usual reports of long strikes, high inflation, and of England's chances when the second Test Match at Lord's resumed after the rest day almost made him feel he was already back home, and then he nearly swerved off the road and into a tree.

The news reader reported matter-of-factly that a young RAF pilot had been found dead in a field off the Auxerre/Dijon road after his plane had crashed in mysterious circumstances. No more details were available at the present time. Adam cursed and slammed his fist on the steering wheel at the thought of Alan Banks becoming another victim of Romanov. He tapped the icon and cursed again.

"It was foolish of you to contact me, young man," said the old banker.

"You're not exactly a hero of the Soviet Union at the present time."

"Listen, old man, I don't have to be a hero any longer because I may never come back to the Soviet Union."

"Be warned: Mother Russia has extremely long finger nails."

"And because of my grandfather's foresight, I can afford to cut them off," the caller said, touching the gold medallion he wore beneath his shirt. "I just need to be sure you don't let them know where I keep the scissors."

"Why should I remain silent?" asked Poskonov.

"Because if I haven't got my hands on St George within the next twenty-four hours, I'll phone again with the details of how you can hope to collect a larger golden handshake than you could have expected from your present employers." The banker offered no comment.

The Ambassador's secretary rushed into the room without knocking. "I told you no interruptions," shouted Romanov, covering the mouthpiece with his hand.

"But we've located Scott."

Romanov slammed the phone down. In Moscow, the old Russian banker wound the tape back. Poskonov smiled and listened to Romanov's words a second time and came to the conclusion that Romanov had left him with only one choice. He booked a flight to Geneva.

"Robin?"

"Batman. Where have you got to?"

"I'm just outside Paris on my way back home," Adam said. "Are you sticking to the schedule you outlined on the bus?"

"Sure am. Why, are you still desperate to spend the night with me?"

"Sure am," said Adam, mimicking her. "But when do you get back home?"

"The orchestra is taking the ferry from Dunkerque at six thirty tonight. Can you join us?"

"No," said Adam. "I have to return by another route. But, Robin, when I reach London can you put me up for the night?"

"Sounds like an offer I can't refuse," she said, and then repeated her address to be sure he had time to write it down. "When shall I expect you?" she asked.

"Around midnight tonight."

"Do you always give a girl so much notice?"

The young KGB officer standing in the adjoining box had caught most of the conversation. He smiled when he recalled Major Romanov's words: "The man who brings me the Tsar's icon need have no fear for his future in the KGB."

Adam jumped back in the car and drove on until he reached the outskirts of Beauvais, where he decided to stop at a wayside *routier* for a quick lunch.

According to the timetable he had picked up from the Hertz counter, the ferry he wanted to catch was due to leave Boulogne at three o'clock, so he felt confident he would still make it with about an hour to spare.

He sat hidden in an alcove by the window enjoying what might have been described in any English pub as a ploughman's lunch. With each mouthful he became aware that the French ploughmen demanded far higher standards of their innkeepers than any English farmworker was happy to settle for.

As he waited for his coffee he took out Albert Tomkins's papers from his inside pocket and began to scrutinise them carefully. He was interested to discover that he had been a private in the Green Jackets, and exactly how many weeks he had been claiming unemployment benefit.

Through the window of the inn he watched the first of the cyclists as they pedalled by. The athletes' muscles strained in their determination to remain among the leading group. As they shot through Beauvais, Adam was amused by the fact that they were all breaking the speed limit. The sight of the competitors reminded him that he was expected to attend the final part of his medical for the Foreign Office tomorrow afternoon.

Romanov read the decoded message a second time. "Scott returned Geneva. Check German girl and bank." He looked up at the senior KGB officer who had handed him the missive.

"Does Mentor think I'm that naïve?" said Romanov to his Parisian colleague. "We already know from our agent in Amsterdam that he's now on his way towards the French coast."

"Then why should Mentor want to send you in the opposite direction?"

"Because it must be him who's been briefing the Americans," said Romanov coldly.

Romanov turned to the colonel who was standing by his side. "We know it can't be Dunkerque, so how many other possibilities are we left with?"

"Cherbourg, Le Havre, Dieppe, Boulogne, or Calais," replied the colonel, looking down at the map laid out on the table in front of him. "My bet would be Calais," he added.

"Unfortunately," said Romanov, "Captain Scott is not quite *that* simple. And as the motorway takes you direct to Calais, the captain will expect us to have that part of his route well covered. I think our friend will try Boulogne or Dieppe first."

He checked the timetable the Second Secretary had supplied him with. "The first boat he could hope to catch leaves Boulogne for Dover at three, and then there's one from Dieppe to Newhaven at five."

Romanov also checked Calais and Le Havre. "Good. Calais left at twelve this morning, and as he phoned the girl after twelve he had no hope of catching that one. And Le Havre doesn't leave until seven fifteen tonight, and he won't risk leaving it that late. Assuming we can beat him to the coast, Colonel, I think Captain Scott is once again within our grasp."

Once Adam had left the *relais routier* it was ony minutes before he began to catch up with the straggling cyclists as they pedalled on towards Abbeville. His thoughts reverted to Romanov. Adam suspected that his agents would have the airports, stations, autoroute and ports well covered. But even the KGB could not be in fifty places at once.

Adam took the Boulogne route out of Abbeville but had to remain in the centre of the road to avoid the bobbing cyclists. He even had to slam his brakes on once when an Italian and a British rider collided in front of him. The two men, both travelling at some speed, were thrown unceremoniously to the ground. The British rider remained ominously still on the side of the road.

Adam felt guilty about not stopping to help his fellow countryman but feared that any hold-up might prevent him catching his boat. He spotted the British team van ahead of him and speeded up until he was alongside. Adam waved at the driver to pull over.

The man behind the steering wheel looked surprised but stopped and wound down the window. Adam pulled up in front of him, leaped out of his car and ran to the van.

"One of your chaps has had an accident about a mile back," shouted Adam, pointing towards Paris.

"Thanks, mate," said the driver who turned round and sped quickly back down the road.

Adam continued to drive on at a sedate speed until he had passed all the leaders. Then, once again, he put the car into top gear. A signpost informed him that it was now only thirty-two kilometres to Boulogne: he would still make the three o'clock sailing comfortably. He began to imagine what it might be like if he could survive beyond Monday. Would his life ever be routine again? Jogs in the park, Foreign Office interviews, workouts with the sergeant major and even the acknowledgment of the part he had played in delivering the icon into safe hands. The problem was that he hadn't yet decided who had safe hands.

A helicopter looking like a squat green bullfrog swept over him; now that would be the ideal way to get back to England, Adam considered. With help like that he could even make it to Harley Street in time for his medical for the Foreign Office.

He watched as the helicopter turned and swung back towards him. He assumed that there must be a military airport somewhere nearby, but couldn't remember one from his days in the army. A few moments later he heard the whirl of the blades as the helicopter flew across his path at a considerably lower level. Adam gripped the wheel of the car until his knuckles went white as an impossible thought crossed his mind. As he did so the helicopter swung back again, and this time flew straight towards him.

Adam wound the window up and crouching over the top of the steering wheel, stared into the sky. He could see the silhouetted outline of three figures sitting in the helicopter cockpit. He banged his fist on the steering wheel in anger as he realised how easy it must have been for them to trace a car signed for in the one name they would immediately recognise. He could sense Romanov's smile of triumph as the chopper hovered above him.

Adam saw a signpost looming up ahead of him and swung off the main road towards a village called Fleureville. He pushed the speed-ometer well over ninety causing the little car to skid along country lanes. The helicopter likewise swung to the right, and dog-like followed his path.

Adam took a hard left and only just avoided colliding with a tractor coming out of a newly ploughed field. He took the next right and headed back towards the Boulogne road, desperately trying to think what he could do next. Every time he looked up the helicopter was there above him: he felt like a puppet dancing on the end of Romanov's string.

A road sign depicting a low tunnel ahead flashed past them and Adam dismissed the melodramatic idea of trying to make them crash; he didn't need reminding that it was he who was proving to be the novice.

When he first saw the tunnel he estimated it to be sixty or seventy yards in length. Although it was quite wide, a double-decker bus could not have entered it without the upstairs passengers ending up walking on the bridge.

For a brief moment Adam actually felt safe. He slammed on the little Citroën's brakes and skidded to a halt about thirty yards from the end of the tunnel. The car ended up almost scraping the side of the wall. He switched on his side lights and they flashed brightly in the darkness. For several seconds he watched as approaching cars slowed down before safely overtaking him.

At last he jumped out of the car and ran to the end of the tunnel where he pinned himself against the wall. The helicopter had travelled on some way, but was already turning back, and heading straight towards the tunnel. Adam watched it fly over his head, and moments later heard it turn again. As he waited, two hitch-hikers passed by on the other side, chatting away to themselves, oblivious to Adam's predicament.

He looked across desperately at the two young men and shouted,

"Were you hoping to thumb a lift?"

"Yes," they called back in unison. Adam staggered across the road to join them.

"Are you all right?" Adam heard one of them ask but he could hardly make out which one as his eyes had not yet become accustomed to the darkness.

"No, I'm not," Adam explained simply. "I drank too much wine at lunch and because of a cycle race the road is just crawling with police. I'm sure to be picked up if I go much further. Can either of you drive?"

"I only have my Canadian licence," said the taller of the two youths. "And in any case we are heading for Paris and your car is facing the opposite direction."

"It's a Hertz Rent-a-Car," Adam explained. "I picked it up on the Rue St Ferdinand this morning, and I have to return it by seven tonight. I don't think I can make it in my present state."

The two young men looked at him apprehensively. "I will give you both one hundred francs if you will return it safely for me. You see I can't afford to lose my licence, I'm a commercial traveller," Adam explained. Neither of them spoke. "My papers are all in order, I can assure you." Adam handed them over to the taller man who crossed back over the road and used the car lights to study Albert Tomkins's licence and insurance before carrying on a conversation with his friend.

Adam could hear the helicopter blades whirling above the tunnel entrance.

"We don't need the hundred francs," the taller one said eventually. "But we will need a note from you explaining why we are returning the car to Hertz in Paris on your behalf." Adam pulled out the colonel's pen and, feeling remarkably sober, he bent over the hood of the car and scribbled on the back of the Hertz agreement.

"Do you want to come back to Paris with us?"

Adam hesitated fractionally. Couldn't they hear the noise too? "No. I have to get to Boulogne."

"We could drive you to Boulogne and still have enough time to take the car to Paris."

"No, no. That's very considerate. I can take care of myself as long as I feel confident that the car will be delivered back as soon as possible."

The taller one shrugged while his companion opened a rear door and threw their rucksacks on the back seat. Adam remained in the tunnel while they started up the engine. He could hear the purr of the helicopter blades change cadence: it had to be descending to land in a nearby field.

Go, go, for God's sake go, he wanted to shout as the car shot forward towards Boulogne. He watched them travel down the road for about a hundred yards before turning in at a farm entrance, reversing, and heading back towards the tunnel. They tooted as they passed him in the dark, disappearing in the direction of Paris. Adam sank down on to his knees with relief and was about to pick himself up and start walking towards Boulogne when he saw two figures silhouetted at the far entrance of the tunnel. Against the clear blue sky he could make out the outline of two tall, thin men. They stood peering into the tunnel. Adam didn't move a muscle, praying they hadn't spotted him.

And then suddenly one of them started walking towards him, while the other remained motionless. Adam knew he could not hope to escape again. He knelt there cursing his own stupidity. In seconds they would be able to see him clearly.

"Don't let's waste any more valuable time, Marvin, we already know that the limey bastard's heading back to Paris."

"I just thought perhaps . . ." began the one called Marvin in a Southern drawl.

"Leave the thinking to me. Now let's get back to the chopper before we lose him."

When Marvin was only twenty yards away from Adam he suddenly stopped, turned around and began running back.

Adam remained rooted to the spot for several minutes. A cold, clammy sweat had enveloped his body the moment he realised his latest pursuer was not Romanov. If one of them hadn't referred to him as a 'limey bastard', Adam would have happily given himself up. Suddenly he had become painfully aware of the difference between fact and fiction: he had been left with no friends.

Adam did not move again until he heard the helicopter rise above him. Peering out, he could see outlined against the arc of the tunnel the Americans heading back in the direction of Paris.

He staggered outside and put a hand across his eyes. The sunlight seemed much fiercer than a few minutes before. What next? He had less than an hour to catch the boat but no longer had any transport. He wasn't sure whether to thumb lifts, search for a bus stop, or simply get as far away from the main road as possible. His eyes were continually looking up into the sky. How long before they reached the car, and realised it was not him inside?

Cyclists began to pass him again as he jogged slowly towards Boulogne. He kept on moving, and even found enough strength to cheer the British competitors as they pedalled by. The British team van followed close behind and Adam gave it the thumbs-up sign. To his surprise the van came to a halt in front of him.

The driver wound down the window. "Weren't you the fellow who stopped me back in Abbeville?"

"That's right," said Adam. "Has your man recovered?"

"No, he's resting in the back – pulled ligament. What happened to your car?"

"Broke down about a mile back," said Adam, shrugging philosophically.

"Bad luck. Can I give you a lift?" the man asked. "We're only going as far as Boulogne in this stage, but jump in if it will help."

"Thank you," said Adam, with the relief of a bearded beatnik who has found the one person willing to stop to pick him up. The driver leaned across and pushed open the door for him.

Before climbing in, Adam shielded his eyes and once more looked up into the sky. The helicopter was nowhere to be seen – although he knew it couldn't be long before it returned. They would quickly work out that there was only one place where the switch could possibly have been made.

"My name's Bob," said the tracksuited driver, thrusting out his free hand. " I'm the British team manager."

"Mine's Adam." He shook the other's hand warmly.

"Where are you heading?"

"Boulogne," said Adam, "and with luck I could still make my crossing by three."

"We should be there about two thirty," said Bob. "We have to be: the afternoon stage starts at three."

"Will your man be able to ride?" asked Adam, pointing over his shoulder.

"No, he won't be competing in this race again," said the team manager. "He's pulled a ligament in the back of his leg, and they always take a couple of weeks to heal properly. I shall have to leave him in Boulogne and complete the last leg myself. You don't ride by any chance, do you?" Bob asked.

"No," said Adam. "Run a little, but haven't done a lot on wheels since my sister crashed the family tricycle."

"We're still in with a chance for the bronze," Bob said, as they overtook the British riders once more.

Adam gave them the thumbs-up sign and then looked over his shoulder through the back window. He was thankful to see that there was still no sign of the helicopter as they drove into the outskirts of Boulogne. Bob took him all the way up to the dockside. "Hope you get that bronze medal," said Adam as he jumped out of the van. "And thanks again. Good luck with the next stage."

Adam checked his watch: twenty minutes before the boat was due to sail. He wondered if it was too much time. He walked over to the booking office and waited in a short line before buying a passenger ticket. He kept looking round to check if anyone was watching him, but no one seemed to be showing the slightest interest. Once he had purchased his ticket he headed towards the ship and had just begun to start whistling a tuneless version of 'Yesterday' when a black speck appeared in the distance. There was no mistaking it – the sound was enough.

Adam looked up at the gangway which led to the deck of the ship now only yards away from him, and then back to the speck as it grew larger and larger in the sky. He checked his watch: the ship was due to leave in twelve minutes – still time enough for his pursuers to land the helicopter and get on board. If he climbed on and the Americans followed, they were bound to discover him. But if the Americans got on and he stayed off that would still give him enough time to reach Dieppe before the next sailing . . .

Adam jogged quickly back towards the large crowd that was hanging about waiting for the start of the next stage of the road race. As he did so the helicopter swept overhead and started hovering, like a kestrel that is looking for a mouse.

"I thought you said you were desperate to be on that ship."

Adam swung round, his fist clenched, only to face the British team manager now dressed in riding gear.

"Changed my mind," said Adam.

"Wouldn't care to drive the van for us on the next stage?" said Bob hopefully.

"Where does the next stage go?" Adam asked.

"Dunkerque," said the team manager.

Adam tried to remember what time Robin had said her boat left from Dunkerque.

"*Six minutes,*" a voice said over the loudspeaker.

"Okay," said Adam.

"Good," said the team manager. "Then follow me."

Adam ran behind the team manager as he headed towards the van.

"*Quatre minutes,*" Adam heard clearly as Bob unlocked the van and handed him the keys. He stared towards the ship. The two Americans were emerging from the ticket office.

"*Deux minutes.*"

Adam jumped up into the driver's seat, looked over towards the boat and watched Marvin and his colleague stride up the gang- plank.

"*Une minute.*"

"Just get the van to Dunkerque and leave the keys at the British checkpoint. We'll see you when we get there."

"Good luck," said Adam.

"Thank you," said Bob, and ran to the starting line to join his team mates who were anxiously holding his bike.

"*Trente secondes.*"

Adam watched the gangplank being hoisted up as the starter raised his gun.

"On your marks, set . . ."

The ship's fog horn belched out a droning note and the two Americans started their journey to Dover. A second later, the gun went off as Adam put the van into second gear and headed towards Dunkerque.

CHAPTER TWENTY-FOUR

Adam sat in the little dockside café waiting for the coach to appear. The team van had been left at the checkpoint and he was now ready to board the ship but he still needed to be sure Robin was on it. The coach trundled in with only ten minutes to spare and Adam greeted her as she stepped off.

"Just couldn't keep away from me, could you?" said Robin.

Adam burst out laughing and threw his arms almost round her.

"It's good to see you," he said.

"I thought you were going back to England by some mysterious route, you know, spy rocket or something even more exotic."

"I wanted to," said Adam, "but the Americans were sitting at the controls just as I decided to climb aboard."

"The Americans?" she said.

"I'll explain everything once we're on board," said Adam. Neither of them noticed the young agent who had trailed Robin from Berlin. He sat in a phone booth on the far side of the dock and dialled an overseas number.

"I wouldn't have believed a word of it a week ago," she said, "but for two things."

"Namely?"

"First, a senior official of the Foreign Office returned Dudley Hulme's passport to him in Amsterdam. Which reminds me to give you yours back." She rummaged around in her bag for a few moments before taking out a dark blue passport and handing it to him.

"And what's the second thing?" said Adam, taking the passport gratefully.

"I had the doubtful pleasure of coming face to face with Comrade Romanov, and I have no desire to do so again."

"I intend to meet him again," said Adam.

"Why?" asked Robin.

"Because I'm going to kill him."

Romanov and Pollard arrived in Dover a few minutes before the ferry was due to dock. They waited expectantly. Romanov stationed himself so that he could look through the customs hall window and watch the ferry as it sailed into Dover harbour. He had found the perfect spot behind a coffee-vending machine from which he could observe everyone who entered or left the customs hall, while at the same time remaining hidden from view.

"Just in case he should act out of character for a change," said Romanov, "and fails to go in a straight line, you will cover the car exit and report back to me if you notice anything unusual."

The colonel left Romanov secreted behind the coffee machine while he selected a place for himself on the dockside where he could watch the cars as they entered the customs area some fifty yards from the exit gate. If Scott did leave the ferry in a car Pollard would easily have enough time to run back and warn Romanov before Scott could hope to clear customs and reach the main gate. At least this would be the one place Scott couldn't risk hiding in the trunk. Both men waited.

The captain switched on his ship-to-shore radio to channel nine and spoke clearly into the small microphone. "This is the MV *Chantilly* calling the Dover Harbour Master. Are you receiving me?" He waited for a moment, flicked up the switch in front of him and then heard: "Harbour Master to MV *Chantilly*. Receiving you loud and clear, over."

"This is the captain speaking. We have an emergency. A male passenger has fallen out of a lifeboat on to the deck and contracted multiple injuries to his arms and legs." Adam groaned as the captain continued. "I shall need an ambulance to be standing by at the quayside to take him to the nearest hospital once we have docked. Over."

"Message received and understood, Captain. An ambulance will be waiting for you when the ship docks. Over and out."

"Everything will be all right, my dear," said Robin in a gentle voice that Adam had not heard before. "As soon as we arrive, they are going to see you are taken straight to a hospital."

"I must get back to the bridge," said the captain gruffly. "I shall instruct two stewards to bring a stretcher down for your brother."

"Thank you, Captain," said Robin. "You have been most helpful."

"It's quite all right, miss. You did say your brother?"

"Yes, Captain," said Robin.

"Well, you might advise him in future that it's in his best interests to drink less before he comes on board."

"I've tried," said Robin, sighing. "You couldn't believe how many times I've tried, Captain, but I'm afraid he takes after my father."

Adam held on to his leg and groaned again.

"Um," said the captain, looking down at the gash across Adam's shoulder. "Let's hope it turns out not to be serious. Good luck," he added.

"Thank you again, Captain," said Robin as she watched the cabin door close behind them.

"So far, so good," said Robin. "Now let's hope the second part of the plan works. By the way, your breath smells foul."

"What do you expect after making me swirl whisky round in my mouth for twenty minutes and then forcing me to spit it out all over my own clothes?"

Adam was lifted carefully on to the stretcher, then carried out on to the deck by two stewards. They waited at the head of the gangplank and placed Adam gently on the deck while a customs officer, accompanied by an immigration officer, ran up to join them. Robin handed over his passport. The immigration officer flicked through the pages and checked the photograph.

"Quite a good likeness for a change," said Robin, "but I'm afraid they may have to include this under 'unusual scars' in the next edition." She threw back the blanket dramatically and revealed the deep gash on Adam's shoulder. Adam looked suitably crestfallen.

"Is he bringing anything in with him that needs to be declared?" asked the customs official. Adam couldn't stop himself from touching the icon.

"No, I wouldn't let him buy any more booze on this trip. And I'll be responsible for checking his personal belongings through with mine when I leave the ship."

"Right. Thank you, miss. Better see he gets off to the hospital then," said the officer, suddenly aware that a restless mob of people were waiting at the top of the gangplank to disembark.

The two stewards carried Adam down the gangplank. An attendant was on hand to check his wound. Adam waved gamely at Robin as they placed him in the ambulance.

Romanov spotted her as she came through customs. "Now I know exactly how Captain Scott hopes to get off the ship, and we will be waiting for him when he least expects it. Go and hire a car to take us to London," he barked at the colonel.

The ambulance shot out through the customs gates with its lights full on and bells ringing. By the time they had arrived at The Royal Victoria Hospital the attendant had watched his patient's remarkable recovery en route with disbelief. He was beginning to feel that the captain might have exaggerated the scale of the emergency.

Romanov stood by the gate and smiled as he watched the coach carrying the musicians emerge from the deep black hole of the ship and take its turn in the queue for customs.

As Romanov's eyes ranged up and down the coach he quickly picked out Robin Beresford. Just as he had anticipated, the double bass was propped up by her side, making it impossible to see who was seated next to her.

"You won't pull that one on me a second time," Romanov muttered, just as the colonel appeared by his side, red in the face.

"Where's the car?" the Russian demanded, not taking his eye from the coach.

"I've booked one provisionally," said the colonel, "but they'll need your international licence. I forgot Scott has got mine, along with all my other papers."

"You stay put," said Romanov, "and make sure Scott doesn't try to get off that coach." Romanov ran to the Avis desk at the same time as Adam was being wheeled into a little cubicle to be examined by the duty registrar.

The young doctor leant over his patient for several minutes. He had never seen a wound quite like it before. He examined him carefully, before making any comment. "Nasty lacerations," he said finally, cleaning Adam's shoulder wound. "Can you circle your arm?" Adam turned the arm in a full circle and straightened it again. "Good. No break, at least." He continued to clean the wound.

"I'm going to put some iodine on the open cut and it may sting a little," said the doctor. He cleaned up both elbows before placing a plaster on them.

"That didn't happen today, did it?" he asked, staring at Adam's half-healed shoulder.

"No," said Adam, without offering any explanations.

"You have been in the wars lately. I'm going to give you an anti-tetanus injection." Adam turned white. "Funny how many grown men don't care for the sight of a needle," said the doctor. Adam groaned.

"Now that wasn't so bad, was it?" he coaxed as he placed a large bandage over the top of the shoulder. "Do you have someone to collect you?" the doctor asked finally.

"Yes, thank you," said Adam. "My wife is waiting for me."

"Good, then you can go now, but please report to your GP the moment you get home."

Romanov sat in the driver's seat and watched the coach clear customs. He followed it out of the main gate and on to the A2 in the direction of London.

"Are we going to intercept them on the way?" asked Pollard nervously.

"Not this time," said Romanov without explanation. He never once allowed the coach out of his sight all the way into the capital.

Adam walked out of the hospital and checked to see that no one was following him. The only people in sight were a man in a blue duffle coat walking in the opposite direction, and a nurse scurrying past him, looking anxiously at her watch. Satisfied, he took a taxi to Dover Priory station and purchased a single ticket to London.

"When's the next train?" he asked.

"Should be in any moment," said the ticket collector, checking his watch. "The ship docked about forty minutes ago, but it always takes a bit of time to unload all the passengers." Adam walked on to the platform, keeping a wary eye out for anyone acting suspiciously. He didn't notice the dark-haired man in a blue duffle coat leaning against the shutters of the W.H. Smith's stall reading the *Evening Standard*.

Adam's thoughts returned to Robin getting safely home. The London train drew in, packed with passengers who had been on the boat. Adam moved out of the shadows and jumped on, selecting a carriage full of teddy-boys who were apparently returning from a day at the seaside. He thought it would be unlikely anyone else would wish to join them. He took the only seat left in the far corner and sat silently but not in silence looking out of the window.

By the time the train had pulled into Canterbury no one had entered the carriage other than the ticket collector, who discreetly ignored the fact that one of the youths only presented him with a platform ticket for his inspection. Adam felt strangely safe in the corner of that particular compartment even when he noticed a dark haired man in a blue duffle coat pass by the compartment door and look in carefully.

Adam was jolted out of his thoughts by a noisy claim made by one of the gang who during the journey had given every appearance of being its leader.

"There's a foul smell in this compartment," he declared, sniffing loudly.

"I agree, Terry," said his mate who was sitting next to Adam and also began imitating the sniff. "And I think it's quite close to me." Adam glanced towards the young man whose black leather jacket was covered in small shiny studs. The words 'Heil Hitler' were printed right across his back. He got up and pulled open the window. "Perhaps some fresh air will help," he said as he sat back down. In moments all four of them were sniffing. "Sniff, sniff, sniff, sniff, I think the smell's getting worse," their leader concluded.

"It must be me," said Adam.

The sniffing stopped and the youths stared towards the corner in disbelief – momentarily silenced by Adam's offensive.

"I didn't have time to take a shower after my judo lesson," Adam added before any of them had found time to recover their speech.

"Any good at judo, are you?" asked the one sitting next to him.

"Passable," said Adam.

"What belt are you?" demanded Terry belligerently. "Go on, tell me, a black belt, I knew it," he added, sniggering.

"I haven't been a black belt for nearly eight years," said Adam casually, "but I've been recently awarded my second Dan."

A look of apprehension came over three of the four faces.

"I was thinkin' about taking up judo myself," continued the leader, straightening his arm. "How long does it take to get any good at it?"

"I've been working at it three hours a day for nearly twelve years and I'm still not up to Olympic standard," replied Adam as he watched the dark-haired man in the duffle coat pass by the compartment again. This time he stared directly at Adam before quickly moving on.

"Of course," continued Adam, "the only quality you really need if you are thinking of taking up judo seriously is nerve, and no one can teach you that. You've either got it or you haven't."

"I've got nerve," said Terry belligerently. "I'm not frightened of nothin'. Or nobody," he added, staring straight at Adam.

"Good," said Adam. "Because you may be given the chance to prove your claim before this journey is over."

"What're you getting at?" said the 'Heil Hitler' clad youth. "You trying to pick a fight or somethin'?"

"No," said Adam calmly. "It's just that at this moment I'm being followed by a private detective who is hoping to catch me spending the night with his client's wife."

The four of them sat still for the first time during the journey and stared at Adam with something approaching respect.

"And are you?" asked the leader.

Adam nodded conspiratorially.

"Nice bit of skirt when you've got it in the hay?" Terry asked, leering.

"Not bad," said Adam, "not bad at all."

"Then just point out this detective git and we'll sew him up for the night," said the leader, thrusting his left hand on his right bicep while pulling up his clenched fist with gusto.

"That might turn out to be overkill," said Adam. "But if you could delay him for a little when I get off at Waterloo East, that should at least give me enough time to warn the lady."

"Say no more, squire," said the leader. "Your friend the Peeping Tom will be delivered to Charing Cross all trussed up like a British Rail parcel."

The other three youths burst out laughing and Adam was beginning to realise that it had taken Romanov only one week to turn him into a storyteller almost in the class of Robin's late father.

"That's him," whispered Adam as the duffle-coated man passed by a third time. They all looked out into the corridor but only saw his retreating back.

"The train is due to arrive at Waterloo East in eleven minutes' time," said Adam, checking his watch. "So what I suggest we do is . . . if you think you're up to it, that is." All four of his new-found team leaned forward in eager anticipation.

A few minutes later Adam slipped out of the compartment, leaving the door wide open. He started to walk slowly in the direction opposite to that in which the man in the blue duffle coat had last been seen going. When Adam reached the end of the carriage, he turned to find the man was now following quickly behind. As he passed the open compartment the man smiled and raised a hand to attract Adam's attention but two leather-clad arms shot out and the man disappeared inside the compartment with a muffled cry. The door was slammed and the blinds pulled quickly down.

The train drew slowly into Waterloo East station.

Robin remained tense as the bus drew into Wigmore Street and came to a halt outside the RPO headquarters. A dark green Ford had been following them for at least thirty miles, and once she had become aware of it she had not dared to move from her seat.

As she dragged her double bass off the bus she looked back to see that the Ford had stopped about fifty yards down the road and turned off its headlights. Romanov was standing on the pavement looking like a caged animal that wanted to spring. Another man that Robin did not recognise remained seated behind the wheel. Adam had warned her not to turn around at any time but to walk straight into the RPO headquarters without stopping. Even so, she couldn't resist looking Romanov in the eye and shaking her head. Romanov continued to stare impassively ahead of him.

When the last musician had left the bus Romanov and 'the Colonel' searched up and down the inside of the vehicle and then finally the trunk, despite noisy protests from the driver. Robin eyed them nervously from an upstairs window, as the two of them jumped back into the green Ford and drove off. She continued watching the car until the back lights had faded away in the darkness.

The colonel swung out of Wigmore Street towards Baker Street, bringing the car to a halt opposite Baker Street station. Romanov jumped out, walked into a vacant telephone booth and started thumbing through the A–D directory. Only one Robin Beresford was listed and it was the same address as the young agent had read over to him. He dialled the number and after ten unanswered rings smiled at the realisation that she lived alone. He was not surprised.

"What now?" asked the colonel, once Romanov was back at the car.

"Where's Argyle Crescent, NW3?"

"Must be out towards Hampstead," said the colonel. "But I'll first check in the London A to Z roadmap. What's the plan?"

"Rather than waiting for Miss Beresford to come out we will be waiting for her to come in," said Romanov.

Robin slipped out of the back of the RPO headquarters about thirty minutes later. She zig-zagged around Portman Square then walked as quickly as she knew how up to the corner. She kept telling herself that Romanov was not coming back, but she found it impossible to stop herself from shaking all the same. She hailed a taxi and was relieved to see one draw up to her side almost immediately. She checked the driver and the back seat, as Adam had advised her, then climbed in.

Romanov arrived at Robin's front door a few moments after she had hailed the taxi. The name holder on the side wall indicated that Miss Beresford resided on the fourth floor.

The door itself would have proved no problem to any self-respecting petty thief in Moscow and Romanov had secured entry within moments. The colonel quickly joined him before they proceeded silently up the dark staircase to the fourth floor.

Romanov slipped the Yale lock faster than Robin could have opened it with her own key. Once inside he quickly checked the layout of the room and assured himself no one else was in the flat.

The colonel stood around fidgeting. "Settle down, Colonel. I don't expect the lady will keep us waiting too long." The colonel laughed nervously.

The taxi drew up outside the house that Robin pointed to. She then jumped out and tipped the cabbie extra because the bewitching hour had long passed and at last she felt safe. It seemed ages since she had been home. All she was looking forward to now was a hot bath and a good night's sleep.

Adam stepped off the train at Waterloo East a little after midnight and was pleased to find the underground was still running. He had avoided going on to Charing Cross, as he couldn't be sure which side would have a reception committee waiting for him. He produced a season ticket for the West Indian on the ticket barrier and waited around on the underground platform for some time before the train eventually drew in.

There were several stations between Waterloo and his destination, and even at this time of night there seemed to be a prolonged stop at every one. Several late-night revellers got in at the Embankment, more still at Leicester Square. Adam waited nervously at each station, now aware that he must have caught the last train. He only hoped Robin had carried out his instructions faithfully. He looked around the carriage he was sitting in. It was full of night people, waiters, nurses, party returners, drunks – even a traffic warden. The train eventually pulled into his station, at twelve forty.

The ticket collector was able to give him the directions he needed. It was a relief to reach his final destination so quickly because there was no one else around to ask the way at that time of night. He moved slowly towards number twenty-three. There were no lights on in the house. He opened the swinging gate and walked straight up the path, removed the bunch of keys from his pocket, putting the Chubb one in the lock. Adam pushed open the door cautiously and then closed it noiselessly behind him.

A little after twelve ten the last train from Dover pulled into Charing Cross station. As Adam was nowhere to be seen, Lawrence instructed his driver to take him back to Cheyne Walk. He couldn't understand why the agent whom he had hand-picked hadn't reported in. When Lawrence arrived back at the flat he put the key in his lock, hoping to find Adam was already waiting for him.

CHAPTER TWENTY-FIVE

He pushed open the swinging gate and made his way slowly up the path in the pitch darkness. Once he reached the corner of the house he searched for the third stone on the left. When he located the correct stone where he always left his spare key, he pulled it up with his fingers and felt around in the dirt. To his relief the key was still in place. Like a burglar he pushed it into the lock quietly.

He crept into the hall and closed the door behind him, switched the light and began to climb the stairs. Once he had reached the landing he switched off the hall light, turned the knob of his bedroom door and pushed.

As he stepped in an arm circled his throat like a whiplash and he was thrown to the ground with tremendous force. He felt a knee pressed hard against his spine and his arm was jerked up behind his back into a half nelson. He lay on the floor, flat on his face, hardly able to move or even breathe. The light switch flashed on and the first thing Adam saw was the colonel.

"Don't kill me, Captain Scott sir, don't kill me," he implored.

"I have no intention of doing so, Mr Tomkins," said Adam calmly.

"But first, where is your esteemed employer at this moment?"

Adam kept his knee firmly in the middle of the colonel's back and pressed his arm a few inches higher before the colonel bleated out, "He went back to the Embassy once he realised the girl wasn't going to return to the flat."

"Just as I planned," said Adam, but he didn't lessen the pressure on the colonel's arm as he described in vivid detail everything that would now be expected of him.

The colonel's face showed disbelief. "But that will be impossible," he said. "I mean, he's bound to noti – Ahhh."

The colonel felt his arm forced higher up his back. "You could carry out the whole exercise in less than ten minutes, and he need never be any the wiser," said Adam. "However, I feel that it's only fair that you should be rewarded for your effort."

"Thank you, sir," said the fawning colonel.

"If you succeed in delivering the one item I require and carry out my instructions to the letter you will be given in exchange your passport, driving licence, papers, wallet and a guarantee of no prosecution for your past treachery. But if, on the other hand, you fail to turn up by nine thirty tomorrow morning with the object of my desire," said Adam, "all those documents will be placed thirty minutes later on the desk of a Mr Lawrence Pemberton of the FO, along with my report on your other sources of income which you have failed to declare on your tax return."

"You wouldn't do that to me, would you, Captain Scott?"

"As ten o'clock chimes," said Adam.

"But think what would then happen to me, Captain Scott, sir, if you carried out such a threat," moaned the colonel.

"I have already considered that," said Adam, "and I have come to two conclusions."

"And what are they, Captain Scott?"

"Spies," continued Adam, not loosening his grip, "at the present time seem to be getting anything from eighteen to forty-two years at Her Majesty's pleasure, so you might, with good behaviour, be out before the turn of the century, just in time to collect your telegram from the Queen."

The colonel looked visibly impressed. "And the other conclusion?" he blurted out.

"Oh, simply that you could inform Romanov of my nocturnal visit and he in return would arrange for you to spend the rest of your days in a very small dacha in a suitably undesirable suburb of Moscow. Because, you see, my dear Tomkins, you are a very small spy. I personally am not sure when left with such an alternative which I would view with more horror."

"I'll get it for you, Captain Scott, you can rely on me."

"I'm sure I can, Tomkins. Because if you were to let Romanov into our little secret, you would be arrested within minutes. So at best, you could try to escape on the Aeroflot plane to Moscow. And I've checked, there isn't one until the early evening."

"I'll bring it to you by nine thirty on the dot, sir. You can be sure of that. But for God's sake have yours ready to exchange."

"I will," said Adam, "as well as all your documents, Tomkins."

Adam lifted the colonel slowly off the ground and then shoved him towards the landing. He switched on the light and then pushed the colonel on down the stairs until they reached the front door.

"The keys," said Adam.

"But you've already got my keys, Captain Scott, sir."

"The car keys, you fool."

"But it's a hire car, sir," said the colonel.

"And I'm about to hire it," said Adam.

"But how will I get myself back to London in time, sir?"

"I have no idea, but you still have the rest of the night to come up with something. You could even walk it by then. The keys," Adam repeated, jerking the colonel's arm to shoulder-blade level.

"In my left hand pocket," said the colonel, almost an octave higher.

Adam put his hand into the colonel's new jacket and pulled out the car keys.

He opened the front door, shoved the colonel on to the path, and then escorted him to the pavement.

"You will go and stand on the far side of the road," said Adam, "and you will not return to the house until I have reached the end of the road. Do I make myself clear, Tomkins?"

"Abundantly clear, Captain Scott, sir."

"Good," said Adam releasing him for the first time, "and just one more thing, Tomkins. In case you think of double-crossing me, I have already instructed the Foreign Office to place Romanov under surveillance and put two extra lookouts near the Soviet Embassy with instructions to report the moment anyone suspicious turns up or leaves before nine tomorrow morning." Adam hoped he sounded convincing.

"Thought of everything, haven't you, sir?" said the colonel mournfully.

"Yes, I think so," said Adam. "I even found time to disconnect your phone while I was waiting for you to return." Adam pushed the colonel across the road before getting into the hire car. He wound the window down. "See you at nine thirty tomorrow morning. Prompt," he added, as he put the Ford into first gear.

The colonel stood shivering on the far pavement, nursing his right shoulder, as Adam drove to the end of the road. He was still standing there when Adam took a left turn back towards the centre of London.

For the first time since Heidi's death, Adam felt it was Romanov who was on the run.

"What a great honour for our little establishment," said Herr Bischoff, delighted to see the most important banker in the East sitting in his boardroom sharing afternoon tea.

"Not at all, my dear Bischoff," said Poskonov. "After all these years the honour is entirely mine. And kind of you to be so understanding about opening the bank on a Sunday. But now to business. Did you manage to get Romanov to sign the release form?"

"Oh, yes," said Bischoff, matter-of-factly. "He did it without even reading the standard clauses, let alone the extra three you asked us to put in."

"So his inheritance automatically returns to the Russian state?"

"That is so, Mr Poskonov, and we in return . . ."

". . . will represent us in all the currency exchange transactions we carry out in the West."

"Thank you," said Herr Bischoff. "And we shall be delighted to assist you in your slightest requirement, but what happens when Romanov returns to the bank and demands to know what has become of his inheritance?" asked the chairman of the bank anxiously.

"He will not return," the Russian banker said emphatically. "You can have my word on it. Now, I would like to see what is in those boxes."

"Yes, of course," said Herr Bischoff. "Will you please accompany me?"

The two banking chairmen took the private lift to the basement and Herr Bischoff accompanied his guest to the underground vault.

"I will unlock the five boxes now in your name with the bank's key but only you can open them with your key."

"Thank you," said Poskonov, and left Herr Bischoff to open the five locks and return to the entrance of the vault.

"Do take as long as you like," said Herr Bischoff, "but at six o'clock the great door is automatically locked until nine o'clock tomorrow morning, and nothing less than a nuclear weapon would prise it open. At five forty-five, an alarm goes off to warn you that you only have fifteen minutes left."

"Excellent," said the man who through his entire banking career had never been given a fifteen-minute warning of anything.

Herr Bischoff handed Comrade Poskonov the envelope with Romanov's key inside it.

As soon as the massive steel door had been swung closed behind him the Russian checked the clock on the wall. They had left him with over two hours to sort out what could be transported to Brazil and what would have to be left behind. A state pension and the Order of Lenin (second class) hadn't seemed much of an alternative to Poskonov.

He turned the key and opened the first of the small boxes and found the deeds to lands the State had owned for decades. He growled. The second box contained the shares of companies once brilliantly successful, now shells in every sense of the word. And to Poskonov's disappointment the third of the small boxes only held a will proving everything belonged to Romanov's father and his immediate heirs. Had he waited all these years to discover the stories the old man had told him of gold, jewels and pearls were nothing but a fantasy? Or had Romanov already removed them?

Poskonov opened the first of the large boxes and stared down at the twelve little compartments. He removed the lid of the first one tentatively, and when he saw the array of gems and stones that shone in front of him his legs felt weak. He put both hands into the box and let the gems slip through his fingers like a child playing with pebbles on a beach.

The second box produced pearls and the third gold coins and medallions that could make even an old man's eyes sparkle. He hadn't realised how long it had taken him to go through the remaining boxes but when the alarm went off he was five thousand miles away already enjoying his new found wealth. He glanced at the clock. He had easily enough time to get everything back into the compartments and then he would return the following day and remove once and for all what he had earned from fifty years of serving the State.

When the last lid had been placed back on he checked the clock on the wall: six minutes to six. Just enough time to glance in the other box and see if he could expect the same again.

He turned the key and licked his lips in anticipation as he pulled the large box out. Just a quick look, he promised himself as he lifted the lid. When he saw the decaying body with its grey skin and eyes hanging in their sockets he reeled backwards from the sight and, falling to the floor, clutched his heart.

Both bodies were discovered at nine the next morning.

The phone rang and Adam grabbed at it before the shrill tone could deafen him a second time.

"Your alarm call, sir," said a girl's voice gently. "It's eight o'clock."

"Thank you," Adam replied and replaced the receiver. The call had proved unnecessary because he had been sitting up in bed considering the implications of his plan for nearly an hour. Adam had finally worked out exactly how he was going to kill Romanov.

He jumped out of bed, threw back the curtains and stared down at the Soviet Embassy. He wondered how long the Russian had been awake.

He returned to the side of the bed and picked up the phone to dial the number Robin had given him. The phone rang several times before it was answered by an elderly voice saying, "Mrs Beresford."

"Good morning, Mrs Beresford. My name is Adam Scott, I'm a friend of Robin's. I was just phoning to check that she reached home safely last night."

"Oh, yes, thank you," said Robin's mother. "It was a pleasant surprise to see her before the weekend. She usually spends the night in the flat when she gets back that late. I'm afraid she's still asleep. Would you like me to wake her?"

"No, no, don't disturb her," said Adam. "I only rang to fix a lunch date. Can you tell her I'll call back later?"

"I certainly will," she replied. "Thank you for phoning, Mr Scott."

Adam replaced the receiver and smiled. Each piece of the jigsaw was fitting neatly into place but without the colonel's help he still lacked the vital corner-piece. Adam began to put everything Tomkins needed, including his passport, personal papers and wallet into a large envelope. He removed the icon from his jacket pocket, turned it over and carefully examined the little silver crest of the Tsar. He then flicked open the colonel's penknife and began the slow and delicate task of removing the crown.

Thirty minutes later, Adam was in the lift on the way to the hotel basement. When he stepped out, he walked across to the space where he had parked the green Cortina earlier that morning. He unlocked the door and threw the colonel's old jacket on to the seat, then locked the car, checking all the doors before taking the lift back up to the ground floor.

The manager of the men's shop in the arcade had just flicked over the 'closed' sign and Adam took his time selecting a white shirt, grey flannels and a blue blazer, trying them on in their little changing room.

At nine twenty-three he settled his bill with the Royal Garden Hotel and asked the doorman to bring the green Ford up from the parking lot. He waited by the hotel entrance.

As the minutes passed, he began to fear that the colonel wouldn't turn up. If he failed to, Adam knew that the next call would have to be to Lawrence and not Romanov.

His reverie was disturbed by a honk on a car horn; the colonel's rented car had been left by the entrance.

"Your car is waiting on the ramp," said the doorman, as he returned the keys to Adam.

"Thank you," said Adam and handed over the last of the colonel's pound notes. He dropped the wallet into the large envelope, which he sealed, before checking his watch again.

He stood waiting anxiously for another two minutes before he spotted the colonel puffing up the slope leading to the hotel entrance. He was clinging on to a small carrier bag.

"I've done it, Captain Scott, sir, I've done it," said the colonel, before he had reached Adam's side. "But I must return immediately or he's bound to notice it's gone."

He passed the carrier bag quickly to Adam who opened the top and stared down at the object inside.

"You're a man of your word," said Adam, "and as promised you'll find everything you need in there." He passed over his own package along with the car keys without speaking. He pointed to the hire car.

The colonel ran to it, jumped in and drove quickly down the ramp of the Royal Garden Hotel before turning left into Kensington Palace Gardens.

Adam checked his watch: nine thirty-five.

"Could you call me a taxi?" he asked the doorman.

The driver pulled the window down and gave Adam an inquiring look.

"Chesham Place, SW1. A carpenter's shop."

Adam spent twenty minutes looking around the shop while the craftsman carried out his unusual request. Adam studied the result with satisfaction, paid him two half crowns and then walked back on to Kings Road, to hail another taxi.

"Where to, guv'nor?"

"The Tower of London."

Everyone was in their place for the D4 meeting at nine thirty and Busch had gone on the attack even before Lawrence had had the chance to sit down.

"How in hell did you manage to lose him this time?"

"I must take the blame myself," said Lawrence. "We had every port from Newhaven to Harwich covered, but the moment my man saw Romanov and his henchman leave the quayside at Dover and chase off down the motorway after the coach he assumed he must have seen Scott. I had already instructed the senior immigration officer at the port," he continued, "to allow Scott to disembark without a fuss. It had been my intention to take over once he passed through customs. There seemed no reason to change that plan while we had Romanov under close surveillance. Scott then proceeded to fool both Romanov and our man at Dover."

"But we were given a second chance when Scott got on the train," persisted Busch. Lawrence stared at the American waiting to see if he would admit that his two CIA agents had also lost Scott at Dover.

"My man was on the train," said Lawrence emphatically, "but had only the one opportunity to make contact with Scott while he was on his own, and at just that moment he was grabbed and badly beaten up by a bunch of drunken louts – teenagers, apparently – who were on their way back from a day trip to the seaside."

"Perhaps we're recruiting our agents from the wrong class of person," said Matthews, staring down at his briefing papers.

Lawrence made no attempt to reply.

"So, as far as we can tell, Scott, the Tsar's icon and Romanov are still holed up somewhere in London?" said Snell.

"It looks that way," admitted Lawrence.

"Perhaps all is not lost then," suggested Snell. "Scott may still try and get in touch with you again."

"I think not," said Lawrence quietly.

"How can you be so sure?" asked Busch.

"Because Scott knows that one of us in this room is a traitor and he thinks it's me."

"Good morning. Soviet Embassy."

"My name is Adam Scott and I need to get in contact with a Major Romanov."

"Good morning, Mr Scott. We do not have a Major Romanov working at the Embassy," came back the polite reply.

"I'm sure you don't."

"But if you would like to leave your number, I will make further inquiries."

"I'll wait. Wouldn't surprise me if you find him very quickly once he knows who it is calling."

There was a long silence at the other end, and Adam only hoped the shilling he had pressed into the call box would prove to be enough. At last there was a click, and then Adam heard a voice.

"Who is this?" said the voice, unable to mask its incredulity.

"You know very well who it is," said Adam curtly. "I want to make a deal."

"A deal?" Romanov repeated, his voice changing from one of disbelief to surprise.

"I'll swap you my icon – which as you so vividly pointed out is worthless to me – in exchange for your copy, which is not. But I also require the papers that prove my father's innocence."

"How do I know you're not setting me up?"

"You don't," said Adam. "But you're the one with nothing to lose."

The pips began to sound across the line.

"Tell me your number," said Romanov.

"738–9121," said Adam.

"I'll phone you back," said Romanov as the line went dead.

"How quickly can we find out where 738–9121 is located?" Romanov asked the local KGB operative who sat opposite him.

"About ten minutes," the aide replied. "But it could be a trap."

"True, but with nineteen hours to go before the icon has to be in America I don't have a lot of choice."

Romanov turned back to the KGB agent. "What's the traffic like in

London on a Friday morning?"

"One of the busiest times in the week. Why do you ask?"

"Because I'll need a motorbike and a superb driver," was all Romanov said.

Adam could do nothing about the middle-aged lady who was now occupying his phone booth. He had nervously walked out to check the bridge when she slipped in. She must have been puzzled as to why the young man didn't use the empty box that stood next to it.

He checked his watch anxiously: ten forty-five. He knew he couldn't risk waiting a minute after eleven but was confident that Romanov would have traced where he'd made the call from long before then.

The talkative woman was another twelve minutes before she eventually put the phone down. When she stepped out of the box she gave Adam a warm smile.

Three more minutes and he would have to phone Lawrence and abort his original plan. He began to watch the Beefeaters as they patrolled under Traitors' Gate. Traitors' Gate – how appropriate, Adam thought. He had chosen the spot because he could see clearly up and down the path leading to the drawbridge and felt he could not be taken by surprise. And in desperation there was always the moat that surrounded them on all sides.

For the first time in his life, Adam discovered exactly how long five minutes could be. When the phone rang, it sounded like an alarm bell. He picked it up nervously, his eyes never leaving the main road.

"Scott?"

"Yes."

"I can now see you clearly as I am less than one minute away. I will be standing at the edge of the bridge until the end of that minute. Be sure you're there with the icon. If you're not, I shall burn the papers that prove your father's innocence in front of you."

The phone went dead.

Adam was delighted that another piece of the jigsaw had fallen into place. He stepped out of the phone booth and checked up and down the road. A BMW motorcycle swerved to a halt at the end of the bridge. A rider dressed in a leather jacket sat astride the bike but only seemed interested in watching the flow of traffic as it passed by the Tower. It was the man seated behind him who stared directly at Adam.

Adam began to walk slowly towards the end of the bridge. He put a hand in his pocket to be sure the icon was still in its place.

He was about thirty yards from the end of the bridge when the second figure got off the bike and started walking towards him. When their eyes met, Romanov stopped in his tracks and held up a small, square frame. Adam did not respond in kind, but simply tapped the side of his pocket and continued walking. Both men advanced towards each other like knights of old until they were only a few paces apart. Almost simultaneously they stopped and faced one another.

"Let me see it," said Romanov.

Adam paused, then slowly removed the icon from his pocket and held it to his chest for his adversary to see St George staring at him.

"Turn it over," said Romanov.

Adam obeyed, and the Russian could not hide his delight when he saw the little silver crown of the Tsar embedded in the back.

"Now you," said Adam. Romanov held his icon away from his body, as if brandishing a sword. The masterpiece shone in the summer sun.

"And the documents," said Adam, forcing himself to speak calmly.

The Russian pulled out a package from within his jacket and slowly unfolded them. Adam stared at the official court verdict for a second time.

"Go to the wall," said Adam, pointing with his left hand to the side of the bridge, "and leave the icon and the documents on it."

It was Romanov who now obeyed as Adam proceeded to the wall on the other side of the bridge and placed his icon in the middle of it.

"Cross slowly," called Adam. The two men moved sideways back across the bridge, never getting closer than a couple of yards from each other until they had come to a halt at each other's icon. The moment the painting was within his reach, Romanov grabbed it, ran and jumped on to the motorcycle without looking back. Within seconds the BMW had disappeared into the dense traffic.

Adam did not move. Although it had only been out of his sight for just over an hour, he was relieved to have the original back. Adam checked the papers that would establish his father's innocence and placed them in his inside pocket. Ignoring the tourists, some of whom had stopped to stare at him, Adam began to relax when suddenly he felt a sharp prod in the middle of his back. He jumped round in fright.

A little girl was staring up at him.

"Will you and your friend be performing again this morning?"

When the BMW motorcycle drew up outside the Soviet Embassy in Kensington Palace Gardens, Romanov leapt off and ran up the steps and straight into the Ambassador's office without knocking. The Ambassador didn't need to ask if he had been successful.

"It worked out just as I planned. He was taken completely by surprise," said Romanov, as he handed the icon over to the Ambassador.

The Ambassador turned the painting over and saw the little silver crown of the Tsar. Any doubts that he might have had were also dispelled.

"I have orders to send the icon to Washington in the diplomatic pouch immediately. There is no time to be lost."

"I wish I could deliver it in person," said Romanov.

"Be satisfied, Comrade Major, that you have carried out your part of the operation in an exemplary fashion."

The Ambassador pressed a button on the side of his desk. Two men appeared immediately. One held open the diplomatic pouch while the other stood motionless by his side. The Ambassador handed over the icon and watched it being placed into the pouch. The two couriers looked as if they would have had no trouble in carrying out the Ambassador's desk as well, thought Romanov.

"There is a plane standing by at Heathrow to take you both direct to Washington," said the Ambassador. "All the necessary documentation for customs has already been dealt with. You should touch down at National airport around five o'clock Washington time, easily giving our comrades in America enough time to fulfil their part of the contract."

The two men nodded, sealed the diplomatic pouch in the Ambassador's presence and left. Romanov walked over to the window and watched the official car drive the two men out into Kensington High Street and off in the direction of Heathrow.

"Vodka, Comrade Major?"

"Thank you," Romanov replied, not moving from the window until the car was out of sight.

The Ambassador went over to a side cabinet and took out two glasses and a bottle from the fridge before pouring Romanov a large vodka.

"It would not be exaggerating to say that you have played your part in establishing the Soviet Union as the most powerful nation on earth," he said as he handed over the drink. "Let us therefore drink to the repatriation of the people of Aleuts as full citizens of the Union of Soviet Socialist Republics."

"How is that possible?" asked Romanov.

"I think the time has come to let you know," said the Ambassador, "the significance of your achievement." He then went on to tell Romanov of the briefing he had received from Moscow that morning.

Romanov was thankful he had never known how much was at stake.

"I have made an appointment to see the Foreign Secretary at three o'clock this afternoon in order to brief him. We can be sure the British will only be interested in fair play," the Ambassador continued. "I am told he is not at all pleased as he had hoped to be in his constituency to open some fete; the British have some strange ideas about how to keep their party system going."

Romanov laughed. "To Aleuts," he said, raising his glass. "But what is happening in Washington at this moment?"

"Our Ambassador has already requested a meeting with the American Secretary of State to be scheduled for eight this evening. He is also setting up a press conference at the Embassy to follow that meeting. It may amuse you to know that President Johnson had to cancel his visit to Texas this weekend and has requested that the networks should allow him to address 'his fellow Americans' at peak time on Monday as a matter of national importance."

"And we achieved it with only hours to spare," said Romanov, pouring himself another vodka.

"Touch and go, as the English would say. Let us also be thankful for the time difference between here and the United States because without that we would never have been able to beat the deadline."

Romanov shuddered at the thought of how close it had been and downed his second vodka in one gulp.

"You must join me for lunch, Comrade. Although your orders are to return to Moscow immediately my secretary assures me that the first plane leaving Heathrow for Moscow does not depart until eight this evening. I envy you the reception you will receive when you arrive back in the Kremlin tomorrow."

"I still need the £1000 for . . ."

"Ah, yes," said the Ambassador, "I have it ready for you." He unlocked the little drawer of his desk and passed over a slim wad of notes in a small cellophane wrapper.

Romanov slipped the tiny packet in his pocket and joined the Ambassador for lunch.

Busch barged into Lawrence's office.

"Romanov's got the icon," he shouted.

Lawrence's jaw dropped. A look of desperation appeared on his face. "How can you be so sure?" he demanded.

"I've just had a message from Washington. The Russians have requested an official meeting with the Secretary of State to be arranged for eight this evening."

"I don't believe it," said Lawrence.

"I do," said Busch. "We've always known that God-damned friend of yours, like his father, was a lousy traitor. There's no other explanation."

"He could be dead," said Lawrence quietly.

"I hope he is, for his sake," said Busch.

The phone on Lawrence's desk rang. He grabbed it as if it were a lifeline. "A Dr John Vance wants a word with you, sir," said his secretary. "He said you had asked him to call."

Vance? Vance? Lawrence recalled the name but couldn't quite place it. "Put him on," he said.

"Good morning, Mr Pemberton," said a voice.

"Good morning, Dr Vance. What can I do for you?"

"You asked me to call you after I had examined Scott."

"Scott?" repeated Lawrence, not believing what he was hearing.

"Yes, Adam Scott. Surely you remember? You wanted him to

complete a medical for your department."

Lawrence was speechless.

"I've given him a clean bill of health," continued the doctor. "Some cuts and a nasty bruise, but nothing that won't heal in a few days."

"Cuts and bruises?" said Lawrence.

"That's what I said, old chap. But don't worry about Scott. He's fit enough to start work whenever you want him. That's if you still want him."

"If I still want him," repeated Lawrence. "Mr Scott isn't there with you at this moment, by any chance?"

"No," said Vance. "Left my surgery about ten minuters ago."

"He didn't happen to tell you where he was going?" asked Lawrence.

"No, he wasn't specific. Just said something about having to see a friend off at the airport."

Once the coffee had been cleared away, Romanov checked his watch. He had left easily enough time to keep the appointment and still catch his plane. He thanked the Ambassador for all his help, left him, ran down the Embassy steps and climbed into the back of the anonymous black car.

The driver moved off without speaking as he had already been briefed as to where the major wanted to go.

Neither of them spoke on the short journey, and when the driver drew into Charlotte Street he parked the car in a lay-by. Romanov stepped out, walked quickly across the road to the door he was looking for and pressed the buzzer.

"Are you a member?" said a voice through the intercom.

"Yes," said Romanov, who heard a metallic click as he pushed the door open and walked down the dark staircase. Once he had entered the club it took a few seconds for his eyes to become accustomed to the light. But then he spotted Mentor seated on his own at a little table near a pillar in the far corner of the room.

Romanov nodded and the man got up and walked across the dance floor and straight past him. Romanov followed as the member entered the only lavatory. Once inside, Romanov checked that they were alone. Satisfied, he led them both into a little cubicle and slipped the lock to engaged. Romanov removed the thousand pounds from his pocket and handed it over to the man who sat down on the lavatory seat. Mentor greedily ripped open the packet, leaned forward and began to count. He never even saw Romanov straighten his fingers; and when the hand came down with a crushing blow on the back of Mentor's neck he slumped forward and fell to the ground in a heap.

Romanov yanked him up; it took several seconds to gather the ten-pound notes that had fallen to the floor. Once he had all hundred, he stuffed them into the member's pocket. Romanov then undid the member's fly buttons one by one and pulled down his trousers until they fell around his ankles. He lifted the lid and placed the man on the lavatory seat. The final touch was to pull his legs as wide open as the fallen trousers would allow, the feet splayed apart. Romanov then slipped under the large gap at the bottom of the door leaving the cubicle locked from the inside. He quickly checked his handiwork. All that could be seen from the outside was the splayed legs and fallen trousers.

Sixty seconds later, Romanov was back in the car on his way to Heathrow.

Adam arrived at Heathrow two hours before the Aeroflot flight was due to depart. He stationed himself with a perfect view of the forty-yard stretch Romanov would have to walk to board the Russian aircraft. He felt confident he would never reach the Aeroflot steps.

Romanov checked in at the BEA desk a little after six. He couldn't resist taking the BEA flight rather than Aeroflot even though he knew Zaborski would frown at such arrogance; he doubted if anyone would comment on this of all days.

Once he had been given his boarding card, he took the escalator to the executive lounge and sat around waiting to be called. It was always the same – the moment any operation had been completed, all he wanted to do was get home. He left his seat to pour himself some coffee and, passing a table in the centre of the room, caught the headline on the London *Evening Standard*. Exclusive. 'Johnson Texas Weekend Cancelled – Mystery.' Romanov grabbed the paper from the table and read the first paragraph but it contained no information he couldn't have already told them. None of the speculation in the paragraphs that followed even began to get near the truth.

Romanov couldn't wait to see the front page of *Pravda* the next day in which he knew the true story would be emblazoned. By Western standards it would be an exclusive.

"BEA announce the departure of their flight 117 to Moscow. Would all first class passengers now board through gate No. 23." Romanov left the lounge and walked the half mile long corridor to the plane. Romanov strolled across the tarmac to the waiting plane a few minutes after six fifty. The plane carrying the icon would be touching down in Washington in about two hours. Romanov would arrive back in Moscow well in time to see Dynamo play Spartak at the Lenin Stadium on Tuesday. He wondered if they would announce his arrival to the crowd over the loudspeakers as they always did when a member of the Politburo attended a match. Romanov walked up the steps and on board, stepping over the feet of the passenger placed next to him, thankful he had been given the window seat.

"Would you care for a drink before take-off?" the stewardess asked.

"Just a black coffee for me," said his neighbour. Romanov nodded his agreement.

The stewardess arrived back a few minutes later with the two coffees and helped the man next to Romanov pull out his table from the armrest. Romanov flicked his over as the stewardess passed him his coffee.

He took a sip but it was too hot so he placed it on the table in front of him. He watched his neighbour take out a packet of saccharines from his pocket and flick two pellets into the steaming coffee.

Why did he bother, thought Romanov. Life was too short.

Romanov stared out of the window and watched the Aeroflot plane start to taxi out on to the runway. He smiled at the thought of how much more comfortable his own flight would be. He tried his coffee a second time: just as he liked it. He took a long gulp and began to feel a little drowsy which he didn't find that strange as he had hardly slept for the last week.

He leaned back in his seat and closed his eyes. He would now take every honour the State could offer him. With Valchek conveniently out of the way, he could even position himself to take over from Zaborski. If that failed, his grandfather had left him another alternative.

He was leaving London with only one regret: he had failed to kill Scott. But then he suspected that the Americans would take care of that. For the first time in a week he didn't have to stop himself falling asleep . . .

A few moments later the passenger seated next to Romanov picked up the Russian's coffee cup and put it next to his own. He then flicked Romanov's table back into the armrest and placed a woollen blanket over Romanov's legs. He quickly slipped the BEA eye shades over the Russian's head, covering his open eyes. He looked up to find that the stewardess was standing by his side.

"Can I help?" she asked, smiling.

"No, thank you. All he said was that he did not want to be disturbed during the flight as he has had a very hard week."

"Of course, sir," said the stewardess. "We'll be taking off in a few minutes," she added, and picked up the two coffee cups and whisked them away.

The man tapped his fingers impatiently on the little table. At last the chief steward appeared at his side.

"There's been an urgent call from your office, sir. You're to return to Whitehall immediately."

"I had been half expecting it," he admitted.

Adam stared up at the Russian plane as it climbed steeply and swung in a semi-circle towards the East. He couldn't understand why Romanov hadn't boarded it. Surely he wouldn't have taken the BEA flight. Adam slipped back into the shadows the moment he saw him. He stared in disbelief. Lawrence was striding back across the tarmac, a smile of satisfaction on his face.

EPILOGUE

SOTHEBY'S,
NEW BOND STREET, LONDON W1

October 18, 1966

EPILOGUE

"Sold to the gentleman in the centre of the room for five thousand pounds.

"We now move on to Lot no. 32," said the auctioneer, looking down from the raised platform at the front of the crowded room. "An icon of St George and the Dragon," he declared as an attendant placed a little painting on the easel next to him. The auctioneer stared down at the faces of experts, amateurs and curious onlookers. "What am I bid for this magnificent example of Russian art?" he asked, expectantly.

Robin gripped Adam's hand. "I haven't felt this nervous since I came face to face with Romanov."

"Don't remind me," said Adam.

"It is, of course, not the original that hangs in the Winter Palace," continued the auctioneer, "but it is nevertheless a fine copy, probably executed by a court painter circa 1914," he added, giving the little painting an approving smile. "Do I have an opening bid? Shall I say eight thousand?" The next few seconds seemed interminable to Robin and Adam. "Thank you, sir," said the auctioneer, eventually looking towards an anonymous sign that had been given somewhere at the front of the room.

Neither Adam nor Robin were able to make out where the bid had come from. They had spent the last hour seated at the back of the room watching the previous items coming under the hammer and had rarely been able to work out whose hands they had ended up in.

"How much did the expert say it might go for?" Robin asked again.

"Anywhere between ten and twenty thousand," Adam reminded her.

"Nine thousand," said the auctioneer, his eyes moving to a bid that appeared to come from the right-hand side of the room.

"I still think it's amazing," said Robin, "that the Russians ever agreed to the exchange in the first place."

"Why?" asked Adam. "They got theirs back, the Americans extracted the treaty and I ended up with mine. As an example of diplomatic ingenuity it was Lawrence at his most brilliant."

"Ten thousand from the front of the room. Thank you, sir," said the auctioneer.

"What are you going to do with all that money?"

"Buy a new double bass, get a wedding present for my sister and hand over the rest to my mother."

"Eleven thousand, a new bid on the centre aisle," said the auctioneer. "Thank you, madam."

"No amount of money can bring back Heidi," said Robin quietly. Adam nodded thoughtfully.

"How did the meeting with Heidi's parents turn out?"

"The Foreign Secretary saw them personally last week. It couldn't help, but at least he was able to confirm that I had only been telling them the truth."

"Twelve thousand." The auctioneer's eye returned to the front of the room.

"Did you see the Foreign Secretary yourself?"

"Good heavens, no, I'm far too junior for that," said Adam. "I'm lucky if I get to see Lawrence, let alone the Foreign Secretary."

Robin laughed. "I consider you were *lucky* to have been offered a place at the Foreign Office at all."

"Agreed," said Adam chuckling to himself, "but a vacancy arose unexpectedly."

"What do you mean, 'unexpectedly'?" asked Robin, frustrated by how few of her questions had been answered directly in the past half hour.

"All I can tell you is that one of Lawrence's old team was 'retired early'," said Adam.

"Was that also true of Romanov?" asked Robin, still desperately trying to discover all that had taken place since they had last met.

"Thirteen thousand," said the auctioneer, his eyes returning to the lady on the centre aisle.

"After all he can't have survived for long once they discovered you had done a switch that gave the Russians back the copy while Romanov ended up presenting you with the original," said Robin.

"He's never been heard of since," admitted Adam innocently.

"And all our information leads us to believe that his boss Zaborski is soon to be replaced by someone called Yuri Andropov."

"Fourteen thousand," said the auctioneer, his eye settling on the gentleman at the front once again.

"What happened when you produced the papers proving that it was not your father who had smuggled the poison into Goering's cell?"

"Once they had been authenticated by the Russians," Adam said, "Lawrence paid an official visit to the Colonel of the Regiment and furnished him with the conclusive evidence."

"Any reaction?" probed Robin.

"They're going to hold a memorial service in Pa's memory and have commissioned some fellow called Ward to paint his portrait for the regimental mess. Mother has been invited to unveil it in the presence of all those officers who served with my father."

"Fourteen thousand for the first time then," said the auctioneer raising the little gavel a few inches in the air.

"She must have been over the moon," said Robin.

"Burst into tears," said Adam. "All she could say was 'I wish Pa could have lived to see it.' Ironic, really. If only he had opened that letter."

"Fourteen thousand for the second time," said the auctioneer, the gavel now hovering.

"How do you fancy a celebration lunch at the Ritz?" said Adam, delighted with how well the sale was turning out.

"No thank you," said Robin.

Adam looked across at his companion in surprise.

"It won't be much fun if every time I ask you a question I only get the official Foreign Office briefing."

Adam looked sheepish. "I'm sorry," he said.

"No, that wasn't fair," said Robin. "Now you're on the inside it can't be easy, so I suppose I will have to go to my grave wondering what treaty was inside that icon."

Adam looked away from the girl who had saved his life.

"Or perhaps I'll find out the truth in 1996 when the cabinet papers are released."

He turned slowly to face her.

"Alas . . ." he began as the auctioneer's hammer came down with a thud. They both looked up.

"Sold to the gentleman at the front for fourteen thousand pounds."

"Not a bad price," said Adam, smiling.

"A bargain in my opinion," replied Robin quietly.

Adam turned to her a quizzical look on his face.

"After all," she said in a whisper, "imagine what the forty-ninth state would have fetched if it had come up for auction."

SHALL WE TELL THE PRESIDENT?

To Adrian and Anne

Author's Note to Revised Edition

When I first wrote *Shall We Tell the President?* I set the story six or seven years in the future. Now that that future date lies in the past, some of the story's credibility becomes impaired.

Since that time too I have written *The Prodigal Daughter* in which the chief character, Florentyna Kane, becomes the first woman President of the United States. It therefore seems logical to me, in recasting *Shall We Tell the President?*, to introduce my fictional president rather than keep the real-life name of Edward M. Kennedy who was the focus of the original novel. This gives it a natural link to *The Prodigal Daughter* and also to *Kane and Abel*.

I have not altered the essential story of *Shall We Tell the President?* but a number of significant changes as well as minor ones, have been made in this revised, re-set edition.

Tuesday afternoon, 20 January. 12:26 pm

"I, Florentyna Kane, do solemnly swear . . ."
"*I, Florentyna Kane, do solemnly swear . . .*"
". . . that I will faithfully execute the office of the President of the United States . . ."
"*. . . that I will faithfully execute the office of the President of the United States . . .*"
". . . and will to the best of my ability, preserve, protect and defend the Constitution of the United States. So help me God."
"*. . . and will to the best of my ability, preserve, protect and defend the Constitution of the United States. So help me God.*".

Her hand still resting on the Douay Bible, the forty-third President smiled at the First Gentleman. It was the end of one struggle and the beginning of another. Florentyna Kane knew about struggles. Her first struggle had been to be elected to Congress, then the Senate and finally four years later when she had become the first woman Vice President of the United States. After a fierce primary campaign, she had only narrowly managed to defeat Senator Ralph Brooks on the fifth ballot at the Democratic National Convention in June. In November she survived an even fiercer battle with the Republican candidate, a former congressman from New York. Florentyna Kane was elected President by 105,000 votes, a mere one per cent, the smallest margin in American history, smaller even than the 118,000 that John F. Kennedy had gained over Richard Nixon back in 1960.

While the applause died down, the President waited for the twenty-one gun salute to come to an end. Florentyna Kane cleared her throat and faced fifty thousand attentive citizens on the Capitol Plaza and two hundred million more somewhere out there beyond the television transmitters. There was no need today for the blankets and heavy coats which normally accompanied these occasions. The weather was unusually mild for late January, and the crowded grassy area facing the east front of the Capitol, although soggy, was no longer white from the Christmas snow.

"Vice President Bradley, Mr Chief Justice, President Carter, President Reagan, Reverend clergy, fellow citizens."

The First Gentlemen looked on, smiling occasionally to himself as he recognised some of the words and phrases he had contributed to his wife's speech.

Their day had begun at about 6:30 am. Neither had slept very well after the splendid pre-Inaugural concert given in their honour the previous evening. Florentyna Kane had gone over her presidential address for the final time, underlining the salient words in red, making only minor changes.

When she rose that morning, Florentyna wasted no time in selecting a blue dress from her wardrobe. She pinned on the tiny brooch her first husband, Richard, had given her just before he had died.

Every time Florentyna wore that brooch she remembered him; how he had been unable to catch the plane that day because of a strike by maintenance workers but still hired a car to be sure he could be by Florentyna's side when she addressed the Harvard commencement.

Richard never did hear that speech, the one *Newsweek* described as a launching pad for the Presidency – because by the time she had reached the hospital he was dead.

She snapped back into the real world of which she was the most powerful leader on earth. But still without enough power to bring Richard back. Florentyna checked herself in the mirror. She felt confident. After all, she had already been President for nearly two years since the unexpected death of President Parkin. Historians would be surprised to discover that she had learned of the President's death while trying to sink a four-foot putt against her oldest friend and future husband, Edward Winchester.

They had both stopped their match when the helicopters had circled overhead. When one of them had landed a Marines Captain had jumped out and run towards her, saluted and said, "Madam President, the President is dead." Now the American people had confirmed that they were willing to continue living with a woman in the White House. For the first time in its history, the United States had elected a woman to the most coveted position in its political life in her own right. She glanced out of the bedroom window at the broad placid expanse of the Potomac River, glinting in the early-morning sunlight.

She left the bedroom and went straight to the private dining-room where her husband Edward was chatting to her children William and Annabel. Florentyna kissed all three of them before they sat down to breakfast.

They laughed about the past and talked about the future but when the clock struck eight the President left them to go to the Oval Office. Her Chief of Staff, Janet Brown, was sitting outside in the corridor waiting for her.

"Good morning, Madam President."

"Good morning, Janet. Everything under control?" She smiled at her.

"I think so, Madam."

"Good. Why don't you run my day as usual? Don't worry about me, I'll just follow your instructions. What do you want me to do first?"

"There are 842 telegrams and 2,412 letters but they will have to wait, except for the Heads of State. I'll have replies ready for them by twelve o'clock."

"Date them today, they'll like that, and I'll sign every one of them as soon as they are ready."

"Yes, Madam. I also have your schedule. You start the official day with coffee at eleven with the former Presidents Reagan and Carter, then you will be driven to the Inauguration. After the Inauguration, you'll attend a luncheon at the Senate before reviewing the Inaugural Parade in front of the White House."

Janet Brown passed her a sheaf of three-by-five index cards, stapled together, as she had done for fifteen years since she joined her staff when Florentyna had first been elected to Congress. They summarised the President's hour-by-hour schedule; there was rather less on them than usual. Florentyna glanced over the cards, and thanked her Chief of Staff. Edward Winchester appeared at the door. He smiled as he always did, with a mixture of love and admiration, when she turned towards him. She had never once regretted her almost impulsive decision to marry him after the eighteenth hole on that extraordinary day she was told of President Parkin's death, and she felt for certain that Richard would have approved.

"I'll be working on my papers until eleven," she told him. He nodded and left to prepare himself for the day ahead.

A crowd of well-wishers was already gathering outside the White House.

"I wish it would rain," confided H. Stuart Knight, the head of the Secret Service, to his aide; it was also one of the most important days of his life. "I know the vast majority of people are harmless, but these occasions give me the jitters."

The crowd numbered about one hundred and fifty; fifty of them belonged to Mr Knight. The advance car that always goes five minutes ahead of a President was already meticulously checking the route to the White House; Secret Service men were watching small gatherings of people along the way, some waving flags; they were there to witness the Inauguration, and would one day tell their grandchildren how they had seen Florentyna Kane being inaugurated as President of the United States.

At 10:59 the butler opened the front door and the crowds began to cheer.

The President and her husband waved to the smiling eyes and only sensed by experience and professional instinct that fifty people were not looking towards them.

Two black limousines came to a noiseless stop at the North Entrance of the White House at 11:00 am. The Marine Honour Guard stood at attention and saluted the two ex-Presidents and their wives as they were greeted by President Kane on the Portico, a privilege normally accorded only to visiting Heads of State. The President herself guided them through the library for coffee with Edward, William and Annabel.

The older of the ex-Presidents was grumbling that if he were frail it was because he had had to rely on his wife's cooking for the past eight years. "She hasn't dirtied a frying pan in ages, but she's improving every day. To make sure, I've given her a copy of *The New York Times Cook Book*; it's about the only one of their publications that didn't criticise me." Florentyna laughed nervously. She wanted to get on with the official proceedings, but she was conscious that the ex-Presidents were enjoying being back in the White House so she pretended to listen attentively, donning a mask that was second nature to her after nearly twenty years in politics.

"Madam President . . ." Florentyna had to think quickly to prevent anyone noticing her instinctive response to the words. "It's one minute past midday." She looked up at her press secretary, rose from her chair, and led the ex-Presidents and their wives to the steps of the White House. The Marine band struck up "Hail to the Chief" for the last time. At one o'clock they would play it again for the first time.

The two former Presidents were escorted to the first car of the motorcade, a black, bubble-topped, bullet-proof limousine. The Speaker of the House, Jim Wright, and the Senate Majority Leader, Robert Byrd, representing the Congress, were already seated in the second car. Directly behind the limousine there were two cars filled with Secret Service men. Florentyna and Edward occupied the fifth car in line. Vice President Bradley of New Jersey and his wife rode in the next car.

H. Stuart Knight was going through one more routine check. His fifty men had now grown to a hundred. By noon, counting the local police and the FBI contingent, there would be five hundred. Not forgetting the boys from the CIA, Knight thought ruefully. They certainly didn't tell him whether they were going to be there or not, and even he could not always spot them in a crowd. He listened to the cheering of the onlookers reaching a crescendo as the presidential limousine pulled out, on its way to the Capitol.

Edward chatted amiably but Florentyna's thoughts were elsewhere. She waved mechanically at the crowds lining Pennsylvania Avenue, but her mind was once again going over her speech. The renovated

Willard Hotel, seven office buildings under construction, the tiered housing units that resembled an Indian cliff-dwelling, the new shops and restaurants and the wide landscaped sidewalks passed by. The J. Edgar Hoover Building, which housed the FBI, still named after its first Director, despite several efforts by certain senators to have the name changed. How this street had been transformed in fifteen years.

They approached the Capitol and Edward interrupted the President's reverie. "May God be with you, darling." She smiled and gripped his hand. The six cars came to a stop.

President Kane entered the Capitol on the ground floor. Edward waited behind for a moment as he thanked the chauffeur. Those who stepped out of the other cars were quickly surrounded by Secret Service agents and, waving to the crowd, they made their way separately to their seats on the platform. Meanwhile the chief usher was taking President Kane quietly through the tunnel into the reception area, Marines saluting at every ten paces. There she was greeted by Vice President Bradley. The two of them stood talking of nothing, neither of them taking in the other's reply.

The two ex-Presidents came through the tunnel smiling. For the first time the older President was looking his age, his hair seemed to have turned grey overnight. Once again, he and Florentyna went through the formality of shaking hands with one another; they were to do it seven times that day. The chief usher guided them through a small reception room on to the platform. For this, as for all Presidential inaugurations, a temporary platform had been erected on the east steps of the Capitol. The crowds rose and cheered for over a minute as the President and the ex-Presidents waved; finally they sat in silence and waited for the ceremony to begin.

"My fellow Americans, as I take office the problems facing the United States across the world are vast and threatening. In South Africa, pitiless civil war rages between black and white; in the Middle East the ravages of last year's battles are being repaired, but both sides are rebuilding their armaments rather than their schools, their hospitals or their farms. On the borders between China and India, and between Russia and Pakistan, there is the potential for war among four of the most populous nations on earth. South America veers between extreme right and extreme left, but neither extreme seems to be able to improve the living conditions of their peoples. Two of the original signatories of the North Atlantic Treaty Organisation, France and Italy, are on the verge of withdrawing from that pact.

"In 1949, President Harry S. Truman announced that the United States stood ready with all its might and resources to defend the forces of freedom wherever they might be endangered. Today, some would say that this act of magnanimity has resulted in failure, that America was, and is, too weak to assume the full burden of world leadership. In the face of repeated international crises, any American citizen might well ask why he should care about events so far from home, and why he should feel any responsibility for the defence of freedom outside the United States.

"I do not have to answer these doubts in my own words. 'No man is an island,' John Donne wrote more than three and a half centuries ago. 'Every man is a piece of the continent.' The United States stretches from the Atlantic to the Pacific and from the Arctic to the Equator. 'I am involved in mankind; and therefore never send to know for whom the bell tolls; it tolls for thee.' "

Edward liked that part of the speech. It expressed so well his own feelings. He had wondered, though, whether the audience would respond with the same enthusiasm as they had greeted Florentyna's flights of rhetoric in the past. The thunderous applause assaulting his ears in wave after wave reassured him. The magic was still working.

"At home, we will create a medical service that will be the envy of the free world. It will allow all citizens an equal opportunity for the finest medical advice and help. No American must be allowed to die because he cannot afford to live."

Many Democrats had voted against Florentyna Kane because of her attitude towards Medicare. As one hoary old GP had said to her, "Americans must learn to stand on their own two feet." "How can they if they're already flat on their backs?" retorted Florentyna. "God deliver us from a woman President," replied the doctor, and voted Republican.

"But the main platform of this administration will be in the field of law and order, and to this end I intend to present to Congress a bill that will make the sale of firearms without a licence illegal."

The applause from the crowd was not quite so spontaneous.

Florentyna raised her head. "And so I say to you, my fellow citizens, let the end of this century be an era in which the United States leads the world in justice as well as in power, in care as well as enterprise, an era in which the United States declares war – war on disease, war on discrimination, and war on poverty."

The President sat down; in a single motion, the entire audience rose to its feet.

The sixteen-minute speech had been interrupted by applause on ten occasions. But as the nation's Chief Executive turned from the microphone, now assured that the crowd was with her, her eyes were no longer on the cheering mass. She scanned the dignitaries on the platform for the one person she wanted to see. She walked over to her husband, kissed him on the cheek, and then took his arm before they were accompanied from the platform by the briskly efficient usher.

H. Stuart Knight hated things that didn't run on schedule, and today nothing had been on time. Everybody was going to be at least thirty minutes late for the lunch.

Seventy-six guests stood as the President entered the room. These were the men and women who now controlled the Democratic party. The Northern establishment who had decided to back the lady were now present, with the exception of those who had supported Senator Ralph Brooks.

Some of those at the luncheon were already members of her cabinet, and everyone present had played some part in returning her to the White House.

The President had neither the opportunity nor the inclination to eat her lunch; everyone wanted to talk to her at once. The menu had been specially made up of her favourite dishes, starting with lobster bisque and going on to roast beef. Finally, the chef's *pièce de résistance* was produced, an iced chocolate cake, in the form of the White House. Edward watched his wife ignore the neat wedge of the Oval Office placed in front of her. "That's why she never needs to slim," commented Marian Edelman, who was the surprise appointment as Attorney General. Marian had been telling Edward about the importance of children's rights. Edward tried to listen; perhaps another day.

By the time the last wing of the White House had been demolished and the last hand pumped, the President and her party were forty-five minutes late for the Inaugural Parade. When they did arrive at the reviewing stand in front of the White House, the most relieved to see them among the crowd of two hundred thousand, was the Presidential Guard of Honour, who had been standing at attention for just over an hour. Once the President had taken her seat the parade began. The State contingent in the military unit marched past, and the United States Marine Band played everything from Sousa to "God Bless America". Floats from each state, some, like that of Illinois, commemorating events from Florentyna's Polish background, added colour and a lighter touch to what for her was not only a serious occasion but a solemn one.

She still felt this was the only nation on earth that could entrust its highest office to the daughter of an immigrant.

When the three-hour-long parade was finally over and the last float had disappeared down the avenue, Janet Brown, Florentyna Kane's Chief of Staff, leaned over and asked the President what she would like to do between now and the first Inaugural Ball.

"Sign all those cabinet appointments, the letters to the Heads of State, and clear my desk for tomorrow," was the immediate reply. "That should take care of the first four years."

The President returned directly into the White House. As she walked through the South Portico, the Marine band struck up "Hail to the Chief". The President had taken off her coat even before she reached the Oval Office. She sat herself firmly behind the imposing oak and leather desk. She paused for a moment, looking around the room. Everything was as she wanted it; behind her there was the picture of Richard and William playing touch football. In front of her, a paperweight with the quotation from George Bernard Shaw which Annabel quoted so often: "Some men see things as they are and say, why; I dream things that never were and say, why not." On Florentyna's left was the Presidential flag, on her right the flag of the United States. Dominating the middle of the desk was a replica of the Baron Hotel, Warsaw, made out of papier mâché by William when he was fourteen. Coal was burning in the fireplace. A portrait of Abraham Lincoln stared down at the newly sworn-in President while outside the bay windows, the green lawns swept in an unbroken stretch to the Washington Monument. The President smiled. She was back at home.

Florentyna Kane reached for a pile of official papers and glanced over the names of those who would serve in her cabinet; there were over thirty appointments to be made. The President signed each one with a flourish. The final one was Janet Brown as Chief of Staff. The President ordered that they be sent down to the Congress immediately. Her press secretary picked up the pieces of paper that would dictate the next four years in the history of America and said, "Thank you, Madam President," and then added, "What would you like to tackle next?"

"Always start with the biggest problem is what Lincoln advised, so let's go over the draft legislation for the Gun Control bill."

The President's press secretary shuddered, for she knew only too well that the battle in the House over the next two years was likely to be every bit as vicious and hard-fought as the Civil War Lincoln had faced. So many people still regarded the possession of arms as their inalienable birthright. She only prayed that it all would not end the same way, as a House Divided.

Thursday evening, 3 March (two years later) 5:45 pm

Nick Stames wanted to go home. He had been at work since seven that morning and it was already 5:45 pm. He couldn't remember if he had eaten lunch; his wife, Norma, had been grumbling again that he never got home in time for dinner, or, if he did, it was so late that her dinner was no longer worth eating. Come to think of it, when did he last find time to finish a meal? Norma stayed in bed when he left for the office at 6:30 am. Now that the children were away at school, her only real task was to cook dinner for him. He couldn't win; if he had been a failure, she would have complained about that, too, and he was, goddamn it, by anybody's standards, a success; the youngest special agent in charge of a Field Office in the FBI and you don't get a job like that at the age of forty-one by being at home on time for dinner every night. In any case, Nick loved the job. It was his mistress; at least his wife could be thankful for that.

Nick Stames had been head of the Washington Field Office for nine years. The third largest Field Office in America, although it covered the smallest territory – only sixty-one square miles of Washington, DC – it had twenty-two squads; twelve criminal, ten security. Hell, he was policing the capital of the world. Of course, he must be expected to be late sometimes. Still, tonight he intended to make a special effort. When he had the time to do so, he adored his wife. He was going to be home on time this evening. He picked up his internal phone and called his Criminal Coordinator, Grant Nanna.

"Grant."

"Boss."

"I'm going home."

"I didn't know you had one."

"Not you, too."

Nick Stames put the phone down, and pushed his hand through his long dark hair. He would have made a better movie criminal than FBI agent, since everything about him was dark – dark eyes, dark skin, dark hair, even a dark suit and dark shoes, but the last two were true of any special agent. On his lapel he wore a pin depicting the flags of the United States and of Greece.

Once, a few years ago, he had been offered promotion and a chance to cross the street to the Bureau Headquarters and join the Director as one of his thirteen assistants. Being an assistant chained to a desk wasn't his style, so he stayed put. The move would have taken him from a slum to a palace; the Washington Field Office is housed on floors four, five, and eight of the Old Post Office Building on Pennsylvania Avenue, and the rooms are a little like railroad coaches. They would have been condemned as slums if they had been sited in the ghetto.

As the sun began to disappear behind the tall buildings, Nick's gloomy office grew darker. He walked over to the light switch. "Don't Be Fuelish," commented a fluorescent label glued to the switch. Just as the constant movement of men and women in dark sober suits in and out of the Old Post Office Building revealed the location of the FBI Washington Field Office, so this government graffito served notice that the czars of the Federal Energy Administration inhabited two floors of the cavernous building on Pennsylvania Avenue.

Nick stared out of his window across the street at the new FBI Headquarters, which had been completed in 1976, a great ugly monster with elevators that were larger than his office. He didn't let it bother him. He'd reached Grade 18 in the service, and only the Director was paid more than he was. In any case, he was not going to sit behind a desk until they retired him with a pair of gold handcuffs. He wanted to be in constant touch with the agent in the street, feel the pulse of the Bureau. He would stay put at the Washington Field Office and die standing up, not sitting down. Once again, he touched the intercom. "Julie, I'm on my way home."

Julie Bayers looked up and glanced at her watch as if it were lunchtime.

"Yes, sir," she said, sounding disbelieving.

As he passed through the office he grinned at her. "Moussaka, rice pilaf, and the wife; don't tell the Mafia." Nick managed to get one foot out of the door before his private phone rang. One more step and he would have made it to the open lift, but Nick never could resist the ring of a phone. Julie rose and began to walk towards his office. As she did so Nick admired, as he always did, the quick flash of leg. "It's all right, Julie. I'll get it." He strode back into his room and picked up the ringing telephone.

"Stames."

"Good evening, sir. Lieutenant Blake, Metropolitan Police."

"Hey, Dave, congratulations on your promotion. I haven't seen you in . . ." he paused, ". . . it must be five years, you were only a sergeant. How are you?"

"Thank you, sir, I'm doing just fine."

"Well, Lieutenant, moved into big-time crime, now have you? Picked up a fourteen-year-old stealing a pack of chewing gum and need my best men to find where the suspect has hidden the goods?"

Blake laughed. "Not quite that bad, Mr Stames. I have a guy in Woodrow Wilson Medical Center who wants to meet the head of the FBI, says he has something vitally important to tell him."

"I know the feeling, I'd love to meet him myself. Do you know whether he's one of our usual informers, Dave?"

"No, sir."

"What's his name?"

"Angelo Casefikis." Blake spelled out the name for Stames.

"Any description?" asked Stames.

"No. I only spoke to him on the phone. All he would say is it will be worse for America if the FBI doesn't listen."

"Did he now? Hold on while I check the name. He could be a nut."

Nick Stames pressed a button to connect him with the Duty Officer. "Who's on duty?"

"Paul Fredericks, boss."

"Paul, get out the nut box."

The nut box, as it was affectionately known in the Bureau, was a collection of white index cards containing the names of all the people who liked to call up in the middle of the night and claim that the Martians had landed in their back yards, or that they had discovered a CIA plot to take over the world.

Special Agent Fredericks was back on the line, the nut box in front of him.

"Right, boss. What's his name?"

"Angelo Casefikis," said Stames.

"A crazy Greek," said Fredericks. "You never know with these foreigners."

"Greeks aren't foreigners," snapped Stames. His name, before it was shortened, had been Nick Stamatakis. He never did forgive his father, God rest his soul, for anglicising a magnificent Hellenic surname.

"Sorry , sir. No name like that in the nut box or the informants' file. Did this guy mention any agent's name that he knows?"

"No, he just wanted the head of the FBI."

"Don't we all?"

"No more cracks from you, Paul, or you'll be on complaints duty for more than the statutory week."

Each agent in the Field Office did one week a year on the nut box, answering the phone all night, fending off canny Martians, foiling dastardly CIA coups, and, above all, never embarrassing the Bureau. Every agent dreaded it. Paul Fredericks put the phone down quickly. Two weeks on this job and you could write out one of the little white cards with your own name on it.

"Well, have you formed any view?" said Stames to Blake as he wearily took a cigarette out of his left desk drawer. "How did he sound?"

"Frantic and incoherent. I sent one of my rookies to see him, but he couldn't get anything out of him other than that America ought to listen to what he's got to say. He seemed genuinely frightened. He's got a gunshot wound in his leg and there may be complications. It's infected; apparently he left it for some days before he went to the hospital."

"How did he get himself shot?"

"Don't know yet. We're still trying to locate witnesses, but we haven't come up with anything so far, and Casefikis won't give us the time of day."

"Wants the FBI, does he? Only the best, eh?" said Stames. He regretted the remark the moment he said it; but it was too late. He didn't attempt to cover himself. "Thank you, Lieutenant," he said. "I'll put someone on it immediately and brief you in the morning." Stames put the telephone down. Six o'clock already – why had he turned back? Damn the phone. Grant Nanna would have handled the job just as well and he wouldn't have made that thoughtless remark about wanting the best. There was enough friction between the FBI and the Metropolitan Police without his adding to it. Nick picked up his intercom phone and buzzed the head of the Criminal Section.

"Grant."

"I thought you said you had to be home."

"Come into my office for a moment, will you?"

"Sure, be right there, boss."

Grant Nanna appeared a few seconds later along with his trademark cigar. He had put on his jacket which he only did when he saw Nick in his office.

Nanna's career had a storybook quality. He was born in El Campo, Texas, and received a BA from Baylor. From there, he went on to get a law degree at SMU. As a young agent assigned to the Pittsburgh Field Office, Nanna met his future wife, Betty, an FBI stenographer. They had four sons, all of whom had attended Virginia Polytechnic Institute: two engineers, a doctor, and a dentist. Nanna had been an agent for over thirty years. Twelve more than Nick. In fact, Nick had been a rookie agent under him. Nanna held no grudge, since he was head of the Criminal Section, and greatly respected Nick – as he called him in private.

"What's the problem, boss?"

Stames looked up as Nanna entered the office. He noted that his five-feet-nine, fifty-five-year-old, robust, cigar-chewing Criminal Co-ordinator was certainly not "desirable", as Bureau weight requirements demanded. A man of five-feet-nine was required to keep his weight between a hundred and fifty-four and a hundred and sixty-one pounds. Nanna had always cringed when the quarterly weigh-in of all FBI agents came due. Many times he had been forced to purge his body of excess pounds for that most serious transgression of Bureau rules, especially during the Hoover era, when "desirability" meant lean and mean.

Who cares, thought Stames. Grant's knowledge and experience were worth a dozen slender, young athletic agents who can be found in the Washington Field Office halls every day. As he had done a hundred times before, he told himself he would deal with Nanna's weight problem another day.

Nick repeated the story of the strange Greek in Woodrow Wilson Medical Center as it had been relayed to him by Lieutenant Blake. "I want you to send down two men. Who's on duty tonight?"

"Aspirin, but if you suspect it might be an informer, boss, I certainly can't send him."

"Aspirin" was the nickname of the oldest agent still employed in the WFO. After his early years under Hoover, he played everything by the book, which gave most people a headache. He was due to retire at the end of the year and exasperation was now being replaced by nostalgia.

"No, don't send Aspirin. Send two youngsters."

"How about Calvert and Andrews?"

"Agreed," replied Stames. "If you brief them right away, I can still make it in time for dinner. Call me at home if it turns out to be anything special."

Grant Nanna left the office, and Nick smiled a second flirtatious goodbye to his secretary. She was the only attractive thing in the WFO. Julie looked up and smiled nonchalantly. "I don't mind working for an FBI agent, but there is no way I would ever marry one," she told her little mirror in the top drawer.

Grant Nanna returned to his office and picked up the extension phone to the Criminal Room.

"Send in Calvert and Andrews."

"Yes, sir."

There was a firm knock on the door. Two special agents entered. Barry Calvert was big by anybody's standards, six-feet-six in his stockinged feet and not many people had seen him that way. At thirty-two, he was thought to be one of the most ambitious young men in the Criminal Section. He was wearing a dark green jacket, dark nondescript trousers, and clumpy black leather brogues. His brown hair was cut short and parted neatly on the right. His tear-drop aviator glasses had been his sign of non-conformity. He was always on duty long after the official check-out time of 5:30 and not just because he was fighting his way up the ladder. He loved the job. He didn't love anybody else, so far as his colleagues knew, or at least not on more than a temporary basis. Calvert was a Midwesterner by birth and he had entered the FBI after leaving college with a BA in sociology from Indiana University and then took the fifteen-week course at Quantico, the FBI Academy. From every angle, he was the archetypal FBI man.

By contrast, Mark Andrews had been one of the more unusual FBI entrants. After majoring in history at Yale he finished his education at Yale Law School, and then decided he wanted some adventure for a few years before he joined a law firm. He felt it would be useful to learn about criminals and the police from the inside. He didn't give this as his reason for applying to the Bureau – no one is supposed to regard the Bureau as an academic experiment. In fact, Hoover had regarded it so much as a career that he did not allow agents who left the service ever to return. At six feet Mark Andrews looked small next to Calvert. He had a fresh, open face with clear blue eyes and a mop of curly fair hair long enough to skim his shirt collar. At twenty-eight he was one of the youngest agents in the department. His clothes were always smartly fashionable and sometimes not quite regulation. Nick Stames had once caught him in a red sports jacket and brown trousers and relieved him from duty so that he could return home and dress properly. Never embarrass the Bureau. Mark's charm got him out of a lot of trouble in the Criminal Section, but he had a steadiness of purpose which more than made up for the Ivy League education and manner. He was self-confident, but never pushy or concerned about his own advancement. He didn't let anyone in the Bureau know about his career plan.

Grant Nanna went over the story of the frightened man waiting for them in Woodrow Wilson.

"Black?" queried Calvert.

"No, Greek."

Calvert's surprise showed in his face. Eighty per cent of the inhabitants of Washington were black, and ninety-eight per cent of those arrested on criminal charges were black. One of the reasons the infamous break-in at the Watergate had been suspicious from the beginning to those who knew Washington at all well was the fact that no blacks were involved, though no agents had admitted it.

"Okay, Barry, think you can handle it?"

"Sure, you want a report on your desk by tomorrow morning?"

"No, the boss wants you to contact him direct if it turns out to be anything special, otherwise just file a report overnight." Nanna's telephone rang. "Mr Stames on the radio line from his car for you, sir," said Polly, the night switchboard operator.

"He never lets up, does he?" Grant confided to the two junior agents, covering the mouthpiece of the phone with his palm.

"Hi, boss."

"Grant, did I say that the Greek had a bullet wound in his leg, and it was infected?"

"Yes, boss."

"Right, do me a favour will you? Call Father Gregory at my church, Saint Constantine and Saint Helen, and ask him to go over to the hospital and see him."

"Anything you say."

"And get yourself home, Grant. Aspirin can handle the office tonight."

"I was just going, boss."

The line went dead.

"Okay, you two – on your way." The two special agents headed down the dirty grey corridor and into the service elevator. It looked as always, as if it required a crank to start it. Finally outside on Pennsylvania Avenue, they picked up a Bureau car.

Mark guided the dark blue Ford sedan down Pennsylvania Avenue past the National Archives and the Mellon Gallery. He circled around the lush Capitol grounds and picked up Independence Avenue going towards the south-east section of Washington. As the two agents waited for a light to change at 1st Street, near the Library of Congress, Barry scowled at the rush-hour traffic and looked at his watch.

"Why didn't they put Aspirin on this damn assignment?"

"Who'd send Aspirin to a hospital?" replied Mark.

Mark smiled. The two men had established an immediate rapport when they first met at the FBI Academy at Quantico. On the first day of the training course, every trainee received a telegram confirming his appointment. Each new agent was then asked to check the telegram of the person on his right and his left for authenticity. The manoeuvre was intended to emphasise the need for extreme caution. Mark had glanced at Barry's telegram and handed it back with a grin. " I guess you're legit," he said, "if FBI regulations allow King Kong in the ranks."

"Listen," Calvert had replied, reading Mark's telegram intently. "You may just need King Kong one day, Mr Andrews."

The light turned green, but a car ahead of Mark and Barry in the inside lane wanted to make a left turn on 1st Street. For the moment, the two impatient FBI men were trapped in a line of traffic.

"What do you imagine this guy could tell us?"

"I hope he has something on the downtown bank job," replied Barry. "I'm still the case agent, and I still don't have any leads after three weeks. Stames is beginning to get uptight about it."

"No, can't be that, not with a bullet in his leg. He's more likely to be another candidate for the nut box. Wife probably shot him for not being home on time for his stuffed vine leaves."

"You know, the boss would only send a priest to a fellow Greek. You and I could wallow in hell as far as he's concerned."

They both laughed. They knew if either of them were to land in trouble, Nick Stames would move the Washington Monument stone by stone if he thought it would help. As the car continued down Independence Avenue into the heart of south-east Washington, the traffic gradually diminished. A few minutes later, they passed 19th Street and the DC Armory and reached Woodrow Wilson Medical Center. They found the visitors' parking lot and Calvert double-checked the lock on every door. Nothing is more embarrassing for an agent than to have his car stolen and then for the Metropolitan Police to call and ask if he could come and collect it. It was the quickest way to a month on the nut box.

The entrance to the hospital was old and dingy, and the corridors grey and bleak. The girl on night duty at the reception desk told them that Casefikis was on the fourth floor, in Room 4308. Both agents were surprised by the lack of security. They didn't have to show their credentials, and they were allowed to wander around the building as if they were a couple of interns. No one gave them a second look. Perhaps, as agents, they had become too security conscious.

The elevator took them gradually, grudgingly, to the fourth floor. A man on crutches and a woman in a wheelchair shared the elevator, chatting to one another as though they had a lot of time to spare, oblivious to the slowness of the elevator. When they arrived at the fourth floor, Calvert walked over to a nurse and asked for the doctor on duty.

"I think Dr Dexter has gone off duty, but I'll check," the staff nurse said and bustled away. She didn't get a visit from the FBI every day and the shorter one with the clear blue eyes was so good-looking. The nurse and the doctor returned together down the corridor. Dr Dexter came as a surprise to both Calvert and Andrews. They introduced themselves. It must have been the legs, Mark decided. The last time he had seen legs like that was when the Yale Cinema Club had show a re-run of Anne Bancroft in *The Graduate*. It was the first time he had ever really looked at a woman's legs, and he hadn't stopped looking since.

"Elizabeth Dexter, MD" was stamped in black on a piece of red plastic that adorned her starched white coat. Underneath it, Mark could see a red silk shirt and a stylish skirt of black crepe that fell below her knees. Dr Dexter was of medium height and slender to the point of fragility. She wore no make-up, so far as Mark could tell; certainly her clear skin and dark eyes were in no need of any help. This trip was turning out to be worthwhile, after all. Barry, on the other hand, showed no interest whatever in the pretty doctor and asked to see the file on Casefikis. Mark thought quickly for an opening gambit.

"Are you related to Senator Dexter?" he asked, slightly emphasising the word Senator.

"Yes, he's my father," she said flatly, obviously used to the question and rather bored by it – and by those who imagined it was important.

"I heard his lecture in my final year at Yale Law," said Mark, forging ahead, realising he was now showing off, but he realised that Calvert would finish that damn report in a matter of moments.

"Oh, were you at Yale, too?" she asked. "When did you graduate?"

"Three years ago, Law School," replied Mark.

"We might even have met. I left Yale Med last year."

"If I had met you before, Dr Dexter, I would not have forgotten."

"When you two Ivy Leaguers have finished swapping life histories," Barry Calvert interrupted, "this Midwesterner would like to get on with his job."

Yes, thought Mark, Barry will end up as Director one day.

"What can you tell us about this man, Dr Dexter?" asked Calvert.

"Very little, I'm afraid," the doctor replied, taking back the file on Casefikis. "He came in of his own volition and reported a gun wound. The wound was septic and looked as if it had been exposed for about a week; I wish he had come in earlier. I removed the bullet this morning. As you know, Mr Calvert, it is our duty to inform the police immediately when a patient comes in with a gunshot wound, and so we phoned your boys at the Metropolitan Police."

"Not our boys," corrected Mark.

"I'm sorry," replied Dr Dexter rather formally. "To a doctor, a policeman is a policeman."

"And to a policeman, an MD is an MD, but you also have specialties – orthopaedics, gynaecology, neurology – don't you? You don't mean to tell me I look like one of those flatfoots from the Met Police?"

Dr Dexter was not to be beguiled into a flattering response. She opened the manilla folder. "All we know is that he is Greek by origin and his name is Angelo Casefikis. He has never been registered in this hospital before. He gave his age as thirty-eight . . . Not a lot to go on, I'm afraid."

"Fine, it's as much as we usually get. Thank you, Dr Dexter," said Calvert. "Can we see him now?"

"Of course. Please follow me." Elizabeth Dexter turned and led them down the corridor.

The two men followed her, Barry looking for the door marked 4308, Mark looking at her legs. When they arrived, they peered through the small window and saw two men in the room, Angelo Casefikis and a cheerful-looking black, who was staring at a television set which emitted no sound. Calvert turned to Dr Dexter.

"Would it be possible to see him alone, Dr Dexter?"

"Why?" she asked.

"We don't know what he's going to tell us, and he may not wish to be overheard."

"Well, don't worry yourself," said Dr Dexter, and laughed. "My favourite mailman, Benjamin Reynolds, who is in the next bed is as deaf as a post, and until we operate on him next week, he won't be able to hear Gabriel's horn on the Day of Judgement, let alone a state secret."

Calvert smiled for the first time. "He'd make a hell of a witness."

The doctor ushered Calvert and Andrews into the room, then turned and left them. *See you soon, lovely lady,* Mark promised himself. Calvert looked at Benjamin Reynolds suspiciously, but the black mailman merely gave him a big happy smile, waved, and continued to watch the soundless *$25,000 Pyramid*; nonetheless, Barry Calvert stood on that side of the bed and blocked his view of Casefikis in case he could lip-read. Barry thought of everything.

"Mr Casefikis?"

"Yes."

Casefikis was a grey, sick-looking individual of medium build, with a prominent nose, bushy eyebrows, and an anxious expression that never left his face. His hair was thick, dark and unkempt. His hands seemed particularly large on the white bedspread, and the veins stood out prominently. His face was darkened by several days of unshaven beard. One leg was heavily bandaged and rested on the cover of the bed. His eyes darted nervously from one man to the other.

"I am Special Agent Calvert and this is Special Agent Andrews. We are officers with the Federal Bureau of Investigation. We understand you wanted to see us."

Both men withdrew their FBI credentials from their right inside pockets, and displayed them to Casefikis while holding the credentials in their left hands. Even such a seemingly insignificant manoeuvre was carefully taught to all new FBI agents so that their "strong hand" would be free to withdraw and fire when necessary.

Casefikis studied their credentials with a puzzled frown, pressing his tongue over his lips, obviously not knowing what to look for. The agent's signature must pass partly over the seal of the Department of Justice to insure authenticity. He looked at Mark's card number, 3302, and his badge number, 1721. He didn't speak, as if wondering where to start, or perhaps whether to change his mind and say nothing at all. He stared at Mark, clearly the more sympathetic, and began his tale.

"I never been in any trouble with police before," he said. "Not with any of police."

Neither agent smiled or spoke.

"But I in big mess now and, by God, I need help."

Calvert stepped in. "Why do you need our help?"

"I am illegal immigrant and so is wife. We both Greek nationals, we came in Baltimore on ship and we been working here two years. We've nothing to go back to."

It came out in spurts and dashes.

"I have information to trade if we not deported."

"We can't make that sort —" began Mark.

Barry touched Mark's arm. "If it's important and you are able to help us solve a crime, we will speak to the Immigration authorities. We can promise no more than that."

Mark mused; with six million illegal immigrants in the United States, another couple was not going to sink the boat.

Casefikis looked desperate. "I needed job, I needed money, you understand?"

Both men understood. They faced the same problem a dozen times a week behind a dozen different faces.

"When I offered this job as waiter in restaurant, my wife very pleased. On second week I was given special job to serve lunch in a hotel room for big man. The only trouble that the man wanted waiter who not speak English. My English very bad so bossman tell me I could go, keep my mouth shut, speak only Greek. For twenty dollars I say yes. We go in back of van to hotel – I think in Georgetown. When we arrive I sent to kitchen, join staff in basement. I dress and start taking food to private dining-room. There five–six men and I heard big man say I no speak English. So they talk on. I don't listen. Very last cup of coffee, when start talking about President Kane, I like Kane, I listen. I heard say, 'We have to blow her away.' Another man say: 'The best day would still be 10 March, the way we planned it.' And then I heard: 'I agree with Senator, let's get rid of the bitch.' Someone was staring at me, so I left room. When I downstairs washing up, one man came in and shouted, 'Hey, you, catch this.' I looked around put arms up. All at once he start come for me. I run for door and down street. He shoot gun at me, I feel bit pain in leg but I able to get away because he older, big and slower than me. I hear him shout but I knew he couldn't catch me. I scared. I get home pretty damn quick, and wife and I move out that night and hide out of town with friend from Greece. Hoped all would be okay, but my leg got bad after few days so Ariana made me come to hospital and call for you because my friend tell they come around to my place look for me because if they find me they kill me." He stopped, breathing deeply, his unshaven face covered in sweat, and looked at the two men imploringly.

"What's your full name?" said Calvert, sounding about as excited as he would if he were issuing a traffic ticket.

"Angelo Mexis Casefikis."

Calvert made him spell it in full.

"Where do you live?"

"Now at Blue Ridge Manor Apartments, 11501 Elkin Street, Wheaton. Home of my friend, good man, please don't give trouble."

"When did this incident take place?"

"Last Thursday," Casefikis said instantly.

Calvert checked the date. "24 February?"

The Greek shrugged. "Last Thursday," he repeated.

"Where is the restaurant you were working in?"

"A few streets from me. It called Golden Duck."

Calvert continued taking notes. "And where was this hotel you were taken to?"

"Don't know, in Georgetown. Maybe could take you there when out of hospital."

"Now, Mr Casefikis, please be careful about this. Was there anyone else working at this luncheon who might have overheard the conversation in that room?"

"No, sir. I only waiter attend in room."

"Have you told anyone what you overheard? Your wife? The friend whose house you're staying at? Anyone?"

"No, sir. Only you. No tell wife what I hear. No tell no one, too scared."

Calvert continued to interview, asking for descriptions of the other men in the room and making the Greek repeat everything to see if the story remained the same. It did. Mark looked on silently.

"Okay, Mr Casefikis, that's all we can do for this evening. We'll return in the morning and have you sign a written statement."

"But they going to kill me. They going to kill me."

"No need to worry, Mr Casefikis. We'll put a police guard on your room as soon as possible; no one is going to kill you."

Casefikis dropped his eyes, not reassured.

"We'll see you again in the morning," said Calvert, closing his notebook. "You just get some rest. Good night, Mr Casefikis."

Calvert glanced back at a happy Benjamin, still deeply absorbed in *$25,000 Pyramid* with no words, just money. He waved again at them and smiled, showing all three of his teeth, two black and one gold. Calvert and Andrews returned to the corridor.

"I don't believe a word of it," Barry said immediately. "With his English, he could easily have got hold of the wrong end of the stick. It was probably quite innocent. People curse the President all the time. My father does, but that doesn't mean he would kill her."

"Maybe, but what about the gunshot wound? That's for real," said Mark.

"I know. I guess that's the one thing that worries me," Barry said. "It could just be a cover for something completely different. I think I'll speak to the boss to be on the safe side."

Calvert headed for the pay phone by the side of the elevator and took out two quarters. All agents carry a pocketful of quarters; there are no special telephone privileges for members of the Bureau.

"Well, was he hoping to rob Fort Knox?" Elizabeth Dexter's voice startled Mark, although he had half-expected her to return. She was obviously on her way home: the white coat had been replaced by a red jacket.

"Not exactly," replied Mark. "We'll have to come around tomorrow morning to tidy things up; probably get him to sign a written statement and take his fingerprints, then we'll pick up the gold."

"Fine," she said. "Dr Delgado will be on duty tomorrow." She smiled sweetly. "You'll like her, too."

"Is this hospital entirely staffed by beautiful lady doctors?" said Mark. "How does one get to stay the night?"

"Well," she said, "the flu is the fashionable disease this month. Even President Kane has had it."

Calvert looked around sharply at the mention of the President's name. Elizabeth Dexter glanced at her watch.

"I've just completed two hours' unpaid overtime," she said. "If you don't have any more questions, Mr Andrews, I ought to get home now." She smiled and turned to go, her heels tapping sharply against the tiled floor.

"Just one more question, Dr Dexter," said Mark, following her around the corner beyond the range of Barry Calvert's disapproving eyes and ears. "What would you say to having dinner with me later tonight?"

"What would I say?" she said teasingly. "Let me see, I think I'd accept gracefully and not too eagerly. It might be interesting to find out what G-men are really like."

"We bite," said Mark. They smiled at each other. "Okay, it's 7:15 now. If you're willing to take a chance on it, I could probably pick you up by 8:30."

Elizabeth jotted her address and phone number on a page of his diary.

"So you're a left-hander, are you, Liz?"

The dark eyes flashed momentarily up to meet his. "Only my lovers call me Liz," she said, and was gone.

"It's Calvert, boss. I can't make my mind up about this one. I don't know if he's a jerk or for real so I'd like to run it past you."

"Fine, Barry. Shoot."

"Well, it could be serious, or just a hoax. He may even be nothing more than a small-time thief trying to get off the hook for something bigger. But I can't be sure. And if every word he said turned out to be true, I figured you ought to know immediately." Barry relayed the salient parts of the interview without mentioning the Senator, stressing that there was an added factor he did not want to discuss over the phone.

"What are you trying to do, get me in the divorce courts – I suppose I'll have to come back to the office," said Nick Stames, avoiding his wife's expression of annoyance. "Okay, okay. Thank God I got to eat at least some of the moussaka. I'll see you in thirty minutes, Barry."

"Right, boss."

Calvert depressed the telephone cradle with his hand momentarily and then dialled the Metropolitan Police. Two more quarters, leaving sixteen in his pockets. He often thought the quickest way to check out an FBI agent would be to make him turn his pockets inside out; if he produced twenty quarters, he was a genuine member of the Bureau.

"Lieutenant Blake is on the front desk. I'll put you right through."

"Lieutenant Blake."

"Special Agent Calvert. We've seen your Greek and we'd like you to put a guard on his room. He's scared to hell about something so we don't want to take any chances."

"He's not my Greek, damn it," said Blake. "Can't you use one of your own fancy guys?"

"There's no one we can spare at the moment, Lieutenant."

"I'm not exactly overstaffed myself, for God's sake. What do you think we're running, the Shoreham Hotel? Oh hell, I'll do what I can. But they won't be able to get there for a couple of hours."

"Fine. Thanks for your help, Lieutenant. I'll brief my office." Barry replaced the receiver.

Mark Andrews and Barry Calvert waited for the elevator, which was just as slow and reluctant to take them down as it had been to take them up. Neither of them spoke until they were inside the dark blue Ford.

"Stames is coming back to hear the story," said Calvert. "I can't imagine he'll want to take it any further, but we'd better keep him informed. Then maybe we can call it a day."

Mark glanced at his watch; another hour and forty-five minutes' overtime, technically the maximum allowed an agent on any one day.

"I hope so," said Mark. "I just got myself a date."

"Anyone we know?"

"The beautiful Dr Dexter."

Barry raised his eyebrows. "Don't let the boss know. If he thought you picked up someone while you were on duty, he'd send you for a spell in the salt mines in Butte, Montana."

"I didn't realise they had salt mines in Butte, Montana."

"Only FBI agents who really screw it up know there are salt mines in Butte."

Mark drove back to downtown Washington while Barry wrote up his report of the interview. It was 7:40 by the time they had returned to the Old Post Office Building and Mark found the parking lot almost empty. By this time at night most civilised people were at home doing civilised things, like eating moussaka. Stames's car was already there. Goddamn him. They took the elevator to the fifth floor and went into Stames's reception room. It looked empty without Julie. Calvert knocked quietly on the chief's door and the two agents walked in. Stames looked up. He had already found a hundred and one things to do since he'd been back, almost as if he had forgotten that he had specifically come back to see them.

"Right, Barry. Let's have it from the top, slowly and accurately."

Calvert recounted exactly what had happened from the moment they had arrived at Woodrow Wilson to the moment he had asked the Metropolitan Police to put a guard on the room to protect the Greek. Mark was impressed by Barry's total recall. At no point had he exaggerated or revealed any personal prejudice. Stames lowered his head for a few moments and then suddenly turned to Mark.

"Do you want to add anything?" he asked.

"Not really, sir. It was all a bit melodramatic. Although he didn't come over as a liar, he was certainly frightened. Also there's no trace of him in any of our files. I radioed the Night Super for a name check. Negative on Casefikis."

Nick picked up the phone and asked to be put through to Bureau Headquarters. "Give me the National Computer Information Center, Polly." He was put straight through. A young woman answered the phone.

"Stames, Washington Field Office. Would you please have the

following suspect checked out on the computer immediately? – Angelo Casefikis: Caucasian; male; Greek ancestry; height, five feet nine inches; weight, about a hundred and sixty-five pounds; hair, dark brown; eyes, brown; age; thirty-eight; no distinguishing marks or scars known; no identifying numbers known." He was reading from the report Calvert had placed in front of him. He waited silently.

"If his story is true," Mark said, "we should have no listing for him at all."

"If it's true," said Calvert.

Stames continued to wait. The days of waiting to find out who was in the FBI files and who wasn't had long gone. The girl came back on the line.

"We have nothing on a Casefikis, Angelo. We don't even have a Casefikis. The best the computer can offer is a Casegikis who was born in 1901. Sorry I can't help, Mr Stames."

"Thanks very much." Stames put the phone down. "Okay, boys, for the moment let's give Casefikis the benefit of the doubt. Let's assume he is telling the truth and that this is a serious investigation. We have no trace of him in any of our files, so we'd better start believing his story until it's disproved; he just might be on to something, and if he is, then it goes way above me. Tomorrow morning, Barry, I want you back at the hospital with a fingerprint expert; take his prints in case he is giving a false name, put them through the identification computer right away and make sure you get a full written statement, signed. Then check the Met files for any shooting incidents on 24 February he could have been involved in. As soon as we can get him out, I want him in an ambulance showing us where that luncheon took place. Push the hospital into agreeing to that tomorrow morning, if possible. To date, he's not under arrest or wanted for any crime we know about, so don't go too far, not that he strikes me as a man who would know much about his rights.

"Mark," Stames said, turning his head, "I want you to go back to the hospital immediately and make sure the Met are there. If not, stay with Casefikis until they do arrive. In the morning, go round to the Golden Duck and check him out. I'm going to make a provisional appointment for us to see the Director tomorrow morning, at 10:00 am, which will give you enough time to report back to me. And if, when we check the fingerprints through the identification computer, nothing comes up at all, and the hotel and the restaurant exist, we may be in a whole heap of trouble. If that's the case, I'm not taking it one inch further without the Director knowing. For the moment, I want nothing in writing. Don't hand in your official memorandum until tomorrow morning. Above all, don't mention that a senator could be involved to anybody – and that includes Grant Nanna. It's possible tomorrow, after we have seen the Director, that we will do no more than make a full report and hand the whole thing over to the Secret Service. Don't forget the clear division of responsibility – the Secret Service guards the President, we cover federal crime. If a senator is involved, it's us; if the President's involved, it's them. We'll let the Director decide the finer points – I'm not getting involved in Capitol Hill, that's the Director's baby, and with only seven days to play with, we don't have time to sit and discuss the academic niceties."

Stames picked up the red phone which put him straight through to the Director's office.

"Nick Stames, WFO."

"Good evening," said a low, quiet voice. Mrs McGregor, a dedicated servant of the Director of the Federal Bureau of Investigation, was still on duty. It was said that even Hoover had been slightly frightened of her.

"Mrs McGregor, I'd like to make a provisional apointment for myself and Special Agents Calvert and Andrews to see the Director for fifteen minutes, if that's possible. Anytime between 09:00 am and 11:00 am tomorrow. It's likely that after further investigation tonight and early tomorrow, I won't need to bother him."

Mrs McGregor consulted the Director's desk diary. "The Director is going to a meeting of police chiefs at eleven but he is expected in the office at 8:30 and he has nothing marked in his diary before eleven. I'll pencil you in for 10:30, Mr Stames. Do you want me to tell the Director what the subject of your discussion will be?"

"I'd prefer not to."

Mrs McGregor never pressed or asked a second question. She knew if Stames called, it was important. He saw the Director ten times a year on a social basis, but only three or four times a year on a professional basis, and he was not in the habit of wasting the Director's time.

"Thank you, Mr Stames. 10:30 tomorrow morning, unless you cancel beforehand."

Nick put the phone down and looked at his two men.

"Okay, we're fixed to see the Director at 10:30. Barry, why don't you give me a lift home, then you can take yourself off afterwards, and pick me up again first thing in the morning. That'll give us another chance to go over the details again." Barry nodded. "Mark, you get straight back to the hospital."

Mark had allowed his mind to slip away to visualise Elizabeth Dexter walking down the corridor of Woodrow Wilson towards him, red silk collar over the white medical coat, black skirt swinging. He was doing this with his eyes open and the result was quite pleasant. He smiled.

"Andrews, what the hell is so amusing about a reported threat on the President's life?" Stames demanded.

"Sorry, sir. You just shot my social life down in flames. Would it be okay if I use my own car? I was hoping to go directly from the hospital to dinner."

"Yes, that's fine. We'll use the duty car and see you first thing in the morning. Get your tail in gear, Mark, and hope the Met makes it before breakfast." Mark looked at his watch. "Christ, it's already 8:00 pm."

Mark left the office slightly annoyed. Even if the Met were there when he arrived, he would still be late for Elizabeth Dexter. Still, he could always call her from the hospital.

"Like a plate of warmed-up moussaka, Barry, and a bottle of retsina?"

"It was more than I was expecting, boss."

The two men left the office. Stames mentally checked off the items on his nightly routine.

"Barry, will you double-check that Aspirin is on duty, as you go out, and tell him we won't be back again tonight."

Calvert made a detour to the Criminal Room and delivered the message to Aspirin. He was doing the crossword from *The Washington Star*. He had finished three clues; it was going to be a long night. Barry caught up with Nick Stames as he stepped into the blue Ford.

"Yes, boss, he's working away."

They looked at each other, a night of headaches. Barry got in the driver's seat, slid it back as far as it would go, and adjusted the seat belt. They moved quietly up Constitution Avenue, then past the White House on to the E Street Expressway, and on towards Memorial Bridge.

"If Casefikis is on to something, we've got one hell of a week ahead of us," said Nick Stames. "Did he seem sure of the date for the assassination attempt?"

"When I questioned him a second time about the details, he repeated 10 March, in Washington."

"Hum-uh, seven days, not very long. Wonder what the Director will make of it," said Stames.

"Hand it over to the Secret Police, if he's got any sense," Barry said.

"Ah, let's forget it for the moment. Let's concentrate on warmed-over moussaka and deal with tomorrow when tomorrow comes."

The car came to a halt at a traffic light, just beyond the White House, where a bearded, long-haired, dirty youth, who had been picketing the home of the President, stood with a large poster advising the world: BEWARE THE END IS NIGH. Stames glanced at it and nodded to Barry.

"That's all we need tonight."

They passed under Virginia Avenue on the Expressway and sped across Memorial Bridge. A black 3·5 Lincoln passed them at about seventy miles an hour.

"Bet the Met pick him up," said Stames.

"Probably late for Dulles Airport," replied Barry.

The traffic was light, the rush-hour well behind them and when they turned on to George Washington Parkway they managed to stay in top gear. The Parkway, which follows the Potomac along the wooded Virginia shore, was dark and winding. Barry's reflexes were as fast as any man's in the service and Stames, although older, saw exactly what happened at the same time. A Buick, large and black, started to overtake them on their left. Calvert glanced towards it and when he looked forward again an instant later, another car, a black Lincoln, had swung in front of them on the wrong side of the highway. He thought he heard a rifle shot. Barry wrenched the wheel towards the centre of the road but it didn't respond. Both cars hit him at once, but he still managed to take one of them with him down the rocky slope. They gathered speed until they hit the surface of the river with a thud. Nick thought as he struggled in vain to open the door that the sinking seemed grotesquely slow, but inevitable.

The black Buick continued down the highway as if nothing had happened; past a car skidding to a halt, carrying a young couple, two terrified witnesses to the accident. They leapt out of their car and ran to the edge of the slope. There was nothing they could do but watch helplessly for the few seconds it took the blue Ford sedan and the Lincoln to sink out of sight.

"Jee-sus, did you see what happened ahead?" said the young man.

"Not really. I just saw the two cars go over the top. What do we do now, Jim?"

"Get the police fast."

Man and wife ran back to their car.

Thursday evening, 3 March. 8:15 pm

"Hello, Liz."

There was a moment's pause at the other end of the phone.

"Hello, G-man. Aren't you getting a little ahead of yourself?"

"Only wishful thinking. Listen, Elizabeth, I've had to come back to the hospital and keep an eye on your Mr Casefikis until the police arrive. It's just possible that he could be in some danger, so we're having to put a guard on him which means I'm bound to be late for our date. Do you mind waiting?"

"No, I won't starve. I always have lunch with my father on

Thursdays, and he's a big eater."

"That's good. Because I think you need to be fed. You look as though you might be hard to find in the dark. I'm still trying to get the flu, incidentally."

She laughed warmly. "See you later."

Mark put the telephone back on the hook and walked over to the elevator, and pressed the arrow on the Up-button.

He only hoped the Met policeman had arrived and was already on duty. Christ. How long was the elevator going to take to return to the ground floor? Patients must have died just waiting for it. Eventually the doors slid open and a burly Greek Orthodox priest hurried out and past him. He could have sworn it was a Greek Orthodox priest, from the high dark hat and long trailing veil and the Orthodox Cross around his neck, although something about the priest struck Mark as strange, but he couldn't put his finger on it. He stood, puzzling for a moment, staring at his retreating back and only just managing to jump into the elevator before the doors closed. He pressed the fourth-floor button several times. Come on, come on. Get going, you bastard, but it had no ears for Mark, and proceeded upward at the same stately pace as it had earlier in the afternoon. It cared nothing for his date with Elizabeth Dexter. The door opened slowly, and he went through the widening gap sideways and ran down the corridor to Room 4308 but there was no sign of any policeman. In fact, the corridor was deserted. It looked as if he were going to be stuck there for some time. He peered through the little window in the door at the two men, asleep in their beds, the voiceless television set was still on giving out a square of light. Mark left to look for the staff nurse and eventually found her tucked away in the head nurse's office enjoying a cup of coffee. She was pleased to see that it was the better-looking of the two FBI men who had returned.

"Has anyone come from the Metropolitan Police to keep an eye on Room 4308?"

"No, no one's been near the place tonight. Silent as the grave. Were you expecting someone?"

"Yes, damn it. Guess I'll have to wait. Do you think I could take a chair? I'm going to have to stick around till an officer from the Metropolitan Police comes. I hope I won't be in your way."

"You won't be in my way. You can stay as long as you like. I'll see if I can find you a nice comfortable chair." She put her mug down. "Would you like some coffee?"

"I certainly would." Mark looked at her more carefully. It might be an evening with the nurse rather than the doctor. Mark decided he had better go back and check the room first, reassure Casefikis, if he were still awake, and then call the Met and ask where the hell their man was. He walked slowly to the door a second time; he felt no need to hurry now. He opened the door quietly. It was pitch black except for the light from the TV, and his eyes were not quite focused. He glanced at the two of them in bed. They were quite still. He wouldn't have bothered to look any further if it hadn't been for the dripping.

Drip, drip, drip.

It sounded like tap water but he couldn't remember a tap.

Drip, drip.

He moved quietly to the bedside of Angelo Casefikis, and glanced down.

Drip, drip.

Warm fresh blood was flowing over the bottom sheet, trickling from Casefikis's mouth, his dark eyes bulged from their sockets, his tongue was hanging loose and swollen. His throat had been cut, ear to ear, just below the chin line. The blood was starting to make a pool on the floor. Mark was standing in it. He felt his legs sink, and he was barely able to grip the side of the bed and stop himself falling. He lurched over towards the deaf man. Mark's eyes were now focused, and he retched loudly. The postman's head was hanging loose from the rest of his body; only the colour of his skin showed that they were once connected. Mark managed to scramble out of the door and get to the pay phone, his heartbeat thudding madly in his ears. He could feel his shirt clinging to his body. His hands were covered wth blood. He fumbled ineffectually for a couple of quarters. He dialled Homicide and gave the bare outline of what had happened. This time they wouldn't be casual about sending someone. The nurse on duty returned with a cup of coffee.

"Are you okay? You look a bit pale," she said, and then she saw his hands and screamed.

"Don't go into Room 4308 whatever you do. Don't let anyone into that room unless I say so. Send me a doctor immediately."

The nurse thrust the cup of coffee at him, forcing him to take it, and ran down the corridor. Mark made himself go back into Room 4308, although his presence was irrelevant. There was nothing he could do except wait. He switched on the lights and went over to the bathroom; he tried to remove the worst of the blood and vomit from himself and his clothes. Mark heard the swinging door and rushed back into the room. Another young, white-coated female doctor . . . "Alicia Delgado, MD" said her plastic label.

"Don't touch anything," said Mark.

Dr Delgado stared at him and then the bodies, and groaned.

"Don't touch anything," repeated Mark, "until Homicide arrive; they will be here shortly."

"Who are you?" she asked.

"Special Agent Mark Andrews, FBI." He instinctively took out his wallet and showed his credentials.

"Do we just stand here staring at each other or are you going to allow me to do something about this mess?"

"Nothing until Homicide has completed their investigation and given clearance. Let's get out of here." He passed her and pushed the door with his shoulder, not touching anything.

They were back in the corridor.

Mark instructed Dr Delgado to wait outside the door and to allow no one else inside while he phoned the Metropolitan Police again.

She nodded reluctantly.

He went over to the pay phone, two more quarters; he dialled the Metropolitan Police and asked for Lieutenant Blake.

"Lieutenant Blake went home about an hour ago. Can I help you?"

"When had you been planning to send someone over to guard Room 4308 at Woodrow Wilson Medical Center?"

"Who's speaking?"

"Andrews, FBI, Washington Field Office." Mark repeated the details of the double murder.

"Well, our man should be with you now. He left the office over half an hour ago. I'll inform Homicide immediately."

"I've already done that," snapped Mark.

He put the phone down and collapsed into a nearby chair. The corridor was now full of white coats. Two gurneys were being wheeled up to Room 4308. They were all waiting. What was the right thing to do?

Two more quarters, he dialled Nick Stames's home. The phone seemed to ring for a long time. Why didn't he answer? Eventually a female voice came on.

Mustn't show panic, he thought, holding on to the phone box. "Good evening, Mrs Stames. It's Mark Andrews. Can I speak to your husband?" An even tone, no sign of stress.

"I'm afraid Nick is not home, Mark. He went back to the office about two hours ago. Funny, he said he was going to see you and Barry Calvert."

"Yes, we saw him, but he left the office to go back home about forty minutes ago."

"Well, he hasn't arrived yet. He only managed to finish the first course of his dinner and said he would come straight back. Maybe he returned to the office. Why don't you try him there?"

"Yes, of course. Sorry to have bothered you." Mark hung up, looked over to check that no one had gone into Room 4308. He put two more quarters in and phoned the office. Polly was on duty.

"Mark Andrews. Put me through to Mr Stames, quickly, please."

"Mr Stames and Special Agent Calvert left about forty-five minutes ago – on their way home, I think, Mr Andrews."

"That can't be right. It can't be right."

"Yes, they did leave, sir. I saw them go."

"Could you double-check?"

"If you say so, Mr Andrews."

Mark waited, it seemed to him, for an interminable time. What should he be doing? He was only one man, where was everyone else? What was he supposed to do? Christ, nothing in his training covered this – the FBI are meant to arrive twenty-four hours after a crime, not during it.

"There's no answer, Mr Andrews."

"Thanks, Polly."

Mark looked desperately at the ceiling for inspiration. He had been briefed not to tell anybody about the earlier events of the evening, not to say a word whatever the circumstances until after Stames's meeting with the Director. He must find Stames; he must find Calvert. He must find somebody he could talk to. Two more quarters. He tried Barry Calvert. The phone rang and rang. No reply from the bachelor apartment. Same two quarters. He called Norma Stames again. "Mrs Stames, Mark Andrews. Sorry to trouble you again. The moment your husband and Mr Calvert arrive, please have them call me at Woodrow Wilson."

"Yes, I'll tell Nick as soon as he comes in. They probably stopped off on the way."

"Yes, of course, I hadn't thought of that. Maybe the best thing will be for me to go back downtown as soon as the relief arrives. So perhaps they could contact me there. Thank you, Mrs Stames." He hung up the receiver.

As he put the phone down Mark saw the Met policeman jauntily walking towards him down the middle of the now crowded corridor, an Ed McBain novel under his arm. Mark thought of bawling him out for his late arrival, but what was the point. No use crying over spilt blood he thought, morbidly, and began to feel sick again. He took the young officer aside, and briefed him on the killings, giving no details of why the two men were important, only of what had happened. He asked him to inform his chief and added that the Homicide Squad were on their way, again adding no details. The policeman called his own duty officer, and reported all he had been told, matter-of-factly. The Washington Metropolitan Police handled over six hundred murders a year.

The medical personnel were all waiting impatiently; it was going to be a long wait. Professional bustle seemed to have replaced the early panic. Mark still wasn't sure where to turn, what to do. Where was Stames? Where was Calvert? Where the hell was anybody?

He went over to the policeman again, who was explaining in detail why no one must enter the room . . . they were not convinced but waited; Mark told him he was leaving for the Field Office. He still gave him no clue why Casefikis had been important. The Metropolitan policeman felt he had things under control. Homicide would be there at any moment. He told Mark they'd want to talk to him later that night. Mark nodded and left him.

When he arrived back at his car, he took the flashing red light out of the side compartment and fixed it to the roof, placing the switch into its special slot. He was going to get back to the office, at top speed, to people he knew, to reality, to men who would make some sense out of his nightmare.

Mark flicked on the car radio. "WFO 180 in service. Please try and locate Mr Stames and Mr Calvert. Urgent. I am returning to Field Office immediately."

"Yes, Mr Andrews."

"WFO out of service."

Twelve minutes later, he arrived at the Washington Field Office and parked his car. He ran to the elevator. The operator took him up. He rushed out.

"Aspirin, Aspirin. Who the hell's on duty tonight?"

"I'm the only one on tonight, boy. I'm here on my own," said Aspirin, looking over his glasses, rather bored. "What's the matter?"

"Where's Stames? Where's Calvert?" Mark demanded.

"They went home just over an hour ago."

Oh hell, what should he do now? Aspirin was not a man to confide in, but he was the only person Mark could seek any advice from. And although Stames had carefully instructed him not to speak to anyone about the details until they had seen the Director, this was an emergency. He wouldn't give away any of the details, he would just find out what a Hoover man would have done.

"I have to find Stames and Calvert, wherever they are. Any suggestions?"

"Well, first of all, have you tried the car radio stations?" asked Aspirin.

"I asked Polly to check. I'll try her again."

Mark picked up the nearest phone. "Polly, did you locate Mr Stames or Mr Calvert on the car radio?"

"Still trying, sir."

He seemed to wait endlessly, endlessly; and nothing happened. "What's going on, Polly, what's going on?"

"I'm trying as hard as I can, sir. All I can get is a buzzing sound."

"Try One, Two, Three, or Four. Doesn't matter what you try. Try every station."

"Yes, sir. I can only do one at a time. There are four stations and I can only do one at a time."

Mark realised he was panicking. It was time to sit down and think things through. The end of the world hadn't come – or had it?

"They're not on One, sir. Not on Two. Why would they be on Three or Four at this time of night? They're only on their way home."

"I don't care where they're going. Just find them. Try again."

"Okay, okay." She tried Three. She tried Four. She had to have authorisation to break the code for Five and Six . Mark looked at Aspirin. The duty officer was authorised to break the code.

"This is an emergency – I swear to you it's an emergency."

Aspirin told Polly to try Five and Six. Five and Six are Federal Communications Commission to the FBI. They are known by the initial KGB: it always amused FBI men to have KGB as their network call code. But at that moment it didn't seem particularly funny. There was no reply to be had on KGB 5. Then KGB 6 was raised; likewise nothing. Now what, dear God, now what? Where did he turn next? Aspirin looked at him inquiringly, not really wanting to get involved.

"Always remember, son, C-Y-A. That's the ticket. C-Y-A."

"Covering your ass will not help me to locate Mr Stames," said Mark, forcing himself to speak calmly. "It doesn't matter, Aspirin, you get back to your crossword puzzle."

Mark left him and went into the men's room, cupped his hands under the tap and washed his mouth out; he still smelled of vomit and blood. He cleaned up as best he could. He returned to the Criminal Room, sat down, and counted to ten very slowly. He had to make up his mind what to do, and then to carry it out, come what may. Something had probably happened to Stames and Calvert, he knew something had happened to the black postman and the Greek. Perhaps he should try and get in touch with the Director, although it was an extreme course. A man of Mark's rank, two years out of training, didn't just pick up a phone and call the Director. In any case he could still keep Stames's appointment with the Director at 10:30 the next morning. 10:30 the next morning. That was half a day away. More than twelve hours of not knowing what to do. Nursing a secret that he had been told not to discuss with anyone. Holding information he couldn't impart to anybody else.

The phone rang and he heard Polly's voice. He prayed it would be Stames, but his prayer was not answered.

"Hey, Mr Andrews, are you still there? I've got Homicide on the line. Captain Hogan wants to talk to you."

"Andrews?"

"Yes, Captain."

"What can you tell me?"

Mark reported truthfully that Casefikis was an illegal immigrant who had delayed seeking treatment for his leg, and untruthfully that he alleged he had been shot by a crook who had subjected him to blackmail, threatening exposure of his illegal entry into the States. A full written report would be sent around to his office by tomorrow morning.

The detective sounded disbelieving.

"Are you holding out on me, son? What was the FBI doing there in the first place? There's going to be one hell of a scene if I find out you're withholding information. I wouldn't hesitate to roast your ass over the hottest coals in Washington."

Mark thought of Stames's repeated injunctions about secrecy.

"No, I'm not withholding information," he said in a raised voice; he knew he was trembling and could hardly have sounded less convincing. The Homicide detective grumbled to himself, asked a few more questions, and hung up. Mark put the phone down. The receiver was clammy with sweat, his clothes still stuck to him. He tried Norma Stames again; still the boss hadn't reached home. He called Polly again, and asked her to go through the whole routine with the radio channels again; still nothing except a buzzing sound on Channel One. Finally, Mark abandoned the telephone and told Aspirin he was leaving. Aspirin didn't seem interested.

Mark headed for the elevator and walked quickly to his car. Must get on to home ground. Then call the Director. Once again he was speeding through the streets towards his home.

It wasn't the most luxurious part of town, but the renovated south-west section of Washington was home for many young, single professionals. It was on the waterfront near the Arena Stage, conveniently located next to a Metro station. Pleasant, lively, not too expensive – the place suited Mark perfectly.

As soon as he reached his apartment, he ran up the stairs, burst through the door and picked up the phone. After several rings, the Bureau answered. "Director's office. Duty officer speaking."

Mark drew a deep breath.

"My name is Special Agent Andrews, Washington Field Office," Mark began slowly. "I want to speak to the Director, priority and immediate."

The Director, it seemed, was dining with the Attorney General at her home. Mark asked for the telephone number. Did he have special authority to contact the Director at this time of night? He had special authority, he had an appointment with him at 10:30 tomorrow morning and, for God's sake, he had special authority.

The man must have sensed Andrews was desperate.

"I'll call you right back, if you'll give me your number."

Andrews knew that this was simply to check that he was an FBI agent and that he was scheduled to see the Director in the morning. The phone rang after one minute and the duty officer was back.

"The Director is still with the Attorney General. Her private number is 761 - 4386."

Mark dialled the number.

"Mrs Edelman's residence," said a deferential voice.

"This is Special Agent Mark Andrews," he began. "I need to speak to the Director of the Federal Bureau of Investigation."

He said it slowly, he said it clearly, although he was still trembling. The reply came back from a man whose biggest worry that night had been that the potatoes had taken longer than expected.

"Will you hold the line one moment please, sir?"

He waited, he waited, he waited.

A new voice said: "Tyson here."

Mark drew a deep breath and plunged in.

"My name is Special Agent Mark Andrews. I have an appointment to see you with SAC Stames and Special Agent Calvert at 10:30 tomorrow morning. You don't know the details, sir, because it was made through Mrs McGregor after you had left your office. I have to see you immediately, you may wish to call me back. I'm at home."

"Yes, Andrews," said Tyson. "I'll call you back. What is your number?"

Mark gave it.

"Young man," Tyson said, "this had better be a priority."

"It is, sir."

Mark waited again. One minute passed, and then another. Had Tyson dismissed him as a fool? What was going on? Three minutes passed. Four minutes passed; he was obviously checking more thoroughly than his duty officer had done.

The phone rang. Mark jumped.

"Hi, Mark, it's Roger. Want to come out for a beer?"

"Not now, Roger, not now." He slammed the phone down.

It rang again immediately.

"Right, Andrews, what do you have to tell me? Make it quick and to the point."

"I want to see you now, sir. I need fifteen minutes of your time and I need you to tell me what the hell to do."

He regretted "hell" the moment he had said it.

"Very well, if it's that urgent. Do you know where the Attorney General lives?"

"No, sir."

"Take this down: 2942 Edgewood Street, Arlington."

Mark put the phone down, wrote the address carefully in block capitals on the inside of a matchbook advertising life insurance, and called Aspirin, who just couldn't get 7-across.

"If anything happens, I'll be on my car radio; you can get me there. I'll leave the line on Channel Two open the whole time. Something's wrong with Channel One."

Aspirin sniffed: the young agents took themselves far too seriously nowadays. It wouldn't have happened under J. Edgar Hoover, shouldn't be allowed to happen now. Still, he only had one more year and then retirement. He returned to the crossword. 7-across, ten letters: gathering of those in favour of buccaneering. Aspirin started to think.

Mark Andrews was thinking too as he rushed into the elevator, into the street, into his car, and moved off at speed to Arlington. He raced up East Basin Drive to Independence Avenue, past the Lincoln Memorial to get on to Memorial Bridge. He drove as fast as possible through the early night, cursing the people calmly strolling across the road on this mild, pleasant evening, casually on their way to nowhere in particular, cursing the people who took no notice of the flashing red light he had affixed to the car roof, cursing all the way. Where was Stames? Where was Barry? What the hell was going on? Would the Director think he was crazy?

He crossed Memorial Bridge and took the G.W. Parkway exit. A tie-up. He couldn't move an inch. Probably an accident. A goddamn accident right now. That was all he needed. He pulled into the centre lane and leaned on his horn. Most people assumed he was connected with the police rescue team: most people let him by. Eventually he made it to the group of police cars and rescue-squad ambulances. A young Metropolitan policeman approached the car. "Are you on this detail?"

"No. FBI. I've got to get to Arlington. Emergency."

He flashed his credentials. The policeman ushered him through. He raced away from the accident. Goddamn accident. Once he was clear of it, the traffic became light. Fifteen minutes later, he arrived at 2942 Edgewood Street, Arlington. One last check with Polly at the Washington Field Office on the car phone. No, neither Stames nor Calvert had called in.

Mark jumped out of the car. Before he had taken a step, a Secret Service man stopped him. Mark showed his credentials, and said that he had an appointment with the Director. The Secret Service man courteously asked him to wait by his car. After consultation at the door, Mark was shown into a small room just on the right of the hall which was obviously used as a study. The Director came in. Mark stood up.

"Good evening, Director."

"Good evening, Andrews. You've interrupted a very important dinner. I hope you know what you are doing."

The Director was cold and abrupt, clearly displeased at being summoned to a meeting by an unknown junior agent.

Mark went through the whole story from the first meeting with Stames through to his decision to go over everybody's head. The Director's face remained impassive throughout the long recital. It was still impassive when Mark had finished. Mark's only thought was: I've done the wrong thing. He should have gone on trying to reach Stames and Calvert. They were probably home by now. He waited, a little sweat appearing on his forehead. Perhaps this was his last day in the

FBI. The Director's first words took him by surprise.

"You did exactly the right thing, Andrews. I'd have made the same decision in your place. It must have taken guts to bring the whole thing to me." He looked hard at Mark. "You're absolutely certain only Stames, Calvert, you, and I know all the details of what happened this evening? No one from the Secret Service, and no one from the Metropolitan Police Department?"

"That's correct, sir, just the four of us."

"And the three of you already have an appointment with me at 10:30 tomorrow morning?"

"Yes, sir."

"Good. Take this down."

Mark took out a pad from his inside coat pocket.

"You have the Attorney General's number here?"

"Yes, sir,."

"And my number at home is 721 - 4069. Learn them and then destroy them. Now I'll tell you exactly what you do next. Go back to the Washington Field Office. Check on Stames and Calvert again. Call the morgue, call the hospitals, call the highway police. If nothing turns up, I'll see you in my office at 8:30 tomorrow morning, not 10:30. That's your first job. Second, get me the names of the Homicide officers working on this detail with the Metropolitan Police. Now tell me if I have this right – you told them nothing about the reason you went to see Casefikis?"

"Nothing, sir."

"Good."

The Attorney General put her head around the door.

"Everything under control, Halt?"

"Fine, thanks, Marian. I don't think you've met Special Agent Andrews of the Washington Field Office."

"No. Nice to meet you, Mr Andrews."

"Good evening, ma'am."

"Will you be long, Halt?"

"No. I'll be back as soon as I've finished briefing Andrews."

"Anything special?"

"No, nothing to worry about."

The Director had obviously decided nobody was going to be told the story until he got to the bottom of it himself.

"Where was I?"

"You told me to return to the Washington Field Office, sir, and check on Stames and Calvert."

"Yes."

"And then to call the morgue, the hospitals, and the highway police."

"Right."

"And you told me to check on the Homicide officers, get their names."

"Right. Take down the following: check the names of all hospital employees and visitors, as well as any other persons who can be identified as having been in the vicinity of Room 4308 between the time the two occupants were known to be alive and the time you found them dead. Check the names of the two dead men through NCIC and Bureau indexes for any background information we may have. Get fingerprints of all persons on duty and all visitors and all others who can be identified as having been near Room 4308, as well as fingerprints of the two dead men. We will need all these prints both for elimination purposes and possible suspect identification. If you don't find Stames and Calvert, as I said, see me at 8:30 in my office tomorrow morning. If anything else arises tonight, you call me here or at home. Don't hesitate. If it's after 11:30, I'll be home. If you call me on the phone use a code name – now let me think – Julius – let's hope it's not prophetic, and give me your number. Make sure you use a pay phone and I'll call you back immediately. Don't bother me before 7:15 in the morning, unless it's really important. Have you understood all that?"

"Yes, sir."

"Right. I think I'll get back to dinner."

Mark stood up, ready to leave. The Director put a hand on his shoulder.

"Don't worry, young man. These things happen from time to time and you made the right decision. You showed a lot of self-possession in a lousy situation. Now get on with the job."

"Yes, sir."

Mark was relieved that someone else knew what he was going through; someone else with far bigger shoulders was there to share it.

On his way back to the FBI office, he picked up the car microphone. "WFO 180 in service. Any word from Mr Stames?"

"Nothing yet, WFO 180, but I'll keep trying."

Aspirin was still there when he arrived, unaware that Mark had just been talking with the Director of the FBI. Aspirin had met all four directors at cocktail parties, though none of them would have remembered his name.

"Emergency over, son?"

"Yes," Mark said, lying. "Have we heard from Stames or Calvert?" He tried not to sound anxious.

"No, must have dropped in somewhere on the way home. Never you worry. The little sheep will find their way back without you to hold their tails."

Mark did worry. He went to his office and picked up the phone. Polly had still heard nothing. Just a buzz that continued on Channel One. He called Norma Stames, still no news. Mrs Stames asked if there might be anything to worry about.

"Nothing at all." Another lie. Was he sounding too unconcerned? "We just can't find out which bar he's ended up in."

She laughed, but she knew Nick never frequented bars.

Mark tried Calvert; still no reply from the bachelor apartment. He knew in his bones something was wrong. He just didn't know what. At least the Director was there, and the Director knew everything now. He glanced at his watch: 11:15. Where had the night gone? And where was it going? 11:15. What was he supposed to have done tonight? Hell. He had persuaded a beautiful girl to have dinner with him. Yet again, he picked up the telephone. At least she would be safely at home, where she ought to be.

"Hello."

"Hello, Elizabeth, it's Mark Andrews. I'm really sorry about not making it tonight. Something happened that got way out of my control."

The tension in his voice was apparent.

"Don't worry," she said lightly. "You warned me you were unreliable."

"I hope you'll let me take a raincheck. Hopefully, in the morning I can sort things out. I'll probably see you then."

"In the morning?" she said. "If you're thinking of the hospital, I'm off duty tomorrow."

Mark hesitated, thinking quickly of what he could prudently say. "Well, that may be best. I am afraid it's not good news. Casefikis and the other man in his room were brutally murdered tonight. The Met is following it up, but we have nothing to go on."

"Murdered? Both of them? Why? Who? Casefikis wasn't killed without reason, was he?" The words came out in a torrent. "What's going on, for heaven's sake? No, don't answer that. You wouldn't tell me the truth in any case."

"I wouldn't waste my time lying to you, Elizabeth. Look, I've had it for tonight, and I owe you a big steak for messing up your evening. Can I call you some time soon?"

"I'd like that. Murder isn't good for the appetite, though. I hope you catch the men responsible. We see the results of a great deal of violence at Woodrow Wilson, but it isn't usually inflicted within our walls."

"I know. I'm sorry it involves you. Good night, Elizabeth. Sleep well."

"And you, Mark. If you can."

Mark put the phone down, and immediately the burden of the day's events returned. What now? There was nothing practicable he could do before 8:30, except keep in touch on the radio phone until he was home. There was no point just sitting there looking out of the window, feeling helpless, sick, and alone. He went in to Aspirin, told him he was going home, and that he'd call in every fifteen minutes because he was still anxious to speak to Stames and Calvert. Aspirin didn't even look up.

"Fine," he said, his mind fully occupied by the crossword puzzle. He had completed eleven clues, a sure sign it was a quiet evening.

Mark drove down Pennsylvania Avenue towards his apartment. At the first traffic circle, a tourist who didn't know he had the right of way was holding up traffic. Damn him, thought Mark. Visitors to Washington who hadn't mastered the knack of cutting out at the right turn-off could end up circling round and round many more times than originally planned. Eventually, Mark managed to get around the circle and back on Pennsylvania Avenue. He continued to drive slowly towards his home, at the Tiber Island Apartments, his thoughts heavy and anxious. He turned on the car radio for the midnight news; must take his mind off it somehow. There were no big stories that night and the newscaster sounded rather bored; the President had held a press conference about the Gun Control bill, and the situation in South Africa seemed to be getting worse. Then the local news; there had been an automobile accident on the G.W. Parkway and it involved two cars, both of which were being hauled out of the river by cranes, under floodlights. One of the cars was a black Lincoln, the other a blue Ford sedan, according to eyewitnesses, a married couple from Jacksonville vacationing in the Washington area. No other details as yet.

A blue Ford sedan. Although he had not really been concentrating, it kept repeating itself in his brain – a blue Ford sedan? Oh no, God, please no. He veered right off 9th Street on to Maine Avenue, narrowly missing a fire hydrant, and raced back towards Memorial Bridge, where he had been only two hours before. The roads were clearer now and he was back in a few minutes. At the scene of the accident the Metropolitan Police were still thick on the ground and one lane of the G.W. was closed off by barriers. Mark parked the car on the grassy verge and ran up to the barrier. He showed his FBI credentials and was taken to the officer in charge; he explained that he feared one of the cars involved might have been driven by an agent from the FBI. Any details yet?

"Still haven't got them out," the inspector replied. "We only have two witnesses to the accident, if it was an accident. Apparently there was some very funny driving going on. They should be up in about thirty minutes. All you can do is wait."

Mark went over to the side of the road to watch the vast cranes and tiny frogmen groping around in the river under vast klieg lights. The thirty minutes wasn't thirty minutes; he shivered in the cold, waiting and watching. It was forty minutes, it was fifty minutes, it was over an hour before the black Lincoln came out. Inside the car was one body. Cautious man, he was wearing a seat belt. The police moved in immediately. Mark went back to the officer in charge and asked how long before the second car.

"Not long. That Lincoln wasn't your car, then?"

"No," said Mark.

Ten minutes, twenty minutes, he saw the top of the second car, a dark blue car; he saw the side of the car, one of the windows fractionally opened; he saw the whole of the car. Two men were in it. He saw the licence plate. For a second time that night, Mark felt sick. Almost crying, he ran back to the officer in charge and gave the names of the two men in the car, and then ran on to a pay phone at the side of the road. It was a long way. He dialled the number, checking his watch as he did so; it was nearly one o'clock. After one ring he heard a tired voice say, "Yes."

Mark said, "Julius."

The voice said, "What is your number?"

He gave it. Thirty seconds later, the telephone rang.

"Well, Andrews. It's one o'clock in the morning."

"I know, sir, it's Stames and Calvert, they're dead."

There was a moment's hesitation, the voice was awake now.

"Are you certain?"

"Yes, sir."

Mark gave the details of the car crash, trying to keep the weariness and emotion out of his voice.

"Call your office immediately, Andrews," Tyson said, "without releasing any of the details that you gave me this evening. Only tell them about the car crash – nothing more. Then get any further information about it you can from the police. See me in my office at 7:30, not 8:30; come through the wide entrance on the far side of the building; there will be a man waiting there for you. He'll be expecting you; don't be late. Go home now and try to get some sleep and keep yourself out of sight until tomorrow. Don't worry, Andrews. Two of us know, and I'll put agents on the routine checks that I gave you to do earlier."

The phone clicked. Mark called Aspirin, what a night for him to have to be on duty, told him about Stames and Calvert, hanging up abruptly before Aspirin could ask any questions. He returned to his car and drove home slowly through the night. There was hardly another car on the streets and the early-morning mist gave everything an unearthly look.

At the entrance to his apartment garage he saw Simon, the young black attendant, who liked Mark and, even more, Mark's Mercedes. Mark had blown a small legacy from his aunt on the car just after graduating from college, but never regretted his extravagance. Simon knew Mark had no assigned spot in the garage and always offered to park his car for him – anything for a chance to drive the magnificent silver Mercedes SLC 580. Mark usually exchanged a few bantering words with Simon; tonight he passed him the keys without even looking at him.

"I'll need it at seven in the morning," he said, already walking away. "Okay, man," came back the reply.

Mark heard Simon restart the car with a soft whoosh before the elevator door closed behind him. He arrived at his apartment; three rooms, all empty. He locked the door, and then bolted it, something he had never done before. He walked around the room slowly, undressed, throwing his sour-smelling shirt into the laundry hamper. He washed for the third time that night and then went to bed, to stare up at the white ceiling. He tried to make some sense out of the night's events; he tried to sleep. Six hours passed, and if he slept it was never for more than a few minutes.

Someone else who didn't sleep that night for more than a few minutes was tossing and turning in her bed at the White House.

Abraham Lincoln, John F. Kennedy, Martin Luther King, John Lennon and Robert Kennedy. How many citizens distinguished and unknown needed to sacrifice their lives before the House would pass a bill to outlaw such self-destruction?

"Who else must die?" she remarked. "If I myself there is no hour so fit as . . ."

She turned over and looked at Edward whose expression left no doubt that such morbid thoughts were not on his mind.

Friday morning, 4 March. 6:27 am

Eventually Mark could stand it no longer and at 6:30 am he rose, showered, and put on a clean shirt and a fresh suit. From his apartment window, he looked out across the Washington Channel to East Potomac Park and went over in his mind all that had happened yesterday. In a few weeks the cherry trees would bloom. In a few weeks . . .

He closed the apartment door behind him, glad simply to be on the move again. Simon gave him the car keys; he had managed to find a space for the Mercedes in one of the private parking lots.

Mark drove the car slowly up 6th Street, turned left on G and right on 7th. No traffic at this time of morning except trucks. He passed the

Hirshhorn Museum as he crossed into Independence Avenue. At the intersection of 7th and Pennsylvania, next to the National Archives, Mark came to a halt at a red light. He felt an eerie sense of nothing being out of the ordinary, as though the previous day had been a bad dream. He would arrive at the office and Nick Stames and Barry Calvert would be there as usual. The vision evaporated as he looked to his left. At one end of the deserted avenue, he could see the White House grounds and patches of the white building through the trees. To his right, at the other end of the avenue, stood the Capitol, gleaming in the early morning sunshine. And between the two, between Caesar and Cassius, thought Mark, stood the FBI Building. Alone in the middle, he mused, the Director and himself, playing with destiny.

Mark drove the car down the ramp at the back of FBI Headquarters and parked. A young man in a dark blue blazer, grey flannels, dark shoes, and a smart blue tie, the regulation uniform of the Bureau, awaited him. An anonymous man, thought Mark, who looked far too neat to have just got up. Mark Andrews showed him his identification. The young man led him towards the elevator without saying a word; it took them to the seventh floor, where Mark was noiselessly escorted to a small room and asked to wait.

He sat in the reception room, next to the Director's office, with the inevitable out-of-date copies of *Time* and *Newsweek*; he might have been at the dentist's. It was the first time in his life that he would rather have been at his dentist's. He pondered the events of the last fourteen hours. He'd gone from being a man with no responsibility enjoying the second of five eventful years in the FBI to one who was staring into the jaws of a tiger. His only previous trip to the Bureau itself had been for his interview; they hadn't told him that this could happen. They had talked of salaries, bonuses, holidays, a worth-while and fulfilling job, serving the nation, nothing about immigrant Greeks and black post-men with their throats cut, nothing about friends being drowned in the Potomac. He paced around the room trying to compose his thoughts; yesterday should have been his day off, but he had decided he could do with the overtime pay. Perhaps another agent would have got back to the hospital more quickly and forestalled the double murder. Perhaps if he had driven the Ford sedan last night, it would have been he, not Stames and Calvert, in the Potomac. Perhaps . . . Mark closed his eyes and felt an involuntary shiver run down his spine. He made an effort to disregard the panicky fear that had kept him awake all night – perhaps it would be his turn next.

His eyes came to rest on a plaque on the wall, which stated that, in over sixty years of the FBI's history, only thirty-four people had been killed while on duty; on only one occasion had two officers died on the same day. Yesterday made that out-of-date. Mark's eyes continued moving around the wall and settled on a large picture of the Supreme

Court; government and the law hand-in-hand. On his left were the five directors, Hoover, Gray, Ruckelshaus, Kelley, and now the redoubtable H.A.L. Tyson, known to everyone in the Bureau by the acronym Halt. Apparently, no one except his secretary, Mrs McGregor, knew his first name. It had become a long-standing joke in the Bureau. When you joined the FBI, you paid one dollar to Mrs McGregor, who had served the Director for twenty-seven years, and told her what you thought the Director's first name was. If you got it right, you won the pool. The kitty had now reached $3,516. Mark had guessed Hector. Mrs McGregor had laughed and the pool was one dollar the richer. If you wanted a second guess, that cost you another dollar, but if you got it wrong, you paid a ten-dollar fine. Quite a few people tried the second time and the kitty grew larger as each new victim arrived.

Mark had had what he thought was the bright idea of checking the Criminal Fingerprints File. The FBI fingerprints records fall into three categories – military, civil, and criminal, and all FBI agents have their prints in the criminal file. This insures that they are able to trace any FBI agent who turns criminal, or to eliminate an agent's prints at the scene of a crime; these records are very rarely used. Mark had considered himself very clever as he asked to see Tyson's card. The Director's card was handed to him by an assistant from the Fingerprints Department. It read – "Height: 6′1″; Weight: 180 lbs; Hair: brown; Occupation: Director of FBI; Name: Tyson, H.A.L." No forename given. The assistant, another anonymous man in a blue suit, had smiled sourly at Mark and had said, loud enough for Mark to hear, as he returned the card to its file, "One more sucker who thought he was going to make a quick three thousand bucks."

Because the Bureau had become more political during the last decade the appointment of a professional law enforcement officer was a figure whom Congress found very easy to endorse. Law enforcement was in Tyson's blood. His great-grandfather had been a Wells Fargo man, riding shotgun on the stage between San Francisco and Seattle in the other Washington. His grandfather had been mayor of Boston and its chief of police, a rare combination, and his father before his retirement had been a distinguished Massachusetts attorney. That the great-grandson had followed family tradition, and ended up as Director of the Federal Bureau of Investigation, surprised no one. The anecdotes about him were legion and Mark wondered just how many of them were apocryphal.

There was no doubt that Tyson had scored the winning touchdown in his final Harvard–Yale game because it was there on record, as indeed was the fact that he was the only white man to box on the 1956 American Olympic team in Melbourne. Whether he had actually said to the late President Nixon that he would rather serve the devil than direct the FBI under his presidency, no one could be sure, but it was certainly a story the Kane camp made no effort to suppress.

His wife had died five years earlier of multiple sclerosis. He had nursed her for twenty years with a fierce loyalty.

He feared no man and his reputation for honesty and straight talking has raised him above most government employees in the eyes of the nation. After a period of malaise, following Hoover's death, Halt Tyson had restored the Bureau to the prestige it had enjoyed in the 1930s and 1940s. Tyson was one of the reasons Mark had been happy to commit five years of his life to the FBI.

Mark began to fidget with the middle button of his jacket, as all FBI agents tend to do. It had been drummed into him in the fifteen-week course at Quantico that jacket buttons should always be undone, allowing access to the gun, on the hip holster, never on a shoulder strap. It annoyed Mark that the television series about the FBI always got that wrong. Whenever an FBI man sensed danger, he would fiddle with that middle button to make sure his coat was open. Mark sensed fear, fear of the unknown, fear of H.A.L. Tyson, fear which an accessible Smith and Wesson could not cure.

The anonymous young man with the vigilant look and the dark blue blazer returned.

"The Director will see you now."

Mark rose, felt unsteady, braced himself, rubbed his hands against his trousers to remove the sweat from his palms and followed the anonymous man through the outer office and into the Director's inner sanctum. The Director glanced up, waved him to a chair, and waited for the anonymous man to leave the room and close the door. Even seated, the Director was a bull of a man with a large head placed squarely on massive shoulders. Bushy eyebrows matched his careless, wiry brown hair; it was so curly you might have thought it was a wig if it hadn't been H.A.L. Tyson. His big hands remained splayed on the surface as though the desk might try to get away. The delicate Queen Anne desk was quite subdued by the grip of the Director. His cheeks were red, not the red of alcohol, but the red of good and bad weather. Slightly back from the Director's chair stood another man, muscular, clean-shaven, and silent, a policeman's policeman.

The Director spoke. "Andrews, this is Assistant Director Matthew Rogers. I have briefed him on the events following Casefikis's death: we will be putting several agents on the investigation with you." The Director's grey eyes were piercing – piercing Mark. "I lost two of my best men yesterday, Andrews, and nothing – I repeat, nothing – will stop me from finding out who was responsible, even if it was the President herself, you understand."

"Yes, sir," Mark said very quietly.

"You will have gathered from the press releases we gave that the public is under the impression that what happened yesterday evening was just another automobile accident. No journalist had connected the murders in Woodrow Wilson Medical Center with the deaths of my agents. Why should they, with a murder every twenty-six minutes in America?"

A Metropolitan Police file marked "Chief of Metropolitan Police" was by his side; even they were under control.

"We, Mr Andrews . . ."

It made Mark feel slightly royal.

". . . we are not going to disillusion them. I have been going over carefully what you told me last night. I'll summarise the situation as I see it. Please feel free to interrupt me whenever you want to."

Under normal circumstances, Mark would have laughed.

The Director was looking at the file.

"The Greek immigrant wanted to see the head of the FBI," he continued. "Perhaps I should have granted his request, had I known about it." He looked up. "Still, the facts: Casefikis made an oral statement to you at Woodrow Wilson, and the gist of it was that he believed that there was a plot in motion to assassinate the President of the United States on 10 March; he overheard this information while waiting on a private lunch in a Georgetown hotel, at which he thought a US senator was present. Is that correct so far, Andrews?"

"Yes, sir."

Once more the Director looked down at the file.

"The police took prints of the dead man, and he hasn't shown up in our files or in the Metropolitan Police files. So for the moment we must act on the assumption, after last night's four killings, that everything the Greek immigrant told us was in good faith. He may not have got the story entirely accurately, but he certainly was on to something big enough to cause four murders in one night. I think we may also assume that whoever the people are behind these diabolical events, they believe they are now in the clear and that they have killed anyone who might have known of their plans. You may consider yourself lucky, young man."

"Yes, sir."

"I suppose it had crossed your mind that they thought it was you in the blue Ford sedan?"

Mark nodded. He had thought of little else for the past ten hours; he hoped Norma Stames would never think of it.

"I want these conspirators to think they are now in the clear and for that reason, I am going to allow the President's schedule for the week to continue as planned, at least for the moment."

Mark ventured a question. "But, sir, won't that put her in grave danger?"

"Andrews, somebody, somewhere, and it may be a United States senator, is planning to assassinate the President; so far, he has been prepared to murder two of my best agents, a Greek who might have recognised him, and a deaf postman whose only connection with the matter was that he may have been able to identify Casefikis's killer. If we rush in now with the heavy artillery, then we will scare them off. We have almost nothing to go on; we would be unlikely to discover their identities. And if we did, we certainly wouldn't be able to nail them. Our only hope of catching them is to let the bastards think they are in the clear – right up to the last moment. That way, we just might get them. It's possible they have already been frightened off, but I think not. They have used such violent means to keep their intentions secret they must have some overriding reason for wanting the President out of the way within seven days. We must find out what the reason is."

"Shall we tell the President?"

"No, no, not yet. God knows, over the past two years she's had enough problems with the Gun Control bill without having to look over her shoulder trying to figure out which senator is Mark Antony and which is Brutus."

"So what do we do for the next six days?"

"You and I will have to find Cassius. And he may not be the one with the lean and hungry look."

"What if we don't find him?" asked Mark.

"God help America."

"And if we do?"

"You may have to kill him."

Mark thought for a moment. He'd never killed anybody in his life; come to think of it, he hadn't knowingly killed anything at all. He didn't like stepping on insects. And the thought that the first person he might kill could be a US senator was, to say the least, daunting.

"Don't look so worried, Andrews. It probably won't come to that. Now let me tell you exactly what I intend to do. I'm going to brief Stuart Knight, the head of the Secret Service, that two of my officers were investigating a man claiming that the President of the United States was going to be assassinated some time within the next month. However, I have no intention of letting him know that a senator may be involved; and I won't tell him that two of our men died because of it; that's not his problem. It may actually have nothing to do with a senator, and I'm not having a whole bunch of people staring at their elected representatives wondering which one of them is a criminal."

The Assistant Director cleared his throat and spoke for the first time. "Some of us think that anyway."

The Director continued unswervingly. "This morning, Andrews, you will write a report on Casefikis's information and the circumstances of his murder, and you will hand it in to Grant Nanna. Do not include the subsequent murders of Stames and Calvert: no one must connect these two events. Report the threat on the President's life but not the possibility that a senator is involved. Is that how you would play it, Matt?"

"Yes, sir," said Rogers. "If we voice our suspicions to people who don't need to know them, we will run the risk of provoking a security operation that will make the assassins run for cover; then we would simply have to pick up our marbles and start over – if we were lucky enough to get a second chance."

"Right," said the Director. "So this is how we'll proceed, Andrews. There are one hundred senators. One of them provides our only link with the conspirators. It's going to be your task to pinpoint that man. The Assistant Director will have a couple of junior men follow up the few other leads that we have. No need for them to know the details, Matt. To start with, check out the Golden Duck Restaurant."

"And every hotel in Georgetown, to see which one put on a private luncheon party on 24 February," said Rogers. "And the hospital. Maybe someone saw suspicious characters hanging around the parking lot or the corridors; the assassins must have seen our Ford there while Calvert and you, Andrews, were interviewing Casefikis. I think that's about all we can do for the moment."

"I agree," said the Director. "Okay, thanks, Matt, I won't take up any more of your time. Please let me have anything you turn up immediately."

"Sure," said the Assistant Director. He nodded at Mark and left the room.

Mark had sat silently, impressed by the clarity with which the Director had grasped the details of the case; his mind must be like a filing cabinet.

The Director pressed a button on his intercom.

"Coffee for two, please, Mrs McGregor."

"Yes, sir."

"Now, Andrews, you come into the Bureau at seven o'clock every morning and report to me. Should any emergency arise, call me, using the code name Julius. I will use the same code name when calling you. When you hear the word 'Julius', break off whatever you are doing. Do you understand?"

"Yes, sir."

"Now, a most important point. If, in any circumstances, I die or disappear, you brief only the Attorney General, and Rogers will take care of the rest. If you die, young man, you can leave the decision to me." He smiled for the first time – it was not Mark's idea of a joke. "I see from the files that you're entitled to two weeks' leave. Well take it, starting at noon today. I don't want you to exist officially for at least a week. Grant Nanna has already been briefed that you have been seconded to me," continued the Director. "You may have to tolerate me night and day for six days, young man, and no one other than my late wife had had that problem before."

"And you me, sir," was Mark's quick and unthinking reply.

He waited for his head to be bitten off; instead the Director smiled again.

Mrs McGregor appeared with the coffee, served them, and left. The Director drank his coffee in one swallow and began to pace around the room as if it were a cage; Mark did not move, though his eyes never left Tyson. His massive frame and great shoulders heaved up and down, his large head with its bushy hair rocking from side to side. He was going through what the boys called the thought process.

"The first thing you're to do, Andrews, is find out which senators were in Washington on 24 February. As it was near the weekend, most of those dummies would have been floating all over the country, making speeches or vacationing with their pampered children."

What endeared the Director to everyone was not that he said it behind their backs but that he said it even more explicitly to their faces. Mark smiled and began to relax.

"When we have that list, we'll try and figure out what they have in common. Separate the Republicans from the Democrats, and then put them under party headings as to interests, public and private. After that, we have to find out which ones have any connection with President Kane, past or present, friendly or unfriendly. Your report will cover all these details and be ready for our meeting tomorrow morning. Understood?"

"Yes, sir."

"Now there's something else I want you to understand, Andrews. As I am sure you know, for the past decade, the FBI has been in a very sensitive political position. Those watchdogs in Congress are just waiting for us to exceed our legitimate authority. If we in any way cast suspicion upon a member of Congress, without indisputable evidence of his guilt, they will hang, draw and quarter the Bureau. And rightly so, in my opinion. Police agencies in a democracy must prove that they can be trusted not to subvert the political process. Purer than Caesar's wife. Understood?"

"Yes, sir."

"From today, we have six days, from tomorrow five, and I want to catch this man and his friends red-handed. So neither of us will be on statutory overtime."

"No, sir."

The Director returned to his desk and summoned Mrs McGregor.

"Mrs McGregor, this is Special Agent Andrews, who'll be working closely with me on an extremely sensitive investigation for the next six days. Whenever he wants to see me, let him come right in; if I'm with anybody but Mr Rogers, notify me immediately – no red tape, no waiting."

"Yes, sir."

"And I'd appreciate it if you didn't mention this to anybody else."

"Of course not, Mr Tyson."

The Director turned to Mark. "Now you go back to the WFO and start working. I'll see you in this office at seven o'clock tomorrow morning."

Mark stood up. He didn't finish his coffee; perhaps by the sixth day he would feel free to say so. He shook hands with the Director and headed towards the door. Just as he reached it, the Director added: "Andrews, I hope you'll be very careful. Keep looking over both shoulders at once."

Mark shivered and moved quickly out of the room, down the corridor, keeping his back firmly to the wall when he reached the elevator, and walking along the sides of the passage on the ground floor, where he ran into a group of tourists who were studying pictures of the Ten Most Wanted Criminals in America. Next week, would one of them be a senator?

When he reached the street, he dodged the traffic until he arrived at the Washington Field Office, on the other side of Pennsylvania Avenue. It wouldn't quite be like home this morning. Two men were missing, and they weren't going to be able to replace them with a training manual. The flag on the top of the FBI Building and the flag on top of the Old Post Office Building were at half-mast; two of their agents were dead.

Mark went straight into Grant Nanna's office; he had aged ten years overnight. For him, two friends had died, one who worked under him and one who worked above him.

"Sit down, Mark."

"Thank you, sir."

"The Director has already spoken to me this morning. I didn't ask any questions. I understand you're taking a two-week leave as of noon today, and that you are writing me a memorandum on what happened at the hospital. I have to pass it on to higher authorities and that will be the end of it as far as the WFO is concerned, because Homicide will take over. They are also trying to tell me Nick and Barry died in a car accident."

"Yes, sir," said Mark.

"I don't believe a goddamn word of it," said Nanna. "Now you're in the middle of this, somehow, and maybe you can nail the bastards who did it. When you find them, grind their balls into powder and then call me so that I can come help you, because if I lay my hands on those bastards . . ."

Mark looked at Grant Nanna, and then tactfully away again, waiting until his superior had regained control of his face and voice.

"Now, you're not allowed to contact me once you leave this office, but if I can help at any time, just call me. Don't let the Director know, he'd kill us both if he found out. Get going, Mark."

Mark left quickly and went to his office. He sat down and wrote out his report exactly as the Director had instructed, bland and brief. He took it back to Nanna, who flicked through it and tossed it into the out-box. "Neat little white-wash job you've done there, Mark."

Mark didn't speak. He signed out of the Washington Field Office, the one place in which he felt secure. He'd be on his own for six days. Ambitious men always wanted to see a few years ahead, to know the shape of their careers; Mark would have settled for a week.

The Director pressed a button. The anonymous man in the dark blue blazer and light grey trousers entered the room.

"Yes, sir."

"I want a full surveillance on Andrews, night and day; six men on three shifts reporting to me every morning. I want detailed background on him, his education, girl friends, associates, habits, hobbies, religion, organisational affiliations, everything by tomorrow morning, 6:45. Understood?"

"Yes, sir."

Aware that Senate staff members would be suspicious of an FBI agent who asked for information about their employers, Mark began his research at the Library of Congress. As he climbed the long flight of steps, he remembered a scene from *All the President's Men*, in which Woodward and Bernstein had spent innumerable fruitless hours searching for a few slips of paper in the bowels of the building. They had been trying to find proof that E. Howard Hunt had checked out materials on Edward M. Kennedy. And for an FBI agent on the trail of a killer, just as for the investigative reporters, it would be tedious research, not glamorous assignments, that would make the difference between success and failure.

Mark opened the door marked "Readers Only" and strolled into the Main Reading Room, a huge, circular, domed room decorated in muted tones of gold, beige, rust, and bronze. The ground floor was filled with rows of dark, curved wooden desks, arranged in concentric circles around the reference area in the centre of the room. On the second floor, visible from the reading area through graceful arches, were thousands of books. Mark approached the reference desk and, in the hushed tones appropriate to all libraries, asked the Clerk where he could find current issues of the *Congressional Record*.

"Room 244. Law Library Reading Room."

"How do I get there?"

"Go back past the card catalogue to the other side of the building and take an elevator to the second floor."

Mark managed to find the Law Library, a white, rectangular room with three tiers of bookshelves on the left-hand side. After questioning another clerk, he located the *Congressional Record* on one of the dark brown reference shelves along the right-hand wall. He carried the unbound volume marked 24 February, to a long, deserted table and began the tedious weeding-out process.

After leafing through the digest of Senate business for half an hour, Mark realised that he was in luck. Many senators had apparently left Washington for the weekend, because a check of the roll calls on 24 February revealed that, of the one hundred senators, the number present on the floor never exceeded sixty. And the bills which were voted on were sufficiently important to command the presence of those senators who might have been hiding in the nooks and crannies of the Senate or the city. When he had eliminated those senators who were listed by the Whips of each party as "absent because of illness" or "necessarily absent", and added those who were merely "detained on official business", Mark was left with sixty-two senators who were definitely in Washington on 24 February. He then double-checked the other thirty-eight senators, one by one, a long and tiresome task. All of them had for some reason been out of Washington that day.

He glanced at his watch: 12:15. He couldn't afford to take time off for lunch.

Friday afternoon, 4 March. 12.30 pm

Three men had arrived. None of them liked one another; only the common bond of financial reward could have got them into the same room. The first went by the name of Tony; he'd had so many names that nobody could be sure what his real name was, except perhaps his mother, and she hadn't seen him in the twenty years since he had left Sicily to join his father, her husband, in the States. Her husband had left twenty years before that; the cycle repeated itself.

Tony's FBI criminal file described him as five-feet-eight, a hundred and forty-six pounds, medium build, black hair, straight nose, brown eyes, no distinguishing features, arrested and charged once in connection with a bank robbery; first offence, two-year jail sentence. What the rap sheet did not reveal was that Tony was a brilliant driver; he had proved that yesterday and if that fool of a German had kept his head,

there would have been four people in the room now instead of three. He
had told the boss, "If you're going to employ a German, have him build
the damn car, never let him drive it." The boss hadn't listened and the
German had been dragged out of the bottom of the Potomac. Next time
they'd use Tony's cousin Mario. At least then there would be another
human on the team; you couldn't count the ex-cop and the little Jap
who never said a word.

Tony glanced at Xan Tho Huc, who only spoke when asked a direct
question. He was actually Vietnamese, but he had finally escaped to
Japan in 1979. Everyone would have known his name if he had entered
the Los Angeles Olympics, because nobody could have stopped him
from getting the gold medal for rifle shooting, but Xan had decided,
with his chosen career in mind, he had better keep a low profile and
withdraw from the Japanese Olympic trials. His coach tried to get him
to change his mind, but without success. To Tony, Xan remained a
goddamn Jap, though he grudgingly admitted to himself he knew no
other man who could fire ten shots into a three-inch square at eight
hundred yards. The size of Florentyna Kane's forehead.

The Nip sat staring at him, motionless. Xan's appearance helped
him in his work. No one expected that the slight frame, only about five-
feet-two and a hundred and ten pounds, was that of a superlative
marksman. Most people still associated marksmanship with hulking
cowboys and lantern-jawed Caucasians. If you had been told this man
was a ruthless killer, you would have assumed he worked with his
hands, with a garrotte or nunchaki, or even with poison. Among the
three, Xan was the only one who carried a personal grudge. As a child
he had seen his parents butchered by the Americans in Vietnam. They
had spoken warmly of the Yanks and had supported them until the
bullets tore into their bodies. They had left him for dead. A target
almost too small to hit. From that moment he had vowed in silent
torment to avenge his loss. He escaped to Japan and there, for two years
after the fall of Saigon, he had lain low, getting a job in a Chinese
restaurant, and participating in the US Government Program for
Vietnamese refugees. Then he had gone with the offer of practical
assistance to some of his old contacts in the Vietnamese intelligence
community. With the US presence so scaled down in Asia, and the
Communists needing fewer killers, and more lawyers, they had been
sorry but they had no work for him. So Xan had begun freelancing in
Japan, In 1981, he obtained Japanese citizenship, a passport, and
started his new career.

Unlike Tony, Xan did not resent the others he was working with. He
simply didn't think about them. He had been hired, willingly, to
perform a professional task, a task for which he would be well paid and
that would at last avenge, at least in part, the outraged bodies of his
parents. The others had limited roles to play in support of his

operation. Provided they played them with a minimum of foolish error, he would perform his part flawlessly, and within a few days, he would be back in the Orient. Bangkok or Manila, perhaps, Singapore. Xan hadn't decided yet. When this one was over, he would need – and would be able to afford – a long rest.

The third man in the room, Ralph Matson, was perhaps the most dangerous of the three. Six-feet-two tall and broad, with a big nose and heavy chin, he was the most dangerous because he was highly intelligent. After five years as a special agent with the Federal Bureau of Investigation, he found an easy way out after Hoover's death; loyalty to the Chief and all that garbage. By then, he had learned enough to take advantage of everything the Bureau had taught him about criminology. He had started with a little blackmail, men who had not wanted their FBI records made public, but now he had moved on to bigger things. He trusted no man – the Bureau had also taught him that – certainly not the stupid wop, who under pressure might drive backward rather than forward, or the silent slant-eyed yellow hit man.

Still nobody spoke.

The door swung open. Three heads turned, three heads that were used to danger and did not care for surprises; they relaxed again immediately when they saw the two men enter.

The younger of the two was smoking. He took the seat at the head of the table as befits a chairman; the other man sat down next to Matson, keeping the Chairman on his right. They nodded acknowledgment, no more. The younger man, Peter Nicholson on his voter-registration card, Pyotr Nicolaivich by birth certificate, looked for all the world like the reputable head of a successful cosmetics company. His suit revealed that he went to Chester Barrie. His shoes were Loeb's. His tie Ted Lapidus. His criminal record revealed nothing. That was why he was at the head of the table. He didn't look upon himself as a criminal; he looked upon himself as a man who wished to maintain the status quo.

He was one of a small group of Southern millionaires who had made their money in the small-arms trade. Theirs was a giant business: it was the right of every American citizen under Amendment Two of the Constitution to bear arms, and one in every four American males exercised that right. A regular pistol or revolver could be had for as little as $100 but the fancy shotguns and rifles that were a status symbol to many patriots could fetch as much as $10,000. The Chairman and his ilk sold handguns by the millions and shotguns by the tens of thousands. It had not been hard to persuade Ronald Reagan to leave the arms trade alone, but they knew they were never going to convince Florentyna Kane. The Gun Control bill had already squeaked through the House, and unless some drastic action were taken, there was undoubtedly going to be the same result in the Senate. To preserve the status quo, therefore, the Chairman sat at the head of their table.

He opened the meeting formally, as any regular chairman would, by asking for reports from his men in the field. First Matson.

The big nose bobbed, the heavy jaw moved.

"I was tuned into the FBI's Channel One." During his years as an FBI agent, preparing for a career in crime, Matson had stolen one of the Bureau's special portable walkie-talkies. He had signed it out for some routine purpose and then reported that it was lost. He was reprimanded and had to reimburse the Bureau; it had been a small price to pay for the privilege of listening to FBI communications. "I knew the Greek waiter was hiding somewhere in Washington, and I suspected that because of his leg injury, he would eventually have to go to one of D.C.'s five hospitals. I guessed he wouldn't end up with a private doctor, too expensive. Then I heard that bastard Stames come up on Channel One."

"Cut out the profanity, if you please," said the Chairman.

Stames had given Matson four reprimands during his service with the FBI. Matson did not mourn his death. He started again.

"I heard Stames come up on Channel One, on his way to Woodrow Wilson Medical Center, to ask a Father Gregory to go to the Greek. It was a long shot, of course, but I remembered that Stames was a Greek himself, and it wasn't hard to trace Father Gregory. I just caught him as he was about to leave. I told him the Greek had been discharged from the hospital and that his services would no longer be needed. And thanked him. With Stames dead, no one is likely to follow that one up and, if they do, they won't be any the wiser. I then went to the nearest Greek Orthodox church and stole the vestments, a hat, a veil, and a cross and I drove to Woodrow Wilson. By the time I arrived Stames and Calvert had already left. I learned from the receptionist on duty that the two men from the FBI had returned to their office. I didn't ask for too much detail as I didn't want to be remembered. I discovered which room Casefikis was in and it was simple to reach there unnoticed. I slipped in. He was sound asleep. I cut his throat."

The Senator winced.

"There was a nigger in the bed next to him, we couldn't take the risk. He might have overheard everything, and he might have given a description of me, so I cut his throat too."

The Senator felt sick. He hadn't wanted these men to die. The Chairman had showed no emotion, the difference between a professional and an amateur.

"Then I called Tony in the car. He drove to the Washington Field Office and saw Stames and Calvert coming out of the building together. I then contacted you, boss, and Tony carried out your orders."

The Chairman passed over a packet. It was one hundred one-hundred-dollar bills. All American employees are paid by seniority and achievement; it was no different in the criminal world.

"Tony."

"When the two men left the Old Post Office Building, we followed them as instructed. Then went over Memorial Bridge. The German passed them and managed to get well ahead of them. As soon as I realised they were turning up on to the G.W. Parkway, as we thought they would, I informed Gerbach on the walkie-talkie. He was waiting in a clump of trees on the middle strip, with his lights off, about a mile ahead. He turned on his lights and came down from the top of the hill on the wrong side of the divided highway. He swung in front of the Feds' car just after it crossed Windy Run Bridge. I accelerated and overtook on the left-hand side of the car. I hit them with a glancing sideways blow at about seventy miles an hour, just as that damn-fool German hit them head-on. You know the rest, boss. If he had kept his cool," Tony finished contemptuously, "the German would be here today to make his report in person."

"What did you do with the car?"

"I went to Mario's workshop, changed the engine block and the licence plates, repaired the damage to the fender, sprayed it, and dumped it. The owner probably wouldn't recognise his own car if he saw it."

"Where did you dump it?"

"New York. The Bronx."

"Good. With a murder there every four hours, they don't have a lot of time to check on missing cars."

The Chairman flicked a packet over the table. Three thousand dollars in used fifties. "Stay sober, Tony, we'll be needing you again." He refrained from saying what assignment number two would be; he simply said, "Xan". He stubbed out his cigarette and lit another one. All eyes turned to the silent Vietnamese. His English was good, though heavily accentuated. He tended, like so many educated Orientals, to omit the definite article, giving his speech a curious staccato effect.

"I was in car with Tony whole evening when we got your orders to eliminate two men in Ford sedan. We followed them over bridge and up freeway and when German swung across path of Ford, I blew both back tyres in under three seconds, just before Tony bounced them. They had no chance of controlling car after that."

"How can you be so sure it was under three seconds?"

"I'd been averaging two-point-eight in practice all day."

Silence. The Chairman passed yet another packet. Another one hundred fifties, twenty-five hundred dollars for each shot.

"Do you have any questions, Senator?"

The Senator did not look up, but shook his head slightly.

The Chairman spoke. "From the press reports and from our further investigation, it looks as if nobody has connected the two incidents, but the FBI just aren't that stupid. We have to hope that we eliminated everybody who heard anything Casefikis might have said, if he had anything to say in the first place. We may just be oversensitive. One thing's for certain, we eliminated everybody connected with that hospital. But we still can't be sure if the Greek knew anything worth repeating."

"May I say something, boss?"

The Chairman looked up. Nobody spoke unless it was relevant, most unusual for an American board meeting. The Chairman let Matson have the floor.

"One thing worries me, boss. Why would Nick Stames be going to Woodrow Wilson?"

They all stared at him, not quite sure what he meant.

"We know from my inquiries and my contacts that Calvert was there, but we don't actually know that Stames was there. All we know is that two agents went and that Stames asked Father Gregory to go. We know Stames was on his way home with Calvert, but my experience tells me that Stames wouldn't go to the hospital himself; he'd send somebody else –"

"Even if he thought it were a serious matter?" interrupted the Chairman.

"He wouldn't know it was a serious matter, boss. He wouldn't have known until the agents had reported back to him."

The Chairman shrugged. "The facts point to Stames going to the hospital with Calvert. He left the Washington Field Office with Calvert driving the same car that left the hospital."

"I know, boss, but I don't like it; I know that we've covered all the angles, but it's possible that three or more men left the Washington Field Office and that there is still at least one agent running around who knows what actually happened."

"It seems unlikely," said the Senator. "As you will discover when you hear my report."

The lips compressed in the heavy jaw.

"You're not happy are you, Matson?"

"No, sir."

"Very well, check it out. If you come up with anything report back to me."

The Chairman never left a stone unturned. He looked at the Senator.

The Senator despised these men. They were so small-minded, so greedy. They only understood money, and Kane was going to take it away from them. How their violence had frightened and sickened him. He should never have allowed that smooth-talking plausible bastard Nicholson to pump so much into his secret campaign funds, although God knows he would never have been elected without the money. Lots of money, and such a small price to pay at the time: steadfast opposition to any gun control proposals. Hell, he was genuinely opposed to gun control anyway. But assassinating the President to stop the bill, by God, it was lunacy, but the Chairman had him by the balls. "Co-operate, or be exposed, my friend," he had said silkily. The Senator had spent half a lifetime sweating to reach the Senate and what's more, he did a damned good job there. If they stopped him now he would be finished. A public scandal. He couldn't face it. "Cooperate, my friend, for your own good. All we need is some inside information, and your presence at the Capitol on 10 March. Be reasonable, my friend, why ruin your whole life for a Polish woman?" The Senator cleared his throat.

"It is highly unlikely that the FBI knows any details about our plans. As Mr Matson knows, if the Bureau had anything to go on, any reason to think that this supposed threat is any different from a thousand others the President has received, the Secret Service would have been informed immediately. And my secretary has ascertained that the President's schedule for this week remains unchanged. All her appointments will be kept. She will go to the Capitol on the morning of 10 March for a special address to the Senate –"

"But that's exactly the point," Matson interrupted with a contemptuous sneer. "All threats against the President, no matter how far-fetched, are routinely reported to the Secret Service. If they haven't reported anything, it must mean that –"

"It may mean that they don't know a thing, Matson," said the Chairman firmly. "I told you to look into it. Now let the Senator answer a more important question: If the FBI knew the details, would they tell the President?"

The Senator hesitated. "No, I don't think so, or only if they were absolutely certain of danger on a particular day; otherwise they'd go ahead as planned. If every threat or suggestion of a threat were taken seriously, the President would never be able to leave the White House. The Secret Service report to Congress last year showed that there were 1,572 threats against the President's life, but thorough investigations revealed that there were no actual known attempts."

The Chairman nodded. "Either they know everything or they know nothing."

Matson persisted. "I am still a member of the Society of Former Special Agents and I attended a meeting yesterday, and no one there knew a damn thing. Someone would have heard something by now. Later, I had a drink with Grant Nanna, who was my old boss at the Washington Field Office, and he seemed almost uninterested, which I found strange. I thought Stames was a friend of his, but I obviously couldn't push it too far, since Stames was no friend of mine. I'm still worried. It doesn't make sense that Stames went to the hospital and no one in the Bureau is saying anything about his death."

"Okay, okay," said the Chairman. "If we don't get her on 10 March, we may as well quit now. We go ahead as if nothing had happened, unless we hear any rumbles – and that's in your hands, Matson. We'll be there on the day, unless you stop us. Now let's plan ahead. First I'll go over Kane's schedule for that day. Kane" – no one in that room except for the Senator ever called her the President – "leaves the White House at 10 am. She passes the FBI Building at three minutes past, she passes the Peace Monument at the north-west corner of the Capitol grounds at five minutes past. She gets out of her car at the east front of the Capitol at six minutes past. Normally, she would go in the private entrance, but the Senator has assured us that she will milk this visit for all it's worth. It takes her forty-five seconds to walk from the car to the top of the Capitol steps. We know that Xan can easily complete the job in forty-five seconds. I will be watching at the corner of Pennsylvania Avenue when Kane passes the FBI Building. Tony will be there with a car, in case of an emergency, and the Senator will be on the Capitol steps to stall her, if we need more time. The most important part of the operation is Xan's, which we have worked out to a split second. So listen and listen carefully. I have arranged for Xan to be on the construction crew working on the renovation of the front of the Capitol. And, believe me, with that union it was no mean feat to place an Oriental. Take over, Xan."

Xan looked up. He had said nothing since his last invitation to speak.

"Construction on west front of Capitol has been going on for nearly six months. No one is more enthusiastic about it than Kane. She wants it finished in time for her second Inaugural." He grinned. All eyes were upon the little man, intent on his every word. "I have been part of work force now for just over four weeks. I am in charge of checking all supplies that come on to site, which means I am in site office. From there, it has not been hard to discover movements of everybody connected with construction. The guards are not from FBI, Secret Service, or from CIA, but from Government Building Security Service. They are usually a lot older than normal agents, often retired from one of services. There are sixteen in all, and they work in fours on four shifts. I know where they drink, smoke, play cards, everything; no one is very interested in site because at moment it overlooks nothing and it's on least-used side of Capitol. A little petty theft from site but not much else to excite guards." Xan had total silence. "Right in middle of site is biggest American Hoist Co. crane in world, number 11-3-10, specially designed for lifting new parts of Capitol into place. Fully extended, it is 322 feet, almost double regulation height allowed in Washington buildings. Nobody expect us on west side, and nobody figure we can see that far. On top is small covered platform for general maintenance of pulleys, used only when it is flat and parallel to ground, but platform becomes like a small box in effect. It is four feet long, two feet three inches in width, and one foot five inches in height. I have slept there for last three nights. I see everything, no one can see me, not even White House helicopter."

There was a stunned silence.

"How do you get up there?" asked the Senator.

"Like cat, Senator. I climb. An advantage of being very small. I go up just after midnight and come down at five. I overlook all Washington and no one see me."

"Do you have a good view of the Capitol steps from such a small platform?" asked the Chairman.

"Perhaps it will take four seconds," Xan replied. "View allows me to see White House as no one has ever seen it. I could have killed Kane twice last week. When she make official visits, it will be easy. I can't miss —"

"What about the other workers on Thursday? They may want to use the crane," the Senator interrupted.

This time the Chairman smiled. "There will be a strike next Thursday, my friend. Something to do with unfair rates for overtime, no work while Kane is visiting the Capitol to emphasise their point. One thing is certain, with no one on the site other than some ageing guards, nobody will be eager to climb to the top of a crane that is all but open to the world. From the ground it doesn't look as if a mouse could hide up there, let alone a human being." The Chairman paused. "Xan flies to Vienna tomorrow and will be back in time to report the results of his trip at our final meeting next Wednesday. By the way, Xan, have you got your can of yellow paint?"

"Yes, stole one from site."

The Chairman looked around the table — silence. "Good, we seem to be well organised. Thank you, Xan."

"I don't like it," mumbled Matson, "Something's wrong. It's all too easy, it's all too clever."

"The FBI has taught you to be overly suspicious, Matson. You'll discover that we're better prepared than they are, because we know what we're going to do and they don't. Fear not, you'll be able to attend Kane's funeral."

Matson's big chin moved up and down. "You're the guy that wants her dead," he said sourly.

"And you're being paid to see it happens," said the Chairman. "Right, we meet again in five days to go over the final plan. You will be told where to report on Wednesday morning. Xan will have returned from Austria long before then."

The Chairman smiled and lit another cigarette. The Senator slipped out. Five minutes later, Matson left. Five minutes later, Tony left. Five minutes later, Xan left. Five minutes later, the Chairman ordered lunch.

Friday afternoon, 4 March. 4:00 pm

Mark was too hungry to work efficiently any longer, so he left the Library in search of some food. When the elevator stopped, the opening doors provided a view of the card catalogue: "Harrison-Health" confronted him. Some sub-conscious word association triggered in his mind the welcome vision of the beautiful, witty girl he had met the previous day, walking along the corridor in her black skirt and red shirt, heels tapping on the tiles. A big grin spread across Mark's face. It was amazing the pleasure it gave him just to know he could call her and rearrange the date, unusual for him to find just how much he wanted to.

Mark found the snack bar and munched his way through a hamburger, letting his mind recall all the things she had said, and the way she had looked while she was saying them. He decided to call Woodrow Wilson.

"I'm sorry, Dr Dexter is not on duty today," said a nurse. "Can Dr Delgado help?"

"No thank you," said Mark. "I'm afraid she can't."

He took out his diary, and dialled Elizabeth Dexter's home number. He was delighted to find her in.

"Hello, Elizabeth. It's Mark Andrews. Any hope of giving you dinner tonight?"

"Promises, promises. I continue to live in the hope of a real meal."

"Not a laughing matter," said Mark, almost to himself.

"You sound a bit low, Mark. Perhaps you really do have a touch of flu."

"No, I don't think it's flu, just thinking of you makes it hard to breathe. I'd better hang up now, before I turn blue."

It was good to hear her laugh.

"Why don't you come by about eight?"

"Fine. See you around eight, Elizabeth."

"Take care, Mark."

He put the telephone down, suddenly conscious that once again he was smiling from ear to ear. He glanced at his watch: 4:30. Good. Three more hours in the Library, then he could go in pursuit of her. He returned to his reference books and continued to make biographical notes on the sixty-two senators.

His mind drifted for a moment to the President. This wasn't just any President. This was the first woman President. But what could he learn from the last presidential assassination of John F. Kennedy. Were there any senators involved with those deaths? Or was this another lunatic working on his own? All the evidence on this inquiry so far pointed to teamwork. Lee Harvey Oswald, long since dead, and still there was no convincing explanation of his assassination or, for that matter, of Robert Kennedy's.

Some people still claimed the CIA was behind President Kennedy's death because he had threatened to hang them out to dry in 1961, after the Bay of Pigs fiasco. Others said Castro had arranged the murder in revenge; it was known that Oswald had an interview with the Cuban ambassador in Mexico two weeks before the assassination, and the CIA had known about that all along. Thirty years after the event, and still no one could be certain.

A smart guy from LA, Jay Sandberg, who had roomed with Mark at law school, had maintained that the conspiracy reached the top, even the top of the FBI: they knew the truth but said nothing.

Maybe Tyson and Rogers were two of those who knew the truth and had sent him out on useless errands to keep him occupied: he hadn't been able to tell anyone the details of yesterday's events, not even Grant Nanna.

If there were a conspiracy, whom could he turn to? Only one person might listen and that was the President, and there was no way of getting to her. He'd have to call Jay Sandberg, who had made a study of presidential assassinations. If anyone would have a theory, it would be Sandberg. Mark retraced his steps to the pay phone, checked Sandberg's home number in New York, and dialled the ten digits. A woman's voice answered the telephone.

"Hello," she said coolly. Mark could visualise the cloud of cocaine smoke that went with the voice.

"Hello, I'm trying to reach Jay Sandberg."

"Oh." More cocaine smoke. "He's still at work."

"Can you tell me his number?" asked Mark.

After more smoke, she gave it to him, and the phone clicked.

Sheeesh, Mark said to himself, Upper East Side women.

A very different voice, warm Irish–American, answered the phone next.

"Sullivan and Cromwell."

Mark recognised the prestigious New York law firm. Other people were getting ahead in the world.

"Can I speak to Jay Sandberg?"

"I'll connect you, sir."

"Sandberg."

"Hi, Jay, it's Mark Andrews. Glad I caught you. I'm calling from

Washington."

"Hello, Mark, nice to hear from you. How's life for a G-man? Rat-a-tat-tat and all that."

"It can be," said Mark, "sometimes. Jay, I need some advice on where to find the facts on political assassination attempts, particularly the one in Massachusetts in 1979; do you remember it?"

"Sure do. Three people arrested; let me think." Sandberg paused. "All released as harmless. One died in an auto accident in 1980, another was knifed in a brawl in San Francisco, later died in 1981, and the third disappeared mysteriously last year. I tell you it was another conspiracy."

"Who this time?"

"Mafia wanted Edward Kennedy out of the way in '76 so they could avoid an inquiry he was pressing for into the death of those two hoodlums, Sam Giancana and John Rosselli; they don't love President Kane now with the way she is running the Gun Control bill."

"Mafia? Gun Control bill? Where do I start looking for the facts?" asked Mark.

"I can tell you it's not in the Warren Commission Report or any of the later inquiries. Your best bet is *The Yankee and Cowboy Wars* by Carl Oglesby – you'll find it all there."

Mark made a note.

"Thanks for your help, Jay. I'll get back to you if it doesn't cover everything. How are things in New York?"

"Oh, fine, just fine. I'm one of about a million lawyers interpreting the constitution at an exorbitant fee. Let's get together soon, Mark."

"Sure, next time I'm in New York."

Mark went back to the Library thoughtfully. It could be CIA, it could be Mafia, it could be a nut, it could be anyone – even Halt Tyson. He asked the girl for the Carl Oglesby book. A well-thumbed volume beginning to come apart was supplied. Sheed Andrews & McMeel, Inc., 6700 Squibb Road, Mission, Kansas. It was going to make good reading, but for now it was back to the senators' life histories. Mark spent two more hours trying to eliminate senators or find motives for any of them wanting President Kane out of the way: he wasn't getting very far.

"You'll have to leave now, sir," said the young librarian, her arms full of books, looking as if she would like to go home. "I'm afraid we lock up at 7:30."

"Can you give me two more minutes? I'm very nearly through."

"I guess so," she said, staggering away under a load of Senate Reports, 1971–73, which few but herself would ever handle.

Mark glanced over his notes. There were some very prominent names among the sixty-two "suspects", men like Alan Cranston of California, often described as the "liberal whip" of the Senate; Ralph

Brooks of Massachusetts, whom Florentyna Kane had defeated at the Democratic Convention. Majority Leader Robert C. Byrd of West Virginia. Henry Dexter of Connecticut. Elizabeth's father, he shuddered at the thought. Sam Nunn, the respected senator for Georgia, Robert Harrison of South Carolina, an urbane, educated man with a reputation for parliamentary skill; Marvin Thornton, who occupied the seat vacated by Edward Kennedy in 1980. Mark O. Hatfield, the liberal and devout Republican from Oregon; Hayden Woodson of Arkansas, one of the new breed of Southern Republicans; William Cain of Nebraska, a staunch conservative who had run as an independent in the 1980 election; and Birch Bayh of Indiana, the man who had pulled Ted Kennedy from a plane wreck in 1967, and probably saved his life. Sixty-two men under suspicion, thought Mark. And six days. And the evidence must be iron-clad. There was little more he could do that day.

Every government building was closing. He just hoped the Director had covered as much and could bring the sixty-two names down to a sensible number quickly. Sixty-two names; six days.

He returned to his car in the public parking lot. Six dollars a day for the privilege of being on vacation. He paid the attendant, eased the car out on Pennsylvania Avenue, and headed down 9th Street back towards his apartment in N Street, SW, the worst of the rush-hour behind him. Simon was there, and Mark tossed him the car keys. "I'm going out again as soon as I've changed," Mark called over his shoulder as he went up to his eighth-floor apartment.

He showered and shaved quickly and put on a more casual suit than the one he had worn for the Director. Now for the good part of the day.

When he came back down, the car was turned around so that Mark could, to quote Simon, make a quick getaway. He drove to Georgetown, turned right on 30th, and parked outside Elizabeth Dexter's house. A small red-brick town house, very chic. Either she was doing well for herself or her father had bought it for her. Her father, he couldn't help remembering . . .

She looked even more beautiful on the doorstep than she had in his imagination. That was good. She wore a long red dress with a high collar. It set off her dark hair and deep brown eyes.

"Are you going to come in, or are you just going to stand there looking like a delivery boy?"

"I'm just going to stand here and admire you," he said. "You know, Doctor, I've always been attracted to beautiful, clever women. Do you think that says something about me?"

She laughed and led him into the pretty house.

"Come and sit down. You look as though you could do with a drink." She poured him the beer he asked for. When she sat down, her eyes were serious.

"I don't suppose you want to talk about the horrible thing that happened to my mailman."

"No," said Mark. "I'd prefer not to, for a number of reasons."

Her face showed understanding.

"I hope you'll catch the bastard who killed him." Again, those dark eyes flashed to meet his. She got up to turn over the record on the stereo. "How do you like this kind of music?" she asked lightly.

"I'm not much on Haydn," he said. "I'm a Mahler freak. And Beethoven, Aznavour. And you?"

She blushed slightly.

"When you didn't turn up last night, I called your office to see if you were there."

Mark was surprised and pleased.

"Finally I got through to a girl in your department. You were out at the time, and besides she said you were very busy, so I didn't leave a message."

"That's Polly," said Mark. "She's very protective."

"And pretty?" She smiled with the confidence of one who knows she is good-looking.

"Good from far but far from good," said Mark. "Let's forget Polly. Come on, you ought to be hungry by now, and I'm not going to give you that steak I keep promising you. I've booked a table for nine o'clock at Tio Pepe."

"Lovely," she said. "Since you managed to get your car parked, why don't we walk?"

"Great."

It was a clear, cool evening and Mark enjoyed the fresh air. What he didn't enjoy was the continual urge to look over his shoulder.

"Looking for another woman already?" she teased.

"No," said Mark. "Why should I look any further?" He spoke lightly, but he knew he hadn't fooled her. He changed the subject abruptly. "How do you like your work?"

"My work?" Elizabeth seemed surprised, as though she never thought of it in those terms. "My life, you mean? It's just about my entire life. Or has been so far."

She glanced up at Mark with a sombre expression on her face. "I hate the hospital. It's a big bureaucracy, old and dirty and a lot of the people there, petty administrative types, don't really care about helping people. To them it's just another way of earning a living. Only yesterday I had to threaten to resign in order to convince the Utilisation Committee to let an old man remain in the hospital. He had no home to go back to."

They walked down 30th Street, and Elizabeth continued to tell him about her work. She spoke with spirit, and Mark listened to her with pleasure. She showed a pleasant self-assurance, as she told him about a soulful Yugoslav who would sing incomprehensible Slavic songs of love and longing as she inspected his ulcerated armpit and who had finally, in a misplaced gesture of passion, seized her left ear and licked it.

Mark laughed and took her arm as he guided her into the restaurant. "You ought to demand combat pay," he said.

"Oh, I wouldn't have complained, other than to tell him that his singing was always out of tune."

The hostess led them upstairs to a table in the centre of the room, near where the floor show would be performed. Mark rejected it in favour of a table in the far corner. He did not ask Elizabeth which seat she would prefer. He sat down with his back to the wall, making a lame excuse about wanting to be away from the noise so he could talk to her. Mark was sure that this girl would not fall too easily for that sort of blarney; she knew something was wrong and she sensed his edginess, but she did not pry.

A young waiter asked them if they would like a cocktail. Elizabeth asked for a Margarita, Mark for a spritzer.

"What's a spritzer?" asked Elizabeth.

"Not very Spanish, half white wine, half soda, lots of ice. Stirred but not shaken. Sort of a poor man's James Bond."

The pleasant atmosphere of the restaurant helped to dispel some of Mark's tension; he relaxed slightly for the first time in twenty-four hours. They chatted about movies, music, and books, and then about Yale. Her face, often animated, was sometimes serene but always lovely in the candlelight. Mark was enchanted by her. For all her intelligence and self-sufficiency, she had a touching fragility and femininity.

As they ate their paella Mark asked Elizabeth why her father had become a senator, about his career, and her childhood in Connecticut. The subject seemed to make her uneasy. Mark couldn't help remembering that her father was still on the list. He tried to shift the conversation to her mother. Elizabeth avoided his eyes and even, he thought, turned pale. For the first time, a tiny ripple of suspicion disturbed his affectionate vision of Elizabeth, and made him worry momentarily. She was the first beautiful thing that had happened for quite a while, and he didn't want to distrust her. Was it possible? Could she be involved? No, of course not. He tried to put it out of his mind.

The Spanish floor show came on and was performed with enthusiasm. Mark and Elizabeth listened and watched, unable to speak to each other above the noise. Mark was happy enough just to sit and be with her; her face was turned away as she looked at the dancers. When the floor show eventually ended, they had both long finished the paella. They ordered dessert and coffee.

"Would you like a cigar?"

Elizabeth smiled. "No, thanks. We don't have to ape men's vile habits as well as their good ones."

"Like that," said Mark. "You're going to be the first woman Surgeon

General, I suppose?"

"No, I'm not," she said demurely. "I'll probably be the second or third."

Mark laughed. "I'd better get back to the Bureau, and do great things. Just to keep up with you."

"And it may well be a woman who stops you becoming Director of the FBI," Elizabeth added.

"No, it won't be a woman that stops me becoming Director of the FBI," said Mark, but he didn't explain.

"Your coffee, señorita, señor."

If Mark had ever wanted to sleep with a woman on the first date, this was the occasion, but he knew it wasn't going to happen.

He paid the bill, left a generous tip for the waiter, and congratulated the girl from the floor show, who was sitting in a corner drinking coffee.

When they left the restaurant Mark found the night had a chill edge. Once again he began looking nervously around him, trying not to make it too obvious to Elizabeth. He took her hand as they crossed the street, and didn't let it go when they reached the other side. They walked on, chatting intermittently, both aware of what was happening. He wanted to hold on to her. Lately, he had been seeing a lot of women, but with none of them had he held their hand either before or afterwards. Gradually his mood darkened again. Perhaps fear was making him excessively sentimental.

A car was driving up behind them. Mark stiffened with anticipation. Elizabeth didn't appear to notice. It slowed down. It was going slower as it neared them. It stopped just beside them. Mark undid his middle button and fidgeted, more worried for Elizabeth than for himself. The doors of the car opened suddenly and out jumped four teenagers, two girls, two boys. They darted into a Hamburger Haven. Sweat appeared on Mark's forehead. He shook free of Elizabeth's touch. She stared at him. "Something's very wrong, isn't it?"

"Yes," he said. "Just don't ask me about it."

She sought his hand again, held it firmly, and they walked on. The oppression of the horrible events of the previous day bore down on Mark and he did not speak again. When they arrived at her front door, he was back in the world which was shared only by him and the hulking, shadowy figure of Halt Tyson.

"Well, you have been most charming this evening, when you've actually been here," she said smilingly.

Mark shook himself. "I'm really sorry."

"Would you like to come in for coffee?"

"Yes and no. Can I take another raincheck on that? I don't feel like good company right now."

He still had several things to do before he saw the Director at 7:00 am and it was already midnight. Also he hadn't slept properly for a day and a half.

"Can I call you tomorrow?"

"I'd like that," she said. "Be sure to keep in touch, whatever happens."

Mark would carry those few words around with him like a talisman for the next few days. He could recall her every word and its accompanying gesture. Were they said in fun, were they said seriously, were they said teasingly? Lately, it hadn't been very fashionable to fall in love; very few people seemed to be getting married and a lot of people who had were getting divorced. Was he really going to fall madly in love in the middle of all this?

He kissed her on the cheek and turned to leave, his eyes darting up and down the road again. She whispered after him:

"I hope you find the man who killed my mailman and your Greek."

Your Greek, your Greek, Greek Orthodox priest, Father Gregory. God in heaven, why hadn't he thought of it before? He'd forgotten Elizabeth for a moment as he started to run towards his car. He turned to wave; she was staring at him with a puzzled expression, wondering what she had said. Mark leaped into the car and drove as fast as he could to his apartment. He must find Father Gregory's number. Greek Orthodox priest, what did he look like; it was all coming back, there had been something unusual with him: what the hell was it? His clothes? No, they were fine, or was it his face? His face was wrong somehow. Of course. Of course. How could he have been so stupid. When he arrived home, he called the Washington Field Office immediately. Polly, on the switchboard, was surprised to hear him.

"Aren't you on leave?"

"Yes, sort of. Do you have Father Gregory's number?"

"Who is Father Gregory?"

"A Greek Orthodox priest whom Mr Stames used to contact occasionally; I think he was his local priest."

"Yes, you're right. Now I remember."

Mark waited.

She checked Stames's Rolodex and gave him the number. Mark wrote it down, and replaced the phone. Of course, of course, of course. How stupid of him. It was so obvious. Well past midnight, but he had to call. He dialled the number. The telephone rang several times before it was answered.

"Father Gregory?"

"Yes."

"Do all Greek Orthodox priests have beards?"

"Yes, as a rule. Who is this asking such a damn silly question in the middle of the night?"

Mark apologised. "My name is Special Agent Mark Andrews. I worked under Nick Stames."

The man at the other end, who had sounded sleepy, immediately woke up. "I understand, young man. What can I do for you?"

"Father Gregory, last night Mr Stames's secretary called you and asked you to go to Woodrow Wilson to check a Greek who had a bullet wound in his leg?"

"Yes, that's right – I remember, Mr Andrews. But somebody else called about thirty minutes later, just as I was leaving, in fact, to tell me I needn't bother because Mr Casefikis had been discharged from the hospital."

"He'd been what?" Mark's voice rose with each word.

"Discharged from the hospital."

"Did the caller say who he was?"

"No, the man gave no other details. I assumed he was from your office."

"Father Gregory, can I see you tomorrow morning at eight o'clock?"

"Yes, of course, my son."

"And can you be sure you don't talk to anybody else about this phone call, whoever they say they are?"

"If that is your wish, my son."

"Thank you, Father."

Mark dropped the telephone and tried to concentrate. He was taller than I was, so he was over six feet. He was dark, or was that just his priest's robes? No, he had dark hair, he had a big nose, I remember he had a big nose, eyes, no I can't remember his eyes, he had a big nose, a heavy chin, a heavy chin. Mark wrote everything down he could remember. A big heavy man, taller than me, big nose, heavy chin, big nose, heavy . . . he collapsed. His head fell on the desk and he slept.

Saturday morning, 5 March. 6:32 am

Mark had awoken, but he wasn't awake. His head was swimming with incoherent thoughts. The first vision to flash across his mind was Elizabeth; he smiled. The second was Nick Stames; he frowned. The third was the Director. Mark woke with a start and sat up, trying to focus his eyes on his watch. All he could see was the second hand moving: 6:35. Hell. He shot up from the chair, his stiff neck and back hurting him; he was still dressed. He threw off his clothes and rushed into the bathroom and showered, without taking time to adjust the water temperature. Goddamn freezing. At least it woke him up and made him forget Elizabeth. He jumped out of the shower and grabbed a towel: 6:40. After throwing the lather on his face, he shaved too quickly, mowing down the stubble on his chin. Damn it, three nicks; the aftershave lotion stung viciously: 6:43. He dressed: clean shirt, same cuff links, clean socks, same shoes, clean suit, same tie. A quick look in the mirror: two nicks still bleeding slightly, the hell with it. He bundled the papers on his desk into his briefcase and ran for the elevator. First piece of luck, it was on the top floor. Downstairs: 6:46.

"Hi, Simon."

The young black garage attendant didn't move. He was dozing in his little cubbyhole at the garage entrance.

"Morning Mark. Hell, man, is it eight o'clock already?"

"No, thirteen minutes to seven."

"What are you up to? Moonlighting?" asked Simon, rubbing his eyes and handing over the car keys. Mark smiled, but didn't have time to answer. Simon dozed off again.

Car starts first time. Reliable Mercedes. Moves on to the road: 6:48. Must stay below speed limit. Never embarrass the Bureau. At 6th Street, held up by lights: 6:50. Cut across G Street, up 7th, more lights. Cross Independence Avenue: 6:53. Corner of 7th and Pennsylvania. Can see FBI Building: 6:55. Down ramp, park, show FBI pass to garage guard, run for elevator: 6:57; elevator to seventh floor: 6:58. Along the corridor, turn right, Room 7074, straight in, past Mrs McGregor as instructed. She barely glances up; knock on door of Director's office; no reply; go in as instructed. No Director: 6:59; sink into easy chair. Director going to be late; smile of satisfaction. Thirty seconds to seven: glance around room, casually, as if been waiting for hours. Eyes land on grandfather clock. Stikes: one, two, three, four, five, six, seven.

The door opened, and the Director marched in. "Good morning, Andrews." He did not look at Mark, but at the clock on the wall. "It's always a little fast." Silence. The Old Post Office Tower clock struck seven.

The Director settled into his chair, and once again the large hands took possession of the desk.

"We'll start with my news first, Andrews. We have just received some identification on the Lincoln that went into the Potomac with Stames and Calvert."

The Director opened a new manilla file marked "Eyes only" and glanced at its contents. What was in the file that Mark didn't know about and ought to know about?

"Nothing solid to go on. Hans-Dieter Gerbach, German. Bonn has reported that he was a minor figure in the Munich rackets until five years ago, then they lost track of him. There is some evidence to suggest he was in Rhodesia and even hitched up with the CIA for a while. The White-Lightning Brigade. The CIA is not being helpful on him. I can't see much information coming from them before Thursday. Sometimes I wonder whose side they're on. In 1980, Gerbach turned up in New York, but there's nothing there except rumours and street talk, no record to go on. It would have helped if he'd lived."

Mark thought of the slit throats in Woodrow Wilson Medical Centre and wondered.

"The interesting fact to emerge from the car crash is that both back tyres of Stames's and Calvert's car have small holes in them. They could have been the result of the fall down the bank, but our laboratory boys think they are bullet holes. If they are, whoever did the shooting makes Wyatt Earp look like a boy scout."

The Director spoke into his intercom. "Have Assistant Director Rogers join us please, Mrs McGregor."

"Yes, sir."

"Mr Rogers's men have found the catering outfit Casefikis was working for, for what that's worth."

The Assistant Director knocked and entered. The Director indicated a chair. Rogers smiled at Mark and sat down.

"Let's have the details, Matt."

"Well, sir, the owner of the Golden Duck wasn't exactly co-operative. Seemed to think I was after him for contravening employers' regulations. I threatened to shut him down if he didn't talk. Finally he admitted to employing a man matching Casefikis's description on 24 February. He sent Casefikis to serve at a small luncheon party in one of the rooms at the Georgetown Inn on Wisconsin Avenue. The man who made the arrangement was a Lorenzo Rossi. He insisted on a waiter who couldn't speak English. Paid in cash. We've run Rossi through all the computers – nothing. Obviously a false name. Same story at the George-town Inn. The proprietor said the room had been hired for the day of 24 February by a Mr Rossi, food to be supplied, but no service, cash paid in advance. Rossi was about five-feet-eight, dark complexion, no distinguishing features, dark hair, sunglasses. The proprietor thought he "seemed Italian". No one at the hotel knows or cares who the hell went to lunch in that room that day. I'm afraid it doesn't get us very far."

"I agree. I suppose we could pull every Italian answering that description off the street," said the Director. "If we had five years, not five days. Did you turn up anything new at the hospital, Matt?"

"It's a hell of a mess, sir. The place is full of people coming and going, all day and most of the night. The staff all work shifts. They don't even know their own colleagues, let alone outsiders. You could wander around there all day with a torchlight in your hand and no one would stop you unless they wanted a light."

"That figures," said Tyson. "Right, Andrews, what have you been up to for the past twenty-four hours?"

Mark opened his regulation blue plastic portfolio. He reported that there were sixty-two senators left, the other thirty-eight accounted for, most of them having been a long way from Washington on 24 February. He passed the list of names over to the Director, who glanced through them.

"Some pretty big fish still left in the muddy pond, Andrews. Go on."

Mark proceeded to outline his encounter with the Greek Orthodox priest. He expected a sharp reprimand for failing to remember the matter of the beard immediately. He was not disappointed. Chastened, he continued:"I am seeing Father Gregory at eight o'clock this morning, and I thought I would go on to see Casefikis's widow afterwards. I don't think either will have much to offer, but I imagine you want those leads followed up, sir. After that I intended to return to the Library of Congress to try and figure out why those sixty-two senators might wish to see an end of President Kane."

"Well, to start with, put them in categories," said the Director. "First political party, then committees, then outside interests, then their personal knowledge of the President. Don't forget, Andrews, we do know that our man had lunch in Georgetown on 24 February and that should bring the numbers down."

"But sir, presumably they all had lunch on 24 February."

"Exactly, Andrews, but not all in private. Many of them would have been seen in a public place or lunched officially, with constituents or federal employees or lobbyists. You have to find out who did what, without letting the senator we're after get suspicous."

"How do you suggest I go about doing that, sir?"

"Simple," replied the Director. "You call each of the senators' secretaries and ask if the boss would be free to attend a luncheon on –" he paused "– 'The Problems of Urban Environment'. Yes, I like that. Give them a date, say 5 May, then ask if they attended either the one given on," the Director glanced at his calendar, "17 January or 24 February, as some senators who had accepted didn't attend, and one or two turned up without invitations. Then say a written invitation will follow. All the secretaries will put it out of their minds unless you write, and if any of them does remember on 5 May, it will be too late for us to care. One thing is certain: no senator will be letting his secretary know that he is planning to kill the President."

The Assistant Director grimaced slightly. "If he gets caught, sir, all hell will break loose. We'll be back in the dirty-tricks department."

"No, Matt, if I tell the President one of her precious brethren is going to knife her in the back, she won't see anything particularly pleasant in that trick."

"We haven't got any real proof, sir," said Mark.

"Then you had better find it, Andrews, or we'll all be looking for a new job, trust my judgement."

Trust my judgement, Mark thought.

"All we have is one strong lead," the Director continued. "That a
senator may be involved, but we have only five days left. If we fail next
Thursday, there will be enought time during the next twenty years to
study the inquiry and you, Andrews, will be able to make a fortune
writing a book about it."

Mark looked apprehensive.

"Andrews, don't get too worried. I have briefed the head of the
Secret Service. I told him no more and no less than was in your report,
as we agreed yesterday, so that gives us a clear run right through to 10
March. I'm working on a contingency plan, in case we don't know who
Cassius is before then: but I won't bore you with it now. I have also
talked to the boys from Homicide; they have come up with very little
that can help us. It may interest you to know that they have seen
Casefikis's wife already. Their brains seem to work a little faster than
yours, Andrews."

"Perhaps they don't have as much on their minds," said the
Assistant Director.

"Maybe not. Okay, go see her if you think it might help. You may
pick up something they missed. Cheer up, you've covered a lot of
ground. Perhaps this morning's investigation will give us some new
leads to work on. I think that covers everything for now. Right,
Andrews, don't let me waste any more of your time."

"No, sir."

Mark rose.

"I'm sorry, I forgot to offer you coffee, Andrews."

I didn't manage to drink it the last time, Mark wanted to say. He left
as the Director ordered coffee for himself and the Assistant Director. He
decided that he too could do with some breakfast and a chance to collect
his thoughts. He went in search of the Bureau cafeteria.

The Director drank his coffee and asked Mrs McGregor to send in his
personal assistant. The anonymous man appeared almost instantly, a
grey folder under his arm.

He didn't have to ask the Director what it was that he wanted. He
placed the folder on the table in front of him, and left without speaking.

"Thank you, " said the Director to the closing door.

He turned the cover of the folder and browsed through it for twenty
minutes, a chuckle here, and a grunt there, the odd comment to
Matthew Rogers. There were facts in it about Mark Andrews of which
Mark himself would have been unaware. The Director finished his
second cup of coffee, closed the file, and locked it in the personal drawer
of the Queen Anne desk. Queen Anne had never held as many secrets as
that desk.

Mark finished a much better breakfast than he could have hoped for at the Washington Field Office. There, you had to go across the street to Lunch Connection, because the snack bar downstairs was so abominable, much in keeping with the rest of the building. Not that he wouldn't have liked to return to it now instead of the underground garage to pick up his car. He didn't notice the man across the street who watched him leave, but he did wonder whether the blue Ford sedan that stayed in his rear-view mirror so long was there by chance. If it wasn't, who was watching whom, who was trying to protect whom?

He arrived at Father Gregory's church just before 8:00 am and they walked together to the priest's house. The priest's half-rim glasses squatted on the end of a stubby nose. His large, red cheeks and even larger basketball belly led the uncharitable to conclude that Father Gregory had found much to solace him on earth while he waited for the eternal kingdom of heaven. Mark told him that he had already breakfasted, but it didn't stop the Father from frying two eggs and bacon, plus toast, marmalade, and a cup of coffee. Father Gregory could add very little to what he had told Mark on the telephone the previous night, and he sighed deeply when he was reminded of the two deaths at the hospital.

"Yes, I read the details in the *Post*." When they talked about Nick Stames, a light came into his grey eyes; it was clear that priest and policeman had shared a few secrets, this was no jolly old Jesus freak.

"Is there any connection between Nick's death and the accident in the hospital?" Father Gregory asked suddenly.

The question took Mark by surprise. There was a shrewd brain behind the half-rim glasses. Lying to a priest, Greek Orthodox or otherwise, seemed somehow worse than the usual lies which were intended to protect the Bureau from the general public.

"Absolutely none," said Mark. "Just one of those horrible auto accidents."

"Just one of those weird coincidences?" said Father Gregory quizzically, peering at Mark over the top of his glasses. "Is that right?" he sounded almost as unconvinced as Grant Nanna. He continued: "There's one more thing I would like to mention. Although it's hard to remember exactly what the man said when he called me and told me not to bother to go the hospital, I'm fairly certain he was a well-educated man. I feel sure by the way he carried it off that he was a professional man, and I am not sure what I mean by that; it's just the strange feeling that he had made that sort of call before; there was something professional about him."

Father Gregory repeated the phrase to himself – "Something professional about him" – and so did Mark, while he was in the car on the way to the house in which Mrs Casefikis was staying. It was the home of the friend who had harboured her wounded husband.

Mark drove down Connecticut Avenue, past the Washington Hilton and the National Zoo, into Maryland. Patches of bright, yellow forsythia had begun to appear along the road. Connecticut Avenue turned into University Boulevard, and Mark found himself in Wheaton, a suburban satellite of stores, restaurants, gas stations and a few apartment buildings. Stopped by a red light near Wheaton Plaza, Mark checked his notes. 11501 Elkin Street. He was looking for the Blue Ridge Manor Apartments. Fancy name for a group of squat, three-storey faded-brick buildings lining Blue Ridge and Elkin streets. As he approached 11501, Mark looked for a parking space. No luck. He hovered for a moment, then decided to park in front of a fire hydrant. He draped the radio microphone carefully over his rear-view mirror, so that any observant meter maid or policeman would know that this was an official car on official business.

Adriana Casefikis burst into tears at the mere sight of Mark's badge. She looked frail; only twenty-nine, her clothes unkempt, her hair all over the place, her eyes grey and still full of tears. The lines on her face showed where the tears had been running, running for two days. She and Mark were about the same age. She didn't have a country, and now she didn't have a husband. What was going to happen to her? If Mark had felt alone, he was certainly better off than this poor woman.

Mrs Casefikis's English turned out to be rather better than her husband's. She had already seen two policemen. She told them that she knew nothing. First the nice man from the Metropolitan Police who had broken the news to her and been so understanding, then the Homicide lieutenant who had come a little later and been much firmer, wanting to know things she hadn't the faintest clue about, and now a visit from the FBI. Her husband had never been in trouble before and she didn't know who shot him or why anybody would want to. He was a gentle, kind man. Mark believed her.

He also assured her that she had no immediate cause for worry and that he would deal personally with the Immigration Office and the Welfare people about getting her some income. It seemed to cheer her up and make her a little more responsive.

"Now please try to think carefully, Mrs Casefikis. Have you any idea where your husband was working on 23 or 24 February, the Wednesday and Thursday of last week, and did he tell you anything about his work?"

She had no idea. Angelo never told her what he was up to and half the jobs were casual and only for the day, because he couldn't risk staying on without a work permit, being an illegal immigrant. Mark was getting nowhere, but it wasn't her fault.

"Will I be able to stay in America?"

"I'll do everything I can to help, Mrs Casefikis. That I promise you. I'll talk to a Greek Orthodox priest I know about finding some money to tide you over till I've seen the Welfare people."

Mark opened the door, despondent about the lack of any hard information either from Father Gregory or from Ariana Casefikis.

"The priest already give me money."

Mark stopped in his tracks, turned slowly, and faced her. He tried to show no particular interest.

"Which priest was that?" he asked casually.

"He said he help. Man who came to visit yesterday. Nice man, very nice, very kind. He give me fifty dollars."

Mark turned cold. The man had been ahead of him again. Father Gregory was right, there was something professional about him.

"What did he look like?"

"Oh, he was a big man, very dark, I think," she began.

Mark tried to remain offhand. It must have been the man who had passed him in the elevator, the man who had earlier kept Father Gregory from going to the hospital and who, if Mr Casefikis had known anything at all about the plot, would no doubt have dispatched her to join her husband.

"Did he have a beard, Mrs Casefikis?"

"Of course he did," she hesitated, "but I can't remember him having one."

Mark asked her to stay in the house, not to leave under any circumstances. He made an excuse that he was going to check on the Welfare situation and talk to the Immigration officials. He was learning how to lie. The clean-shaven Greek Orthodox priest was teaching him.

He jumped into the car and drove a few hundred yards to the nearest pay phone on Georgia Avenue. He dialled the Director's private line. The Director picked up the phone.

"Julius."

"What is your number?" asked the Director.

Thirty seconds later the phone rang. Mark went over the story carefully.

"I'll send an Identikit man down to you immediately. You go back there and hold her hand. And, Andrews, try to think on your feet. I'd like that fifty dollars. Was it one bill, or several? There may just be a fingerprint on them." The telephone clicked. Mark frowned. If the phony Greek Orthodox priest weren't always two steps ahead of him, the Director was.

Mark returned to Mrs Casefikis and told her that her case would be dealt with at the highest level; he must remember to speak to the Director about it at the next meeting, he made a note about it on his pad. Back to the casual voice again.

"Are you sure it was fifty dollars, Mrs Casefikis?"

"Oh, yes, I don't see a fifty-dollar bill every day, and I was most thankful at the time."

"Can you remember what you did with it?"

"Yes, I went and bought food from the supermarket just before they closed."

"Which supermarket, Mrs Casefikis?"

"Wheaton Supermarket. Up the street."

"When was that?"

"Yesterday evening about six o'clock."

Mark realised that there wasn't a moment to lose. If it weren't already too late.

"Mrs Casefikis, a man will be coming, a colleague of mine, a friend, from the FBI, to ask you to describe the kind Father who gave you the money. It will help us greatly if you can remember as much about him as possible. You have nothing to worry about because we're doing everything we can to help you."

Mark hesitated, took out his wallet and gave her fifty dollars. She smiled for the first time.

"Now, Mrs Casefikis, I want you to do just one last thing for me. If the Greek priest ever comes to visit again, don't tell him about our conversation, just call me at this number."

Mark handed her a card. Ariana Casefikis nodded, but her lacklustre grey eyes followed Mark to his car. She didn't understand, or know which man to trust: hadn't they both given her fifty dollars?

Mark pulled into a parking space in front of the Wheaton Supermarket. A huge sign in the window announced that cases of cold beer were sold inside. Above the window was a blue and white cardboard representation of the dome of the Capitol. Five days, thought Mark. He went into the store. It was a small family enterprise, privately owned, not part of a chain. Beer lined one wall, wine the other, and in between were four rows of canned and frozen foods. A meat counter stretched the length of the rear wall. The butcher seemed to be minding the store alone. Mark hurried towards him, starting to ask the question before he reached the counter.

"Could I please see the manager?"

The butcher eyed him suspiciously. "What for?"

Mark showed his credentials.

The butcher shrugged and yelled over his shoulder, "Hey, Flavio. FBI. Wants to see you."

Several seconds later, the manager, a large red-faced Italian, appeared in the doorway to the left of the meat counter. "Yeah? What can I do for you, Mr, uh . . ."

"Andrews, FBI." Mark showed his credentials once again.

"Yeah, okay. What do you want, Mr Andrews? I'm Flavio Guida. This is my place. I run a good, honest place."

"Yes, of course, Mr Guida. I'm simply hoping you can help me. I'm investigating a case of stolen money, and we have reason to believe that a stolen fifty-dollar bill was spent in this supermarket yesterday and we wonder now if there is any way of tracing it."

"Well, my money is collected every night," said the manager. "It's put into the safe and deposited in the bank first thing in the morning. It would have gone to the bank about an hour ago, and I think –"

"But it's Saturday," Mark said.

"No problem. My bank is open till noon on Saturday. It's just a few doors down."

Mark thought on his feet.

"Would you please accompany me to the bank immediately, Mr Guida?"

Guida looked at his watch and then at Mark Andrews.

"Okay. Give me just half a minute."

He shouted to an invisible woman in the back of the store to keep an eye on the cash register. Together he and Mark walked to the corner of Georgia and Hickers. Guida was obviously getting quite excited by the whole episode.

At the bank Mark went immediately to the chief cashier. The money had been handed over thirty minutes before to one of his tellers, a Mrs Townsend. She still had it in piles ready for sorting. It was next on her list. She hadn't had time to do so yet, she said rather apologetically. No need to feel sorry, thought Mark. The supermarket's take for the day had been just over five thousand dollars. There were twenty-eight fifty-dollar bills. Christ Almighty, the Director was going to tear him apart, or to be more exact, the fingerprint experts were. Mark counted the fifty-dollar notes using gloves supplied by Mrs Townsend and put them on one side – he agreed there were twenty-eight. He signed for them, gave the receipt to the chief cashier, and assured him they would be returned in the very near future. The bank manager came over and took charge of the receipt and the situation.

"Don't FBI men usually work in pairs?"

Mark blushed. "Yes, sir, but this is a special assignment."

"I would like to check," said the manager. "You are asking me to release one thousand four hundred dollars on your word."

"Of course, sir, please do check."

Mark had to think quickly. He couldn't ask the manager of a local bank to ring the Director of the FBI. It would be like charging your gasoline to the account of Henry Ford.

"Why don't you ring the FBI's Washington Field Office, sir, ask for the head of the Criminal Section. Mr Grant Nanna."

"I'll do just that."

Mark gave him the number, but he ignored it and looked it up for himself in the Washington directory. He got right through to Nanna.

Thank God he was there.

"I have a young man from your Field Office with me. His name is Mark Andrews. He says he has the authority to take away twenty-eight fifty-dollar bills. Something to do with stolen money."

Nanna also had to think quickly. Deny the allegation, defy the alligator – Nick Stames's old motto.

Mark, meanwhile, offered up a little prayer.

"That's correct, sir," said Nanna. "He has been instructed by me to pick up those notes. I hope you will release them immediately. They will be returned as soon as possible."

"Thank you, Mr Nanna. I'm sorry to have bothered you. I just felt I ought to check; you never can be sure nowadays."

"No bother, sir, a wise precaution. We wish everybody were as careful." The first truth he'd uttered, thought Grant Nanna.

The bank manager replaced the receiver, put the pile of fifty-dollar bills in a brown envelope, accepted the receipt, and shook hands with Mark apologetically.

"You understand I had to check?"

"Of course," said Mark. "I would have done the same myself."

He thanked Mr Guida and the manager and asked them both not to mention the matter to anybody. They nodded with the air of those who know their duty.

Mark returned to the FBI Building immediately and went straight to the Director's office. Mrs McGregor nodded at him. A quiet knock on the door, and he went in.

"Sorry to interrupt you, sir."

"Not at all, Andrews. Have a seat. We were just finishing."

Matthew Rogers rose and looked carefully at Andrews and smiled.

"I'll try and have the answers for you by lunch, Director," he said, and left.

"Well, young man, do you have our Senator in the car downstairs?"

"No, sir, but I do have these."

Mark opened the brown envelope and put twenty-eight fifty-dollar bills on the table.

"Been robbing a rank, have you? A federal charge, Andrews."

"Almost, sir. One of these notes, as you know, was given to Mrs Casefikis by the man posing as the Greek Orthodox priest."

"Well, that will be a nice little conundrum for our fingerprint boys; fifty-six sides with hundreds, perhaps thousands of prints on them. It's a long shot and it will take a considerable time, but it's worth a try." He was careful not to touch the notes. "I'll have Sommerton deal with it immediately. We'll also need Mrs Casefikis's prints. I'll also put one of our agents on her house in case the big man returns." The Director was writing and talking at the same time. "It's just like the old days when I ran a field office. I do believe I'd enjoy it if it weren't so serious."

"Can I mention just one other thing while I'm here, sir?"

"Yes, say whatever you want to, Andrews." Tyson didn't look up, just continued writing.

"Mrs Casefikis is worried about her status in this country. She has no money, no job, and now no husband. She may well have given us a vital lead and she has certainly been as cooperative as possible. I think we might help."

The Director pressed a button.

"Ask Sommerton from Fingerprints to come up immediately, and send Elliott in."

Ah, thought Mark, the anonymous man has a name.

"I'll do what I can. I'll see you Monday at seven, Andrews. I'll be home all weekend if you need me. Don't stop working."

"Yes, sir."

Mark left. He stopped at the Riggs Bank and changed fifteen dollars into quarters. The teller looked at him curiously.

"Have your own pinball machine, do you?"

Mark smiled.

He spent the rest of the morning and most of the afternoon with a diminishing pile of quarters, calling the weekend-duty secretaries of the sixty-two senators who had been in Washington on 24 February. All of them were most gratified that their senator should be invited to an Environmental Conference; the Director was no fool. At the end of sixty-two phone calls, his ears were numb. Mark studied the results . . . thirty senators had eaten in the office or with constituents, fifteen had not told their secretaries where they were having lunch or had mentioned some vague "appointment", and seventeen had attended luncheons hosted by groups as varied as the National Press Club, Common Cause, and the NAACP. One secretary even thought her boss had been at that particular Environmental Luncheon on 24 February. Mark hadn't been able to think of a reply to that.

With the Director's help he was now down to fifteen senators.

He returned to the Library of Congress, and once again made for the quiet reference room. The librarian did not seem the least bit suspicious of all his questions about particular senators and committees and procedure in the Senate; she was used to graduate students who were just as demanding and far less courteous.

Mark went back to the shelf that held the *Congressional Record*. It was easy to find 24 February: it was the only thumbed number in the pile of unbound latest issues. He checked through the fifteen remaining names. On that day, there had been one committee in session, the Foreign Relations Committee; three senators on his list of fifteen were members of that committee, and all three had spoken in committee that morning, according to the *Record*. The Senate itself had debated two issues that day: the allocation of funds in the Energy Department for solar-energy research, and the Gun Control bill. Some of the remaining twelve had spoken on one or both issues on the floor of the Senate: there was no way of eliminating any of the fifteen, damn it. He listed the fifteen names on fifteen sheets of paper, and read through the *Congressional Record* for every day from 24 February to 3 March. By each name he noted the senator's presence or absence from the Senate on each working day. Painstakingly, he built up each senator's schedule; there were many gaps. It was evident that senators do not spend all their time in the Senate.

The young librarian was at his elbow. Mark glanced at the clock: 7:30. Throwing-out time. Time to forget the senators and to see Elizabeth. He called her at home.

"Hello, lovely lady. I think it must be time to eat again. I haven't had anything since breakfast. Will you take pity on my debilitated state, Doctor, and eat with me?"

"And do what with you, Mark? I've just washed my hair. I think I must have soap in my ears."

"Eat with me, I said. That will do for the moment. I just might think of something else later."

"I just might say no later," she said sweetly. "How's the breathing?"

"Coming on nicely, thank you, but if I go on thinking what I am thinking right now, I may break out in pimples."

"What do you want me to do, pour cold water in the phone?"

"No, just eat with me. I'll pick you up in half an hour, hair wet or dry."

They found a small restaurant called Mr Smith's in Georgetown. Mark was more familiar with it in the summer, when one could sit at a table in the garden at the back. It was crowded with people in their twenties. The perfect place to sit for hours and talk.

"God," said Elizabeth. "This is just like being back at college; I thought we had grown out of that."

"I'm glad you appreciate it," Mark smiled.

"It's all so predictable. Folksy wooden floors, butcher-block tables, plants. Bach flute sonatas. Next time we'll try McDonald's."

Mark couldn't think of a reply, and was saved only by the appearance of a menu.

"Can you imagine, four years at Yale, and I still don't know what *ratatouille* is," said Elizabeth.

"I know what it is, but I wasn't sure how to pronounce it."

They both ordered chicken, baked potato, and salad.

"Look, Mark, there, that ghastly Senator Thornton with a girl young enough to be his daughter."

"Perhaps she is his daughter."

"No civilised man would bring his daughter here." She smiled at him.

"He's a friend of your father's, isn't he?"

"Yes, how do you know that?" asked Elizabeth.

"Common knowledge." Mark already regretted his question.

"Well, I'd describe him as more of a business associate. He makes his money manufacturing guns. Not the most attractive occupation."

"But your father owns part of a gun company."

"Daddy? Yes, I don't approve of that either, but he blames it on my grandfather who founded the firm. I used to argue with him about it when I was at school. Told him to sell his stock and invest it in something socially useful, saw myself as a sort of Major Barbara."

"How is your dinner?" a hovering waiter asked.

"Um, just great, thanks," said Elizabeth looking up. "You know, Mark, I once called my father a war criminal."

"But he was against the war, I thought."

"You seem to know an awful lot about my father," said Elizabeth looking at him suspiciously.

Not enough, thought Mark, and how much could you really tell me? If Elizabeth picked up any sign of his anxiety, she didn't register it but simply continued.

"He voted to approve the MX missile, and I didn't sit at the same table with him for almost a month. I don't think he even noticed."

"How about your mother?" asked Mark.

"She died when I was fourteen, which may be why I'm so close to my father," Elizabeth said. She looked down at her hands in her lap, evidently wanting to drop the subject. Her dark hair shone as it fell across her forehead.

"You have very beautiful hair," Mark said softly. "I wanted to touch it when I first saw you. I still do."

She smiled. "I like curly hair better." She leaned her chin on her cupped hands and looked at him mischievously. "You'll look fantastic when you're forty and fashionably grey at the temples. Provided you don't lose it all first, of course. Did you know that men who lose their hair at the crown are sexy, those who lose it at the temples, think, and those who lose it all over, think they are sexy?"

"If I go bald at the crown, will you accept that as a declaration of intent?"

"I'm willing to wait but not that long."

On the way back to her house he stopped, put his arm around her and kissed her, hesitantly at first, unsure of how she would respond.

"You know, my knees are feeling weak, Elizabeth," he murmured into her soft, warm hair. "What are you going to do with your latest victim?"

She walked on without speaking for a little way.

"Get you some knee pads," she said.

They walked on hand in hand, silently, happily, slowly. Three not very romantic men were following them.

In the pretty living-room, on the cream-coloured sofa, he kissed her again.

The three unromantic men waited in the shadows outside.

She sat alone in the Oval Office going over the clauses in the bill one by one, searching for any line that still might trip her up when the bill was voted on tomorrow.

She looked up suddenly startled to see her husband standing in front of her, a mug of steaming cocoa in his hand.

"An early night won't harm your chances of influencing that lot," he said pointing towards the Capitol.

She smiled, "Darling Edward, where would I be without your common sense?"

Sunday morning, 6 March. 9:00 am

Mark spent Sunday morning putting the finishing touches to his report for the Director. He began by tidying his desk; he could never think clearly unless everything was in place. Mark gathered all his notes together and put them in a logical sequence. He completed the task by two o'clock, without noticing that he had missed lunch. Slowly he wrote down the names of the fifteen senators who were left, six under the heading Foreign Relations Committee, nine under Gun Control bill – Judiciary Committee. He stared at the lists, hoping for inspiration but none came. One of these men was a killer and there were only four days left to find out which one. He put the papers into his briefcase, which he locked in his desk.

He went into the kitchen and made himself a sandwich. He looked at his watch. What could he do that would be useful for the rest of the day? Elizabeth was on duty at the hospital. He picked up the phone and dialled the number. She could only spare a minute, due in the operating theatre at three o'clock.

"Okay, Doctor, this won't take long and it shouldn't hurt. I can't call you every day just to tell you that you are lovely and intelligent and that you drive me crazy, so listen carefully."

"I'm listening, Mark."

"Okay. You are beautiful and bright and I'm crazy about you . . . What, no reply?"

"Oh, I thought there might be more. I'll say something nice in return when I'm three inches away from you, not three miles."

"Better make it soon or I am going to crack up. Off you go, and cut out someone else's heart."

She laughed. "It's an ingrown toenail actually . . ."

She hung up. Mark roamed about the room, his mind jumping from fifteen senators, to Elizabeth, back to one Senator. Wasn't it going just a little too well with Elizabeth? Was one Senator looking for him, rather than the other way around? He cursed and poured himself a Michelob. His mind switched to Barry Calvert; on Sunday afternoons they usually played squash. Then to Nick Stames, Stames who had unknowingly taken his place. If Stames were alive now, what would he do? . . . A remark that Stames had made at the office party last Christmas came flashing across Mark's mind: "If I'm not available, the second best crime man in this goddamn country is George Stampouzis of *The New York Times*" – another Greek, naturally. "He must know more about the Mafia and the CIA than almost anyone on either side of the law."

Mark dialled Information in New York, and asked for the number, not quite sure where it was leading him. The operator gave it to him.

"Thank you."

"You're very welcome."

He dialled it.

"Crime desk, George Stampouzis, please." They put him through.

"Stampouzis," said a voice. They don't waste words on *The New York Times*.

"Good afternoon. My name is Mark Andrews. I'm calling from Washington. I was a friend of Nick Stames; in fact, he was my boss."

The voice changed. "Yes, I heard about the terrible accident, if it was an accident. What can I do for you?"

"I need some inside information. Can I fly up and see you immediately?"

"Does it concern Nick?"

"Yes."

"Then yes. Meet me at eight o'clock, north-east corner of Twenty-first and Park Avenue South?"

"I'll be there," said Mark looking at his watch.

"And I'll be waiting for you."

The Eastern Airlines shuttle flight arrived a few minutes after seven. Mark made his way through the crowd milling around the baggage pickup and headed for the taxi stand. A potbellied middle-aged, unshaven New Yorker with an unlit cigar stub bobbing up and down in his mouth drove him towards Manhattan. He never stopped talking the whole way, a monologue that required few replies. Mark could have used the time to compose his thoughts.

"This country's full of shit," said the bobbing cigar.

"Yes," said Mark.

"And this city is nothing more than a garbage hole."

"Yes," said Mark.

"And that daughter of a bitch Kane's to blame. They ought to string her up."

Mark froze. It was probably said a thousand times a day; someone in Washington was saying it and meaning it.

The cab driver pulled up to the curb.

"Eighteen dollars even," said the bobbing cigar.

Mark put a ten and two fives into the little plastic drawer in the protective screen that divided driver from passenger, and climbed out. A heavy-set man in his mid-fifties and wearing a tweed overcoat, headed towards him. Mark shivered. He had forgotten how cold New York could be in March.

"Andrews?"

"Yes. Good guess."

"When you spend your life studying criminals, you begin to think like them." He was taking in Mark's suit. "G-men are certainly dressing better than they did in my day."

Mark looked embarrassed. Stampouzis must know that an FBI agent was paid almost double the salary of a New York cop.

"You like Italian food?" He didn't wait for Mark's reply. "I'll take you to one of Nick's old favourites." He was already on the move. They walked the long block in silence, Mark's step hesitating as he passed each restaurant entrance. Suddenly, Stampouzis disappeared into a doorway. Mark followed him through a run-down bar full of men who were leaning on the counter and drinking heavily. Men who had no wives to go home to, or if they did, didn't want to.

Once through the bar, they entered a pleasant, brick-walled dining area. A tall, thin Italian guided them to a corner table: obviously Stampouzis was a favoured customer. Stampouzis didn't bother with the menu.

"I recommend the shrimp marinara. After that, you're on your own."

Mark took his advice and added a *piccata al limone* and half a carafe of Chianti. Stampouzis drank Colt 45. They talked of trivia while they ate. Mark knew the residual Mediterranean creed after two years with Nick Stames – never let business interfere with the enjoyment of good food. In any case, Stampouzis was still sizing him up, and Mark needed his confidence. When Stampouzis had finished an enormous portion of zabaglione and settled down to a double espresso with Sambuca on the side, he looked up at Mark and spoke in a different tone.

"You worked for a great man, a rare lawman. If one tenth of the FBI were as conscientious and intelligent as Nick Stames, you would have something to be pleased about in that brick coliseum of yours."

Mark looked at him, about to speak.

"No, don't add anything about Nick; that's why you're here, and don't ask me to change my opinion of the Bureau. I've been a crime reporter for over thirty years and the only change I've seen in the FBI and the Mafia is that they are both bigger and stronger." He poured the Sambuca into his coffee, and took a noisy gulp. "Okay. How can I help?"

"Everything off the record," said Mark.

"Agreed," said Stampouzis. "For both our sakes."

"I need two pieces of information. First, are there any senators with close connections in organised crime and second, what is the attitude of the mob to the Gun Control bill?"

"You don't want much, do you?" said the Greek sarcastically. "Where shall I begin? The first is easier to answer directly, because the truth is that half the senators have loose connections with organised crime, by which I mean the Mafia, however out-of-date that is. Some don't even realise it, but if you include accepting campaign contributions from businessmen and large corporations directly or indirectly associated with crime, then every President is a criminal. But when the Mafia needs a senator they do it through a third party, and even that's rare."

"Why?" queried Mark.

"Tha Mafia needs clout at the state level, in courts, with deals, local by-laws, all that. They're just not interested in foreign treaties and the approval of Supreme Court justices. In a more general way, there are some senators who owe their success to links with the Mafia, the ones who have started as civil court judges or state assembly-men and received direct financial backing from the Mafia. It's possible they didn't even realise it; some people don't check too carefully when they are trying to get elected. Added to this are cases like Arizona and Nevada, where the Mafia runs a legit business, but God help any outsiders who try to join in. Finally, in the case of the Democratic party, there's organised labour, especially the Teamsters Union. There you are, Mark, thirty years' experience in ten minutes."

"Great background. Now can I ask you some specifics. If I name fifteen senators, will you indicate if they could fall into any of the categories you have mentioned?" Mark asked.

"Maybe. Try me. I'll go as far as I feel I can. Just don't push me."

"Bradley."

"Never," said Stampouzis.

"Thornton."

He didn't move a muscle.

"Bayh."

"Not that I have ever heard."

"Harrison."

"No idea. I don't know much about South Carolina politics."

"Nunn."

"Sam Sunday-School? Scout's Honour Nunn? You've got to be kidding."

"Brooks."

"Hates the President but I don't think he'd go that far."

Mark went down the list. Stevenson, Biden, Moynihan, Woodson, Clark, Mathias. Stampouzis shook his head silently.

"Dexter."

He hesitated. Mark tried not to tense.

"Trouble, yes," Stampouzis began. "But Mafia, no."

He must have heard Mark sigh. Mark was anxious to know what the trouble was; he waited but Stampouzis didn't add anything.

"Byrd."

"Majority leader. Not his style."

"Pearson."

"You're joking."

"Thank you," said Mark. He paused. "Now to the Mafia's attitude towards the Gun Control bill."

"I'm not certain at the moment," began Stampouzis. "The Mafia is no longer monolithic. It's too big for that and there has been a lot of internal disagreement lately. The old-timers are dead set against it because of the obvious difficulty of getting guns legally in the future, but they are more frightened by the riders to the bill, like mandatory sentences for carrying an unregistered gun. The Feds will love that; for them it's the best thing since tax evasion. They will be able to stop any known criminal, search him, and if he is carrying an unregistered gun, which he is almost certain to be, wham, he's in the court-house. On the other hand, some of the young Turks are looking forward to it, a modern-day Prohibition for them. They will supply unregistered guns to unorganised hoodlums and any mad radical who wants one, another source of income for the mob. They also believe the police won't be able to enforce the law and the cleaning-up period will take a decade. Does that get near to answering the question?"

"Yes, very near," said Mark.

"Now, my turn to ask you a question, Mark."

"Same rules?"

"Same rules. Are these questions directly connected with Nick's death?"

"Yes," said Mark.

"I won't ask any more then, because I know what to ask and you're going to have to lie. Let's just make a deal. If this breaks into something big, you'll see I get an exclusive over those bastards from the *Post*."

"Agreed," said Mark.

Stampouzis smiled and signed the check; the last comment had made Mark Andrews a legitimate expense.

Mark looked at his watch; with luck he would make the last shuttle from La Guardia. Stampouzis rose and walked to the door; the bar was still full of men drinking heavily, the same men with the same wives. Once on the street, Mark hailed a cab. This time, a young black pulled up beside him.

"I'm halfway there," said Stampouzis, puzzling Mark. "If I pick up anything that I think might help, I'll call you."

Mark thanked him and climbed into the cab.

"La Guardia, please."

Mark rolled down the window, Stampouzis stared in briefly.

"It's not for you, it's for Nick." He was gone.

The journey back to the airport was silent.

When Mark eventually reached his own apartment, he tried to put the pieces together in his mind ready for the Director the following morning. He glanced at his watch. Christ, it was already the following morning.

Monday morning, 7 March. 7:00 am

The Director listened to the results of Mark's research in attentive silence and then added his own unexpected piece of information.

"Andrews, we may be able to narrow your list of fifteen senators even further. Last Thursday morning a couple of agents picked up an unauthorised transmission on one of our KGB channels. Either temporary interference from some commercial station caused us to tune in a different frequency momentarily, or else some guy is in possession of an illegal transmitter for our frequency. The only thing our boys heard was: 'Come in, Tony. I just dropped the Senator back for his committee meeting and I'm . . .' The voice stopped transmitting abruptly and we couldn't find it again. Perhaps the conspirators had been listening in on our conversations, and this time one of them without thinking started to transmit on our frequency as well; it's easy enough to do. The agents who heard it filed a report concerning the illegal use of our frequency without realising its particular significance."

Mark was leaning forward in his chair.

"Yes, Andrews," said the Director. "I know what's going through your mind: 10:30 am. The message was sent at 10:30 am."

"10:30 am, 3 March," said Mark urgently. "Let me just check . . . which committees were already in progress . . ." He opened his file. "Dirksen Building . . . that hour . . . I have the details at hand somewhere, I know," he continued as he flicked through his papers. "Three possibilities, sir. The Foreign Relations and Government Operations committees were in session that morning. On the floor of the Senate they were debating the Gun Control bill: that seems to be taking up a lot of their time right now."

"Now we may be getting somewhere," said the Director. "Can you tell from your records how many of your fifteen were in the Capitol on 3 March and what they were up to?"

Mark leafed through the fifteen sheets of paper and slowly divided them into two piles. "Well, it isn't conclusive, sir, but I have no record of these eight" – he placed his hand on one of the piles – "being in the Senate that morning. The remaining seven were definitely there. None on the Government Operations Committee. Two on Foreign Relations – Pearson and Nunn, sir. The other five are Brooks, Byrd, Dexter, Harrison and Thornton. They were all on the floor. And they were all on the Judiciary Committee, Gun Control bill, as well."

The Director grimaced. "Well, as you say, Andrews, it's hardly conclusive. But it's all we have, so you concentrate on those seven. With only four days, it's a chance we will have to take. Don't get too excited just because we had one lucky break, and double-check that those eight could not have been in Dirksen that morning. Now, I am not going to risk putting seven senators under surveillance. Those folks on the Hill are suspicious enough of the FBI as it is. We'll have to use different tactics. Politically, we can't take a chance on a full-scale investigation. I'm afraid we'll have to find our man by using the only clues we're certain of – where he was on Thursday, 24 February at lunchtime, and this 10:30 Judiciary Committee meeting last week. So don't bother with the motive – we needn't waste time second-guessing that, Andrews. Just keep looking for ways of narrowing the list, and spend the rest of the day at the Foreign Relations Committee and the floor of the Senate. Talk to the staff directors. There is nothing they don't know – public or private – about the senators."

"Yes, sir."

"And one more thing. I'm having dinner with the President tonight so I may be able to glean some information from her which could help us reduce the number of suspects."

"Will you tell the President, sir?"

The Director of the FBI paused. "No, I don't think so. I still believe we have the problem under control. I see no reason for worrying her at this stage, certainly not before I'm convinced we're likely to fail."

Finally the Director passed over an Identikit picture of the Greek priest. "Mrs Casefikis's version," he said. "What do you think of it?"

"It's not a bad likeness at all," said Mark. "Maybe a little fleshier around the jaws than that. Those men really know their job."

"What worries me," said the Director, "is that I've seen that damn face before. So many criminals have come across my path that to remember one of them is almost impossible. Maybe it will come to me."

"I hope it comes before Thursday, sir," said Mark, without thinking.

"So do I," Tyson replied grimly.

"And to think I was only twenty-four hours behind him. It hurts."

"Think yourself lucky, young man. If you had been ahead of him, I think Ariana Casefikis would now be dead and so might you. I've still got a man on Mrs Casefikis's home just in case he returns, but I think he is far too professional a bastard to risk that."

Mark agreed. "Professional bastard," he repeated.

The red light on the internal telephone winked.

"Yes, Mrs McGregor?"

"You'll be late for your appointment with Senator Hart."

"Thank you, Mrs McGregor." He put the phone down. "I'll see you at the same time tomorrow, Mark." It was the first time he called him Mark. "Leave no stone unturned; only four days left."

Mark took the elevator down and left the building by his usual route. He didn't notice he was being followed from the other side of the street. He went to the Senate Office Building and made appointments to see the staff directors of the Foreign Relations and Judiciary committees. The earliest either could manage was the following morning. Mark returned to the Library of Congress to research more thoroughly the personal histories of the seven senators left on his list. They were a rather varied bunch, from all over the country, with little in common; one of them had nothing in common with the other six, but which one? Nunn – it didn't add up. Thornton – Stampouzis obviously didn't care for him but what did that prove. Byrd – surely not the majority leader? Harrison – Stampouzis said he was against the Gun Control bill, but so was almost half the Senate. Dexter – what was the trouble Stampouzis wouldn't tell him about? Perhaps Elizabeth would enlighten him tonight. Ralph Brooks, a strangely intense, driven man and certainly lacking any affection for Kane, that was for sure. Pearson – if he turned out to be the villain, no one would believe it: thirty-three years in the Senate, and always playing honest Casca in public and private.

Mark sighed – the long weary sigh of a man who has come to an impasse. He glanced at his watch: 10:45; he must leave immediately if he were to be on time. He returned the various periodicals, *Congressional Records*, and Ralph Nader reports to the librarian, and hurried across the street to the parking lot to pick up his car. He drove quickly down Constitution Avenue and over Memorial Bridge – how many times had he done that this week? Mark glanced in his rear-view mirror and thought he recognised the car behind him, or was it just the memory of last Thursday?

Mark parked his car at the side of the road. Two Secret Service men stopped him. He produced his credentials and walked slowly down the path just in time to join a hundred and fifty other mourners standing around two graves, freshly dug to receive two men who a week ago were more alive than most of the people attending their burial. The Vice President, former Senator Bill Bradley, was representing the President. He stood next to Norma Stames, a frail figure in black, being supported by her two sons. Hank, the eldest, stood next to a giant of a man, who must have been Barry Calvert's father. Next was the Director, who glanced around and saw Mark, but didn't acknowledge him. The game was being played out even at the graveside.

Father Gregory's vestments fluttered slightly in the cold breeze. The hem was muddy, for it had rained all night. A young chaplain in white surplice and black cassock stood silently at his side.

"I am the image of Thine inexpressible glory, even though I bear the wounds of sin," Father Gregory intoned.

His weeping wife bent forward and kissed Nick Stames's pale cheek and the coffin was closed. As Father Gregory prayed, Stames's and Calvert's coffins were lowered slowly, slowly into their graves. Mark watched sadly: it might have been him going down, down; it should have been him.

"With the saints give rest, O Christ, to the souls of Thy servants, where there is neither sickness or sorrow, nor sighing, but Life everlasting."

The final blessing was given, the Orthodox made the sign of the cross and the mourners began to disperse.

After the service Father Gregory was speaking warmly of his friend Nick Stames and expressed the hope that he and his colleague Barry Calvert had not died without purpose; he seemed to be looking at Mark as he said it.

Mark saw Nanna, Aspirin, Julie, and the anonymous man, but realised he mustn't speak to them. He slipped quietly away. Let the others mourn the dead: his job was to find their living murderers.

Mark drove back to the Senate, more determined than ever to find out which senator should have been present at the poignant double funeral. Had he stayed a little longer, he would have seen Matson talking casually to Grant Nanna, saying what a good man Stames was and what a loss he would be to law enforcement.

Mark spent the afternoon at the Foreign Relations Committee listening to Pearson and Nunn. If it were either of them, they were cool customers, going about their job without any outward signs of anxiety. Mark wanted to cross their names off the list but he needed one more fact confirmed before he could. When Pearson finally sat down, Mark felt limp. He also needed to relax tonight if he were going to survive the next three days. He left the committee room and called Elizabeth to confirm their dinner date. He then called the Director's office and gave Mrs McGregor the telephone numbers at which he could be reached: the restaurant, his home, Elizabeth's home. Mrs McGregor took the numbers down without comment.

Two cars tailed him on his way back: a blue Ford sedan and a black Buick. When he arrived home, he tossed the car keys to Simon, dismissed the oppressive but familiar sensation of being continually watched, and started thinking of more pleasant things, an evening with Elizabeth.

6:30 pm

Mark walked down the street thinking about the evening ahead of him. Already I adore that girl. That's the one thing I am certain of at the moment. If only I could get rid of the nagging doubt about her father – even about her.

He went into Blackistone's and ordered a dozen roses, eleven red, one white. The girl handed him a card and an envelope. Quickly, he wrote Elizabeth's name and address on the envelope, and he pondered the blank card, fragments of sentences and poems flashing through his mind. Finally, he smiled. He wrote, carefully:

> Happly I think on thee, and then my state,
> Like to the lark at break of day arising
> From sullen earth, sings hymns at heaven's gate.
> P.S. Modern version. Is it at long last love?

"Have them sent at once, please."
"Yes, sir."
Good. Back home. What to wear? A dark suit? Too formal. The light blue suit? Too much like a gay, should never have bought it in the first place. The double-breasted suit – latest thing. Shirt. White, casual, no tie. Blue, formal, tie. White wins. Too virginal? Blue wins. Shoes: black slip-on or laces? Slip-on wins. Socks: simple choice, dark blue. Summing up: denim suit, blue shirt, dark blue tie, dark blue socks, black

slip-on shoes. Leave clothes neatly on bed. Shower and wash hair – I like curly hair better. Damn, soap in eyes. Grope for towel, soap out, drop towel, out of shower. Towel around waist. Shave; twice in one day. Shave very carefully. No blood. Aftershave. Dry hair madly with towel. Curls all over the place. Back to bedroom. Dress carefully. Get tie exactly – that won't do, tie again. Better, this time. Pull up zipper – could stand to lose inch around waist. Check in mirror. Seen worse. To hell with modesty, have been a whole lot worse. Check money, credit cards. No gun. All set. Bolt door. Press button for elevator.

"Can I have my keys, please, Simon?"

"Well, goddamn." Simon's eyes opened very wide. "Found yourself a new fox!"

"You better not wait up, because if I fail, Simon, I'll probably jump on top of you."

"Thanks for the warning, Mark. Tough it out, man."

Beautiful evening, climb into car, check watch: 7:34.

The Director checked his dinner jacket again.

I miss Ruth. Housekeeper does a great job, but not the same thing at all. Pour a scotch, check clothes. Tuxedo just pressed – a little out of fashion. Dress shirt back from the cleaners. Black tie to be tied. Black shoes, black socks, white handkerchief – all in order. Turn on shower. Ah, how to get something useful out of the President? Damn, where's the soap? Have to get out of shower and soak bathmat and towel. Only one towel. Grab soap, revolting smell. Nowadays, they must only make it for gays. Wish I could still get army surplus. Out of the shower. Overweight; I need to lose about fifteen pounds. Body too white. Hide it quickly and forget. Shave. Good old trusty cutthroat. Never shave twice a day except when dining with the President. Good. No damage. Get dressed. Fly buttons; hate zippers. Now to tie black tie. Damn it. Ruth could always do it the first time, perfectly. Try again. At last. Check wallet. Don't really need money, credit cards, or anything else. Unless the President's going through hard times. Tell housekeeper I'll be back about eleven. Put on overcoat. Special agent there with car, as always.

"Good evening, Sam, beautiful evening."

The only chauffeur in the employ of the FBI opened the back door of the Ford sedan.

Climb into car, check watch: 7:45.

Drive slowly – lots of time – don't want to be there early – never seems to be any traffic when you have all the time in the world – hope roses have arrived – take longer route to Georgetown, past Lincoln Memorial and up Rock Creek and Potomac Parkway – it's prettier – at least con yourself that's why you're doing it. Don't run yellow lights, even though man behind you is obviously late and gesticulating. Obey the law – con yourself again – you'd shoot through the lights if you were running late for her. Never embarrass the Bureau. Careful of trolley lines in Georgetown, so easy to skid on them. Turn right at end of street and find parking space. Circle slowly looking for perfect spot – no such thing. Double-park and hope no traffic cop's around. Stroll nonchalantly towards house – bet she's still in the tub. Check watch: 8:04. Perfect. Ring doorbell.

"We're running a bit late, Sam." Perhaps unwise to say that because he'll break the speed limit and might embarrass the Bureau. Why is there so much traffic when you're in a hurry? Damn Mercedes in front of us at the circle, stopping even before the lights turned red. Why have a car that can do 120 mph if you don't even want to do thirty? Good, the Mercedes has turned off towards Georgetown. Probably one of the beautiful people. Down Pennsylvania Avenue. At last the White House in sight. Turn on to West Executive Avenue. Waved on by guard at gate. Pull up to West Portico. Met by Secret Service man in dinner jacket. His tie looks better than mine. Bet it's a clip-on. No, come to think of it, it's regulation to have to tie them in the White House. Damn it, the man must be married. Didn't do it himself. Follow him through foyer to West Wing Reception Room past Remington sculpture. Met by another Secret Service man also in dinner jacket. Also better tie. I give up. Escorted to elevator. Check watch: 8:06. Not bad. Enter West Sitting Hall.

"Good evening, Madam President."

"Hello, lovely lady."

She looks beautiful in that blue dress. Fantastic creature. How could I have any suspicions about her?

"Hello, Mark."

"That's a terrific dress you're wearing."

"Thank you. Would you like to come in for a minute?"

"No, I think we'd better go, I'm double-parked."

"Fine, I'll just grab my coat."

Open car door for her. Why didn't I just take her by the hand into the bedroom and make mad passionate love to her? I would have happily settled for a sandwich. That way we could do what we both want to do and save a lot of time and trouble.

"Did you have a good day?"

"Very busy. How about you, Mark?"

Oh, managed to think about you for a few hours while I got some work done, but it wasn't easy.

"Busy as all hell. I wasn't sure I was going to be able to make it."

Start car, right on M Street to Wisconsin. No parking spaces. Past

Roy Rogers' Family Restaurant. Let's just get some chicken legs and head back home.

"Aah, success."

Hell, where did that Volkswagen come from?

"What lousy luck. You'll find another one."

"Yes, but four hundred yards away from the restaurant."

"The walk will do us good."

Did the roses come? I'll put that florist's girl in jail in the morning if she forgot to send them.

"Oh, Mark, how thoughtless of me not to mention it before; thank you for those glorious roses. Are you the white one? And the Shakespeare?"

"Think nothing of it, lovely lady."

Liar. So you liked the Shakespeare, but what was your answer to the Cole Porter? Enter supersmooth French restaurant, Rive Gauche. Gauche is right. A Fed in a place like this? Bet it'll cost an arm and a leg. Full of snotty waiters with their hands out. What the hell, it's only money.

"Did you know that this place is responsible for making Washington the French-restaurant capital of America?"

Trying to impress her with a little inside dope.

"No, why?"

"Well, the owner keeps bringing his chefs over from France. One by one they quit and go off to start their own restaurants."

"You G-men really do carry around a store of useless information."

Look for the maître d'.

"Table in the name of Andrews."

"Good evening, Mr Andrews. How nice to see you."

Damn man's never seen me before and probably will never see me again. Which table is he going to give me? Not too bad. She might even believe I've been here before. Slip him a five-dollar bill.

"Thank you, sir. Enjoy your dinner."

They settled back in the deep red leather chairs. The restaurant was crowded.

"Good evening. Would you care for an aperitif, sir?"

"What will you have, Elizabeth?"

"Campari and soda, please."

"One Campari and soda and I'll have a spritzer."

Glance at menu. Chef Michel Laudier. The restaurant motto: *Fluctuat nec mergitur*. Oh, I'll *mergitur*, all right, cover charges, service charges. Ouch. And she has no way of knowing. This is one of those sexy places where the man is given a menu with the prices.

"I'll have a first course, but only if you'll join me."

"Of course, I'm going to have one, lovely lady."

"Good, I'll have the avocado . . ."

Without prawns?

". . . with prawns, and then . . ."

. . . Caesar salad?

". . . the filet mignon Henri IV – rare, please."

$20.50. To hell with it, she's worth every penny. I think I'll have the same.

"Have you decided, sir?"

"Yes, we'll both have the avocado with prawns and the filet mignon Henri IV, rare."

"Would you care to look at the wine list?"

No, thank you, I'll have a beer.

"Would you like some wine, Elizabeth?"

"That would be lovely, Mark."

"A bottle of Hospice de Beaune, *soixante-dix-huit*, please."

I bet he can tell the only damn French I learned at school was the numbers.

"Very good, sir."

The first course arrived and so did the sommelier with the wine.

If you think you're going to sell us two bottles, you damn frog, think again.

"Shall I serve the wine, sir?"

"Not yet, thank you. Open it and then serve it with the main course."

"Certainly, sir."

"Your avocado, Mademoiselle."

Prawns go before the fall.

"Good evening, Halt. How's life at the Bureau?"

"We're surviving, Madam."

What banal remarks the mighty make to each other.

The Director glanced around the pleasant blue and gold room. H. Stuart Knight, the head of the Secret Service, stood alone at the far end. On the sofa, by the window overlooking the West Wing and the Executive Office Building, sat the Attorney General, Marian Edelman, talking to Senator Birch Bayh, the man who had succeeded Ted Kennedy as chairman of the Judiciary Committee. The hackneyed phrase "boyish good looks", which had been applied to Bayh constantly during his campaigning in the 1976 Democratic presidential primaries, was still an accurate description. The thin, gaunt senator from Texas, Marvin Thornton, hovered over his colleague and Marian Edelman.

My God, let me have men about me that are fat . . .

"You see I've invited Thornton."

"Yes, Madam."

"We must try and talk him round on the Gun Control bill."

The West Sitting Hall was a comfortable room on the family floor of the White House, adjacent to the First Gentleman's dressing-room. It was an honour to be entertained in this part of the White House. And to eat in the small dining-room, rather than the President's dining-room downstairs, was a special privilege, since the former was usually reserved for strictly family dining. The fact that the President's husband was absent only confirmed how private this occasion had to be.

"What will you drink, Halt?"

"Scotch on the rocks."

"Scotch on the rocks for the Director and an orange juice for me. I'm watching my weight."

Doesn't she know orange juice is the last thing to drink if you're dieting?

"How are the votes stacking up, Madam?"

"Well, the numbers are forty-eight for and forty-seven against at the moment, but it's got to go through on the tenth or I'll have to forget the whole thing until the next session. That's my biggest worry at the moment, what with my European tour and the New Hampshire primary less than a year off. I would have to drop the bill until I was re-elected and I can't afford it to be the main election issue. I want it out of the way and seen to be working before then."

"Then let's hope it passes on the tenth, because it would certainly make my job easier, Madam President."

"Marian's too. Another drink, Halt?"

"No, thank you, Madam."

"Shall we go in to dinner?"

The President led her five guests into the dining-room. The wall-paper in the room depicted scenes from the American Revolution. It was furnished in the Federal style of the early nineteenth century.

I never get bored with the beauty of the White House.

The Director gazed at the plaster-composition mantel designed by Robert Welford of Philadelphia in 1815. It bore the famous report of Commodore Oliver Hazard Perry after the Battle of Lake Erie during the War of 1812: "We have met the enemy, and they are ours."

"Five thousand people passed through this building today," H. Stuart Knight was saying. "Nobody really grasps the security problems. This building may be the home of the President, but it still belongs to the people and that makes one continuous democratic headache."

If he knew everything . . .

The President sat at the head of the table, the Attorney General at the other end, Bayh and Thornton on one side, the Director and Knight on the other. The first course was avocado with prawns.

I always get sick when I eat prawns.

"It's good to see my law officers together," said the President. "I want to take this opportunity to discuss the Gun Control bill, which I remain determined will pass on 10 March. That's why I invited Birch and Marvin here tonight, because their support will influence the fate of this bill."

10 March again. Perhaps Cassius has to keep to a deadline. Seem to remember Thornton being firmly against this bill, and he's on Andrews' list of seven.

"The rural states are going to be a problem, Madam President," Marian Edelman was saying. "They won't be willing to hand over their guns all that readily."

"A long amnesty period, say about six months, might be the answer," the Director offered. "So the law remains unaffected for a statutory period. It's what always happens after a war. And the public relations boys can keep announcing that hundreds of weapons have been handed in to local police stations."

"Good thinking, Halt," said the President

"It's going to be a hell of an operation," said the Attorney General, "with seven million members of the National Rifle Association and probably fifty million firearms in America."

No one disagreed with that conclusion. The second course arrived. Dover sole. Obviously the President is serious about her diet.

"Coffee or brandy, sir?"

"Don't let's bother," said Elizabeth, touching Mark's hand gently. "Let's have it at home."

"Nice idea."

He smiled into her eyes and tried to guess what was going on in her mind . . .

"No, thank you. Just the check."

The waiter scurried away obediently.

They always scurry away obediently when you ask for the check. She hasn't let go of my hand.

"A delicious meal, Mark. Thank you very much."

"Yes, we must come here again sometime."

The check arrived. Mark glanced at it in rueful bemusement.

$87.20, plus tax. If you can understand how a restaurant gets to its final figure you deserve to be Secretary of the Treasury. Hand over the American Express Card. The little piece of blue paper comes back to sign. Make it up to $100.00 and forget it until the envelope marked American Express arrives in the mail.

"Good night, Mr Andrews." Much bowing and scraping. "I hope we will see you and Mademoiselle again soon."

"Yes, indeed."

You'll need a very good memory to recognise me next time I come. Open car door for Elizabeth. Will I do this when we're married? Christ,

I'm thinking about marriage.

"I think I must have eaten too much. I'm rather sleepy."

Now what does that mean? You could take that about twenty different ways.

"Oh, really, I feel ready for anything."

A bit clumsy, maybe. Look for parking space again. Good. There's one right in front of the house and no Volkswagen to stop me grabbing it. Open car door for Elizabeth. She fumbles with front door keys. Into kitchen. Kettle on.

"What a nice kitchen."

Silly remark.

"I'm glad you like it."

Equally silly.

Into living-room.

Good, there are the roses.

"Hello, Samantha. Come and meet Mark."

Christ Almighty, she has a roommate.

Samantha rubbed up against Mark's leg and purred.

Relief. Samantha is Siamese, not American.

"Where shall I sit?"

"Anywhere."

She's no help at all.

"Black or with cream, darling?"

"Darling." The odds must be better than 50–50.

"Black, please, with one sugar."

"Amuse yourself till the water boils. I'll only be a few minutes."

"More coffee, Halt?"

"No thank you, Madam, I have to be getting home, if you'll excuse me."

"I'll walk you to the door. There are one or two things I'd like to discuss with you."

"Yes, of course, Madam President."

The Marines at the West Entrance came to attention. A man in a dinner jacket hovered in the shadows behind the pillars.

"I'll need your backing a hundred per cent for this Gun Control bill, Halt. The committee is bound to be pushing for your views. And although the numbers are just with us on the floor of the House, I don't want any last-minute hiccups; I'm running out of time."

"I'll be with you, Madam. I've wanted it ever since the death of John F. Kennedy."

"Have you any particular worries about it, Halt?"

"No, Madam. You deal with the politics and sign the bill, and I'll see that the law is enforced."

"Any advice, perhaps?"

"No, I don't think so . . ."

Beware the Ides of March.

". . . although it's always puzzled me, Madam President, why in the end you left the bill this late. If something goes wrong on 10 March and if you were to lose next year's election, we would all be back at square one."

"I know, Halt, but I had to decide between my Medicare bill, which was a controversial enough way to start an administration, and pushing a Gun Control bill through at the same time; I might have ended up losing both. To tell you the truth, it had been my intention to start the bill in committee a year earlier, but no one could have anticipated Nigeria attacking South Africa without warning, and America finally having to decide where she stood on that continent."

"You sure stuck your neck out on that one, Madam President, and I confess at the time I thought you were wrong."

"I know, Halt. I had a few sleepless nights myself. But, getting back to the Gun Control bill: don't ever forget that Dexter and Thornton have run the most successful two-man filibuster in the history of the Senate. By 10 March, this damn bill will have been going the rounds for nearly two years despite the tacit support of Senator Byrd as Majority Leader. But I'm not too worried. I still believe we'll pull it off. I can't foresee anything that can stop it now, can you, Halt?"

The Director hesitated. "No, Madam."

The first lie I have ever told the Chief. Would an investigating commission believe my reasons if the President is assassinated in three days' time?

"Good night, Halt, and thank you."

"Good night, Madam President, and thank you for an excellent dinner."

The Director stepped out, and into his car. The special agent in the driver's seat looked around at him.

"An important message has just come in for you, sir. Could you return to the Bureau immediately?"

Not again.

"All right, but it might be simpler to keep a bed in the place, except someone would accuse me of trying to live rent-free on taxpayers' money."

The driver laughed; the Director had obviously had a good dinner, which was more than he had.

Elizabeth brought the coffee in and sat down by him.

Only the brave deserve the fair. Lift arm casually, place at the back of the couch, touch her hair lightly.

Elizabeth rose. "Oh, I nearly forgot. Would you like a brandy?"

No, I don't want a brandy. I want you to come back.

"No, thank you."

She settled back into Mark's shoulder.

Can't kiss her while she's got the coffee cup in her hand. Ah, she's put the cup down. Hell, she's up again.

"Let's have some music."

No thank you.

"Great idea."

"How about 'In Memory of Sinatra'?"

"Great."

. . . "This time we almost made the pieces fit . . . didn't we . . . gal?"

It's got to be absolutely the wrong song. Ah, she's back. Try the kiss again. Damn, still more coffee. The cup's down at last. Gentle. Yes, very nice. Christ, she's beautiful. Long kiss – are her eyes open? – no, closed. She's enjoying it – good – longer and even better.

"Would you like some more coffee, Mark?"

No no no no no no no.

"No, thank you."

Another long kiss. Start moving hand across back – I've been this far before with her – can't possibly be any objection – move hand to leg – pause – what fabulous legs and she's got two of them. Take hand off leg and concentrate on kissing.

"Mark, there's something I have to tell you."

Oh, Christ! It's the wrong time of the month. That's all I need now.

"Uh-mh?"

"I adore you."

"I adore you too, darling."

He unzipped her skirt, and began to caress her gently.

She began to move her hand up his leg.

Heaven is about to happen.

Ring, ring, ring, ring.

Jee-sus!

"It's for you, Mark."

"Andrews?"

"Sir."

"Julius."

Shit.

"I'm coming."

Tuesday morning, 8 March. 1:00 am

The man standing at the corner of the churchyard was trying to keep warm in the chill of the early March morning by slapping himself on the back. He had once seen Gene Hackman do it in a movie and it had worked. It wasn't working. Perhaps he needed the big Warner Brothers arc light Hackman had had to help him. He considered the matter, while he continued slapping.

There were actually two men on surveillance, Special Agent Kevin O'Malley and Assistant Field Supervisor Pierce Thompson, both selected by Tyson for their ability and discretion. Neither had shown any sign of surprise when the Director had instructed them to tail a fellow FBI man and report back to Elliott. It had been a long wait for Mark to emerge from Elizabeth's house, and O'Malley didn't blame him. Pierce left the churchyard and joined his colleague.

"Hey, Kevin, have you noticed that someone else is tailing Andrews for us?"

"Yeah. Matson. Why?"

"I thought he was retired."

"He is, I just assumed old Halt was making sure."

"I guess you're right but I wonder why Tyson didn't tell us."

"Because the whole operation's pretty irregular. No one seems to be telling anyone anything. You could always ask Elliott."

"You ask Elliott. You might as well ask the Lincoln Memorial."

"Or you could ask the Director."

"No, thank you."

A few minutes passed by.

"Think we should talk to Matson?"

"You remember the special orders. No contact with anyone. He probably has the same orders, and he would report us without thinking about it. He's that sort of bastard."

O'Malley was the first to see Mark leaving the house and could have sworn he was carrying one shoe. He was right and Mark was running, so he began to follow him. Must avoid getting burned, thought O'Malley. Mark stopped at the pay phone; his pursuer disappeared into some new shadows, to continue his vain attempts to keep warm. He was thankful for the brisk walk, which had helped a little.

Mark had only two quarters; the others were all lying uselessly on the floor by the side of Elizabeth's couch. Where had the Director phoned from? Could it have been the Bureau? That didn't make sense, what would he be doing there at this time of night? Wasn't he supposed to be with the President? Mark looked at his watch. Hell, 1:15. He must be at home; if he isn't I'll be out of quarters. Mark put on his other shoe. Easy slip-on. He cursed, and tossed one of the quarters; George Washington, I call the Bureau. *E pluribus unum*, then I call him at home. The coin landed – George Washington. Mark dialled the Director's private number at the Bureau.

"Yes."

God bless George Washington.

"Julius?"

"Come in immediately."

That didn't sound very friendly. Perhaps he had just returned from the President with some important new information, or maybe something at the dinner had given him indigestion.

Mark walked quickly to his car, checking his shirt buttons and tie as he went. His socks felt uncomfortable, as if one of the heels were in the arch of his foot. He passed the man in the shadows, who watched as Mark returned to his car and hesitated. Should he return to Elizabeth and say, say what? He looked up at the light in the window, took a deep breath, cursed again, and fell into the bucket seat of the Mercedes. There hadn't even been time for a cold shower.

It took only a few minutes to reach the Bureau. There was very little traffic, and with the streets so quiet, the computerised lights meant no stopping.

Mark parked the car in the basement garage of the FBI and immediately there was the anonymous man, the anonymous man who obviously was waiting for him. Didn't he ever go to bed? A harbinger of bad tidings, probably, but he didn't let him know, because as usual he didn't speak. Perhaps he's a eunuch, Mark thought. Lucky man. They shared the elevator to the seventh floor. The anonymous man led him noiselessly to the Director's office; wonder what he does for a hobby, thought Mark. Probably a prompter at the National Theater for the Deaf.

"Mr Andrews, sir."

The Director offered no greeting. He was still in evening clothes and looked as black as thunder.

"Sit down, Andrews."

Back to Andrews, thought Mark.

"If I could take you out into the parking lot, stick you up against the wall, and shoot you, I would."

Mark tried to look innocent; it had usually worked with Nick Stames. It didn't seem to cut any ice with the Director.

"You stupid, unthinking, irresponsible, reckless idiot."

Mark decided he was more frightened of the Director than he was of those who might be trying to kill him.

"You've compromised me, the Bureau, and the President," continued the Director. Mark could hear his heart pounding. If he could have counted it, it would have been a hundred and twenty. Tyson was still in full cry. "If I could suspend you or just dismiss you, if only I could do something as simple as that. How many senators are there left, Andrews?"

"Seven, sir."

"Name them."

"Brooks, Harrison, Thornton, Byrd, Nunn, Dex . . . Dexter, and . . ." Mark went white.

"*Summa cum laude* at Yale, and you have the naïvete of a boy scout. When we first saw you with Dr Elizabeth Dexter, we, in our stupidity, knowing she was the doctor on duty on the evening of 3 March at Woodrow Wilson, assumed in our stupidity" – he repeated it even more pointedly – "that you were on to a lead, but now we discover that not only is she the daughter of one of the seven senators whom we suspect of wanting to murder the President but, as if that's not enough, we find out you're having an affair with her."

Mark wanted to protest but couldn't get his lips to move.

"Can you deny you've slept with her, Andrews?"

"Yes, sir, I can," Mark said very quietly.

The Director was momentarily dumbfounded. "Young man, we wired the place; we know exactly what went on."

Mark leaped out of his chair, stunned dismay yielding to fierce anger. "I couldn't have denied it," he cried, "if you hadn't interrupted me. Have you forgotten what it feels like to love someone, if you ever knew? Fuck your Bureau, and I don't use that word that often, and fuck you. I've been working sixteen hours a day and I'm not getting any sleep at night. Someone may be trying to murder me and I find that you, the only man I've trusted, have ordered your anonymous pimps to play Peeping Tom at my expense. I hope you all roast in hell. I'd rather join the Mafia because I'm sure they let their people have it off occasionally."

Mark was angrier than he had ever been in his life. He collapsed back into the chair, and waited for the consequences. His only strength was that he no longer cared. The Director was equally silent. He walked to the window and stared out. Then he turned slowly; the heavy shoulders, the large head were turning towards him. This is it, thought Mark.

The Director stopped about a yard away from him, looking him square in the eyes, the way he had done from the first moment they had met.

"Forgive me," said the Director. "I've been thoughtless, but I'm becoming paranoid about the whole problem. I've just left the President, healthy, fit, full of plans for the future of this country, only to be told that her one hope of carrying out those dreams is sleeping with the daughter of one of the seven men who might at this very moment be planning to assassinate her. I didn't think much further than that."

A big man, thought Mark.

The Director's eyes hadn't left him.

"Let's pray it's not Dexter. Because if it is, Mark, you may well be in considerable danger." He paused again. "By the way, those anonymous pimps have been guarding you night and day, also on a sixteen-hour day, without a break. Some of them even have wives and children. Now we both know the truth. Let's get back to work, Mark, and let's try and stay sane for three more days. Just remember to tell me everything."

Mark had won. No, Mark had lost.

"There are seven senators left." The words were slow and tired, the man was still on edge. Mark had never seen him like this and doubted that many members of the Bureau had.

"My discussions with the President have confirmed my suspicion that the link between 10 March and the Senator is the Gun Control bill. The chairman of the Judiciary Committee, who handled the planning stages of the bill, was there – Senator Bayh. He's still on the list. You had better see what he and our other suspects on that committee had to say about the bill – but keep your eye on Pearson and Nunn at Foreign Relations as well." He paused. "Only three days to go. I intend to stick to my original plan and let things run just as they are for the moment. I'm still in a position to cancel the President's schedule for the tenth at the very last minute. Do you wish to add anything, Mark?"

"No, sir."

"What are your plans?"

"I am seeing the staff directors of both the Foreign Relations and Judiciary committees tomorrow, sir. I may have a clearer idea then on how to approach the problem and what to be looking for."

"Good. Follow them both up meticulously, just in case I've missed something."

"Yes, sir."

"We've had our fingerprint men working overtime on those twenty-eight bills; at the moment, they are only looking for the prints of Mrs Casefikis. That way at least we will know which one might have our man's on it. They have found over a thousand prints, so far, but none fit Mrs Casefikis's. I'll brief you the moment I hear anything. Now let's call it a day, we're both bushed. Don't bother to come in at seven tomorrow" – the Director looked at his watch – "I mean today. Make it 7:00 am on Wednesday and make it on time because then we'll have only one full day left."

Mark knew he was being invited to leave but there was something he wanted to say. The Director looked up and sensed it immediately.

"Save it, Mark. Go home and get some rest. I'm a tired old man, but I would like those bastards, each and every one of them, behind bars on Thursday night. For your sake, I hope to God Dexter isn't involved. But don't close your eyes to anything, Mark. Love may be blind, but let's hope it's not deaf and dumb."

A very big man, thought Mark.

"Thank you, sir. I'll see you on Wednesday morning."

Mark drove his car quietly out of the FBI's garage. He was drained. There was no sign of the anonymous man. He stared in the rear-view mirror. A blue Ford sedan was following him, and this time it seemed obvious. How could he ever be sure whose side they were on? In three more days, he might know. This time next week he'd know everything or nothing. Would the President be alive or dead?

Simon, still on duty at the entrance to the apartment house, gave Mark a cheerful grin. "Make it, man?"

"Not exactly," he replied.

"I could always call up my sister, if you're desperate."

Mark tried to laugh.

"A generous offer, but not tonight, Simon." He tossed the car keys over and headed for the elevator. Once locked and bolted into his apartment, he strode into his bedroom, pulled off his shirt and tie, picked up the phone and dialled seven digits slowly. A gentle voice answered.

"You still awake?"

"Very much so."

"I love you." He put the phone down and slept.

Tuesday morning, 8 March. 8:04 am

The phone was ringing, but Mark was still in a deep sleep. It continued to ring. Eventually he awoke, focused on his watch: 8:05. Damn, probably the Director asking where the hell he was; no, he hadn't wanted to see him this morning, isn't that what they agreed? He grabbed the phone.

"You're awake?"

"Yes."

"I love you, too."

He heard the phone click. A good way to start the day, though if she knew he was going to spend it investigating her father . . . And almost certainly the Director was investigating her.

Mark let the cold shower run on and on until he was fully awake. Whenever he was awakened suddenly, he always wanted to go back to sleep. Next week, he promised himself he would. There was one hell of a lot of things he was going to do next week. He glanced at his watch: 8:25. No Wheaties this morning . He flicked on the television to see if he had missed anything going on in the rest of the world; he was sitting on a news story that would make Barbara Walters fall off her CBS chair. What was the man saying?

". . . and now one of the greatest achievements of mankind, the first pictures ever taken from the planet Jupiter by an American spacecraft. History in the making, but first, this message from Jell-O, the special food for special children."

Mark turned it off, laughing. Jupiter, along with Jell-O, would have to wait until next week.

Because he was running late, he decided to return to taking the Metro from the Waterfront Station next to his apartment. It was different when he had been going in early and had the roads to himself, but at 8:30, the cars would be bumper to bumper the whole way.

The entrance to the subway was marked with a bronze pylon sporting an illuminated M. Mark stepped on to the escalator, which took him from street level down to the Metro station. The tunnel-like station reminded him of a Roman bath, grey and dark with a honey-combed, curved ceiling. One dollar. Rush-hour fare. And he needed a transfer. Another dollar. Mark fumbled in his pockets for the exact fare. Must remember to stock up on quarters when I get to the centre of town, he thought, as he stepped on to another escalator and was deposited at track level. During rush-hour, 6:30–9:00 am, the trains drew in every five minutes. Round lights on the side of the platform began to flash to indicate the train was approaching. The doors opened automatically. Mark joined the crowd in a colourful, brightly lit car, and five minutes later heard his destination announced on the public address system: Gallery Place. He stepped out on to the platform and waited for a red line train. The green line worked perfectly on mornings when he was going to the Washington Field Office, but to get to Capitol Hill he had to switch. Four minutes later, he emerged into the sunshine at Union Sation Visitors' Center, the bustling command post for bus, train, and subway travel in and out of Washington. The Dirksen Senate Office Building was three blocks away, down 1st Street, at the corner of Constitution. That was quick and painless, thought Mark, as he went in the Constitution Avenue entrance. Why do I ever bother with a car at all?

He walked past two members of the Capitol police who were inspecting briefcases and packages at the door, and pressed the Up-button at the public elevator.

"Four, please," he said to the elevator operator.

The Foreign Relations Committee hearing was scheduled to begin shortly. Mark pulled the list of "Today's Activities in the House and Senate", which he had torn out of *The Washington Post*, from his coat pocket. "Foreign Relations: 9:30 am. Open. Hearing on US policy towards the Common Market; administration representatives. 4229 DOB." As Mark walked down the hall, Senator Ralph Brooks of Massachusetts stepped into Suite 4229, and Mark followed him into the hearing room.

The senator, a tall man with rugged, almost film star good looks, had dogged every step of President Kane's political career until finally she had replaced him as Secretary of State when she took over after President Parkin's death.

He had quickly won her seat back in the Senate and then stood against Florentyna Kane as the Democratic candidate and only lost on the seventh ballot. He had gone on to be chairman of the Senate Foreign Relations Committee.

Did he now intend to kill the President in order to reach the highest office himself? It didn't add up because if Kane were assassinated the Vice President Bill Bradley, who was younger than he was, would take her place and then Brooks would be left with no chance. No, the senator didn't look a serious threat but Mark still needed proof before he could cross him off the list.

The hearing room had light-coloured wood panelling, accented by green marble on the lower part of the wall and around the door. At the end of the chamber, there was a semi-circular desk of the same light wood, which was raised one step above the rest of the room. Fifteen burnt-orange chairs. Only about ten of them were occupied. Senator Brooks took his seat, but the assorted staff members, aides, newsmen, and administrative officials continued to mill around. On the wall behind the senators hung two large maps, one of the world, the other of Europe. At a desk immediately in front of and below the senators sat a stenotypist, poised to record the proceedings verbatim. In front, there were desks for witnesses.

More than half the room was given over to chairs for the general public, and these were nearly all full. An oil painting of George Washington dominated the scene. The man must have spent the last ten years of his life posing for portraits, thought Mark.

Senator Brooks whispered something to an aide, and rapped his gavel for silence. "Before we begin," he said, "I'd like to notify Senate staff members and the press of a change in schedule. Today and tomorrow, we will hear testimony from the State Department concerning the European Common Market. We will then postpone the continuation of these hearings until next week, so the committee may devote its attention to the pressing and controversial issue of arms sales to Africa."

By this time, almost everyone in the room had found a seat, and the government witnesses were glancing through their notes. Mark had worked on Capitol Hill one summer during college, but even now he could not help feeling annoyed at the small number of senators who showed up at these hearings. Because each senator served on three or more committees and innumerable sub- and special committees, they were forced to specialise, and to trust the expertise of fellow senators and staff members in areas outside their own speciality. So it was not at all unusual for committee hearings to be attended by three or two or sometimes even only one senator.

The subject under debate was a bill to dismantle the North Atlantic Treaty Organisation. Portugal and Spain had gone Communist and left the Common Market, like two well-behaved dominoes, at the turn of the decade. The Spanish bases went soon after; King Juan Carlos was living in exile in England. NATO had been prepared for the Communist takeover in Portugal, but when Italy finally installed a Fronte Popolare government in the Quirinal, things began to fall apart. The Papacy, trusting to tried and proven methods, locked itself behind its gates, and American Catholic opinion forced the United States to cut off financial aid to the new Italian government. The Italians retaliated by closing her NATO bases.

The economic ripples of the Italian collapse were thought to have influenced the French elections, which had led to a victory for Chirac and the Gaullists. The more extreme forms of socialism had recently been repudiated in Holland and some Scandinavian countries. The Germans were happy with their social democracy. But as the west entered the last decade of the twentieth century, Senator Pearson was declaring that America's only real ally in NATO was Britain, where a Tory government had recently won an upset victory in the February general election.

The British Foreign Secretary, Kenneth Clarke, had argued force-fully against the formal breakup of NATO. Such a move would sever Great Britain from her alliance with the United States, and commit her solely to the EEC, seven of whose fifteen members were now Communist or close to it. Senator Pearson thumped the table. "We should take the British view seriously in our considerations and not be interested only in immediate strategic gains."

After an hour of listening to Brooks and Pearson questioning State Department witnesses about the political situation in Spain, Mark slipped out of the door and went into the Foreign Relations Committee suite down the hall. The secretary informed him that Lester Kenneck, the committee staff director, was out of the office. Mark had telephoned him the day before, leaving the impression that he was a student doing research for his dissertation.

"Is there someone else who could give me some information about the committee?"

"I'll see if Paul Rowe, one of our staff members, might be able to help you." She picked up the telephone and, several moments later, a thin bespectacled man emerged from one of the back rooms.

"What can I do for you?"

Mark explained that he would like to see other members of the committee in action, particularly Senator Nunn. Rowe smiled patiently. "No problem," he said. "Come back tomorrow afternoon or Thursday for the discussion about arms sales to Africa. Senator Nunn will be here, I guarantee. And you'll find it much more interesting than the Common Market stuff. In fact, the meeting may be closed to the public. But I'm sure if you come by here and talk to Mr Kenneck, he'll arrange for you to sit in."

"Thank you very much. Would you by any chance happen to know if Nunn and Pearson were present at the hearing on 24 February, or last Thursday?"

Rowe raised his eyebrows. "I have no idea. Kenneck might know."

Mark thanked him. "Oh, one more thing. Can you give me a pass for the Senate gallery?" The secretary stamped a card and wrote in his name. Mark headed for the elevator. Arms sales. Africa, he thought. Thursday's too late. Damn. How the hell am I supposed to know why one of these guys would want to kill President Kane? Could be some crazy military thing, or a severe case of racism. It doesn't make any sense. Not why, but who, he reminded himself. As he walked, Mark almost knocked over one of the Senate pages, who was running down the corridor clutching a package. The Congress operates a page school for boys and girls from across the nation who attend classes and work as "gophers" in the Capitol. They all wear dark blue and white and always give the impression of being in a hurry. Mark stopped just in time and the boy scooted around him without even breaking stride.

Mark took the elevator to the ground floor and walked out of the Dirksen Building on to Constitution Avenue. He made his way across the Capitol grounds, entered the Capitol on the Senate side, underneath the long marble expanse of steps, and waited for the public elevator.

"Busy day," the guard informed him. "Lots of tourists here to watch the gun control debate."

Mark nodded. "Is there a long wait upstairs?"

"Yes, sir, I think so."

The elevator arrived, and on the gallery level a guard ushered Mark into line with a horde of gaping visitors. Mark was impatient. He beckoned to one of the guards.

"Listen, officer," he said, "I have a regular public pass for the gallery, but I'm a student from Yale doing research. Think there is any way you could get me in?"

The guard nodded sympathetically.

A few minutes later, Mark was seated in the chamber. He could see only part of the floor. The senators were seated at desks in semi-circular rows facing the Chair. Even while someone was speaking, staff members and senators wandered around, giving the impression that the really significant manoeuvring took place in hushed tones, not in dramatic debate.

The Judiciary Committee had reported out the bill two weeks before, after prolonged hearings and discussion. The House had already passed similar legislation, which would have to be reconciled with the stricter Senate version if it were to be approved.

Senator Dexter was speaking. My future father-in-law? Mark wondered. He certainly didn't look like a killer, but then which senator did? He had given his daughter her glorious dark hair, although there was a little white at his temples. Not as much as there ought to be, thought Mark – a politician's vanity. And he had also given her his dark eyes. He seemed fairly contemptuous of most of the people around him, tapping the desk with his long fingers to emphasise a point.

"In our discussion about this bill, we have side-stepped a critical, perhaps the most crucial, consideration. And that is the principle of Federalism. For the past fifty years, the federal government has usurped many of the powers once wielded by the states. We look to the President, the Congress, for answers to all our problems. The Founding Fathers never intended the central government to have so much power, and a country as wide and diverse as ours cannot be governed democratically or effectively on that basis. Yes, we all want to reduce crime. But crime differs from place to place. Our constitutional system wisely left the business of crime control to state and local jurisdiction, except for those federal criminal laws which deal with truly national matters. But crimes committed with guns are of a local nature. They ought to be legislated against and enforced at the local level. Only at the state and local levels can the attitudes of the people and the specific characteristics of the crime problem be understood and dealt with by public officials.

"I know that some of my colleagues will argue that, since we require registration of cars and drivers, we ought also to register guns. But gentlemen, we have no national car- or driver-registration law. These matters are left to the states to determine. Each state should be allowed to decide for itself, taking into account the interests of its people, what is reasonable and necessary."

Senator Dexter monopolised the floor for twenty minutes before yielding to the Chair, occupied today by Senator Kemp, who recognised Senator Brooks. When Brooks had finished his preliminary remarks, he launched into a prepared speech:

". . . have consistently decried the killing in the Middle East, in Africa, in Northern Ireland, in Chile. We ended the bloodshed in Vietnam. But when are we going to confront the killing that takes place in our own communities, our own streets, our own homes, every day of every year?" Brooks paused and looked at Senator Harrison from South Carolina, one of the leading opponents of the bill. "Are we waiting for another national tragedy to compel us to take action? Only after the assassination of John F. Kennedy was Senator Thomas Dodd's Handgun Control bill taken seriously by a Senate committee. No legislation was passed. After the Watts riots of August 1965, in which purchased, not looted guns were used, the Senate held hearings about control of handguns. No action was taken. It took the slaying of Martin Luther King, before the Judiciary Committee passed legislation, controlling interstate sale of handguns as a rider to the omnibus Crime Control bill. The Senate approved the bill. The House concurred after Robert Kennedy was murdered too. In response to the violence of 1968, we enacted the Handgun Control act. But the act, gentlemen, contained a huge loophole – it did not regulate domestic production of these weapons, because at that time eighty per cent of available handguns were manufactured overseas. In 1972, after George Wallace was shot with a Saturday-Night Special, the Senate finally acted to close the loophole. But the bill died in a House Committee.

"Now, some twenty years or more later, having disregarded the fact that President Reagan was seriously wounded in 1981 by a man wielding a handgun in the streets of Washington, even with all that history someone in America is killed or injured by gunfire every two minutes, and we are still without an effective gun control law. What are we waiting for? Someone to try again to assassinate the President?" He paused for effect. "The American people favour gun control legislation. Every poll indicates that this is the case, and it has been true for a decade. Why do we allow the National Rifle Association to manipulate us, to persuade us that they and their views are compelling when in fact they are hollow? What has happened to our capacity for the clear weighing of alternatives, and for outrage at the violence in our society?"

Mark, along with many other observers, was astonished by this impassioned outburst. His impression from informed political journalists was that Brooks would not support the President as, quite apart from personal animosity, he had been a key figure on a number of constitutional issues and in the fight against two of Kane's Supreme Court appointees, Haynsworth and Carswell.

Senator Harrison of South Carolina, an urbane, quietly distinguished man, asked to be recognised. "Will the distinguished
Senator from Massachusetts yield?"

Brooks nodded to the Chair.

Harrison addressed his colleagues in a soft, firm voice.

"This bill completely negates the concept of self-defence. It asserts
that the only legitimate reason for owning a handgun, a shotgun, or a
rifle is for sporting purposes. But I would like to ask my distinguished
colleagues from the urban states to consider for a moment – just a
moment – the plight of a family on a farm in Iowa or on a homestead in
Alaska which needs a gun in the house to protect itself. Not for sport,
but for self-defence. In my estimation, they have a right to take that
step. For what we face in this country, in urban as well as rural areas, is
increasing lawlessness. That is the root problem – lawlessness – not the
number of guns in circulation. Increased lawlessness means more
crimes involving guns, to be sure. But guns do not cause crimes, people
cause crimes. If we want to fight crime, we should investigate its root
causes instead of trying to take guns away from people who would use
them legally. As many a bumper sticker in this great land proclaims, 'If
guns are outlawed, only outlaws will have guns'."

Senator Thornton of Texas, thin and gaunt, with greasy black hair,
whom Mark remembered from Mr Smith's Restaurant, had only just
begun to express his agreement with the views of Senator Dexter and
Senator Harrison when six lights around the numbers on the clock at
Mark's end of the chamber came alive. A buzzer sounded six times to
signal that morning business was concluded. The "morning hour" on
the floor of the Senate, from midday until no later than 2:00 pm, was set
aside for the presentation of petitions and memorials, reports of
standing and select committees, and introduction of bills and
resolutions.

Senator Kemp looked at his watch. "Excuse me, Senator Thornton,
but it is noon and now that morning business is over, a number of us are
expected to appear in committee to debate the Clean Air bill which is
on the calendar for this afternoon. Why don't we reconvene at 2:30? As
many of us who can get away from the committee at that time can meet
back here to discuss this bill. It's important that we move as quickly as
possible on this legislation, as we are still hoping to vote on it in this
session."

The Senate floor was cleared in a minute. The actors had said their
lines and left the stage. Only those who had to get the theatre ready for
the afternoon performance remained. Mark asked the guard which was
Henry Lykham, the other staff director he had to see. The doorman in
the official blue uniform of the Senate Security Staff pointed to a short
fat man with a thin moustache and a jolly open face sitting firmly in a
large seat at the far side of the gallery, making notes and checking

papers. Mark strolled over to him, unaware that a pair of eyes behind dark glasses was following his every movement.

"My name is Mark Andrews, sir."

"Ah, yes, the graduate student. I'll be free in a moment, Mr Andrews."

Mark sat down and waited. The man in dark glasses left the chamber by the side door.

"All right, Mr Andrews, how about some lunch?"

"Great," replied Mark. He was taken to the ground floor, to G-211, the Senators' Dining-Room. They found a table at the side of the room. Mark chatted convincingly about the hard work a committee staff director must have to do, while others get the praise and publicity. Henry Lykham readily agreed. They both chose their meal from the fixed menu; so did the man three tables away, who was watching them both carefully. Mark told the committee staff director that he intended to write his thesis on the Gun Control bill if it became law, and that he wanted some interesting inside information that the general public wouldn't get from the newspapers. "Therefore, Mr Lykham," he concluded, "I have been advised to speak to you."

The fat man beamed; he was duly flattered, as Mark had hoped, and he began.

"There is nothing I can't tell you about this bill or the bunch of politicians involved in it."

Mark smiled, he had studied the Watergate hearings in an elective seminar at Yale and he recalled a particular remark of Anthony Ulasewicz, a retired NYPD detective. "Why bother to bug the place? Politicians and officials will tell you anything you want to know, over the phone, they'll even want to send it to you in the mail, whoever you are."

Senator Sam Irvin of North Carolina, the committee chairman, had reprimanded him for treating the committee lightly and turning the matter into a joke. "It's no joke – it's the truth," was Ulasewicz's reply.

Mark asked which of the eleven senators on the committee were for the bill. Only four of them had been present at the morning discussion. From his research, Mark was fairly certain about the opinions of most of them but he wanted his assessments confirmed.

"Among the Democrats, Brooks, Burdick, Stevenson, and Glenn will vote for the measure. Abourezk, Byrd, and Moynihan are keeping their own counsel, but will probably come through in support of the Administration position. They voted for the bill in committee. Thornton is the only Democrat who may vote against it. You heard him start to speak in favour of Dexter's states' rights position. Well, for Thornton, young man, it's not a matter of principle. He wants it both ways. Texas has a strong state gun control measure, so he can claim that his stance means that states can take whatever action they deem necessary to protect their citizens. But Texas also has a number of firearms companies – Smith and Wesson, GKN Powdermet, Harrington and Richardson – which would be seriously affected by a federal gun control act. The spectre of unemployment again. As long as those companies can sell their wares outside Texas, they're okay. So Thornton fools his constituents into thinking they can control guns and manufacture them at the same time. Strange games are being played by that particular man. As for the Republicans, Mathias of Maryland will vote for the bill. He's a very liberal guy – I'll never understand why he stays in the GOP. McCollister of Nebraska is against, along with Woodson of Arkansas. Harrison and Dexter you heard. No question where they stand.

"Harrison despite being a Democrat knows damn well that his constituents wouldn't tolerate gun control and will vote him out if he goes with it. Hard to tell if he's been brainwashed by the National Rifle Association, because he seems to be sincere when he talks about the idea of self-defence. He's a strange guy. Everyone in this place regards him as a dyed-in-the-wool conservative, but no one really knows him. He hasn't been here all that long. He succeeded Sparkman when he retired – bit of an unknown quantity."

Mark let him talk on. Lykham was enjoying the role of the expert, the man who knew everything. Normally, he sat for hours in the hearing room, unable to say a word, listening and making notes and occasionally whispering a suggestion in the ear of the chairman. Only his wife listened to his opinions and she never understood their significance. Lykham was delighted to have found an academic who had come to him for the facts.

"Dexter talks a good game – smooth character, that one. He beat the guy who was appointed to fill Ribicoff's term when Abe was picked by the President for a roving ambassadorship. Surprise winner. Wouldn't have thought that Connecticut would be represented by two Republicans. Guess all those rich New Yorkers moving to Stamford are making a difference. Anyway, just between the two of us, Mark, I have my suspicions about the purity of his principles. Do you know how many gun companies there are in Connecticut? Remington, Colt, Olin, Winchester, Marlin, Sturm-Ruger. Now, that never stopped Senator Ribicoff from voting for gun control, but Dexter . . . well, he owns a big slice of one of them, that's no secret. Something's biting him at the moment, he's as grouchy as hell, and he hasn't missed a session yet."

Mark had a sick feeling in his stomach. My God, Elizabeth's father? He just didn't want to believe it.

"So you think the bill will be passed?" said Mark in a conversational tone.

"No question, while the Democrats remain in control of both Houses. The minority report was vicious, but it'll get a majority on 10

March. There wasn't much doubt about that after the House put it through. By Thursday, nothing can stop it. The Majority Leader is only too aware of the importance the President attaches to this bill."

Byrd, thought Mark. He's on the list. "Could you tell me a little about the Majority Leader? He was on the Judiciary Committee, right? Where does he stand?"

"That's an interesting question, Andrews. Senator Byrd is a humourless, driven, ambitious individual. He has ulcers. He was born in poverty, always makes a point of emphasizing his origins, so much so that some of his colleagues call him Uriah Heep. In the 1940s, when he was only nineteen, he belonged to the Ku Klux Klan; yet he managed to overcome that handicap and rise to the most powerful post in the Senate in a party dominated by liberals. He got where he is because he's a team player. He does favours for other senators, and always has. He's diligent, conscientious about meeting their needs. His attention to detail has paid off in spades. He had always supported the Democratic – with a capital D – position. And he's a very effective Majority Leader.

"No love lost in that relationship, but since Byrd has become Majority Leader he has fallen into line. With his background, it's unlikely that he's genuinely in favour of gun control, but he hasn't spoken out against the bill, naturally, because he has been shepherding it through the Senate for the President. He's done it very efficiently. He's scheduled it early, avoided recesses –"

"Sorry to interrupt you, Mr Lykham, but what do you mean he's avoided recesses? The committee didn't sit round the clock, surely?"

"No, young man, I was referring to a technical, procedural distinction between adjournment and recess. You see, the Senate usually recesses from one day to the next. The day after a recess, the unfinished business of the previous day is in order; the morning business can be dispensed with. Whenever the Majority Leader opts for a recess rather than adjournment, he thereby lengthens the 'legislative day'. And since bills reported from committee must lay over one legislative day before a motion to consider is in order, the recess can be used to delay action on a particular measure. The so-called legislative day can extend for days, weeks, conceivably even months now she only has two years left. This bill has been put through in the minimum possible time. If the President doesn't get support on 10 March, she will not have time to put it up again before she goes for re-election. It will be a victory for those against the bill. And she may not be re-elected if the polls are to be believed. Americans get sick of their presidents very quickly nowadays. So it's 10 March or forget it."

"What could stop it on 10 March?"

"Nothing I can think of offhand, except the death of the President, which could recess the Senate for seven days. Still the President looks pretty fit to me, perhaps a little tired, not that I'm one to comment."

Mark was about to question Lykham about Brooks, when the staff director glanced at his watch.

"Look at the time," Lykham expostulated, "I must get back. I have to be the first, you know, get everything in order, so those senators think that we haven't been away at all."

Mark thanked him. Lykham picked up the check and signed it.

"Any time you want more help or information, don't hesitate to get in touch."

"I certainly will," said Mark.

The fat staff director waddled away at what for him was full speed. Mark pondered over his coffee. The man three tables away had finished his and was waiting for Mark's next move. Those damn bells were ringing again. Only one this time, indicating that the yeas and nays were being tallied on the Senate floor. As soon as the vote was over, the senators would be flocking back to committee meetings. The bell brought Mark sharply out of his thoughts.

Once again he returned to the Dirksen Building and the Foreign Relations Committee Suite, where he asked if he could see Mr Kenneck.

"Who shall I say is asking for him?" the receptionist inquired.

"Andrews, I'm a Yale student."

She picked a phone up and pressed two digits, informed the listener of what Mark had told her.

"He's in Room 4491."

Mark thanked her and left for Room 4491, which was only a few doors down the corridor.

"Well, Andrews, what can I do for you?" he asked, even before Mark had closed the door.

Mark was taken aback by the suddenness of his question; he recovered.

"I'm doing some research for a thesis, Mr Kenneck, on the work of senators, and Mr Lykham said you were the man to speak to. I wondered if Senators Nunn and Pearson were in the Senate on Thursday, 3 March, at 10:30, for the Foreign Relations Committee?"

Kenneck bent over a red leather-bound book. "Nunn – no," he paused. "Pearson – no. Anything else, Mr Andrews?" He obviously hadn't any time to waste.

"No, thank you," said Mark and left.

Mark headed for the Library. Suddenly he was down to five senators, if the Bureau were right about what they had overheard on the illegal radio transmission when their man must have been in the Senate on the morning of 3 March. He checked his notes: each one of the remaining suspects – Brooks, Byrd, Dexter, Harrison, and Thornton – had sat on the Judiciary Committee on the Gun Control bill and was in the Senate for the debate. Five men and a motive?

He was followed out of the room and into the elevator that took him to the ground floor. He used the pay phone across the hall from the elevator, near the Constitution Avenue entrance, to call the Director.

He dialled the Director's private number.

"Julius."

"What's your number?"

Mark gave it. A few seconds later the Director called him back.

"Nunn and Pearson are off. I'm down to five and the one thing they have in common is that all of them were on the committee of the Gun Control bill."

"Good," said the Director. "Much as I had expected. Getting better, Mark, but your time is running out, we've only about forty-eight hours left."

"Yes, sir."

The phone clicked.

He waited for a moment and then dialled Woodrow Wilson. There was the usual interminable wait while they found Elizabeth. What could he say about last night? What if the Director were right and her father –

"Dr Dexter."

"When do you finish work tonight, Liz?"

"Five o'clock, lover," she said mockingly.

"May I pick you up?"

"If you like, now that I know your intentions are pure and honourable."

"Listen, one day, but not today, I'll be able to explain about that."

"See you at five, Mark."

"See you at five, Liz."

Mark put Elizabeth out of his mind by a conscious effort of will, and walked across the street to the Capitol grounds. He sat down under a tree on the grassy area between the Supreme Court and the Capitol. Protected, he thought, by law and legislature, bounded by Constitution and Independence. Who would dare to confront him here in front of the Capitol, the favoured haunt of Senate staff, law clerks, and the Capitol police? A blue and white sight-seeing tourmobile passed by on 1st Street, blocking his view of the fountains in front of the Supreme Court. Tourists gaped at Washington's white-marbled splendour. "And on your right, ladies and gentlemen, the United States Capitol. The cornerstone of the original building was laid in 1793. The British burned the Capitol building on 24 August, 1814 . . ."

And some crazy senator is going to defile it on 10 March, added Mark silently as the tourmobile moved on. Foreboding oppressed him; it really is going to happen, we can't stop it. Comes Caesar to the Capitol . . . Blood on the steps.

He forced himself to look at his notes. Brooks, Byrd, Dexter, Harrison, Thornton. He had two days to transform five into one. The conspirator he sought was Cassius, not Brutus. Brooks, Byrd, Dexter, Harrison, and Thornton. Where were they at lunchtime on 24 February? If he knew the answer, he would know which four men were innocent and which man was so desperate that he would plot to assassinate the President. Even if we find out which man is behind this, he thought, as he stood up and brushed the grass from his trousers, how do we stop the murder? Obviously, the Senator isn't going to commit the killing himself. We must keep the President away from the Capitol. The Director must have a plan, he surely wouldn't let it go that far. Mark closed his file and walked to the Metro.

Once home, he picked up his car and drove slowly to Woodrow Wilson. He looked in the rear-view mirror. A different car was following him today, a black Buick. Someone looking after me again, he thought. He arrived at the hospital at 4:45 but Elizabeth wasn't free yet, so he went back to his car and turned on the evening news. An earthquake in the Philippines that had killed 112 people was the lead story. President Kane was still confident of support for the Gun Control bill. The Dow-Jones index had moved up three points to 1,411. The Yankees beat the Dodgers in a spring training game, what's new?

Elizabeth came out of the hospital looking depressed and jumped in beside him.

"What can I say about last night?" Mark asked.

"Nothing," said Elizabeth. "It was like reading a book with the last chapter torn out. Who tore it out, Mark?"

"Perhaps I've brought the last chapter with me," said Mark, avoiding the question.

"Thanks, but I don't think I'll be in the mood for another bedtime story for a while," she replied. "The last one gave me a bad dream."

Elizabeth was very quiet and Mark could get little response from her. He turned right off Independence and stopped the car on one of the side streets on the Mall, facing the Jefferson Memorial and the sunset.

"Is it last night?" asked Mark.

"Partly," she said. "You made me feel pretty silly walking off like that. I don't suppose you're going to tell me what it was all about?"

"I can't do that," said Mark uneasily. "But believe me, it had nothing to do with you. At least that's almost –" He stopped abruptly.

Never embarrass the Bureau.

" 'At least that's almost' what? Almost true? Why was that call so important?"

"Let's stop this and go eat."

Elizabeth didn't reply.

He started the car again. Two cars pulled out at the same time as he did. A blue Ford sedan and a black Buick. They're certainly making sure today, he thought. Perhaps one of them is just looking for a parking space. He glanced at Elizabeth to see if she'd noticed them too; no, why should she, only he could see in the rear-view mirror. He drove to a small, warm Japanese restaurant in Wisconsin Avenue. He couldn't take her home, while the damned Bureau had the place bugged. Deftly, the Oriental waiter sliced the fat shrimps, cooked them on the metal slab in the centre of their table. He flicked each shrimp as he finished it on to their plates, giving them small, delicious bowls of sauces in which to dip the pieces. Elizabeth brightened under the influence of the hot sake.

"I'm sorry to react so strongly. I have a lot on my mind at the moment."

"Like to tell me about it?"

"I can't, I'm afraid. It's personal and my father has asked me not to discuss it with anyone yet."

Mark froze. "Can't you tell me?"

"No. I guess we'll both have to be patient."

They went to a drive-in movie and sat in the comfortable semi-darkness, arms companionably intertwined. Mark sensed she didn't wish to be touched, and indeed he was in no mood to do so. They were both concerned about the same man, but for different reasons – or was it the same reason? And how would she react if she discovered that he had been investigating her father since the day after they met? Maybe she knew. Damn it, why couldn't he simply believe in her? Surely, she wasn't setting him up. He could remember very little about the film, and when it ended he took her home and left immediately. Two cars were still following him.

A figure jumped out of the shadows. "Hi, stud!" Mark swung around and checked his holster nervously.

"Oh, hi, Simon."

"Listen, man, I can show you some dirty postcards if you're still desperate, 'cause it seems that you're just not good enough, man. I had a black one last night, I'm having a white one tonight."

"How can you be so sure?" asked Mark.

"I check in advance, man. I ain't got time to waste with my pretty body." Simon burst out laughing. "Think about me when you go to bed tonight, all alone, Mark, 'cause I sure will have forgotten you. Cool your jets, man."

Mark threw him the keys and watched him as he walked towards the Mercedes swinging his hips, dancing and laughing.

"You ain't got it, baby, whatever it is."

"Bullshit! You're a jive-ass bastard," Mark said, and laughed.

"Now, you're just jealous, man, or prejudiced," said Simon, as he revved up the car and moved to a parking space. As he passed Mark, he shouted, "Either way, I'm the winner."

Mark wondered if he ought to apply for a job as a garage attendant at the apartment building. It seemed to have its compensations. He looked around; something moved; no, it was just his nerves or his imagination. Once in his room, he wrote his report for the morning session with the Director and fell into bed.

Two days to go.

Wednesday morning, 9 March. 1:00 am

The phone rang. Mark was just falling asleep, still in that world between sleeping and waking. The phone insisted. Try to answer it, it could be Julius.

"Hello," he said, yawning.

"Mark Andrews?"

"Yes," he said wearily, shifting himself to a more comfortable position in the bed, fearing if he woke up fully he would never get back to sleep.

"It's George Stampouzis. Sorry to wake you, but I've come up with something I thought you would want to know about immediately."

Stampouzis's statement acted like cold water. Mark was wide awake instantly.

"Right, don't say anything else, I'll call you from a pay phone. What's your number?" Mark wrote it down on the back of a Kleenex box, the only thing he could reach. He threw on a bathrobe, forced his feet into a pair of tennis shoes, and started for the door. He opened the door, looked both ways. Hell, he was getting paranoid. There was no sound in the hall; there wouldn't be even if someone were waiting for him. He took the elevator down to the garage level, where there was a pay phone. Simon was asleep on the chair – how did he manage it? Mark had found it hard enough to sleep in bed.

He dialled the 212 area code.

"Hello, Stampouzis. Mark Andrews."

"Do you G-men always play games at one in the morning? I would have thought you'd figured out a better system by now."

Mark laughed; the sound echoed in the garage; Simon twitched.

"What can I do for you?"

"I traded some information today, now you owe me two stories." Stampouzis paused. "The Mafia had nothing to do with Stames's death, and they are not going overboard for the Gun Control bill, although they basically oppose it. So you can eliminate them. I wouldn't have gone this far for anyone but Nick, so make sure you handle it right."

"I'm doing my best," Mark replied. "Thanks for your help."

He put the phone back on the hook and walked back to the elevator, thinking about the tousled bed which he hoped was still warm. Simon was still asleep.

Wednesday morning, 9 March. 5:50 am

"It's for you, sir."

"What?" mumbled the Director, still half-asleep.

"The phone, sir, it's for you." His housekeeper was standing by the doorway in her dressing-gown.

"Ugh. What time is it?"

"Ten to six, sir."

"Who is it?"

"Mr Elliott, sir."

"Right, switch it through."

Elliott had woken him up. A decision he would never have taken unless it was urgent.

"Good morning, Elliott, what is it?" He paused. "Can you be sure? That changes the whole situation. What time is he due in? 7:00, of course. I'll see you at 6:30."

The Director put the phone down, and sat on the edge of the bed, and said very loudly: "Damn," which by the Director's standards was extreme. His big feet placed firmly on the floor, his large hands splayed on his equally large thighs, he was deep in thought. Eventually he rose, put on a dressing-gown, and disappeared into the bathroom, repeating the expletive several times.

Mark also had a phone call, not from the anonymous man, but from Elizabeth. She needed to see him urgently. They agreed to meet at eight o'clock in the lobby of the Mayflower. He felt sure no one would recognise him there, but he wondered why Elizabeth had chosen that particular meeting place.

Mark took off his dressing-gown and returned to the bathroom.

The Senator took an early-morning phone call as well, not from the anonymous man or from Elizabeth, but from the Chairman, who was confirming their midday meeting for the final briefing at the Sheraton Hotel in Silver Spring. The Senator agreed, replaced the phone, and roamed around the room in his dressing-gown thinking.

"Coffee for three, Mrs McGregor. Are they both here?" the Director asked as he passed her.

"Yes, sir."

Mrs McGregor looked very chic in a new turquoise, two-piece suit, but the Director didn't notice. He strolled into his office.

"Good morning, Matt. Good morning, Mark." When should he drop the bomb? He decided to let Andrews speak first. "Right, let's hear what you've found out."

"As I told you yesterday, sir, I think I've cut the list of senators down to five – Brooks of Massachusetts, Byrd of West Virginia, Dexter of Connecticut, Harrison of South Carolina, and Thornton of Texas. The only common factor is their interest in the Gun Control bill, which as we know, sir, is likely to become law on 10 March. Assassination of the President would now be about the only way of holding that bill up."

"I would have thought," said Rogers, "that that could be the one act that would make certain the bill passed through both Houses."

"You tell that to two Kennedys, Martin Luther King, George Wallace and Ronald Reagan and see what they all have to say," responded the Director. "Continue, Mark."

Mark summarised what Lykham and Stampouzis had briefed him on each man, and explained how he was able to eliminate two other men from the list of seven – namely Pearson and Nunn. "That completes my report, sir, unless, of course, we are approaching this thing in the wrong way and I'm heading down a blind alley. And as far as I'm concerned that is entirely possible, as I seem to be boxing with shadows."

The Director nodded and waited.

Mark continued: "I was going to spend today trying to hear each one of them in action in the Senate. I wish I could think of a good way of finding out where they were at lunchtime on 24 February, short of asking them outright, that is."

"Don't go anywhere near any of them. That would be the surest way to shut down the whole plot. Now, Mark, I must warn you my news is not good, so settle back and prepare for the worst. We are beginning to think the man we are after is Dexter," said the Director.

Mark went cold. "Why, sir?" he managed to get out.

The Assistant Director leaned forward to speak. "I have had some men checking out the Georgetown Inn, very unobtrusively. We didn't expect to turn anything up. We questioned all the day staff but they couldn't help. Early this morning, just to be thorough, we interviewed the night staff. Turned out that one of the night porters, who was off duty during the day, of course, is pretty sure he saw Senator Dexter hurrying away from the hotel some time like 2:30 in the afternoon on 24 February."

Mark was stunned. "How did he know it was Senator Dexter?"

"The man was born and raised in Wilton, Connecticut; he knows his face well. I'm afraid there's something else, too; he was accompanied by a young woman whose rough description tallies with his daughter."

"That's not proof," said Mark. "It's all circumstantial. It wouldn't stand up in a court of law."

"I'm sure you're right," said the Director, "but it's an unfortunate coincidence for Senator Dexter. Remember his involvement in the arms business; it won't do his finances any good if the Gun Control bill goes through; in fact our inquiries show he stands to lose a personal fortune, so we have a motive as well."

"But, sir," Mark argued, carried away by the desire to believe in Elizabeth, "do you really think that a senator would plot to kill the President just to keep one of his companies afloat? There are so many less drastic ways to stall the bill. He could try to tie it up in committee. Or organise a filibuster . . ."

"He already has tried – and failed, Mark," Matthew Rogers interrupted.

"The other four senators may have more powerful motives we don't happen to know about. It doesn't have to be Dexter," continued Mark, sounding unconvinced.

"Mark, I understand what you're saying and you do have a point. Under ordinary circumstances I'd agree that it seems unlikely, but we have to go on the evidence we have, even if it's slim and at present no more than circumstantial. And there's something else. On the night of 3 March, when Casefikis and the postman were killed, Dr Dexter's name was not marked on the duty register. She should have finished work at five, but for some inexplicable reason she stayed an extra two hours, treated the Greek – who was not her patient – and then went home. Now it's possible that she was just conscientious and working overtime, or that she was filling in for a colleague, but there are a hell of a lot of coincidences here, Mark. I'm bound to say if one is dispassionate about it, the odds are stacked heavily against Senator Dexter – and his daughter."

Mark did not reply.

"Now listen and listen carefully," the Director went on. "I know you want to believe that all this is circumstantial and that it's one of the other four – but I only have twenty-six hours left before the President leaves the White House, and I have to live with the facts as they present themselves. I want to catch the man involved, whoever he is, and I'm not willing to risk the life of the President to do it. When are you seeing the girl next?"

Mark looked up. "At eight, at the Mayflower."

"Why?"

"I have no idea, sir. She just said that it was important."

"Um, well I think you still ought to go but then report back to me immediately you're through."

"Yes, sir."

"I can't understand why, Andrews. Be careful."

"Yes, sir."

"It's twenty to eight now, you'd better be on your way. Incidentally, we're still having no luck with those fifty-dollar bills. We're down to the last eight, but still no prints from Mrs Casefikis. Better news on the German, Gerbach, however. We've established beyond a doubt that he had no connection with the CIA during his stay in Rhodesia or at the time of his death, so that's one more problem out of the way."

Mark didn't give a damn about the fifty-dollar bills, the German driver, the Mafia, or the CIA. All his hard work appeared to be leading them straight to Dexter. He left the office even more despondent than he had been when he came in.

Once back on the street, he decided to walk to the Mayflower in the hope of clearing his head. He didn't notice that two men followed him down Pennsylvania Avenue, past the White House, and on towards the hotel.

At the press of a button, Elliott entered the Director's office.

"Elliott, you were right about the Mayflower. What have you done about it?"

"There are two men already there, sir, and one following Andrews."

"It's the first time in thirty-six years that I've hated my job," said the Director. "You've done very well, Elliott, and all too soon I'll be able to tell you what this whole damn thing is about."

"Yes, sir."

"Follow up these five names. Leave no stone unturned."

"Yes, sir."

"Thank you."

Elliott slid out of the room.

Damn man has no heart. Can't have a right-hand man without a heart. Makes him damn useful in a strange situation like this though. When this operation's all over, I'll transfer him back to Idaho and –

"You said something, sir?"

"No, Mrs McGregor, I'm just going quietly mad. Don't worry about me. When the men in the white coats come to take me away, just sign the forms in triplicate and look relieved."

Mrs McGregor smiled.

"I like your new suit," the Director said.

She blushed. "Thank you, sir."

Mark pushed through the revolving doors of the Mayflower Hotel, his eyes searching the lobby for Elizabeth. How he wanted to see her and how he wanted to stop being devious and tell her the truth. It's all circumstantial, he continued to insist. He couldn't spot her so chose a comfortable seat which had a good view of the lobby.

On the far side of the lobby, a man was buying *The Washington Post* from the newspaper stand. Mark didn't notice that he made no attempt to read it. Suddenly he saw Elizabeth heading towards him with Senator Dexter by her side. Hell, that was all he needed.

"Hello, Mark." She kissed him gently on the cheek.

Judas showing the Pharisees which one was to be killed? The unkindest cut of all.

"Mark, I'd like you to meet my father."

"Good morning, sir."

"Good morning, Mark, it's good to meet you. Elizabeth has told me quite a bit about you."

And what should you be able to tell me, thought Mark. Where were you on 24 February? Where will you be tomorrow?

"Mark, are you all right?" Elizabeth inquired.

"Yes, fine. I'm sorry, Senator, it's good to meet you too."

The Senator was staring at him strangely.

"Well, I must be getting along, dear – I have a busy schedule. I look forward to our usual lunch tomorrow."

"See you then, Father. Thanks for the breakfast and the chat."

"Goodbye, Mark. See you again soon, I hope." Senator Dexter still looked at him quizzically.

"Perhaps," replied Mark quietly.

They watched him leave. So did three other people. One of them left to make a phone call.

"Mark, what's come over you? Why were you so brusque with my father? I especially wanted you to meet him."

"I'm sorry, I'm just tired."

"Or is there something you're not telling me?" said Elizabeth.

"I could ask you the same question."

"What are you talking about?"

"Oh, I don't know, let's forget it," said Mark. "Why did you want to see me so urgently?"

"Simply because I wanted you to meet my father. What's so strange about that? Why the hell did I bother?"

She began to walk away down the corridor, pushing her way quickly through the revolving door at the entrance to the hotel. Three men saw her leave. One followed her, two stuck with Mark. He walked slowly towards the doors. The doorman saluted him punctiliously.

"Cab, sir?"

"No, thanks. I'll walk."

The Director was on the phone when Mark returned and waved him into the large leather chair by his desk. He sank down in it, his mind fuzzy. The Director put the phone down and looked directly at him.

"So now you've met Senator Dexter, and I must tell you that either Dr Dexter knows nothing or she deserves an Oscar for her performance at the Mayflower."

"You saw everything," said Mark.

"Of course, and more. She was just involved in an automobile accident, two minutes ago. That phone call was the details."

Mark jumped out of his seat.

"She's all right. A couple of hundred dollars' worth of damage to the front of her little Fiat and not a mark on the bus she hit. Sensible girl. She's on her way to work now in a cab, or rather, she thinks it's a cab."

Mark sighed, resigned to whatever would happen next. "Where is Senator Dexter?" he asked.

"He's gone to the Capitol. Made one phone call when he got there, but it didn't turn out to be of any significance."

Mark was beginning to feel like a puppet. "What do you expect me to do now?"

There was a knock on the door and the anonymous man appeared. He handed a note to the Director, who read it quickly.

"Thank you."

The anonymous man left. Mark feared the worst. The Director placed the note on the desk and looked up.

"Senator Thornton has called a press conference at 10:30 in the Senate Committee Room 2228. Better get down there immediately. Phone me as soon as he has said his piece. The questions from the press afterwards will be irrelevant; they always are."

Mark walked to the Senate, once again hoping it would clear his head. It didn't. He wanted to ring Elizabeth and ask if she were all right after the accident; he wanted to ask her a hundred questions, but he only wanted one answer. Three men also walked to the Senate, two of them taking a half of the route each, and the third walking the whole way. All three of them arrived eventually in Room 2228; none of them was interested in Senator Thornton's statement.

The room was already well lit by the large Idreg lights especially set up for the television cameras, and the members of the press were chatting among themselves. It was a packed house, even though Senator Thornton had not yet arrived. Mark wondered what he had to say, whether it would throw any light on his own questions. Point the guilty finger at Thornton perhaps, supply a motive he could return with to the Director. He thought, as he looked at the senior reporters, that they might have a shrewd idea or even a tip from one of Thornton's staff as to the contents of his statement. But he didn't want to ask them any questions for fear of being remembered. With an entrance that would have pleased Caesar himself, Senator Thornton came in, accompanied by three aides and a private secretary. He certainly was making the most of it. His dark hair was covered with grease, and he had put on what he obviously imagined to be his best suit, green with a blue pinstripe. No one had briefed him on what to wear when facing colour television – only dark clothes, as plain as possible – or if he had been briefed, he hadn't listened.

He sat in a large throne of a chair at the far end of the room, his feet only just touching the ground. He was now surrounded by arc lights and the TV acoustics men put microphones all around him and in front of him. Suddenly, three more vast Idreg lights were switched on. Thornton was sweating already, but still smiling. The three television networks agreed that they were ready for the Senator. Thornton cleared his throat.

"Ladies and gentlemen of the press . . ."

"That's a pompous start," said a correspondent in front of Mark, writing every word down in shorthand. Mark looked more closely, he thought he recognised the face. It was Bernstein of *The Washington Post*. Senator Thornton now had complete silence from the room.

"I have just left the White House after a private session with the President of the United States and because of that meeting, I wish to make a statement for press and television." He paused. "My criticisms of the Gun Control bill and my vote against it in committee were motivated by a desire to represent my constituents and their genuine fear of unemployment . . ."

". . . and *your* own genuine fear of unemployment," remarked Bernstein, *sotto voce*. "What bribe did the President offer you at dinner on Monday?"

The Senator cleared his throat again. "The President has assured me that if this piece of legislation is passed, and domestic production of guns is prohibited, she will sponsor legislation to give immediate financial assistance to gun manufacturers and their employees, in the hope that the facilities of the gun industry can be turned to other, less dangerous uses than the production of weapons of destruction. The President's concern has made it possible for me to vote in favour of the Gun Control bill. I have for some considerable time been in two minds . . ."

"True enough," said Bernstein.

". . . concerning this bill, because of my genuine fear of the freedom and ease with which criminals can obtain firearms."

"It didn't worry you yesterday. Just what contracts did the President promise," murmured the correspondent, "or did she say she would help you win re-election next year?"

"And the problem for me has always been in the balance . . ."

". . . and a little bribe tipped that balance."

Bernstein now had his own audience, which was enjoying his offerings far more than those of the Senator from Texas.

"Now that the President has shown such consideration, I feel able to announce with a clear conscience . . ."

". . . so clear we can see right through it," more Bernstein.

". . . that I am now able to support my party's position over gun control. I will, therefore, not be opposing the President on the floor of the Senate tomorrow."

Wild applause from scattered parts of the room, sounding – and looking – suspiciously like aides placed in strategic spots.

'I shall, ladies and gentlemen," Senator Thornton continued, "rest an easier man tonight . . ."

"And a re-elected one," added Bernstein.

"I should like to end by thanking the members of the press for attending . . ."

"We had to; it was the only show in town."

Laughter broke out around the *Post* correspondent, but it didn't reach Thornton.

"And I would like to say that I will be delighted to answer any questions. Thank you."

"Bet you don't answer any of mine."

Most of the other reporters left the room immediately, in order to catch the early editions of the afternoon papers, already going to press right across the country. Mark joined them but glanced over the famous journalist's shoulder. He had been scribbling in longhand.

"Friends, Romans, country bumpkins, lend me your jeers; I come to bury Kane, not to praise her." Not exactly front-page material.

Three other men who had attended the press conference followed Mark out of the room, as he ran to the nearest pay telephones, halfway down the hall. Mark found them all occupied by newspapermen anxious to get their copy in first, and there was a long line behind those already dictating. Another line had formed by the two phones at the other end of the hall. Mark took the elevator to the ground floor; same problem; his only chance would be the pay phone in the Russell Building across the street. He ran all the way; so did three other men. When he reached there, a middle-aged woman stepped into the booth a pace ahead of him, and put her quarter in.

"Hello . . . it's me. I got the job . . . Yeah, pretty good . . . Mornings only. Start tomorrow . . . But I can't complain, money's not bad."

Mark paced up and down while the three men caught their breath. At last, the woman finished talking and, with a big smile all over her face, she walked away, oblivious of Mark or the nation's problems. At least someone is confident about tomorrow, thought Mark. He glanced around to be sure that there was no one near him, though he could have sworn he recognised a man standing by the Medicare poster; perhaps it was one of his colleagues from the FBI. He had seen that face behind the dark glasses somewhere. He was getting better protection than the President. He dialled the Director's private line and gave him his pay phone number. The phone rang back almost immediately.

"Thornton's off the list, sir, because he has –"

"I know, I know," said the Director. "I've just been briefed on what Thornton said. It's exactly what I would have expected him to say if he were involved. It certainly does not get him off my list; if anything, I'm a little more suspicious. Keep working on all five this afternoon and contact me the moment you come up with anything; don't bother to come in."

The phone clicked. Mark felt despondent. He depressed the cradle and waited for the dial tone, put in a quarter and dialled Woodrow Wilson. The nurse on duty went on a search for Elizabeth, but returned and said that no one had seen her all day. Mark hung up, forgetting to say thank you or goodbye. He took the elevator down to the basement cafeteria to have lunch. His decision gained the restaurant two more customers; the third man already had a lunch date, for which he was running late.

Wednesday afternoon, 9 March. 1:00 pm

Only Tony and Xan were on time for the meeting at the Sheraton Hotel in Silver Spring. They had spent many hours together but seldom spoke; Tony wondered what the Nip thought about all the time. Tony had had a busy schedule checking the routes for the final day, getting the Buick perfectly tuned – and chauffeuring the Chairman and Matson; they all treated him like a damn cab driver. His skill was equal to theirs anytime, and where the hell would they be without him? Without him those FBI men would still be around their necks. Still, the whole damn thing would be over by tomorrow night and he could then get away and spend some of his hard-earned money. He couldn't make

up his mind whether it would be Miami or Las Vegas. Tony always
planned how to spend his money before he got it. The Chairman came
in, a cigarette hanging from his mouth as always. He looked at them,
and asked brusquely where Matson was. Both shook their heads.
Matson always worked alone. He trusted no one. The Chairman was
irritated and made no attempt to hide it. The Senator arrived, just a few
moments later, looking equally annoyed, but he didn't even notice that
Matson wasn't there.

"Why don't we start?" demanded the Senator. "I find this meeting
inconvenient as it is, since it's the final day of debate on the bill."

The Chairman looked at him with contempt. "We're missing Matson and his report is vital."

"How long will you wait?"

"Two minutes."

They waited in silence. They had nothing to say to each other; each
man knew why he was there. Exactly two minutes later, the Chairman
lit another cigarette and asked Tony for his report.

"I've checked the routes, boss, and it takes a car going at twenty-two
miles per hour three minutes to get from the south exit of the White
House on to E Street and down Pennsylvania Avenue to the FBI
Building and another three minutes to reach the Capitol. It takes forty-
five seconds to climb the steps and be out of range. On average six
minutes forty-five seconds in all. Never under five minutes thirty
seconds, never over seven minutes. That's trying it at midnight, one
o'clock, and two o'clock in the morning, remembering the routes are
going to be even clearer for Kane."

"What about after the operation is over?" asked the Chairman.

"It's possible to get from the crane through basement passageways
to the Rayburn Building and from there to the Capitol South Metro
Station in two minutes at best and three minutes fifteen seconds at
worst – depends on elevators and congestion. Once the VC –" He
stopped himself. "Once Xan is in the Metro, they'll never find him; in a
few minutes, he can be on the other side of Washington."

"How can you be sure they won't pick him up in under three minutes
fifteen seconds?" asked the Senator, whose personal interest in Xan
was non-existent, but he didn't trust the little man not to sing if he were
caught.

"Assuming they know nothing, they also won't know which way to
turn for at least the first five minutes," answered the Chairman.

Tony continued: "If it goes as planned, you won't even need the car
so I'll just dump it and disappear."

"Agreed," said the Chairman. "but nevertheless I trust the car is in
perfect condition?"

"Sure is, it's ready for Daytona."

The Senator mopped his brow, which was surprising, since it was a cold March day.

"Xan, your report," said the Chairman.

Xan went over his plan in detail; he had rehearsed it again and again during the last two days. He had slept at the head of the crane for the last two nights and the gun was already in place. The men would be going on a twenty-four-hour strike starting at six that evening. "By six tomorrow evening, I will be on other side of America and Kane will be dead."

"Good," said the Chairman, stubbing out his cigarette and lighting another one. "I shall be on the corner of 9th and Pennsylvania and will contact you on my watchband radio when I arrive at 9:30 and again when Kane's car passes me. When your watch starts vibrating, she will be three minutes away, giving you three minutes and forty-five seconds in all. How much warning do you need?"

"Two minutes and thirty seconds will be enough," said Xan.

"That's cutting it a bit close, isn't it?" inquired the Senator, still sweating.

"If that turns out to be the case you will have to delay her on the steps of the Capitol because we don't want to expose Xan more than necessary," said the Chairman. "The longer he is in view, the greater the chance the Secret Service helicopters will have of spotting him."

The Senator turned his head towards Xan. "You say you've been rehearsing every day?"

"Yes," replied Xan. He never saw any reason to use more words than necessary, even when addressing a United States Senator.

"Then why don't people notice you carrying a rifle or at least a gun box?"

"Because gun has been taped to platform on top of crane three hundred and twenty feet out of harm's way ever since I returned from Vienna."

"What happens if the crane comes down? They'll spot it right away."

"No, I am in yellow overalls and rifle is in eight parts and has been painted yellow and is taped to underpart of platform. Even with strong field glasses, it looks like part of crane. When I picked up latest sniper rifle from Dr Schmidt of Helmut, Helmut, and Schmidt, even he was surprised by can of yellow paint."

They all laughed except the Senator.

"How long does it take you to assemble it?" continued the Senator, probing for a flaw, something he always did when questioning so-called experts in Senate committees.

"Two minutes to put rifle together and thirty seconds to get into perfect firing position; two more minutes to dismantle gun and retape it. It's a 5·6 by 61 millimetre Vomhofe Super Express rifle, and I'm using a ·77 grain bullet with a muzzle speed of 3,480 feet per second, which is 2,000 foot-pounds of muzzle energy which, in layman's language, Senator, means if there is no wind, I will aim one and one half inches above Kane's forehead at two hundred yards."

"Are you satisfied?" the Chairman asked the Senator.

"Yes, I suppose so," he said, and sank into a brooding silence, still wiping his brow. Then he thought of something else and was about to start his questioning again, when the door flew open and Matson rushed in.

"Sorry, boss, I've been following something up."

"It'd better be good," snapped the Chairman.

"It could be bad, boss, very bad," said Matson between breaths. They all looked anxiously at him.

"Okay, let's have it."

"His name is Mark Andrews," said Matson, as he fell into the unoccupied seat.

"And who is he?" asked the Chairman.

"The FBI man who went to the hospital with Calvert."

"Could we start at the beginning?" the Chairman asked calmly.

Matson took a deep breath. "You know I've always been bothered about Stames going to the hospital with Calvert – it never made sense, a man of his seniority."

"Yes, yes," said the Chairman impatiently.

"Well, Stames didn't go. His wife told me. I went by to visit her to offer my condolences, and she told me everything Stames had done that evening, right down to eating half his moussaka. The FBI told her not to say anything to anyone but she thinks that I'm still with the Bureau, and she doesn't remember, or maybe she never knew, that Stames and I were not exactly friends. I've checked up on Andrews and I've been following him for the last forty-eight hours. He's listed in the Washington Field Office as on leave for two weeks, but he's been spending his leave in a very strange way. I've seen him at FBI Headquarters, going around with a female doctor from Woodrow Wilson, and nosing around at the Capitol."

The Senator flinched.

"The good doctor was on duty the night that I got rid of the Greek and the black bastard."

"So if they know everything," said the Chairman quickly, "why are we still here?"

"Well, that's the strange part. I arranged to have a drink with an old buddy from the Secret Service; he's on duty details tomorrow with Kane and nothing has been changed. It is painfully obvious that the Secret Service has no idea what we have planned for tomorrow, so either the FBI know one hell of a lot or nothing, but if they do know everything, they're not letting the Secret Service in on it."

"Did you learn anything from your contacts in the FBI?" asked the Chairman.

"Nothing. Nobody knows anything, even when they're blind drunk."

"How much do you think Andrews knows?" continued the Chairman.

"I think he's fallen for our friend the doctor and knows very little. He's running around in the dark," Matson replied. "It's possible he's picked up something from the Greek waiter. If so, he's working on his own, and that's not FBI policy."

"I don't follow," said the Chairman.

"Bureau policy is to work in pairs or threes, so why aren't there dozens of men on it? Even if there were only six or seven, I would have heard about it and so would at least one of my contacts in the FBI," said Matson. "I think they may believe there is going to be an attempt on the President, but I don't think they have a clue when – or where."

"Did anyone mention the date in front of the Greek?" asked the Senator nervously.

"I can't remember, but there's only one way of finding out if they know anything," said the Chairman.

"What's that, boss?" asked Matson.

The Chairman paused, lit another cigarette, and said dispassionately, "Kill Andrews."

There was silence for a few moments. Matson was the first to recover. "Why, boss?"

"Simple logic. If he is connected with an FBI investigation, then they would immediately change tomorrow's schedule. They would never risk allowing Kane to leave the White House if they believed such a threat existed. Just think of the consequences involved; if the FBI knew of an assassination attempt on the President and they haven't made an arrest to date and they didn't bother to inform the Secret Service . . ."

"That's right," said Matson. "They would have to come up with some excuse and cancel at the last minute."

"Exactly, so if Kane comes out of those gates, we will still go ahead because they know nothing. If she doesn't, we're going to take a long holiday, because they know far too much for our health."

The Chairman turned to the Senator, who was now sweating profusely.

"Now, you just make sure that you're on the steps of the Capitol to stall her if necessary and we'll take care of the rest," he said harshly. "If we don't get her tomorrow, we have wasted one hell of a lot of time and money, and we sure aren't going to get another chance as good as this."

The Senator groaned. "I think you're insane, but I won't waste time arguing. I have to get back to the Senate before somebody notices that I'm missing."

"Settle down, Senator. We have it all under control; now we can't lose either way."

"Maybe you can't, but at the end of the day I might end up the fall guy."

The Senator left without another word. The Chairman waited in silence for the door to close.

"Now we've got that little funk out of the way, let's get down to business. Let's hear all about Mark Andrews and what he's been up to."

Matson gave a detailed description of Mark's movements during the past forty-eight hours. The Chairman took in every detail without writing down a word.

"Right, the time has come to blow away Mr Andrews, and then we'll sit back and monitor the FBI's reaction. Now listen carefully, Matson. This is the way it will be done: you will return to the Senate immediately and . . ."

Matson listened intently, taking notes and nodding from time to time.

"Any questions?" the Chairman asked when he had finished.

"None, boss."

"If they let the bitch out of the White House after that, they know nothing. One more thing before we finish. If anything does go wrong tomorrow, we all take care of ourselves. Understood? No one talks; compensation will be made at a later date, in the usual way."

They all nodded.

"And one final point: if there should be a foul-up, there's one man who certainly won't take care of us, so we must be prepared to take care of him. I propose we do it in the following way. Xan, when Kane . . ."

They all listened in silence; no one disagreed.

"Now I think it's time for lunch. No need to let that bitch in the White House spoil our eating habits. Sorry you'll be missing it, Matson; just make sure it's Andrews' last lunch."

Matson smiled. "It will give me a good appetite," he said, and left.

The Chairman picked up the phone. "We're ready for lunch now, thank you." He lit another cigarette.

Wednesday afternoon, 9 March. 2:15 pm

Mark finished his lunch. Two other men finished their sandwiches and also rose to leave. Mark quickly returned to the Senate, as he wanted to catch Henry Lykham before the floor debate started. He hoped that Lykham would have something new to reveal after having had a night to sleep on it. He also needed copies of the Judiciary Committee Gun Control Hearings so that he could study the questions asked by Brooks, Byrd, Dexter, Harrison, and Thornton. Perhaps they would reveal another missing piece of the jigsaw. But somehow Mark doubted it. He was becoming convinced that politicians rarely revealed anything. He arrived a few minutes before the session was scheduled to begin, and aked a page if he could locate Lykham in the ante-chamber.

Lykham bustled out a few moments later. It was obvious he didn't want a chat ten minutes before a full session. So he had no real chance to tell him anything new even if he had thought of something. All Mark did manage to find out was where to obtain transcripts of the committee hearings and discussions.

"You can get them from the committee office at the end of the corridor."

Mark thanked him and walked upstairs to the gallery, where his new friend, the guard, had saved him a seat. The place was already packed. Senators were entering the chamber and taking their places, so he decided to pick up the transcripts later.

The Vice President, Bill Bradley, called for order and the tall figure of Senator Dexter looked around the room slowly and dramatically, sweeping the chamber with his eyes to be assured of everyone's attention. When his eyes alighted on Mark he looked a little surprised, but he quickly recovered and began his final arguments against the bill.

Mark was embarrassed and wished he had taken a seat nearer the back, beyond the range of Dexter's piercing glance. The debate dragged on. Brooks, Byrd, Dexter, Harrison, Thornton. They all wanted a final word before tomorrow's vote. Before tomorrow's death.

Mark listened to them all but he learned nothing new. He seemed to have come to a dead end. All that was left for him to do that day was to go and pick up transcripts of the hearings. He would have to read them through the night and he doubted, having listened to the five speak twice already, that they would reveal anything. But what other lead did he have left? Everything else was being covered by the Director. He walked down the hall to the elevator, left the Capitol by the ground-floor exit, and made his way across the Capitol grounds to the Dirksen Building.

"I would like the transcripts of the Gun Control Hearings, please."

"All of them?" asked the disbelieving secretary.

"Yes," replied Mark.

"But there were six all-day sessions."

Oh, hell, he thought, it will be worse than all night; still, it would be only the questions and statements of Brooks, Byrd, Dexter, Harrison and Thornton.

"Sign or pay?"

"I wish I could sign," he said jokingly.

"Well, are you an official of any kind?"

Yes, thought Mark. But I can't admit it.

"No," said Mark, and took out his wallet.

"If you asked for these through one of the senators from your state, you could probably get them for nothing. Otherwise that'll be ten dollars, sir."

"I'm in a hurry," said Mark. "Guess I'll have to pay."

He handed over the money. Senator Stevenson appeared in the doorway connecting the hearing room to the committee office.

"Good afternoon, Senator," said the secretary, turning away from Mark.

"Hi, Debbie. Would you happen to have a copy of the Clean Air bill as it was reported out of the sub-committee, before the committee markup?"

"Certainly, Senator, just a moment." She disappeared into a back room. "It's the only copy we have at the moment. Can I trust you with it, Senator?" She laughed. "Or should I make you sign for it?"

Even senators sign, thought Mark. Senators sign for everything. Henry Lykham signs for everything, even lunch. No wonder my taxes are so high. But I imagine they have to pay for the food later. The food. My God, why didn't I think of it before. Mark started running.

"Sir, sir, you've left your hearings," a voice shouted. But it was too late.

"Some kind of nut," said the secretary to Senator Stevenson.

"Anyone who wants to read all those hearings must be crazy to begin with," said Senator Stevenson, staring at the pile of paper Mark had left behind him.

Mark went straight to Room G-211, where he had lunched with Lykham the previous day. The door was marked "Official's Dining-Room". There were only two or three attendants in evidence.

"Excuse me, I wonder if you could tell me, is this where the senators eat?"

"I'm sorry, I don't know. You'd have to talk to the hostess. We're just cleaning up."

"Where might I find the hostess?"

"She's not here. Gone for the day. If you come back tomorrow, maybe she can help you.

"Okay." Mark sighed. "Thanks. But can you tell me – is there another Senate dining-room?"

"Yeah, the big one in the Capitol. S-109, but you won't be able to get in there."

Mark ran back to the elevator and waited impatiently. When he reached the basement level, he jumped out and walked past the entrance to the labyrinthine tunnels which connect all the office buildings on Capitol Hill. Past the door marked "Tobacco Shop", he raced towards the large sign – "Subway Cars to Capitol". The subway car, actually just an open train with compartments, was about to leave. Mark stepped into the last compartment and sat down opposite a couple of Senate staffers who were jabbering away about some bill or other, with an air of "we belong".

A few moments later, a bell signalled their arrival and the train came to a stop at the Senate side of the Capitol. Easy life, thought Mark. These guys need never even wander out into the cold, cruel world. They just shuttle back and forth between votes and hearings. The basement on this side was a replica of the basement on the other side, a dull yellow, with exposed plumbing, and the inevitable Pepsi machine; it must have made Coca-Cola mad that Pepsi had the concession for the Senate. Mark bounded up the small escalator and waited for the public elevator, while a couple of men with a certain air of importance were ushered into the elevator marked "Senators Only".

Mark got off on the ground floor, and looked around, perplexed. Nothing but marble arches and corridors. Where was the Senate Dining-Room? he asked one of the Capitol policemen.

"Just walk straight ahead, take the first corridor on the left. It's the narrow one, the first entrance you get to." He pointed.

Mark tossed a thank-you over his shoulder and found the narrow corridor. He passed the kitchens and a sign which announced "Private – Press Only". Straight ahead, in large letters on a wooden sign, he saw another "Senators Only". An open door on the right led into the anteroom, decorated with a chandelier, a rose-coloured, patterned carpet, and green leather furniture, all dominated by the colourful, crowded painting on the ceiling. Through another door, Mark could see white tablecloths, flowers, the world of gracious dining. A matronly woman appeared in the doorway.

"What can I do for you?" she asked, raising her eyebrows inquisitively.

"I'm doing a thesis on the working life of a senator for my Ph.D."
Mark took out his wallet and showed his Yale ID card, covering the
expiration date with his thumb.

The lady was not visibly impressed.

"I really only want to look at the room. Just to get the atmosphere of
the place."

"Well, there are no senators in here at the moment, sir. There almost
never are this late on a Wednesday. They start going back to their home
states on Thursdays for a long weekend. The only thing that is keeping
them here this week is that Gun Control bill."

Mark had managed to edge himself into the centre of the room. A
waitress was clearing a table. She smiled at him.

"Do senators sign for their meals? Or do they pay cash?"

"Almost all of them sign, and then they pay at the end of the month."

"How do you keep track?"

"No problem. We keep a daily record." She pointed to a large book
marked *Accounts*. Mark knew that twenty-three senators had lunched
that day because their secretaries had told him so. Had any other
senator done so without bothering to inform his secretary? He was a
yard away from finding out.

"Could I just see a typical day? Just out of interest," he asked with an
innocent smile.

"I'm not sure I'm allowed to let you look."

"Only a glance. When I write my thesis, I want people to think that I
really know what I'm talking about, that I've seen for myself.
Everyone's been so kind to me."

He looked at the woman pleadingly.

"Okay," she said grudgingly, "but please be quick."

"Thank you. Why don't you pick any old day, let's say 24 February."

She opened the book and thumbed through to 24 February. "A
Thursday," she said. Stevenson, Nunn, Moynihan, Heinz, names rang
one after the other. Dole, Hatfield, Byrd. So Byrd lunched at the Senate
that day. He read on. Templeman, Brooks – Brooks as well. More
names. Barnes, Reynolds, Thornton. So his statement this morning
was for real. The hostess closed the book. No Harrison, no Dexter.

"Nothing very special about that, is there?" she said.

"No," said Mark. He thanked the woman and left quickly.

In the street he hailed a taxi. So did one of the three men following
him; the other two went off to pick up their car.

Mark arrived at the Bureau a few moments later, paid the driver,
showed his credentials at the entrance, and took the elevator to the
seventh floor. Mrs McGregor smiled. The Director must be alone,
thought Mark. He knocked and went in.

"Well, Mark?"

"Brooks, Byrd, and Thornton are not involved, sir."

"The first two don't surprise me," said the Director. "It never made any sense that they were, but I'd have put a side bet on Thornton. Anyway, how did you dispose of those three?"

Mark described his brainstorm about the Senate dining-room, and wondered what else he had overlooked.

"You should have worked all of that out three days ago, shouldn't you, Mark?"

"Yes, sir."

"So should I," said the Director. "So we're down to Dexter and Harrison. It will interest you to know that both men, along with almost all of the senators, intend to be in Washington tomorrow and both are down to attend the ceremony at the Capitol. Amazing," he mused, "even at that level, men like to watch their crimes enacted.

"Let's go over it once again, Andrews. The President leaves the south entrance of the White House at 10:00 am unless I stop her, so we have seventeen hours left and one last hope. The boys in Fingerprints have isolated the bill with Mrs Casefikis's prints on it. The twenty-second, we may be lucky – with still another half dozen to go we shouldn't have had a hope before ten o'clock tomorrow. There are several other prints on the bill, and they will be working on them all through the night. I expect to reach home by midnight. If you come up with anything before then, call me. I want you here in the office at 8:15 tomorrow. There's very little you can do now. But don't worry too much; I have twenty agents still working on it, though none of them knows all the details. And I'll only let the President into the danger zone if we have a fix on these villains."

"I'll report at 8:15 then, sir," said Mark.

"And, Mark, I strongly advise you not to see Dr Dexter. I don't want to blow this whole operation at the last moment, because of your love life. No offence intended."

"No, sir."

Mark left, feeling slightly superfluous. Twenty agents now assigned to the case. How long had the Director had them working round the clock without telling him? Twenty men trying to find out whether it was Dexter or Harrison, without knowing why. Still, only he and the Director knew the whole story, and he feared the Director knew more than he did. Perhaps it would be wiser to avoid Elizabeth until the following evening. He picked up his car, and drove back to the Dirksen Building and then remembered he had left the hearings' transcripts at the Committee Office. When he got there he found himself drawn towards the telephone booths. He had to call her, he had to find out how she was after her accident. He dialled Woodrow Wilson.

"Oh, she left the hospital – some time ago."

"Thank you," said Mark. He could feel his heart beat as he dialled her Georgetown number.

"Elizabeth?"

"Yes, Mark." She sounded – cold? frightened? tired? A hundred questions were racing through his mind.

"Can I come and see you right now?"

"Yes." The telephone clicked.

Mark left the booth, conscious of the sweat on the palms of his hands. One more job to do before he could drive off to Elizabeth, pick up those damned papers from the Senate Gun Control Hearings.

Mark walked towards the elevator and thought he could hear footsteps behind him. Of course he could hear footsteps behind him; there were several people behind him. When he reached the elevator, he pressed the Up-button and glanced around at the footsteps. Among the crowd of Senate staffers, congressmen, and sightseers, two men were watching him – or were they protecting him? There was a third man in dark glasses staring at a Medicare poster, even more obviously an agent, to Mark's quick eyes, than the other two.

The Director had said that he had put twenty agents on the case, and three of them must have been allocated to watch Mark. Hell. Soon they would be following him back to Elizabeth and Mark did not doubt that the Director would learn about it immediately. Mark resolved that no one was going to follow him back to Elizabeth's. It was none of their damned business. He'd shake the three of them off. He needed to see her in peace, without prying eyes and malicious tongues. He thought quickly as he waited to see which of the two elevators would arrive first. Two of the agents were now walking towards him, but the one by the Medicare poster remained motionless. Perhaps he wasn't an operative after all, but there certainly was something familiar about him. He had the aura of an agent; other agents can sense it with their eyes shut.

Mark concentrated on the elevator. The arrow on his right lit up and the doors opened slowly. Mark shot in and stood facing the buttons and stared out at the corridor. The two operatives followed him into the elevator, and stood behind him. The man by the Medicare poster started walking towards the elevator. The doors were beginning to close. Mark pressed the Open-button, and the doors parted again. Must give him a chance to get in, and have all three of them together, Mark thought, but the third man did not respond. He just stood, staring as if waiting for the next elevator. Perhaps he wanted to go down and wasn't an agent at all. Mark could have sworn . . . The doors began to close and at what Mark thought was the optimum point, he jumped back out. Wrong. O'Malley managed to squeeze himself out as well, while his partner was left to travel slowly but inevitably up to the eighth floor. Now Mark was down to two tails. The other elevator arrived. The third agent stepped into it immediately. Very clever or innocent, Mark thought, and waited outside. O'Malley was at his shoulder – which one next?

Mark strolled into the elevator and pressed the Down-button, but O'Malley was able to get in easily. Mark pressed the Open-button and sauntered back out. O'Malley followed him, face impassive. The third man remained motionless in the elevator. They must be working together. Mark jumped back in and jabbed the Close-button hard. The doors closed horribly slowly, but O'Malley had walked two paces away and was not going to make it. As the doors slammed together, Mark smiled. Two gone, one standing on the ground floor helpless, the other heading for the roof, while he was descending to the basement alone with the third.

O'Malley caught up with Pierce Thompson on the fifth floor. Both were out of breath.

"Where is he?" cried O'Malley.

"What do you mean, where is he? I thought he was with you."

"No, I lost him on the first floor."

"Shit, he could be anywhere," said Thompson. "Whose side does the smart-ass think we are on? Which one of us is going to tell the Director?"

"Not me," O'Malley said. "You're the senior officer, you tell him."

"No way I'm telling him," Thompson said. "And let that bastard Matson take all the credit – you can be sure he's still with him. No, we're going to find him. You take the first four floors and I'll take the top four. Bleep immediately when you spot him."

When Mark reached the basement, he stayed in the elevator. The third man walked out and seemed to hesitate. Mark's thumb was jammed on the Close-button again. The door responded. He was on his own. He tried to make the elevator bypass the ground floor but he couldn't; someone else wanted to get in. He prayed it was not one of the three men. He had to risk it. The doors opened and he walked out immediately. No agents in sight, no one studying the Medicare poster. He ran towards the revolving doors at the end of the corridor. The guard on duty looked at him suspiciously and fingered the holster of his gun. Through the revolving doors and out into the open, running hard. He glanced around. Everyone was walking, no one was running. He was safe.

Pennsylvania Avenue – he dodged in and out of the traffic amid screeching tyres and angry expletives. He reached the parking lot and jumped into his car, fumbling for some change. Why did they make trousers that you couldn't get your hands into when you sat down? He quickly paid for his ticket and drove towards Georgetown – and Elizabeth. He glanced in the rear-view mirror. No Ford sedan in sight. He'd done it. He was on his own. He smiled. For once he had beaten the Director. He drove past the lights at the corner of Pennsylvania and

14th just as they were changing. He began to relax.

A black Buick ran the lights. Lucky there were no traffic cops around.

When Mark arrived in Georgetown, his nervousness returned, a new nervousness associated with Elizabeth and her world, not with the Director and his world. When he pressed the bell on her front door, he could still hear his heart beating.

Elizabeth appeared. She looked drawn and tired and didn't speak. He followed her into the living-room.

"Have you recovered from your accident?"

"Yes, thank you. How did you know I'd had an accident?" she asked.

Mark thought quickly. "Called the hospital. They told me there."

"You're lying, Mark. I didn't tell them at the hospital, and I left early after a phone call from my father."

Mark couldn't look her in the eyes. He sat down and stared at the rug. "I . . . I don't want to lie to you, Elizabeth. Please don't."

"Why are you following my father?" she demanded. "He thought you looked familiar when he met you at the Mayflower. You've been haunting his committee meetings and you've been watching the debates in the Senate."

Mark didn't answer.

"Okay, don't explain. I'm not completely blind. I'll draw my own conclusions. I'm part of an FBI assignment. My, you've been working late hours, haven't you, Agent Andrews? For a man singled out to work a senators' daughters' beat, you're pretty goddamn inept. Just how many daughters have you seduced this week? Did you get any good dirt? Why don't you try the wives next? Your boyish charm might be more effective on them. Although, I must confess, you had me fooled, you lying bastard."

Despite a considerable effort to maintain the icy control with which she had launched her attack, Elizabeth bit her lip. Her voice caught. Mark still couldn't look at her. He heard the anger and the tears in her voice. In a moment, the chilling frost had covered her emotion again.

"Please leave now, Mark. Now. I've said my piece and I hope I never lay eyes on you again. Perhaps then I can recover some of my self-respect. Just go; crawl back into the slime."

"You've misunderstood, Elizabeth."

"I know, you poor misunderstood agent, and you love me for myself. There's no other girl in your life," she said bitterly. "At least not until you're transferred to a new case. Well, this case has just finished. Go find somebody else's daughter to seduce with your lies about love."

He couldn't blame her for her reaction, and left without another word.

He drove home in a daze. The occupants of the car following him were fully alert. When he arrived, Mark left the car keys with Simon and took the elevator to his apartment.

The black Buick was parked a hundred yards from the building. The two men could see the light in Mark's apartment. He dialled six of the seven digits of her number, but then he put the phone back on the hook and turned off the light. One of the men in the Buick lit another cigarette, inhaled, and checked his watch.

After months of bargaining, bullying, cajoling and threatening the Gun Control bill was at last to be presented to the House for their final approval.

This was to be the day when Florentyna made an indelible mark on American history. If she achieved nothing else during her term of office she would live to be proud of this single act.

What could prevent it now? she asked for the thousandth time. And for the thousandth time the same dreadful thought flashed across her mind.

She dismissed it once again.

Thursday morning, 10 March. 5:00 am

The Director woke suddenly. He lay there, frustrated; there was nothing he could do at this hour except look at the ceiling and think, and that didn't help much. He went over and over in his mind the events of the past six days, always leaving until last the thought of cancelling the whole operation, which would probably mean even now that the Senator and his cohorts would get away scot-free. Perhaps they already knew and had disappeared to lick their wounds and prepare for another day. Either way it would remain his problem.

The Senator woke at 5:35 in a cold sweat – not that he had really slept for more than a few minutes at any one time. It had been an evil night, thunder and lightning and sirens. It was the sirens that had made him sweat. He was even more nervous than he had expected to be; in fact just after he heard three chime he had nearly dialled the Chairman to say that he couldn't go through with it, despite the consequences that the Chairman had so delicately, but so frequently, adumbrated. But the vision of President Kane dead beside him reminded the Senator that everybody even now could remember exactly where he was when John F. Kennedy was assassinated, and he himself was never going to be able to forget where he was when Florentyna Kane died. Even that seemed less appalling than the thought of his own name in the headlines, his public image irreparably damaged, and his career ruined. Even so, he nearly called the Chairman as much for reassurance as anything, despite their agreement that they had contacted each other for the last time until late the following morning, when the Chairman would be in Miami.

Five men had already died and that had caused only a ripple: President Kane's death would reverberate around the world.

The Senator stared out of the window for some time, focusing on nothing, then turned away. He kept looking at his watch, wishing he could stop time. The second hand moved relentlessly – relentlessly towards 10:56. He busied himself with breakfast and the morning paper. The *Post* informed him that many buildings had caught fire during the night in one of the worst storms in Washington's history, and the Lubber Run in Virginia had overflowed its banks, causing heavy property damage. There was little mention of President Kane. He wished he could read tomorrow's papers today.

The first call the Director received was from Elliott, who informed him that the recent activities of Senators Dexter and Harrison revealed nothing new about the situation – not that the anonymous man knew exactly what the situation was. The Director grumbled to himself, finished his egg – sunny-side up – and read the *Post*'s description of the demonic weather that had assailed Washington during the night. He glanced out of the window at the day, now clear and dry. A perfect day for an assassination, he thought. The bright day that brings forth the adder. How late could he leave it before letting everyone know everything? The President was scheduled to leave the White House at 10:00 am. The Director would have to brief the head of the Secret Service, H. Stuart Knight, long before then and, if necessary, the President at least one hour before that. To hell with it, he would leave it to the last minute and make a full explanation afterwards. He was willing to risk his career to catch this pernicious Senator red-handed. But risking the President's life . . .

He drove to the Bureau soon after 6:00. He wanted to be there a full two hours before Andrews to study all the reports he had ordered the evening before. Not many of his senior aides would have had much sleep last night, though they were probably still wondering why. They would know soon enough. His deputy Associate Director for Investigation, his Assistant Director for Planning and Evaluation, and the head of the Criminal Section of that division would help him decide if he should go ahead or cancel. His Ford sedan slid down the ramp to the underground parking lot and his reserved parking place.

Elliott was there to meet him at the elevator – he was always there, never late. He's not human, he'll have to go, thought the Director, if I don't have to go first. He suddenly realised that he could be handing his resignation in to the President that night. Which President? He put it out of his mind – that would all take care of itself in its own time, he must now take care of the next five hours.

Elliott had nothing useful to say. Dexter and Harrison had both received and made phone calls during the night and early morning, but nothing incriminating had been picked up. No other information was forthcoming. The Director asked where the two senators were at that moment.

"Both eating breakfast at their homes. Dexter in Kensington, Harrison in Alexandria. Six agents have been watching them since five o'clock this morning and have been detailed to follow them all day."

"Good. Report back to me immediately if anything unusual happens."

"Of course, sir."

The fingerprint man was next. When he arrived, the Director first apologised for keeping him up all night, though the man's face and eyes looked more alight and alive than his own had been in the shaving mirror that morning.

Five feet four inches tall, slight and rather pale, Daniel Sommerton began his report. He was like a child with a toy. For him, working with prints had always been a passion as well as a job. The Director remained seated while Sommerton stood. If the Director had stood, he would not have been head and shoulders above him, but head, shoulders, and chest above him.

"We have found seventeen different fingers, and three different thumbs, Director," he said gleefully. "We're putting them through the Ninhydrin rather than the iodine-fume process, since we were unable to do them one at a time for technical reasons that I won't bother you with."

He waved his arm imperiously to imply that he would not waste a scientific explanation on the Director, who would have been the first to acknowledge such a pointless exercise.

"We think there are two more prints we might identify," Sommerton continued, "and we will have a read-out for you on all twenty-two of them within two, at the most three hours."

The Director glanced at his watch – already 6:45.

"Well done. That won't be a minute too soon. Get me the results – even if they are negative – as quickly as possible, and please thank all of your staff for working through the night."

The fingerprint expert left the Director, anxious to return to his seventeen fingers, three thumbs and two unidentified marks. The

Director pressed a button and asked Mrs McGregor to send in the Assistant Director for Planning and Evaluation.

Two minutes later, Walter Williams was standing in front of him.

Five feet eleven, fair with a thin pallid face, dominated by a magnificent high-domed forehead, lined with amusement not grief, Williams was known in the Bureau either as the Brain or W.W. His primary responsibility was to head the Bureau's think tank of six lesser but still impressive brains. The Director often confronted him with hypothetical situations to which W.W. would later provide an answer which often proved, in retrospect, to be the right one. The Director placed great faith in his judgement, but he could not take any risks today. W.W. had better come up with a convincing answer to his hypothetical question of last night or his next call would be to the President.

"Good morning, Director."

"Good morning, W.W. What is your decision concerning my little problem?"

"Most interesting, Director . . . I feel, to be fair, the answer is simple, even when we look at the problem from every angle."

For the first time that morning a trace of a smile appeared on the Director's face.

"Assuming I haven't misunderstood you, Director."

The Director's smile broadened slightly; W.W. neither missed nor misunderstood anything, and was so formal that he didn't address the Director even in private as Halt. W.W. continued, his eyebrows moving up and down like the Dow-Jones index in an election year:

"You asked me to assume that the President would be leaving the White House at X hundred hours and then travelling by car to the Capitol. That would take her six minutes. I'm assuming her car is bullet-proof and well covered by the Secret Service. Under these conditions would it be possible to assassinate her. The answer is, it's possible but almost impossible, Director. Nevertheless, following the hypothesis through to its logical conclusion, the assassination team could use three methods: (a) explosives; (b) a handgun at close range; (c) a rifle."

W.W. always sounded like a textbook. "The bomb can be thrown at any point on the route, but it is never used by professionals, because professionals are paid for results, not attempts. If you study bombs as a method of removing a President, you will find there hasn't been a successful one yet, despite the fact that we have had four Presidents assassinated in office. Bombs inevitably end up killing innocent people and quite often the perpetrator of the crime as well. For that reason, since you have implied that the people involved would be professionals, I feel they must rely on the handgun or the rifle. Now the short-range gun, Director, is not a possible weapon on the route itself because it is unlikely that a pro would approach the President and shoot him at close range, thereby risking his own life. It would take an elephant gun or an anti-tank gun to pierce the President's limousine, and you can't carry those around in the middle of Washington without a permit."

With W.W., the Director could never be sure if it were meant to be a joke or just another fact. The eyebrows were still moving up and down, a sure signal not to interrupt him with foolish questions.

"When the President arrives at the steps of the Capitol, the crowd is too far away from her for a handgun to (a) be accurate and (b) give the assassin any hope of escape. So we must assume that it's the best-tested and most successful method of assassination of a Head of State – the rifle with telescopic sights for long range. Therefore, the only hope the assassin would have must be at the Capitol itself. The assassin can't see into the White House, and in any case the glass in the windows is four inches thick, so he must wait until the President actually leaves the limousine at the steps of the Capitol. This morning we timed a walk up the Capitol steps and it takes around fifty seconds. There are very few vantage points from which to make an assassination attempt, but we have studied the area carefully and you will find them all listed in my report. Also the conspirators must be convinced that we know nothing about the plot, because they know we can cover every possible shooting site. We think an assassination here in the heart of Washington unlikely, but nevertheless just possible by a man or team daring and skilful enough."

"Thank you, W.W. I'm sure you're right."

"A pleasure, sir. I do hope it's only hypothetical."

"Yes, W.W."

W.W. smiled like the only schoolboy in the class who can answer the teacher's questions. The Brain left the room to return to other problems. The Director paused and called for his other Assistant Director.

Matthew Rogers knocked and entered the room, waiting to be asked to take a seat. He understood authority. Like W.W. he would never become the Director, but no one who did would want to be without him.

"Well, Matt?" said the Director, pointing to the leather chair.

"I read Andrews' latest report last night, Director, and I really think the time has come for us to brief the Secret Service."

"I will be doing so in about an hour," said the Director. "Don't worry. Have you decided how you'll deploy your men?"

"It depends where the maximum risk is, sir."

"All right, Matt, let's assume that the point of maximum risk is the Capitol itself, at 10:06, right on the steps – what then?"

"First, I would surround the area for about a quarter of a mile in every direction. I'd close down the Metro, stop all traffic, public and private, pull aside for interrogation anyone who has a past record of making threats, anyone who's on the Security Index. I'd get assistance from the Met to provide perimeter security. We'd want as many eyes and ears in the area as possible. We could get two to four helicopters from Andrews Air Force Base for close scanning. In the immediate vicinity of the President, I'd use the full Secret Service Presidential detail in tight security."

"Very good, Matt. How many men do you need for such an operation, and how long would it take them to be ready if I declared an emergency procedure now?"

The Assistant Director looked at his watch – just after 7:00. He considered the matter for a moment. "I need three hundred special agents briefed and fully operational in two hours."

"Right, go ahead," said the Director crisply. "Report to me as soon as they're ready but leave the final briefing to the last possible moment, and, Matt, I want no helicopters until 10:01. I don't want there to be a chance of a leak of any sort; it's our one hope of catching the assassin."

"Why don't you simply cancel the President's visit, sir? We're in enough deep water as it is, and it's not entirely your responsibility in the first place."

"If we pull out now, we only have to start all over again tomorrow," said the Director, "and I may never get another chance like this."

"Yes, sir."

"Don't let me down, Matt, because I am going to leave the ground operations entirely in your hands."

"Thank you, sir."

Rogers left the room. The Director knew his job would be done as competently as it could be by any professional law-enforcement officer in America.

"Mrs McGregor."

"Yes, sir."

"Get me the head of the Secret Service at the White House."

"Yes, sir."

The Director glanced at his watch: 7:10. Andrews was due at 8:15. The phone rang.

"Mr Knight on the line, sir."

"Stuart, can you call me on my private line and be sure you're not overheard?"

H. Stuart Knight knew Halt well enough to realise that he meant what he said. He called back immediately on his special scrambler.

"Stuart, I'd like to see you immediately, usual place, take about thirty minutes, no more. Top priority."

Damned inconvenient, thought Knight, with the President leaving for the Capitol in two hours, but Halt only made this request two or three times a year, and he knew that other matters must be put to one side for the moment. Only the President and the Attorney General took priority over Halt.

The Director of the FBI and the head of the Secret Service met at a line of cabs in front of Union Station ten minutes later. They didn't take the first cab in the line, but the seventh. They climbed in the back without speaking or acknowledging each other. Elliott drove the Max's Yellow Cab off to circle the Capitol. The Director talked and the head of the Secret Service listened.

Mark's alarm woke him at 6:45. He showered and shaved and thought about those transcripts he had left in the Senate, trying to convince himself that they would have thrown no light on whether it was Dexter or Harrison. He silently thanked Senator Stevenson for indirectly disposing of Senators Brooks, Byrd, and Thornton. He would thank anybody who could dispose of Senator Dexter. He was beginning to agree with the Director's reasoning – it all pointed to Dexter. His motive was particularly compelling, but . . . Mark looked at his watch; he was a little early. He sat on the edge of his bed; he scratched his leg which was itching; something must have bitten him during the night. He continued trying to figure out if there was anything he had missed.

The Chairman got out of bed at 7:20 and lit his first cigarette. He couldn't remember exactly when he had woken. At 6:10 he had phoned Tony, who was already up and waiting for his call. They weren't to meet that day unless the Chairman needed the car in an emergency. The next time they would speak to each other would be on the dot of 9:30 for a check-in to confirm they were all in position.

When he had completed the call, the Chairman dialled room service and ordered a large breakfast. What he was about to do that morning was not the sort of work to be tackled on an empty stomach. Matson was due to ring him any time after 7:30. Perhaps he was still asleep. After that effort last night, Matson deserved some rest. The Chairman smiled to himself. He went into the bathroom and turned on the shower; a feeble trickle of cold water emerged. Goddamn hotels. One hundred dollars a night and no hot water. He splashed around ineffectively and began to think about the next five hours, going over the plan again carefully to be sure he had not overlooked even the smallest detail. Tonight, Kane would be dead and he would have $2,000,000 in the Union Bank of Switzerland, Zurich, account number AZL–376921–B, a small reward from his grateful friends in the gun trade. And to think Uncle Sam wouldn't even get the tax.

The phone rang. Damn. He dripped across the floor, his heartbeat quickened. It was Matson.

Matson and the Chairman had driven back from Mark's apartment at 2:35 that morning, their task completed. Matson had overslept by thirty minutes. The damned hotel had forgotten his wake-up call; you couldn't trust anyone nowadays. As soon as he had woken, he phoned the Chairman and reported in.

Xan was safely in the top of the crane and ready – probably the only one of them who was still asleep.

The Chairman, although dripping, was pleased. He put the phone down and returned to the shower. Damn, still cold.

Matson masturbated. He always did when he was nervous and had time to kill.

Florentyna Kane did not wake until 7:35. She rolled over, trying to recall the dream she had just had, but none of it would come back to her, so she let her mind wander. Today, she would be going to the Capitol to plead her case for the Gun Control bill before a special session of the Senate and then on to have lunch with all the key supporters and opponents of the bill. Since the bill had been approved in committee, as she had been confident it would be, she had concentrated on her strategy for the final day of floor battle; at least the odds now seemed to be with her. She smiled at Edward, although he had his back to her. It had been a busy session, and she was looking forward to going to Camp David and spending more time with her family. Better get moving, more than half of America is already up, she thought, and I am still lying in bed . . . Still, that waking half of America had not had to dine the previous evening with the four-hundred-pound King of Tonga, who wasn't going to leave the White House until he was virtually thrown out. The President wasn't absolutely certain she could pinpoint Tonga on the map. The Pacific was after all a large ocean. She had left her Secretary of State, Abe Chayes, to do the talking; he at least knew exactly where Tonga was.

She stopped thinking about the overweight king and put her feet on the floor – or to be more exact, on the Presidential Seal. The damned thing was on everything except the toilet paper. She knew that when she appeared for breakfast in the dining-room across the hall, she would find the third edition of the *New York Times*, the third edition of the *Washington Post*, the first editions of the *Los Angeles Times* and the *Boston Globe*, all ready for her to read, with the pieces referring to her marked in red, plus a prepared digest of yesterday's news. How did they get it all completed before she was even dressed? Florentyna went to the bathroom and turned on the shower; the water pressure was just right. She began to consider what she could say finally to convince the waverers in the Senate that the Gun Control bill must become law. Her train of thought was interrupted by her efforts to reach the middle of her back with the soap. Presidents still do that for themselves, she thought.

Mark was due to be with the Director in twenty minutes. He checked his mail – just an envelope from American Express, which he left on the kitchen table unopened.

A yawning O'Malley was sitting in the Ford sedan a hundred yards away. He was relieved to be able to report that Mark had left the apartment building and was talking to the black garage attendant. Neither O'Malley nor Thompson had admitted to anybody that they had lost Mark for several hours the previous evening.

Mark walked around the side of the building and disappeared from the view of the man in the blue Ford. It didn't worry him. O'Malley had checked the location of the Mercedes an hour earlier; there was only one way out.

Mark noticed a red Fiat as he came around the corner of the building. Looks like Elizabeth's, he thought to himself, except for the damage to a bumper. He stared at it again and was taken by surprise to see Elizabeth sitting in it. He opened the door. If he were to be Ragani and she were Mata Hari, he was now past caring. He climbed in beside her. Neither of them spoke until they both spoke at once and laughed nervously. She tried again. Mark sat in silence.

"I've come to say I'm sorry about being so touchy last night. I should have at least given you a chance to explain. I really don't want you to sleep with any other senator's daughter," she said, trying to force a smile.

"I'm the one who should be sorry, Liz. Trust me, as they say in Hollywood. Whatever happens, let's meet this evening and then I'll try to explain everything. Don't ask me anything before then and promise that whatever happens you will see me tonight. If after that you never want to see me again I promise I'll leave quietly."

Elizabeth nodded her agreement. "But not as abruptly as you left once before, I hope."

Mark put his arm around her and kissed her quickly. "No more nasty cracks about that night. I've spent every night since looking forward to a second chance."

They both laughed. He started to get out.

"Why don't I drive you to work, Mark? It's on my way to the hospital and we won't have to bother with two cars this evening."

Mark hesitated. "Why not?"

He wondered if this were the final set-up.

As she drove around the corner, Simon waved them down. "Apartment Seven's car won't be back until late this morning, Mark. I'll have to park the Mercedes on the street for now, but don't worry, I'll keep an eye on it." Simon looked at Elizabeth and grinned. "You won't be needing my sister after all, man."

Elizabeth pulled out and joined the traffic on 6th Street. A hundred yards away, O'Malley was chewing gum.

"Where shall we have dinner tonight?"

"Let's go back to that French restaurant and try the whole evening again. This time we'll complete the final act of the play."

I hope it begins, "This was the noblest Roman of them all. All the conspirators, save only he . . ." Mark thought.

"This time it's my treat," said Elizabeth.

Mark accepted, remembering his unopened bill from American Express. The lights turned red at the corner of G Street. They stopped and waited. Mark started scratching his leg again, it really felt quite painful.

The cab was still circling the Capitol but Halt was coming to the end of his briefing for H. Stuart Knight.

"We believe that the attempt will be made when the President gets out of her car at the Capitol. We'll take care of the Capitol itself if you can manage to get her into the building unharmed. I'll have my men cover the buildings and roofs of buildings and every elevated vantage point from which it would be possible to shoot."

"It would make our job a lot easier if the President didn't insist on walking up the steps. Ever since Carter took his little stroll up Pennsylvania Avenue in '77 . . ." His voice trailed off in exasperation. "By the way, Halt, why didn't you tell me about this earlier?"

"There's a strange quirk to it, Stuart. I still can't give you all the details, but don't worry, they're not relevant to the task of protecting the President."

"Okay. I'll buy that. But are you sure my men can't help at your end?"

"No, I'm happy as long as I know you're keeping a close watch on the President. It will give me the freedom I need to catch the bastards red-handed. They mustn't be allowed to get suspicious. I want to catch the killer while he still has the weapon in his hand."

"Shall I tell the President?" asked Knight.

"No, just inform her that it's a new security measure you are putting into practice from time to time."

"She's had so many of those she's bound to believe it," said Knight.

"Stick to the same route and timetable and I'll leave the finer points to you, Stuart. And I don't want any leaks. I'll see you after the President's lunch. We can bring each other up-to-date then. By the way, what's today's code name for the President?"

"Julius."

"Good God, I don't believe it."

"You are telling me everything I need to know, aren't you, Halt?"

"No, of course I'm not, Stuart. You know me, Machiavelli's younger brother."

The Director tapped Elliott on the shoulder and the cab slipped back into the seventh place in line. The two passengers got out and walked in opposite directions, Knight to catch the Metro to the White House, the Director a cab to the Bureau. Neither looked back.

Lucky Stuart Knight, thought the Director, he's gone through the last seven days without the information I have. Now the meeting was over, the Director's confidence in his own stratagem was renewed, and he was resolved that only he and Andrews would ever know the full story – unless they had conclusive proof on which to secure the Senator's conviction. He had to catch the conspirators alive, get them to testify against the Senator. The Director checked his watch with the clock on the Old Post Office Tower over the Washington Field Office. It was 7:58. Andrews would be due in two minutes. He was saluted as he went through the revolving doors of the Bureau. Mrs McGregor was standing outside his office, looking agitated.

"It's Channel Four, sir, asking for you urgently."

"Put them through," said the Director. He moved quickly into his office and picked up the extension.

"It's Special Agent O'Malley from the patrol car, sir."

"Yes, O'Malley?"

"Andrews has been killed, sir, and there must have been another person in the car."

The Director couldn't speak.

"Are you there, Director?" O'Malley waited. "I repeat are you there, Director?"

Finally the Director said, "Come in immediately." He put the phone down, and his great hands gripped the Queen Anne desk like a throat he wanted to strangle. The fingers then curled and clenched slowly into the palms of his hands until they made massive fists, the nails digging into the skin. Blood trickled slowly down on to the leather-work on the desk, leaving a dark stain. Halt Tyson sat alone for several minutes. Then he instructed Mrs McGregor to get the President at the White House. He was going to cancel the whole damned thing; he'd already gone too far. He sat silently waiting. The bastards had beaten him. They must know everything.

It took Special Agent O'Malley ten minutes to reach the Bureau, where he was ushered straight into the Director.

My God, he looks eighty, thought O'Malley.

The Director stared at him. "How did it happen?" he asked quietly.

"He was blown up in a car; we think someone else was with him."

"Why? How?"

"Must have been a bomb attached to the ignition. It blew up right there in front of us. Made an unholy mess."

"I don't give a fuck for the mess," began the Director on a slowly rising note, when the door opened.

Mark Andrews walked in. "Good morning, sir. I hope I'm not interrupting something. I thought you said 8:15."

Both men stared at him.

"You're dead."

"Excuse me, sir?"

"Well, who the hell," said Special Agent O'Malley, "was driving your Mercedes?"

Mark stared at him uncomprehending.

"My Mercedes?" he said quickly. "What are you talking about?"

"Your Mercedes has just been blown to smithereens. I saw it with my own eyes. My colleague down there is trying to put the pieces together; he's already reported finding the hand of a black man."

Mark steadied himself against the wall. "The bastards have killed Simon," he cried in anger. "There will be no need to call Grant Nanna to screw their balls off. I'll do it myself."

"Please explain yourself," said the Director.

Mark steadied himself again, turned around and faced them both. "I came in with Elizabeth Dexter this morning; she came by to see me. I came in with her," he repeated, not yet coherent.

"Simon moved my car because it was occupying a reserved daytime parking space and now the bastards have killed him."

"Sit down, Andrews. You too, O'Malley."

The telephone rang. "The President's Chief of Staff, sir. The President will be with you in about two minutes."

"Cancel it and apologise. Explain to Janet Brown, that it was nothing important, just wanted to wish the President luck on the Gun Control bill today."

"Yes, sir."

"So they think you're dead, Andrews, and they have now played their last card. So we must hold ours back. You're going to remain dead – for a little while longer."

Mark and O'Malley looked at each other, both puzzled.

"O'Malley, you return to your car. You say nothing, even to your partner. You have not seen Andrews alive, do you understand?"

"Yes, sir."

"Get going."

"Mrs McGregor, get me the head of External Affairs."

"Yes, sir."

The Director looked at Mark. "I was beginning to miss you."

"Thank you, sir."

"Don't thank me, I'm just about to kill you again."

A knock on the door, and Bill Gunn came in. He was the epitome of the public relations man, better dressed than anyone else in the building, with the biggest smile and a mop of fair hair that he washed every two days. His face as he entered was unusually grim.

"Have you heard about the death of one of our young agents, sir?"

"Yes, Bill. Put out a statement immediately that an unnamed special agent was killed this morning and that you will brief the press fully at eleven o'clock."

"They'll be hounding me long before then, sir."

"Let them hound you," said the Director sharply.

"Yes, sir!"

"At eleven, you will put out another statement saying the agent is alive . . ."

Bill Gunn's face registered surprise.

". . . and that a mistake has been made, and the man who died was a young garage attendant who had no connection with the FBI."

"But sir, our agent?"

"No doubt you would like to meet the agent who is supposed to be dead. Bill Gunn – this is Special Agent Andrews. Now not a word, Bill. This man is dead for the next three hours and if I find a leak, you can find a new job."

Bill Gunn looked convincingly anxious. "Yes, sir."

"When you've written the press statement, call me and read it over to me."

"Yes, sir."

Bill Gunn left, dazed. He was a gentle, easy-going man and this was way above his head, but he like so many others trusted the Director.

The Director was becoming very aware just how many men did trust him and how much he was carrying on his own shoulders. He looked back at Mark, who had not recovered from the realisation that Simon had died instead of him – the second man to do so in eight days.

"Right, Mark, we have under two hours left, so we will mourn the dead later. Have you anything to add to yesterday's report?"

"Yes, sir. It's good to be alive."

"If you get past eleven o'clock, young man, I think you have a good chance for a long and healthy life, but we still don't know if it's Dexter or Harrison. You know I think it's Dexter." The Director looked at his watch again: 8:29 – ninety seven minutes left. "Any new ideas?"

"Well, sir, Elizabeth Dexter certainly can't be involved, she saved my life by bringing me in this morning. If she wanted me dead, that sure was a funny way of going about it."

"I'll accept that," said the Director, "but it doesn't clear her father."

"Surely he wouldn't kill a man he thought might marry his daughter," said Mark.

"You're sentimental, Andrews. A man who plans to assassinate a President doesn't worry about his daughter's boy friends."

The phone rang. It was Bill Gunn from Public Relations.

"Right, read it over." The Director listened carefully. "Good. Issue it immediately to radio, television, and the papers, and release the second statement at eleven o'clock, no earlier. Thank you, Bill." The Director put the phone down.

"Congratulations, Mark, you're the only dead man alive and, like Mark Twain, you will be able to read your own obituary. Now, to bring you quickly up to date. I have three hundred field agents already out covering the Capitol and the area immediately surrounding it. The whole place will be sealed off the moment the Presidential car arrives."

"You're letting her go to the Capitol?" said Mark in astonishment.

"Listen carefully, Mark. I'll have a minute-by-minute briefing on where the two senators are from 9:00 am on and six men are tailing both of them. At 9:15, we're going into the street ourselves. When it happens, we're going to be there. If I'm going to carry the ultimate responsibility, I may as well carry it in person."

"Yes, sir."

The intercom buzzed.

"It's Mr Sommerton. He wants to see you urgently, sir." The Director looked at his watch: 8:45. On the minute, as promised.

Daniel Sommerton rushed in, looking rather pleased with himself. He came straight to the point. "One of the prints has come up on the criminal file, it's a thumb, his name is Matson – Ralph Matson."

Sommerton produced a photograph of Matson, an Identikit picture, and an enlarged thumbprint.

"And here's the part you're not going to like, sir. He's an ex-FBI agent." He passed Matson's card over for the Director to study. Mark looked at the photo. It was the Greek Orthodox priest, big nose, heavy chin.

"Something professional about him," said the Director and Mark simultaneously.

"Well done, Sommerton, make three hundred copies of the picture immediately and get them to the Assistant Director in charge of the Investigation Division – and that means immediately."

"Yes, sir." The fingerprint expert scurried away, pleased with himself. They wanted his thumb.

"Mrs McGregor, get me Mr Rogers."

The Assistant Director was on the line; the Director briefed him.

"Shall I arrest him on sight?"

"No, Matt. Once you've spotted him, watch him and keep your boys well out of sight. He could still call everything off if he got suspicious. Keep me briefed all the time. Move in on him at 10:06. I'll let you know if anything changes."

"Yes, sir. Have you briefed the Secret Service?"

"Yes, I have." He slammed the phone down.

The Director looked at his watch: 9:05. He pressed a button and Elliott came in. "Where are the two senators?"

"Harrison's still in his Alexandria town house, Dexter has left Kensington and is heading towards the Capitol, sir."

"You stay here in this office, Elliott, and keep in radio contact with me and the Assistant Director on the street. Never leave this room. Understood?"

"Yes, sir."

"I'll be using my walkie-talkie on Channel Four. Let's go, Andrews." They left the anonymous man.

"If anybody calls me, Mrs McGregor, put them through to Special Agent Elliott in my office. He will know where to contact me."

"Yes, sir."

A few moments later, the Director and Mark were on the street walking up Pennsylvania Avenue towards the Capitol. Mark put on his dark glasses and pulled his collar up. They passed several agents on the way. None of them acknowledged the Director. On the corner of Pennsylvania Avenue and 9th Street, they passed the Chairman, who was lighting a cigarette and checking his watch: 9:30. He moved to the edge of the sidewalk, leaving a pile of cigarette butts behind him. The Director glanced at the cigarette butts: litter bug, ought to be fined a hundred dollars. They hurried on.

"Come in, Tony. Come in, Tony."

"Tony, boss. The Buick's ready. I've just heard it announced on the car radio that pretty boy Andrews bought it."

The Chairman smiled.

"Come in, Xan."

"Ready, await your signal."

"Come in, Matson."

"Everything's set, boss. There's a hell of a lot of agents around."

"Don't sweat, there's always a lot of Secret Service men around when the President is travelling. Don't call again unless there's a real problem. All three keep your lines open. When I next call, I will only activate the vibrators on the side of your watches. Then you have three minutes forty-five seconds, because Kane will be passing me. Understood?"

"Yes."

"Yes."

"Yes."

The Chairman broke the circuit and lit another cigarette: 9:40.

The Director spotted Matthew Rogers in a special squad car and went quickly over to him. "Everything under control, Matt?"

"Yes, sir. If anybody tries anything, no one will be able to move for half a mile."

"Good; what time do you have?"

"Nine-forty-five."

"Right, you control it from here. I'm going to the Capitol."

Halt and Mark left the Assistant Director and walked on.

"Elliott calling the Director."

"Come in, Elliott."

"They have spotted Matson at the junction of Maryland Avenue and 1st Street, other side of the Garfield statue, south-west corner of the Capitol grounds, near the west front renovation site."

"Good. Observe and post fifty men around the area, don't move in yet, brief Mr Rogers and tell him to keep his men out of Matson's field of vision."

"Yes, sir."

"What the hell is he doing on that side of the Capitol?" said Mark softly. "You couldn't shoot anyone on the Capitol steps from the north-west side unless you were in a chopper."

"I agree, it beats me," said the Director.

They reached the police cordon surrounding the Capitol. The Director showed his credentials to get himself and Andrews through. The young Capitol policeman double-checked them; he couldn't believe it; he was looking at the real live object. Yes, it was the Director of the FBI. H.A.L. Tyson himself.

"Sorry, sir. Please come through."

"Elliott to the Director."

"Yes, Elliott?"

"Head of the Secret Service for you, sir."

"Stuart."

"The advance car is leaving the front gate now. Julius will leave in five minutes."

"Thank you, Stuart. Keep your end up and surprise me."

"Don't worry, Halt. We will."

Five minutes later, the Presidential car left the South Entrance and turned left on to E Street. The advance car passed the Chairman on the corner of Pennsylvania Avenue and 9th. He smiled, lit another cigarette and waited. Five minutes later, a large Lincoln, flags flying on both front fenders, the Presidential Seal on the doors, passed by the Chairman. Through the misty grey windows, he could see three figures in the back. A limousine known as the "gun car" and occupied by Secret Service agents and the President's personal physician, followed the President's car. The Chairman pressed a button on his watch. The vibrator began to tickle his wrist. After ten seconds, he stopped it, walked one block north and hailed a taxi.

"National Airport," he said to the cab driver, fingering the ticket in his inside pocket.

The vibrator on Matson's watch was touching his skin. After ten seconds, it stopped. Matson walked to the side of the construction site, bent down and tied his shoelace.

Xan started to take off the tape, He was glad to be moving; he had been bent double all night. First he screwed the barrel into the sight finder.

"Assistant Director to Director. Matson is approaching the construction site. Now he has stopped to tie his shoe. No one on the construction site but I'm asking a helicopter to check it out. There's a huge crane in the middle of the site which looks deserted."

"Good. Stay put until the last minute. I'll give you the timing the moment the President's car arrives. You must catch them red-handed. Alert all agents on the roof of the Capitol."

The Director turned to Mark, more relaxed. "I think it's going to be all right."

Mark's eyes were on the steps of the Capitol. "Have you noticed, sir, both Senator Dexter and Senator Harrison are in the welcoming party for the President?"

"Yes," said the Director. "The car is due to arrive in two minutes; we'll catch the others even if we can't figure out which Senator it is. We'll make them talk in due course. Wait a minute – that's odd."

The Director's finger was running down a couple of closely typed sheets he held in his hand.

"Yes, that's what I thought. The President's detailed schedule shows that Dexter will be there for the special address to Congress but isn't attending the luncheon with the President. Very strange: I'm sure all the key leaders of the opposition were invited to lunch. Why won't Dexter be present?"

"Nothing strange about that, sir. He always has lunch with his daughter on Thursdays. Good God 'I always have lunch with my father on Thursdays.' "

"Yes, Mark, I heard you the first time."

"No, sir, 'I always have lunch with my father on Thursdays.' "

"Mark, the car will be here in one minute."

"It's Harrison, sir. It's Harrison. I'm a fool – Thursday, 24 February, in Georgetown. I always thought of it as 24 February, not as Thursday. Dexter was having lunch with Elizabeth. 'I always have lunch with my father on Thursdays.' That's why he was seen in Georgetown that day, must be. They never miss it."

"Are you sure? Can you be certain? There's a hell of a lot riding on it."

"It's Harrison, sir. It can't be Dexter. I should have realised it on the first day. Christ, I'm stupid."

"Right, Mark. Up those steps quickly, watch Harrison's every move and be prepared to arrest him whatever the consequences."

"Yes, sir."

"Rogers."

The Assistant Director came in. "Sir?"

"The car is pulling up. Arrest Matson immediately; check the roof of the Capitol." The Director stared up into the sky. "Oh my God, it's not a helicopter, it's that damn crane. It has to be the crane."

Xan nestled the butt of the yellow rifle into his shoulder and watched the President's car. He had attached a feather to a piece of thread on the end of the gun barrel, a trick he had picked up when training for the Olympics – no wind. The hours of waiting were coming to an end. Senator Harrison was standing there on the Capitol steps. Through the thirty-power Redfield scope he could even see the beads of sweat standing out on the man's forehead.

The President's car drew up on the north side of the Capitol. All was going according to plan. Xan levelled the telescopic sight on the car door and waited for Kane. Two Secret Service men climbed out, scanned the crowd, and waited for the third. Nothing happened. Xan put the sight on the Senator, who looked anxious and bemused. Back at the car, still no Kane. Where the hell was she, what was going on? He checked the feather; still no wind. He moved his sight back on the President's car. Good God, the crane was moving and Kane wasn't in the car. Matson had been right all along, they knew everything. Xan knew exactly what had to be done in these circumstances. Only one man could ditch them and he wouldn't hesitate to do it. Xan moved his sight up the Capitol steps. One and one-half inches above the forehead. A moment's hesitation before he squeezed the trigger once . . . twice, but the second time he didn't have a clear shot, and a fraction of a second later he could no longer see the Capitol steps. He looked down from the moving crane. He was surrounded by fifty men in dark suits, fifty guns were pointing up at him.

Mark was about a yard away from Senator Harrison when he heard him cry out and fall. Mark jumped on top of the Senator and the second bullet grazed his shoulder. There was a panic among the other senators and officials on the top steps. The welcoming party scurried inside. Thirty FBI men moved in quickly. The Director was the only man who remained on the Capitol steps, steady and motionless, staring up at the crane. They hadn't nicknamed him Halt by mistake.

"May I ask where I'm going, Stuart?"

"Certainly, Madam President. To the Capitol."

"But this isn't the normal route to the Capitol."

"No, Madam. We're going down Constitution Avenue to the Russell Building. We hear there has been a little trouble at the Capitol. A demonstration of some kind. The National Rifle Association."

"So I'm avoiding it, am I? Like a coward, Stuart."

"No, Madam, I'm slipping you through the basement. Just as a safety precaution and for your own convenience."

"That means I'll have to go on that damned subway. Even when I was a senator, I preferred to walk outside."

"We've cleared the way for you, Madam. You'll still be there bang on time."

The President grumbled as she looked out of the window and saw an ambulance race in the opposite direction.

Senator Harrison died before he reached the hospital and Mark had his wound patched up by a house doctor. Mark checked his watch and laughed. It was 11:04 – he was going to live.

"Phone for you, Mr Andrews. The Director of the FBI."

"Sir?"

"Mark, I hear you're fine. Good. I am sorry to say the Senate went into recess out of respect for Senator Harrison. The President is shocked but feels this is precisely the moment to emphasise the significance of gun control, so we're all now going into lunch early. Sorry you can't join us. And we caught three of them – Matson, a Vietnamese sharpshooter, and a petty crook called Tony Loraido. There may still be more, I'll let you know later. Thank you, Mark."

The telephone clicked before Mark could offer any opinion.

Thursday evening, 10 March. 7:00 pm

Mark arrived in Georgetown at seven that evening. He had gone to Simon's wake and paid his respects to the bewildered parents that afternoon. They had five other children, but that never helped. Their grief made Mark long for the warmth of the living.

Elizabeth was wearing the red silk shirt and black skirt in which he had first seen her. She greeted him with a cascade of words.

"I don't understand what's been going on. My father called earlier and told me you tried to save Senator Harrison's life. What were you doing there anyway? My father is very upset about the shooting. Why have you been following him around? Was he in any danger?"

Mark looked at her squarely. "No, he wasn't involved in any way so let's try and start over again."

Still she didn't understand.

When they arrived at the Rive Gauche, the maître d' welcomed them with open arms.

'Good evening, Mr Andrews, how nice to see you again. I don't remember your booking a table."

"No, it's in my name. Dr Dexter," said Elizabeth.

"Oh, yes, Doctor, of course. Will you come this way?"

They had baked clams, and, at last, a steak with no fancy trimmings and two bottles of wine.

Mark sang most of the way home. When they arrived, he took her firmly by the hand and led her into the darkened living-room.

"I'm going to seduce you. No coffee, no brandy, no music, just straightforward seduction."

"I should be so lucky."

They fell on the couch.

"You're too drunk," Elizabeth added.

"Wait and see." He kissed her fully on the lips for a long time and started to unbutton her shirt.

"Are you sure you wouldn't like some coffee?" she asked.

"Yes, quite sure," he said as he pulled the shirt slowly free from her skirt and felt her back, his other hand moving on to her leg.

"What about some music?" she said lightly. "Something special." Elizabeth touched the start button on the hi-fi. It was Sinatra again, but this time it was the right song:

> Is it an earthquake or simply a shock
> Is it the real turtle soup or merely the mock,
> Is it a cocktail, this feeling of joy,
> Or is what I feel – the real –McCoy?
>
> Is it for all time or simply a lark,
> Is it Granada I see or only Asbury Park,
> Is it a fancy not worth thinking of,
> Or is it at . . . long . . . last . . . love ?

She settled back into Mark's arms.

He unzipped her skirt. Her legs were slender and beautiful in the dim light. He caressed her gently.

"Are you going to tell me the truth about today, Mark?"

"Afterwards, darling."

"When you've had your way with me," she said.

He slipped his shirt off. Elizabeth stared at the bandage on his shoulder.

"Is that where you were wounded in the line of duty?"

"No, that's where my last lover bit me."

"She must have had more time than I did."

They moved closer together.

He took the phone off the hook – not tonight, Julius.

"I can't get through, sir," Elliott said, "just a continual busy signal."

"Try again, try again. I'm sure he's there."

"Shall I go through the operator?"

"Yes, yes," said the Director testily.

The Director waited, tapping his fingers on the Queen Anne desk, staring at the red stain and wondering how it had got there.

"The operator says the phone is off the hook, sir. Shall I ask her to bleep him; that'll certainly get his attention."

"No, Elliott, just leave it and go home. I'll have to call him in the morning."

"Yes, sir. Good night, sir."

He'll have to go – back to Idaho or wherever he came from, thought the Director, as he switched off the lights and made his own way home.

Friday morning, 11 March. 7:00 am

Mark woke first; perhaps because he was in a strange bed. He turned over and looked at Elizabeth. She never wore make-up and was just as beautiful in the morning as she was on the other side of a dinner table. Her dark hair curled in towards the nape of her neck and he stroked the soft strands gently. She stirred, rolled over, and kissed him.

"Go and brush your teeth."

"What a romantic way to start the day," he said.

"I'll be awake by the time you get back." She groaned a little and stretched.

Mark picked up the Pepsodent – that was one thing that would have to change, he preferred Macleans – and tried to figure out which part of the bathroom he was going to be able to fit his things into. When he returned, he noticed the phone was still off the hook. He looked at his watch: 7:05. He climbed back into bed. Elizabeth slipped out.

"Only be a minute," she said.

It was never like this in the movies, thought Mark.

She returned and lay down beside him. After a moment she said, "Your chin is hurting my face. You're not as clean-shaven as you were the first time."

"I shaved very carefully that first evening," said Mark. "Funny, I was never so sure of anything. Didn't happen quite the way I intended."

"What did you intend?"

"It was never like this in the movies." This time he stated the sentiments clearly. "Do you know what the Frenchman said when accused of raping a dead woman?"

"No."

"I didn't realise she was dead; I thought she was English."

After she had proved she wasn't English Elizabeth asked Mark what he would like for breakfast.

After Mark had told her, he disappeared into the shower.

Mark turned on the shower, getting the temperature just right.

"Disappointing, I thought we would take a bath together," said Elizabeth.

"I never bathe with the domestic staff. Just give me a call when breakfast is ready," Mark replied from under the shower and started to sing "At Long Last Love" in several different keys.

A slim arm appeared through the falling water and turned off the hot water tap. The singing stopped abruptly. Elizabeth was nowhere to be seen.

Mark dressed quickly and put the phone back on the hook. It rang almost immediately. Elizabeth appeared in a brief slip.

Mark wanted to go back to bed.

She picked up the phone. "Good morning. Yes, he's here. It's for you. A jealous lover, I shouldn't wonder."

She put on a dress and returned to the kitchen.

"Mark Andrews."

"Good morning, Mark."

"Oh, good morning, sir."

"I've been trying to get you since eight o'clock last night."

"Oh, really, sir. I thought I was on vacation. If you look in the official book in the WFO, I think you'll find I've signed out."

"Yes, Mark, but you are going to have to interrupt that vacation because the President wants to see you."

"The President, sir?"

"Of the United States."

"Why would she want to see me, sir?"

"Yesterday I killed you, but today I've made you a hero and she wants to congratulate you personally on trying to save Senator Harrison's life."

"What?"

"You'd better read the morning papers. Say nothing for now; I'll explain my actions later."

"Where do I go, what time, sir?"

"You'll be told." The line clicked.

Mark replaced the phone and thought about the conversation. He was just about to call Elizabeth to ask if the morning paper had come when the phone rang again.

"Answer it will you, Mark darling. Now that the lovers have found your whereabouts, it's bound to be for you."

Mark picked it up.

"Mr Andrews?"

"Speaking."

"Hold the line one moment, please. The President will be with you in one moment."

"Good morning. Florentyna Kane. I just wanted to know if you could find time to drop into the White House this morning at about ten o'clock. I'd like to meet you and have a chat."

"I'd be honoured, Madam."

"Then I'll look forward to it, Mr Andrews, and the chance to meet you and congratulate you personally. If you come to the West Entrance, Janet Brown will be there to meet you."

"Thank you, Madam."

One of those legendary phone calls that the press so often wrote about. The Director had only been checking where he was. Had the President been trying to reach him since eight last night?

"Who was it, darling?"

"The President of the United States."

"Tell her you'll call back; she's always on the line, usually calls collect."

"No, I'm serious."

"Yes, of course you are."

"She wants to see me."

"Yes, darling, your place or hers?"

Mark went into the kitchen and attacked some Wheaties. Elizabeth came in brandishing the *Post*.

"Look," she said. "It's official. You're not a villain, you're a hero."

The headline read: SENATOR HARRISON KILLED ON STEPS OF CAPITOL.

"It was the President, wasn't it?" she said.

"Yes, it was."

"Why didn't you tell me?"

"I did, but you didn't choose to listen."

"I'm sorry," said Elizabeth.

"I love you."

"I love you too, but let's not go through this every week."

She continued to read the paper. Mark munched his Wheaties.

"Why would someone want to kill Senator Harrison, Mark?"

"I don't know. What does the *Post* say?"

"They haven't figured out a reason yet; they say he was known to have many enemies both here and abroad." She began to read from the paper:

"Senator Robert Harrison (D-South Carolina) was shot by an assassin on the steps of the Capitol yesterday morning at 10:06.

"The assassination took place only moments before President Kane was due to arrive for her final assault on behalf of the Gun Control bill, which had been scheduled for a vote in the Senate yesterday. Because they had been warned of a demonstration on the steps of the Capitol, the Secret Service diverted the President's car to the Russell Senate Office Building.

"The bullet lodged in Senator Harrison's brain and he was pronounced dead on arrival at Woodrow Wilson Medical Center. A second bullet grazed the shoulder of FBI Agent Mark Andrews, 28, who threw himself on the Senator in an effort to save his life. Andrews was treated at the same hospital and later released.

"There was no immediate explanation of the fact that a second presidential motorcade did arrive at the Capitol steps a few moments before the assassination, without the President.

"Vice President Bradley ordered an immediate recess of the Senate out of respect for Senator Harrison. The House then voted unanimously to extend the recess for seven days.

"The President, who arrived at the Capitol via the congressional subway from the Russell Building, first learned the news of Harrison's assassination when she reached the Senate. Visibly shaken, she announced that the luncheon to discuss gun control would continue as planned but asked the assembled Senators to observe a minute of silence in honour of their dead colleague.

"The President went on to say, 'I know we are all shocked and saddened by the tragic and horrifying event which has just occurred. This senseless killing of a good and decent man must, however, only strengthen our determination to work together in making our country safe from the easy access of arms.'

"The President plans to address the nation at nine o'clock tonight."

"So now you know everything, Liz."
   "I know nothing," she replied.
   "I didn't know very much of that myself," Mark admitted.
   "Living with you is going to be difficult."
   "Who said I was going to live with you?"
   "I took it for granted from the way you're eating my eggs."

At the Fontainebleau Hotel a man was sitting by the side of the swimming pool reading the *Miami Herald* and drinking coffee. At least Senator Harrison could cause no more trouble which made him feel a little safer. Xan had kept his part of the bargain.

He sipped the coffee, a little hot, it didn't matter, he was in no hurry. He had already given new orders; he couldn't afford any further risks. Xan would be dead by the evening; that had been arranged. Matson and Tony would be freed for lack of evidence, so his lawyer, who had never let him down yet, had assured him, and he would not be visiting Washington for a while. He relaxed and settled back in his beach chair to let the Miami sun warm him. He lit another cigarette.

At 9:45, the Director was met at the White House by Janet Brown, the President's Chief of Staff. They waited and chatted. The Director briefed her on Special Agent Andrews' background. Brown made careful notes.

Mark arrived just before 10:00. He had only just managed to get home and change into a new suit.

"Good morning, Director," he said nonchalantly.

"Good morning, Mark. Glad you could make it." Slightly quizzical but not disapproving. "This is the President's Chief of Staff, Janet Brown."

"Good morning, ma'am," said Mark.

Janet Brown took over. "Will you be kind enough to come through to my office, where we can wait. The President will be videotaping her address to the nation for this evening's television broadcast so that she can fly to Camp David at 11:15. I imagine you and the Director will have about fifteen minutes with her."

Janet Brown took them to her office, a large room in the West Wing with a fine view of the Rose Garden through a bow window.

"I'll get us some coffee," she said.

"That'll be a change," murmured Mark.

"I'm sorry?" said Janet Brown.

"Nothing."

The Director and Mark settled down in comfortable chairs where they could watch a large liquid-crystal monitor screen on one of the walls, already alive with comings and goings in the Oval Office.

The President's forehead was being powdered in preparation for her speech and the cameramen were wheeling around her. Janet Brown was on the phone.

"CBS and NBC can roll, Janet, but ABC is still fixing things up with their OB unit," said an agitated female voice.

Janet Brown got the producer of ABC on the other line.

"Get a move on, Harry, the President doesn't have all day."

"Janet."

Florentyna Kane was on the middle of the screen.

She looked up. "Yes, Madam President?"

"Where's ABC?"

"I'm just chasing them, Madam President."

"Chasing them? They've had four hours' warning. They couldn't get a camera to the Second Coming."

"No, ma'am. They're on their way now."

Harry Nathan, ABC's producer, appeared on the screen. "We're all set now, Janet. Ready to record in five minutes."

"Fine," said Florentyna Kane and looked at her watch. It was 10:11. The digits changed – and were replaced by the rate of her heartbeat – 72; normal, she thought. They disappeared again, to be replaced by her blood pressure, 140/90; a little high; she'd get it checked by her doctor this weekend. The digits were replaced by the Dow-Jones index, showing an early fall of 1·5 to 1,409. This disappeared and the watch showed 10:12. The President rehearsed the opening line of her speech for the last time. She'd gone over the final draft with Edward that morning, and she was satisfied with it.

"Mark."

'Sir?"

"I want you to report back to Grant Nanna at the WFO this afternoon."

"Yes, sir."

"Then I want you to take a vacation. I mean a real vacation, some time in May. Mr Elliott is leaving me at the end of May to take up the post of Special Agent in Charge of the Columbus Field Office. I'm going to offer you his job, and enlarge it to your being my personal assistant."

Mark was stunned. "Thank you very much, sir. I would be delighted." Bang goes the five-year plan.

"You said something, Mark?"

"No, sir."

"In private, Mark, you must stop calling me 'sir', if we're going to work together all the time; it's more than I can stand. You can call me Halt or Horatio – I don't mind which."

Mark couldn't help laughing.

"You find my name amusing, Mark?"

"No, sir. But I just made $3,516."

"Testing: one, two, three. Loud and clear. Could you give us a voice test, please, Madam President?" asked the floor producer, now less agitated. "What did you have for breakfast?"

"Toast and coffee," said the President resonantly.

"Thank you, Madam. That's fine. Ready to roll."

All the cameras were focused on the President, who sat behind her desk, sombre and serious.

"When you're ready, Madam President."

The President looked into the lens of Camera One.

"My fellow Americans, I speak to you tonight from the Oval Office in the wake of the bloody assassination of Senator Harrison on the steps of the Capitol. Robert Everard Harrison was my friend and colleague, and I know we will all feel his loss greatly. Our sympathy goes out to his family in their distress. This evil deed only strengthens my determination to press for legislation early in the new session strictly limiting the sale and the unauthorised ownership of guns. I will do this in memory of Senator Robert Harrison, so that we may feel he did not die in vain."

The Director looked at Mark; neither of them spoke. The President continued, repeating her belief in the importance of gun control and why the measure deserved the full support of the American people.

"And so I leave you, my fellow citizens, thanking God that America can still produce men who are willing to risk their own lives for public service. Thank you and good night."

The camera panned to the Presidential Seal. Then the Outside Broadcast units took over and switched to a picture of the White House with the flag at half-mast.

"It's a wrap, Harry," said the female floor producer.

"Let's do a re-run and see what it looks like."

The President in the Oval Office, and the Director and Mark in Janet Brown's room watched the re-run. It was good. The Gun Control bill will sail through, thought Mark.

The chief usher arrived at Janet Brown's door. He addressed the Director.

"The President wonders if you and Mr Andrews would be kind enough to join her in the Oval Office."

Both men rose from their chairs and followed in silence down the long marble corridor of the West Wing, passing pictures of former presidents, intermingled with oil paintings commemorating famous incidents in American history. They passed the bronze bust of Lincoln. When they reached the East Wing, they stopped at the massive white semi-circular doors of the Oval Office, dominated by the great Presidential Seal. A Secret Service man was sitting behind a desk in the hallway. He looked up at the chief usher, neither spoke. Mark watched the Secret Service agent's hand go under the desk, and he heard a click. The Seal split as the doors opened. The usher remained in the entrance.

Someone was unclipping a tiny microphone from under the President's collar, and the remnants of make-up were being removed by an attentive young woman. The television cameras had already gone. The usher announced, "The Director of the Federal Bureau of Investigation, Mr H.A.L. Tyson, and Special Agent Mark Andrews, Madam President."

The President rose from her seat at the far end of the room and

waited to greet them. They walked towards her slowly.
"Sir," said Mark under his breath.
"Yes, Mark?"
"Shall we tell the President?"

FIRST
AMONG
EQUALS

PROLOGUE

Wednesday 10 April 1931

If Charles Gurney Seymour had been born nine minutes earlier he would have become an earl, inherited a castle in Scotland, 22,000 acres in Somerset, and a thriving merchant bank in the City of London.

It was to be several years before young Charles worked out the full significance of coming second in life's first race.

His twin brother, Rupert, only just came through the ordeal, and in the years that followed contracted not only the usual childhood illnesses but managed to add scarlet fever, diphtheria and meningitis, causing his mother, Lady Seymour, to fear for his survival.

Charles, on the other hand, *was* a survivor, and had inherited enough Seymour ambition for both his brother and himself. Only a few years passed before those who came into contact with the brothers for the first time mistakenly assumed Charles was the heir to the earldom.

As the years passed Charles's father tried desperately to discover something at which Rupert might triumph over his brother – and failed. When they were eight the two boys were sent away to Summerfields where generations of Seymours had been prepared for the rigours of Eton. During his first month at the Oxford prep school Charles was voted form captain and no one hindered his advance *en route* to becoming head boy at the age of twelve, by which time Rupert was looked upon as Seymour Minor. Both boys proceeded to Eton, where in their first half Charles beat Rupert at every subject in the classroom, outrowed him on the river and nearly killed him in the boxing ring.

When in 1947 their grandfather, the thirteenth Earl of Bridgwater, finally expired, the sixteen-year-old Rupert became Viscount Seymour while Charles inherited a meaningless prefix.

The Hon. Charles Seymour felt angry every time he heard his brother deferentially addressed by strangers as "My Lord".

At Eton, Charles continued to excel and ended his schooldays as President of Pop before being offered a place at Christ Church, Oxford, to read History. Rupert covered the same years without over-burdening the examiners, internal or external. At the age of eighteen the young viscount returned to the family estate in Somerset to pass the rest of his days as a landowner. No one destined to inherit 22,000 acres could be described as a farmer.

At Oxford, Charles, free of Rupert's shadow, progressed with the air of a man who found the university something of an anticlimax. He would spend his weekdays reading the history of his relations and the weekends at house parties or riding to hounds. As no one had suggested for one moment that Rupert should enter the world of high finance, it was assumed once Charles had left Oxford that he would succeed his father at Seymour's Bank: first as a director and then in time as its chairman: although it would be Rupert who would eventually inherit the family shareholding.

This "best laid plan" changed, however, when one evening the Hon. Charles Seymour was dragged off to the Oxford Union by a nubile undergraduate from Somerville, who demanded he should listen to the Eights Week motion. "I would rather be a commoner than a lord". The President of the Union had achieved the unique coup of having the motion proposed by the Prime Minister, Sir Winston Churchill.

Charles sat at the back of a hall packed with eager students mesmerised by the elder statesman's performance. Never once did he take his eyes off the great war leader during his witty and powerful speech, although what kept flashing across his mind was the realisation that, but for an accident of birth, Churchill would have been the ninth Duke of Marlborough. Here was a man who had dominated the world stage for three decades and then turned down every hereditary honour a grateful nation could offer, including the title of Duke of London.

From that moment Charles never allowed himself to be referred to as "the Hon." again: his ultimate ambition was now above mere titles.

Another undergraduate who listened to Churchill that night was also considering his future. But he did not view proceedings crammed between his fellow students at the back of the crowded hall. The tall young man dressed in white tie and tails sat alone in a large chair on a raised platform, for such was his right as President of the Oxford Union.

Although Simon Kerslake *was* the first-born, he had otherwise few of Charles Seymour's advantages. The only son of a family solicitor, he had come to appreciate how much his father had denied himself to ensure that his son should remain at the local public school. Simon's father had died during his son's last year at Lancing College, leaving his widow a small annuity and a magnificent MacKinley grandfather clock. Simon's mother sold the clock a week after the funeral in order that her son could complete his final year with all the 'extras' the other boys took for granted. She also hoped that it would give Simon a better chance of going on to university.

From the first day he could walk Simon had always wanted to outdistance his rivals. The Americans would have described him as "an achiever", while many of his contemporaries thought of him as pushy, or even arrogant, according to their aptitude for jealousy. During his last term at Lancing Simon was passed over for head of school and he still found himself unable to forgive the headmaster his lack of foresight. Later that year, some weeks after he had completed his S-levels and been interviewed by Magdalen, a circular letter informed him that he would not be offered a place at Oxford; it was a decision Simon was unwilling to accept.

In the same mail Durham University offered him a scholarship, which he rejected by return of post. "Future Prime Ministers aren't educated at Durham," he informed his mother.

"How about Cambridge?" she inquired, continuing to wipe the dishes.

"No political tradition," replied Simon.

"But if there is no chance of being offered a place at Oxford, surely – ?"

"That's not what I said, Mother," replied the young man. "I shall be an undergraduate at Oxford by the first day of term."

After eighteen years of forty-yard goals Mrs Kerslake had learned to stop asking her son, "How will you manage that?"

Some fourteen days before the start of the Michaelmas Term at Oxford Simon booked himself into a small guest house just off the Iffley Road. On a trestle table in the corner of lodgings he intended to make permanent he wrote out a list of all the colleges, then divided them into five columns, planning to visit three each morning and three each afternoon until his question had been answered positively by a resident Tutor for Admissions: "Have you accepted any freshmen for this year who are now unable to take up their places?"

It was on the fourth afternoon, just as doubt was beginning to set in and Simon was wondering if after all he would have to travel to Cambridge the following week, that he received the first affirmative reply.

The Tutor for Admissions at Worcester College removed the glasses from the end of his nose and stared at the tall young man with a mop of dark hair falling over his forehead. Alan Brown was the twenty-second don Kerslake had visited in four days.

"Yes," he replied. "It so happens that a young man from Nottingham High School, who had been offered a place here, was tragically killed in a motor cycle accident last month."

"What course – what subject was he going to read?" Simon's words were unusually faltering. He prayed it wasn't Chemistry, Anthropology or Classics. Alan Brown flicked through a rotary index on his desk, obviously enjoying the little cross-examination. He peered at the card in front of him. "History," he announced.

Simon's heartbeat reached 120. "I just missed a place at Magdalen to read Politics, Philosophy and Economics," he said. "Would you consider me for the vacancy?"

The older man was unable to hide a smile. He had never in twenty-four years come across such a request.

"Full name?" he said, replacing his glasses as if the serious business of the meeting had now begun.

"Simon John Kerslake."

Dr Brown picked up the telephone by his side and dialled a number. "Nigel?" he said. "It's Alan Brown here. Did you ever consider offering a man called Kerslake a place at Magdalen?"

Mrs Kerslake was not surprised when her son went on to be President of the Oxford Union. After all, she teased, wasn't it just another stepping stone on the path to Prime Minister – Gladstone, Asquith . . . Kerslake?

Ray Gould was born in a tiny, windowless room above his father's butcher's shop in Leeds. For the first nine years of his life he shared that room with his ailing grandmother until she died at the age of sixty-one.

Ray's close proximity to the old woman who had lost her husband in the Great War at first appeared romantic to him. He would listen enraptured as she told him stories of her hero husband in his smart Khaki uniform – a uniform now folded neatly in her bottom drawer, but still displayed in the fading sepia photograph at the side of her bed. Soon, however, his grandmother's stories filled Ray with sadness, as he became aware that she had been a widow for nearly thirty years. Finally she seemed a tragic figure as he realised how little she had experienced of the world beyond that cramped room in which she was surrounded by all her possessions and a yellowed envelope containing 500 irredeemable war bonds.

There had been no purpose in Ray's grandmother making a will, for all he inherited was the room. Overnight it became his study – full of ever-changing library and school books, the former often returned late, using up Ray's meagre pocket money in fines. But as each school report was brought home it became increasingly apparent to Ray's father that he would not be extending the sign above the butcher's shop to proclaim "Gould and Son".

Shortly after his eleventh birthday Ray won the top scholarship to Roundhay School. Wearing his first pair of long trousers – turned up several inches by his mother – and horn-rimmed spectacles that didn't quite fit, he set off for the opening day at his new school. Ray's mother hoped there were other boys as thin and spotty as her son, and that his wavy red hair would not cause him to be continually teased.

By the end of his first term Ray was surprised to find he was far ahead of his classmates, so far in fact that the headmaster considered it prudent to put him up a form – "to stretch the lad a little", as he explained to Ray's parents.

By the end of that year, one spent mainly in the classroom, Ray managed to come third in the form, and top in Latin and English. Only when it came to selecting teams for any sport did Ray find he came bottom in anything. However brilliant his mind might have been, it never seemed to coordinate with his body. His single greatest academic achievement during the year, though, was to be the youngest winner of the prize essay competition in the school's history.

Each year the winner of the essay was required to read his entry to the assembled pupils and parents on Speech Day. Even before he handed in his entry Ray rehearsed his efforts out loud several times in the privacy of his study-bedroom, fearing he would not be properly prepared if he waited until the winner was announced.

Ray's form master had told all his pupils that the subject of the essay could be of their own choosing, but that they should try to recall some experience that had been unique to them. Thirty-seven entries arrived on his desk by nine o'clock on the closing date six weeks later. After reading Ray's account of his grandmother's life in the little room above the butcher's shop the form master had no inclination to pick up another script. When he had dutifully struggled through the remainder he did not hesitate in recommending Gould's essay for the prize. The only reservation, he admitted to its author, was the choice of title. Ray thanked him for the advice but the title remained intact.

On the morning of Speech Day the school hall was packed with 700 pupils and their parents. After the headmaster had delivered his speech and the applause had died down, he announced, "I shall now call upon the winner of the prize essay competition to deliver his entry: Ray Gould."

Ray left his place in the hall and marched confidently up on to the stage. He stared down at the 2,000 expectant faces but showed no sign of apprehension, partly because he found it difficult to see beyond the third row. When he announced the title of his essay some of the younger children began to snigger, causing Ray to stumble through his first few lines. But by the time had had reached the last page the packed hall was still, and after he had completed the final paragraph he received the first standing ovation of his career.

Twelve-year-old Ray Gould left the stage to rejoin his parents in the body of the hall. His mother's head was bowed but he could still see tears trickling down her cheeks. His father was trying not to look too proud. Even when Ray was seated the applause continued, so he too lowered his head to stare at the title of his prize-winning essay: 'The first changes I will make when I become Prime Minister'.

Andrew Fraser attended his first political meeting in a pram. True, he was left in the corridor while his parents sat on the stage inside another draughty hall, but he quickly learned that applause signalled his mother would soon be returning. What Andrew did not know was that his father, who had made his name as Scotland's finest scrum-half since the Great War, had delivered yet another speech to the citizens of Edinburgh Carlton in his efforts to capture a marginal seat on the City Council. At that time few believed Duncan Fraser was more than a rugby hero, and consequently he failed to win the seat for the Conservatives, if only by a few hundred votes. Three years later Andrew, a sturdy four-year-old, was allowed to sit at the back of several sparsely filled halls as once again he and his mother trailed round the city to support their candidate. This time Duncan Fraser's speeches were almost as impressive as his long pass, and he won his place on the City Council by 207 votes.

Hard work and consistent results on behalf of his constituents ensured that the marginal seat remained in the hands of Councillor Fraser for the next nine years. By the age of thirteen, Andrew, a stocky wee lad with straight black hair and a grin that no one seemed to be able to remove from his face, had learned enough about local politics to help his father organise a fifth campaign, by which time neither party considered Edinburgh Carlton a marginal seat.

At the Edinburgh Academy it came as no surprise to his fellow pupils that Andrew was chosen to captain the school debating society; however, they were impressed when under his leadership the team went on to win the Scottish Schools debating trophy. Although Andrew was destined to be no taller than five-foot-nine it was also widely accepted that he was the most complete scrum-half the Academy had produced since his father had captained the school side in 1919.

On matriculating from the Academy Andrew took up a place at Edinburgh University to read Politics, and by his third year he had been elected President of the Union and captain of rugby.

When Duncan Fraser became Lord Provost of Edinburgh he made one of his rare visits to London, to receive a knighthood from the Queen. Andrew had just completed his final exams and, along with his mother, attended the investiture at Buckingham Palace. After the ceremony Sir Duncan travelled on to the House of Commons to fulfil an engagement with his local member, Ainsley Munro. Over lunch Munro informed Sir Duncan that he had contested the Edinburgh Carlton seat for the last time, so they had better start looking for a new candidate. Sir Duncan's eyes lit up as he savoured the thought of his son succeeding Munro as his Member of Parliament.

After Andrew had been awarded an honours degree at Edinburgh, he remained at the university to complete a thesis entitled "The history of the Conservative party in Scotland". He planned to wait for his father to complete the statutory three years as Lord Provost before he informed him of the most significant outcome the research for his doctorate had produced. But when Ainsley Munro announced officially that he would not be contesting the next election Andrew knew he could no longer hide his true feelings if he wanted to be considered for the seat.

'Like father, like son', read the headline in the centre-page of the *Edinburgh Evening News*, who considered that Andrew Fraser was the obvious candidate if the Conservatives hoped to hold on to the marginal seat. Sir Duncan, fearing the local burghers would consider Andrew too young, reminded them at the first selection meeting that eight Scots had been Prime Ministers and every one had been in the House before the age of thirty. He was pleased to find members nodding their agreement. When Sir Duncan returned home that night he phoned his son and suggested that they should have lunch at the New Club the following day to discuss a plan of campaign.

"Think of it," said Sir Duncan, after he had ordered a second whisky. "Father and son representing the same constituency. It will be a great day for the Edinburgh Conservative party."

"Not to mention the Labour party," said Andrew, looking his father in the eye.

"I am not sure I take your meaning," said the Lord Provost.

"Precisely that, Father. I do not intend to contest the seat as a Conservative. I hope to be selected as the Labour candidate – if they'll adopt me."

Sir Duncan looked disbelieving. "But you've been a Conservative all your life," he declared, his voice rising with every word.

"No, Father," replied Andrew quietly. "It's you who have been a Conservative all my life."

BOOK ONE

THE BACK BENCHES

1964 – 1966

CHAPTER ONE

Thursday 10 December 1964

Mr Speaker rose and surveyed the Commons. He tugged at his long black silk gown, then nervously tweaked the full-bottomed wig that covered his balding head. The House had almost got out of control during a particularly rowdy session of Prime Minister's questions, and he was delighted to see the clock reach three-thirty. Time to pass on to the next business of the day.

He stood shifting from foot to foot waiting for the 500-odd members present to settle down before he intoned solemnly, "Members desiring to take the oath." The packed assembly switched its gaze from the Speaker to the far end of the Chamber, like a crowd watching a tennis match. There, standing at the bar of the Commons, was the victor of the first by-election since the Labour party had taken office some two months before.

The new member, flanked by his proposer and seconder, took four paces forward. Like well-drilled guardsmen, they stopped and bowed. The stranger stood at six-foot-four. He looked like a man born with the Tory party in mind, his patrician head set on an aristocratic frame, a mane of fair hair combed meticulously into place. Dressed in a dark grey, double-breasted suit and wearing a Guards' tie of maroon and blue, he advanced once again towards the long table that stood in front of the Speaker's chair between the two front benches which faced each other a mere sword's length apart.

Leaving his sponsors in his wake, he passed down the Government side, stepping over the legs of the Prime Minister and Foreign Secretary before being handed the oath by the Clerk of the House.

He held the little card in his right hand and pronounced the words as firmly as if they had been his marriage vows.

"I, Charles Seymour, do swear that I will be faithful, and bear true allegiance to Her Majesty Queen Elizabeth, her heirs and successors according to law, so help me God."

"Hear, hear," rose from his colleagues on the benches opposite as the new MP leaned over to subscribe the Test Roll, a parchment folded into book-shape. Charles was introduced to the Speaker by the Clerk. The new member then proceeded towards the chair where he stopped and bowed.

"Welcome to the House, Mr Seymour," said the Speaker, shaking his hand. "I hope you will serve this place for many years to come."

"Thank you, Mr Speaker," said Charles, and bowed for a final time before continuing on behind the Speaker's chair. He had carried out the little ceremony exactly as the Tory Chief Whip had rehearsed it with him in the long corridor outside his office.

Waiting for him behind the Speaker's chair and out of sight of the other members was the leader of the Opposition, Sir Alec Douglas-Home, who also shook him warmly by the hand.

"Congratulations on your splendid victory, Charles. I know you have a great deal to offer to our party and indeed your country."

"Thank you," replied the new MP, who after waiting for Sir Alec to return to take his place on the Opposition front bench made his way up the steps of the side gangway to find a place in the back row of the long green benches.

For the next two hours Charles Seymour followed the proceedings of the House with a mixture of awe and excitement. For the first time in his life he had found something that wasn't his by right or by effortless conquest. Glancing up at the Strangers' Gallery he saw his wife Fiona, his father the fourteenth Earl of Bridgwater and his brother, the Viscount Seymour, peering down at him with pride. Charles settled back on the first rung of the ladder. He smiled to himself: only six weeks ago he had feared it would be many more years before he could hope to take a seat in the House of Commons.

At the general election a mere two months before Charles had contested a South Wales mining seat with an impregnable Labour majority. "Good for the experience, not to mention the soul," the vice-chairman in charge of candidates at Conservative Central Office had assured him. He had proved to be right on both counts, for Charles had relished the contest and brought the Labour majority down from 22,300 to 20,100. His wife had aptly described it as a "dent", but it had turned out to be enough of a dent for the party to put Charles's name forward for the Sussex Downs seat when Sir Eric Koops had died of a heart attack only a few days after Parliament had assembled. Six weeks later Charles Seymour sat in the Commons with a 20,000 majority of his own.

Charles listened to one more speech before leaving the Chamber. He stood alone in the Members' Lobby not quite certain where to begin. Another young member strode purposefully towards him. "Allow me to introduce myself," the stranger said, sounding to Charles every bit like a fellow Conservative. "My name is Andrew Fraser. I'm the Labour member for Edinburgh Carlton and I was hoping you hadn't yet found yourself a pair." Charles admitted that so far he hadn't found much more than the Chamber. The Tory Chief Whip had already explained to him that most members paired with someone from the opposite party for voting purposes, and that it would be wise for him to select someone of his own age. When there was a debate on less crucial issues a two-line whip came into operation, pairing made it possible for members to miss the vote and return home to their wife and family before midnight. However, no member was allowed to miss the vote when there was a "three-line whip".

"I'd be delighted to pair with you," continued Charles. "Am I expected to do anything official?"

"No," said Andrew, looking up at him. "I'll just drop you a line confirming the arrangement. If you'd be kind enough to reply letting me have all the phone numbers where you can be contacted we'll just take it from there. Any time you need to miss a vote just let me know."

"Sounds a sensible arrangement to me," said Charles as a rotund figure wearing a light grey three-piece suit, blue shirt and a pink-spotted bow tie trundled over towards them.

"Welcome to the club, Charles," said Alec Pimkin. "Care to join me for a drink in the Smoking Room and I'll brief you on how this bloody place works."

"Thank you," said Charles, relieved to see someone he knew. Andrew smiled when he heard Pimkin add, "It's just like being back at school, old chum," as the two Tories retreated in the direction of the Smoking Room. Andrew suspected that it wouldn't be long before Charles Seymour was showing his "old school chum" just how the bloody place really worked.

Andrew also left the Members' Lobby but not in search of a drink. He had to attend a meeting of the Parliamentary Labour party at which the following week's business was due to be discussed. He hurried away.

Andrew had been duly selected as the Labour candidate for Edinburgh Carlton and had gone on to capture the seat from the Conservatives by a majority of 3,419 votes. Sir Duncan, having completed his term as Lord Provost, continued to represent the same seat on the City Council. In six weeks Andrew – the baby of the House – had quickly made a name for himself and many of the older members found it hard to believe that it was his first Parliament.

When Andrew arrived at the party meeting on the second floor of the Commons he found an empty seat near the back of the large committee room and settled down to listen to the Government Chief Whip go over the business for the following week. Once again it seemed to consist of nothing but three-line whips. He glanced down at the piece of paper in front of him. The debates scheduled for Tuesday, Wednesday and Thursday all had three thick lines drawn under them: only Monday and Friday had two-liners which at last after his agreement with Charles Seymour he could arrange to miss. The Labour party might have returned to power after thirteen years but, with a majority of only four and a full legislative programme, it was proving almost impossible for members to get to bed much before midnight during the week.

As the Chief Whip sat down the first person to jump to his feet was Tom Carson, the new member for Liverpool Dockside. He launched into a tirade of abuse against the Government, complaining that they were looking more like Tories every day. The under-the-breath remarks and coughing that continued during his speech showed how little support there was for his views. Tom Carson had also made a name for himself in a very short time, for he had openly attacked his own party from the first day he had arrived.

"*Enfant terrible*," muttered the man sitting on the right of Andrew.

"Those aren't the words I'd use to describe him," muttered Andrew. "Altogether too many letters." The man with wavy red hair smiled as they listened to Carson ranting on.

If Raymond Gould had acquired any reputation during those first six weeks it was as one of the party's intellectuals, and for that reason older members were immediately suspicious of him, although few doubted he would be among the first from the new intake to be promoted to the front bench. Not many of them had really got to know Raymond as the north countryman appeared remarkably reserved for someone who had chosen a career in public life. But with a majority of over 10,000 in his Leeds constituency he looked destined for a long career.

Leeds North had chosen Raymond to be their candidate from a field of thirty-seven, when he showed himself to be so much better informed than a local trade-union official whom the press had tipped as favourite for the seat. Yorkshire folk like people who stay at home and Raymond had been quick to point out to the selection committee – in an exaggerated Yorkshire accent – that he had been educated at Round-hay School on the fringes of the constituency. But what really tipped the vote in his favour had been Raymond's refusal of an open scholarship to Cambridge. He had preferred to continue his education at Leeds University, he explained.

Raymond took a first-class honours degree in Law at Leeds before moving to London to complete his studies for the bar at Lincoln's Inn. At the end of his two-year course Raymond joined a fashionable London chambers to become a much sought-after junior counsel. From that moment he rarely mentioned his family background to his carefully cultivated circle of Home Counties friends, and those comrades who addressed him as Ray received a sharp "Raymond" for their familiarity.

When the last question had been asked, the party meeting broke up, and Raymond and Andrew made their way out of the committee room – Andrew for his tiny office on the second floor to finish off the day's mail, Raymond to return to the Chamber as he hoped to deliver his maiden speech that day. He had waited patiently for the right moment to express his views to the House on the subject of widows' pensions and the redemption of war bonds, and the debate in progress on the economy was an obvious opportunity. The Speaker had dropped Raymond a note earlier in the day saying he expected to call him some time that evening.

Raymond had spent many hours in the Chamber, carefully studying the techniques demanded by the House and noting how they differed from those of the law courts. F. E. Smith had been right in his assessment of his colleagues when he had described the Commons as nothing more than a noisy courtroom with over 600 jurors and absolutely no sign of a judge. Raymond was dreading the ordeal of his maiden speech; the dispassionate logic of his arguments had always proved more appealing to judges than to juries.

As he approached the Chamber an attendant handed him a note from his wife Joyce. She had just arrived at the Commons and had been found a seat in the Strangers' Gallery so that she could be present for his speech. After only a cursory glance Raymond scrunched up the note, dropped it into the nearest waste-paper basket and hurried on towards the Chamber.

The door was held open for him by a Conservative member who was on his way out.

"Thank you," said Raymond. Simon Kerslake smiled back, trying in vain to recall the man's name. Once Simon was in the Members' Lobby he checked the message board to see if the light under his name was lit up. It wasn't, so he continued on through the swing doors to the right of the lobby on his way down past the cloisters to the Members' Car Park. Once he had found his car he headed off in the direction of St Mary's, Paddington, to pick up his wife. They had seen little of each other during Simon's first six weeks in Parliament which made the thought of tonight even more enjoyable. Simon couldn't see any easing of the pressure until there was another general election and one party had gained a sensible working majority. But what he feared most – having won his seat by the slimmest of margins – was that such a working majority would not include him and he might end up with one of the shortest political careers on record. After such a prolonged stretch of Tory rule the new Labour Government was looking fresh, idealistic and certain to increase their numbers whenever the Prime Minister chose to go to the country.

Once Simon had reached Hyde Park Corner he headed on up towards Marble Arch thinking back over how he had become a member. On leaving Oxford he had completed two years' national service with the Sussex Light Infantry, finishing his military days as a second lieutenant. After a short holiday he had joined the BBC as a general trainee. He spent five years moving from drama, to sport, to current affairs before being appointed a producer on "Panorama".

During those early days in London he had rented a small flat in Earl's Court and continued his interest in politics by becoming a member of the Tory Bow Group. When he became the Group's secretary he helped to organize meetings, and had then progressed to writing pamphlets and speaking at weekend conferences before being invited to work at Central Office as personal assistant to the chairman during the 1959 election campaign.

Two years later Simon met Elizabeth Drummond when "Panorama" carried out an investigation into the National Health Service and she had been invited to be a participant. Over drinks before the programme Elizabeth made it perfectly clear to Simon that she distrusted media men and detested politicians. They were married a year later. Elizabeth had since given birth to two sons, and with only a small break on each occasion she had continued her career as a doctor.

Simon had left the BBC somewhat abruptly when, in the summer of 1964, he had been offered the chance to defend the marginal constituency of Coventry Central. He held on to the seat at the general election by a majority of 918.

Simon drove up to the gates of St Mary's and checked his watch. He was a few minutes early. He pushed back the mop of brown hair from his forehead and thought about the evening ahead. He was taking Elizabeth out to celebrate their fourth wedding anniversary, and had prepared one or two surprises for her. Dinner at Mario & Franco, followed by dancing at the Establishment Club, and then home together for the first time in weeks.

"Um," he said, savouring the thought.

"Hi, stranger," said the lady who jumped in beside him and gave him a kiss. Simon stared at the woman with a perfect smile and long fair hair that turned up at the shoulder. He had stared at her when she had first arrived at the "Panorama" studio that night nearly three years before and he had hardly stopped staring since.

He switched on the ignition. "Want to hear some good news?" he asked, and answered his own question before she could reply. "I'm paired for tonight. That means dinner at Mario & Franco, dancing at the Establishment, home and . . ."

"Do you want to hear the bad news?" asked Elizabeth, also not waiting for a reply. "There's a shortage of staff because of the flu epidemic. I have to be back on duty by ten o'clock."

Simon switched off the ignition. "Well, which would you prefer?" he asked. "Dinner, dancing or straight home?"

Elizabeth laughed. "We've got three hours," she said. "So we might even find time for dinner."

CHAPTER TWO

Raymond Gould stared down at the invitation. He had never seen the inside of No. 10 Downing Street. During the last thirteen years few Socialists had. He passed the embossed card across the breakfast table to his wife.

"Should I accept or refuse, Ray?" she asked in her broad Yorkshire accent.

She was the only person who still called him Ray, and even her attempts at humour now annoyed him. The Greek tragedians had based their drama on "the fatal flaw", and he had no doubt what his had been.

He had met Joyce at a dance given by the nurses of Leeds General Hospital. He hadn't wanted to go but a second-year undergraduate friend from Roundhay convinced him it would make an amusing break. At school he had shown little interest in girls as his mother kept reminding him that there would be occasion enough for that sort of thing once he had taken his degree. By the time he graduated he felt certain that he was the only virgin left at the university.

He had ended up sitting on his own in the corner of a room decorated with wilting balloons and day-glow orange crêpe paper. He sucked disconsolately at a shandy through a bent straw. Whenever his school friend turned round from the dance floor – each time with a different partner – Raymond would smile broadly back. With his National Health spectacles tucked away in an inside pocket, he couldn't always be certain he was smiling at the right person. He began contemplating at what hour he could possibly leave without having to admit the evening had been a total disaster. He wouldn't even have answered her question if it hadn't been for that familiar accent.

"You at the university as well?"

"As well as what?" he asked, without looking directly at her.

"As well as your friend," she said.

"Yes," he replied, looking up at a girl he guessed was about his age.

"I'm from Bradford."

"I'm from Leeds," he admitted, aware he was going redder by the second.

"My name is Joyce," she volunteered.

"Mine's Ray – Raymond," he said.

"Like to dance?"

He wanted to tell her that he had rarely been on a dance floor before in his life but he didn't have the courage. Like a puppet he found himself standing up and being guided by her towards the jivers. So much for his assumption that he was one of nature's leaders.

Once they were on the dance floor he looked at her properly for the first time. She wasn't half bad, any normal Yorkshire boy might have admitted. She was about five feet seven, and her auburn hair was tied up in a pony tail, matching the dark brown eyes that had a little too much make-up round them. She wore pink lipstick, the same colour as her short skirt from which emerged two very attractive legs. They looked even more attractive when she twirled to the music of the four-piece student band. Raymond discovered that if he twirled Joyce very fast he could see the tops of her stockings, and he remained on the dance floor for longer than he would ever have thought possible. After the quartet had put their instruments away Joyce kissed him goodnight. He walked slowly back to his small room above the butcher's shop.

The following Sunday, in an attempt to gain the upper hand, he took Joyce rowing on the Aire, but his performance was no better than his dancing, and everything on the river overtook him including a hardy swimmer. He watched out of the side of his eyes for a mocking laugh but Joyce only smiled and chatted about missing Bradford and wanting to return home to nurse. After only a few weeks at university Raymond knew he wanted to get away from Leeds, but he didn't admit it to anyone. When he eventually returned the boat Joyce invited him back to her digs for tea. He went scarlet as they passed her landlady. Joyce hustled him up the worn stone staircase to her room.

Raymond sat on the end of the narrow bed while Joyce made two milkless mugs of tea. After they had both pretended to drink she sat beside him, her hands in her lap. He found himself listening intently to an ambulance siren as it faded away in the distance. She leaned over and kissed him, taking one of his hands and placing it on her knee.

She parted his lips and their tongues touched: he found it a peculiar sensation, an arousing one; his eyes remained closed as she gently led him through each new experience, until he was unable to stop himself committing what he felt sure his mother had once described as a mortal sin.

"It will be easier next time," she said shyly, manoeuvring herself from the narrow bed to sort out the crumpled clothes spread across the floor. She was right: he wanted her again in less than an hour, and this time his eyes remained wide open.

It was another six months before Joyce talked about their future and by then Raymond was bored with her and had his sights set on a bright little mathematician in her final year. The mathematician hailed from Surrey.

Just at the time Raymond was summoning up enough courage to let her know the affair was over Joyce told him she was pregnant. His father would have taken a meat axe to him had he suggested an illegal abortion. His mother was only relieved that she was a Yorkshire girl; like the county cricket selection committee, Mrs Gould did not approve of outsiders.

Raymond and Joyce were married at St Mary's in Bradford during the long vacation. When the wedding photos were developed Raymond looked so distressed and Joyce so happy they resembled father and daughter rather than husband and wife. After a reception given at the church hall the newly-married couple travelled to Dover to catch the night ferry. Their first night as Mr and Mrs Gould was a disaster. Raymond turned out to be a particularly bad sailor. Joyce only hoped that Paris would prove to be memorable – and it was. She had a miscarriage on the second night of their honeymoon.

"Probably caused by all the excitement," his mother said on their return. "Still, you can always have another, can't you? And this time folk won't be able to call it a little . . ." She checked herself.

Raymond showed no interest in having another. Ten years had passed since that memorable honeymoon; he had escaped to London and become a barrister, but had long since accepted that he was tethered to her for life. Although Joyce was only thirty-two she already needed to cover those once-slim legs that had first so attracted him. How could he be so punished for such a pathetic mistake? Raymond wanted to ask the gods. How mature he had thought he was: how immature he had turned out to be. Divorce made sense, but it would have meant the end of his political ambitions: Yorkshire folk would not have considered selecting a divorced man. To be fair, it hadn't all been a disaster: he had to admit that the locals adored her, and his parents semed every bit as proud of Joyce as they did of their son. She mixed with the trade unionists and their frightful wives far better than he ever managed. He also had to acknowledge that Joyce had been a major factor in his winning the seat by over 10,000 votes. He wondered how she could sound so sincere the whole time: it never occurred to him that it was natural.

"Why don't you buy yourself a new dress for Downing Street?" Raymond said as they rose from the breakfast table. She smiled: he had not volunteered such a suggestion for as long as she could remember. Joyce had been left with no illusions about her husband and his feelings for her, but hoped that eventually he would realise she could help him achieve his unspoken ambition.

On the night of the reception at Downing Street Joyce made every effort to look her best. She had spent the morning at Harvey Nichols searching for an outfit appropriate for the occasion, finally returning to a suit she had liked the moment she had walked in to the store. It was not the perfect fit but the sales assistant assured Joyce "that Modom looked quite sensational in it". She only hoped that Raymond's remarks would be half as flattering. By the time she reached home she realised she had nothing to match the unusual colour.

Raymond was late returning from the Commons and was pleased to find Joyce ready when he leaped out of the bath. He bit back a remark about the incongruity of her shoes and new suit. As they drove towards Westminster he rehearsed the names of every member of the Cabinet with her, making Joyce repeat them as if she were a child.

The air was cool and crisp that night so Raymond parked his Sunbeam in New Palace Yard and they strolled across Whitehall together to No. 10. A solitary policeman stood guard at the door. Seeing Raymond approach, the officer banged the brass knocker once and the door was opened for the young member and his wife.

Raymond and Joyce stood awkwardly in the hall as if they were waiting outside a headmaster's study. Eventually they were directed to the first floor. They walked slowly up the staircase, which turned out to be less grand than Raymond had anticipated, passing photographs of former Prime Ministers. "Too many Tories," muttered Raymond as he passed Chamberlain, Churchill, Eden, Macmillan and Home, with Attlee the only framed compensation.

At the top of the stairs stood Harold Wilson, pipe in mouth, waiting to welcome his guests. Raymond was about to introduce his wife when the Prime Minister said, "How are you, Joyce? I'm so glad you could make it."

"Make it? I've been looking forward to the occasion all week." Her frankness made Raymond wince; he failed to notice that it made Wilson chuckle.

Raymond chatted to the Prime Minister's wife about the difficulty of getting poetry published until she turned away to greet the next guest. He then moved off into the drawing-room and was soon talking to Cabinet ministers, trade-union leaders and their wives, always keeping a wary eye on Joyce, who seemed engrossed in conversation with the General Secretary of the Trades Union Congress.

Raymond moved on to the American Ambassador, who was telling Andrew Fraser how much he had enjoyed the Edinburgh Festival that summer. Raymond envied Fraser his relaxed clubbable manner and had already worked out that the Scotsman would be a formidable rival among his contemporaries.

"Good evening, Raymond," said Andrew. "Do you know David Bruce?" he asked, as if they were old friends.

"No," Raymond replied, rubbing his palm on his trousers before shaking hands. "Good evening, Your Excellency," he said, glad to see Andrew slipping away. "I was interested to read Johnson's latest communiqué on Vietnam and I must confess the escalation . . ."

Andrew had spotted the Minister of State for Scotland arriving and
went over to chat to him.

"How are you, Andrew?" Hugh McKenzie asked.

"Never better."

"And your father?"

"In great form."

"I'm sorry to hear that," said the minister, grinning. "He's giving
me a lot of trouble over the Highlands and Islands Development
Board."

"He's a sound chap basically," said Andrew, "even if his views are a
little misguided." They both laughed as a slight, attractive woman with
long brown hair came up to the minister's side. She wore a white silk
blouse and a McKenzie tartan skirt.

"Do you know my daughter Alison?"

"No," Andrew said, holding out his hand. "I've not had that
pleasure."

"I know who you are," she said, in a slight lowland accent, her eyes
flashing. "Andrew Fraser, the man who makes Campbells look trust-
worthy. The Tories' secret mole."

"It can't be much of a secret if the Scottish Office know about it,"
said Andrew.

A waiter, wearing the smartest dinner-jacket in the room,
approached them carrying a silver tray of thinly-cut sandwiches.

"Would you care for a smoked salmon sandwich?" Alison asked
mockingly.

"No, thank you. I gave them up with my Tory background. But
beware – if you eat too many you won't appreciate your dinner
tonight."

"I wasn't thinking of having dinner."

"Oh, I thought you might enjoy a bite at Sigie's," teased Andrew.

Alison hesitated, then said, "It'll be the first time anyone's picked me
up at No. 10."

"I hate to break with tradition," said Andrew. "But why don't I
book a table for eight?"

"Is Sigie's one of your aristocratic haunts?"

"Good heavens no, it's far too good for that lot. Why don't we leave
in about fifteen minutes? I must have a word with one or two people
first."

"I'll bet." She grinned as she watched Fraser comb the room. His
years as a Tory party fellow-traveller had taught Andrew all he needed
to know about how to make the best use of a cocktail party. His trade-
union colleagues would never understand that it was not in pursuit of
endless smoked salmon sandwiches drowned by whisky. When he
arrived back at Alison McKenzie's side she was chatting to Raymond
Gould about Johnson's landslide victory at the polls.

"Are you trying to pick up my date?" asked Andrew.

Raymond laughed nervously and pushed his spectacles back up his nose. A moment later Andrew was guiding Alison towards the door to say their farewells, and Raymond, watching them, wondered if he would ever learn to be that relaxed. He looked around for Joyce: it might be wise not to be the last to leave.

Andrew was ushered discreetly to a corner table at Sigie's Club and it became quickly evident to Alison that he had been there several times before. The waiters ran around him as if he were a Tory Cabinet minister, and she had to admit to herself that she enjoyed the experience. After an excellent dinner of roast beef that wasn't burnt and a *crème brûlée* that was they strolled over to Annabel's where they danced until the early morning. Andrew drove Alison back to her Chelsea flat a little after two a.m.

"Care for a nightcap?" she asked casually.

"Daren't," he replied. "I'm making my maiden speech tomorrow."

"So this maiden is to be rejected," she said to his retreating back.

The House of Commons was well attended at five o'clock the following afternoon when Andrew rose to address his fellow members. The Speaker had allowed him to follow the front-bench contributions, an honour Andrew would not be granted again for some considerable time. His father and mother looked down over the railings from the Strangers' Gallery as he informed the commoners that the Lord Provost of Edinburgh had spent a lifetime teaching him all he knew about the constituency he was now proud to represent. The Labour party chuckled at the Opposition's obvious discomfort, but they abided by tradition and made no interruption during a maiden speech.

Andrew had chosen as his subject the question of whether Scotland should remain part of the United Kingdom despite the recent oil discoveries. He delivered a well-argued case, assuring members that he saw no future for his country as a tiny independent state. His rhetoric, and his relaxed turn of phrase, had members laughing on both sides of the House. When he came to the end of his argument, never having once referred to a note, he sat down to loud cheers from his own benches and generous acknowledgement from the Tory side. In his moment of glory he glanced up towards the Strangers' Gallery. His father was leaning forward, following every word. To his surprise sitting in front of his mother on the benches reserved for distinguished visitors was Alison McKenzie, her arms folded on the balcony. He smiled.

Andrew's success was considerably enhanced when later that afternoon another member from the Labour benches rose to address the House for the first time. Tom Carson cared nothing for convention and even less for keeping to tradition and made no attempt to avoid controversy in his maiden speech. He began with an attack on what he described as "the Establishment conspiracy", pointing an accusing finger as much at the ministers on his own front bench as at those opposite him, describing them all as "puppets of the capitalist system".

Members present in the Chamber restrained themselves from interrupting the scowling Liverpudlian, but the Speaker stirred several times as the accusing finger appeared to cross his path as well. He was painfully aware that the member from Liverpool Dockside was going to cause all sorts of problems if this was the way he intended to conduct himself in the House.

When Andrew left the Chamber three speeches later he went to look for Alison, but she had already left; so he took the members' lift up to the Public Gallery and invited his parents to join him for tea in the Harcourt Rooms.

"The last time I had tea here was with Ainsley Munro . . ." Sir Duncan began.

"Then it may be a very long time before you're invited again," Andrew interrupted.

"That may depend on whom we select as Tory candidate to oppose you at the next election," retorted his father.

Several members from both sides of the House came up one by one to congratulate Andrew on his speech. He thanked them all individually but kept glancing hopefully over his father's shoulder; but Alison McKenzie did not appear.

After his parents had finally left to catch the last flight back to Edinburgh Andrew returned to the Chamber to hear Alison's father summing up the debate on behalf of the Government. The Minister of State described Andrew's contribution as one of the finest maiden speeches the House had heard in years. "Maiden it may have been but virginal it was not," concluded Hugh McKenzie.

Once the debate was over and the usual ten o'clock division had been declared by the tellers Andrew left the Chamber. One final vote on a prayer detained members for a further forty-five minutes and Andrew found the tea room – the traditional haunt of the Labour party – as crowded as it had been earlier in the afternoon.

Members jostled for the remains of unappetising-looking lettuce leaves that any self-respecting rabbit would have rejected accompanied by blobs of plastic-covered sweating cheese, described optimistically on the bill board as salad. Andrew contented himself with a cup of Nescafé.

Raymond Gould sat alone, slumped in an armchair in the far corner of the tea room, apparently engrossed in a week-old copy of the *New Statesman*. He stared impassively as several of his colleagues went over to Andrew to congratulate him. His own maiden speech the previous week had not been as well received and he knew it. He believed just as passionately about war widows' pensions as Andrew did about the future of Scotland but reading from a prepared manuscript he had been unable to make members hang on his every word. He consoled himself with the thought that Andrew would have to choose the subject for his next speech very carefully as the Opposition would no longer treat him with kid gloves.

Andrew was not concerning himself with such thoughts as he slipped into one of the many internal telephone booths and after checking in his diary dialled a London number. Alison was at home, washing her hair.

"Will it be dry by the time I arrive?"

"It's very long," she reminded him.

"Then I'll have to drive slowly."

When Andrew appeared on the Chelsea doorstep he was greeted by Alison in a housecoat, her newly-dry hair falling down well below shoulder level.

"The victor come to claim his spoils?"

"No, only last night's coffee," he said.

"But won't that keep you awake?"

"I certainly hope so."

By the time Andrew left Alison's home at eight the next morning he had already decided he wanted to see a lot more of Hugh McKenzie's daughter. He returned to his own flat in Cheyne Walk, showered and changed before making breakfast for himself and going over his mail. There were several more messages of congratulations including one from the Secretary of State for Scotland, while *The Times* and the *Guardian* carried brief but favourable comments.

Before leaving for the Commons Andrew checked over an amendment he wanted to move in committee that morning. When he had reworded his efforts several times he picked up his papers and headed off towards Westminster.

Arriving a little early for the ten-thirty committee meeting, Andrew found time to collect his mail from the Members' Post Office just off the Central Lobby. He set off head down along the corridor towards the library, flicking through the envelopes to see if he recognized any familiar hand or official-looking missive that demanded to be opened immediately.

As he turned the corner he was surprised to find the House ticker-tape machine surrounded by Conservative members, including the man who had agreed to be his "pair" for voting purposes.

Andrew stared up at the tall figure of Charles Seymour, who, although standing on the fringe of the crowd, still found it possible to read the tapped-out message on the telex machine.

"What's causing so much interest?" he asked, prodding Seymour's elbow.

"Sir Alec has just announced the timetable that'll be followed when we select the new Tory leader."

"We all await with bated breath," said Andrew.

"As well you might," said Charles, ignoring the sarcasm, "since the next announcement will undoubtedly be his resignation. Then the real politics will begin."

"Be sure you back the winner," said Andrew, grinning.

Charles Seymour smiled knowingly but made no comment.

CHAPTER THREE

Charles Seymour drove his Daimler from the Commons to his father's bank in the City. He still thought of Seymour's of Cheapside as his father's bank although for two generations the family had been only minority shareholders, with Charles himself in possession of a mere two per cent of the stock. Nevertheless as his brother Rupert showed no desire in representing the family interests the two per cent guaranteed Charles a place on the board and an income sufficient to ensure that his paltry parliamentary salary of £1,750 a year was adequately supplemented.

From the day Charles had first taken his place on the board of Seymour's he had no doubt that the new chairman, Derek Spencer, considered him a dangerous rival. Spencer had lobbied to have Rupert replace his father on retirement and only because of Charles's insistence had Spencer failed to move the old earl to his way of thinking.

When Charles went on to take his seat in Parliament Spencer at once raised the problem of his burdensome responsibilities at the House preventing him from carrying out his day-to-day duties for the board. However, Charles was able to convince a majority of his fellow directors of the advantages of having someone on the board at Westminster, although he knew that would cease if he was ever invited to be a minister.

As Charles left the Daimler in Seymour's courtyard it amused him to consider that his parking space was worth twenty times the value of the car. The area at the front of Seymour's was a relic of his great-grandfather's day. The twelfth Earl of Bridgwater had insisted on an entrance large enough to allow a complete sweep for his coach and four. That conveyance had long disappeared, to be replaced by twelve car spaces for Seymour directors. The bank's new management-conscious chairman, despite all his grammar school virtues, had never suggested the land be used for any other purpose.

The young girl seated at the reception desk abruptly stopped polishing her nails in time to say "Good morning, Mr Charles," as he came through the revolving doors and disappeared into a waiting lift. A few moments later Charles was seated behind a desk in his small oak-panelled office, a clean white memo pad in front of him. He pressed a button on the intercom and told his secretary that he did not want to be disturbed during the next hour.

Sixty minutes later the white pad had twelve names pencilled on it, but ten already had lines drawn through them. Only the names of Reginald Maudling and Edward Heath remained.

Charles tore off the piece of paper and the indented sheet underneath and put them both through the shredder by the side of his desk. He tried to summon up some interest in the agenda for the bank's weekly board meeting; only one item, item seven, seemed to be of importance. Just before eleven, he gathered up his papers and headed towards the boardroom. Most of his colleagues were already seated when Derek Spencer called item number one as the boardroom clock chimed the hour.

During the ensuing predictable discussion on bank rates, the movement in metal prices, Eurobonds and client investment policy Charles's mind kept wandering back to the forthcoming leadership election and the importance of backing the winner if he were to be quickly promoted from the back benches.

By the time they reached item seven on the agenda Charles had made up his mind. Derek Spencer opened a discussion on the proposed loans to Mexico and Poland, and most of the board members agreed with him that the bank should participate in one but not risk both.

Charles's thoughts, however, were not in Mexico City or Warsaw. They were far nearer home and when the chairman called for a vote, Charles didn't register.

"Mexico or Poland, Charles. Which of the two do you favour?"

"Heath," he replied.

"I beg your pardon," said Derek Spencer.

Charles snapped back from Westminster to Cheapside to find everyone around the boardroom table staring at him. With the air of a man who had been giving the matter considerable thought Charles said firmly, "Mexico", and added, "The great difference between the two countries can best be gauged by their attitudes to repayment. Mexico might not want to repay, but Poland won't be able to, so why not limit our risks and back Mexico? If it comes to litigation I'd prefer to be against someone who won't pay rather than someone who can't." The older members round the table nodded in agreement; the right son of Bridgwater was sitting on the board.

When the meeting was over Charles joined his colleagues for lunch in the directors' dining-room. On the walls hung two Hogarths, a Brueghel, a Goya and a Rembrandt that could distract even the most indulgent gourmet: just another reminder of his great-grandfather's ability to select winners. Charles did not wait to make a decision between the Cheddar and the Stilton as he wanted to be back in the Commons for question time.

On arrival at the House he immediately made his way to the smoking room, long regarded by the Tories as their preserve. There in the deep leather armchairs and cigar-laden atmosphere the talk was entirely of who would be Sir Alec's successor.

Charles could not avoid overhearing Pimkin's high-pitched voice. "As Edward Heath is Shadow Chancellor while we debate the Finance Bill on the floor of the House, it is he who is bound to be the centre of attention."

Later that afternoon Charles returned to the Commons Chamber. He wanted to observe Heath and his Shadow team deal with the Government's amendments one by one.

He was about to leave the Chamber when Raymond Gould rose to move an amendment. Charles listened with grudging admiration as Raymond's intellectual grasp and force of argument easily compensated for his lack of oratorical skill. Although Gould was a cut above the rest of his intake on the Labour benches he didn't frighten Charles. Twelve generations of shrewd business acumen had kept large parts of Leeds in the hands of the Bridgwater family without the likes of Raymond Gould even being aware of it.

Charles took supper in the Members' Dining-room that night and sat at the large table in the centre of the room frequented by Tory back-benchers. There was only one topic of conversation and as the same two names kept emerging it was obvious that it was going to be a very close run thing.

When Charles arrived back at his Eaton Square home after the ten o'clock division Fiona was already tucked up in bed reading Philip Larkin's *The Whitsun Weddings*.

"They let you out early tonight."

"Not too bad," said Charles, and began regaling her with how he had spent his day, before disappearing into the bathroom.

If Charles imagined he was cunning, his wife, Lady Fiona, only daughter of the Duke of Falkirk, was in a different league. She and Charles had been selected for each other at an early age and neither had questioned or doubted the wisdom of the choice. Although Charles had squired numerous girl-friends before their marriage in between he had always assumed he would return to Fiona. Charles's grandfather always maintained that the aristocracy was becoming far too lax and sentimental about marriage. "Women," he declared, "are for bearing children and ensuring a continuation of the male line." The old earl became even more staid in his convictions when he was made aware that Rupert showed little interest in the opposite sex, and was rarely to be found in the company of women. Fiona would never have dreamed of disagreeing with the old man to his face as she was determined that it would be a son of hers that would inherit the earldom. But despite enthusiastic and then contrived efforts Charles seemed unable to sire an heir. Fiona was later assured by a Harley Street physician that there was no reason *she* could not bear children. The specialist had suggested that perhaps her husband pay the clinic a visit. She shook her head, knowing Charles would dismiss such an idea out of hand, and never mentioned the subject to anyone again.

Fiona spent a considerable amount of her spare time in their Sussex Downs constituency furthering Charles's political career. She had learned to live with the fact that theirs was not destined to be a romantic marriage and resigned herself to its other advantages. Although many men confessed covertly and overtly that they found the tall elegant lady desirable she either ignored their overtures or pretended not to notice them.

By the time Charles returned from the bathroom in his blue silk pyjamas Fiona had formed a plan, but first she needed some questions answered.

"Whom do you favour?"

"I'd like Sir Alec to carry on: after all, the Homes have been friends of our two families for over 400 years."

"But that's a non-starter," said Fiona. "Everyone knows Alec is on the way out."

"I agree, and that's exactly why I spent the entire afternoon observing the worthwhile candidates."

"Did you come to any serious conclusions?" Fiona asked.

"Heath and Maudling are out on their own, though to be honest I've never had a conversation with either of them that lasted for more than five minutes."

"In that case we must turn a disadvantage into an advantage."

"What do you mean, old girl?" Charles asked as he climbed into bed beside his wife.

"Think back. When you were President of Pop at Eton, could you have put a name to any of the first-year boys?"

"Certainly not," said Charles.

"Exactly. And I'd be willing to bet that neither Heath nor Maudling could put a name to twenty of the new intake on the Tory benches."

"Where are you leading me, Lady Macbeth?"

"No bloody hands will be needed for this killing. Simply, having chosen your Duncan you volunteer to organise the new intake for him. If he becomes leader, he's bound to feel it would be appropriate to select one or two new faces for his team."

"You could be right."

"Well, let's sleep on it," said Fiona, turning out the light on her side of the bed.

Charles didn't sleep on it but lay restless most of the night turning over in his mind what she had said. When Fiona awoke the next morning she carried on the conversation as if there had been no break in between. "Do you have to be rushed into a decision?"

"No, but if I let it drift I could be accused of jumping on the bandwagon and then I would have lost my chance to be seen as a leader among the new intake."

"Better still," she continued, "before the man you choose announces he is a candidate demand that he stand on behalf of the new members."

"Clever," said Charles.

"Whom have you decided on?"

"Heath," Charles replied without hesitation.

"I'll back your political judgement," said Fiona. "Just trust me when it comes to tactics. First, we compose a letter."

In dressing-gowns, on the floor at the end of the bed, the two elegant figures drafted and redrafted a note to Edward Heath. At nine-thirty it was finally composed and sent round by hand to his rooms in Albany.

The next morning Charles was invited to the small, bachelor flat for coffee. They talked for over an hour and later, as the two men stood below a Piper landscape in the drawing-room, the deal was struck.

Charles thought Sir Alec would announce his resignation in the late summer which would give him eight to ten weeks to carry out a campaign. Fiona typed out a list of all the new members and during the next eight weeks every one of them was invited to their Eaton Square flat for drinks. Fiona was subtle enough to see that members of the Lower House were outnumbered by other guests, often from the House of Lords. Heath managed to escape from his front-bench duties on the Finance Bill to spend at least an hour with the Seymours once a week. As the day of Sir Alec Douglas-Home's resignation drew nearer Charles realised the leadership result could be almost as important to him as it would be to Heath, but he also remained confident that he had carried out his plan in a subtle and discreet way. He would have been willing to place a wager that no one other than Edward Heath had worked out how deeply he was involved.

One man who attended the second of Fiona's soirées saw exactly what was going on. While many of the guests spent their time admiring the Seymour art collection Simon Kerslake kept a wary eye on his host and hostess. Kerslake was not convinced that Edward Heath would win the forthcoming election and felt confident that Reginald Maudling would turn out to be the party's natural choice. Maudling was, after all,

Shadow Foreign Secretary, a former Chancellor and far senior to
Heath. More important, he was a married man. Simon doubted the
Tories would ever pick a bachelor to lead them.

As soon as Kerslake had left the Seymours he jumped into a taxi and
returned immediately to the Commons. He found Reginald Maudling
in the Members' Dining-room seated at the table frequented only by
the Shadow Cabinet. He waited until Maudling had finished his meal
before asking if they could have a few moments alone. The tall
shambling figure – not altogether certain of the name of the new
member – leaned over and invited Simon to join him for a drink in his
room.

Maudling listened intently to all the enthusiastic young man had to
say and accepted the judgement of the well-informed member without
question. It was agreed that Simon should try to counter the Seymour
campaign and report back his results twice a week.

While Seymour could call on all the powers and influence of his
Etonian background, Kerslake could rely on the knowledge and arm-
twisting skills gained from his time as President of the Oxford Union.
Simon weighed up the advantages and disadvantages he possessed. He
did not own a palatial home in Eaton Square in which Turners,
Constables and Holbeins were not to be found in books but on the
walls. He also lacked a glamorous society wife. Simon lived in a small
house in Beaufort Street in Chelsea and Elizabeth was a gynaecologist
at St Mary's Hospital, Paddington. Although Elizabeth gave Simon's
political aspirations her full backing she still considered her own career
every bit as important, an opinion with which Simon concurred. The
local Coventry press had on several occasions recalled in their columns
how Elizabeth had left her three-day-old child to help perform a
Caesarian section on a mother in the adjoining ward and, two years
later, had to be dragged off night duty just as she went into labour with
their second child.

This independence of character was one of the reasons Simon had
admired Elizabeth when they first met, but he realised she was no
match for Lady Fiona Seymour as a hostess and he never wanted her to
be. He despised pushy political wives.

Simon spent the following days trying to work out the certain
Maudling and certain Heath supporters, although many members
claimed they would favour both candidates, according to who asked
them. These he listed as doubtfuls. When Enoch Powell threw his cap
into the ring Simon could not find a single new member other than Alec
Pimkin who openly supported him. That left forty members from the
new intake who still had to be followed up. He estimated twelve certain
Heath, eleven certain Maudling and one Powell, leaving sixteen
undecided. As the day of the election drew nearer it became obvious
that few of the remaining sixteen actually knew either candidate well,

and were still not sure for whom they should vote.

Simon realised that he could not invite them all round to Beaufort Street between Elizabeth's ward duties, so he would have to go to them. During the last eight weeks he accompanied his chosen leader as he addressed the party faithfuls in twenty-three new members' constituencies. Simon travelled from Bodmin to Glasgow, from Penrith to Great Yarmouth, briefing Maudling studiously before every meeting.

Gradually it became obvious to everyone that Charles Seymour and Simon Kerslake were the chosen lieutenants among the new intake. Some members resented the whispered confidences at the Eaton Square cocktail parties, or the discovery that Simon Kerslake had visited their constituencies under false pretences, while others were simply envious of the reward that would inevitably be heaped on the victor.

"But why do you support Maudling?" Elizabeth had asked him one evening over dinner.

"Reggie has a great deal more experience of Government than Heath – and in any case he's more caring about those around him."

"But Heath appears to be so much more professional," Elizabeth insisted, pouring her husband a glass of wine.

"That may well be the case, but the British have always preferred good amateurs to preside over their affairs."

"If you believe all that stuff about amateurs why become so involved yourself?"

Simon considered her question for some time before answering. "Because I don't come from the type of background that automatically commands the centre of the Tory stage," he admitted.

"Neither does Heath," commented Elizabeth dryly.

Although everyone inside and outside of Parliament knew it could not be long before Sir Alec formally announced his resignation it did not become official until 22 July 1965, when he addressed the 1922 Committee of Tory back-benchers.

The date chosen for the leadership election was just five days later. During that time Simon Kerslake and Charles Seymour worked almost round the clock but, despite many national papers' commissioned polls, columns of newsprint offering statistics and opinions, no one seemed certain of the outcome, other than to predict that Powell would come third.

Charles and Simon began avoiding each other and Fiona started referring to Kerslake, first in private then in public, as "that pushy self-made man". She stopped using the expression when Alec Pimkin asked in all innocence whether she was referring to Edward Heath.

On the morning of the secret ballot Simon and Charles voted early and spent the rest of the day pacing the corridors of the Commons trying to assess the result. By lunchtime they were both outwardly exuberant, while inwardly despondent.

At two-fifteen they were seated in the large committee room to hear the chairman of the 1922 Committee make the historic announcement:

"The result of the first election for leader of the Conservative parliamentary party," said Sir William Anstruther-Gray, "is as follows:

Edward Heath	150 votes
Reginald Maudling	133 votes
Enoch Powell	15 votes."

An hour later Reginald Maudling, who had been lunching in the City, telephoned Heath to say he would be happy to serve under him as the new leader. Charles and Fiona opened a bottle of Krug while Simon took Elizabeth to the Old Vic to see *The Royal Hunt of the Sun*. He slept the entire way through Robert Stephens' brilliant performance, before Elizabeth drove him home.

"How come you didn't fall asleep? After all, you've been just as busy as I have the last few weeks," Simon asked.

Elizabeth smiled. "It was my turn to want to be involved with what was happening on the centre of the stage."

Two weeks later, on 4 August, Edward Heath announced his Shadow team. Reggie Maudling was to be deputy leader. Sir Alec accepted the Foreign Office brief while Powell went to Defence. Charles Seymour received an invitation to join the Shadow Environment team as its junior spokesman, thus becoming the first of the new intake to be given front-bench responsibilities.

Simon Kerslake received a handwritten note from Reggie Maudling thanking him for his valiant efforts.

BOOK TWO

JUNIOR OFFICE

1966–1974

CHAPTER FOUR

When Alison McKenzie moved into Andrew Fraser's Cheyne Walk flat everyone, including her father, the Minister of State for Scotland, assumed they would soon announce their engagement.

For the previous three months Andrew had had his head down in committee helping out with the public bills relating exclusively to Scotland which were referred to the committee from the House itself. He found much of the committee work boring, as so many members repeated the views of their colleagues, less and less articulately, and for some time only his doodling improved. Even so, Andrew's energy and charm made him a popular companion through the long summer months and he quickly gained enough confidence to suggest first minor and later major changes to amendments considered by the committee. The disparity between penalties under English and Scottish law had long worried him, and he pressed hard for changes that would bring the two systems closer together. He soon discovered that the Scottish Labour members were more traditional and clannish than even the most hide-bound of Tories.

When the session came to an end Andrew invited Alison to spend a long weekend with his parents at their country home in Stirling at the end of the recess.

"Do you expect me to sleep under the same roof as a former Conservative Lord Provost of Edinburgh?" she demanded.

"Why not? You've been sleeping with his son for the past six months."

"Well, the same roof perhaps, but there's one weekend we won't be able to sleep in the same bed."

"Why not? The Tories may be snobs but they're not hypocrites."

Alison didn't want to admit that she was actually quite nervous about spending the weekend with Andrew's father, as she had heard him continually maligned at her parents' breakfast table for over twenty years.

When she did meet "Old Dungheap", as her father referred to the former Lord Provost, Alison liked him immediately. He reminded her so much of her own father, while Lady Fraser was not at all the snobbish little battle-axe her mother had prepared her for.

It was immediately agreed that during the weekend nobody would
talk politics. Andrew and Alison spent most of the Friday afternoon
walking through the heather-covered hills and discussing in detail how
they saw their future. On the Saturday morning the minister
telephoned Sir Duncan and invited them over to Bute House – the
official residence of the Secretary of State for Scotland – for dinner.

After so many years of opposing each other both families were
nervous of the social get-together, but it seemed the children were to
bridge the political gap they had failed to build for themselves. The
McKenzies had invited two other Edinburgh families to dinner in the
hope that it would ease the tension of the occasion, a branch of the
Forsyths who owned the departmental store in Princes Street, and the
Menzies, who ran the largest chain of newsagents in the country.

Andrew had decided to use the gathering to make an announcement
at the end of dinner, and having spent longer shopping than he
originally intended was the last to arrive at Bute House.

After they had all found their place cards around the long dining-
room table the fourteen guests remained silent as a lone piper played a
lament before the chef entered carrying a silver salver which bore on it a
large haggis for the minister's inspection. Sir Duncan's opinion was
sought: "Warm – reekin rich!" he declared. It was the first occasion the
two men had wholeheartedly agreed on anything.

Andrew did not eat as much as the others because he couldn't take
his eyes off the guest who had been placed opposite him. She didn't pay
much attention to Andrew, but seemed always to be smiling or
laughing, making those around her enjoy her company. When Andrew
had last seen Louise Forsyth it had been scoring goals on a hockey
pitch. She had been a dumpy little girl with long pigtails and a tendency
to go for one's ankles rather than for the ball. Now the jet black hair was
short and curly, while the body had become slim and graceful. After
dinner Andrew mixed among the guests and it was well after one
o'clock when the party broke up: he never managed a moment alone
with her. Andrew was relieved to discover that Alison wanted to spend
the night with her parents at Bute House while the Frasers travelled
back to their home in Stirling.

"You're very silent for a Socialist," his father said in the car on the
way home.

"He's in love," said his mother fondly.

Andrew made no reply.

The next morning he rose early and travelled into Edinburgh to see
his agent. The minister had caught the first flight back to London but
had left a message asking if Andrew would be kind enough to see him at
ten o'clock in Dover House, the London headquarters of the Scottish
Office, the following day, "on an official matter".

Andrew was delighted but it didn't change his attitude.

Having answered his local post and dealt with some constituents' problems he left his office and made his way over to the New Club to make a private phone call. He was relieved to find her still at home. She reluctantly agreed to join him for lunch. Andrew sat alone for forty minutes, checking the grandfather clock every few moments while pretending to read the *Scotsman*. When she was eventually ushered in by the steward Andrew knew this was the woman with whom he wanted to spend the rest of his life. He would have laughed, if he had been told – before the previous evening – that he could change his well-ordered plans on what was nothing more than a casual meeting. But then he had never met anyone like Louise before and was already convinced he never would again.

"Miss Forsyth," said the man wearing the green livery uniform of the Club. He inclined his head slightly and left them alone.

Louise smiled and Andrew guided her to a table in the corner.

"It was kind of you to come at such short notice," he said nervously.

"No," she said. "It was very stupid of me."

Over a lunch which he ordered but didn't eat Andrew learned that Louise Forsyth was engaged to an old friend of his from university days and that they planned to be married the following spring. By the end of lunch he had convinced her they should at least meet again.

Andrew caught the five-ten flight back to London and sat alone in his flat and waited. Alison returned a little after nine o'clock and asked why he hadn't travelled down from Scotland with her or at least phoned. Andrew immediately told her the truth. She burst into tears while he stood helplessly by. Within the hour she had moved all her possessions out of Andrew's flat and left.

At ten-thirty he phoned Louise again.

The next morning Andrew dropped into the Commons to collect his mail from the Members' Post Office, and to check with the Whips' office as to what time they were anticipating the votes that day.

"One at six and two at ten," shouted a junior Whip from behind his desk. "And we could lose the second so be certain you're not far away if we need you."

Andrew nodded and turned to leave.

"By the way, congratulations."

"On what?" queried Andrew.

"Oh hell, another indiscretion to start the week on. It's pencilled in on the morning sheet," said the Whip, tapping a piece of paper in front of him.

"What is?" asked Andrew impatiently.

"Your appointment as Parliamentary Private Secretary to Hugh McKenzie. For pity's sake don't let him know I told you."

"I won't," promised Andrew, breathing a sigh of relief. He checked his watch: perfect timing to stroll over to Dover House and keep his appointment with the minister.

He whistled as he walked down Whitehall and the doorman saluted as he entered the ministry. They had obviously been briefed as well. He tried not to show too much anticipation. He was met at the top of the stone steps by the minister's secretary.

"Good morning," Andrew said, trying to sound as if he had no idea what was in store for him.

"Good morning, Mr Fraser," replied the secretary. "The minister has asked me to apologise for not being available to see you, but he has been called away to a Cabinet committee to discuss the new IMF standby credit."

"I see," said Andrew. "Has the minister rearranged my appointment?"

"Well, no, he hasn't," replied the secretary, sounding a little surprised. "He simply said that it was no longer important, and he was sorry to have wasted your time."

Charles Seymour was enjoying the challenge of his new appointment as a junior Opposition spokesman. Even if he was not actually making decisions on future policy he was listening to them, and at least he felt he was near the centre of affairs. Whenever a debate on housing took place in the Commons he was allowed to sit on the front bench along with the rest of the team. He had already caused the defeat of two amendments on the Town and Country Planning Bill in standing committee, and had added one of his own, relating to the protection of trees, during the report stage of the bill on the floor of the House. "It isn't preventing a world war," he admitted to Fiona, "but in its own way it's quite important because if we win the election I'm confident of being offered junior office and then I'll have a real chance to shape policy."

Fiona continued to play her part, hosting monthly dinner parties at their Eaton Square house. By the end of the year every member of the Shadow Cabinet had dined with the Seymours at least once and Fiona never wore the same dress twice or allowed a menu to be repeated.

When the parliamentary year began again in October Charles was one of the names continually dropped by the political pundits. Here was someone to watch. "He makes things happen," was the sentiment that was expressed again and again. He could barely cross the Members' Lobby without a correspondent trying to solicit his views on everything from butter mountains to rape. Fiona cut out of the papers every mention of her husband and couldn't help noticing that, if any new member was receiving more press coverage than Charles, it was a young Socialist from Leeds called Raymond Gould.

Raymond's name began to disappear from political columns soon after his success on the budget debate; his colleagues assumed it was because he was busy building a career at the bar. Had they passed his room at the Temple they would have heard the continual tap of a typewriter and been unable to contact him on his off-the-hook phone.

Each night Raymond could be found in chambers writing page after page, checking then rechecking his proofs, and often referring to the piles of books that cluttered his desk. When his *Full Employment at any Cost? Reflections of a worker educated after the Thirties* was published it caused an immediate sensation. The suggestion that the unions would become impotent and the Labour party would need to be more radical to capture the young vote was never likely to endear him to the party activists. Raymond had anticipated that it would provoke a storm of abuse from union leaders, and even among some of his more left-wing colleagues. But A. J. P. Taylor suggested in *The Times* that it was the most profound and realistic look at the Labour party since Anthony Crosland's *The Future of Socialism*, and had given the country a politician of rare honesty and courage. Raymond soon became aware that his strategy and hard work was paying dividends. He found himself a regular topic of conversation at political dinner-parties in London.

Joyce thought the book a magnificent piece of scholarship and she spent a considerable time trying to convince trade unionists who had only read out-of-context quotations from it in the *Sun* or *Daily Mirror* that it in fact showed a passionate concern for the trade-union movement, while at the same time realistically considering the Labour party's future in the next decade.

The Labour Chief Whip took Raymond on one side and told him, "You've caused a right stir, lad. Now keep your head down for a few months and you'll probably find every Cabinet member quoting you as if it was party policy."

Raymond took the Chief Whip's advice, but he did not have to wait months. Just three weeks after the book's publication the Prime Minister quoted a whole passage at the Durham Miners' Rally. A few weeks later Raymond received a missive from No. 10 requesting him to check over the Prime Minister's speech to the TUC conference and add any suggestions he might have.

Simon Kerslake had sulked for about twenty-four hours after Maudling's defeat for the leadership. He then decided to turn his anger and energy towards the Government benches. It hadn't taken him long to work out that there was a fifteen-minute period twice a week when someone with his skills of oratory could command notice. At the beginning of a new session each week he would carefully study the order paper and in particular the first five questions listed for the Prime Minister on the Tuesday and Thursday. Every Monday morning he would prepare a supplementary for at least three of them. These he worded, then reworded, so that they were biting and witty and always likely to embarrass the Government. Although preparation of such supplementary questions could take several hours Simon would make them sound as though they had been jotted down on the back of the order paper during question time – and in fact would even do so. Elizabeth teased him about how long he took on something she considered trivial. He reminded her of Churchill's comment after being praised for a brilliant rejoinder, "All my best off-the-cuff remarks had been worked on days before."

Even so Simon was surprised at how quickly the House took it for granted that he would be there on the attack, probing, demanding, harrying the Prime Minister's every move. Whenever he rose from his seat the party perked up in anticipation, and many of his interruptions reached the political column of the daily newspapers the following day.

Unemployment was the subject of that day's question. Simon was on his feet leaning forward jabbing a finger in the direction of the Government front bench.

"With the appointment of four extra Secretaries of State this week the Prime Minister can at least claim he has full employment – in the Cabinet."

The Prime Minister sank lower into his seat, looking forward to the recess.

CHAPTER FIVE

When the Queen opened Parliament the talk was not of the contents of her speech, which traditionally lists the aims of the Government of the day, but of how much of the legislation could possibly be carried out while the Labour party retained a majority of only four. Any contentious legislation was likely to be defeated at the committee stage and everyone knew it. The Conservatives were convinced they could win the forthcoming election whatever date the Prime Minister chose until the by-election held in Hull increased the Labour majority from 1,100 to 5,350. The Prime Minister couldn't believe the result and asked the Queen to dissolve Parliament immediately and to call a general election. The date announced from Buckingham Palace was 31 March.

Simon Kerslake began spending most of his spare time in his Coventry constituency. The local people seemed pleased with the apprenticeship of their new member, but the disinterested statisticians pointed out that a swing of less than one per cent would remove him from the House for another five years. By then his rivals would be on the second rung of the ladder.

The Tory Chief Whip advised Simon to stay put in Coventry and not to participate in any further parliamentary business. "There'll be no more three-line whips between now and the election," he assured him. "The most worthwhile thing you can do is pick up votes in Coventry, not give them in Westminster."

Elizabeth could only manage two weeks' leave of absence from St Mary's, and yet between the two of them they covered the entire constituency before election day. Simon's opponent was the former member, Alf Abbott, who became progressively confident of victory as the national swing to Labour accelerated during the campaign. The slogan "You know Labour Government works" was sounding convincing after only eighteen months in power. The Liberals fielded a third candidate, Nigel Bainbridge, but he admitted openly that he only hoped to save his deposit.

Alf Abbott felt assured enough to challenge Simon to a public debate. Although it was usual for the sitting member to refuse to be drawn on such occasions Simon jumped at his opponent's challenge and prepared for the encounter with his usual diligence. Seven days before the election Simon and Elizabeth stood in the wings behind the stage of Coventry town hall with Alf Abbott, Nigel Bainbridge and their wives. The three men made stilted conversation while the women eyed each other's outfits critically. The political correspondent of the *Coventry Evening Telegraph*, acting as chairman, introduced each of the protagonists as they walked on to the stage, to whipped-up applause from different sections of the hall. Simon spoke first and held the attention of the large audience for over twenty minutes. Those who tried to heckle him ended up regretting having brought attention to themselves. Without once referring to his notes, he quoted figures and clauses from Government bills with an ease that impressed even Elizabeth. Abbott followed him and made a bitter attack on the Tories, accusing them of still wanting to tread down the workers at any cost, and was greeted by large cheers from his section of the audience. Bainbridge claimed that neither understood the real issues and went into an involved dissertation on the problem of the local sewers. During the questions that followed Simon once again proved to be far better informed than Abbott or Bainbridge, but he was aware that the packed hall only held 700 that cold March evening while elsewhere in Coventry were 50,000 more voters, most of them glued to "Coronation Street".

Although the local press proclaimed Simon the victor of a one-sided debate he remained downcast by the national dailies which were now predicting a landslide for Labour.

On election morning Simon and Elizabeth were up by six and among the first to cast their votes at the local primary school. They spent the rest of the day travelling from polling station to committee room to party checking posts, trying to keep up the morale of their supporters. Everywhere they went the committed believed in his victory but Simon knew that the national swing would be impossible to ignore. A senior Conservative back-bencher had once told him that an outstanding member could be worth a thousand personal votes and a weak opponent might sacrifice another thousand. It wasn't going to be enough.

By nine o'clock the last polling station had been locked and Simon and Elizabeth collapsed into a local pub and ordered two halves of bitter. They sat and watched the television above the bar. The commentator was saying that during the day a straw poll had been taken outside six constituencies in London and from those figures they were predicting a Labour majority of sixty to seventy seats. Up on the screen flashed the seventy seats most vulnerable to siege by Labour. Ninth on the list was Coventry Central: Simon ordered the other half.

"We should be off to watch the count soon," said Elizabeth.

"There's no hurry."

"Don't be such a wimp, Simon. And remember you're still the member," she said, surprisingly sharply. "You owe it to your supporters to remain confident after all the work they've put in."

In the town hall black boxes were being delivered by police vehicles from every ward in the constituency. Their contents were tipped on to trestle tables which made up three sides of a square on the vast cleared floor. The town clerk and his personal staff stood alone in the well made by the tables, while council workers sat around the outside carefully stacking up the votes into little piles of ten. These in turn were checked by party scrutineers who hovered over them, hawk-like, often demanding that a particular ten be rechecked.

The little piles grew into large stacks which were then placed next to each other, and as the hours passed it became obvious even to a casual observer that the outcome was going to be extremely close.

The tension on the floor mounted as each hundred, then each thousand, was handed over to the clerk. Rumours that began at one end of the room had been puffed up like *soufflés* long before they had reached the waiting crowd standing in a chill wind outside the hall. By midnight, several constituencies' results around the country had been declared. The national swing seemed to be much as predicted, around three per cent to Labour, which would give them the promised majority of seventy or over.

At twelve-twenty-one the Coventry town clerk invited all three candidates to join him in the centre of the room. He told them the result of the count.

A recount was immediately demanded. The town clerk agreed, and each pile of voting slips was returned to the tables and checked over again.

An hour later the town clerk called the three candidates together again and briefed them on the result of the recount; it had changed by only three votes.

Another recount was requested and the town clerk reluctantly acquiesced. By two o'clock in the morning Elizabeth felt she had no nails left. Another hour passed, during which Heath conceded defeat while Wilson gave an extended interview to ITN spelling out his programme for the new Parliament.

At two-twenty-seven the town clerk called the three candidates together for the last time and they all accepted the result. The town clerk walked up on to the stage accompanied by the rivals. He tapped the microphone to check the speaker was working, cleared his throat and said:

"I, the undersigned, being the acting returning officer for the constituency of Coventry Central, hereby announce the total number of votes cast for each candidate to be as follows:

Alf Abbott	19,716
Nigel Bainbridge	7,002
Simon Kerslake	19,731

I therefore declare Simon Kerslake to be the duly elected Member of Parliament for the constituency of Coventry Central."

Even though the Labour party ended up with an overall majority in the House of ninety-seven, Simon had still won by fifteen votes.

Raymond Gould increased his majority to 12,413 in line with the national swing, and Joyce was ready for a week's rest.

Andrew Fraser improved his vote by 2,468 and announced his engagement to Louise Forsyth on the night after the election.

Charles Seymour could never recall accurately the size of his majority because, as Fiona explained to the old earl the following morning, "They don't count the Conservative vote in Sussex Downs, darling, they weigh it."

CHAPTER SIX

In most democratic countries a newly elected leader enjoys a transitional period during which he is able to announce the policies he intends to pursue and whom he has selected to implement them. In Britain MPs sit by their phones and wait for forty-eight hours immediately after the election result has been declared. If a call comes in the first twelve hours they will be asked to join the Cabinet, the second twelve given a position as a Minister of State, the third twelve made an Under-Secretary of State, and the last twelve as Parliamentary Private Secretary to a Cabinet minister. If the phone hasn't rung by then, they remain on the back benches.

Andrew Fraser had not bothered to be anywhere near a phone when the BBC midday news announced that Hugh McKenzie had been promoted from Minister of State to Secretary of State for Scotland, with a seat in the Cabinet. Andrew and Louise Forsyth decided to spend a quiet weekend at Aviemore, he to relax and climb other mountains before returning to the House, she to make plans for their forthcoming wedding.

It had taken Andrew countless trips to Edinburgh to convince Louise what had happened to him at Bute House that night had not been mere infatuation that would soon pass, but held long-term conviction. When the one weekend he couldn't travel to the Scottish capital and she came down to London he knew she no longer doubted his resolve. Andrew had found in the past that once the conquest was achieved interest soon waned. For him, though, his love for "the wee slip of a thing", as his mother had come to describe Louise, grew and grew.

Although Louise was only five foot three she was so slim she appeared far taller, and her short black hair, blue eyes and laughing smile had many tall men bending down to take a closer look.

"You eat like a pig and look like a rake. I don't know how you manage it," grumbled Andrew over dinner one night. He played regular games of squash and swam three times a week to keep his own heavy frame in trim. He stared in admiration and not a little envy as Louise's eyes twinkled mischievously before she devoured another portion of Black Forest gâteau.

Although she had been brought up in a strict Calvinist household in which politics were never discussed Louise quickly learnt about the machinery of Government and soon found herself debating long into the night with Sir Duncan. At first he scored points off her with ease, but it was not long before he had to answer her demands with more and more reasoned argument, and sometimes even that was not enough.

By the time the election had taken place Louise had become a total convert to Andrew's views. The squalor in some of the parts of the Edinburgh Carlton constituency, which she had never set foot in before, made her sick at heart. Like all converts, she became zealous and began by trying to reform the entire Forsyth clan. She even paid twelve shillings to join the Scottish Labour party.

"Why did you do that?" asked Andrew, trying not to show his pleasure.

"I'm against mixed marriages," she replied.

Andrew was delighted and surprised by the interest she took, and the local constituency suspicions of "the wealthy lady" soon turned to affection.

"Your future husband will be Secretary of State for Scotland one day," many of them shouted, as she walked down the narrow cobbled streets.

"It's Downing Street, not Bute House, that I want to live in," he had once confided to her. "And in any case I've still got to become a junior minister."

"That could change in the very near future."

"Not while Hugh McKenzie is Secretary of State," he said, not under his breath.

"To hell with McKenzie," she said. "Surely one of his Cabinet colleagues has the guts to offer you the chance to be his PPS?" But despite Louise's sentiments the phone did not ring that weekend.

Raymond Gould returned from Leeds the moment the count was over, leaving Joyce to carry out the traditional "thank you" drive around the constituency.

When he wasn't sitting by the phone the following day he was walking around it, nervously pushing his glasses back up his nose. The first call came from his mother who had rung to congratulate him.

"On what?" he asked. "Have you heard something?"

"No, love," she said, "I just rang to say how pleased I was about your increased majority."

"Oh."

"And to add how sorry we were not to see you before you left the constituency, especially as you have to pass the shop on the way to the A1."

Not again, Mother, he wanted to say.

The second call was from a colleague inquiring if Raymond had been offered a job.

"Nothing so far," he said before learning of his contemporary's promotion.

The third call was from one of Joyce's friends.

"When will she be back?" another Yorkshire accent inquired.

"I've no idea," said Raymond, desperate to get the caller off the line.

"I'll call again this afternoon, then."

"Fine," said Raymond, putting the phone down quickly.

He went into the kitchen to make himself a cheese sandwich, but there wasn't any cheese, so he ate stale bread smeared with three-week-old butter. He was half-way through a second slice when the phone rang.

"Raymond?"

He held his breath.

"Noel Brewster."

He exhaled in exasperation as he recognised the vicar's voice.

"Can you read the second lesson when you're next up in Leeds? We had rather hoped you would read it this morning – your dear wife . . ."

"Yes," he promised. "The first weekend I am back in Leeds." The phone rang again as soon as he placed it back on the receiver.

"Raymond Gould?" said an anonymous voice.

"Speaking," he said.

"The Prime Minister will be with you in one moment."

Raymond waited. The front door opened and another voice shouted, "It's only me. I don't suppose you found anything to eat, poor love." Joyce joined Raymond in the drawing-room.

Without looking at his wife he waved his hand at her to keep quiet.

"Ray," said a voice on the other end of the line.

"Good afternoon, Prime Minister," he replied, rather formally in response to the more pronounced Yorkshire accent.

"I was hoping you would feel able to join the new team as Under-Secretary for Employment?"

Raymond breathed a sigh of relief. It was exactly what he'd hoped for. "I'd be delighted, Prime Minister."

"Good, that will give the trade-union leaders something new to think about." The phone went dead.

Raymond Gould, Under-Secretary of State at the Department of Employment, sat motionless on the third rung of the ladder.

As Raymond left the house the next morning he was greeted by a driver standing next to a gleaming black Austin Westminster. Unlike his second-hand Sunbeam, it glowed in the morning light. The rear door was opened and Raymond climbed in to be driven off to the department. Thank God he knows where my office is, thought Raymond as he sat alone in the back. By his side on the back seat was a red leather box the size of a very thick briefcase with gold lettering running along the edge: "Under-Secretary of State for Employment". Raymond turned the small key, knowing what Alice must have felt like on her way down the rabbit hole. The inside was crammed with buff files. He opened the first to see, "A five-point plan for discussion by Cabinet on how to keep unemployment under one million". He immediately started to read the closely-typed documents.

When Charles Seymour returned to the Commons on the Tuesday there was a note from the Whips' office waiting for him on the Members' Letter-board. One of the Environment team had lost his seat in the general election and Charles had been promoted to number two on the Opposition bench. "No more preservation of trees. You'll be on to higher things now," chuckled the Chief Whip. "Pollution, water shortage and exhaust fumes . . ."

Charles smiled with pleasure as he walked through the Commons, acknowledging old colleagues and noticing a considerable number of new faces. He didn't stop and talk to any of the newcomers as he could not be certain if they were Labour or Conservative and, given the election result, most of them had to be Socialist. A doorkeeper in white tie and black tail-jacket handed him a message to say that a constituent was waiting to see him in the Central Lobby. He hurried off to find out what the problem was, passing some of his older colleagues who wore forlorn looks on their faces. For some it would be a considerable time before they were offered the chance of office again, while others knew they had served as ministers for the last time. In politics, he'd quickly learned, the luck of age and timing could play a vital part in any man's career, however able he might be.

But at thirty-five Charles dismissed such thoughts as he marched towards the waiting constituent. He turned out to be a red-faced Master of Hounds who had travelled up to London to grumble about the proposed private member's bill banning hare coursing. Charles listened to a fifteen-minute monologue before assuring his constituent that any such bill was doomed through lack of parliamentary time. The Master of Hounds went away happy and Charles returned to his room to check over the constituency mail. Fiona had reminded him of the 800 letters of thanks to the party workers that had been franked but still needed topping and tailing after every election. He groaned.

"Mrs Blenkinsop, the chairman of Sussex Ladies' Luncheon Club, wants you to be their guest speaker this year," his secretary told him once he had settled.

"Reply yes – what's the date?" asked Charles, reaching for his diary.

"16 June."

"Stupid woman, that's Ladies Day at Ascot. Tell her that I'm delivering a speech at an Environmental Conference, but I'll be certain to make myself free for the function next year."

The secretary looked up anxiously.

"Don't fuss, she'll never know any better."

She moved on to the next letter. "Mr Heath wonders if you can join him for a drink on Thursday, six o'clock?"

Simon Kerslake also knew it was going to be a long slog. He was aware the Tories would not change their leader until Heath had been given a second chance at the polls, and that could take every day of five years with a Government which had a ninety-seven majority.

He began writing articles for the *Spectator* and for the *Sunday Express* centre pages, in the hope of building a reputation outside the House while at the same time supplementing his parliamentary salary of £3,400. Even with Elizabeth's income as a consultant he was finding it difficult to make ends meet, and soon their two young sons would have reached prep school age. He envied the Charles Seymours of this world who did not have to give a second thought about their next pay cheque. Simon wondered if the damn man had any problems at all. He ran a finger down his own bank account: as usual there was a figure around £500 in the right-hand margin, and as usual it was in red. Many of his Oxford contemporaries had already established themselves in the City or at the bar and on a Friday evening could be seen being driven to large houses in the country. Simon laughed whenever he read that people went into politics to make money.

He pressed on with demanding questions to the Prime Minister, and tried not to show how frustrated he was by the expectations of his colleagues whenever he rose each Tuesday and Thursday. Even after it became routine he prepared himself thoroughly, and on one occasion he even elicited praise from his normally taciturn leader. But as the weeks passed he found that his thoughts continually returned to money – or to his lack of it.

That was before he met Ronnie Nethercote.

Andrew Fraser had often read that the anger or jealousy of one man could block the advance of a political career but he still found it hard to accept that it could apply to him. What annoyed him even more was that Hugh McKenzie's tentacles seemed to have spread through every other department.

Andrew's marriage to Louise Forsyth had been expansively covered in the national papers and the absence of the Secretary of State at the wedding did not escape the notice of the *Daily Express*'s William Hickey. They even published an out-of-date photograph of Alison McKenzie looking sorrowful.

Sir Duncan reminded his son that politics was for long-distance runners, not sprinters, and that he still had a few more laps to complete yet. "An unfortunate analogy," considered Andrew as he had been a member of the Edinburgh University 4 × 110 relay team. Nevertheless he prepared himself for the marathon.

"Don't forget, Harold Macmillan spent fourteen years on the back benches before holding office," Sir Duncan added.

Louise accompanied Andrew all over the country for his speeches 'of major importance', usually to an audience of less than twenty; she only stopped travelling to Scotland every week when she discovered she was pregnant.

To Louise's surprise, Andrew turned out to be a keen anticipatory father, determined his son would not think of him only as a politician. Single-handed, he converted one of the upstairs bedrooms in Cheyne Walk into a nursery and sought her approval for a variety of blue decorative schemes.

Louise was anxious that Andrew should extend the same feelings to their unborn child, if they had a daughter.

Raymond Gould quickly gained a reputation at the Department of Employment. He was thought of as extremely bright, demanding, hard working and, not that it was ever reported to him, arrogant. His ability to cut a junior civil servant off in mid-sentence or to correct his principal Private Secretary on matters of detail did not endear him even to his closest staff, who always want to be loyal to their master.

Raymond's work load was prodigious and even the Permanent Secretary experienced Gould's unrelenting 'Don't make excuses' when he tried to trim one of the minister's private schemes. Soon senior civil servants were talking of when, not whether, he would be promoted. His Secretary of State, like all men who were expected to be in six places at once, often asked Raymond to stand in for him, but even Raymond was surprised when he was invited to represent the department as guest of honour at the annual CBI dinner.

Joyce checked to see that her husband's dinner-jacket was well brushed, his shirt spotless and his shoes shining like a guards officer's. His carefully worded speech – a combination of civil-servant draughtsmanship and a few more forceful phrases of his own to prove to the assembled capitalists that not every member of the Labour party was a "raving commie" – was safely lodged in his inside pocket. His driver ferried him from his Lansdowne Road home towards the West End.

Raymond enjoyed the occasion; although he was nervous when he rose to represent the Government in reply to the toast of the guests, by the time he had resumed his seat he felt it had been one of his better efforts. The ovation that followed was certainly more than polite from what had to be classified as a naturally hostile audience.

"That speech was dryer than the Chablis," one guest whispered in the chairman's ear but he had to agree that, with men like Gould in high office, it was going to be a lot easier to live with the Socialists.

The man on Simon Kerslake's left was far more blunt in voicing his opinion of Gould. "Bloody man thinks like a Tory, talks like a Tory, so why isn't he a Tory?" he demanded.

Simon grinned at the prematurely balding man who had been expressing his equally vivid views throughout dinner. Corpulent and ruddy-faced, Ronnie Nethercote looked as if he was trying to escape from every part of his bulging dinner-jacket.

"I expect," said Simon in reply, "that Gould would have found it hard to join the Young Conservatives, born in the thirties and living in Leeds."

"Balls," said Ronnie. "I managed it and I was born in the East End of London without any of his advantages. Now tell me, Mr Kerslake, what do you do when you're not wasting your time in the House of Commons?"

Raymond stayed on after dinner and chatted for some time to the captains of industry. A little after eleven he left to return to Lansdowne Road.

As his chauffeur drove slowly away from Grosvenor House down Park Lane, the Under-Secretary waved expansively back to his host. Someone else waved in reply. At first Raymond only glanced across, assuming it was another dinner guest, until he saw her legs. Standing on the corner outside the petrol station on Park Lane stood a young girl smiling at him invitingly, her white leather mini skirt so short it might have been better described as a handkerchief. Her long legs reminded him of Joyce ten years before except that they were black. Her finely curled hair and the set of her hips remained firmly implanted in Raymond's mind all the way home.

When they reached Lansdowne Road Raymond climbed out of the official car and said "Goodnight" to his driver before walking slowly towards his front door, but he did not take out his latch key. He awaited until he was sure the driver had turned the corner before looking up and checking the bedroom window. All the lights were out. Joyce must be asleep.

He crept down the path and back on to the pavement, then looked up and down the road, finally spotting the space where Joyce had parked the Sunbeam. He checked the spare key was on his key-ring and fumbled about, feeling like a car thief. It took three attempts before the car spluttered into life, and Raymond wondered if he would wake up the whole road as he moved off and headed back to Park Lane, not certain what to expect. When he reached Marble Arch he travelled slowly down in the centre stream of traffic. A few dinner guests in evening dress were still spilling out of Grosvenor House. He passed the petrol station: she hadn't moved. She smiled again and he accelerated, nearly running into the car in front of him. Raymond travelled back up to Marble Arch but, instead of turning towards home, he drove down Park Lane again, this time not as quickly and on the inside lane. He took his foot off the accelerator as he approached the petrol station and she waved again. He returned to Marble Arch before repeating his detour down Park Lane, this time even more slowly. As he passed Grosvenor House for a third time he checked to be sure that there were no stragglers still chatting on the pavement. It was clear. He touched the brakes and his car came to a stop just beyond the petrol station. He waited.

The girl looked up and down the street before strolling over to the car, opening the passenger door and taking a seat next to the Under-Secretary of State for Employment.

"Looking for business?"

"What do you mean?" asked Raymond hoarsely.

"Come on, darling. You can't imagine I was standing out there hoping to get a sun tan."

Raymond turned to look at the girl more carefully and wanted to touch her despite the aura of cheap perfume. Her black blouse had three buttons undone; a fourth would have left nothing to the imagination.

"It's ten pounds at my place."

"Where's your place?" he heard himself say.

"I use a hotel in Paddington."

"How do we get there?" he asked, putting his hand nervously through his red hair.

"Just head up to Marble Arch and I'll direct you."

Raymond pulled out and went off towards Hyde Park Corner, and drove round before travelling on up towards Marble Arch once again.

"I'm Mandy," she said, "what's your name?"

Raymond hesitated. "Malcolm."

"And what do you do, Malcolm, in these hard times?"

"I . . . I sell second-hand cars."

"Haven't picked out a very good one for yourself, have you?" She laughed.

Raymond made no comment. It didn't stop Mandy.

"What's a second-hand car salesman doing dressed up like a toff, then?"

Raymond had quite forgotten he was still in evening dress.

"I've . . . just been to a convention . . . at the . . . Hilton Hotel."

"Lucky for some," she said, and lit a cigarette. "I've been standing outside Grosvenor House all night in the hope of getting some rich feller from that posh party." Raymond's cheeks nearly turned the colour of his hair. "Slow down and take the second on the left."

He followed her instructions until they pulled up outside a small dingy hotel. "I'll get out first, then you," she said. "Just walk straight through reception and follow me up the stairs.'' As she got out of the car he nearly drove off and might have done so if his eye hadn't caught the sway of her hips as she walked back towards the hotel.

He obeyed her instructions and climbed several flights of narrow stairs until he reached the top floor. As he approached the landing, a large bosomy blonde passed him on the way down.

"Hi, Mandy,'' she shouted back at her friend.

"Hi, Sylv. Is the room free?''

"Just,'' said the blonde sourly.

Mandy pushed open the door and Raymond followed her in. The room was small and narrow. In one corner stood a tiny bed and a threadbare carpet. The faded yellow wallpaper was peeling in several places. There was a wash basin attached to the wall; a dripping tap had left a brown stain on the enamel.

Mandy put her hand out, and waited.

"Ah, yes, of course,'' said Raymond, taking out his wallet to find he only had nine pounds on him.

She scowled. "Not going to get overtime tonight, am I, darling?'' she said, tucking the money carefully away in the corner of her bag before matter-of-factly taking off all her clothes.

Although the act of undressing had been totally sexless he was still amazed by the beauty of her body. Raymond felt somehow detached from the real world. He watched, eager to feel the texture of her skin, but made no move. She lay down on the bed.

"Let's get on with it, darling. I've got a living to earn.''

The minister undressed quickly, keeping his back to the bed. He folded his clothes in a neat pile on the floor as there was no chair. Then he laid down on top of her. It was all over in a few minutes.

"Come quickly, don't you, darling?'' said Mandy, grinning.

Raymond turned away from her and started washing himself as best he could in the little basin. He dressed hurriedly, realising he must get out of the place as rapidly as possible.

"Can you drop me back at the petrol station?'' Mandy asked.

"It's exactly the opposite direction for me,'' he said, trying not to sound anxious as he made a bolt for the door. He passed Sylv on the stairs accompanied by a man. She stared at him more closely the second time. Raymond was back in his car a few moments later. He drove home quickly but not before unwinding the windows in an attempt to get rid of the smell of stale tobacco and cheap perfume.

Back in Lansdowne Road he had a long shower before creeping into bed next to Joyce; she stirred only slightly.

CHAPTER SEVEN

Charles drove his wife down to Ascot early to be sure to avoid the bumper-to-bumper traffic that always developed later in the day. With his height and bearing, Charles Seymour was made for tails and a topper and Fiona wore a hat which on anyone less self-assured would have looked ridiculous. They had been invited to join the McAlpines for the afternoon and when they arrived they found Sir Robert awaiting them in his private box.

"You must have left home early," said Charles.

"About thirty minutes ago," he said, laughing. Fiona looked politely incredulous.

"I always come here by helicopter," he explained.

They lunched on lobster and strawberries accompanied by a fine vintage champagne which the waiter kept pouring and pouring. Charles might not have drunk quite as much had he not picked the winners of the first three races. He spent the fifth race slumped in a chair in the corner of the box and only the noise of the crowd kept him from nodding off.

If they hadn't waited for a farewell drink after the last race Charles might have got away with it. He had forgotten that his host was returning by helicopter.

The long tail of cars across Windsor Great Park all the way back to the M4 made Charles very short-tempered. When he eventually reached the motorway he put his Daimler into fourth gear. He didn't notice the police car until the siren sounded and he was directed to pull over.

"Do be sensible, Charles," whispered Fiona.

"Don't worry, old girl, I know exactly how to deal with the law," he said, and wound down his window to address the policeman who stood by the car. "Do you realise who I am, officer?"

"No, sir, but I would like you to accompany me – "

"Certainly not, officer, I am a Member of . . ."

"Do be quiet," said Fiona, "and stop making such a fool of yourself."

". . . Parliament and I will not be treated . . ."

"Have you any idea how pompous you sound, Charles?"

"Perhaps you will be kind enough to accompany me to the station, sir?"

"I want to speak to my solicitor."

"Of course, sir. As soon as we reach the station."

When Charles arrived at the constabulary he proved quite incapable of walking in a straight line and refused to provide a blood sample.

"I am the Conservative MP for Sussex Downs."

Which will not help you, Fiona thought, but he was past listening and only demanded that she phone the family solicitor at Speechly, Bircham and Soames.

After Ian Kimmins had spoken first gently, then firmly to Charles his client eventually cooperated with the police.

Once Charles had completed his written statement Fiona drove him home, praying that his stupidity would pass unnoticed by the press the following day.

Andrew even bought a football but hid it from Louise.

As the months passed Louise's slight frame expanded alarmingly. Andrew would rest his head on the bulge and listen for the heartbeat. "It's a scrum-half," he declared.

"Perhaps she's a centre forward," Louise suggested, "and will want to emulate the distaff side of the family."

"If he has to be a centre forward he will play for Hearts," Andrew assured her.

"Male chauvinist pig," she called to his back as he headed off to the Commons that morning. Andrew toyed with the names of Jamie, Robert, Hector and Iain and had settled on Robert before he had reached Westminster. On arrival at New Palace Yard he hailed the policeman on the gate and was surprised to see the familiar figure immediately rush towards him.

Andrew wound down the window. "What's the problem, officer?"

"Your wife's been taken to St Mary's, Paddington, sir. Emergency wing."

Andrew would have broken the speed limit all the way to Marble Arch if it hadn't been for the traffic. He kept praying he would be there in time, but he couldn't help remembering that Louise was only six months pregnant. When he arrived the doctor on duty would not allow him to see her.

"How is Louise?" were Andrew's first words.

The young doctor hesitated, then said, "Your wife's fine, but I'm afraid she's lost the baby."

Andrew felt his whole body go limp. "Thank God she's all right," he said.

"I'm afraid I can't let you see her until she has come out of sedation."

"Of course, Doctor," said Andrew, glancing at the lapel badge on her white coat.

"But I can see no reason why you shouldn't have more children in the future," she added gently, before he had the chance to ask the question.

Andrew smiled with relief and began pacing up and down the corridor, unaware of the passing of time, until the doctor returned and said it would now be all right for him to see his wife.

"I hope you're not too disappointed?" were Louise's first words when eventually he was allowed to see her.

"Don't be silly – we'll have a dozen before we're through," he said, taking her hand.

She tried to laugh. "Do you know my doctor's husband?"

"Not that I'm aware of," said Andrew.

"Simon Kerslake."

"Good heavens, yes. Very capable fellow. Look aye, lass," said Andrew, putting on a deep brogue, "you'll be a new woman after a couple of days' rest, I'll guarantee it."

"And if I'm not?"

"I'll stick with the old one. And I'll tell you what: as soon as they let you out of this place we'll go down to the South of France for the weekend."

"You don't like him because he comes from the East End," said Simon, after she had read the letter.

"That's not true," replied Elizabeth. "I don't like him because I don't trust him."

"But you've only met him twice."

"Once would have been quite enough."

"Well, I can tell you I'm impressed by the not inconsiderable empire he's built up over the last ten years, and frankly it's an offer I can't refuse," said Simon, pocketing the letter.

"I know we could do with a little more money," said Elizabeth, "but surely not at any cost."

"I won't be offered many chances like this," continued Simon, "and frankly we could use the money. The belief people have that every Tory MP has some lucrative sinecure and two or three non-executive directorships is plain baloney and you know it. Not one other serious propositon has been put to me since I've been in the House, and another £2,000 a year for a monthly board meeting would come in very handy."

"And what else?"

"What do you mean, what else?"

"What else does Mr Nethercote expect for his £2,000? Don't be naive, Simon, he's not offering you that kind of money on a plate unless he's hoping to receive some scraps back."

"Well, maybe I have a few contacts and a little influence with one or two people . . ."

"I'll bet."

"You've just taken against him, Elizabeth."

"I'm against anything that might in the long term harm your career, Simon. Struggle on but never sacrifice your integrity, as you're so fond of reminding the people of Coventry."

On Friday morning, two weeks later, Andrew and Louise set out for London airport with one suitcase between them. As Andrew locked the front door the phone rang.

"No one's in," he shouted at the door knob, "but we'll be back on Monday."

He had booked a suite at the Colombe d'Or nestled in the hills of St Paul in the south of France. He was determined to prise Louise away from London and see she had some sun and rest.

The famous old hotel was everything the brochure had promised. On the walls hung paintings by Picasso, Monet, Manet, Utrillo – all of which the patroness, Madame Reux, had accepted many years before in place of payment from artists who needed lodging and a square meal. On the way up the winding staircase Louise was nearly knocked out by a Calder mobile and a Courbet hung above the bed in their room. But it was the bed itself, a sixteenth-century four-poster, that they both coveted. They were soon to discover it possessed a mattress so comfortable that visitors always overslept.

The food was memorable and they walked through the green hills each day to be sure they could tackle another full dinner at night. Three days of no radio, no television, no papers and no telephone ensured that by Monday morning they were ready to face London. They swore they would return again soon.

Once their plane had landed at Heathrow they were made aware that the holiday was over. Twenty minutes passed before someone pushed the waiting steps up to the Vanguard's door. Then a crowded bus to the terminal that seemed miles away was followed by a route-march to customs. Despite their first-class tickets their bags were among the last off. By the time the taxi had crawled through the morning rush hour to their front door in Cheyne Walk all Louise could say was, "I need another holiday." As Andrew put his latch key in the door the telephone started ringing.

"I hope they haven't been trying all weekend," Louise said.

Andrew put the phone to his ear as it went dead.

"Just missed whoever it was," said Andrew, picking up several brown envelopes from the floor. "France already seems about a week ago." He kissed his wife. "Must get changed and be off to the House," he said, checking his watch.

"How has the nation managed to survive without you?" mocked

Louise.

When the phone rang again Andrew was just stepping out of the bath.

"Can you take it, Louise?" he shouted. A moment later he heard her rushing up the stairs.

"Andrew, it's the Prime Minister's office."

He ran dripping and naked to the bedroom phone and picked up the extension.

"Andrew Fraser," he said.

"This is No. 10," said an official-sounding voice, "the Prime Minister has been wanting to contact you since Friday morning."

"I'm sorry, I took my wife to Provence for the weekend."

"Really, sir?" said the voice, not sounding at all interested. "May I tell the Prime Minister you are now free to speak to him?"

"Of course," said Andrew, frowning at his nude reflection in the mirror. He must have put on half a stone; it would have to be four games of squash this week and no more wine at lunch.

"Andrew."

"Good morning, Prime Minister."

"Sad news about Hugh McKenzie."

"Yes, sir," said Andrew, automatically.

"They warned me about his heart before the last election but he insisted he wanted to carry on. I've asked Bruce to be the new Secretary of State and Angus to take his place as minister. They both want you to be the new Under-Secretary – how do you feel about it?"

"I'd be delighted, Prime Minister," Andrew stammered, trying to take in the news.

"Good. And by the way, Andrew, when you open your first red box you won't find any tickets for Colombe d'Or, so I do hope Louise is fully recovered." The phone clicked.

They had tracked him down, but the Prime Minister had left him in peace.

The first official function Andrew Fraser attended as Her Majesty's Under-Secretary of State at the Scottish Office was Hugh McKenzie's funeral.

"Think about it, Simon," said Ronnie, as they reached the boardroom door. "Two thousand pounds a year may be helpful but if you take shares in my property company it would give you a chance to make some capital."

"What did you have in mind?" asked Simon, doing up the middle button of his blazer and trying not to sound too excited.

"Well, you've proved damned useful to me. Some of those people who you bring to lunch wouldn't have allowed me past their front doors. I'd let you buy in cheap . . . you could get hold of 50,000 shares at one pound so when we go public you'll make a killing."

"Raising £50,000 won't be that easy, Ronnie."

"When your bank manager has checked over my books he'll be only too happy to lend you the money, you see."

After the Midland Bank had studied the authorised accounts of Nethercote and Company and the area manager had interviewed Simon, they agreed to his request, on the condition that Simon lodge the shares with the bank.

How wrong Elizabeth was proving to be, Simon thought, and when Nethercote and Company went on to double their profits for the year he brought home a copy of the annual report for his wife to study.

"Looks good," she had to admit. "But that still doesn't mean I have to trust Ronnie Nethercote."

When Charles Seymour's drink-driving charge came up in front of the Reading Bench he listed himself as C. G. Seymour – no mention of MP. Under profession he entered "Banker".

He came sixth in the list that morning, and on behalf of his absent client Ian Kimmins apologised to the Reading magistrates and assured them it would not happen again. Charles received a fifty-pound fine and was banned from driving for six months. The whole case was over in four minutes.

When Charles was told the news by telephone later that day he was appreciative of Kimmins's sensible advice and felt he had escaped lightly. He couldn't help remembering how many column inches George Brown, the Labour Foreign Secretary, had endured after a similar incident outside the Hilton Hotel.

Fiona kept her own counsel.

At the time Fleet Street was in the middle of "the silly season", that period in the summer when the press are desperate for news. There had only been one cub reporter in the court when Charles's case came up, and even he was surprised by the interest the nationals took in his little scoop. The pictures of Charles taken so discreetly outside the Seymours' country home were now glaring from the pages the following morning. Headlines ranged from "Six months' ban for drink-drive son of earl" to "MP's Ascot binge ends in heavy fine". Even *The Times* mentioned the case on its home news page.

By lunchtime the same day every Fleet Street newspaper had tried to contact Charles – and so had the Chief Whip. When he did track Charles down his advice was short and to the point. A junior Shadow minister can survive that sort of publicity once, not twice.

"Whatever you do, don't drive a car during the next six months and don't ever drink and drive again."

Charles concurred, and after a quiet weekend hoped he had heard the last of the case. Then he caught the headline on the front page of the

Sussex Gazette, "Member faces no confidence motion": Mrs Blenkinsop, the chairman of the Ladies Luncheon Club, was proposing the motion – not for the drunken driving but for deliberately misleading her about why he had been unable to fulfil a speaking engagement at their annual luncheon.

Raymond had become so used to receiving files marked "Strictly Private", "Top Secret", or even "For Your Eyes Only" in his position as a Government Under-Secretary that he didn't give a second thought to a letter marked "Confidential and Personal" even though it was written in a scrawled hand. He opened it while Joyce was boiling his eggs.

"Four minutes and forty-five seconds, just the way you like them," she said as she returned from the kitchen and placed two eggs in front of him. "Are you all right, dear? You're white as a sheet."

Raymond recovered quickly, pushing the letter into a pocket before checking his watch. "Haven't the time for the other egg," he said. "I'm already late for Cabinet committee, I must dash."

Strange, thought Joyce, as her husband hurried to the door. Cabinet committees didn't usually meet until ten and he hadn't even cracked open his first egg. She sat down and slowly ate her husband's breakfast, wondering why he had left all his post behind.

Once he was in the back of his official car Raymond read the letter again. It didn't take long.

DEAR "MALCOLM",

I enjoid our little get together the other evening and five hundrud pounds would help me to forget it once and for all.

LOVE, MANDY.

PS. I'll be in touch again soon.

He read the letter once more and tried to compose his thoughts. There was no address on the top of the notebook paper. Neither letter nor envelope gave any clue as to where they had come from.

After he had arrived outside the Department of Employment Raymond remained in the back seat for several moments.

"Are you feeling all right, sir?" his driver asked.

"Fine, thank you," he replied, and jumped out of the car and ran all the way up to his office. As he passed his secretary's desk he barked at her, "No interruptions."

"You won't forget Cabinet committee at ten o'clock, will you, Minister?"

"No," replied Raymond sharply and slammed his office door. Once at his desk he tried to calm himself and recall what he would have done had he been approached by a client as a barrister at the bar: first instruct a good solicitor. Raymond considered the two most capable lawyers in England to be Arnold Goodman and Sir Roger Pelham. Goodman was getting too high a profile for Raymond's liking whereas Pelham was just as sound but virtually unknown to the general public. He called Pelham's office and made an appointment to see him that afternoon.

Raymond hardly spoke in Cabinet committee, but as most of his colleagues wanted to express their own views nobody noticed. As soon as the meeting was over Raymond hurried out and took a taxi to High Holborn.

Sir Roger Pelham rose from behind his large Victorian desk to greet the junior minister.

"I know you're a busy man, Gould," Pelham said as he fell back into his black leather chair, "so I shan't waste your time. Tell me what I can do for you."

"It was kind of you to see me at such short notice," Raymond began and without further word handed the letter over.

"Thank you," the solicitor said courteously and, pushing his half-moon spectacles higher up his nose he read the note three times before he made any comment.

"Blackmail is something we all detest," he began, "but it will be necessary for you to tell me the whole truth, and don't miss out any details. Please remember I am on your side. You'll recall only too well from your days at the bar what a disadvantage one labours under when one is in possession of only half the facts."

The tips of Pelham's fingers touched, forming a small roof in front of his nose as he listened intently to Raymond's account of what had happened that night.

"Could anyone else have seen you?" was Pelham's first question.

Raymond thought back and then nodded. "Yes," he said. "Yes, I'm afraid there was another girl who passed me on the stairs."

Pelham read the letter once more. "My immediate advice," he said, looking Raymond in the eye and speaking slowly and deliberately, "and you won't like it, is to do nothing."

"But what do I say if she contacts the press?"

"She will probably get in touch with someone from Fleet Street anyway, even if you pay the £500, or however many other £500s you can afford. Don't imagine you're the first minister to be blackmailed, Mr Gould. Every homosexual in the House lives in daily fear of it. It's a game of hide and seek. Very few people other than saints have nothing to *hide*, and the problem with public life is that a lot of busybodies want to *seek*." Raymond remained silent, trying not to show his anxiety. "Phone me on my private line immediately the next letter arrives," said Pelham, scribbling a number on a piece of paper.

"Thank you," said Raymond, at least relieved that his secret was now shared with someone else. Pelham rose from behind his desk and accompanied Raymond to the door. "You'll be glad to see Yorkshire back as county champions," said the solicitor as he walked down the long passage with the minister. Raymond did not reply. When they reached the outer door they shook hands formally. "I'll wait to hear from you," said Pelham. A pity that the man showed no interest in cricket.

Raymond left the solicitor's office feeling better, but he found it hard to concentrate on his work the rest of that day and slept only in fits and starts during the night. When he read the morning papers he was horrified to see how much space was being given to Charles Seymour's peccadillo. What a field day they would be able to have with him. When the post came, he searched anxiously for the scrawled handwriting. It was hidden under an American Express circular. He tore it open. The same hand was this time demanding that the £500 should be deposited at a newsagent in Pimlico. Sir Roger Pelham saw the minister one hour later.

Despite the renewed demand the solicitor's advice remained the same.

Andrew Fraser never stopped moving from one city to another because the Scottish Office had to show a presence in Edinburgh and Glasgow as well as in London. Louise did not complain; she had never seen her husband so happy. The only moment of light relief during his first three months as a minister came when Andrew found it necessary to send a letter to his father addressed, "Dear Sir Duncan," which went on to explain why he had to reject his offered advice on a Highlands and Islands Board project. Andrew was particularly pleased with the line, "I have for some considerable time listened to both sides of the argument."

Once he had settled in his favourite chair that night with a large whisky in his hand Louise told him she was pregnant again. "When did I find the time?" he asked, taking her in his arms.

"Maybe the half-hour between your meeting with the Norwegian Fishing Minister and the address to the Oil Conference in Aberdeen?"

When the AGM of the Sussex Downs Conservative Association came round in October Charles was pleased to learn that Mrs Blenkinsop's "no confidence" motion had been withdrawn. The local press tried to build up the story but the nationals were full of the Aberfan coal-tip disaster, in which 116 schoolchildren had lost their lives. No editor could find space for Sussex Downs.

Charles delivered a thoughtful speech to his association which was well received. During question time he was relieved to find no embarrassing questions directed at him.

When the Seymours finally said goodnight, Charles took the chairman to one side and inquired: "How did you manage it?"

"I explained to Mrs Blenkinsop," replied the chairman, "that if her motion of no confidence was discussed at the AGM it would be awfully hard for the member to back my recommendation that she should receive an OBE in the New Year's Honours for service to the party. That shouldn't be too hard for you to pull off, should it, Charles?"

Every time the phone rang Raymond assumed it would be the press asking him if he knew someone called Mandy. Often it was a journalist, but all that was needed was a quotable remark on the latest unemployment figures, or a statement of where the minister stood on devaluation of the pound.

It was Mike Molloy, a reporter from the *Daily Mirror*, who was the first to ask Raymond what he had to say about a statement phoned in to his office by a girl with a West Indian accent called Mandy Page.

"I have nothing to say on the subject. Please speak to my solicitor, Sir Roger Pelham," was the Under-Secretary's succinct reply. The moment he put the phone down he felt queasy.

A few minutes later when the phone rang again Raymond still hadn't moved. He picked up the receiver, his hand still shaking. Pelham confirmed that Molloy had been in touch with him.

"I presume you made no comment," said Raymond.

"On the contrary," replied Pelham. "I told him the truth."

"*What?*" exploded Raymond.

"Be thankful she hit on a fair journalist because I expect he'll let this one go. Fleet Street are not quite the bunch of shits everyone imagines them to be," Pelham said uncharacteristically, and added, "they also detest two things, bent policemen and blackmailers. I don't think you'll see anything in the press tomorrow."

Sir Roger Pelham was wrong.

Raymond was standing outside his local newsagent the next morning when it opened at five-thirty and he surprised the proprietor by asking for a copy of the *Daily Mirror*. Raymond Gould was plastered all over page five saying, "Devaluation is not a course I can support while the unemployment figures remain so high." The photograph by the side of the article was unusually flattering.

Simon Kerslake read a more detailed account of what the minister had said on devaluation in *The Times*, and noted Raymond Gould's firm stand against what was beginning to look like inevitable Government policy.

Simon looked up from his paper and started to consider a ploy that might trap Gould. If he could make the minister commit himself again and again on devaluation in front of the whole House he knew that when the inevitable happened Gould would be left with no choice but to resign. Simon pencilled a question on the top of the paper before returning to the political columns.

The devaluation news had caused a Tory lead in the opinion polls of eight per cent, and despite a majority of ninety-five in the Commons the Government had actually lost a vote on the floor of the House the previous day. Nevertheless, Simon still could not envisage a general election for at least another two years.

On the business front Simon had advised Ronnie Nethercote not to allow his company shares to be traded on the Stock Exchange until the Tories returned to power. "The climate," he assured Ronnie, "should be much easier then."

Charles Seymour was glad to be behind the wheel again after his driving ban had been completed, and he had the grace to smile when Fiona showed him the photograph of the happy Mrs Blenkinsop displaying her OBE outside Buckingham Palace to a reporter from the *Sussex Gazette*.

It was six months to the day of his first meeting with Sir Roger Pelham that Raymond Gould received an account from the solicitor for services rendered – £500. He sent the cheque by return of post in a parcel that also contained a copy of the recently published edition of *Wisden*.

CHAPTER EIGHT

Andrew had been warned by his ministerial colleagues that the first day answering questions at the dispatch box would be an experience he was unlikely to forget.

Questions for the Scottish Office appear on the order paper once every four or five weeks, and each minister answers on behalf of his own department between two-thirty-five and three-fifteen. There are usually four or five ministers of the Crown, not including the law officer available to represent each great department of state. During the forty-minute to one-hour period the ministers would expect to reply to about twenty-five questions, but it is rarely the questions that are the problem; it is the supplementaries.

Any member can place a question through the table office to any minister, and can word it in a seemingly innocuous way. "When does the minister hope next to visit Aberdeen?" to which the minister concerned may reply anything from "next week" to "I have no plans to do so in the foreseeable future", – but when the member who put down the question rises from his seat to ask his supplementary he can change the subject completely. "Does the minister realise that Aberdeen has the highest rate of unemployment in the United Kingdom, and what new ideas does his department have to deal with this problem?" The hapless minister must then come up with a convincing reply on the spot.

In an attempt to see that a minister is adequately briefed, his department will spend the morning scrutinising each tabled question and looking for pitfalls he might encounter. A variety of possible supplementaries will be placed in his brief with appropriate answers. Ministers can, of course, always ask colleagues on their own side what they are hoping to find out from their tabled questions, but Opposition members use question time to test a minister in the hope of discovering some weakness in his armoury, thus making the Government appear incompetent.

Andrew spent a considerable time in preparation for his first encounter at the dispatch box although the more senior and experienced ministers in the Scottish Office had agreed to handle any questions that looked hostile.

He ended up having to respond to only one question from the Opposition benches, while fielding four from his own. Added to which, the timing was such that question number twenty-three from the Opposition member seemed unlikely to be reached by three-fifteen, when the Prime Minister would have to start answering questions himself.

Andrew's first four answers to questions numbers five, nine, eleven and fourteen, went smoothly enough. He opened his red file and was pleased to confirm the well-prepared briefs to everything that was thrown at him. By three-ten, when question number nineteen was being answered, Andrew sat back on the front bench and began to relax for the first time that day.

Harold Wilson entered a now packed Commons and, moving alongside the table in the centre of the Chamber, he crouched slightly to be sure he did not obscure the Speaker's view of the Government benches on his right. The Prime Minister had been left a place between the Chancellor and the Foreign Secretary and waited for the clock to reach three-fifteen.

The Speaker called question number twenty-one but the member was not present. He called number twenty-two and once again the member was absent. Each had obviously considered that their question had little chance of being reached before three-fifteen. At three-thirteen the Speaker called question twenty-three – Andrew's heart sank – which read on the order paper, "Had the minister been invited to visit the Kinross Nursing Home?"

Andrew rose, opened his folder and said, "No, sir."

"No one in the House will be surprised by the minister's reply," said George Younger, the member for Ayr, "because the nursing home has forty-nine occupants, forty-seven of whom have their own television sets and yet the minister demands forty-seven separate licence fees. If they were to congregate in one room, he would only expect one fee. Is this another example of the Labour Party's 'Care for the Aged' programme that we hear so much about nowadays?"

Andrew rose to the dispatch box to cries of "Answer, answer," from the Opposition benches. He had checked his crib sheet while sitting on the edge of his seat. Andrew had a prepared answer for medical facilities, old-age pensions, supplementary benefits, food allowances, medical charges – but nothing on TV licences. As he stood stranded at the dispatch box he was aware for the first time of the pitfalls that a minister encounters when he is not fully prepared. Such a system might appear wonderfully democratic to onlookers, he thought, until you are the Christian facing the 300 hungry lions.

A handwritten note was quickly passed along the front bench to him from one of the civil servants who sit in the official box to the left behind the Speaker's chair. With no time to consider its implications Andrew crossed his fingers and read the note out to the House.

"This was a decision taken by the last administration, of which the Honourable Gentleman was a member. We have seen no reason to reverse that decision," he read, thinking how much like a parrot he sounded. He sat down to polite Government murmurs and some considerable relief.

Mr Younger rose again and was allowed a second supplementary.

"Mr Speaker, this is the sort of inaccuracy we have grown to expect from this Government. The decision he refers to was made by his Right Honourable friend, the Secretary of State, only last year, and I think the minister will find, if he does his research more fastidiously, that his party was in power at the time." The Opposition howled their delight.

Andrew rose again and gripped the sides of the dispatch box to avoid anyone seeing that he was shaking in fear. Several members of the Government front bench had their heads bowed. The Opposition had drawn blood and were baying in triumph. Lord Attlee's words came back to Andrew. "When you are caught out by the House admit it, apologise, and sit down."

Andrew waited for the noise to subside before he replied. "The Secretary of State warned me that a new minister will never forget his first question time and I feel bound to agree with him." Andrew, who knew how the atmosphere in the House can change in a moment, felt such a moment now, and before it could turn back added, "On the question of television licences in the Kinross Nursing Home, I apologise to the Honourable Gentleman for Ayr for my mistake and I will look into the case immediately and send him a written reply within twenty-four hours." "Hear, hears" could now be heard from his own benches and the Opposition benches were quietened. Mr Younger was trying to interrupt again but as Andrew didn't give way he had to resume his seat, knowing the Speaker would not call on him again once the clock had passed three-fourteen. Andrew waited for silence before adding, "And I blame my grandmother for this who, as President of the Kinross Nursing Home and a staunch Conservative, has always believed in increasing old-age pensions rather than looking for false subsidies that can never be fair to everyone." By now the Labour members were laughing and all the heads on the front bench were looking towards the new minister, who remained at the dispatch box until the House was silent again. "My grandmother would be delighted to learn that this administration has raised that old-age pension by fifty per cent in the three years since we have taken office." The Labour back-benchers were now cheering and waving their order papers as Andrew resumed his seat, while the Opposition were silent and glum.

The hands of the clock touched three-fifteen and the Speaker said, "Prime Minister's questions."

Andrew Fraser had made a political reputation, and as the laughter echoed round the House the intense figure sitting on the end of the front bench put a hand through his red hair and wondered if he could ever match Andrew's skill at the dispatch box. On the Opposition back benches Simon Kerslake made a mental note to be cautious if he ever thought of putting a sharp question to Andrew Fraser.

As soon as Prime Minister's questions were over Simon left the House and drove himself to Whitechapel Road. He arrived a few minutes after the four o'clock board meeting of Nethercote and Company had begun, quietly took his seat and listened to Ronnie Nethercote describing another coup.

Ronnie had signed a contract that morning to take over a major city block at a cost of fifteen million pounds with a guaranteed rental income of over 1.1 million per annum for the first seven years of a twenty-one year lease with seven-year rent reviews.

Simon formally congratulated him and asked if this made any difference to the company's timing for going public.

"Why do you ask?" said Ronnie.

"Because I still feel it might be wise to wait until we know the result of the next general election. If the Conservatives return to power, as the opinion polls forecast, that could change the whole atmosphere for launching a new company."

"If they don't, I shan't hold up going public much longer."

"I wouldn't disagree with that decision either, Mr Chairman," said Simon.

When the meeting was over he joined Nethercote in his office for a drink.

"I want to thank you," Ronnie said, "for that introduction to Harold Samuel and Louis Freedman. It made the deal go through much more smoothly."

"Does that mean you'll allow me to purchase some more shares?"

Ronnie hesitated. "Why not? You've earned them. But only another 10,000. Don't get ahead of yourself, Simon, or the other directors may become jealous."

In the car on the way to pick up Elizabeth Simon decided to take a second mortgage out on the house in Beaufort Street to raise the extra cash needed for the new shares. He thought it might be wise not to trouble her with the details. He savoured the prospect of the Conservatives winning the next election, perhaps being given office in the Government and selling his shares for a sum that would make it possible for him to stop the continual worries of how he would finance his children's education. Perhaps he could even give Elizabeth that holiday in Venice she had talked about so often.

When he drove up to the hospital Elizabeth was waiting outside the gates. "We won't be late, will we?" were her first words.

"No," said Simon, checking the clock on the dashboard as he turned the car round in the direction of Beaufort Street.

They arrived at the hall five minutes before the curtain was due to rise. The occasion was their sons' pantomime, and both Peter and Michael had assured their parents that they had major parts. It was Charles Kingsley's *The Water Babies*, and Michael turned out to be a crab, who although he never left the stage lay on his stomach throughout the entire performance and never uttered a word. Peter, who had spent the week learning his words off by heart, was an unconvincing water baby standing at the end of a row of twelve. His speaking part turned out to be one sentence: "If grown-ups go on eating all the fish in the sea there will be none left for me." King Neptune fixed his imperial eye on Peter and said, "Don't blame us, it's your father who's the MP," upon which Peter bowed his head and blushed, though not as deeply as Elizabeth when the audience in front of them turned round and smiled at Simon, who felt more embarrassed than if he had been in the centre of a raging debate in the Commons.

At coffee afterwards the headmaster admitted that the sentence had been added without the approval of the late Charles Kingsley. When Simon and Elizabeth took the children home that night they insisted on repeating Peter's one line again and again.

"If the Government did an about-turn and devalued the pound, would the Under-Secretary find it possible to remain in office?"

Raymond Gould stiffened when he heard Simon Kerslake's question. His grasp of the law and his background knowledge of the subject made all except the extremely articulate or highly experienced wary of taking him on. Nevertheless Raymond had one Achilles' heel arising from his firmly stated views in *Full Employment at any Cost?*: any suggestion that the Government would devalue. Time and again eager back-benchers would seek to tackle him on the subject but once more it was Simon Kerslake who felled his opponent.

Andrew, sitting on the front bench, composed in his mind a sharp reply about his colleagues' collective responsibility, but Raymond Gould said rather ponderously: "The policy of Her Majesty's Government is one hundred per cent against devaluation, and therefore the question does not arise."

"Wait and see," shouted Kerslake.

"Order," said the Speaker, rising from his seat and turning towards Simon as Raymond sat down. "The Honourable Member knows all too well he must not address the House from a sedentary position. The Under-Secretary of State."

Raymond rose again. "This Government believes in a strong pound, which still remains our best hope for keeping unemployment figures down."

"But what would you do if Cabinet does go ahead and devalue?" Joyce asked him when she read her husband's reply to Kerslake's question reported in *The Times* the next morning.

Raymond was already facing the fact that devaluation looked more likely every day. A strong dollar causing imports to reach record levels coupled with a run of strikes during the summer of sixty-seven was causing foreign bankers to ask when, not if.

"I'd have to resign," he said in reply to Joyce's question.

"Why? No other minister will."

"I'm afraid Kerslake is right. I'm on the record and he's made sure everybody knows it. Don't worry, Harold will never devalue. He's assured me of that many times."

"He only has to change his mind once."

Pressure on the pound increased during the following weeks and Raymond began to fear that Joyce might turn out to be right.

Andrew Fraser had read *Full Employment at any Cost?* and considered it a succinctly argued case although he did not agree with all the small print. He personally was in favour of devaluation but felt it should have been pushed through in the Labour Party's first week in office, so that the blame could be left at the door of the Tories. After three years and a second election victory any such suggestion would rightly be considered outrageous.

As Louise's time of delivery approached she was getting larger by the day. Andrew helped to take pressure off her as much as he could, but this time he did not prepare so obviously for the birth, as he felt his unbridled enthusiasm might have contributed to her previous anxiety. He tried as often as possible to bring the red boxes home each night, but it remained an exception if he returned to Cheyne Walk before eleven o'clock.

"Voting every night at ten o'clock and sometimes on through the night into the next day is one system the rest of the world has *not* considered worth emulating," Andrew had told Louise after one particularly gruelling session. He couldn't even remember what he had been voting on – although he didn't admit that to her. "But as no Government of whatever party has ever seriously considered the idea of limiting the time for ending business 'the troops', as back-benchers are known, go on charging through the lobbies day in and day out. That's why the press refer to us as 'lobby fodder'."

"More like a bunch of unruly children," she chided.

When Louise went into hospital one week early Elizabeth Kerslake assured her there was nothing to be worried about, and two days later Louise gave birth to a beautiful girl.

Andrew was in a departmental meeting discussing Glasgow's high-rise housing programme when the hospital staff nurse rang to congratulate him. He went straight to his fridge and took out the bottle of champagne his father had sent him the day he joined the Scottish Office. He poured a plastic mug of Krug for each of his team of advisers.

"Just better than drinking it out of the bottle," he suggested as he left his civil servants to go to the hospital.

On arrival at St Mary's Andrew was relieved to find Elizabeth Kerslake was on duty. She warned him that his wife was still under sedation after a particularly complicated Caesarian delivery. Elizabeth took him to see his daughter who remained under observation in an isolation unit.

"Nothing to fret about," Elizabeth assured him. "We always take this precaution after any Caesarian birth as there are a number of routine tests we still have to carry out."

She left Andrew to stare at his daughter's large blue eyes. Although he knew it might change in time the soft down on the crown of her head was already dark.

He slipped out an hour later when she had fallen asleep to return to Dover House, where he had a second celebration in the Secretary of State's office, but this time the champagne was served in crystal glasses.

When Andrew climbed into bed that night the champagne helped him fall into a deep sleep with the only problem on his mind being what they should call their daughter. Claire had always been the name Louise favoured.

The phone had rung several times before he answered it and as soon as he had replaced the receiver he dressed and drove to the hospital as quickly as possible. He parked the car and ran to the now-familiar ward. Elizabeth Kerslake was standing waiting by the door. She looked tired and dishevelled, and even with all her training and experience she found it hard to explain to Andrew what had happened.

"Your daughter died forty minutes ago when her heart stopped beating. Believe me, we tried everything."

Andrew collapsed on the bench in the corridor and didn't speak for several moments. "How's Louise?" was all he could eventually manage.

"She hasn't been told yet. She's still under sedation. Be thankful she never saw the baby."

Andrew thumped his leg until it was numb. He stopped suddenly. "I'll tell her myself," he said quietly and remained on the bench, tears coursing down his cheeks. Elizabeth sat down beside him but didn't speak. When she left it was only to check that Mrs Fraser was ready to see her husband.

Louise knew the moment Andrew walked in. It was over an hour before she managed to speak.

"I bet Alison McKenzie would have given you a dozen sons," she said, trying to make him smile.

"No doubt about that," said Andrew, "but they would have all been ugly and stupid."

"I agree with you," said Louise. "But that wouldn't have been her fault."

They both tried to laugh.

Andrew returned to Cheyne Walk a little after four o'clock, but he didn't sleep again that night.

The great orator Iain Macleod once remarked that it was the first two minutes of a speech that decided one's fate. One either grasps the House and commands it or dithers, and loses it, and once the House is lost it can rarely be brought to heel. When Charles Seymour was invited to present the winding-up speech for the Opposition during the Economic debate, he felt he had prepared himself well, and although he knew he could not expect to convert Government back-benchers to his argument he hoped the press would acknowledge the following day that he had won the argument and embarrassed the Government. The Administration was already rocking over daily rumours of devaluation and economic trouble, and Charles was confident that this was the chance to make his name.

Full parliamentary debates usually start at three-thirty, after question time, but can be delayed if there are ministerial statements to be made. The senior minister in the department concerned makes the opening speech for approximately thirty minutes and then the Opposition spokesman addresses the House for the same period of time. Between four-thirty and nine the debate is thrown open to the floor and the Speaker tries to be scrupulously fair in calling a cross-section of back-benchers who have demonstrated an interest in the subject, as well as preserving a party and regional balance. These back-bencher speeches are frowned on if they last for more than fifteen minutes. Some of the most memorable speeches delivered in the House have lasted eight or nine minutes, some of the worst over thirty.

At nine o'clock the Opposition spokesman makes his final comments, and at nine-thirty a Government minister winds up.

When Charles rose and stood at the dispatch box he intended to press home the Tory case on the Government's economic record, the fatal consequences of devaluation, the record inflation, coupled with record borrowing and a lack of confidence in Britain unknown in any member's lifetime.

He stood his full height and stared down belligerently at the Government benches.

"Mr Speaker," he began, "I can't think . . ."

"Then don't bother to speak," someone shouted from the Labour benches. Laughter broke out as Charles tried to compose himself, cursing his initial over-confidence. He began again.

"I can't imagine . . ."

"No imagination either," came another voice. "Typical Tory."

". . . why this motion was ever put before the House."

"Certainly not for you to give us a lesson in public speaking."

"Order," growled the Speaker, but it was too late.

The House was lost and Charles stumbled through thirty minutes of embarrassment until no one but the Speaker was listening to a word he said. Several members of his own front bench had their feet up on the table and their eyes closed. Back-benchers on either side sat chattering amongst themselves waiting for the ten o'clock division: the ultimate humiliation the House affords to its worst debaters. The Speaker had to call for order several times during Charles's speech, once rising to rebuke noisy members, "The House does its reputation no service by behaving in this way." But his plea fell on deaf ears as the conversations continued. At nine-thirty Charles sat down in a cold sweat. A few of his own back-benchers managed to raise an unconvincing "Hear, hear."

When the Government minister opened his speech by describing Charles's offering as among the most pathetic he had heard in a long political career he may well have been exaggerating, but from the expressions on the Tory front benches not many Opposition members were going to disagree with him.

CHAPTER NINE

The decision was finally made by the inner Cabinet of twelve on Thursday 16 November 1967. By Friday every bank clerk in Tokyo was privy to the inner Cabinet's closest secret, and by the time the Prime Minister made the announcement official on Saturday afternoon the Bank of England had lost 600 million dollars of reserves on the foreign exchange market.

At the time of the Prime Minister's statement Raymond was in Leeds conducting one of his fortnightly constituency "surgeries". He was in the process of explaining the new housing bill to a young married couple when Fred Padgett, his agent, burst into the room.

"Raymond, sorry to interrupt you, but I thought you'd want to know immediately. No. 10 have just announced that the pound has been devalued from two dollars eighty to two dollars forty." The sitting member was momentarily stunned, the local housing problem driven from his mind. He stared blankly across the table at the two constituents who had come to seek his advice.

"Will you please excuse me for a moment, Mr Higginbottom," Raymond asked courteously, "but I must make a phone call." The moment turned out to be fifteen minutes, in which time Raymond had made contact with a senior civil servant from the Treasury and had all the details confirmed. He called Joyce and told her not to answer the phone until he arrived back home. It was several minutes before he felt composed enough to put his head round the office door.

"How many people are still waiting to see me, Fred?" he asked.

"After the Higginbottoms there's only the mad major, still convinced that Martians are about to land on the roof of Leeds town hall."

"Why would they want to come to Leeds first?" asked Raymond, trying to hide his anxiety with false humour.

"Once they've captured Yorkshire, the rest would be easy."

"Hard to find fault with that argument. Nevertheless, tell the major I'm deeply concerned but I need to study his claim in more detail and to seek further advice from the Ministry of Defence. Make an appointment for him to see me at the next surgery and by then I should have a strategic plan ready for him."

Fred Padgett grinned. "That will give him something to tell his friends about for at least two weeks."

Raymond returned to Mr and Mrs Higginbottom and assured them he would have their housing problem sorted out within a few days. He made a note on his file to ring the Leeds Borough Housing Officer.

"What an afternoon," exclaimed Raymond after the door had closed behind them. "One wife-beating, one electricity turned off by the YEB with four children under ten in the house, one pollution of the Aire river and one appalling housing problem – never forgetting the mad major and his itinerant Martians. And on top of all of that the devaluation news."

"How can you remain so calm?" asked Fred Padgett.

"Because I can't afford to let anyone know how I really feel."

After his surgery Raymond would normally have gone round to the local pub for a pint and an obligatory natter with the locals. This always gave him the chance to catch up on what had been happening in Leeds during the past fortnight. But on this occasion he bypassed the pub and returned quickly to his parents' home.

Joyce told him that the phone had rung so often that she had finally taken it off the hook, without letting his mother know the real reason.

"Very sensible," said Raymond.

"What are you going to do?" she asked.

"I shall resign, of course."

"Why do that, Raymond? It will only harm your career."

"You may turn out to be right, but that won't stop me going."

"But you're only just beginning to get on top of your work."

"Joyce, without trying to sound pompous, I know I have many failings but I'm not a coward and I'm certainly not so self-seeking as totally to desert any principles I might have."

"You know, you just sounded like a man who is destined to become Prime Minister."

"A moment ago you said it would harm my chances. Make up your mind."

"I have," she said.

Raymond smiled wanly before retreating to his study to write a short handwritten letter.

Saturday, 18 November 1967

Dear Prime Minister,

After your announcement this afternoon on devaluation and the stand I have continually taken on the issue I am left with no choice but to resign my position as Under-Secretary of State at the Department of Employment.

I would like to thank you for having given me the opportunity to serve in your administration. Be assured that I shall continue to

support the Government on all other issues from the back
benches.

> Yours,
> Raymond Gould.

When the red box arrived at the house that Saturday night Raymond
instructed the messenger to deliver the letter to No. 10 immediately. As
he opened the box for the last time he reflected that his department was
answering questions on employment in the House that Monday. He
wondered who would take his place.

Because of the paraphernalia surrounding devaluation, the Prime
Minister did not get round to reading Raymond's letter until late
Sunday morning. The Goulds' phone was still off the hook when an
anxious Fred Padgett was heard knocking on the front door later that
day.

"Don't answer it," said Raymond. "It's bound to be another
journalist."

"No, it's not, it's only Fred," said Joyce, peeping through an opening
in the curtain.

She opened the door. "Where the hell's Raymond?" were Fred's first
words.

"Right here," said Raymond, appearing from the kitchen holding
the Sunday newspapers.

"The Prime Minister has been trying to contact you all morning."
Raymond turned round and replaced the phone on the hook, picked it
up a few seconds later and checked the tone before dialling London
WHI4433. The Prime Minister was on the line in moments. He
sounded calm enough, thought Raymond.

"Have you issued any statement to the press, Ray?"

"No, I wanted to be sure you had received my letter first."

"Good. Please don't mention your resignation to anyone until we've
met. Could you be at Downing Street by eight o'clock?"

"Yes, Prime Minister."

"Remember, not a word to the press."

Raymond heard the phone click.

Within the hour he was on his way to London, and arrived at his
house in Lansdowne Road a little after seven. The phone was ringing
again. He wanted to ignore the insistent *burr-burr* but thought it might
be Downing Street.

He picked the phone up. "Hello."

"Is that Raymond Gould?" said a voice.

"Who's speaking?" asked Raymond.

"Walter Terry, *Daily Mail*."

"I am not going to say anything," said Raymond.

"Do you feel the Prime Minister was right to devalue?"

"I said nothing, Walter."

"Does that mean you are going to resign?"

"Walter nothing."

"Is it true you have already handed in your resignation?"

Raymond hesitated.

"I thought so," said Terry.

"I said nothing," spluttered Raymond and slammed down the phone – before lifting it back off the hook.

He quickly washed and change his shirt before leaving the house. He nearly missed the note that was lying on the doormat, and he wouldn't have stopped to open it had the envelope not been embossed with large black letters across the left-hand corner – "Prime Minister". Raymond ripped it open. The handwritten note from a secretary asked him on his arrival to come by the rear entrance of Downing Street and not the front door. A small map was enclosed. Raymond was becoming weary of the whole exercise.

Two more journalists were waiting by the gate and followed him to his car.

"Have you resigned, Minister?" asked the first.

"No comment."

"Are you on your way to see the Prime Minister?"

Raymond did not reply and leaped into his car. He drove off so quickly that the pursuing journalists were left with no chance of catching him.

Twelve minutes later, at five to eight, he was seated in the ante-room of No. 10 Downing Street. As eight struck he was taken through to Harold Wilson's study. He was surprised to find the Secretary of State for Employment seated in the corner of the room.

"Ray," said the Prime Minister. "How are you?"

"I'm well, thank you, Prime Minister."

"I was sorry to receive your letter and thoroughly understand the position you are in, but I hope perhaps we can work something out."

"Work something out?" Raymond repeated, puzzled.

"Well, we all realise devaluation is a problem for you after *Full Employment at any Cost?* but I felt perhaps a move to the Foreign Office as Minister of State might be a palatable way out of the dilemma. It's a promotion you've well earned."

Raymond hesitated. The Prime Minister continued. "It may interest you to know that the Chancellor of the Exchequer has also resigned, but will be moving to the Home Office."

"I am surprised," said Raymond.

"What with the problems we are about to tackle in Rhodesia and Europe your legal skills would come in very useful."

Raymond remained silent as he listened to the Prime Minister; he knew what decision he must now make.

Monday usually gets off to a quiet start in the Commons. The Whips never plan for any contentious business to be debated, remembering that members are still arriving back from their constituencies all over the country. The House is seldom full before the early evening. But the knowledge that the Chancellor of the Exchequer would be making a statement on devaluation at three-thirty ensured that the Commons would be packed long before that hour.

The green benches accommodating just 427 members, had deliberately been restored as they were after the Germans had bombed the Palace of Westminster on 10 May 1941. The intimate theatrical atmosphere of the House had remained intact. Sir Giles Gilbert Scott could not resist highlighting some of the Gothic décor of Barry, but he concurred with Churchill's view that to enlarge the Chamber would only destroy the packed atmosphere of great occasions.

The Commons filled up quickly, and by two-forty-five there was not a seat to be found. Members huddled up on the steps by the Speaker's canopied chair and around the legs of the chairs of the clerks at the table. One or two even perched like unfed sparrows on the empty petition bag behind the Speaker's chair. The galleries to the side and above the Chamber, which normally resembled empty benches at the Oval on a rainy day, had taken on the look of a crucial last Test match against Australia.

The chief doorkeeper checked his supply of snuff that it had been his office to keep since those days when "unpleasant odours" wafted through London.

Raymond Gould rose to answer question number seven on the order paper, an innocent enough inquiry concerning supplementary benefits for women. As soon as he reached the dispatch box the first cries of "Resign" came from the Tory benches. Raymond couldn't hide his embarrassment. Even those seated on the back benches could see he had gone scarlet. It didn't help that he hadn't slept the previous night following the agreement he had come to with the Prime Minister. He answered the question, but the calls for his resignation did not subside. The Opposition fell silent as he sat down only waiting for him to rise for a further question. The next question on the order paper for Raymond to answer was from Simon Kerslake; it came a few minutes after three. "What analysis has been made by his department of the special factors contributing to increasing unemployment in the Midlands?"

Raymond checked his brief before replying. "The closure of two large factories in the area, one in the Honourable Member's constituency, has exacerbated local unemployment. Both of these factories specialised in car components which have suffered from the Leyland strike."

Simon Kerslake rose slowly from his place to put his supplementary.

The Opposition benches waited in eager anticipation. "But surely the minister remembers informing the House, in reply to my adjournment debate last April, that devaluation would drastically increase unemployment in the Midlands, indeed in the whole country. If the Honourable Gentleman's words are to carry any conviction, why hasn't he resigned?" Simon sat down as the Tory benches demanded, "Why, why, why?"

"My speech to the House on that occasion is being quoted out of context, and the circumstances have since changed."

"They certainly have," shouted a number of Conservatives and the benches opposite Raymond exploded with demands that he give up his office.

"Order, order," shouted the Speaker into the tide of noise.

Simon rose again, while everyone on the Conservative benches remained seated to ensure no one else was called. They were now hunting as a pack. Everyone's eyes switched back and forth between the two men, watching the dark, assured figure of Kerslake once again jabbing his forefinger at the bowed head of Raymond Gould who was now only praying for the clock to reach three-thirty.

"Mr Speaker, during the debate, which he now seems happy to orphan, the Honourable Gentleman was only echoing the views he so lucidly expressed in his book *Full Employment at any Cost?* Can those views have altered so radically in three years, or is his desire to remain a minister so great that he now realises that *his* employment can be retained at any cost?"

"This question has nothing to do with what I said to the House on that occasion," retorted Raymond angrily. His last few words were lost in Opposition shouts of "Resign, resign!"

Simon was up in a flash and the Speaker called him for a third time.

"Is the Honourable Gentleman telling the House that he has one set of moral standards when he speaks, and yet another when he writes?"

The House was now in total uproar and few members heard Raymond say, "No, sir, I try to be consistent."

The Speaker rose and the noise subsided slightly. He looked about him with an aggrieved frown. "I realise the House feels strongly on these matters, but I must ask the Honourable Member for Coventry Central to withdraw his remark suggesting that the minister has behaved dishonourably."

Simon rose and retracted his statement at once, but the damage had been done. Nor did it stop members from calling "Resign" until Raymond left the Chamber a few minutes later.

Simon sat back smugly as Gould left the Chamber. Conservative members turned to nod their acknowledgement of his professional demolition of the Government's Under-Secretary of State. The Chancellor of the Exchequer rose to deliver his prepared statement on devaluation. Simon felt sick as he listened with horror to the Chancellor's opening words. "The Honourable Member for Leeds North handed in his resignation to the Prime Minister on Saturday evening but graciously agreed not to make this public until I had had an opportunity to address the House."

The Chancellor went on to praise Raymond for his work in the Department of Employment, and to wish him well on the back benches.

Andrew visited Raymond in his room immediately after the Chancellor had finished answering questions. He found him slumped at his desk, a vacant look on his face. Andrew had never considered Raymond a natural friend but he wanted to express his admiration for the way he had conducted himself.

"It's kind of you," said Raymond, who was still shaking from the experience. "Particularly as you would have demolished the lot of them."

"Well, they're all demolished now," said Andrew. "Simon Kerslake must feel the biggest shit in town."

"There's no way he could have known," said Raymond. "He'd certainly done his homework and the questions were spot on. I suspect we would have approached the situation in much the same way given the circumstances."

Several other members dropped in to commiserate with Raymond after which he returned to his old department to say farewell to his team before he went home to spend a quiet evening with Joyce. There was a long silence before the Permanent Secretary ventured an opinion: "I hope, sir, it will not be long before you return to Government. You have certainly made our lives hard but for those you ultimately serve you have undoubtedly made life easier." The sincerity of the statement touched Raymond, especially as the civil servant was already serving a new master.

It felt strange to sit down and watch television, read a book, even go for a walk and not be perpetually surrounded by red boxes and ringing phones. Within forty-eight hours he missed it all.

He was to receive over a hundred letters from colleagues in the House but he kept only one.

Monday, 20 November 1967

Dear Gould,

I owe you a profound apology. We all in our political life make monumental mistakes about people and I certainly made one today.

I believe that most members of the House have a genuine desire to serve the country, and there can be no more honourable way of proving it than by resigning when one feels one's party has taken a wrong course.

I envy the respect in which the whole House now holds you.
                              Yours sincerely,
                              Simon Kerslake.

When Raymond returned to the Commons that afternoon, he was cheered by the members of both sides from the moment he entered the Chamber. The minister who had been in the middle of addressing the House at the time had no choice but to wait until Raymond had taken his seat on the back benches.

CHAPTER TEN

Simon had already left when Edward Heath called his home. It was another hour before Elizabeth was able to pass on the message that the party leader wanted to see him at two-thirty.

Charles was at the bank when the Chief Whip called, asking if they could meet at two-thirty that afternoon before Commons business began. Charles felt like a schoolboy who had been told the headmaster expected him to be in his study after lunch. The last time the Chief Whip had phoned was to ask him to make the winding-up speech and they had hardly spoken since. Charles remained apprehensive; he always preferred to be told what a problem was immediately.

He decided to skip lunch at the bank and join his colleagues in the House, to be certain he wouldn't be late for the afternoon appointment.

Charles did not enjoy eating at the House as the food, with the exception of the *hors d'oeuvres* trolley, was only a little better than Paddington station and rather worse than London airport.

He joined some of his colleagues at the large table in the centre of the Members' Dining-room and took the only seat available, next to Simon Kerslake. The two men had not really been on good terms since the Heath–Maudling leadership contest. Charles did not care much for Kerslake: he had once told Fiona that he was one of the new breed of Tories who tried a little too hard and he had not been displeased to see him embarrassed over the Gould resignation. Not that he allowed anyone other than Fiona to know his true feelings.

Simon watched Charles sit down and wondered how much longer the party could go on electing Etonian guardsmen who spent more time making money in the City and spending it at Ascot than they did working in the House – not that it was an opinion he would have expressed to anyone but his closest friend. The discussion over lunch centred on the remarkable run of by-election results the Tories had had at Acton, Meriden and Dudley. It was obvious that most of those around the table could not wait for a general election, although the Prime Minister did not have to call one for at least another three years.

Neither Charles nor Simon ordered coffee.

At two-twenty-five Charles watched the Chief Whip leave his private table in the corner of the room and turn to walk towards his office. Charles checked his watch and waited a moment before leaving his colleagues to begin a heated discussion about entry into the Common Market.

He strolled past the smoking room before turning left at the entrance to the library. Then he continued down the old Ways and Means corridor until he passed the Opposition Whips' office on his left. Once through the swing doors he entered the Members' Lobby which he crossed to reach the Government Whips' office. He put his head round the secretary's door. Miss Norse OBE, the Chief's invaluable secretary, stopped typing.

"I have an appointment with the Chief Whip," said Charles.

"Yes, Mr Seymour, he is expecting you. Please go through." The typing recommenced immediately.

Charles walked on down the corridor and found the Chief Whip blocking his own doorway.

"Come on in, Charles. Can I offer you a drink?"

"No, thank you," replied Charles, not wanting to delay the news any longer.

The Chief Whip poured himself a gin and tonic before sitting down.

"I hope what I'm about to tell you will be looked upon as good news." The Chief Whip paused and took a gulp of his drink. "The leader thinks you might benefit from a spell in the Whips' office, and I must say I would be delighted if you felt able to join us . . ."

Charles wanted to protest but checked himself. "And give up my Environment post?"

"Oh yes, and more of course, because Mr Heath expects all Whips to forgo outside commitments. Working in this office is not a part-time occupation."

Charles needed a moment to compose his thoughts. "And if I turn it down, will I keep my post at Environment?"

"That's not for me to decide,' said the Chief Whip, "but it is no secret that Ted Heath is planning several changes in the run-up to the election."

"How long do I have to consider the offer?"

"Perhaps you could let me know your decision by question time tomorrow."

"Yes, of course. Thank you," said Charles. He left the Chief Whip's office and drove to Eaton Square.

Simon arrived at two-twenty-five, five minutes before his meeting with the party leader. He had tried not to speculate as to why Heath wanted to see him, in case the meeting only resulted in disappointment. Douglas Hurd, the head of the private office, ushered him straight through to the Conservative leader.

"Simon, how would you like to join the Environment team in the run-up to the election?" It was typical of Heath not to waste any time on small talk and the suddenness of the offer stunned Simon. He recovered quickly.

"Thank you very much," he said. "I mean er . . . yes . . . thank you."

"Good, let's see you put your back into it, and be sure the results at the dispatch box are as effective as they have been from the back benches."

The door was opened once again by the private secretary; the interview was clearly over. Simon found himself back in the corridor at two-thirty-three. It was several moments before the offer sank in. Then he suddenly felt elated and made a dash for the nearest phone. He dialled the St Mary's switchboard and asked if he could be put through to Dr Kerslake. As he spoke, his voice was almost drowned by the sound of the division bells, signalling the start of the day's business at two-thirty-five following prayers. A woman's voice came on the line.

"Is that you, darling?" asked Simon above the din.

"No, sir. It's the switchboard operator. Dr Kerslake's in the operating theatre."

"Is there any hope of getting her out?"

"Not unless you're expecting a baby, sir."

"What brings you home so early?" asked Fiona as Charles came charging through the front door.

"I need to talk to someone." Fiona could never be sure if she ought to be flattered, but she didn't express any opinion as it was all too rare these days to have his company at all.

Charles repeated to his wife as nearly verbatim as possible his conversation with the Chief Whip. Fiona remained silent when Charles had come to the end of his monologue. "Well, what's your opinion?" he asked anxiously.

"All because of one bad speech from the dispatch box," Fiona commented wryly.

"I agree," said Charles, "but nothing can be gained by tramping over that ground again."

"We'll miss the salary you earn as a director of the bank," said Fiona. "The tax on my private income has made the amount I now receive derisory."

"I know, but if I turn it down, and we win the next election . . .?"

"You'll be left out in the cold."

"More to the point, stranded on the back benches."

"Charles, politics has always been your first love," said Fiona, touching him gently on the cheek. "So I don't see that you have a choice, and if that means some sacrifices you'll never hear me complain."

Charles rose from his seat saying, "Thank you. I'd better go and see Derek Spencer immediately."

As Charles turned to leave, Fiona added, "And don't forget, Ted Heath became leader of the party via the Whips' office."

Charles smiled for the first time that day.

"A quiet dinner at home tonight?" suggested Fiona.

"Can't," said Charles. "I've got a late vote."

Fiona sat alone wondering if she would spend the rest of her life cohabiting with three-line whips.

At last they put him through.

"Let's have a celebration dinner tonight."

"Why?" asked Elizabeth.

"Because I've been invited to join the front-bench team to cover the Environment."

"Congratulations, darling, but what does Environment consist of?"

"Housing, urban land, transport, devolution, water, historic buildings, Stansted or Maplin airport, the Channel tunnel, royal parks . . ."

"Have they left anything for anyone else to do?"

"That's only half of it, if it's out of doors it's mine. I'll tell you the rest over dinner."

"Oh, hell, I don't think I can get away until eight tonight, and we'd still have to get a baby-sitter. Does that come under Environment, Simon?"

"Sure does," he said, laughing. "I'll fix it and book a table at the Grange for eight-thirty."

"Have you got a ten o'clock vote?"

"Afraid so."

"I see, coffee with the baby-sitter," she said. She paused. "Simon."

"Yes, darling."

"I'm very proud of you."

Derek Spencer sat behind his massive partner's desk in Cheapside and listened intently to what Charles had to say.

"You will be a great loss to the bank," were the chairman's first words. "But no one here would want to hold up your political career, least of all me."

Charles noticed that Spencer could not look him in the eye as he spoke.

"Can I assume that I would be invited back on the board if for any reason my situation changed at the Commons?"

"Of course," said Spencer. "There was no need for you to ask such a question."

"That's kind of you," said Charles, genuinely relieved. He stood up, leaned forward and shook hands rather stiffly.

"Good luck, Charles," were Spencer's parting words.

"Does that mean you can no longer remain on the board?" asked Ronnie Nethercote when he heard Simon's news.

"No, not while I'm in Opposition and only a Shadow spokesman. Only the Chief Whip receives a salary and is therefore disqualified, but if we win the next election and I'm offered a job in Government I would have to resign immediately."

"So I've got your services for another three years?"

"Unless the Prime Minister goes earlier, or we lose the next election."

"No fear of the latter," said Ronnie. "I knew I'd picked a winner the day I met you, and I don't think you'll ever regret joining my board."

Over the months that followed Charles was surprised to find how much he enjoyed working in the Whips' office, although he had been unable to hide from Fiona his anger at Kerslake taking over his shadow post at Environment. The order, discipline and *camaraderie* of the job brought back memories of his days in the Grenadier Guards. His duties were manifold and ranged from checking that members were all present in their committees to sitting on the front bench in the Commons and picking out the salient points members made in their speeches to the House. He also had to keep an eye out for any signs of dissension or rebellion on his own benches while remaining abreast of what was happening on the other side of the House. In addition he had fifty of his own members from the Midlands area to shepherd, and had to be certain that they never missed a vote unless paired, and only then when the Whips' office had been informed.

As Whips are never called on to make speeches in the House at any time Charles seemed to have discovered a role for which he was best cut out. Fiona reminded him once again that Ted Heath had jumped from the Whips' office to become Shadow Chancellor. She was delighted to see how involved her husband had become with Commons life but still hated going to bed alone each night and regularly falling asleep before he had even arrived home.

Simon also enjoyed his new appointment from the first moment. As the junior member of the Environment team he was given transport as his special subject. During the first year he read books, studied pamphlets, held meetings with national transport chairmen from air, sea and rail and frequently worked long into the night trying to master his new brief. Simon was one of those rare members who, after only a few weeks, looked as if he had always been on the front bench.

Both parties were surprised by the fourteen per cent swing to the Conservatives at the Louth by-election towards the end of 1969. It began to look as if the Labour party did not have enough time to recover before they had to call an election. But in March 1970 the Labour party had a surprisingly good result in the Ayrshire South by-election; it caused the press to speculate that the Prime Minister might go to the country early. The May local elections in England and Wales showed a further swing to Labour, which was contrary to every other political trend of the previous two years. Talk of a general election was suddenly in the air.

When the following month's opinion polls confirmed the swing to Labour Harold Wilson visited the Queen at Buckingham Palace and asked her to dissolve Parliament. The date of the general election was set for 18 June 1970.

The press were convinced that Wilson had got it right again, and would lead his party to victory for the third time in a row, a feat no man in political history had managed. Every Conservative knew that would spell the end of Edward Heath's leadership of his party.

Andrew and Louise returned to Edinburgh as soon as the Queen had made the announcement. Parliament went into a limbo period while members dispersed all over the country only in order to try and return to Westminster.

Andrew found his local committee had been taken by surprise by the PM's announcement, and realised he only had a matter of days to prepare himself.

The evening he arrived back in Edinburgh he called his General Purposes Committee together and over coffee and sandwiches mapped out a demanding three-week timetable which would allow him to reach every part of the constituency not once but several times. Street cards were pinned on to an old trestle table, soon to be filled in with crayon of various colours according to the canvassing returns: a red line through a definite Labour vote, a blue line through a Conservative one, a yellow through a Liberal and a black line through the growing Scottish Nationalist party.

Andrew began each day of the campaign with a press conference at which he discussed local matters that affected his constituents, answered criticisms made by the other candidates and dealt with any national issues that had arisen during the previous twenty-four hours. He then spent the rest of the morning touring the constituency with a loudspeaker van, entreating people to "Send Fraser back to Westminster". He and Louise would fit in a pub lunch together before the dreaded door-to-door canvassing began.

"You'll enjoy this," said Andrew as they walked up to the first door on a cold Monday morning. The street list of names was on a card in his pocket. Andrew pressed the door bell, and a little jingle could be heard. A woman still in her dressing-gown answered it a few moments later.

"Good morning, Mrs Foster," he began. "My name is Andrew Fraser. I'm your Labour candidate."

"Oh, how nice to meet you. I have so much I need to discuss with you – won't you come in and have a cup of tea?"

"It's kind of you, Mrs Foster, but I have rather a lot of ground to cover during the next few days." When the door closed, Andrew put a blue line through her name on his card.

"How can you be sure she's Conservative?" demanded Louise, "she seemed so friendly."

"The Conservatives are trained to ask all the other candidates in for tea and waste their time. Your own side will always say, 'You have my vote, don't spend your time with me,' and let you get on to those who are genuinely uncommitted."

"I always vote for Fraser," said Mrs Foster's next-door neighbour. "Labour for parliament, Tory for the local council."

"But don't you feel Sir Duncan should be removed from the council?" asked Andrew, grinning.

"Certainly not, and that's what I told him when he suggested I shouldn't vote for you."

Andrew put a red line through the name and knocked on the next door.

"My name is Andrew Fraser and I –"

"I know who you are, young man, and I'll have none of your politics, or your father's for that matter."

"May I ask who you will be voting for?" asked Andrew.

"Scottish Nationalist."

"Why?" asked Louise.

"Because the oil belongs to us, not those bloody Sassenachs."

"Surely it's better for the United Kingdom to remain as one body?" suggested Andrew. "At least that way –"

"Never. The Act of 1707 was a disgrace to our nation."

"But –" began Louise enthusiastically. Andrew put a hand on her arm. "Thank you, sir, for your time," and prodded his wife gently down the path.

"Sorry, Louise," said Andrew, when they were back on the pavement. "Once they mention the 1707 Act of Union we have no chance; some Scots have remarkably long memories."

He knocked on the next door. A fat man answered it, a dog lead in his hand.

"My name is Andrew Fraser, I –"

"Get lost, creep," came back the reply.

"Who are you calling creep?" Louise retaliated as the door was slammed in their faces. "Charming man."

"Don't be offended, darling. He was referring to me, not you."

"What will you put by his name?"

"A question mark. No way of telling who he votes for. Probably abstains."

He tried the next door.

"Hello, Andrew," said a lady before he could open his mouth. "Don't waste your time on me, I always vote for you."

"Thank you, Mrs Irvine," said Andrew, checking his house list. "What about your next-door neighbour?" he asked, pointing back.

"Ah, he's an irritable old basket, but I'll see he gets to the polls on the day and puts his cross in the right box. He'd better, or I'll stop keeping an eye on his greyhound for him when he's out."

"Thank you very much, Mrs Irvine," said Andrew, laughing.

"One more red," he told Louise as they returned to the pavement.

"And you might even pick up the greyhound vote."

They covered four streets during the next three hours, and Andrew put red lines through those names he was certain would support him on polling day.

"Why do you have to be so sure?" asked Louise.

"Because when we pick them up to vote on election day we don't want to remind the opposition, let alone arrange a lift for someone who then takes pleasure in voting Tory."

Louise laughed. "Politics is so dishonest."

"Be relieved you're not married to an American senator," said Andrew, putting a red line through the last name in the street. "At least we don't have to be millionaires to stand. Time for a quick bite before the evening meeting," he added, taking his wife's hand. On their way back to their headquarters they came across their Conservative opponent, but Andrew didn't respond when Hector McGregor tried to engage him in conversation, again holding him up.

Louise never joined her husband again on these sessions, deciding she could be of more use working back in the Committee Rooms.

In the public meetings held each evening, Andrew made the same speech thirty-two times in twenty-four days with only slight variations to account for national developments. Louise sat loyally through every one of them, always laughing at his punch lines and starting the clapping whenever he made a telling point. Somehow she managed to remain fresh and lively even at the end of the day when she drove her husband home.

By the eve of the election all the press were predicting a clear majority for Labour, but Andrew observed the gleam in his father's eye when he passed him in the street canvassing for McGregor.

At five-thirty on the morning of the election Louise woke Andrew with a cup of tea. He didn't see another cup that day. To his relief the sun was shining when he pulled back the curtains after he had had his bath: bad weather invariably helped the Tories with their never-ending pool of cars, ferrying voters to the polling booths. He returned to the bedroom to find his wife pinning to the lapel of his jacket a vast red rosette bearing the exhortation, "Send Fraser back to Westminster".

He was strolling through the streets of Edinburgh shaking hands, chatting to well-wishers, trying to convince last-minute "don't knows" when he spotted his father heading towards him. They ended up facing each other in the middle of the street.

"It's going to be a close-run thing," said Sir Duncan.

"Then I'll know who to blame if I lose by one vote," said Andrew.

Sir Duncan looked conspiratorially about him, then lowered his voice. "If you win by one vote you'll have me to thank, laddie." He marched away entreating the citizens of Edinburgh to remove the turncoat Fraser.

The next time father and son met was at the count that evening. As the little piles of votes began to grow it became obvious that Andrew would be returned to Parliament, and Hector McGregor was soon shaking his head in disappointment.

But when the first result was announced in Guildford and showed a four per cent swing to the Tories all the previous predictions of a strong Labour victory began to look unrealistic. As each return was announced from town hall platforms all over the country it became progressively more obvious that the Tories were going to end up with a large enough majority to govern.

"I would have thought," Sir Duncan said to his son as the trend was confirmed across the nation, "that you'll be in for a wee spell of Opposition."

"Wee is the important word," was all that Andrew replied.

Andrew retained his seat, keeping the swing against him down to one per cent and his majority a safe 4,009. Scotland wasn't as sure about Heath as the rest of the country, which showed an average swing against Labour of 4.7 per cent.

Simon Kerslake managed a four-figure majority for the first time when he won Coventry Central by 2,118.

When Fiona was asked by the old earl how many votes Charles had won by, she said she couldn't be certain but she did recall Charles telling a journalist it was more than the other candidates put together.

Raymond Gould suffered an adverse swing of only two per cent and was returned with a 10,416 majority. The people of Leeds admire independence in a member, especially when it comes to a matter of principle.

The Conservatives captured Parliament with an overall majority of thirty. Her Majesty the Queen called for Edward Heath and asked him to form a Government. He kissed the hands of his sovereign and accepted her commission.

CHAPTER ELEVEN

When Simon awoke on the morning after the election he felt both exhausted and exhilarated. He lay in bed trying to imagine how those Labour ministers, who only the previous day had assumed they would be returning to their departments, would be feeling now.

Elizabeth stirred, let out a small sleep-filled sigh. Simon stared down at his wife. In the seven years of their marriage she had lost none of her attraction for him, but he still took pleasure in just looking at her sleeping form. Her long fair hair rested on her shoulders and her slim, firm figure curved gently beneath the silk nightgown. He started stroking her back and watched her slowly come out of sleep. When she finally awoke she turned over and he took her in his arms.

"I admire your energy," she said. "If you're still fit after three weeks on the trail I can hardly claim to have a headache."

He smiled, delighted to catch a moment of privacy between the seeming lunacy of electioneering and the anticipation of office. No voter was going to interrupt this rare moment of pleasure.

"Mum," said a voice, and Simon quickly turned over to see Peter standing at the door in his pyjamas. "I'm hungry."

On the way back to London in the car Elizabeth asked, "What do you think he'll offer you?"

"Daren't anticipate anything," said Simon. "But I would hope – Under-Secretary of State for the Environment."

"But you're still not certain to be offered a post?"

"Not at all. One can never know what permutations and pressures a new Prime Minister has to consider."

"Like what?" asked Elizabeth.

"Left and right wings of the party, north and south of the country – countless debts to be cleared with those people who can claim they played a role in getting him into No. 10." Simon yawned.

"Are you saying he could leave you out?"

"Oh yes. But I'll be livid if he does, and I'd certainly want to know who had been given my job – and why."

"And what could you do about it?"

"Nothing. There is absolutely nothing one can do and every back-bencher knows it. The Prime Minister's power of patronage is absolute."

"It won't matter, if you continue driving on the centre line," she said. "Are you sure you wouldn't like me to take a turn at the wheel?"

Louise let Andrew lie in on the Friday morning. She knew he had been expecting to return to a higher ministerial office and had been shattered by the election result.

By the time Andrew woke it was nearly eleven. He sat in silence in his dressing-gown, unshaven, and tapped a hard-boiled egg that refused to crack. An unopened *Times* lay by his side.

"Thank you for all your hard work," he said once the second cup of coffee had taken effect. She smiled.

An hour later, dressed in sports jacket and grey flannels, he toured the constituency in a loudspeaker van, thanking his supporters for returning him to Westminster. Louise was by his side, often able to jog his memory on names he couldn't recall.

After they had shaken the last hand they spent a quiet weekend with Sir Duncan in Stirling – who found it extremely hard to remove the smirk from his face.

Raymond was astonished by the election result. He couldn't believe that the opinion polls had been so wrong. He didn't confide in Joyce that he had hoped a Labour victory would bring him back into office after languishing on the back benches for what seemed an interminable time.

"There's nothing for it," he told her, "but to rebuild a career at the bar. We may be out of office for years."

"But surely that won't be enough to keep you fully occupied?"

"I have to be realistic about the future," he said slowly. "Although I don't intend to let Heath drag us into Europe without putting up one hell of a fight."

"Perhaps they'll ask you to Shadow someone?"

"No, there are always far fewer jobs available in Opposition, and in any case they always give the orators like Fraser the dispatch box when all you can do is to sit and make noises while we wait for another election."

Raymond wondered how he would broach what was really on his mind and tried to sound casual when he said, "Perhaps it's time we considered having our own home in the constituency."

"That seems an unnecessary expense," said Joyce, "especially as there's nothing wrong with your parents' home. And, in any case, wouldn't they be offended?"

"My first interest should be my duty to the constituents and this would be a chance to prove a long-term commitment to them. Naturally my parents will understand."

"But we can't afford the cost of two houses," said Joyce uncertainly.

"I realise that, but it's you who have always wanted to live in Leeds, and this will give you the chance to stop commuting from London every week. After I've done the rounds why don't you stay up, contact a few local estate agents and see what's on the market?"

"All right, if that's what you really want," said Joyce. "I'll start next week."

Charles and Fiona spent a quiet weekend at their cottage in Sussex. Charles tried to do some gardening while he kept one ear open for the telephone. Fiona began to realise how anxious he was when she looked through the French windows and saw her finest delphinium being taken for a weed.

Charles eventually gave the weeds a reprieve and came in and turned on the television to catch Maudling, Macleod, Thatcher and Carrington enter No. 10 Downing Street looking pensive, only to leave smiling. The senior appointments had been made: the Cabinet was taking shape. The new Prime Minister came out and waved to the crowds before being whisked away in his official car.

Would he remember who had organised the young vote for him before he was even the party leader?

"When do you want to go back to Eaton Square?" Fiona inquired from the kitchen.

"Depends," said Charles.

"On what?"

"On whether the phone rings."

Simon sat staring at the television. All those hours of work on Environment, and the PM had offered the portfolio to someone else. He had left the set on all day but didn't learn who it was, only that the rest of the Enviroment team had remained intact.

"Why do I bother?" he said out loud. "The whole thing's a farce."

"What were you saying, darling?" asked Elizabeth as she came into the room.

The phone rang again. It was the newly appointed Home Secretary,

Reginald Maudling.

"Simon?"

"Reggie, many congratulations on your appointment – not that it came as a great surprise."

"That's what I'm calling about, Simon. Would you like to join me at the Home Office as Under-Secretary?"

"Like to? I'd be delighted."

"Thank heavens for that," said Maudling. "It took me a dickens of a time to convince Ted Heath that you should be released from the Environment team."

When Andrew and Louise arrived back at Cheyne Walk after the weekend a red box was waiting for him in the drawing-room. "Under-Secretary of State for Scotland" was printed in gold on the side.

"They'll be round to collect that later today," he told Louise. He turned the key to find the box was empty: and then he saw the small envelope in one corner. It was addressed to "Andrew Fraser Esquire, MP". He tore it open. It contained a short handwritten note from the Permanent Secretary, the senior civil servant at the Scottish Office.

"In keeping with a long tradition, ministers are presented with the last red box from which they worked. *Au revoir*. No doubt we will meet again."

"I suppose it could be used as a lunch box," said Louise, standing by the door.

"Or perhaps an overnight case," offered Andrew.

"Or a very small cot," added his wife, trying to make her words casual.

Andrew looked up to see Louise looking radiant.

"I let your parents know last night, but I wasn't going to tell you until dinner this evening."

Andrew threw his arms around her.

"By the way," Louise added, "we've already decided on her name."

When Raymond arrived back at Lincoln's Inn he let his clerk know that he wanted to be flooded with work. Over lunch with Sir Nigel Hartwell, the head of chambers, he explained that he thought it unlikely that the Labour party would be in Government again for some considerable time.

"Age is on your side, Raymond. Another full Parliament and you'll be barely forty, so you can still look forward to many years in the Cabinet."

"I wonder," said Raymond, uncharacteristically hesitant.

"Well, you needn't worry about briefs. Solicitors have been calling constantly since it was known you were back on a more permanent basis."

Raymond began to relax.

Joyce phoned him after lunch with the news that she hadn't found anything suitable, but the estate agent had assured her that they were expecting a lot more on the market in the autumn.

"Well, keep looking," said Raymond.

"Don't worry, I will," said Joyce, sounding as if she was enjoying the whole exercise. "If we find something perhaps we can think of starting a family," she added tentatively.

"Perhaps," said Raymond brusquely.

Charles eventually received a call on the Monday night, not from No. 10 Downing Street but from No. 12, the office of the Chief Whip. Because the Chief Whip's is not an official post, he is paid as the Third Lord of the Treasury and he works from No. 12. The Prime Minister and the Chancellor of the Exchequer, being the first and second Lords of the Treasury, live at Nos. 10 and 11 Downing Street respectively.

The Chief Whip had phoned to say he hoped that Charles would be willing to soldier on as a junior Whip. When he heard the disappointment in Charles's voice he added, "For the time being."

"For the time being," repeated Charles and put the phone down.

"At least you're a member of the Government. You haven't been left out in the cold," said Fiona gamely.

"True," he replied.

"People are sure to come and go during the next five years."

Charles had to agree with his wife but it didn't lessen his disappointment. Returning to the Commons as a member of the Government, however, turned out to be far more rewarding than he had expected. This time it was his party that were making the decisions.

The Queen travelled early that November morning to the House of Lords in the Irish State Coach. An escort of the Household Cavalry accompanied her, preceded by a procession of lesser state carriages in which the King Edward III Crown and other royal trappings were transported. Charles could remember watching the ceremony from the streets when he was a boy. Now he was taking part in it. When the Queen arrived at the Upper House she was accompanied by the Lord Chancellor through the Sovereign's entrance to the robing room, where her ladies-in-waiting began to prepare her for the ceremony.

Charles always considered the State opening of Parliament a special occasion for members of both Houses. As a Whip he watched the members take their seats in the Commons and await the arrival of Black Rod. Once the Queen was seated on the throne the Lord Great Chamberlain commanded the Gentleman Usher of Black Rod to inform the Commons that: "It is Her Majesty's pleasure they attend her immediately in this House." Black Rod, wearing his black topcoat, black waistcoat, black knee-breeches, black stockings and black shoes, resembled the devil's advocate rather than the Queen's messenger. He marched alone across the great tiled floor joining the two Chambers until he reached the doors of the House of Commons which were slammed in his face when he was just two paces away from them.

He struck the door three times with the silver knob of his long thin black rod. In response a little window in the door was flicked back to check on who it was – not unlike a sleazy nightclub, Charles's father had once observed. Black Rod was then allowed admittance to the Lower House. He advanced towards the table and made three obeisances to the chair before saying, "Mr Speaker, the Queen commands this Honourable House to attend Her Majesty immediately in the House of Peers."

With that, the Serjeant-at-Arms, bearing the mace, led Mr Speaker, in full court dress, a gold embroidered gown of black satin damask, back towards the Lords. They were followed by the Clerk of the House and the Speaker's chaplain, behind whom came the Prime Minister, accompanied by the leader of the Opposition, then Government ministers with their opposite numbers, and finally as many back-benchers as could squeeze into the rear of the Lords' Chamber.

The Lords themselves were waiting in the Upper House, dressed in red capes with ermine collars, looking somewhat like benevolent Draculas, accompanied by peeresses glittering in diamond tiaras and wearing long evening dresses. The Queen was seated on the throne, in her full Imperial robes, the King Edward the Third Crown on her head. She waited until the procession had filled the Chamber and all was still.

The Lord Chancellor shuffled forward and, bending down on one knee, presented her with a printed document. It was the speech, written by the Government of the day, and although she had read over a copy of the script earlier that morning she had made no personal contribution to its contents, as her role on this occasion was only ceremonial. She looked up at her subjects and began to read.

Charles stood at the back of the cramped gathering, but with his height he had no trouble in following the entire proceedings. Their lordships were all in their places for the Queen's speech, with the law lords seated in their privileged position in the centre of the Chamber, an honour bestowed upon them by an Act of 1539. The Lord Chancellor sat stockily alone on the Woolsack, which was stuffed with wool from the days when it was the staple commodity of England. When the Lords are in session he acts much as the Speaker does for the Commons.

Charles could spot his elderly father, the Earl of Bridgwater, nodding off during the Queen's speech, which promised that Britain would make a determined effort to become a full member of the EEC. "My Government also intends to bring in a bill to enact trade union reform," she declared. Charles, along with everyone else from the Commons, was counting the likely number of bills that would be presented during the coming months and soon worked out that the Whips' office were going to be in for a busy session.

As the Queen finished her speech Charles took one more look at his father, now sound asleep. How Charles dreaded the moment when he would be standing there watching his brother Rupert in ermine. The only compensation would be if he could produce a son who would one day inherit the title, as it was now obvious Rupert would never marry.

It was not as if he and Fiona had not tried. He was beginning to wonder if the time had not come to suggest that she visit a specialist. He dreaded finding out she was unable to bear a child.

The speech delivered, the Sovereign left the Upper House followed by Prince Philip and Prince Charles to a fanfare of trumpets. At the other end of the Chamber the procession of MPs, led again by the Speaker, made their way back in pairs from the red benches of the Lords to the green of the Commons.

The leader of the Opposition, having formed his own team, invited Andrew to cover the Home Office brief as number two. Andrew was delighted by the challenge of this new responsibility, especially when he discovered Simon Kerslake was to be his opposite number in Government.

Louise once again became very large in a short period, but Andrew tried to keep his mind off the pregnancy, as he dreaded her going through that amount of pain and sorrow for a third time. He telephoned Elizabeth Kerslake and they agreed to meet privately.

"That's a hard question to answer without ifs and buts," she told Andrew over coffee in her room the following day.

"But what would your advice be if Louise were to lose the third child?"

Elizabeth took a long time considering her reply. "If that happened I cannot believe it would be wise to put her through the same ordeal again," she said flatly. "The psychological repercussions alone might affect her for the rest of her life."

Andrew sat staring in front of him.

"Enough of this morbid talk," Elizabeth added. "I checked Louise last week and I can see no reason why this shouldn't turn out to be a routine birth."

As the first weeks of the new Tory administration took shape, Simon and Andrew became locked in battle over several issues and were soon known as "the mongoose and the rattlesnake". When either of the names "Kerslake" or "Fraser" was cranked up on the old-fashioned wall machines indicating one of them had risen to speak, members drifted back into the Chamber. Andrew found himself a constant visitor to the table office, a tiny room in the corridor behind the Speaker's chair where members tabled their questions, usually scribbled on yellow sheets, but still acceptable to the omniscient clerks had they been written on postage stamps.

The clerks often helped Andrew reword a question so that it would be acceptable to the chair, a function they carried out for any member, even Tom Carson, who had once accused them of political bias when they suggested one of his questions was out of order. When Carson was finally referred to the Speaker, he was called for and reprimanded, and his question deposited in one of the mock-Gothic waste-paper baskets in the Order office.

Once behind the Speaker's chair, Simon and Andrew would good-humouredly discuss the issues on which they were crossing swords. The opportunity to be out of sight of the Press Gallery above them was often taken by the two opposing members, but once they had both returned to the dispatch box they would tear into each other, looking for any weakness in the other's argument.

On one subject they found themselves in total accord. Ever since August 1969, when the troops had first been sent in, Parliament had been having another of its periodic bouts of trouble with Northern Ireland. In February 1970 the House devoted a full day's business to listen to members' opinions in the never-ending effort to find a solution to the growing clash between the Protestant extremists and the IRA. The motion before the House was to allow emergency powers to be renewed in the province.

Andrew rose from his seat on the front bench to deliver the opening speech for the Opposition. He said he took no side in this unhappy affair, but he felt sure the House was united in condemning violence. Yet however hard he searched for the answer he found neither faction willing to give an inch. 'Goodwill' and 'trust' were words that might as well have been left out of any dictionary printed in Ulster. It was not long before Andrew came to the conclusion that Gladstone was right when he had said, "Every time I find the solution to the Irish question, they change the question."

When Andrew had finished he surprised members by leaving the Chamber and not returning for several minutes.

Simon had been selected to wind up for the Government and had prepared his speech with meticulous care. Although both sides appeared in agreement on the main issue, the mood as always could change in a moment if an unfortunate view was expressed by a Government minister.

During the debate, much to everyone's surprise, Andrew Fraser kept leaving the Chamber. Simon left only twice before three-thirty and the ten o'clock division, once to take a call from his wife, and then again at seven-thirty for a quick supper.

When Simon came back Andrew was still absent from the Chamber, and he had not returned by the time the Shadow Home Secretary began to sum up. Andrew did eventually take his seat on the front bench but Simon had already begun his speech.

As Andrew entered the Chamber and took his place on the front bench, an elderly Conservative rose from his seat.

"On a point of order, Mr Speaker."

Simon sat down immediately and turned his head to listen to the point his colleague wanted to make.

"Is it not a tradition of this House, sir," began the elder statesman rather ponderously, "for a front-bench spokesman to have the courtesy to remain in his seat during the debate in order that he may ascertain views other than his own?"

"That is not a point of order," replied the Speaker above the cries of "Hear, hear" from the Conservative benches. Andrew scribbled a quick note and hurriedly passed it over to Simon. On it was written a single sentence.

"I accept the point my Right Honourable friend makes," Simon began, "and would have complained myself had I not known that the Honourable Gentleman, the member for Edinburgh Carlton, has spent most of the afternoon in hospital." Simon paused to let the effect sink in. "Where his wife was in labour. I am not given to accepting as necessarily accurate all the Opposition tells me," he continued, "but I am able to confirm this statement because it was my wife who delivered the baby." The House began to laugh. "I can assure my Honourable friend that my wife has spent her entire afternoon indoctrinating the infant in the value of Conservative policies as understood by his grandfather, which is why the Honourable Gentleman has found it necessary to be absent himself from so much of the debate." Simon waited for the laughter to subside. "For those members of the House who thrive on statistics, it's a boy and he weighs four pounds three ounces."

There are times in the House when affection is displayed on both sides, thought Andrew, who considered it was ironic that during an Irish debate an Englishman had demonstrated such affection for a Scotsman.

There was no challenge when the Speaker "collected the voices" at ten o'clock so the matter was decided "on the nod" and Simon joined Andrew behind the Speaker's chair.

"Just over four pounds doesn't sound very big to me. I thought I'd take a second opinion from the Minister of Health."

"I agree," said Andrew, "the little blighter is stuck in an incubator, but your wife is doing everything she can to fatten him up. I'm off to watch him now."

"Good luck," said Simon.

Andrew sat by the incubator all night, hating the drip, drip, drip of the little plastic tube that passed up the child's nose and down into his stomach. He feared that when he woke his son would be dead and continually went to the wash basin and put a damp, cold cloth over his eyes to ensure he remained awake. He finally lost the battle and dozed off in a "dad's bed" in the corner.

When his father woke, Robert Bruce Fraser was very much alive. The crumpled father rose from his bed to admire his crumpled offspring, who was receiving milk down the plastic tube from a night nurse.

Andrew stared down at the crinkly face. The boy had inherited his square jaw, but he had his mother's nose and hair colouring. Andrew chuckled at the time Louise had wasted over girls' names. Robert it would be.

Robert Bruce Fraser travelled to Cheyne Walk with his mother and father three weeks later, having topped the scales earlier that morning at five pounds ten ounces.

Elizabeth Kerslake had told them to be thankful: the post-natal examination had shown that it would not be possible for Louise to bear another child.

CHAPTER TWELVE

The Chief Whip looked round at his colleagues, wondering which of them would volunteer for such a thankless task.

A hand went up, and he was pleasantly surprised.

"Thank you, Charles."

Charles had already warned Fiona that he was going to volunteer to be the Whip responsible for the issue that had most dominated the last election: Britain's entry into the EEC. Everyone in that room realised that it would be the most demanding marathon of the entire Parliament, and there was an audible sigh of relief when Charles volunteered.

"Not a job for anyone with a rocky marriage," he heard one Whip whisper. At least that's something I don't have to worry about, thought Charles, but he made a note to take home some flowers that night.

"Why was it the bill everyone wanted to avoid?" asked Fiona as she arranged the daffodils.

"Because many of our side don't necessarily back Edward Heath in his lifelong ambition to take Britain into Europe, while quite a few of the Opposition do," said Charles, accepting a large brandy. "Added to that, we have the problem of presenting a bill to curb the trade unions at the same time which may well influence many members of the Labour Party from voting with us on Europe. Because of this problem, the Prime Minister requires a regular "state of play" assessment on Europe even though legislation may not be presented on the floor of the Commons for at least another year. He'll want to know periodically how many of our side are still against entry, and how many from the Opposition we can rely on to break ranks when the crucial vote is taken."

"Perhaps I should become Member of Parliament and then at least I could spend a little more time with you."

"Especially on the European issue if you were a 'don't know'."

The "Great Debate" was discussed by the media to the point of boredom. Members were nevertheless conscious that they were playing a part in history. And, because of the unusual spectacle of the Whips not being in absolute control of the voting procedure, the Commons sprang to life, and excitement began to build up over the weeks and months of debate.

Charles retained his normal task of watching over fifty members on all normal Government bills, but because of the priority given to the issue of entry into Europe he had been released from all other duties. He knew that this was his chance to atone for his disastrous winding-up speech on the economy which he sensed his colleagues had still not completely forgotten.

"I'm gambling everything on this one," he told Fiona. "And if we lose the final vote I will be sentenced to the back benches for life."

"And if we win?"

"It will be hard to keep me off the front bench," replied Charles.

Robert Fraser was one of those noisy children who after only a few weeks sounded as if he was on the front bench.

"Perhaps he's going to be a politician after all," concluded Louise, staring down at her son.

"What has changed your mind?" asked Andrew.

"He never stops shouting at everyone, he's totally preoccupied with himself and he falls asleep as soon as someone else offers an opinion," she replied.

"At last I think I've found it." After Raymond heard the news he took the train up to Leeds the following Friday. Joyce had selected four houses for him to consider, but he had to agree with her that the one in Chapel Allerton was exactly what they were looking for. It was also by far the most expensive.

"Can we afford it?" asked Joyce anxiously.

"Probably not, but one of the problems of seeing four houses is that you end up only wanting the best one."

"I could go on looking."

"No, you've found the right house; now I'll have to work out how we can pay for it, and I think I may have come up with an idea."

Joyce said nothing, waiting for him to continue.

"We could sell our place in Lansdowne Road."

"But where would we live when you're in London?"

"I could rent a small flat somewhere between the law courts and the Commons while you set up our real home in Leeds."

"But wouldn't you get lonely?"

"Of course I will," said Raymond, trying to sound convincing. "But almost every member north of Birmingham is parted from his wife during the week. In any case, you've always wanted to settle in Yorkshire, and this might be our best chance. If my practice continues to grow we can buy a second house in London at a later date."

Joyce looked apprehensive.

"One added bonus," said Raymond, "your being in Leeds will ensure I never lose the seat."

She smiled, as she always felt reassured whenever Raymond showed the slightest sign of needing her.

On Monday morning Raymond put in a bid for the house in Chapel Allerton before returning to London. After a little bargaining over the phone during the week, he and the owner settled on a price. By Thursday Raymond had put his Lansdowne Road house on the market and was surprised by the amount the estate agent thought it would fetch.

All Raymond had to do now was find himself a flat.

Simon sent a note to Ronnie expressing his thanks for keeping him so well informed about what was happening at Nethercote and Company. It had been eight months since he had resigned from the board because of his appointment as a minister, but Ronnie saw that the minutes of each meeting were posted to him to study in his own time. "His own time": Simon had to laugh at the thought.

His overdraft at the bank now stood at a little over £72,000, but as Ronnie intended the shares should be offered at five pounds each when they went public Simon felt sure there was still a fair leeway, as his personal holding should realise £300,000. Elizabeth warned him not to spend a penny of the profit until the money was safely in the bank. He was thankful she didn't know the full extent of his borrowing.

Over one of their occasional lunches at the Ritz Ronnie spelt out to Simon his plans for the future of the company.

"Now that the Tories are in I think I'll go public in eighteen months' time. This year's profits are up again and next year's look even better. So 1973 looks a perfect bet."

Simon looked apprehensive and Ronnie responded quickly. "If you're having any problem, Simon, I'll be happy to take the shares off your hands at their market value. At least that way you'd show a small profit."

"No, no," said Simon. "I'll hang in there now that I've waited this long."

"Suit yourself," said Ronnie. "Now tell me – how are you enjoying the Home Office?"

Simon put down his knife and fork. "Of the three great offices of state, it's the one most involved with people, so there's a new challenge at a personal level every day, although it can be depressing too. Locking people up in prisons, banning immigrants and deporting harmless aliens isn't my idea of fun. The Home Office never seems to want anyone to enjoy too much freedom."

"And what about Ireland?"

"What about Ireland?" said Simon, shrugging his shoulders.

"I'd give the north back to Eire," said Ronnie, "or let them go independent and give them a large cash incentive to do so. At the moment the whole exercise is money down the drain."

"We're discussing people," said Simon, "not money."

"Ninety per cent of the voters would back me," said Ronnie, lighting a cigar.

"Everyone imagines ninety per cent of the people support their views, until they stand for election," said Simon. "The issue of Ireland is far too important to be glib about. I repeat, we're discussing people, eight million people, all of whom have the same right to justice as you and I. And as long as I work in the Home Office I intend to see that they get it."

Ronnie remained silent.

"I'm sorry, Ronnie," continued Simon. "Too many people have an easy solution to Ireland. If there *was* an easy solution the problem wouldn't have lasted over two hundred years."

"Don't be sorry," said Ronnie. "I'm so stupid, I've only just worked out for the first time why you're in public office."

"You're a typical self-made Fascist," said Simon, teasing his companion once again.

"You may be right, but you won't change my mind on hanging. Your lot should bring back the rope; the streets aren't safe any longer."

"For property developers like you, hoping for a quick killing?"

Both men laughed.

"Andrew, do you want lunch?"

"In a moment, in a moment."

"That's what you said half an hour ago."

"I know, but he's nearly got it. Just give me a few more minutes." Louise waited and watched, but Robert collapsed in a heap again.

"No doubt you're expecting him to play soccer for England by the time he's two."

"No, certainly not," said Andrew, carrying his son back into the house. "Rugby for Scotland."

Louise was touched by the amount of time Andrew spent with Robert. She told her disbelieving friends that he regularly fed and bathed the baby and even changed his nappy.

"Don't you think he's good-looking?" asked Andrew, strapping his son carefully into his chair.

"Yes," said Louise, laughing.

"That's because he looks like me," said Andrew, putting his arms round his wife.

"He most certainly does not," said Louise firmly.

Crash. A bowlful of porridge had been deposited on the floor, leaving just a lump left in the spoon, which Robert was now smearing across his face and hair.

"He looks as if he has just stepped out of a concrete mixer," said Andrew.

Louise stared at her son. "Perhaps you're right. There *are* times when he looks like you."

"How do you feel about rape?" asked Raymond.

"I can't see that it's relevant," Stephanie Arnold replied.

"I think they'll go for me on it," said Raymond.

"But why?"

"They'll be able to pin me in a corner, damage my character."

"But where does it get them? They can't prove lack of consent."

"Maybe, but they will offer it as background to prove the rest of the case."

"Because you raped someone doesn't prove you murdered them."

Raymond and Stephanie Arnold, who was new to chambers, continued discussing their first case together on the way to the Old Bailey, and she left Raymond in no doubt that she was delighted to be led by him. They were to appear together to defend a labourer accused of the rape and murder of his step-daughter.

"Open and shut case unfortunately," said Raymond, "but we're going to make the Crown prove their argument beyond anyone's doubt."

When the case stretched into a second week Raymond began to believe that the jury were so gullible they might even get their client off. Stephanie was sure they would.

The day before the judge's summing up Raymond invited Stephanie to dinner at the House of Commons. "That'll make them turn their heads," he thought to himself. "They won't have seen anything in a white shirt and black stockings that looks like that for some time, certainly not Mr Speaker."

Stephanie seemed flattered by the invitation and sat through the stodgy meal served in the Strangers' Dining-room, obviously impressed as former Cabinet ministers flitted in and out, all of them acknowledging him.

"How's the new flat?" asked Stephanie.

"Worked out well," replied Raymond. "The Barbican is so convenient for Parliament and the law courts."

"Does your wife like it?" she asked, lighting a cigarette but not looking at him directly.

"She's not in town that much nowadays. She spends most of her time in Leeds – doesn't care much for London."

The awkward pause that followed was interrupted by a sudden clanging of bells.

"Are we on fire?" said Stephanie, quickly stubbing out her cigarette.

"No," said Raymond laughing. "Just the ten o'clock division. I have to leave you and vote. I'll be back in about fifteen minutes."

"Shall I order coffee?"

"No, don't bother," said Raymond. "It's foul. Perhaps . . . perhaps you'd like to come back to the Barbican? Then you can give a verdict on my flat."

"Maybe it's an open and shut case," she smiled.

Raymond returned the smile before joining his colleagues as they flooded out of the dining-room down the corridor towards the Commons Chamber. He didn't have time to explain to Stephanie that he had only six minutes to get into the right lobby. As Raymond had no idea what they were voting on that night he followed the surge of Labour members into the Noes lobby. The bells stopped and the doors were bolted.

Whenever the vote is called for at the end of the debate the Speaker puts the question and the moment he reaches the words, "I think the Ayes have it," the roar of "No" from those opposed to the motion ensures a vote at ten o'clock. Bells peal out over the Palace of Westminster, and in some nearby restaurants and members' homes in the division-bell area.

Members then scurry into the Ayes or Noes division lobby before the cry of "Lock the doors" is heard. Once the doors have been secured each member then files past two clerks seated at a high desk at the far end of the corridor who tick off his name. As Raymond stepped past the clerks he came towards the exit doors which were angled so as to make a funnel through which only one member at a time could pass. The Whip acting as teller shouted out the mounting vote. "Seventy-three," he called as Raymond passed him. The only particular rule relating to voting was that members could not wear a hat or overcoat while in the lobby. A clerk had once told Raymond that this dated from the days when lazy members sent their driver off in the hansom cab, hats over ears, coat buttoned up to the nose, to march through the corridors and give their masters' names. Some of them would have been a damn sight better MPs than their employers, Raymond had often thought.

While in the corridor he discovered that they were voting on a clause of the Trade Union Bill concerning the validity of closed shops. He was in no doubt that he supported his party on that subject.

When he returned to the Strangers' Dining-room after the vote he found Stephanie checking her face in a compact mirror, a small round face with green eyes and brunette hair. She was replacing the trace of lipstick. He suddenly felt conscious of being a little overweight for a man not yet forty.

"Shall we go?" he suggested, after he had signed the bill.

Once they had reached the flat Raymond put on a Charles Aznavour record and retired to the small kitchen to prepare coffee. He was totally oblivious to the fact that women were beginning to find him attractive. A little extra weight and a few grey hairs had not harmed his appearance, if anything giving him an air of authority.

"There's no doubting this is a bachelor flat," Stephanie remarked as she took in the one comfortable leather chair, the pipe stand, and the Spy cartoons of turn-of-the-century judges and politicians.

"I suppose that's because that's what it is," he mused, setting down a tray laden with coffee and two brandy balloons generously filled with cognac.

"Don't you get lonely?" she asked.

"From time to time," he said, pouring the coffee.

"And between times?"

"Black?" he said, not looking at her.

"Black," she said.

"Sugar?"

"For a man who has served as a minister of the Crown and who, it's rumoured, is about to become the youngest QC in the country, you're still very unsure of yourself with women."

Raymond blushed, but raised his head and stared into her eyes.

In the silence he caught Aznavour's words, "You've let yourself go . . ."

"Would my Honourable friend care to dance?" she said quietly.

Raymond could still remember the last occasion he had danced. This time he was determined it would be different. He held Stephanie so that their bodies touched and they swayed rather than danced to the music of Marcel Stellman. She didn't notice Raymond slipping off his glasses and putting them into his jacket pocket. He bent over and kissed her neck. She gave a long sigh, and when they parted, she said, "Let's hope this is between times."

Charles studied his chart of 330 Conservatives. He felt confident of 217, not sure about fifty-four and had almost given up on fifty-nine. On the Labour side the best information he could glean was that fifty Socialists were expected to defy the Whip and join the Government's ranks when the great vote took place.

"The main fly in the ointment," Charles reported to the Chief Whip, "is still the Trade Union Reform Bill. The left are trying to convince those Socialists who still support the bill that there is no cause so important for which they should enter the same lobby as those Tory trade union bashers." He went on to explain his fear that unless the Government were willing to modify the Trade Union Bill they might lose Europe on the back of it. "Alec Pimkin doesn't help matters by trying to gather the waverers in our party round him."

"There's no chance of the Prime Minister modifying one sentence of the Trade Union Bill," said the Chief Whip, draining his gin and tonic. "He promised it in his speech at the party conference, and he intends to deliver by the time he goes to Blackpool at the end of this year. I can also tell you he isn't going to like your conclusions on Pimkin, Charles. He cares almost as passionately about trade union reform as he does about Europe." Charles was about to protest. "I'm not complaining, you've done damn well so far. Just keep working on the fifty waverers. Threaten, cajole, bully, bribe. Try anything, but get them in the right lobby come the night, Pimkin included."

"How about sex?" asked Charles.

"You've been seeing too many American films," said the Chief Whip, laughing. "In any case I don't think we've got anyone other than Miss Norse to offer them."

Charles returned to his office and went over the list once again. His forefinger stopped at the letter "P". Charles strolled out into the corridor and looked around; his quarry wasn't there. He checked the Chamber: no sign of him. He passed the library. "No need to look in there," he thought, and moved on to the smoking room where he found his man, about to order another gin.

"Alec," said Charles expansively.

The rotund figure of Pimkin looked round.

May as well try bribery first, thought Charles. "Let me get you a drink."

"That's good of you, old fellow," said Pimkin, nervously fingering his bow tie.

"Now, Alec, what's this about your voting against the European Bill?"

Simon was horrified when he read the initial document. Its implications were all too evident.

The report of the new Boundary Commission had been left in the red box for him to study over the weekend. He had agreed at a meeting of Home Office officials that he would steer it through the House as quickly as possible so that it would make the basis for the seats to be contested at the next election. As the Secretary of State reminded him: there must be no hold-ups.

Simon had read the document carefully. In essence the changes made sense and, because of the movement of families from urban to rural areas, it would undoubtedly create more winnable seats for the Conservatives overall. No wonder the party wanted no hold-ups. But what could he do about the decision the Commission had come to on his own constituency, Coventry Central? His hands were tied. If he suggested any change from the Boundary Commission's recommendations he would rightly be accused of jerrymandering.

Because of the city's dwindling population the Commission had recommended that the four constituencies of Coventry become three. Coventry Central was to be the one to disappear, its voters distributed among Coventry West, Coventry East and Coventry North. Simon realised this would leave one safe seat for his sitting colleague and two safe Labour seats. It had never been far from his mind how marginal a constituency he represented. Now he was on the verge of being without one at all. He would have to traipse around the country all over again looking for a new seat to fight at the next election, while at the same time taking care of his constituents in the moribund one; and at the stroke of a pen – *his* pen – they would pass on their loyalties to someone else. If only he had remained in Enviroment he could have put up a case for keeping all four seats.

Elizabeth was sympathetic when he explained the problem but told him not to concern himself too much until he had spoken to the vice-chairman of the party, who advised candidates which constituencies were likely to become available.

"It may even work out to your advantage," she added.

"What do you mean?" said Simon.

"You could get a safer seat nearer London."

"With my luck I'll end up with a marginal in Newcastle."

Elizabeth prepared his favourite meal and spent the evening trying to keep up his spirits. After three portions of shepherd's pie Simon fell asleep almost as soon as he put his head on the pillow. But she stayed awake long into the night.

The casual conversation with the head of Gynaecology at St Mary's kept running through her mind. Although she hadn't confided in Simon, she could recall her supervisor's every word.

"I notice from the roster that you've had far more days off than you are entitled to, Dr Kerslake. You must make up your mind if you want to be a doctor or the wife of an MP.''

Elizabeth stirred restlessly as she considered the problem, but came to no conclusion except not to bother Simon while he had so much on his mind.

''Do these boundary changes affect you?'' Louise asked, looking up from her copy of *The Times*.

Andrew was bouncing a small rubber ball on Robert's head.

''You'll give him brain damage,'' said Louise.

''I know, but think of the goals he'll score – and it won't be long before I can start him on rugby.''

Robert started to cry when his father stopped to answer his mother's question. ''No, Edinburgh isn't affected. There's such a small movement in the population that the seven city seats will remain intact. The only real changes in Scotland will be in Glasgow and the Highlands.''

''That's a relief,'' said Louise. ''I should hate to have to look for another constituency.''

''Poor old Simon Kerslake is losing his seat altogether and he daren't do anything about it.''

''Why not?'' asked Louise.

''Because he's the minister in charge of the bill, and if he tried anything clever we would crucify him.''

''So what will he do?''

''Have to shop around for a new seat, or convince an older colleague to stand down in his favour.''

''But surely ministers find it easy to pick up a plum seat?''

''Not necessarily,'' said Andrew. ''Many constituencies don't like to have someone foisted on them and want to choose their own man. And some actually prefer a local man who will never be a minister, because they feel he can devote more time to them.''

''Andrew, can you revert to being some use in Opposition?''

''What are you suggesting?'' asked Andrew.

''Just keep throwing that ball at your stupid son's head or he'll be crying all day.''

''Take no notice of her, Robert. She'll feel differently when you score your first goal against England.''

CHAPTER THIRTEEN

At exactly the time Raymond was ready to stop the affair Stephanie began leaving a set of court clothes in the flat. Although the two had gone their separate ways at the conclusion of the case they continued to see one another a couple of evenings a week. Raymond had had a spare key made so that Stephanie didn't have to spend her life checking when he had a three-line whip.

At first he began simply to avoid her, but she would then seek him out. When he did manage to give her the slip he would often find her back in his flat when he returned from the Commons. When he suggested they should be a little more discreet she began to make threats, subtle at first, but after a time more direct.

During the period of their affair Raymond conducted three major cases for the Crown, all of which had successful conclusions and which added to his reputation. On each occasion his clerk made certain Stephanie was not assigned to be with him. Now that his residency problem had been sorted out Raymond's only worry was how to end their relationship. He quickly discovered that getting rid of Stephanie Arnold was going to prove considerably more difficult than picking her up.

Simon was on time for his appointment at Central Office. He explained his dilemma to Sir Edward Mountjoy – vice-chairman of the party responsible for candidates – in graphic detail.

"What bloody bad luck," said Sir Edward. "But perhaps I may be able to help," he added, opening the green folder on the desk in front of him. Simon could see that he was studying a list of names. It made him feel once again like an undergraduate who needed someone to die.

"There seem to be about a dozen safe seats that will fall vacant at the next election, caused either by retirement or redistribution."

"Anywhere in particular you could recommend?"

"I fancy Littlehampton."

"Where's that?" said Simon.

"It will be a new seat, safe as houses. It's in Sussex, on the borders of Hampshire." He studied an attached map. "Runs proud to Charles Seymour's constituency which remains unchanged. Can't think you would have many rivals there," said Sir Edward. "But why don't you have a word with Charles? He's bound to know everyone involved in taking the decision."

"Anything else that looks promising?" asked Simon, only too aware that Seymour might not prove altogether cooperative.

"Let me see. Can't afford to put all your eggs in one basket, can we? Ah, yes – Redcorn, in Northumberland." Again the vice-chairman studied the map. "Three hundred and twenty miles from London and no airport within eighty miles, and their nearest main line station is forty miles. I think that one's only worth trying for if you get desperate. My advice would be to speak to Charles Seymour about Little-hampton. He must know the lay of the land in that neck of the woods."

Two clichés in one sentence, thought Simon. Thank heavens Sir Edward would never have to make a speech from the dispatch box.

"I'm sure you're right, Sir Edward," he said.

"Selection committees are being formed already," continued Sir Edward, "so you shouldn't have to wait too long."

"I appreciate your help," said Simon. "Perhaps you could let me know if anything else comes up in the meantime."

"Of course, delighted. The problem is that if one of our side were to die during the sessions you couldn't desert your present seat because that would cause two by-elections. We certainly don't want a by-election in Coventry Central with you being accused of being a carpetbagger somewhere else."

"Don't remind me," said Simon.

Charles had whittled down the fifty-nine anti-Common Market members to fifty-one, but he was now dealing with the hard kernel who seemed quite immunue to future advancement or bullying. When he made his next report to the Chief Whip Charles assured him that the Conservatives who would vote against entry into Europe were outnumbered by the Socialists who had declared they would support the Government. The Chief Whip seemed pleased, but asked if Charles had made any progress with Pimkin's disciples.

"Those twelve mad right-wingers?" said Charles sharply. "They seem to be willing to follow Pimkin even into the valley of death. I've tried everything but they're still determined to vote against Europe whatever the cost."

"The maddening thing is that that bloody nuisance Pimkin has nothing to lose," said the Chief Whip. "His seat disappears at the end of this Parliament in the redistribution. I can't imagine anyone with his extreme views would find a constituency to select him, but by then he'll have done the damage." The Chief Whip paused. "If his twelve would even abstain I would feel confident of advising the PM of victory."

"The problem is to find a way of turning Pimkin into Judas and then urging him to lead the chosen twelve into our camp," said Charles.

"You achieve that, and we'd certainly win."

Charles returned to the Whips' office to find Simon Kerslake waiting by his desk.

"I dropped by on the off-chance, hoping you might be able to spare me a few moments," said Simon.

"Of course," said Charles, trying to sound welcoming. "Take a pew."

Simon sat down opposite him. "You may have heard that I lose my constituency as a result of the Boundary Commission report and Edward Mountjoy suggested I have a word with you about Little-hampton, the new seat that borders your constituency."

"It does indeed," said Charles, masking his surprise. He had not considered the problem as his own seat remained intact. He recovered quickly. "And how wise of Edward to send you to me. I'll do everything I can to help."

"Littlehampton would be ideal," said Simon. "Especially while my wife is still working in Paddington."

Charles raised his eyebrows.

"I don't think you've met Elizabeth. She's a doctor at St Mary's," Simon explained.

"Yes, I can see how convenient Littlehampton would be. Why don't I start by having a word with Alexander Dalglish, the constituency chairman, and see what I can come up with?"

"That would be extremely helpful."

"Not at all. I'll call him at home this evening and find out what stage they've reached over selection, and then I'll put you in the picture."

"I'd appreciate that."

"While I've got you, let me give you the whip for next week," said Charles, passing over a sheet of paper. Simon folded it up and put it in his pocket. "I'll call you the moment I have some news."

Simon left feeling happier and a little guilty about his past prejudice concerning Charles, whom he watched disappear into the Chamber to carry out his bench duty.

The European issue had been given six days for debate by back-benchers, the longest period of time allocated to one motion in living memory.

Charles strolled down the aisle leading to the front bench and took a seat on the end to check on another set of speeches. Usually he listened intently to see if he could spot a member wavering in his position; but on this occasion his thoughts were in Littlehampton. Andrew Fraser was on his feet, and Charles was delighted to be able to confirm the tick alongside his name before he drifted into deep thought.

"I for one shall vote for entry into Europe," Andrew was telling the House. "When my party was in power I was a pro-European, and now we are in Opposition I can see no good reason to do a volte-face. The principles that held true two years ago hold true today. Not all of us . . ."

Tom Carson leaped up and asked if his Honourable friend would give way. Andrew resumed his seat immediately.

"Would my Honourable friend really support the peasant farmers of France before the sheep farmers in New Zealand?" asked Carson.

Andrew rose and explained to his colleague that he would certainly expect safeguards for New Zealand, but the initial vote on the floor of the House was on the principle of entry. The details could and should be dealt with in committee. He went on to express the view that had his Honourable friend talked of wogs or Jews in such a context the House would have been in uproar. "Why is it therefore acceptable to the anti-marketeers to describe French farmers as peasants?"

"Perhaps it's you who is the peasant," Carson shouted back, in seven words thus ruining his case for the lamb farmers of New Zealand.

Andrew ignored the jibe and went on to tell the House that he believed in a united Europe as a further insurance against a third world war. He concluded with the words:

"Britain has for a thousand years written history, even the history of the world. Let us decide with our votes whether our children will read that history, or continue to write it." Andrew sat down to acclamation from both sides.

By the time Andrew had resumed his seat Charles had formed a plan and left the Chamber when one of his own colleagues started what promised to be a long, boring and predictable speech.

Instead of returning to the Whips' office which afforded no privacy, Charles disappeared into one of the telephone booths near the cloisters above the Members' Cloakroom. He checked the number and dialled it.

"Alexander, it's Charles. Charles Seymour."

"Good to hear from you, Charles, it's been a long time. How are you?"

"Well. And you?"

"Can't complain. What can I do for a busy man like you?"

"Wanted to chew over the new Sussex constituency with you, Littlehampton. How's your seletion of a candidate going?"

"They've left me to draw up a short list of six for final selection by the full committee in about ten days' time."

"Have you thought of standing yourself, Alexander?"

"Many times," came back the reply. "But the old lady wouldn't allow it, neither would the bank balance. Do you have any ideas?"

"Might be able to help. Why don't you come and have a quiet dinner at my place early next week?"

"That's kind of you, Charles."

"Not at all, it will be good to see you again. It's been far too long. Next Monday suit you?"

"Absolutely."

"Good, let's say eight o'clock, 27 Eaton Square."

Charles put the phone down, returned to the Whips' Office and pencilled a note in his diary.

Raymond had just finished making his contribution to the European debate when Charles returned to take a seat on a half-empty Treasury bench. Raymond had made a coherent economic case for remaining free of the other six European countries and for building stronger links with the Commonwealth and America. He doubted that Britain could take the financial burden of entering a club that had been in existence for so long. If the country had joined at its inception it might have been different, he argued, but he would have to vote against this risky, unproven venture that he suspected could only lead to higher unemployment. When Raymond sat down he did not receive the acclamation that Andrew had and, worse, what praise he did elicit came from the left wing of the party who had spent so much time in the past criticising *Full Employment at any Cost?* Charles put a cross by the name Gould.

A note was being passed along the row to Raymond from one of the House Badge messengers, dressed in white tie and black tails. It read, "Please ring head of chambers as soon as convenient."

Raymond left the floor of the House and went to the nearest telephone in the corner of the Members' Lobby. He was immediately put through to Sir Nigel Hartwell.

"You wanted me to phone?"

"Yes," said Sir Nigel. "Are you free at the moment?"

"I am," said Raymond. "Why? Is it something urgent?"

"I'd rather not talk about it over the phone," said Sir Nigel ominously.

Raymond took a tube from Westminster to Temple and was in chambers fifteen minutes later. He went straight to Sir Nigel's office, sat down in the comfortable chair in the corner of the spacious club-like room, crossed his legs and watched Sir Nigel pace about in front of him. He was clearly determined to get something off his chest.

"Raymond, I have been asked by those in authority about you taking silk. I've said I think you'd make a damn good QC." A smile came over Raymond's face, but it was soon wiped off. "But I need an undertaking from you."

"An undertaking?"

"Yes," said Sir Nigel. "You must stop having this damn silly er . . . relationship with another member of chambers." He rounded on Raymond and faced him.

Raymond turned scarlet but before he could speak the head of chambers continued.

"Now I want your word on it," said Sir Nigel, "that it will end, and end immediately."

"You have my word," said Raymond quietly.

"I'm not a prig," said Sir Nigel, pulling down on his waistcoat, "but if you are going to have an affair for God's sake make it as far away from the office as possible and, if I may advise you, that should include the House of Commons and Leeds. There's still a lot of the world left over and it's full of women."

Raymond nodded his agreement: he could not fault the head of chambers' logic.

Sir Nigel continued, obviously embarrassed. "There's a nasty fraud case starting in Manchester next Monday. Our client has been accused of setting up a series of companies that specialise in life insurance but avoid paying out on the claims: I expect you remember all the publicity. Miss Arnold has been put on the case as a reserve junior. They tell me it could last several weeks."

"She'll try and get out of it," said Raymond glumly.

"She already has, but I made it quite clear that if she felt unable to take the case on she would have to find other chambers."

Raymond breathed a sigh of relief. "Thank you," he said.

"Sorry about this. I know you've earned your silk, old boy, but I can't have members of chambers going around with egg on their faces. Thank you for your cooperation: I can't pretend I enjoyed that."

"Got time for a quiet word?" asked Charles.

"You're wasting your time, dear thing, if you imagine the disciples will change their minds at this late stage," said Alec Pimkin. "All twelve of them will vote against the Government on Europe. That's final."

"I don't want to discuss Europe this time, Alec. It's far more serious, and on a personal level. Let's go and have a drink on the terrace."

Charles ordered the drinks, and the two men strolled out on to the quiet end of the terrace towards the Speaker's house. Charles stopped as soon as he was certain there was no longer anyone within earshot.

"If it's not Europe, what is it?" asked Pimkin, staring out at the Thames.

"What's this I hear about you losing your seat?"

Pimkin turned pale and touched his bow tie nervously. "It's this bloody boundary business. My constituency is swallowed up, and no one seems willing to interview me for a new one."

"What's it worth if I secure you a safe seat for the rest of your life?"

Pimkin looked suspiciously up at Charles. "Almost anything up to a pound of flesh," he added with a false laugh.

"No, I won't need to cut that deep."

The colour returned to Pimkin's cheeks. "Whatever it is, you can rely on me, old fellow."

"Can you deliver the disciples,' said Charles.

Pimkin turned pale again.

"Not on the small votes in committee," said Charles, before Pimkin could reply. "Not on the clauses even, just on the second reading, the principle itself. Standing by the party in their hour of need, no desire to cause an unnecessary general election, all that stuff – you fill in the details for the disciples. I know you can convince them, Alec."

Pimkin still didn't speak.

"I deliver a copper-bottomed seat, you deliver twelve votes. I think we can call that a fair exchange."

"What if I get them to abstain?" said Pimkin.

Charles waited, as if giving the idea considerable thought. "It's a deal," he said, never having hoped for anything more.

Alexander Dalglish arrived at Eaton Square a little after eight. Fiona met him at the door and explained that Charles had not yet returned from the Commons.

"But I expect him any moment," she added. "May I offer you a drink?"

Another thirty minutes passed before Charles hurried in.

"Sorry I'm late, Alexander," he said, grasping his guest by the hand. "Hoped I might make it just before you." He kissed his wife on the forehead.

"Not at all," said Alexander. "I couldn't have asked for more pleasant company."

"What will you have, darling?" asked Fiona.

"A strong whisky, please, and can we go straight into dinner? I've got to be back at the talkshop by ten."

Charles guided his guest towards the dining-room and seated him at the side of the table before taking his place below the Holbein portrait of the first Earl of Bridgwater, an heirloom his grandfather had left him. Fiona took a seat opposite her husband. During the meal of Beef Wellington, Charles spent a great deal of time catching up on what Alexander had been doing since they had last met. Although they had spent three years together in the Guards as brother officers they rarely saw each other outside of regimental reunions since Charles had entered the House. He made no mention of the real purpose behind the meeting until Fiona provided the opportunity when she served coffee.

"I know you two have a lot to talk about, so I'll leave you to get on with it."

"Thank you," said Alexander. He looked up at Fiona and smiled. "For a lovely dinner."

She smiled back and left them alone.

"Now, Charles," said Alexander, picking up the file he had left on the floor by his side. "I need to pick your brains."

"Go ahead, old fellow," said Charles, "only too delighted to be of assistance."

"Sir Edward Mountjoy has sent me a pretty long list for us to consider, among them a Home Office minister and one or two other Members of Parliament who'll be losing their present seats. What do you think of . . .?"

Dalglish opened the file in front of him as Charles poured him a generous glass of port and offered him a cigar from a gold case that he picked up from the sideboard.

"What a magnificent object," said Alexander, staring in awe at the crested box and the engraved C.G.S. along its top.

"A family heirloom," said Charles. "Should have been left to my brother Rupert, but I was lucky enough to have the same initials as my grandfather."

Alexander handed it back to his host before returning to his notes. "Here's the man who impresses me," he said at last. "Kerslake, Simon Kerslake."

Charles remained silent.

"You don't have an opinion, Charles?"

"Yes."

"So what do you think of Kerslake?"

"Strictly off the record?"

Dalglish nodded, but said nothing.

Charles sipped his port. "Very good," he said.

"Kerslake?"

"No, the port. Taylor's '35. I'm afraid Kerslake is not the same vintage. Need I say more?"

"Well, no, I follow your drift but it's most disappointing. He looks so good on paper."

"On paper is one thing," said Charles, "but having him as your member for twenty years is quite another. You want a man you can rely on. And his wife – never seen in the constituency, you know." He frowned. "I'm afraid I've gone too far."

"No, no," said Alexander. "I've got the picture. Next one is Norman Lamont."

"First class but he's already been selected for Kingston, I'm afraid," said Charles.

Dalglish looked down at his file once again. "Well, what about Pimkin?"

"We were at Eton together. His looks are against him, as my grandmother used to say, but he's a sound man, and very good in the constituency, so they tell me."

"You would recommend him then?"

"I should snap him up before another constituency adopts him."

"That popular is he?" said Alexander. "Thanks for the tip. Pity about Kerslake."

"That was strictly off the record," said Charles.

"Of course. Not a word. You can rely on me."

"Cigar to your liking?"

"Excellent," said Alexander, "but your judgement has always been so good. You only have to look at Fiona to realise that."

Charles smiled.

Most of the other names Dalglish produced were either unknown, unsuitable or easy to dismiss. When Alexander left shortly before ten Fiona asked him if the chat had been worthwhile.

"Yes, I think we've found the right man."

Raymond had the locks on his flat changed that afternoon. It turned out to be more expensive than he had bargained for, and the carpenter had insisted on cash in advance.

The carpenter grinned as he pocketed the money. "I make a fortune doing this job, Guv'nor, I can tell you. At least one gentleman a day, always cash, no receipt. Means the wife and I can spend a month in Ibiza every year, tax free."

Raymond smiled at the thought. He checked his watch; he could just catch the Thursday seven-ten from King's Cross and be in Leeds by ten o'clock for a long weekend.

Alexander Dalglish phoned Charles a week later to tell him Pimkin had made the short list, and that they hadn't considered Kerslake.

"Pimkin didn't go over very well with the committee at the first interview."

"No, he wouldn't," said Charles. "I warned you his looks were agin' him and he may come over a bit right wing at times but he's as sound as a bell and will never let you down, take my word."

"I'll have to, Charles. Because by getting rid of Kerslake we've removed his only real challenger."

Charles put the phone down and dialled the Home Office.

"Simon Kerslake, please."

"Who's calling?"

"Seymour, Whips' office." He was put straight through.

"Simon, it's Charles. I thought I ought to give you an update on Littlehampton."

"That's thoughtful of you," said Simon.

"Not good news, I'm afraid. It turns out the chairman wants the seat for himself. He's making sure the committee only interviews idiots."

"How can you be so certain?"

"I've seen the short list and Pimkin's the only sitting member they're considering."

"I can't believe it."

"No, I was pretty shocked myself. I pressed the case for you, but it fell on deaf ears. Didn't care for your views on hanging or some such words. Still, I can't believe you'll find it hard to pick up a seat."

"I hope you're right, Charles, but in any case thanks for trying."

"Any time. Let me know of any other seats you put your name in for. I have a lot of friends up and down the country."

"Thank you, Charles. Can you pair me for next Thursday?"

Two days later Alec Pimkin was invited by the Littlehampton Conservatives to attend a short-list interview for the selection of a Tory candidate for the new constituency.

"How do I begin to thank you?' he asked Charles when they met up in the bar.

"Keep your word – and I want it in writing," replied Charles.

"What do you mean?"

"A letter to the Chief Whip saying you've changed your mind on the main European vote, and you and the disciples will be abstaining on Thursday."

Pimkin looked cocky. "And if I don't play ball, dear thing?"

"You haven't got the seat yet, Alec, and I might find it necessary to phone Alexander Dalglish and tell him about that awfully nice little boy you made such a fool of yourself over when you were up at Oxford."

Three days later the Chief Whip received the letter from Pimkin. He immediately summoned his junior Whip.

"*Well done*, Charles. How did you manage to succeed where we've all failed – and the disciples as well?"

"Matter of loyalty," said Charles. "Pimkin saw that in the end."

On the final day of the Great Debate on "the principle of entry" into Europe the Prime Minister delivered the winding-up speech. He rose at nine-thirty to cheers from both sides. At ten o'clock the House divided and voted in favour of "the principle" by a majority of 112. Sixty-nine Labour MPs, led by Roy Jenkins, had helped to swell the Government's majority.

Raymond Gould voted against the motion in accordance with his long-held beliefs. Andrew Fraser joined Simon Kerslake and Charles Seymour in the Ayes lobby. Alec Pimkin and the twelve disciples remained in their places on the Commons benches while the vote took place.

When Charles heard the Speaker read out the final result he felt a moment of triumph, although he realised that he still had the committee stage to go through. Hundreds of clauses, any of which could go wrong and turn the bill into a farce. Nevertheless the first round belonged to him.

Ten days later Alec Pimkin defeated a keen young Conservative just down from Cambridge and a local woman councillor to be selected as prospective candidate for Littlehampton.

CHAPTER FOURTEEN

Andrew studied the case once again and decided to make his own inquiries. Too many constituents had in the past demonstrated that they were willing to lie to him in surgery as happily as they would in the witness box to any judge.

Robert was trying to climb up on to his lap. Andrew hoisted him the remainder of the way in one tug and attempted to return to his papers. "Whose side are you on?" Andrew demanded as his son dribbled all over his freshly written notes. He stopped to pat his bottom. "Ugh," he said, putting the case file by his side on the floor. A few minutes later Robert had been changed and left with his mother.

"I'm afraid your son is not over-anxious to help me in my desire to secure the release of an innocent man," Andrew shouted over his shoulder.

He settled down to go over the papers once more, something about the case didn't ring true . . . Andrew dialled the Procurator Fiscal's number. There was one man who could cut his work in half with a sentence.

"Good morning, Mr Fraser. What can I do for you, sir?"

Andrew had to smile. Angus Sinclair was a contemporary of his father and had known Andrew all his life, but once he was in his office he treated everyone as a stranger, making no exception.

"He even calls his wife 'Mrs Sinclair' when she rings the office," Sir Duncan once told him. Andrew was willing to join in the game.

"Good morning, Mr Sinclair. I need your advice as Procurator Fiscal."

"Always happy to be of service, sir."

"I want to talk to you off the record about the Paddy O'Halloran case. Do you remember it?"

"Of course, everyone in this office remembers that case."

"Good," said Andrew. "Then you'll know what a help you can be to me in cutting through the thicket."

"Thank you, sir," the slight burr came back down the telephone.

"A group of my constituents, whom I wouldn't trust further than I could toss a caber, claim O'Halloran was framed for the Princes Street bank robbery last year. They don't deny he has criminal tendencies" – Andrew would have chuckled if he hadn't been speaking to Angus Sinclair – "but they say he never left a pub called the Sir Walter Scott the entire time the robbery was taking place. All you have to tell me, Mr Sinclair, is that you have no doubt that O'Halloran was guilty and I'll drop my inquiries. If you say nothing, I shall dig deeper."

Andrew waited, but he received no reply.

"Thank you, Mr Sinclair." Although he knew it would elicit no response, he couldn't resist adding: "No doubt I'll see you at the golf club some time over the weekend." The silence continued.

"Goodbye, Mr Sinclair."

"Good day, Mr Fraser."

Andrew settled back: it was going to be a lengthy exercise. He started by checking with all the people who had confirmed O'Halloran's alibi that night but after interviewing the first eight he came to the reluctant conclusion that none of them could be trusted as a witness. Whenever he came across another of O'Halloran's friends the expression "anyone's for a pint" kept crossing his mind. The time had come to talk with the landlord of the Sir Walter Scott.

"I couldn't be sure, Mr Fraser, but I think he was here that evening. Trouble is, O'Halloran came almost every night. It's hard to recall."

"Do you know anyone who might remember? Someone you could trust with your cash register?"

"That'd be pushing your luck in this pub, Mr Fraser." The landlord thought for a moment. "However, there's old Mrs Bloxham," he said at last, slapping the drying-up cloth over his shoulder. "She sits in that corner every night." He pointed to a small round table that would have been crowded had it seated more than two people. "If she says he was here, he was."

Andrew asked the landlord where Mrs Bloxham lived and then, hoping she was in, made his way to 43 Mafeking Road, neatly sidestepping a gang of young children playing football in the middle of the street. He climbed some steps that badly needed repairing and knocked on the door of number forty-three.

"Is it another general election already, Mr Fraser?" asked a dis-believing old lady as she peered through the letter-box.

"No, it's nothing to do with politics, Mrs Bloxham," said Andrew, bending down. "I came round to seek your advice on a personal matter."

"A personal matter? Better come on in out of the cold then," she said, opening the door to him. "There's a terrible draft rushes through this corridor."

Andrew followed the old lady as she shuffled down the dingy corridor in her carpet slippers to a room that he would have said was colder than it had been outside on the street. There were no ornaments in the room save a crucifix that stood on a narrow mantelpiece below a pastel print of the Virgin Mary. Mrs Bloxham beckoned Andrew to a wooden seat by a table yet unlaid. She eased her plump frame into an ancient stuffed armchair. It groaned under her weight and a strand of horsehair fell to the floor. Andrew looked more carefully at the old lady. She was wearing a black shawl over a dress she must have worn a thousand times. Once settled in her chair, she kicked off her slippers.

"Feet still giving you trouble, then?" he inquired.

"Doctor doesn't seem to be able to explain the swellings," she said, without bitterness.

Andrew leaned on the table and noticed what a fine piece of furniture it was, and how incongruous it looked in its present surroundings. He was struck by the craftsmanship of the carved Georgian legs. She noticed he was admiring it. "My great-grandfather gave that to my great-grandmother the day they were married, Mr Fraser."

"It's magnificent," said Andrew.

She didn't seem to hear because all she said was, "What can I do for you, sir?" The second time that day he had been addressed by an elder in that way.

Andrew went over the O'Halloran story again. Mrs Bloxham listened intently, leaning forward slightly and cupping her hand round her ear to be sure she could hear every word.

"That O'Halloran's an evil one," she said, "not to be trusted. Our Blessed Lady will have to be very forgiving to allow the likes of him to enter the kingdom of heaven." Andrew smiled. "Not that I'm expecting to meet all that many politicians when I get there either," she added, giving Andrew a toothless grin.

"Could O'Halloran possibly have been there that Friday night as all his friends claim?" Andrew asked.

"He was there all right," said Mrs Bloxham. "No doubt about that – saw him with my own eyes."

"How can you be so sure?"

"Spilled his beer over my best dress, and I knew something bad would happen on the thirteenth, especially with it being a Friday. I won't forgive him for that. I still haven't been able to get the stain out despite what those washing-powder ads tell you on the telly."

"Why didn't you inform the police immediately?"

"Didn't ask," she said simply. "They've been after him for a long time for a lot of things they couldn't pin on him, but for once he was in the clear."

Andrew finished writing his notes and then rose to leave. Mrs Bloxham heaved herself out of the chair, dispensing yet more horsehair on to the floor. They walked to the door together. "I'm sorry I couldn't offer you a cup of tea but I'm right out at the moment," she said. "If you had come tomorrow it would have been all right."

Andrew paused on the doorstep.

"I get the pension tomorrow, you see,' she replied to his unasked question.

It took Elizabeth some time to find a locum to cover for her so that she could travel to Redcorn for the interview. Once again the children had to be left with a baby-sitter. The local and national press had made him the hot favourite for the new seat. Elizabeth put on what she called her best Conservative outfit, a pale blue suit with a dark blue collar that hid everything on top and reached well below her knees.

The journey from King's Cross to Newcastle took three hours and twenty minutes, on what was described in the timetable as 'the express'. At least Simon was able to catch up with a great deal of the paper work that had been stuffed into his red box. Civil servants, he reflected, rarely allowed politicians time to involve themselves in politics. They wouldn't have been pleased to learn that he spent an hour of the journey reading the last four weekly copies of the *Redcorn News*.

At Newcastle they were met by the wife of the Association treasurer, who had volunteered to escort the minister and Mrs Kerslake to the constituency to be sure they were in time for the interview. "That's very thoughtful of you," said Elizabeth, as she stared at the mode of transport that had been chosen to take them the next forty miles.

The ancient Austin Mini took a further hour and a half through the winding B-roads before they reached their destination, and the treasurer's wife never drew breath once throughout the entire journey. When Simon and Elizabeth piled out of the car at the market town of Redcorn they were physically and mentally exhausted.

The treasurer's wife took them through to the constituency headquarters and introduced them both to the agent.

"Good of you to come," he said. "Hell of a journey, isn't it?"

Elizabeth felt unable to disagree with his judgement. But on this occasion she made no comment, feeling that if this was to be Simon's best chance of returning to Parliament she had already decided to give him every support possible. Nevertheless she dreaded the thought of her husband making the journey to Redcorn twice a month as she feared they would see even less of each other than they did at present, let alone the children.

"Now the form is," began the agent, "that we are interviewing six potential candidates and they'll be seeing you last." He winked knowingly.

Simon and Elizabeth smiled uncertainly.

"I'm afraid they won't be ready for you for at least another hour, so you have time for a stroll round the town."

Simon was glad of the chance to stretch his legs and take a closer look at Redcorn. He and Elizabeth walked slowly round the pretty market town, admiring the Elizabethan architecture that had somehow survived irresponsible or greedy town planners. They even climbed the hill to take a look inside the magnificent perpendicular church which dominated the surrounding area.

As he walked back past the shops in the high street Simon nodded to those locals who appeared to recognise him.

"A lot of people seem to know who you are," said Elizabeth, and then they saw the paper rack outside the local newsagent. They sat on the bench in the market square and read the lead story under a large picture of Simon.

"Redcorn's next MP?" ran the headline.

The story volunteered the fact that although Simon Kerslake had to be considered the favourite, Bill Travers, a local farmer who had been chairman of the county council the previous year, was still thought to have an outside chance.

Simon began to feel a little sick in the stomach. It reminded him of the day he had been interviewed at Coventry Central nearly eight years before. Now that he was a minister of the Crown he wasn't any less nervous.

When he and Elizabeth returned to constituency headquarters they were informed that only two more candidates had been seen and the third was still being interviewed. They walked around the town once again, even more slowly this time, watching the shopkeepers put up their coloured shutters and turn "Open" signs to "Closed".

"What a pleasant market town," said Simon, trying to find out how his wife was feeling.

"And the people seem so polite after London," she added.

Simon smiled as they headed back to the party headquarters. As they passed Simon and Elizabeth they bid the strangers "Good evening", courteous people whom Simon felt he would have been proud to represent. But although they walked slowly Elizabeth and he could not make their journey last more than thirty minutes.

When they returned a third time to constituency headquarters the fourth candidate was leaving the interview room. She looked very despondent. "It shouldn't be long now," said the agent, but it was another forty minutes before they heard a ripple of applause, and a man dressed in a Harris tweed jacket and brown trousers left the room. He didn't seem happy either.

The agent ushered Simon and Elizabeth through, and as they entered everyone in the room stood. Ministers of the Crown did not visit Redcorn often.

Simon waited for Elizabeth to be seated before he took the chair in the centre of the room facing the committee. He estimated that there were about fifty people present and they were all staring at him, showing no aggression, merely curiosity. He looked around at the weather-beaten faces. Most of them, male and female, were dressed in tweed. In his dark striped London suit Simon felt out of place.

"And now," said the chairman, "we welcome the Right Honourable Simon Kerslake, MP."

Simon had to smile at the mistake so many people made in thinking that all ministers were automatically members of the Privy Council, and therefore entitled to the prefix "Right Honourable" instead of the plain "Honourable" accorded to all MPs – and then only when they were present in the House.

"Mr Kerslake will address us for twenty minutes, and he has kindly agreed to answer questions after that," added the chairman.

Simon felt confident he had spoken well, but even his few carefully chosen quips received no more than a smile, and his more serious comments elicited little response. This was not a group of people given to showing their emotions. When he had finished he sat down to respectful clapping and murmurs.

"Now the minister will take questions," said the chairman.

"Where do you stand on hanging?" said a scowling middle-aged woman in a grey suit seated in the front row.

Simon explained his reasons for being a convinced abolitionist. The scowl did not move from the questioner's face and Simon thought to himself how much happier she would be with Ronnie Nethercote as her member.

A man in a hacking jacket asked: "How do you feel, Mr Kerslake, about this year's farm subsidy?"

"Good on eggs, tough on beef, and disastrous for pig farmers. Or at least that's what I read on the front page of *Farmer's Weekly* yesterday." Some of them laughed for the first time. "It hasn't proved necessary for me to have a great knowledge of farming in Coventry Central, but if I am lucky enough to be selected for Redcorn I shall try to learn quickly, and with your help I shall hope to master the farmers' problems." Several heads nodded their approval.

"Miss Pentecost, chairman of the Women's Advisory," announced a tall, thin spinsterish woman who had stood up to catch the chairman's eye. "May I be permitted to ask Mrs Kerslake a question? If your husband were offered this seat, would you be willing to come and live in Northumberland?"

Elizabeth had dreaded the question because she knew that if Simon was offered the constituency she would be expected to resign her post at the hospital. Simon turned and looked towards his wife.

"No," she replied directly. "I am a doctor at St Mary's Hospital,

Paddington, where I practise gynaecology. I support my husband in his career but, like Margaret Thatcher, I believe a woman has the right to a good education and then the chance to use her qualifications to their best advantage."

A ripple of applause went round the room and Simon smiled at his wife.

The next question was on Europe, and Simon gave an unequivocal statement as to his reasons for backing the Prime Minister in his desire to see Britain as part of the Common Market.

Simon continued to answer questions on subjects ranging from trade union reform to violence on television before the chairman asked, "Are there any more questions?"

There was a long silence and just as he was about to thank Simon the scowling lady in the front row, without being recognised by the chair, asked what Mr Kerslake's views were on abortion.

"Morally, I'm against it," said Simon. "At the time of the Abortion Act many of us believed it would stem the tide of divorce. We have been proved wrong: the rate of divorce has quadrupled. Nevertheless, in the cases of rape or fear of physical or mental injury arising from birth I would have to support the medical advice given at the time. Elizabeth and I have two children and my wife's job is to see that babies are safely delivered," he added.

The lips moved from a scowl to a straight line.

"Thank you," said the chairman. "It was good of you to give us so much of your time. Perhaps you and Mrs Kerslake would be kind enough to wait outside."

Simon and Elizabeth joined the other hopeful candidates, their wives and the agent in a small dingy room at the back of the building. When they saw the half-empty trestle table in front of them they both remembered they hadn't had any lunch and devoured what was left of the curling cucumber sandwiches and the cold sausage rolls.

"What happens next?" Simon asked the agent between mouthfuls.

"Nothing out of the ordinary. They'll have a discussion, allowing everyone to express their views, and then vote. It should all be over in twenty minutes."

Elizabeth checked her watch: it was seven o'clock and the last train was at nine-fifteen.

"Ought to make the train comfortably," said Simon.

An hour later when no smoke had emerged from the chimney the agent suggested to all the candidates who had a long journey ahead of them that they might like to check into the Bell Inn just over the road.

When Simon looked around the room it was clear that everyone else had done so in advance.

"You had better stay put in case you're called again," Elizabeth said. "I'll go off and book a room and at the same time call and see how the children are getting on."

"Probably eaten the poor baby-sitter by now," said Simon.

Elizabeth smiled before slipping out and making her way to the small hotel.

Simon opened his red box and tried to complete some work. The man who looked like a farmer came over and introduced himself.

"I'm Bill Travers, the chairman of the new constituency," he began. "I only wanted to say that you'll have my full support as chairman if the committee select you."

"Thank you," said Simon.

"I had hoped to represent this area, as my grandfather did. But I shall understand if Redcorn prefers to choose a man destined for the Cabinet rather than someone who would be happy to spend his life on the back benches."

Simon was touched by his opponent's goodwill, and would have liked to respond in kind but Travers quickly added, "Forgive me, I'll not waste any more of your time. I can see" – he looked down at the red box – "that you have a lot of work to catch up on."

Simon felt guilty as he watched the man walk away. A few minutes later Elizabeth returned and tried to smile. "The only room left is smaller than Peter's and it faces the main road, so it's just about as noisy."

"At least no children to say 'I'm hungry'," he said, touching her hand.

It was a little after nine when a weary chairman came out and asked all the candidates if he could have their attention. Husbands and wives all faced him. "My committee want to thank you for going through this grim procedure. It has been hard for us to decide something that we hope not to have to discuss again for twenty years." He paused. "The committee are going to invite Mr Bill Travers to fight the Redcorn seat at the next election."

In a sentence it was all over. Simon's throat went dry.

He and Elizabeth didn't get much sleep in their tiny room at the Bell Inn, and it hadn't helped that the agent told them the final vote had been twenty-five – twenty-three.

"I don't think Miss Pentecost liked me," said Elizabeth, feeling guilty. "If I had told her that I would have been willing to live in the constituency I think you'd have been offered the seat."

"I doubt it," said Simon. "In any case it's no use agreeing to their terms at the interview and then imposing your own when you have been offered the constituency. My guess is you'll find Redcorn has chosen the right man."

Elizabeth smiled at her husband, grateful for his support.

"There will be other seats," said Simon, only too aware that time was now running out. "You'll see."

Elizabeth prayed that he would prove right, and that next time the choice of a constituency would not make her have to face the dilemma she had so far managed to avoid.

When Raymond took silk and became a Queen's Counsel Joyce made one of her periodic trips to London. The occasion she decided warranted another visit to Harvey Nichols. She recalled her first trip to the store so many years before when she had accompanied her husband to meet the Prime Minister. Raymond had come so far since then although their relationship seemed to have progressed so little. She had given up hope of being a mother, but still wanted him to believe she was a good wife. She couldn't help thinking how much better-looking Raymond had become in middle age, and feared the same could not be said of her.

She enjoyed watching the legal ceremony as her husband was presented in court before the judges. Latin words spoken but not understood. Suddenly her husband was Raymond Gould, QC, MP.

She and Raymond arrived late in chambers for the celebration party. Everyone seemed to have turned out in her husband's honour. Raymond felt full of *bonhomie* and was chatting to the chief clerk when Sir Nigel handed him a glass of champagne. Then he saw a familiar figure by the mantelpiece and remembered that the trial in Manchester was over. He managed to circle the room speaking to everyone but Stephanie Arnold. To his horror he turned to see her introducing herself to his wife. Every time he glanced towards them they seemed deeper in conversation.

"Ladies and gentlemen," said Sir Nigel, banging a table. He waited for silence. "We are always proud in chambers when one of our members takes silk. It is a comment not only on the man but also on his chambers. And when it is the youngest silk – still under forty – it adds to that pride. All of you, of course, know that Raymond also serves in another place in which we expect him to rise to even greater glory. May I add finally how pleasant it is to have his wife Joyce among us tonight. Ladies and gentlemen," he concluded. "The toast is Raymond Gould, QC."

"Raymond Gould, QC," said everyone in chorus. Then, "Speech, speech."

"I would like to thank all those people who made this great honour possible," began Raymond. "My producer, my director, the other stars and not forgetting the criminals, without whom I would have no profession to profess. And finally," he said, "to those of you who want to see the back of me, I direct you all to work tirelessly to ensure the return of a Labour Government at the next election. Thank you."

The applause was sustained and genuine and many of his colleagues were impressed by how relaxed Raymond had become of late. As they came up to congratulate him Raymond couldn't help noticing that Stephanie and Joyce had resumed their conversation. Raymond was handed another glass of champagne just as an earnest young pupil called Patrick Montague who had recently joined them from chambers in Bristol engaged him in conversation. Although Montague had been with them for some weeks Raymond had never spoken to him at length before. He seemed to have very clear views on criminal law and the changes that were necessary. For the first time in his life Raymond felt he was no longer a young man.

Suddenly both women were at his side.

"Hello, Raymond."

"Hello, Stephanie," he said awkwardly and looked anxiously towards his wife. "Do you know Patrick Montague?" he asked, absent-mindedly.

The three of them burst out laughing.

"What's so funny," asked Raymond.

"You do embarrass me sometimes, Raymond," said Joyce. "Surely you realise Stephanie and Patrick are engaged?"

CHAPTER FIFTEEN

'With or without civil servants?" asked Simon as Andrew entered the minister's office.

"Without, please."

"Fine," said Simon and pressed a switch on the intercom by his desk.

"I don't want to be disturbed while I'm with Mr Fraser," he said and ushered his colleague towards a comfortable seat in the corner. "Elizabeth was asking me this morning to find out how Robert was getting on."

"It's his second birthday next month and he's overweight for a scrum-half," replied Andrew. "And how's your search for a seat working out?"

"Not too good. The last three constituencies to come up haven't even asked to see me. I can't put a finger on why, except they all seem to have selected local men."

"It's still a long time to the next election. You're sure to find a seat before then."

"It might not be so long if the Prime Minister decides to go to the country and test his strength against the unions."

"That would be a foolish thing to do," said Andrew. "He might defeat us but he still wouldn't defeat the unions."

A young woman came into the room with two cups of coffee, put them on the low Formica table and left the two men alone.

"Have you had time to look at the file?" Andrew continued.

"Yes, I went over it last night between checking over Peter's prep and helping Michael to build a model galleon."

"And how do you feel?" Andrew asked.

"Not very good. I can't get to grips with this new maths they're now teaching, and my mast was the only one that fell off when Elizabeth launched the galleon in the bath."

Andrew laughed.

"I think you've got a case," said Simon, sounding serious.

"Good," said Andrew. "Now the reason I wanted to see you privately is because I feel there are no party political points to be made out of this case for either of us. I've no plans to try to embarrass your department, and I consider it's in the best interest of my constituent to cooperate as closely as I can with you."

"Thank you," said Simon. "So where do you want to go from here?"

"I'd like to table a planted question for your department in the hope that you would consider opening an inquiry. If the inquiry comes to the same conclusion as I have, I would expect you to order a re-trial."

Simon hesitated. "And if the inquiry goes against you will you agree to no reprisals for the Home Office?"

"You have my word on it."

"Shall I ask the civil servants to come in now?"

"Yes, please do."

Simon returned to his desk and pressed a button. A moment later three men in almost identical suits, white shirts with stiff collars and discreet ties entered the room. Between them they could have ruined any police identification parade.

"Mr Fraser," began Simon, "is asking the Home Office to consider . . ."

"Can you explain why Simon Kerslake missed a vote yesterday?"

Charles looked across the table at the Chief Whip.

"No, I can't," he said. "I've been distributing the weekly whip to him the same as every member of my group."

"What's behind it then?"

"I think the poor man has been spending a lot of his time traipsing around the country looking for a seat to fight at the next election."

"That's no excuse," said the Chief Whip. "Duties in the House must come first, every member knows that. He missed a vote on a vital clause during the European Bill last Thursday while everyone else in your group has proved reliable. Despite our majority we seem to be in single figures for almost every clause. Perhaps I should have a word with him?"

"No, no, I'd rather you didn't," said Charles, fearing he sounded a little too insistent. "I consider it my responsibility. I'll speak to him and see that it doesn't happen again."

"All right, Charles, if that's the way you want to play it. Thank God it can't last much longer and the damn thing will soon be law, but we must remain vigilant over every clause. The Labour Party know only too well that if they defeat us on certain key clauses they can still scupper the whole bill, and if I lost one of those by a single vote I would cut Kerslake's throat. Or anyone else's who was responsible."

"I'll make sure he gets the message," said Charles.

"How's Fiona reacting to all these late nights?" the Chief Whip asked, finally relaxing.

"Very well, considering. In fact now that you mention it I have never seen her looking better."

"Can't say my wife is enjoying 'the prep school antics', as she describes our continual late-night sittings. I've had to promise to take her to the West Indies this winter to make up for it. Well, I'll leave you to deal with Kerslake then. Be firm, Charles. Just remember, we can't afford to lose a vote at this late stage."

"Norman Edwards?" repeated Raymond in disbelief. "The General Secretary of the Haulage Union?"

"Yes," said Fred Padgett, getting up from behind his desk.

"But he burnt *Full Employment at any Cost?* on a public bonfire with every journalist he could lay his hands on to witness the conflagration."

"I know," said Fred, returning a letter to the filing cabinet. "I'm only your agent, I'm not here to explain the mysteries of the universe."

"When does he want to see me?" asked Raymond.

"As soon as possible."

"Better ask him if he can come for a drink back at the house round six o'clock."

Raymond had had a heavy Saturday morning surgery and thanks to the still imminent Martians had only found time to grab a sandwich at the pub before going off to pursue his favourite pastime. This week Leeds were playing Liverpool at Elland Road. Sitting in the directors' box every other week in full view of his constituents while he supported his local football team killed 30,000 birds with one stone. Later, when talking to the lads in the dressing-room after the match, he found himself lapsing into a pronounced Yorkshire accent that bore no resemblance to the one he used to address high court judges during the week.

Leeds won three–two and after the match Raymond joined the directors for a drink in the boardroom. He became so impassioned about an off-side decision that could have lost them a point that he nearly forgot about his meeting with Norman Edwards.

Joyce was in the garden showing the union leader her early snow-drops when Raymond returned.

"Sorry I'm late," he shouted, as he hung up his yellow and blue scarf. "I've been to the match."

"Who won?" asked Edwards.

"Leeds, of course, three–two."

"Damn," said Norman, his accent leaving the other in no doubt that he had not spent many nights outside of Liverpool.

"Come on in and have a beer," said Raymond.

"I'd prefer a vodka."

The two men went into the house while Joyce continued with her gardening.

"Well," said Raymond, pouring his guest a Smirnoff. "What brings you all the way from Liverpool if it wasn't to watch the football? Perhaps you want a signed copy of my book for your next union bonfire."

"Don't give me any hassle, Ray. I came all this way because I need your help, simple as that."

"I'm all ears."

"We had a full meeting of the General Purposes Committee yesterday, and one of the brothers has spotted a clause in the European Bill which could put us all out of work."

Norman passed over a copy of the bill to Raymond with the relevant clause marked in red. It gave the minister power to make new haulage and lorry regulations which would come before the House as statutory instruments and thus could not be amended.

"If that gets through the House my boys are in deep trouble."

"Why?" said Raymond.

"Because those bloody Frogs know only too well that there's a Channel between us and them, and if my lads are forced by law to sleep a night each side the only people who'll end up making money on the deal will be the guest-house proprietors."

"What's behind it?" asked Raymond.

"They want us to drop the stuff our end, so they can pick it up on the other side."

"But wouldn't that also be true when they need to deliver goods to us?"

"No. Their journeys are much longer to the coast, and they have to stay overnight anyway, not to mention the fact that there are eight of them to one of us. It's diabolical, nothing less."

Raymond studied the wording in detail while Edwards helped

himself to another vodka.

"The clause doesn't stop you from going over the next day."

"And how much do you think that will add to your costs?" asked Raymond.

"I'll tell you, enough to make us uncompetitive, that's how much," replied the trade-union leader.

"Point taken," said Raymond. "So what's wrong with asking your own member to put the case?"

"Don't trust him. He's pro-European at any price."

"And what about your sponsored trade-union representative in the House?"

"Tom Carson? You must be joking. He's so far to the left that even his own side are suspicious when he supports a cause. We lost the 'tachograph' clause because he championed it. In any case I only put him in the House to get him off my back." Raymond laughed. "Now, all my General Purposes Committee want to know is: would you be willing to fight this clause in the House for us? Not that we can afford the sort of fees you're used to at the bar," he added.

"There would be no fee involved," said Raymond, "but I'm sure you'll be able to repay me in kind sometime in the future."

"Got the picture," said Edwards, touching the side of his nose with a forefinger. "What do I do next?"

"You go back to Liverpool and hope that I am better on an away pitch than your team."

Norman Edwards put on an old raincoat and started to button it up. He smiled at Raymond. "I may have been appalled by your book, Ray. But it doesn't mean I didn't admire it."

The Speaker looked down at the front bench. "Mr Andrew Fraser."

"Number seventeen, sir," said Andrew.

The Speaker looked down to check over the question, seeking a Home Office answer.

Simon rose to the dispatch box, opened his file and said, "Yes, sir."

"Mr Andrew Fraser," called the Speaker again.

Andrew rose from his place on the Opposition front bench to put his supplementary.

"May I thank the minister for agreeing to an inquiry so quickly, and ask him that, if he discovers an injustice has been done to my constituent Mr Paddy O'Halloran, that the Home Secretary will order a re-trial immediately?"

Simon rose again.

"Yes, sir."

"I am grateful to the Honourable Gentleman," said Andrew, half-rising from his place.

All over in less than a minute, but older members who listened to the

brief exchange between Fraser and Kerslake in the House that day had
no doubt that considerable preparation had gone into that minute from
both sides.

"The damn man missed another three-line whip, Charles. It must be
the last time. You've been protecting him for far too long."

"It won't happen again," promised Charles convincingly. "I would
like to give him one more chance. Allow him that."

"You're very loyal to him," said the Chief Whip. "But next time I'm
going to see Kerslake myself and get to the bottom of it."

"It won't happen again," repeated Charles.

"Hm," said the Chief Whip. "Next problem is, are there any clauses
on the European Bill that we should be worried about next week?"

"Yes," replied Charles. "This haulage clause that Raymond Gould
is fighting. He made a brilliant case on the floor of the House, and got
all his own side and half of ours backing him."

"He's not the sponsored MP for the Haulage Union," said the Chief
Whip, surprised.

"No, the unions obviously felt Tom Carson wouldn't help the cause
and he's hopping mad at the slight."

"Clever of them to pick Gould. He improves as a speaker every time I
hear him, and no one can fault him when it comes to a point of law."

"So we'd better face the fact that we're going to lose the clause?"

"Never. We'll redraft the damn thing so that it's acceptable and *seen*
to be compassionate. It's not a bad time to be the defender of the union
interests. That way we'll keep Gould from getting all the credit. I'll
speak to the PM tonight – and don't forget what I said about
Kerslake."

Charles returned to his office and realised that in future he would
have to be more careful about telling Simon Kerslake when he was
paired for the European Bill. He suspected he had carried this ploy as
far as he could for now.

Simon had read the final report prepared by his department on the
O'Halloran case while Elizabeth was trying to get to sleep. He only had
to go over the details once to realise that he would have to order a re-
trial and institute a full investigation into the past record of the police
officers who had been involved in the case.

When Andrew heard the news, and that the re-trial would be held in
London, he asked Raymond Gould to represent O'Halloran.

"Praise indeed," said Raymond, who still considered Andrew
among the Commons' finest orators. He somehow managed to fit
O'Halloran into his busy schedule.

The trial was in its third day when Mr Justice Comyns, after
listening to Mrs Bloxham's evidence, stopped proceedings and instruc-

ted the jury to return a verdict of not guilty.

Andrew received praise from all quarters of the House, but he was quick to acknowledge the support given him by Simon Kerslake and the Home Office. *The Times* even wrote a leader the next day on the proper use of influence by a constituency MP.

Some months later the court awarded O'Halloran £25,000 in compensation. The only drawback Andrew's success caused was that every convict's mother north of Hadrian's wall queued to tell him about her innocent son at his fortnightly surgery. But during the year he took only one seriously and once again began to check into the details.

During the long hot summer of 1972 clause after clause of the European Bill was voted on, often through the night. On some occasions the Government managed majorities of only five or six but somehow the bill remained intact.

Charles would often arrive home at Eaton Square at three in the morning to find Fiona asleep, only to leave again before she had woken. Veterans of the House, both servants and elected, confirmed they had never experienced anything like it since the Second World War.

And, just as suddenly, the last vote was taken and the marathon was over. The European Bill was through the Commons and on its way to the Upper House to receive their lordship's approval. Charles wondered what he would do with all the hours that were suddenly left him in the day.

When the bill finally received the Royal Assent in October the Chief Whip held a celebration lunch at the Carlton Club in St James's to thank all his team. "And in particular, Charles Seymour," he said, raising his glass during an impromptu speech. When the lunch broke up the Chief Whip offered Charles a lift back to the Commons in his official car. They travelled along Piccadilly, down Haymarket, through Trafalgar Square and into Whitehall. Just as the Commons came into sight the black Rover turned into Downing Street, as Charles assumed, to drop the Chief Whip at No. 12. But as the car stopped the Chief Whip said, "The Prime Minister is expecting you in five minutes."

"What? Why?" said Charles, as he joined his colleague outside No. 10.

"Timed it rather well, didn't I?" said the Chief Whip – and headed off towards No. 12.

Charles stood alone in front of No. 10. The door was opened by a man in a long black coat. "Good afternoon, Mr Seymour."

The Prime Minister saw Charles in his study and, as ever, wasted no time on small talk.

"Thank you for all the hard work you have put in on the European Bill."

"It was a tremendous challenge," said Charles, searching for words.

"As will be your next job," said Mr Heath. "I want you to take over as one of the Ministers of State at the Department of Trade and Industry."

Charles was speechless.

"With all the problems we are going to encounter with the trade unions during the next few months, that should keep you fully occupied."

"It certainly will," said Charles.

He still hadn't been asked to sit down, but as the Prime Minister was now rising from behind his desk it was clear that the meeting was over.

"You and Fiona must come and have dinner at No. 10 as soon as you've settled into your new department," said the Prime Minister as they walked towards the door.

"Thank you," Charles said.

As he stepped back on to Downing Street a driver opened the back door of a shiny Austin Westminster. It was several moments before Charles realised the car was his.

"The Commons, sir?"

"No, I'd like to return to Eaton Square for a few minutes," he said, sitting back and enjoying the thought of tackling his new job.

The car drove past the Commons, up Victoria Street and on to Eaton Square. He wanted to tell Fiona that all the hard work had been rewarded. He felt guilty about how little he had seen of her lately, although he could not believe it would be much better now that he was to be involved in trade union legislation. How much he still hoped for a son, perhaps even that would prove possible now. The car came to a halt outside the Georgian house. Charles ran up the steps and into the hall. He could hear his wife's voice from the first floor. He took the wide staircase in bounds of two and three at a time, and threw open the bedroom door.

"I'm the new Minister of State at the Department of Trade and Industry," he announced to Fiona, who was lying in bed.

Alexander Dalglish looked up. He showed no sign of interest in Charles's elevation.

When Andrew rang Angus Sinclair at the Procurator Fiscal's office to find that nothing was known of Ricky Hodge and that Sinclair was able to confirm that he had no criminal record, Andrew felt he had stumbled on a case with international implications.

As Ricky Hodge was in a Turkish jail any inquiries had to be made through the Foreign Office. Andrew did not have the same relationship with the Foreign Secretary as he did with Simon, so he felt the direct approach would be best and put down a question to be answered in the House. He worded it carefully: "What action does the Foreign Secretary intend to take over the confiscation of a British passport from a constituent of the Honourable member for Edinburgh Carlton, details of which have been supplied to him?"

When the question came in front of the House on the following Wednesday the Foreign Secretary rose to answer the question himself. He stood at the dispatch box and peered over his half-moon spectacles and said:

"Her Majesty's Government are pursuing this matter through the usual diplomatic channels."

Andrew was quickly on his feet. "Does the Right Honourable Gentleman realise that my constituent has been in a Turkish prison for six months and has still not been charged?"

"Yes, sir," replied the Foreign Secretary. "I have asked the Turkish Embassy to supply the Foreign Office with more details of the case."

Andrew leaped up again. "How long will my constituent have to be forgotten in Ankara before the Foreign Secretary does more than ask for the details of his case?"

The Foreign Secretary rose again showing no sign of annoyance. "I will report those findings to the Honourable Member as quickly as possible."

"When? Tomorrow, next week, next year?" Andrew shouted angrily.

"When?" joined in a chorus of Labour back-benchers, but the Speaker called for the next question above the uproar.

Within the hour Andrew received a handwritten note from the Foreign Office. It read: "If Mr Fraser would be kind enough to telephone, the Foreign Secretary would be delighted to make an appointment to see him."

Andrew phoned from the Commons and was invited to join the Foreign Secretary in Whitehall immediately.

The Foreign Office, known as "The Palazzo" by its inmates, has an atmosphere of its own. Although Andrew had worked in a Government department as a minister he was still struck by its grandeur. He was met at the courtyard entrance and guided along yards of marble corridors before climbing a fine double staircase at the top of which he was greeted by the Foreign Secretary's Principal Private Secretary.

"Sir Alec will see you immediately, Mr Fraser," he said, and led Andrew past the magnificent pictures and tapestries which lined the way. He was taken into a beautifully proportioned room. The Foreign Secretary stood in front of an Adam fireplace over which hung a portrait of Lord Palmerston.

"Fraser, how kind of you to come at such short notice. I do hope it has not caused you any inconvenience." Platitudes, thought Andrew. Next the silly man will be mentioning my father. "I don't think we have met before, but of course I have known your father for many years. Won't you sit down?"

"I realise you are a busy man. Can we get down to the point at issue, Foreign Secretary?" Andrew demanded.

"Of course," Sir Alec said courteously. "Forgive me for taking up so much of your time." Without a further word, he handed Andrew a file marked "Richard M. Hodge – Confidential". "Although Members of Parliament are not subject to the Official Secrets Act I know you will respect the fact that this file is classified."

Another bluff, thought Andrew. He flicked back the cover. It was true: exactly as he had suspected, Ricky Hodge had never been arrested or charged. He turned the page. "Rome, child prostitution; Marseilles, narcotics; Paris, blackmail;" Page after page, ending in Turkey, where Hodge had been found in possession of four pounds of heroin which he had been selling in small packets on the black market. In his twenty-nine years Ricky Hodge had spent eleven of the last fourteen in foreign jails.

Andrew closed the file and could feel the sweat on his forehead. It was some moments before he spoke. "I apologise, Foreign Secretary," he said. "I have made a fool of myself."

"When I was a young man," said Sir Alec, "I made a similar mistake on behalf of a constituent. Ernie Bevin was Foreign Secretary at the time. He could have crucified me in the House with the knowledge he had. Instead he revealed everything over a drink in this room. I sometimes wish the public could see members in their quiet moments as well as in their rowdy ones."

Andrew thanked Sir Alec and walked thoughtfully back to the House. The *Evening Standard* poster outside the Commons caught his eye. 'O'Halloran arrested again.' He bought a copy, stood by the railings and began reading. Paddy O'Halloran had been detained in a Glasgow police station and charged with robbing the Bank of Scotland in Sauchiehall Street. Andrew wondered if his friends would allege it was another "frame up" by the police until he read the next paragraph. "O'Halloran was arrested leaving the bank in possession of a shotgun and £25,000 in used notes. He said when apprehended by the police, 'I've just been clearing my account.' "

At home, Louise told him that Ricky Hodge had done him a favour.

"How's that possible?" asked Andrew.

"You won't take yourself so seriously in future," she smiled.

When Andrew conducted his next surgery in Edinburgh two weeks later he was surprised to see that Mrs Bloxham had made an appointment.

As he greeted her at the door he was even more surprised. She was wearing a bright crimplene dress and a new pair of squeaky brown leather shoes. She also looked as if "Our Blessed Lady" might have to wait a few more years to receive her after all. Andrew motioned her to a seat.

"I came to thank you, Mr Fraser," she said, once she was settled.
"What for?" asked Andrew.

"For sending that nice young man round from Christ–ies. They auctioned great-grandma's table for me. I couldn't believe my luck – it fetched £1,400." Andrew smiled. "So it don't matter about the stain on the dress any more." She paused. "It even made up for having to eat off the floor for three months."

Simon steered the new Boundary Commission recommendations unspectacularly through the House as an order in Council, and suddenly he had lost his own constituency. His colleagues in Coventry were understanding, and nursed those wards that would become theirs at the next election in order that he might spend more time searching for a new seat.

Seven seats became available during the year but Simon was only interviewed for two of them. Both were almost on the Scottish border and both put him in second place. He began to appreciate what it must feel like for an Olympic favourite to be awarded the silver medal.

Ronnie Nethercote's monthly board reports began to paint an increasingly sombre picture, thus reflecting in real life what the politicians were decreeing in Parliament. Ronnie had decided to postpone going public until the climate was more advantageous. Simon couldn't disagree with the judgement, but when he checked his special overdraft facility the interest on his loans had pushed the figure in red to over £90,000.

When unemployment first passed the million mark and Ted Heath ordered a pay and prices freeze strikes broke out all over the country.

The new parliamentary session in the autumn was dominated by the issue of a Prices and Incomes policy. Charles Seymour became involved in putting the case for the Government. While he didn't always win every argument, he was now so well-briefed on his subject that he no longer feared making a fool of himself at the dispatch box. Raymond Gould and Andrew Fraser both made passionate speeches on behalf of the unions, but the Conservative majority beat them again and again.

However, the Prime Minister was moving inexorably towards a head-on clash with the unions and an early general election.

When all three party conferences were over members returned to the Commons aware that it was likely to be their last session before the general election. It was openly being said in the corridors that all the Prime Minister was waiting for was a catalyst. The miners provided it. In the middle of a bleak winter they called an all-out strike for more pay in defiance of the Government's new trade union legislation.

In a television interview the Prime Minister told the nation that with unemployment at an unprecedented 2,294,448 and the country on a three-day week he had to call an election to ensure that the rule of law be maintained. The inner Cabinet advised Heath to plump for 28 February 1974.

'Who runs the country?' became the Tory theme but seemed only to emphasize class differences, rather than uniting the country as Edward Heath had hoped.

Andrew Fraser had his doubts but he faced a different threat in his own constituency, where the Scottish Nationalists were using the quarrel between the two major parties to promote their own cause. He returned to Scotland, to be warned by his father that the Scottish Nationalists were no longer a joke and that he would be facing a hard campaign against the robust local candidate, Jock McPherson.

Raymond Gould travelled back to Leeds, confident that the north-east industrial area would not tolerate Heath's high-handedness.

Charles felt sure that the people would back any party which had shown the courage to stand up to the unions, although the left wing, led vociferously by Tom Carson, made a great play of the "two nations" issue, insisting that the Government were out to crush the Labour movement once and for all.

Charles drove down to Sussex to find his supporters glad of the chance to put those "lazy trade unionists" in their place.

Simon, with no seat to fight, worked on in the Home Office right up to the day of the election, convinced that his career was facing only a temporary setback.

"I'll fight the first by-election that comes up," he promised Elizabeth.

"Even if it's a mining seat in South Wales?" she replied.

Many months had passed before Charles had found it possible even to sustain a conversation with Fiona for any length of time. Neither wanted a divorce, both citing the ailing Earl of Bridgwater as their reason, although inconvenience and loss of face were nearer the truth. In public it would have been hard to detect the change in their relationship since they had never been given to overt affection.

Charles gradually became aware that it was possible for marriages to have been over for years without outsiders knowing it. Certainly the old earl never found out, because even on his death bed he told Fiona to hurry up and produce an heir.

"Do you think you'll ever forgive me?" Fiona once asked her husband.

"Never," he replied, with a finality that encouraged no further discourse.

During the three-week election campaign in Sussex they both went about their duties with a professionalism that masked their true feelings.

"How is your husband bearing up?" someone would inquire.

"Much enjoying the campaign and looking forward to returning to Government," was Fiona's stock reply.

"And how is dear Lady Fiona?" Charles was continously asked.

"Never better than when she's helping in the constituency," was his.

On Sundays, at one church after another, he read the lesson with confidence while she sang "Fight the good fight" in a clear contralto.

The demands of a rural constituency are considerably different from those of a city. Every village, however small, expects the member to visit them and to recall the local chairmen's names. Subtle changes were taking place: Fiona no longer whispered the names in Charles's ear. Charles no longer turned to her for advice.

During the campaign Charles would ring the photographer on the local paper to discover which events his editor had instructed him to cover that day. With the list of places and times in his hand Charles would arrive on each occasion a few minutes before the photographer. The Labour candidate complained officially to the local editor that Mr Seymour's photograph was never out of the paper.

"If you were present at these functions we would be only too happy to publish your photo," said the editor.

"But they never invite me," cried the Labour candidate.

They don't invite Seymour either, the editor wanted to say, but he somehow manages to be there. It was never far from the editor's mind that his proprietor was a Tory peer so he kept his mouth shut.

All the way up to election day Charles and Fiona opened bazaars, attended dinners, drew raffles and only just stopped short of kissing babies.

Once, when Fiona asked him, Charles admitted that he hoped to be moved to the Foreign Office as a Minister of State, and perhaps to be made a Privy Councillor.

On the last day of February they dressed in silence and went off to their local polling station to vote. The photographer was there on the steps to take their picture. They stood closer together than they had for some weeks, looking like a smart register office couple. Charles knew it would be the main photograph on the front page of the *Sussex Gazette* the following day, as surely as he knew the Labour candidate would be relegated to a half-column mention on the inside page not far from the obituaries.

The count in a rural seat is always taken the following morning at a more leisurely pace than is customary for its city cousins. So Charles anticipated that by the time he arrived in the town hall the Conservative majority in the House would already be assured. But it was not to be, and the result still hung in the balance that Friday morning.

Edward Heath did not concede when the newscasters predicted he would fail to be given the overall majority he required. Charles spent the day striding around the town hall with an anxious look on his face. The little piles of votes soon became larger and it was obvious that he would hold the seat with at least his usual 21,000 – or was it 22,000 – ? majority. He never could remember the exact figure. But as the day progressed it became more and more difficult to assess the national verdict.

The last result came in from Northern Ireland a little after four o'clock that afternoon and a BBC commentator announced –

Labour	301
Conservative	296
Liberal	14
Ulster Unionists	11
Scottish Nationalists	7
Welsh Nationalists	2
Others	4

Ted Heath invited the Liberal leader to join him at Downing Street for talks in the hope that they could form a coalition. The Liberals demanded a firm commitment to electoral reform and, in particular, to proportional representation by the next election. Heath knew he could never get his back-benchers to deliver. On the Monday morning he told the Queen in her drawing-room at Buckingham Palace that he was unable to form a Government. She called for Harold Wilson. He accepted her commission and drove back to Downing Street to enter the front door. Heath left by the back.

By the Tuesday afternoon every member, having watched the drama unfold, had returned to London. Raymond had increased his majority and now hoped that the Prime Minister had long since forgotten his resignation and would offer him a job.

Andrew had had the hard and unpleasant fight with Jock McPherson, just as his father had predicted, and held on to his seat by only 2,229.

Charles, still unsure of the exact majority by which he had won, drove back to London, resigned to Opposition. The one compensation was that he would be reinstated on the board of Seymour's where the knowledge he had gained as a Minister of Trade and Industry could only be of value.

Simon left the Home Office on 1 March 1974 with little more than an empty red box to show for nine years as a parliamentarian.

BOOK THREE

MINISTERS OF STATE

1974 – 1977

CHAPTER SIXTEEN

"His diary looks rather full at the moment, Mr Charles."

"Well, as soon as it's convenient," Charles replied over the phone. He held on as he heard the pages being turned.

"12 March at ten-thirty, Mr Charles?"

"But that's nearly a fortnight away," he said, irritated.

"Mr Spencer has only just returned from the States and –"

"How about a lunch, then – at my club?" Charles interrupted.

"That couldn't be until after 19 March."

"Very well, then," said Charles. "12 March, at ten-thirty."

During the fourteen-day wait Charles had ample time to become frustrated by his seemingly aimless role in Opposition. No car came to pick him up and whisk him away to an office where real work had to be done. Worse, no one sought his opinion any longer on matters that affected the nation. He was going through a sharp bout of what is known as "ex-ministers' blues".

He was relieved when the day for the appointment with Derek Spencer at last came round. But although he arrived on time he was kept waiting for ten minutes before the chairman's secretary took him through.

"Good to see you after so long," said Spencer, coming round his desk to greet him. "It must be nearly six years since you've visited the bank."

"Yes, I suppose it is," said Charles. "But looking around the old place it feels like yesterday. You've been fully occupied, no doubt?"

"Like a Cabinet minister, but I hope with better results."

They both laughed.

"Of course I've kept in touch with what's been happening at the bank."

"Have you?" said Spencer.

"Yes, I've read all the reports you've sent out over the past years, not to mention the *Financial Times*'s coverage."

"I hope you feel we've progressed satisfactorily in your absence."

"Oh. Yes," said Charles, still standing. "Very impressive."

"Well, now what can I do for you?" asked the chairman, returning to his seat.

"Simple enough," said Charles, finally taking an unoffered chair. "I wish to be reinstated on the board."

There was a long silence.

"Well, it's not quite that easy, Charles. I've just recently appointed two new directors and . . ."

"Of course it's easy," said Charles, his tone changing. "You have only to propose my name at the next meeting and it will go through, especially as you haven't a member of the family on the board at the present time."

"We have, as a matter of fact. Your brother the Earl of Bridgwater has become a non-executive director."

"What? Rupert never told me," said Charles. "Neither did you."

"True, but things have changed since –"

"Nothing has changed except my estimation of the value of your word," said Charles, suddenly realising that Spencer had never intended he should return to the board. "You gave me your assurance –"

"I won't be spoken to like this in my own office."

"If you're not careful, the next place I shall do it will be in your boardroom. Now, will you honour your undertaking or not?"

"I don't have to listen to threats from you, Seymour. Get out of my office before I have you removed. I can assure you that you will never sit on the board again as long as I'm chairman."

Charles turned and marched out, slamming the door as he left. He wasn't sure with whom to discuss the problem and returned immediately to Eaton Square to consider a plan of campaign.

"What brings you home in the middle of the afternoon?" asked Fiona.

Charles hesitated, considered the question and then joined his wife in the kitchen and told her everything that had happened at the bank. Fiona continued to grate some cheese as she listened to her husband.

"Well, one thing is certain," she said, not having spoken for several minutes but delighted that Charles had confided in her. "After that fracas, you can't both be on the board."

"So what do you think I ought to do, old girl?"

Fiona smiled; it was the first time he had called her that for nearly two years. "Every man has his secrets," she said. "I wonder what Mr Spencer's are?"

"He's such a dull middle-class fellow I doubt if –"

"I've just had a letter from Seymour's Bank," interrupted Fiona.

"What about?"

"Only a shareholder's circular. It seems Margaret Trubshaw is retiring after twelve years as the board secretary. Rumour has it she wanted to do five more years, but the chairman has someone else in mind. I think I might have lunch with her."

Charles returned his wife's smile.

Andrew's appointment as Minister of State at the Home Office came as no surprise to anyone except his three-year-old son, who quickly discovered how to empty any red boxes that were left unlocked, refilling them with marbles or sweets, and even managing to fit a football into one. As Robert didn't fully understand "For Your Eyes Only", it didn't seem to make a lot of difference that Cabinet committee papers were sometimes found glued together with old bubble-gum.

"Can you remove that latest stain in the red box?"

"Good heavens, what caused it?" asked Louise, staring down at a jelly-like blob.

"Frog spawn," said Andrew, grinning.

"He's a brain-washed Russian spy," warned Louise, "with a mental age about the same as most of your colleagues in the House. Yes, I'll remove the stain if you sit down and write that letter."

Andrew nodded his agreement.

Among the many letters of commiseration Simon received when he did not return to the House was one from Andrew Fraser. Simon could imagine him sitting in his old office and implementing the decisions he had been involved in making just a few weeks before.

There was also a letter from Ronnie Nethercote inviting him to return to the board of Nethercote and Company at £5,000 a year, which even Elizabeth acknowledged as a generous gesture.

It was not long before Ronnie Nethercote had made Simon an executive director of the company. Simon enjoyed negotiating with the trade unions at a level he had not experienced before. Ronnie made it clear how he would have dealt with the "Commie bastards" given half a chance. "Lock them all up until they learn to do a day's work."

"You would have lasted about a week in the House of Commons," Simon told him.

"After a week with those windbags I'd have been only too happy to return to the real world."

Simon smiled. Ronnie, he felt, was like so many others – imagining all Members of Parliament were unemployable except the one they knew.

Raymond waited until the last Government appointment was announced before he finally gave up any hope of a job. Several leading political journalists pointed out that he had been left on the back benches while lesser men had been given Government posts but it was scant comfort. Reluctantly he returned to Lincoln's Inn to continue his practice at the bar.

Harold Wilson, starting his third administration, made it clear that he would govern as long as possible before calling an election. But as he did not have an overall majority in the House few members believed that he could hold out for more than a matter of months.

Fiona returned home after her lunch with Miss Trubshaw with a large Cheshire Cat grin on her face. It remained firmly in place during the hours she had to wait for Charles to get back from the Commons after the last division.

"You look pleased with yourself," said Charles, shaking out his umbrella before closing the front door. His wife stood in the hallway, her arms crossed.

"How has your day been?" she asked.

"So-so," said Charles, wanting to hear the news. "But what about you?"

"Oh, pleasant enough. I had coffee with your mother this morning. She seems very well. A little cold in the head, otherwise –"

"To hell with my mother. How did your lunch with Miss Trubshaw go?"

"I wondered how long it would take you to get round to that."

She continued to wait just as long as it took for them to walk into the drawing-room and sit down. "After seventeen years as secretary to your father and twelve years as secretary to the board there isn't much Miss Trubshaw doesn't know about Seymour's or its present chairman," Fiona began.

"So what did you discover?"

"Which do you want to hear about first, the name of his mistress or the number of his Swiss bank account?"

Fiona revealed everything she had learned over her two-hour lunch, explaining that Miss Trubshaw usually only drank fortified wine but on this occasion she had downed most of a vintage bottle of Pommard. Charles's smile grew wider and wider as each fact came pouring out. To Fiona he looked like a boy who has been given a box of chocolates and keeps discovering another layer underneath.

"Well done, old girl," he said when she had come to the end of her tale. "But how do I get all the proof I need?"

"I've made a deal with our Miss Trubshaw."

"You've what?"

"A deal. With Miss Trubshaw. You get the proof if she remains as secretary to the board for a further five years, and no loss of benefit to her pension."

"Is that all she wants?" said Charles, guardedly.

"And the price of another lunch at the Savoy Grill when you're invited back on the board."

Unlike many of his Labour colleagues Raymond now enjoyed dressing up in white tie and tails and mixing with London society. An invitation to the annual bankers' banquet at the Guildhall was no exception. The Prime Minister was the guest of honour and Raymond wondered if he would drop a hint as to how long he expected the parliamentary session to last before he felt he had to call an election.

At the pre-dinner drinks Raymond had a quick word with the Lord Mayor before becoming involved in a conversation with a circuit court judge on the problems of the parity of sentencing.

When dinner was announced Raymond found his seat on one of the long fingers stretching away from the top table. He checked his place card. Raymond Gould QC, MP. On his right was the chairman of Chloride, Michael Edwardes, and on his left an American banker who had just taken up an appointment in the City.

Raymond found Michael Edwardes's views on how the Prime Minister should tackle the nationalized industries fascinating, but he devoted far more of his attention to the Euro Bond manager from Chase Manhattan. She must have been thirty, Raymond decided, if only because of her elevated position at the bank and her claim to have been an undergraduate at Wellesley at the time of Kennedy's death. He would have put Kate Garthwaite at far younger and was not surprised to learn she played tennis in the summer and swam every day during the winter – to keep her weight down, she confided. She had a warm, oval face, and her dark hair was cut in what Raymond thought was a Mary Quant style. Her nose turned up slightly at the end and would have cost a lot of money for a plastic surgeon to reproduce. There was no chance of seeing her legs as they were covered by a long dress, but what he could see left Raymond more than interested.

"I see there's an 'MP' behind your name, Mr Gould. May I ask which party you represent?" she asked, in an accent heard more often in Boston.

"I'm a Socialist, Mrs Garthwaite. Where do your sympathies lie on this occasion?"

"I would have voted Labour at the last election if I had been qualified," she declared.

"Should I be surprised?" he teased.

"You certainly should. My ex-husband is a Republican congress-man."

He was about to ask his next question when the toastmaster called for silence. For the first time Raymond turned his eyes to the top table and the Prime Minister. Harold Wilson's speech stuck firmly to economic problems and the role of a Labour Government in the City and gave no clue as to the timing of the next election. Nevertheless, Raymond considered it a worthwhile evening. He had made a useful contact with the chairman of a large public company. And he had acquired Kate's telephone number.

The chairman of Seymour's reluctantly agreed to see him a second time, but it was obvious from the moment Charles walked in when no hand was proffered that Derek Spencer intended it to be a short interview.

"I thought I ought to see you personally," said Charles as he settled back in the comfortable leather chair and slowly lit a cigarette, "rather than raise my query at the AGM next month."

The first sign of apprehension began to show on the chairman's face, but he said nothing.

"I'm rather keen to discover why the bank should pay out a monthly cheque of £400 to an employee called Miss Janet Darrow, whom I have never come across, although it appears she has been on the payroll for over five years. The cheques, it seems, have been going to a branch of Lloyds in Kensington."

Derek Spencer's face became flushed.

"What I am at a loss to discover," continued Charles after he had inhaled deeply, "is what services Miss Darrow has been supplying to the bank. They must be quite impressive to have earned her £25,000 over the last five years. I appreciate that this is a small amount when you consider the bank's turnover of 123 million last year, but my grandfather instilled in me at an early age the belief that if one took care of the pennies the pounds would take care of themselves."

Still Derek Spencer said nothing, although beads of sweat had appeared on his forehead. Suddenly Charles's tone changed. "If I find I am not a member of the board by the time of the Annual General Meeting I feel it will be my duty to point out this slight discrepancy in the bank's accounts to the other shareholders present."

"You're a bastard, Seymour," the chairman said quietly.

"Now that is not accurate. I am the second son of the former chairman of this bank and I bear a striking resemblance to my father, although everyone says I have my mother's eyes."

"What's the deal?"

"No deal. You will merely keep to your original agreement and see that I am reinstated on the board before the AGM. You will also cease any further payments to Miss Janet Darrow immediately."

"If I agree, will you swear never to mention this matter to anyone again?"

"I will. And, unlike you, I am in the habit of keeping my word."

Charles rose from his chair, leaned over the desk and stubbed out his cigarette in the chairman's ashtray.

Andrew Fraser was surprised when he heard that Jock McPherson wanted to see him. The two men had never been on good terms since

McPherson had failed to be elected to the Scottish Labour Party Executive Committee and had then left the party to stand against him at Edinburgh Carlton. Since McPherson had switched his allegiance they had barely been on speaking terms. However, Andrew realized it would be foolish not to see him after the SNP's sweeping successes in the election.

Andrew was even more surprised when McPherson asked if all seven SNP Members of Parliament could also attend the meeting, not in Andrew's office but somewhere private. He agreed, even more mystified.

McPherson and his band of renegade Scots arrived together at Cheyne Walk, looking as though they had already held a meeting between themselves. Andrew offered them a variety of seats, including the dining-room chairs, a pouffe and even the kitchen stool, apologising that his London flat had never been intended to accommodate nine men in the drawing-room.

While the men settled themselves Andrew remained standing by the mantelpiece, facing Jock McPherson who had obviously been chosen to act as their spokesman.

"I'll get straight to the point," McPherson began. "We want you to fight under the SNP banner at the next election."

Andrew tried not to show his disbelief, and began, "I don't feel . . ."

"Hear me out," said McPherson, raising his massive palms. "We want you to contest the Edinburgh Carlton seat not just as a Scottish Nationalist candidate but as leader of the party."

Andrew still couldn't believe what he was hearing but remained silent.

"We're convinced you'll lose your seat in any case if you stand as a Socialist," McPherson continued, "but we realise that there are many people in Scotland who, whatever their political views, admire what you have achieved in the nine years you have been in the House. After all, man, you were brought up and educated in Edinburgh. With you as leader, we believe we could capture forty to fifty of the seventy-one seats in Scotland. And I may add that your own party is moving inexorably to the left, a state of affairs that I can't believe you are altogether happy about."

Andrew still made no comment. He listened as each one of the MPs put his own view, which became predictable long before the last one had spoken. Every Scottish tone from a Highland lilt to a Glasgow growl was represented in the voices. It became clear that they had given the matter considerable thought and were obviously sincere. "I am very flattered, gentlemen," he began when the last one had said his piece. "And I assure you I will give your offer my serious consideration."

"Thank you," said McPherson. They all stood up like clan leaders in the presence of a new chief.

"We'll wait to hear from you then," said McPherson. One by one they shook hands with their host before filing out.

As soon as they had left Andrew went straight into the kitchen where Robert was still waiting impatiently to play football before going to bed.

"In a moment, in a moment," he said in response to his son's noisy demands. "I'll join you in the garden."

"And what did that lot want?" inquired Louise, as she continued to peel the potatoes.

Andrew went over the details of their proposition.

"And how did you respond?"

"I didn't. I shall wait a week and then decline as gracefully as possible."

"What made you decide against the offer so quickly?"

"I don't like being told by Jock McPherson, or anyone else for that matter, that I will lose my seat at the next election if I don't fall in with their plans." He headed towards the kitchen door. "I'll be back to the red box as soon as I've scored a couple of goals against MacPele." A moment later he had joined Robert in the garden.

"Now listen, clever boots, I'm going to teach you how to feint a pass so that your opponent goes one way while you go the other."

"Sounds just like politics to me," muttered Louise, watching them out of the window.

> 27 EATON SQUARE,
> LONDON, SW1
> 23 APRIL 1974

DEAR DEREK,

Thank you for your letter of 18 April and your kind invitation to rejoin the board of Seymour's. I am delighted to accept and look forward to working with you again.

> YOURS SINCERELY,
> CHARLES SEYMOUR.

Fiona checked the wording and nodded. Short and to the point. "Shall I post it?"

"Yes, please," said Charles as the phone rang.

He picked it up. "730–9712. Charles Seymour speaking."

"Oh, hello, Charles. It's Simon Kerslake."

"Hello, Simon," said Charles, trying to sound pleased to hear from his former colleague. "What's it like out there in the real world?"

"Not much fun, which is exactly why I'm phoning. I've been short-listed for Pucklebridge, Sir Michael Harbour-Baker's seat. He's nearly seventy and has decided not to stand again at the next election. As his constituency touches the south border of yours, I thought you might be able to put in a word for me again."

"Delighted," said Charles. "I'll speak to the chairman tonight. You can rely on me, and good luck. It would be nice to have you back in the House."

Simon gave him his home number which Charles repeated slowly, as if he were writing it down.

"I'll be in touch," said Charles.

"I really appreciate your help."

Simon put down the phone.

Elizabeth looked up from her copy of *The Lancet*.

"I don't trust that man," she said.

"A woman's intuition again?" said Simon smiling. "You were wrong about Ronnie Nethercote."

"That's yet to be proved."

It was several days before Kate Garthwaite agreed to see Raymond again. And when she eventually joined him for dinner at the House she was not overwhelmed or flattered and she certainly didn't hang on his every word.

She was lively, fun, intelligent and well informed and they began to see each other regularly. As the months passed Raymond found himself missing her at weekends when he was in Leeds with Joyce. Kate enjoyed her independence and made none of the demands on him that Stephanie had, never once suggesting he spend more time with her or that she might leave clothes behind in the flat.

Raymond sipped his coffee. "That was a memorable meal," he said, falling back into the sofa.

"Only by the standards of the House of Commons," replied Kate.

Raymond put an arm round her shoulder before kissing her gently on the lips.

"What! Rampant sex as well as cheap Beaujolais?" she exclaimed, stretching over and pouring herself some more coffee.

"I wish you wouldn't always make a joke of our relationship," said Raymond, stroking the back of her hair.

"I have to," said Kate quietly.

"Why?" Raymond turned to face her.

"Because I'm frightened of what might hapen if I take it seriously."

Raymond leant over and kissed her again. "Don't be frightened. You're the best thing that's happened to me in my whole life."

"That's what I'm worried about," said Kate, turning away.

Charles sat through the Annual General Meeting in silence. The chairman made his report for the year ending March 1974 before welcoming two new directors to the board and the return of Charles Seymour.

There were several questions from the floor which Derek Spencer had no trouble in handling. As Charles had promised, there was not even a hint of Miss Janet Darrow. Miss Trubshaw had let Fiona know that the payment had been stopped and also mentioned that she was still worried that her contract was coming to an end on 1 July.

When the chairman brought the AGM to a close Charles asked courteously if he could spare him a moment.

"Of course," said Spencer, looking relieved that the meeting had gone through without a hitch. "What can I do for you?"

"I think it might be wiser to talk in the privacy of your office."

The chairman glanced at him sharply but led him back to his room.

Charles settled himself comfortably in the leather chair once more and removed some papers from his inside pocket. Peering down at them he asked, "What does BX41207122, Bank Rombert, Zurich, mean to you?"

"You said you would never mention –"

"Miss Darrow," said Charles. "And I shall keep my word. But now, as a director of the bank, I am trying to find out what BX41207122 means to you?"

"You know damn well what it means," said the chairman, banging his clenched fist on the desk.

"I know it's your *private*" – Charles emphasized the last word – "account in Zurich."

"You could never prove anything," said Derek Spencer defiantly.

"I agree with you, but what I am able to prove," said Charles, shuffling through the papers that were resting on his lap, "is that you have been using Seymour's money to do private deals, leaving the profit in your Zurich account without informing the board."

"I've done nothing that will harm the bank, and you know it."

"I know the money has been returned with interest, and I could never prove the bank had suffered any loss. Nevertheless, the board might take a dim view of your activities remembering they pay you £40,000 a year to make profits for the bank, not for yourself."

"When they saw all the figures they would at worst rap me over the knuckles."

"I doubt if the Director of Public Prosecutions would take the same lenient attitude if he saw these documents," said Charles, holding up the papers that had been resting on his lap.

"You'd ruin the bank's name."

"And you would probably spend the next ten years in jail. If, however, you did get away with it you would be finished in the City, and by the time your legal fees had been paid there wouldn't be much left of that nest-egg in Zurich."

"So what do you want this time?" demanded Spencer, sounding exasperated.

"Your job," said Charles.

"My job?" said Spencer in disbelief. "Do you imagine because you've been a junior minister you're capable of running a successful merchant bank?" he added scornfully.

"I didn't say I would run it. I can buy a competent chief executive to do that."

"Then what will you be doing?"

"I shall be the chairman of Seymour's which will convince City institutions that we wish to continue in the traditions of generations of my family."

"You're bluffing," stammered Spencer.

"If you are still in this building in twenty-four hours' time," said Charles, "I shall send these to the DPP."

There was a long silence.

"If I agreed," said Spencer at last, "I would expect two years' salary as compensation."

"One year," said Charles. Spencer hesitated, then nodded slowly. Charles rose to his feet and put the papers resting on his lap back into his inside pocket.

They consisted of nothing more than the morning mail from Sussex Downs.

Simon felt the interview had gone well but Elizabeth was not so sure. They sat huddled in a room with five other candidates and their wives, patiently waiting.

He thought back to his answers, and to the eight men and four women on the committee.

"You must admit it's the most ideal seat I've been considered for," said Simon.

"Yes, but the chairman kept eyeing you suspiciously."

"But Millburn mentioned that he had been at Eton with Charles Seymour."

"That's what worries me," whispered Elizabeth.

"A 15,000 majority at the last election and only forty minutes from London. We could even buy a little cottage . . ."

"If they invite you to represent them."

"At least this time you were able to tell them you would be willing to live in the constituency."

"So would anyone in their right mind," said Elizabeth.

The chairman came out and asked if Mr and Mrs Kerslake would be kind enough to return once more to see the committee.

"Oh, God," thought Simon. "What else can they want to know?"

"It's too near London to be my fault this time," chuckled Elizabeth.

The committee sat and stared at them with long faces.

"Ladies and gentlemen," said the chairman. "After our lengthy deliberations, I formally propose that Mr Simon Kerslake be invited to contest Pucklebridge at the next election. Those in favour . . .?"

All twelve hands went up.

"Those against . . .?"

"Carried unanimously," said the chairman. He then turned to Simon. "Do you wish to address your committee?"

The prospective Conservative Member of Parliament for Pucklebridge rose. They all waited expectantly.

"I don't know what to say, except that I'm very happy and honoured and I can't wait for a general election."

They all laughed and came forward and surrounded them. Elizabeth dried her eyes before anyone reached her.

About an hour later the chairman accompanied Simon and Elizabeth back to their car and bade them goodnight. Simon wound down his window.

"I knew you were the right man," Millburn said, "as soon as Charles Seymour phoned" – Simon smiled – "and warned me to avoid you like the plague."

"Could you tell Miss Trubshaw to come in?" Charles asked his secretary.

Margaret Trubshaw arrived a few moments later and remained standing in front of his desk. She couldn't help but notice the change of furniture in the room. The modern Conran suite had been replaced by a leather club-like sofa. Only the picture of the eleventh Earl of Bridgwater remained in place.

"Miss Trubshaw," began Charles, "since Mr Spencer has felt it necessary to resign so suddenly I think it important for the bank to keep some continuity now that I'm taking over as chairman."

Miss Trubshaw stood like a Greek statue, her hands hidden in the sleeves of her dress.

"With that in mind, the board has decided to extend your contract with the bank for a further five years. Naturally, there will be no loss in your pension rights."

"Thank you, Mr Charles."

"Thank you, Miss Trubshaw."

Miss Trubshaw almost bowed as she left the room.

"And Miss Trubshaw?"

"Yes, Mr Charles," she said, holding on to the door knob.

"I believe my wife is expecting a call from you. Something about inviting you to lunch at the Savoy Grill."

CHAPTER SEVENTEEN

"A blue shirt," said Raymond, looking at the Turnbull and Asser label with suspicion. "A *blue* shirt," he repeated.

"A fortieth-birthday present," shouted Kate from the kitchen.

I shall never wear it, he thought, and smiled to himself.

"And what's more, you'll wear it," she said, her Boston accent carrying a slight edge.

"You even know what I'm thinking," he complained as she came in from the kitchen. He always thought how elegant she looked in her tailored office suit.

"It's because you're so predictable, Carrot Top."

"Anyway, how did you know it was my birthday?"

"A massive piece of detective work," said Kate, "with the help of an outside agent and a small payment."

"An outside agent. Who?"

"The local paper shop, my darling. In the *Sunday Times* they tell you the name of every distinguished person celebrating a birthday in the following seven days. In a week during which only the mediocre were born, you made it."

Raymond had to laugh.

"Now listen, Carrot Top."

Raymond pretended to hate his new nickname. "Do you have to call me by that revolting name?"

"Yes. I can't stand Raymond."

He scowled. "In any case, carrot tops are green."

"No comment. Try on your shirt."

"Now?"

"Now."

He took off his black coat and waistcoat, removed his white shirt and eased the stud on his stiff collar, leaving a small circle above his Adam's apple. Curly red hairs stuck up all over his chest. He quickly put on the new gift. The fabric had a pleasant soft feel about it. He started to do up the buttons, but Kate walked over and undid the top two.

"You know what? You've brought a whole new meaning to the word 'uptight'."

Raymond scowled again.

"But in the right clothes you could even pass for good looking. Now. Where shall we go to celebrate your birthday?"

"The House of Commons?" suggested Raymond.

"Good God," said Kate. "I said celebrate, not hold a wake. What about Annabel's?"

"I can't afford to be seen in Annabel's."

"With me, you mean?"

"No, no, you silly woman, because I'm a Socialist."

"If members of the Labour Party are not allowed to indulge in a good meal then perhaps it's time for you to change parties. In my country one only sees the Democrats in the best restaurants."

"Oh, do be serious, Kate."

"I intend to be. Now what have you been up to in the House lately?"

"Not a lot," said Raymond sheepishly. "I've been snowed under in court and . . ."

"Precisely. It's time you did something positive before your colleagues in Parliament forget you exist."

"Have you anything particular in mind?" asked Raymond, folding his arms across his chest.

"As a matter of fact, I have," said Kate. "I read in the same Sunday paper as the one in which I discovered your best-kept secret that it is proving difficult for the Labour party to repeal the Tories' trade-union legislation. It appears there are long-term legal implications which the front bench are still trying to find a way round. Why don't you set that so-called 'first class' mind of yours to working out the legal niceties?"

"Not such a stupid idea." Raymond had become used to Kate's political sense, and when he had remarked on it she had only said, "Just another bad habit I picked up from my ex-husband."

"Now, where do we celebrate?" she asked.

"Compromise," said Raymond.

"I'm all ears."

"The Dorchester."

"If you insist," said Kate, not sounding over-enthusiastic.

Raymond started to change his shirt.

"No, no, no, Carrot Top, people have been known to wear blue shirts at the Dorchester."

"But I haven't got a tie to match," said Raymond triumphantly.

Kate thrust her hand into the Turnbull and Asser bag and drew out a dark blue silk tie.

"But it's got a pattern on it," said Raymond in disgust. "What will you expect next?"

"Contact lenses," said Kate.

Raymond stared at her, and blinked.

On the way out of the door Raymond's gaze fell upon the brightly wrapped package that Joyce had posted from Leeds earlier in the week.

He had completely forgotten to open it.

"Damn," said Charles, putting down *The Times* and draining his coffee.

"What's the problem?" asked Fiona as she poured out another cup.

"Kerslake's been selected for Pucklebridge, which means he's back in the House for life. Obviously my chat to Archie Millburn had no effect."

"Why have you got it in for Kerslake?" asked Fiona.

Charles folded the paper and considered the question. "It's quite simple really, old girl. I think he's the only one of my contemporaries who could stop me leading the party."

"Why him in particular?"

"I first came across him when he was President of the Union at Oxford. He was damn good then, and now he's better. He had rivals, but he brushed them aside like flies. No, despite his background, Kerslake's the one man left who frightens me."

"It's a long race yet, my darling, and he could still stumble."

"So could I, but what he doesn't realise is that I shall be putting out some of his hurdles."

Andrew worded the letter very carefully. He assured Jock McPherson and his colleagues that he had been flattered by their approach, but explained that he had decided his loyalties were still firmly based in the Labour Party.

He accepted the point Jock had made about the left trying to gain control, but felt that every democratic party was bound to have a maverick element within its ranks, which was not necessarily unhealthy. He added that he considered the offer to have been confidential on both sides.

"Why add that postscript?" asked Louise when she had read the letter through.

"It's only fair to Jock," said Andrew. "If it gets around I turned him down it will have the opposite effect to the one they were trying to create."

"I'm not so sure they will act in the same magnanimous way when the next election comes round."

"Ah, Jock will make a lot of noise, but he's all right underneath . . ."

"That isn't what your father says about him," said Louise. "He's sure they'll want revenge."

"Father always sees grubs under even the greenest leaf."

"So if we're not about to celebrate your leadership of the Scottish Nationalists we'll have to be satisfied with celebrating your fortieth birthday."

"But that's not for at least –"

"– another month, a week before Robert's fourth birthday."

"How would you like to commemorate the occasion, darling?"

"I thought we might have a week in the Algarve on our own."

"Why don't we have two weeks? Then we can celebrate your fortieth birthday as well?"

"Andrew Fraser, you just lost yourself one vote in Edinburgh Carlton."

Simon listened intently to Ronnie's report at the monthly board meeting. Two tenants had not paid their quarterly rent, and another quarter date was fast approaching. Ronnie's solicitors had sent firm reminders, followed a month later by writs but this action had also failed to elicit any money.

"It only proves what I feared most," said Ronnie.

"What's that?" asked Simon.

"They just haven't got the cash."

"So we will have to replace them with new tenants."

"Simon, when you next travel from Beaufort Stret to Whitechapel start counting the 'To Let' signs on office blocks along the way. When you've passed a hundred you'll find you still haven't reached the City."

"So what do you think we should do about it?"

"Try and sell one of our larger properties to secure cash flow. We can at least be thankful that even at these prices they are still worth a lot more than our borrowings. It's the companies who are the other way round that have to call in the receiver."

Simon thought about his overdraft, now approaching £100,000, and was beginning to wish he had accepted Ronnie's generous offer to buy back his shares. He accepted reluctantly that the opportunity had now passed.

When the board meeting was over he drove to St Mary's to pick up Elizabeth. It was to be one of their three-times-a-week journeys to Pucklebridge as Simon tried to get round all the villages before Wilson called an election.

Archie Millburn was turning out to be a conscientious chairman who had accompanied them on nearly every trip.

"He's been very kind to us," said Elizabeth, on their way down.

"He certainly has," said Simon. "Remember he also has to run Millburn Electronics. But, as he reminds us so often, once he's introduced us to every village chairman we'll be on our own."

"Have you ever discovered why he and Charles Seymour didn't see eye to eye?"

"No, he hasn't mentioned his name since that night. All I know for certain is that they were at school together."

"So what do you intend to do about Seymour?"

"Not a lot I can do," said Simon. "Except keep my eyes very wide open."

"The man who has deserted Edinburgh once too often" – Andrew read the Scottish Nationalist leaflet that had been sent to him that morning by his father. It was full of half-truths and innuendoes.

"Andrew Fraser, the man who has forgotten Edinburgh, should no longer be allowed to represent a Scottish seat." It went on to declare: "He now lives far away from the problems of his constituents in a smart apartment building in fashionable Chelsea among his Tory friends. He visits the City of Edinburgh only a few times a year to make well-publicised appearances . . . Has being a minister gone to his head?"

"How dare they?" cried Louise in a rage. Andrew had never seen his wife so angry. "How dare they come to my home, offer you the leadership of their dreadful little party and then write such a pack of lies? And did you read this?" she added, pointing to the last paragraph, " 'His wife Louise, née Forsyth'," she read out aloud, " 'comes from one of the wealthiest families in Scotland. She is a close relation of the owners of Forsyth's in Princes Street.' I'm a second cousin once removed, and they don't even give me a discount in the main store."

Andrew started to laugh.

"What's so funny?"

He took her in his arms. "I always suffered under the illusion that you would inherit the Forsyth empire and I would never have to work again," he mocked. "Now we shall have to live off Robert's earnings as a star football player."

"Don't joke, Andrew. It won't seem funny when the election comes round."

"I'm far more concerned about the extreme left trying to infiltrate my General Management Committee," he said, his voice changing, "than I am by Jock McPherson's band of mad little islanders. But at this moment of time my red box is too full to worry about either of them."

Raymond made such a penetrating speech during the second reading of the new Trade Union Bill that the Whips put him on the standing committee, the perfect medium for him to display his skills as the committee debated each clause, point by point. He was able to show his colleagues where the legal pitfalls were and how to find a way round them. The rest of the committee soon learnt from Raymond the meaning of "mastering a brief", and it was not long before trade-union leaders were calling him at the House and even at his flat to learn his views on how their members should react to a host of different legal problems. Raymond showed patience with each of them and, more important, gave them excellent professional advice for the price of a phone call. He found it ironic how quickly they chose to forget that he was the author of *Full Employment at any Cost?* Snippets began to appear

in the national press, ranging from laudatory comments from those
involved with a bill to a pointed suggestion in the *Guardian* that,
whatever had happened in the past, it would be insupportable if
Raymond Gould were not made a member of the Government in the
near future.

"If they were to offer you a job, would it make any difference to our
relationship?" Kate asked.

"Certainly," said Raymond. "I shall have found the perfect excuse
not to wear your blue shirts."

Harold Wilson held the crumbling edifice together for a further six
months before finally having to call a general election. He chose 10
October 1974.

Raymond immediately returned to his constituency to fight his fifth
campaign. When he met Joyce at Leeds City station he couldn't help
remembering that his dumpy wife was only four years older than Kate.
He kissed her on the cheek as one might a distant relative, then she
drove him back to their Chapel Allerton home.

Joyce chatted away on the journey home and it became clear that the
constituency was under control and that this time Fred Padgett was
well prepared for a general election. "He hasn't really stopped since the
last one," she said. As for Joyce, she was undoubtedly better organized
than the agent and the secretary put together. What was more,
Raymond thought, she enjoyed it. He glanced over at her and couldn't
help thinking she even looked prettier at election time.

Unlike his colleagues in rural seats, Raymond did not have to make
speech after speech in little village halls. His votes were to be found in
the high street where he addressed the midday shoppers through a
megaphone, and walked around supermarkets, pubs and clubs, grasping hands before repeating the whole process a few streets away.

Joyce set her husband a schedule that allowed few people in the
Leeds community to escape him. Some saw him a dozen times during
the three-week campaign – most of them at the football match on the
Saturday afternoon before the election.

Once the game was over Raymond was back trooping round the
working men's clubs, drinking pint after pint of John Smith's bitter. He
accepted it was inevitable that he would put on half a stone during any
election campaign. He dreaded what Kate's comments would be when
she saw him. Somehow he always found a few minutes in each day to
steal away and phone her. She seemed so busy and full of news it only
made Raymond feel downcast; she couldn't possibly be missing him.

The local trade unionists backed Raymond to the hilt. They may
have found him stuck up and distant in the past, but they knew "where
his heart was", as they confided to anyone who would listen. They
banged on doors, delivered leaflets, drove cars to polling booths. They

rose before he did in the morning and could still be found preaching to the converted after the pubs had thrown them out at night.

Raymond and Joyce cast their votes in the local secondary school on the Thursday of election day, looking forward to a large Labour victory. The Labour party duly gained a working majority in the House of forty-three over the Conservatives, but only three over all the parties combined. Nevertheless Harold Wilson looked set for another five years when the Queen invited him to form his fourth administration. The count in Leeds that night gave Raymond his biggest majority ever: 12,207 votes.

He spent the whole of Friday and Saturday thanking his constituents, then set out for London on the Sunday evening.

"He must invite you to join the Government this time," said Joyce, as she walked down the platform of Leeds City station with her husband.

"I wonder," said Raymond, kissing his wife on the other cheek. He waved at her as the train pulled out of the station. She waved back enthusiastically.

"I do like your new blue shirt, it really suits you," were the last words he heard her say.

During the election campaign Charles had had to spend a lot of time at the bank because of a run on the pound. Fiona seemed to be everywhere in the constituency at once, assuring voters that her husband was just a few yards behind.

After the little slips were counted the swing against Charles to the Labour candidate didn't amount to more than one per cent in his 22,000 majority. When he heard the overall result he returned to London resigned to a long spell in Opposition. As he began to catch up with his colleagues in the House, he found many of them already saying openly that Heath had to go after two election defeats in a row.

Charles knew then that he would have to make up his mind once again on where he stood over the election of a new party leader, and that once again he must pick the right man.

Andrew Fraser returned to London after a gruelling and unhappy campaign. The Scottish Nationalists had concentrated their attack on him, Jock McPherson sailing close to libel and slander. Sir Duncan advised his son against any legal action. "Only plays into their hands," he warned. "Small parties always benefit from the publicity."

Louise wanted him to inform the press that he had been offered the leadership of the SNP but Andrew felt it would serve no purpose, and might even rebound against him: and he also reminded her that he had given his word. In the last week of the campaign he spent most of his time trying – and failing – to stop Frank Boyle, a Communist, who had recently moved from Glasgow, from being elected to his General Management Committee. On polling day he scraped home by 1,656, Jock McPherson taking second place. At least he looked secure for another five years; but it didn't help that the Scottish Nationalists had increased their overall seats in the House to eleven.

Andrew, Louise and Robert took the plane to London on the Sunday night to find the red box awaiting them and a message that the Prime Minister wanted Andrew to continue as Minister of State at the Home Office.

Simon had a glorious campaign. He and Elizabeth had started moving into their new cottage the day the election was announced, thankful that, now she had to commute, her salary at the hospital had made it possible for them to employ a nanny. A double bed and a couple of chairs sufficed as Elizabeth cooked on an old Aga from provisions still packed in tea chests. They seemed to use the same two forks for everything. During the campaign Simon covered the 200-square-mile constituency for a second time and assured his wife that she need only take the final week off from her duties at St Mary's.

The voters of Pucklebridge sent Simon Kerslake back to Parliament with a majority of 18,419, the largest in the constituency's history. The local people had quickly come to the conclusion that they now had a member who was destined to have a Cabinet career.

Kate kept her remarks very gentle as it became obvious by the Monday night that the Prime Minister was not going to offer Raymond a job in the new administration. She cooked his favourite meal of roast beef – overdone – and Yorkshire pudding in the flat that night, but he didn't comment on it and hardly spoke.

CHAPTER EIGHTEEN

After Simon had been back at the Commons for a week he felt a sense of *déjà vu*, a feeling that most members returning to the House for a second or even third time often experience. The sense was heightened by finding everything unchanged, even the policeman who greeted him at the Members' Entrance. When Edward Heath announced his Shadow team Simon was not surprised that he wasn't included, as he never had been a known supporter of the Tory leader. He was, however, mystified but not displeased to discover Charles Seymour was not among the names to be found in the Shadow Cabinet.

"Do you regret turning him down now the full team has been published?" asked Fiona, looking up from her copy of the *Daily Mail.*

"It wasn't an easy decision but I think it'll prove right in the long run," replied Charles, buttering another piece of toast.

"What did he offer in the end?"

"Shadow Minister of Industry."

"That sounds rather interesting," said Fiona.

"Everything about it was interesting except the salary, which would have been nothing. Don't forget the bank pays me £40,000 a year while I'm chairman."

Fiona folded her paper. "But you've just appointed a full-time chief executive, so your responsibilities at the bank should be only part-time compared with when you took the chair over. So what's the real reason?"

Charles accepted that he could rarely fool Fiona. "The truth is that I'm far from certain Ted will be leading the party at the next election."

"Then who will if he doesn't?" asked Fiona.

"Whoever's got the guts to oppose him."

"I'm not sure I understand," said Fiona, beginning to clear away the plates.

"Everyone accepts that he has to allow his name to go forward for re-election now that he's lost twice in a row."

"That's fair enough," agreed Fiona.

"But as he has appointed all possible contenders to the Cabinet or Shadow Cabinet over the last ten years, someone he has selected in the past will have to oppose him. No one of lesser stature would stand a chance."

"Is there a member of the Shadow Cabinet willing to stand?" asked Fiona, returning to her seat at the end of the table.

"One or two are considering it, but the problem is that if they lose it could easily end their political career," said Charles, folding his napkin.

"But if they win?"

"They will undoubtedly be the next Prime Minister."

"Interesting dilemma. And what are you going to be about it?"

"I'm not supporting anyone at the moment, but I've got my eyes wide open," said Charles, folding his copy of *The Times* and rising from the table.

"Is there a front runner?" asked Fiona, looking up at her husband.

"No, not really. Although Kerslake is trying to rally support for Margaret Thatcher, but that idea is doomed from the start."

"A woman leading the Tory party? Your lot haven't got the imagination to risk it," said Elizabeth, tasting the sauce. "The day that happens I shall eat my one and only Tory hat in full view of all the delegates at the party conference."

"Don't be so cynical, Elizabeth. She's the best bet we've got at the moment."

"But what are the chances of Ted Heath standing down? I always thought the leader of the party stayed on until he was hit by the mythical bus. I don't know Heath very well, but I can never imagine him resigning."

"I agree," said Simon. "So the 1922 Committee will have to change the rules."

"You mean the back-benchers will put pressure on him to go?"

"No, but a lot of the committee in their present mood would be willing to volunteer as driver for that bus."

"If that's true, he must realise that his chances of holding on are slim?"

"I wonder if any leader ever knows that," said Simon.

"You ought to be in Blackpool next week," said Kate, resting her elbow on the pillow.

"Why Blackpool?" Raymond asked, staring up at the ceiling.

"Because, Carrot Top, that's where they are holding this year's Labour party conference."

"What do you imagine I could hope to accomplish there?"

"You'd be seen to be alive. At present you're just a rumour in trade-union circles."

"But if you're not a minister or a trade-union leader all you do at a party conference is spend four days eating foul food, sleeping in seedy guest houses, and applauding second-rate speeches."

"I've no interest in where you put your weary head at night but I do want you to revive your contacts with the unions during the day."

"Why?" said Raymond. "That lot can't influence my career."

"Not at the moment," said Kate. "But I predict that, like my fellow Americans at their conventions, the Labour Party will one day select their leader at the party conference."

"Never," said Raymond. "That is and will always remain the prerogative of elected members of the House of Commons."

"That's the sort of crass, short-sighted, pompous statement I would expect a Republican to make," she said, before plonking a pillow over his head. Raymond feigned death, so she lifted up a corner and whispered in his ear, "Have you read any of the resolutions to be debated at this year's conference?"

"A few," came back Raymond's muffled reply.

"Then it might serve you well to note Mr Anthony Wedgwood Benn's contribution," she said, removing the pillow.

"What's he up to this year?"

"He's calling on 'conference', as he insists on describing your gathering of the brothers, to demand that the next leader be chosen by a full vote of the delegates, making up an electoral college from all the constituencies, the trade-union movement and Parliament – I suspect in that order."

"Madness. But what do you expect? He's married to an American."

"Today's extremist is tomorrow's moderate," said Kate blithely.

"A typical American generalization."

"Benjamin Disraeli, actually."

Raymond placed the pillow back over his head.

Andrew always attended the party conference, although he would never have voted for Tony Benn's resolution on the method of selecting a leader. He feared that if the trade unions were given that sort of power a leader who was totally unacceptable to his colleagues in the House of Commons could be selected. He was relieved when the motion was defeated but he noted that the majority against was far from overwhelming.

Despite being a minister Andrew could only get a small room at Blackpool in a guest house masquerading as a hotel, and that some two miles from the conference centre. Such were the problems created by 4,000 self-important people converging on a seaside resort for a week that many had to forgo the Presidential Suite.

Andrew still had to carry on his job as Minister of State, with red boxes being delivered and taken every morning and afternoon, while making his presence felt at the conference. He spent half his time on a phone in the hotel lobby putting through transfer-charge calls to the Home Office. No one in the Soviet Union would have believed it, especially if they had realised that the Minister of State for Defence, who had the room next to Andrew's, was pacing up and down the corridor waiting for the phone to be free.

Andrew had never addressed the 3,000 delegates at a party conference. Even Cabinet ministers are only allowed a maximum of ten minutes at the rostrum unless they are members of the National Executive. Over half the Labour Cabinet had failed to be elected to this body, which consisted mainly of the leaders of the larger trade unions.

As he left the morning session Andrew was surprised to find Raymond Gould roaming around looking lost. They fell on each other like sane men locked in an asylum and decided to lunch together at the River House, Andrew's favourite restaurant a few miles outside of Blackpool.

Although they had both been in the House for nearly ten years it was the first time they discovered how much they had in common. Andrew had never considered himself a close friend of Raymond's but he had always admired his stand on devaluation.

"You must have been disappointed when the PM didn't ask you to rejoin the Government," Andrew began.

Raymond stared down at the menu. "Very," he finally admitted, as a girl joined them in the bar to take their order.

"Nevertheless, you were wise to come to Blackpool. This is where your strength lies."

"You think so?"

"Come on. Everybody knows you're the trade unions' pin-up boy, and they still have a lot of influence as to who sits in the Cabinet."

"I haven't noticed," said Raymond mournfully.

"You will when they eventually choose the leader."

"That's funny, that's exactly what . . . Joyce said last week."

"Sensible girl, Joyce. I fear it will happen in our time as members."

Bill Scott, the proprietor, told them their table was ready and they went through to the small dining-room.

"Why fear?" asked Raymond, as he took his seat.

"Middle-of-the-road democrats like myself will end up as so many leaves on a bonfire."

"But I'm middle-of-the-road myself, practically right wing on some issues."

"Perhaps. But every party needs a man like you, and at this moment union leaders wouldn't mind if you were a card-carrying Fascist; they'd still back you."

"Then what makes you attend the conference?"

"Thank God it still gives one a chance to keep in touch with the grass roots, and I live in hope that the extreme left will never be much more than an unruly child that the grown-ups have to learn to live with."

"Let's hope you're right," said Raymond, "because they're never going to grow up." Andrew laughed as Raymond continued in a different mood. "I still envy you your job at the Home Office. I didn't go into politics to spend my life on the back benches."

"There may well come a day when I sit and envy you from those same back benches," said Andrew.

As he spoke, the chairman of the Boilermakers' Union shouted across as he passed their table. "Good to see you, Ray." He showed no recognition of Andrew. Raymond turned and smiled at the man and waved back as Caesar might have done to Cassius.

When they had both rejected the choice of date and walnut pudding or Pavlova, Andrew suggested a brandy.

Raymond hesitated.

"You'll see more double brandies drunk here than you will at the Conservative Party conference next week. Ask any waitress."

"Have you decided how you're going to vote in the leadership battle?" asked Fiona over breakfast.

"Yes," said Charles, "and at this point in my career I can't afford to make the wrong choice."

"So who have you decided on?" asked Fiona.

"While there isn't a serious contender to oppose Ted Heath it remains in my best interest to continue backing him."

"Isn't there one Shadow Cabinet minister who has the guts to stand against him?"

"The rumour grows that Margaret Thatcher will act as whipping girl. If she gets close enough to force a second ballot the serious contenders will then join in."

"What if she won the first round?"

"Don't be silly, Fiona," said Charles, taking more interest in his scrambled egg. "The Tory party would never elect a woman to lead them. We're far too traditional. That's the sort of immature mistake the Labour Party would make to prove how much they believe in equality."

Simon was still pushing Margaret Thatcher to throw her hat in the ring.

"She certainly has enough of them," said Elizabeth.

It amused Andrew and Raymond to watch the Tory party leadership struggle while they got on with their respective jobs. Raymond would have dismissed Thatcher's chances if Kate hadn't reminded him that the Tories had been the first party to choose a Jewish leader, and also the first to select a bachelor.

"So why shouldn't they be the first to elect a woman?" she demanded. He would have continued to argue with her but the damn woman had proved to be right so often in the past. "Let's wait and see," was all he said.

The 1922 Committee announced that the election for leader would take place on 4 February 1975.

At a press conference in early January at the House of Commons Margaret Thatcher announced she would allow her name to go forward to contest the leadership. Simon immediately spent his time exhorting his colleagues to support "The Lady" and joined a small committee under Airey Neave that was formed for the purpose. Charles Seymour warned his friends that the party could never hope to win a general election with a woman leading them. As the days passed, nothing became clearer than the uncertainty of the outcome.

At four o'clock on a particularly wet and windy day the chairman of the 1922 Committee announced the figures:

Margaret Thatcher	130
Edward Heath	119
Hugh Fraser	16

According to the 1922 Committee rules, the winner needed a fifteen per cent majority and so a second round was necessary. "It will be held in seven days' time," the Chief Whip announced. Three former Cabinet ministers immediately declared they were candidates, while Ted Heath, having been warned that he would get fewer votes a second time round, withdrew from the ballot.

They were the longest days in Simon's life. He did everything in his power to hold Thatcher's supporters together. Charles meanwhile decided to play the second round very low-key. When the time came to vote he put his cross on the ballot paper next to the former Secretary of State he had served under at Trade and Industry. "A man we can all trust," he told Fiona.

When the votes had been counted and confirmed the chairman of the 1922 Committee announced that Margaret Thatcher was the outright winner with a vote of 146 to 79 from her nearest challenger.

Simon was delighted while Elizabeth hoped he had forgotten about the promise to eat her hat. Charles was dumbfounded. They both wrote to their new leader immediately.

11 FEBRUARY 1975

DEAR MARGARET,

Many congratulations on your victory as the first woman leader of our party. I was proud to have played a small part in your triumph and will continue to work for your success at the next election.

YOURS,
SIMON

27 EATON SQUARE,
LONDON, SW1
11 FEBRUARY 1975

DEAR MARGARET,

I made no secret of backing Ted Heath in the first round of the leadership contest having had the privilege of serving in his administration. I was delighted to have supported you on the second ballot. It illustrates how progressive our party is that we have chosen a woman who will undoubtedly be Britain's next Prime Minister.

Be assured of my loyalty,

YOURS,
CHARLES.

Margaret Thatcher answered all her colleagues' letters within the week. Simon received a handwritten letter inviting him to join the new Shadow team as number two in the Education Department. Charles received a typed note thanking him for his letter of support.

CHAPTER NINETEEN

Seymour's Bank had weathered the Great War, the thirties' crash, and then the Second World War. Charles had no intention of being the chairman who presided over its demise in the seventies. Soon after taking over from Derek Spencer – at the board's unanimous insistence – he had discovered that being chairman wasn't quite the relaxed job he expected, and while he remained confident that the bank could ride the storm he still wasn't taking any risks. The business sections of the newspapers were full of stories of the Bank of England acting as a "lifeboat" and having to step in to assist ailing financial institutions, along with daily reports of the collapse of yet another property company. The time when property values and rents automatically increased each year had become a thing of the past.

When he had accepted the board's offer, Charles insisted that a chief executive be appointed to carry out the day to day business while he remained the man with whom other City chairmen dealt. He interviewed several people for the position but he did not find anyone suitable. Head-hunting seemed to be the next move, the expense of which was saved when he overheard a conversation at the next table at White's that the newly appointed chief executive of the 1st Bank of America was sick of having to report to the board in Chicago every time he wanted to use a first-class stamp.

Charles immediately invited the chief executive to lunch at the House of Commons. Clive Reynolds had come from a similar background to Derek Spencer: London School of Economics, followed by the Harvard Business School and a series of successful appointments which had culminated in his becoming chief executive of the 1st Bank of America. This similarity did not worry Charles, as he made it clear to Mr Reynolds that the appointee would be the chairman's man.

When Reynolds was offered the appointment he drove a hard bargain and Charles looked forward to his doing the same on behalf of Seymour's. Reynolds ended up with £50,000 a year and enough of a profit incentive to ensure that he didn't deal for himself or encourage any other head-hunters to invite him to join their particular jungle.

"He's not the sort of fellow we could invite to dinner," Charles told Fiona, "but his appointment will enable me to sleep at night knowing the bank is in safe hands."

Charles's choice was rubber-stamped by the board at their next meeting, and as the months passed it became obvious that the 1st Bank of America had lost one of its prime assets well below the market value.

Clive Reynolds was a conservative by nature, but when he did take what Charles described as a risk – and Reynolds called a "hunch" – over fifty per cent of them paid off. While Seymour's kept its reputation for caution and good husbandry, they managed a few quite spectacular coups thanks to their new chief executive.

Reynolds had enough sense to treat his new chairman with respect without ever showing deference while their relationship remained at all times strictly professional.

One of Reynolds's first innovations had been to suggest they check on every customer account over £250,000 and Charles had approved.

"When you've handled the account of a company for many years," Reynolds pointed out, "it sometimes is not apparent when one of your traditional customers is heading for trouble as it would be to a newcomer. If there are any 'lame ducks' let's discover them before they hit the ground" – a simile that Charles repeated at several weekend parties.

Charles enjoyed his morning meetings with Clive Reynolds as he picked up a great deal about a profession to which he had previously only brought gut feeling and common sense. In a very short time he learned enough from his new tutor to make him sound like David Rockefeller when he rose to speak in a finance debate on the floor of the House, an unexpected bonus.

Charles knew little of Reynolds's private life except what was on file. He was forty-one, unmarried and lived in Esher, wherever that was. All Charles cared about was that Reynolds arrived each morning at least an hour before him, and left after him every night, even when the House was in recess.

Charles had studied fourteen of the confidential reports on customers with loans over £250,000. Clive Reynolds had already picked out two companies with whom he felt the bank should revise their current position.

Charles still had three more reports to consider before he presented a full assessment to the board.

The quiet knock on the door, however, meant that it was ten o'clock and Reynolds had arrived to make his daily report. Rumours were circulating in the City that the bank rate would go up on Thursday, so Reynolds wanted to go short on dollars and long on gold. Charles nodded. As soon as the announcement had been made about the bank rate, Reynolds continued: "It will be wiser to return to dollars as the new round of pay negotiations with the unions is about to take place. This in turn will undoubtedly start a fresh run on the pound." Charles nodded again.

"I think the dollar is far too weak at two-ten," Reynolds added. "With the unions settling at around twelve per cent the dollar must strengthen, say, to nearer one-ninety." He added that he was not happy about the bank's large holding in Slater Walker and wanted to liquidate half the stock over the next month. He proposed to do so in small amounts over irregular periods. "We also have three other major accounts to consider before we make known our findings to the board. I'm concerned about the spending policy of one of the companies, but the other two appear stable. I think we should go over them together when you have time to consider my reports. Perhaps tomorrow morning, if you could manage that. The companies concerned are Speyward Laboratories, Blackies Limited and Nethercote and Company. It's Speyward I'm worried about."

"I'll take the files home tonight," said Charles, "and give you an opinion in the morning."

"Thank you, Chairman."

Charles had never suggested that Reynolds should call him by his first name.

Archie Millburn held a small dinner party to celebrate Simon's first anniversary as the member for Pucklebridge. Although these occasions had originally been to introduce the party hierarchy to their new member, Simon now knew more about the constituency and its flock than he did, as Archie was the first to admit.

Elizabeth, Peter and Michael had settled comfortably into their small cottage, while Simon, as a member of the Shadow Education team, had visited schools – nursery, primary, public and secondary: universities – red brick, plate glass and Oxbridge; technical colleges, art institutes and even borstals. He had read Butler, Robbins, and Plowden and listened to children and to professors of psychology alike. He felt that after a year he was beginning to understand the subject, and only longed for a general election so that he could once again turn rehearsal into performance.

"Opposition must be frustrating," observed Archie when the ladies had retired after dinner.

"Yes, but it's an excellent way to prepare yourself for Government and do some basic thinking about the subject. I never found time for such luxury as a minister."

"But it must be very different from holding office?" said Archie, clipping a cigar.

"True. In Government," said Simon, "you're surrounded by civil servants who don't allow you to lift a finger or give you a moment to ponder, while in Opposition you can think policy through even if you do often end up having to type your own letters."

Archie pushed the port down to Simon's end of the table. "I'm glad the girls are out," said Archie conspiratorially, "because I wanted you to know I've decided to give up being chairman at the end of the year."

"Why?" said Simon, taken aback.

"I've seen you elected and settled in. It's time for a younger man to have a go."

"But you're only my age."

"I can't deny that, but the truth is that I'm not giving enough time to my electronics company, and the board are continually reminding me of it. No one has to tell you that these are not easy times."

"It's sad," said Simon. "Just as you get to know someone in politics you or they always seem to move on."

"Fear not," said Archie. "I don't intend to leave the area, and I feel confident that you will be my member for at least another twenty years, by which time I will be happy to accept an invitation to dine with you in Downing Street."

"You may find that it's Charles Seymour who is residing at No. 10," said Simon, striking a match to light his cigar.

"Then I won't be getting an invitation," said Archie with a smile.

Charles couldn't sleep that night after his discovery, and his tossing and turning kept Fiona awake. He had opened the Nethercote file when he was waiting for dinner to be served. His first act with any company was to glance down the names of the directors to see if he knew anyone on the board. He recognised no one until his eye stopped at "S. J. Kerslake, MP". The cook felt sure that Mr Seymour had not enjoyed his dinner, because he hardly touched the main course.

On his arrival at Seymour's, only moments after Clive Reynolds, he called for his chief executive. He appeared a few minutes later without his usual armful of files, surprised to see the chairman so early. Once Reynolds was seated Charles opened the file in front of him. "What do you know about Nethercote and Company?"

"Private company. Net asset value approaching £10,000,000, running a current overdraft of £7,000,000 of which we service half.

Efficiently managed with a good board of directors, will ride out the current problems in my view, and should be well oversubscribed when they eventually go public."

"How much of the company do we own?"

"Seven and a half per cent. As you know, the bank never take eight per cent of any company because then we would have to declare an interest under section twenty-three of the Finance Act. It has always been a policy of this bank to invest in a major client without becoming too involved with the running of the company."

"Who are their principal bankers?"

"The Midland."

"What would happen if we put our seven and a half per cent up for sale and did not renew the overdraft facility at the end of the quarter, but called it in instead?"

"They would have to seek finance elsewhere."

"And if they couldn't?"

"They would have to start selling their assets, which under that sort of forced-sale position would be very damaging for any company, if not impossible, in the present climate."

"And then?"

"I would have to check my file and . . ."

Charles passed over the file and Reynolds studied it carefully, frowning. "They already have a cash-flow problem because of bad debts. With a sudden increased demand they might go under. I would strongly advise against such a move, Chairman. Nethercote have proved a reliable risk over the years, and I think we stand to make a handsome profit when they are quoted on the Stock Exchange."

"For reasons I cannot disclose to you," said Charles, looking up from his chair, "I fear that remaining involved with this company may turn out to be a financial embarrassment for Seymour's." Reynolds looked at him, puzzled. "You will inform the Midland Bank that we will not be renewing this loan at the next quarter."

"Then they would have to look for support from another bank. The Midland would never agree to shoulder the entire amount on their own."

"And try to dispose of our seven and a half per cent immediately."

"But that could lead to a crisis of confidence in the company."

"So be it," said Charles, as he closed the file.

"But I do feel —"

"That will be all, Mr Reynolds."

"Yes, Chairman," said the mystified chief executive, who had never thought of his boss as an irrational man. He turned to leave. Had he looked back he would have been even more mystified by the smile that was spread across Charles Seymour's face.

"They've pulled the rug out from under our feet," said Ronnie Nethercote angrily.

"Who?" said Simon, who had just come into the room.

"The Midland Bank."

"Why would they do that?"

"An outside shareholder put all his stock on the market without warning, and the Midland got worried about their position. They wouldn't be prepared to continue such a large overdraft position on their own."

"Have you been to see the manager?" asked Simon, unable to disguise his anxiety.

"Yes, but he can't do anything. His hands are tied by a main board directive," said Ronnie, slumping deeper into his seat.

"How bad is it?"

"They've given me a month to find another bank. Otherwise I'll have to start selling some of our assets."

"What will happen if we don't manage to come up with another bank?" asked Simon desperately.

"The company could be bankrupt within weeks. Do you know any bankers who are looking for a good investment?"

"Only one, and I can assure you he wouldn't help."

Charles put the phone down satisfied. He wondered if there was anything that could still be regarded as secret. It had taken him less than an hour to find out the size of Kerslake's overdraft. "Banker to banker confidentiality," he had assured them. He was still smiling when Reynolds knocked on the door.

"The Midland weren't pleased," he immediately briefed Charles.

"They'll get over it," his chairman replied. "What's the latest on Nethercote?"

"Only a rumour, but everyone now knows they're in trouble and the chairman is searching around for a new backer," said Reynolds impassively. "His biggest problem is that no one is touching property companies at the moment."

"Once they've collapsed, what's to stop us picking up the pieces and making a killing?"

"A clause that was slipped through in the Finance Act which your Government passed three years ago. The penalties range from a heavy fine to having your banking licence taken away."

"Oh, yes, I remember," said Charles. "Pity. So how long do you expect them to last?"

"Once the month is up," said Reynolds stroking a clean-shaven chin, "if they fail to find a backer the creditors will swarm in like locusts."

"Aren't the shares worth anything?" asked Charles innocently.

"Not the paper they are written on at the moment," said Reynolds, watching his chairman carefully.

This time the chief executive couldn't miss the chairman's smile as Charles thought of Simon Kerslake and his overdraft of £108,000 now backed by worthless shares. Pucklebridge would soon be looking for a new member.

At the end of a month during which no bank came to his rescue Ronnie Nethercote caved in and agreed to call in the receiver and file a bankruptcy notice. He still hoped that he could pay off all his creditors even if the shares he and his fellow directors held remained worthless. He felt as worried for Simon and his career as he did for himself, but he knew there was nothing the receiver would allow him to do to help one individual.

When Simon told Elizabeth she didn't complain. She had always feared this could be the eventual outcome of her husband joining the board of Nethercotes.

"Can't Ronnie help?" she asked. "After all, you've supported him enough in the past."

"No, he can't," replied Simon, avoiding telling her where the real responsibility for his downfall lay.

"But do bankrupts automatically have to leave Parliament?" was Elizabeth's next question.

"No, but I shall because I could never be considered for further promotion – I'd always be rightly tainted with 'lack of judgement'."

"It seems so unfair when you weren't personally to blame."

"There are different rules for those who wish to live in the spotlight," Simon said simply.

"But in time, surely –" began Elizabeth.

"I'm not willing to remain on the back benches for another twenty years only to hear whispered in the corner of the smoking room – Would have made the Cabinet if it hadn't been for . . ."

"Does that mean the children will have to be taken away from school?"

"I'm afraid so," said Simon, his hands shaking. "As a bankrupt I can hardly expect the receiver to view the fees for my sons' education as a dire necessity even if I could find the money."

"So we'll have to get rid of the nanny, too?"

"Not necessarily, but we may both have to make sacrifices in order that she can be part-time."

"But my work at the hospital . . ." began Elizabeth but didn't complete the sentence. "What happens next?"

"I'll have to tell Archie Millburn tonight. I've already written my letter of resignation to hand to him. I shall make an appointment to see the Chief Whip on Monday to explain why I am going to apply for the Chiltern Hundreds."

"What does that mean?"

"It's one of the only ways of leaving the House in mid-session – other than dying. Officially it's a nominal office under the Crown which therefore debars you from membership of the House."

"It all sounds rather formal to me."

"I'm afraid it will cause an embarrassing by-election in Pucklebridge," Simon admitted.

"Can nobody help?"

"There aren't a lot of people around who have a spare £108,000 for a worthless bunch of shares."

"Would you like me to come with you when you go to see Archie?" Elizabeth asked, rising from her seat.

"No, darling. It's kind of you to ask, but I'm the one who made such a fool of myself."

Elizabeth leaned over and pushed back the hair that had fallen over his forehead. She couldn't help noticing some grey strands that must have appeared in the last few weeks. "We'll just have to live off my salary while you look for a job."

Simon drove slowly down to Pucklebridge to keep his impromptu appointment with the chairman. Archie Millburn, standing hands on hips in his garden, listened to the tale with a sad face. "It's been happening to a lot of good people in the City lately, but what I can't understand is: if the company owns such prime properties, why has no one made a takeover bid? Sounds as if it's an asset-stripper's dream."

"It appears to be a matter of confidence," said Simon.

"A sacred word in the City," agreed Archie, while he continued to prune his Roosevelts and Red Mistresses.

Simon handed him the prepared letter of resignation, which Millburn read over and reluctantly accepted.

"I won't mention this to anyone until you've seen the Chief Whip on Monday. I'll call a special meeting of the full committee on Tuesday evening and inform them of your decision then. You had better be prepared for an unfriendly barrage from the press on Tuesday night."

The two men shook hands. "Your misfortune is our misfortune," said Archie. "In a very short time you've gained the respect and the affection of the local people. You'll be missed."

Simon drove back to London and, although the car radio was on low, he did not take in the news flash that they kept repeating every thirty minutes.

CHAPTER TWENTY

Raymond was among the first to hear the announcement, and was stunned by it. Harold Wilson was going to resign less than half-way through the five-year Parliament, and for no apparent reason other than that he had just passed his sixtieth birthday. He proposed to remain Prime Minister only so long as the Labour party took to select its new leader. Raymond and Kate sat glued to the television, picking up every scrap of information they could. They discussed the implications far into the night.

"Well, Carrot Top, could this mean rehabilitation for our forgotten hero?"

"Who can say?"

"Well, if you can't, who can?"

"The next leader," said Raymond.

The fight for the leadership was a straight battle between the left and right wings of the party, James Callaghan on the right and Michael Foot on the left. Andrew and Raymond both wanted the same man and it was with some relief that they saw Callaghan, despite losing the first ballot, come through to be elected leader. The Queen duly called Callaghan and asked him to form a new administration.

As tradition demands Andrew sent his resignation to Downing Street, as did every other member of the Government, to allow the new Prime Minister to select his own team.

Raymond was in court listening to the judge's summing up when his junior passed him a note: "Please call 10 Downing Street as soon as possible." The judge took a further thirty minutes, meticulously explaining to the jury the legal definition of manslaughter, before Raymond could escape. He ran down the corridor and stopped at one of the clerks' private boxes to make the call. The plastic dial rotating back into place after each number seemed to take forever.

After he had been passed through three people a voice said, "Good afternoon, Ray": the unmistakable gravelly tones of the new Prime Minister. "I think it's time you rejoined the Government" – Raymond held his breath – "as Minister of State at the Department of Trade." Minister of State: only one place away from the Cabinet."

"You still there, Ray?"

"Yes, Prime Minister, and I'd be delighted to accept."

He put the phone down, immediately picked it up again and dialled the City office of the Chase Manhattan Bank. They put him through to the Euro Bond manager.

Andrew had left his desk at the Home Office and returned to Cheyne Walk. He stayed away from the House of Commons where the lobby correspondents were hanging about like hyenas, scampering off to phone their papers with even the rumour of a rumour. The new Cabinet had been selected, and now it was the turn of the Ministers of State. All Andrew knew for certain was that his old job at the Home Office had been given to someone else.

"Why don't you go and play football with Robert?" Louise suggested. "And stop moping around under my feet?"

"Yes, Dad, yes, Dad, yes, Dad," demanded his son, running upstairs to reappear a few minutes later dressed in the Liverpool kit that he had bought himself from eleven weeks' hard-saved pocket money.

"Go on, Andrew. I can always call you if the phone goes."

Andrew smiled, took off his jacket and put on the pair of old gym shoes Robert was holding out for him. He followed his five-year-old son into the garden to find him already dribbling up and down the thin strip between the flower beds. The little goal he had bought for Robert – or was it for himself? – at Christmas was already set up at the far end of the grass and they took turns defending it. Andrew always had to start in goal. He rubbed his hands together to keep warm as Robert dribbled towards him. He came out of the goal ready to stifle a shot, but Robert kicked the ball to the right and ran to the left, leaving his father spreadeagled on the ground before he pushed the ball gently into the goal. "That's called a feint," he shouted triumphantly, as he ran back past his prostrate father.

Andrew picked himself up. "I know what it's called," he said, laughing. "You seem to have forgotten who taught you the feint in the first place. Let's see if you can do it twice running," he added, returning to defend the goal.

Robert dribbled away from his father until he reached the end of the garden, then turned to face him again. He had begun advancing towards the goal for a second time when there was the sound of the phone ringing. Andrew looked towards the house just as Robert kicked the ball, which rising sharply, struck him in the face. He and the ball fell back into the goal mouth.

Louise opened the kitchen window and shouted, "It's only my mother."

"Wake up, Dad," demanded Robert simultaneously.

Andrew's face was still stinging from the blow. "I'm going to get you for that," he said. "Your turn to defend the goal."

Robert rushed forward to take his place between the posts, jumping up and down trying to touch the crossbar with the tips of his fingers. Andrew took his time as he moved towards his son. When he was about a yard in front of Robert he feinted to the right and ran to the left but Robert had seen the move coming and leaped on the ball shouting, "No goal."

Once again Andrew returned to the end of the garden, thinking over what move he could try next. He suddenly ran straight at Robert and kicked the ball firmly towards the right-hand corner of the goal mouth. But again Robert anticipated the move and caught the ball above his head before pulling it to his chest and shouting, "No goal, Dad, no goal!" He tossed the ball confidently back along the ground to his father's feet.

"Right, the fooling around is over," said Andrew, not quite convinced. He kicked the ball from one foot to the other, trying to look skilful.

"Come on, Dad," Robert complained.

This time Andrew advanced with a look of determination on his face. He tried a change of pace to make his son leave the goal mouth too early. Robert duly came out of the goal; Andrew kicked the ball a little harder and higher than his previous attempt. As he did so he heard the phone ring again and turned his head towards the house. He didn't see his shot cannon against the left-hand corner of the goal post and bounce away.

"It's the Prime Minister," shouted Louise from the window. Andrew turned to walk quickly back towards the house. Out of the corner of his eye he saw the ball bounce on to the path, on its way towards the gate and into the road.

Robert was already running towards the open gate. "I'll save it, Dad, I'll save it."

"No," screamed Andrew at the top of his voice and turned back to run as fast as he could after his son.

Louise froze as she stared out of the window, still holding on to the phone with her rubber gloves. She watched as Andrew turned his back and tore towards the pavement until he was only a yard behind his son. The ball bounced on into the road and Robert dived for it a split second before his father threw himself on his son.

Louise was the only one who saw the driver of the massive Shell tanker slam on its brakes and swerve – too late – to avoid them. Andrew and Robert collided with the corner of the wide metal mudguard and were thrown back together before rolling over and over several times, ending up in the gutter.

"Are you there, Andrew?" asked the Prime Minister.

Louise dropped the phone and ran out of the kitchen towards the open gate. Her husband lay motionless beside the kerb with their son in his arms, the ball still clutched against his chest. She tried to hold on to both of them as Andrew's blood poured down over Robert's red shirt and on to her rubber gloves.

She fell on to her knees by the kerb side. "Let them live, let them live," was all she said.

Robert was crying softly as he held firmly on to the ball and stared at his unconscious father. She had to lean over to hear him repeating, "No goal, Dad, no goal."

When the complete list of ministers was published in *The Times* two days later the only unfilled post left was that of Minister of State for Defence. *The Times*'s political editor, David Wood, surmised that the position was being held open for Mr Andrew Fraser, who was expected to be out of hospital by the end of the week. Wood's final paragraph read:

> Politicians from all parties joined forces in praising Mr Fraser's remarkable courage in diving in front of a moving lorry to rescue his only son, Robert, who was chasing a football. Both father and son were rushed to St Thomas's Hospital with internal injuries where surgeons operated through the night to save Mr Fraser's life.
>
> As was reported in the final edition of yesterday's paper, his five-year-old son Robert died during the night before Mr Fraser regained consciousness.

"My God," exclaimed Elizabeth, "how dreadful."

"What's dreadful?" asked Simon, as he took his seat at the breakfast table. She passed the paper to her husband and pointed to the picture of Robert.

"Poor kid," said Simon before he had finished the article.

"Certainly puts our own problems into perspective. If Peter or Michael were killed we really would have something to worry about."

Neither of them spoke for several minutes. Then Elizabeth asked, "Are you dreading it?"

"Yes, I am," said Simon. "I feel like a condemned man eating his last breakfast, and the worst part of it is that I have to drive myself to the gallows."

"I wonder if we will ever laugh about today?"

"No doubt – when I collect my parliamentary pension."

"Can we live off that?"

"Hardly. I don't get the first payment until I'm sixty-five, so we have a twenty-five-year wait to find out." He got up. "Can I give you a lift to the hospital?"

"No thanks. I intend to savour the joys of being a two-car family for at least another week. Just let's hope the new Marina holds its price as well as Sir Michael Edwardes claimed it would."

Simon laughed, kissed his wife and left for his appointment with the Chief Whip at the House of Commons. As he started the car Elizabeth rushed out. "I forgot to tell you, Ronnie phoned while you were in the bath."

"I'll call him as soon as I reach the House."

Simon made his way to the Commons. He felt sick as he passed Cheyne Walk and thought of Andrew Fraser and all he must be going through. He made a mental note to write to him immediately. At the Commons the policeman on the gate saluted as he drove in. "Good morning, sir," he said.

"Good morning," said Simon. He parked his car on the second level of the new underground car park and took the escalator up to the Members' Entrance. He couldn't help reflecting that ten years ago he would have taken the stairs. He continued through the Members' Cloakroom, up the marble staircase to the Members' Lobby. Habit made him turn left into the little post office to check whether he had any mail.

"Mr Kerslake," the man behind the counter called into an intercom, and a few seconds later a parcel and a packet of letters held together by a thick elastic band thudded into an office basket. Simon left the parcel marked "London School of Economics" and the letters on the desk in his room and checked his watch: over forty minutes before his appointment with the Chief Whip. He went to the nearest phone and dialled Nethercote and Company. Ronnie answered the phone himself.

"Sacked the telephone operator last Friday," he explained. "Only me and my secretary left."

"You called, Ronnie," a millimetre of hope in Simon's voice.

"Yes, I wanted to express how I felt. I tried to write you a letter over the weekend but I'm not very good with words." He paused. "Nor it seems with figures. I just wanted to say how desperately sorry I am. Elizabeth told me you were going to see the Chief Whip this morning. I'll be thinking of you."

"That's kind, Ronnie, but I went into it with my eyes wide open. As an advocate of free enterprise, I can hardly complain when I turn out to be one of its victims."

"A very philosophical attitude for this time of the morning."

"How are things your end?"

"The receiver's checking the books. I stil believe we can get out with all our creditors fully paid. At least that way I'll avoid the stigma of bankruptcy." There was a longer pause. "Oh Christ, that was tactless."

"Don't worry about it, Ronnie, the overdraft was my decision."

Simon already wished he had been as frank with his wife.

"Let's have lunch one day next week."

"It will have to be somewhere that takes luncheon vouchers," said Simon wryly.

"Good luck, mate," said Ronnie.

Simon decided to fill up the remaining thirty minutes at the House by going to the library and glancing over the rest of the morning press. He settled himself in a corner of the "B" Room, next to the fireplace over which hung a notice reminding members not to have overloud or prolonged conversations. He leafed through the papers, which all carried photographs of Andrew Fraser and his wife and son. The same portrait of five-year-old Robert appeared on almost every front page. Elizabeth was right: in so many respects they were lucky.

The story of the probable break-up of Nethercote and Company was detailed on the financial pages. They quoted approvingly Ronnie's view that all creditors ought to be paid in full. Not one of the articles mentioned Simon's name, but he could already anticipate the headlines in tomorrow's paper with another picture of a young MP and his happy family. "The Rise and Fall of Simon Kerslake." Over ten years' work quickly forgotten: he would be old news within a week.

The library clock inched towards the hour that he could no longer put off. Simon heaved himself out of the deep leather chair like an old man and walked slowly towards the Chief Whip's office.

Miss Norse, the Chief's ancient secretary, smiled benignly as he came in.

"Good morning, Mr Kerslake," she said brightly. "I'm afraid the Chief is still with Mrs Thatcher but I did remind him of your appointment so I don't expect him to be long. Would you care to have a seat?"

"Thank you," he said.

Alec Pimkin always claimed that Miss Norse had a set patter for every occasion. His imitation of her saying, "I hope I find you in rude health, Mr Pimkin," had brought chuckles to the Members' Dining-room on many occasions. He must have exaggerated, thought Simon.

"I hope I find you in rude health, Mr Kerslake," said Miss Norse, not looking up from her typing. Simon choked back a laugh.

"Very rude, thank you," he said, wondering how many tragic stories or tales of lost opportunities Miss Norse had had to listen to over the years. She stopped suddenly and looked at her note pad.

"I should have mentioned it to you before, Mr Kerslake, a Mr Nethercote rang."

"Thank you, I've spoken to him already."

Simon was leafing through an out-of-date copy of *Punch* when the Chief Whip strode in.

"I can spare you one minute, Simon, one and a half if you are going to resign," he said, laughing, and marched off towards his office. As Simon followed him down the corridor the phone by Miss Norse's side rang. "It's for you, Mr Kerslake," she shouted to their retreating backs.

Simon turned and said, "Can you take the number?"

"He says it's urgent."

Simon stopped, hesitating. "With you in a moment," he said to the Chief Whip, who disappeared into his office. Simon walked back and took the phone from Miss Norse's outstretched hand.

"Simon Kerslake here. Who is it?"

"It's Ronnie."

"Ronnie," said Simon flatly.

"I've just had a call from Morgan Grenfell. One of their clients has made an offer of one pound twenty-five a share for the company and they're willing to take over the current liabilities."

Simon was trying to do the sums in his head.

"Don't bother working it out," Ronnie said. "At one pound twenty-five your shares would be worth £75,000."

"It won't be enough," said Simon, as he recalled his overdraft of £108,712, a figure etched in his memory.

"Don't panic. I've told them I won't settle for anything less than one pound fifty a share and it has to be within seven days, which will give them ample time to check the books. That would bring you in £90,000 but you would still be £18,000 down the Swanee, which you'll have to learn to live with. If you sell the wife as well as the second car you should just about survive."

Simon could tell by the way his friend was speaking that Ronnie already had a cigar between his lips.

"You're a genius."

"Not me – Morgan Grenfell. And I bet they'll make a handsome profit in the long run for their unnamed client who seemed to have all the inside information. If you're still on for lunch next Tuesday, don't bring your luncheon vouchers. It's on me."

Simon put the phone down and kissed Miss Norse on the forehead. She was completely taken aback by a situation for which she had no set reply. She remained silent as the Chief Whip put his head round the door. "An orgy in the Chief Whip's office? You'll be on page three of the *Sun* next, Miss Norse." Simon laughed. "I've got a crisis on over tonight's vote. The Government are reneging on our agreement for pairing and I have to get a delegation back from Brussels in time for the ten o'clock division. Whatever it is, can it wait, Simon?"

"Yes, of course."

"Can you come to my office, Miss Norse – if I can drag you away from James Double-O-Seven Kerslake?"

Simon left and almost bounced to the nearest phone. First he called Elizabeth and then Archie Millburn at his office. Archie didn't sound all that surprised.

"Don't you think it might be wise for us to stop seeing each other?"

"Why?" said Raymond. "Palmerston had a mistress when he was seventy, and he still beat Disraeli come the election."

"Yes, but that was before the days of a dozen national newspapers *and* investigative journalism. Frankly it wouldn't take a Woodward or Bernstein more than a few hours to discover our little secret."

"We'll be all right. I've destroyed all the tapes."

"Do be serious."

"You're always telling me I'm far too serious."

"Well, I want you to be now. Very."

Raymond turned to face Kate. "I love you, Kate, and I know I always will. Why don't we stop this charade and get married?"

She sighed. "We've been over this a hundred times. I'll want to return to America eventually, and in any case I wouldn't make a very good Prime Minister's wife."

"Three American women have in the past," said Raymond sulkily.

"To hell with your historical precedents – and what's more, I hate Leeds."

"You've never been there."

"I don't need to if it's colder than London."

"Then you'll have to be satisfied with being my mistress." Raymond took Kate in his arms. "You know, I used to think being Prime Minister was worth every sacrifice, but now I'm not so sure."

"It's still worth the sacrifice," said Kate, "as you'll discover when you live at No. 10. Come on, or my dinner will be burnt to a cinder."

"You haven't noticed these," said Raymond smugly, pointing down at his feet.

Kate stared at the fashionable new slip-ons.

"I never thought the day would come," she said. "Pity you're starting to go bald."

When Simon returned home his first words were "We'll survive."

"Thank God for that," Elizabeth said. "But what have you done about your resignation letter?"

"Archie said he would return it the day I became Prime Minister."

"If that's ever to be true I want you to promise me just one thing."

"Anything," said Simon.

"You'll never speak to Ronnie Nethercote again."

For a moment Simon hesitated before saying, "That's not completely fair, Elizabeth, because I haven't been totally straight with you from the beginning." He then sat his wife down on the sofa and told her the whole truth.

It was Elizabeth's turn to remain silent.

"Oh, hell," she said, looking up at Simon. "I do hope Ronnie can forgive me."

"What are you talking about?"

"I phoned him back soon after you had left for the Commons and I spent at least ten minutes telling him why he was the biggest two-faced bastard I'd ever come across, and I didn't want to hear from him again in my life."

It was Simon's turn to collapse on to the sofa. "How did he respond?" he asked anxiously. Elizabeth faced her husband. "That's the strange thing, he didn't even protest. He just apologised."

"Do you think she will ever speak again?"

"God knows, I hope so," said his father, staring at the picture of his grandchild on the mantelpiece. "She's still young enough to have another child."

Andrew shook his head. "No, that's out of the question. The doctor warned me a long time ago that could be dangerous."

He had returned home from hospital ten days after the accident. The first thing he and Louise did was to attend Robert's funeral. With Andrew on crutches, Sir Duncan had to support Louise during the short service. As soon as the burial was over Andrew took his wife back to Cheyne Walk and put her to bed, before returning downstairs to join his parents.

Andrew's mother bowed her head. "Whatever happens, you must move from this place as soon as possible. Every time Louise looks out of that kitchen window she'll relive the tragedy."

"I hadn't thought of that," said Andrew. "I'll start looking for a new house immediately."

"And what do you plan to do about the Prime Minister's offer?" inquired Sir Duncan.

"I haven't finally made up my mind," he said sharply. "He's given me until Monday to come to a decision."

"You must take it, Andrew. If you don't your political career will be finished. You can't sit at home and mourn Robert's death for the rest of your life."

Andrew looked up at his father. "No goal, Dad, no goal," he murmured and left them to go and sit with Louise in the bedroom. Her eyes were open but there was no expression on her face. Little white hairs had appeared at either side of her head that he had not noticed the week before. "Feeling any better, my darling?" he asked.

There was still no reply.

He undressed and climbed into bed beside her, holding her close, but she did not respond. She felt detached and distant. He watched his tears fall on her shoulder and run down on to the pillow. He fell asleep and woke again at three in the morning. No one had closed the curtains and the moon shone in through the windows, lighting the room. He looked at his wife. She had not moved.

Charles paced up and down the room angrily.

"Give me the figures again."

"Nethercote has accepted a bid of £7,500,000, which works out at one pound fifty a share," said Clive Reynolds.

Charles stopped at his desk and scribbled the figures down on a piece of paper. £90,000, leaving a shortfall of only £18,000. It wouldn't be enough. "Damn," he said.

"I agree," said Reynolds, "I always thought we were premature to lose our position in the company in the first place."

"An opinion you will not voice outside this room," said Charles.

Clive Reynolds did not reply.

"What's happened to Nethercote himself?" asked Charles, searching for any scrap of information he could find about Simon Kerslake.

"I'm told he's starting up again in a smaller way. Morgan Grenfell were delighted by the deal and the manner in which he handled the company during the takeover. I must say we let it fall into their laps."

"Can we get any stock in the new company?" asked Charles, ignoring his comment.

"I doubt it. It's only capitalized at one million although Morgan Grenfell are giving Nethercote a large overdraft facility as part of the deal."

"Then all that remains necessary is to see the matter is never referred to again."

Andrew spent the weekend reading over the letters of condolence sent to him and Louise. There were over a thousand, many from people he didn't even know. He selected a few to take into the bedroom and read to Louise; not that he was sure she could even hear him. The doctor had told him not to disturb her unless it was really necessary. After such a severe shock she was now suffering from acute depression and must be nursed slowly back to health. Louise had walked a few paces the previous day but needed to rest today, the doctor explained to him.

He sat by the side of their bed, and quietly read the letters from the Prime Minister, from a contrite Jock McPherson, from Simon Kerslake, from Raymond Gould and from Mrs Bloxham. There was no sign that Louise had taken in anything he had said.

"What shall I do about the PM's offer?" he asked. "Shall I accept it?"

She made no response of any kind.

"He's asked me to be the Minister of State for Defence, but I need to know how you would feel." After sitting with her for a few more minutes and eliciting no response he left her to rest.

Each night he slept with her and tried to infuse her with his love, but he only felt more alone.

On the Monday morning he called his father and told him he had decided to turn down the Prime Minister's offer. He couldn't leave Louise alone for long periods while she was still in this state.

Andrew returned to the bedroom and sat by her side.

He said in a whisper, as if to himself, "Should I have taken the job?"

Louise gave such a slight nod that Andrew nearly missed it but her fingers were moving. He placed his hand between her fingers and palm and she squeezed gently and repeated the nod, then fell asleep.

Andrew phoned the Prime Minister.

Raymond dug deeper into the red box.

"You enjoying yourself, Carrot Top?"

"It's fascinating," said Raymond. "Do you know –"

"No, I don't. You haven't spoken to me in the last three hours, and when you do it's to tell me how you spend the day with your new mistress."

"My new mistress?"

"The Secretary of State for Trade."

"Oh, him."

"Yes, him."

"What sort of day did you have at the bank?" asked Raymond, not looking up from his papers.

"I had a most fascinating day," replied Kate.

"Why, what happened?"

"One of our customers required a loan," said Kate.

"A loan," repeated Raymond, still concentrating on the file in front of him. "How much?"

" 'How much do you want?' I said. 'How much have you got?' they asked. 'Four hundred and seventeen billion at the last count,' I told them. 'That will do fine to start with,' they said. 'Sign here,' I said. But I couldn't close the deal because the lady concerned was only in possession of a £50 banking card."

Raymond burst out laughing and slammed down the lid of the red box. "Do you know why I love you?"

"My taste in men's clothes?" suggested Kate.

"No, no. Just your taste in men."

"I always thought that mistresses were supposed to get fur coats, trips to the Bahamas, the odd solitaire diamond, yet all I ever get is to share you with your red box."

Raymond opened the box once more, took out a small package and handed it to Kate.

"What's this?"

"Why don't you open it and find out?"

Kate slipped off the purple Asprey paper and found inside an exquisitely made miniature, a solid gold replica of a red box on a gold chain. The neat lettering on the side of the lid read, 'For Your Eyes Only'.

"Although they don't announce the birthdays of ministers' mistresses in the *Sunday Times*, I can still remember the day we met."

Andrew made a bid for the house in Pelham Crescent the day he was shown over it, and Louise's mother came down to London immediately to organise the move.

"Let's hope this does the trick," she said.

Andrew prayed for nothing more. The move from Cheyne Walk took about a fortnight, and Louise could still walk only a few paces before she had to sit down. Louise's mother rarely left the house and Andrew began to feel guilty about how much he was enjoying his new job at the Ministry of Defence. Each night and then again in the morning he would try a few words to Louise. She nodded occasionally, touched him once in a while and even began writing notes to him, but never spoke and never cried. The doctor became even more pessimistic. "The crucial time has passed," he explained.

Andrew would sit with her for hours while he worked through the red boxes. Harrier Jump jets for the RAF, Polaris missiles for the Royal Navy, Chieftain tanks for the Army, what should Labour's attitude be to Trident when Polaris was phased out? Should we allow Cruise to be based on British soil? There was so much to learn before he could face the civil servants on their own ground or the members from the dispatch box. As the months passed Andrew was always asking questions; a year had gone by and he was beginning to know some of the answers.

He looked up at his wife once again. She was gazing at the portrait of Robert on the mantelpiece.

On the anniversary of his son's sixth birthday Andrew stayed at Pelham Crescent all day with Louise. For the first time a tear lodged in her eye. As he held her, he kept remembering the lorry. He could see it so clearly now as if in slow motion. If only the phone hadn't gone, if only the gate had been closed, if only he had turned earlier, if only he had run a little faster. "No goal, Dad, no goal."

If only he had scored that goal.

CHAPTER TWENTY ONE

Raymond entered a Washington ablaze with red, white and blue as the Americans prepared for their bicentennial. He was among the three ministers chosen to represent the United Kingdom when they presented a copy of Magna Carta to the United States Congress. He was making his first trip to America on Concorde only a few weeks after its inaugural flight. Tom Carson had complained to the House about the expense of the trip but his words had fallen upon a silent Chamber.

As the plane taxied to a halt at Dulles airport three limousines drew up. The three ministers were given a car each and motorcycle outriders rushed them to the grounds of the British Embassy on Massachusetts Avenue in less than thirty minutes.

Raymond had an immediate love affair with America, perhaps because it reminded him so much of Kate with its bubbling enthusiasm, its spirit and sense of perpetual innovation. During the ten-day visit he managed to forge several useful contacts in the Senate and House, and over the weekend became an unrepentant sightseer of the beautiful Virginia countryside. He concentrated on getting to know those contemporaries whom he felt would be on the American political stage for the next twenty years, while his more senior colleagues dealt with President Ford and his immediate entourage.

Raymond enjoyed starting each day with the *Washington Post* and the *New York Times*. He quickly learned how to reject those sections that seemed full of endless advertisements for non-essentials he couldn't believe anyone really bought. Once he had finished reading both papers he found he had to wash his hands as they were always black with newsprint. The one occasion he kept the Outlook section of the *Washington Post* was when it did profiles on the three ministers from London. He tucked the paper away as he wanted to show Kate the paragraph that read: "The two Secretaries of State are interesting men at the end of their careers, but it is Raymond Gould we should keep our eyes on because he has the look of a future Prime Minister."

As Raymond flew out of Washington on his way back to London he presumed, like any lover, that the affair with America could be continued whenever he chose to return.

Simon was in Manchester as a guest of the Business School when he received Elizabeth's message to call her. It was most unusual for Elizabeth to phone in the middle of the day and Simon assumed the worst: something must have happened to the children. The Principal of the Business School accompanied him to his private office, then left him alone.

Dr Kerslake was not at the hospital, he was told, which made him even more anxious. He dialled the Beaufort Street number.

Elizabeth picked up the receiver so quickly that she must have been sitting by the phone waiting for him to call.

"I've been sacked," she said.

"What?" said Simon, unable to comprehend.

"I've been made redundant – isn't that the modern term meant to lessen the blow? The hospital governors have been instructed by the Department of Health and Social Security to make cut-backs and three of us in gynaecology have lost our jobs. I go at the end of the month." .

"Darling, I'm sorry," he said, knowing how inadequate his words must have sounded.

"I didn't mean to bother you, but I just wanted someone to talk to," she said. "Everyone else is allowed to complain to their MP, so I thought it was my turn."

"Normally what I do in these circumstances is to put the blame on the Labour party." Simon was relieved to hear Elizabeth laugh.

"Thanks for ringing me back so quickly, darling. See you tomorrow," she said and put the phone down.

Simon returned to his group and explained that he had to leave for London immediately. He took a taxi to the airport and caught the next shuttle to Heathrow. He was back at Beaufort Street within three hours.

"I didn't mean you to come home," Elizabeth said contritely when she saw him on the doorstep.

"I've come back to celebrate," Simon said. "Let's open the bottle of champagne that Ronnie gave us when he closed the deal with Morgan Grenfell."

"Why?"

"Because Ronnie taught me one thing. You should always celebrate disasters, not successes."

Simon hung up his coat and went off in search of the champagne. When he returned with the bottle and two glasses Elizabeth asked, "What's your overdraft looking like nowadays?"

"Down to £16,000, give or take a pound."

"Well, that's another problem then, I won't be giving any pounds in the future, only taking."

"Don't be silly. Someone will snap you up," he said, embracing her.

"It won't be quite that easy," said Elizabeth.

"Why not?" asked Simon, trying to sound cheerful.

"Because I had already been warned about whether I wanted to be a politician's wife or a doctor."

Simon was stunned. "I had no idea," he said. "I'm so sorry."

"It was my choice, darling, but I will have to make one or two decisions if I want to remain in medicine, especially if you're going to become a minister."

Simon remained silent: he had always wanted Elizabeth to make this decision herself and he was determined not to try to influence her.

"If only we weren't so short of money."

"Don't worry about the money," said Simon.

"I do worry, but it may just be an excuse because I worry more about becoming bored when the children have grown up. I just wasn't cut out to be a politician's wife," she added. "You should have married someone like Fiona Seymour and you'd be Prime Minister by now."

"If that's the only way I can be sure of getting the job I'll stick with you," said Simon, taking Elizabeth in his arms. Simon couldn't help thinking of all the support his wife had given him during their marriage and even more so since his financial crisis. He knew exactly what his wife must do.

"You mustn't be allowed to give up being a doctor," he said. "It's every bit as important as wanting to be a minister. Shall I have a word with Gerry Vaughan? As Shadow spokesman for Health he might –"

"Certainly not, Simon. If I am to get another job, it'll be without anyone doing you or me a favour."

Louise was now coping on her own, and had almost returned to a normal life except she still couldn't speak. She seemed to be self-sufficient within her own world and the doctor agreed that she no longer needed a full-time nurse.

The day the nurse left Andrew decided to take Louise off for a week's holiday abroad. He wanted to return to the South of France and the Colombe d'Or, but the specialist had advised against it, explaining that any past association might trigger off a memory that in itself could cause a further relapse.

"Witch doctors' mumbo jumbo," Andrew complained but nevertheless took her to Venice, not Colombe d'Or. Once there, he was delighted by the interest Louise showed in the beautiful and ancient city. Her eyes lit up at the sight of the Torcello and she appeared to revel in the trip on a gondola down the twisting waterways past irreplaceable Italian architecture. Again and again she squeezed his hand. As they sat on a piazza for an evening drink, she inclined her head and listened to a quintet playing on St Mark's Square. Andrew was confident that she could now hear everything he told her. The night before they flew back to England he woke to find her reading James

Morris's *Venice* which he had left by his side of the bed. It was the first time she had opened a book since the accident. When he smiled at her she grinned back. He laughed wanting to hear her laugh.

Andrew returned to the Ministry of Defence on Monday. On his desk there was a general directive from the Chancellor of the Exchequer, requiring the budget estimates for all the big-spending Departments of State. Andrew fought hard to keep the Polaris missile after being convinced by the Joint Chiefs of its strategic importance to the nation's defence. He was, however, continually reminded by his colleagues in the House that it was party policy to rid themselves of "the warmongers' toy".

When the Secretary of State returned from Cabinet he told Andrew, "We've had our way: the Cabinet were impressed by the case. But I can promise you one thing – you won't be the golden boy at this year's party conference."

"It will make a change for them even to notice me," replied Andrew.

He breathed a sigh of relief while the Joint Chiefs were delighted, but a week later he lost – by default – the same argument with his own General Purposes Committee in Edinburgh. In his absence, they passed a resolution deploring the retention of the Polaris missile and demanded that all the ministers involved should reconsider their decision. They stopped short of naming Andrew, but everyone knew whose scalp they were after. His case was not helped by Tom Carson making yet another inflammatory speech in the House, claiming that Andrew had been browbeaten by the Joint Chiefs and was nothing more than a Polaris puppet.

Andrew's trips to Edinburgh had become less frequent over the past year because of his commitments to Louise and the Defence Department. During the year three members of his General Management Committee had been replaced with a new group calling themselves "Militant Tendency" led by Frank Boyle. It wasn't just Edinburgh Carlton that was facing the problem of a left-wing insurgence – as Andrew learned from colleague after colleague who was beginning to work out why the left were pushing a resolution at the party conference proposing that members should be re-selected for each election. Some of his more right-wing colleagues had already been replaced, and it didn't take a Wrangler to work out that once a majority of the Trotskyites had secured places on his Management Committee Andrew could be removed at their whim, whatever his past experience or record.

Whenever Andrew was in Edinburgh the local people continually assured him of their support and their confidence in him, but he could not forget, despite their avowals, that it would still take only a handful of votes to remove him. Andrew feared what the outcome would be if many other members were facing the same problem as he faced in

Edinburgh.

"Dad, can I have a new cricket bat, please?"

"What's wrong with the old one?" asked Simon, as they came out of the house.

"It's too small," he said, waving it around as if it was an extension to his arm.

"It will have to do, I'm afraid."

"But Martin Henderson's dad has given him a new bat to start the season."

"I'm sorry, Peter, the truth is that Martin's father is far better off than I am."

"I'll tell you one thing," said Peter with feeling. "I'm sure not going to be an MP when I grow up." Simon smiled as his son removed an old cricket ball from his trouser pocket and tossed it over to his father. "Anyway, I bet you can't get me out even though I've only got a small bat."

"Don't forget we still have the junior size stumps left over from last year," said Simon, "so it will be just as hard to hit them."

"Stop making excuses, Dad. Just admit you're past it."

Simon burst out laughing. "We'll see," he said, with more bravado than conviction. Simon always enjoyed a few overs in the garden against his elder son although at the age of thirteen Peter was already able to play his best deliveries with a confidence that was beginning to look ominous.

It was several overs before Simon removed Peter's middle stump and took his turn at the crease.

Michael ran out of the house to join them in the field and Simon couldn't help noticing that he was wearing a pair of jeans that were far too short and had once belonged to Peter.

"Get behind the wicket, nipper," shouted Peter at his eleven-year-old brother. "Because that's where most of the balls will be going." Michael happily obeyed without comment.

A colleague in the House had recently warned Simon that by fourteen they began to beat you and by sixteen they hoped not to show they weren't trying their hardest any longer.

Simon gritted his teeth as he watched his elder son's fastest ball safely on to the middle of the bat. The way he was going Peter wouldn't have to wait much longer before he could clean bowl him.

He managed to keep his wicket intact for a further five minutes before he was rescued by Elizabeth who came out to tell them that supper was ready.

"What, hamburgers and chips again?" said Michael as his mother put a plate in front of him.

"You're lucky to get anything," Elizabeth snapped back.

Simon cursed again at the damage his own selfish greed had brought upon his family, and marvelled at how little they all complained. He said nothing, only too aware that the previous day Elizabeth had completed her last week at the hospital and was already missing St Mary's.

"How did you all get on?" she asked cheerily.

"I'll survive," said Simon, still thinking about his overdraft.

Once the Chancellor had presented his mini budget, in November 1976, the long process of the Finance Bill, confirming all the new measures proposed, fully occupied the House. Charles, although not a member of the front-bench finance team, regularly took the lead among back-benchers on clauses on which he had specialist knowledge.

He and Clive Reynolds studied the new Finance Bill meticulously and between them picked out the seven clauses that would have an adverse effect on banking.

Reynolds guided Charles through each clause, suggesting changes, rewording, and on some occasions presenting an argument for deleting whole sections of the bill. Charles learned quickly and was soon adding his own ideas; one or two even made Clive Reynolds reconsider. After Charles had put forward amendments to the House on three of the clauses both front benches became respectfully attentive whenever he rose to present a case. One morning, after the Government's defeat on a clause relating to banking loans, he received a note of congratulation from Margaret Thatcher.

The clause Charles most wanted to see removed from the bill concerned a client's right to privacy when dealing with a merchant bank. The Shadow Chancellor was aware of Charles's specialised knowledge on this subject and invited him to oppose clause 110 from the front bench. Charles realised that if he could defeat the Government on this clause he might be invited to join the Shadow finance team in the run-up to the general election.

Judging by the chairman of Ways and Means' selection of amendments the Whips estimated that clause 110 on banking privacy would be reached some time on Thursday afternoon.

On Thursday morning Charles rehearsed his arguments thoroughly with Clive Reynolds, who only had one or two minor amendments to add before Charles set off for the House. When he arrived at the Commons there was a note on the message board asking him to phone the Shadow Chancellor urgently.

"The Government are going to accept a Liberal amendment tabled late last night," the Shadow Chancellor told him.

"Why?" said Charles.

"Minimum change is what they're really after, but it gets them off the hook and at the same time keeps the Liberal vote intact. In essence nothing of substance has changed, but you'll need to study the wording carefully. Can I leave you to handle the problem?"

"Certainly," said Charles, pleased with the responsibility with which they were now entrusting him.

He walked down the long corridor to the vote office and picked up the sheet with clause 110 on it and the proposed Liberal amendment. He read them both through half a dozen times before he started to make notes. Parliamentary counsel, with their usual expertise, had produced an ingenious amendment. Charles ducked into a nearby phone booth and rang Clive Reynolds at the bank. Charles dictated the amendment over the phone to him and then remained silent while Reynolds considered its implications.

"Clever bunch of sharpies. It's a cosmetic job, but it won't change the power it invests in the Government one iota. Were you thinking of returning to the bank? That would give me time to work on it."

"No," said Charles. "Are you free for lunch?"

Clive Reynolds checked his diary: a Belgian banker would be lunching in the boardroom but his colleagues could handle that. "Yes, I'm free."

"Good," said Charles. "Why don't you join me at White's around one o'clock?"

"Thank you," said Reynolds. "By then I should have had enough time to come up with some credible alternatives."

Charles spent the rest of the morning rewriting his speech which he hoped would counter the Liberal argument and make them reconsider their position. If it met with Reynolds's imprimatur the day could still be his. He read through the clause once more, convinced he had found a way through the loophole the civil servants couldn't block. He placed his speech and the amended clause in his inside pocket and went down to the Members' Entrance and jumped into a waiting taxi.

As the cab drove up St James's Charles thought he saw his wife coming down the opposite side of the road. He pushed down the window to be sure but she had disappeared into Prunier's. He wondered with which of her girl friends she was lunching.

The cab travelled on up St James's and came to a halt outside White's. Charles found he was a few minutes early so he decided to walk down to Prunier's and ask Fiona if she would like to come to the House after lunch and hear him oppose the clause. Reaching the restaurant he glanced through the pane-glass window. He froze on the spot. Fiona was chatting at the bar with a man whose back was to Charles but he thought he recognised his profile although he couldn't be certain. He noticed that his wife was wearing a dress he had never seen before. He didn't move as he watched a waiter bow, then guide the pair towards a corner table where they were conveniently out of sight. Charles's first instinct was to march straight in and confront them; but he remained outside. For what seemed an interminable time he stood alone, uncertain what to do next. Finally he crossed back over St James's Street and stood in the doorway of the Economist building going over several plans. In the end he decided to do nothing but wait. He stood there so cold and so incensed that he did not consider returning for his lunch appointment with Clive Reynolds a few hundred yards up the road.

An hour and twenty minutes later the man came out of Prunier's alone and headed up St James's. Charles felt a sense of relief until he saw him turn into St James's Place. He checked his watch: Reynolds would have left by now but he would still be well in time for clause number 110. A few minutes later Fiona stepped out of the restaurant and followed in the man's footsteps. Charles crossed the road, causing a cab to swerve while another motorist slammed on her brakes. He didn't notice. He shadowed his wife, careful to keep a safe distance. When she reached the far end of the passage he watched Fiona enter the Stafford Hotel. Once she was through the swing doors Fiona stepped into an empty lift.

Charles came up to the swing doors and stared at the little numbers above the lift, watching them light up in succession until they stopped at four.

Charles marched through the swing doors and up to the reception desk.

"Can I help you, sir?" the hall porter asked.

"Er – is the dining-room in this hotel on the fourth floor?" asked Charles.

"No, sir," replied the hall porter, surprised. "The dining-room is on the ground floor to your left" – he indicated the way with a sweep of his hand – "there are only bedrooms on the fourth floor."

"Thank you," said Charles and marched back outside.

He returned slowly to the Economist building incensed where he waited for nearly two hours pacing up and down St James's before the man emerged from the Stafford Hotel; Alexander Dalglish hailed a taxi and disappeared in the direction of Piccadilly.

Fiona left the hotel about twenty minutes later, and took the path through to the park before setting off towards Eaton Square. On three occasions Charles had to fall back to be certain Fiona didn't spot him; once he was so close he thought he saw a smile of satisfaction come over her face.

He had followed his wife most of the way across St James's Park when he suddenly remembered. He checked his watch, then dashed back to the roadside, hailed a taxi and shouted, "The House of Commons, as fast as you can." The cabby took seven minutes and Charles passed him two pound notes before running up the steps into the Members' Lobby and through to the Chamber out of breath. He stopped by the Serjeant-at-Arms's chair.

From the table where he sat during Committee of the whole House, the Mace lowered on its supports in front of the table, the chairman of Ways and Means faced a packed House. He read from the division list.

"The Ayes to the right 294.

The Noes to the left 293.

The Ayes have it, the Ayes have it."

The Government benches cheered and the Conservatives looked distinctly glum. "What clause were they debating?" a still out of breath Charles asked the Serjeant-at-Arms.

"Clause 110, Mr Seymour."

BOOK FOUR

THE CABINET

1977 – 1989

CHAPTER TWENTY TWO

Raymond's second trip to the States was at the behest of the Secretary of State for Trade: he was asked to present the country's export and import assessment to the International Monetary Fund, following up a loan granted to Britain the previous November. His civil servants went over the prepared speech with him again and again, emphasizing to their minister the responsibility that had been placed on his shoulders. Even the Governor of the Bank of England's private office had been consulted.

"A chance to impress a few people beyond the boundaries of Leeds," Kate assured him.

Raymond's speech was scheduled for the Wednesday morning. He flew into Washington on the Sunday and spent Monday and Tuesday listening to the problems of other nations' trade ministers while trying to get used to the dreadful earphones and the female interpreter.

The conference was attended by most of the leading industrial nations and the British Ambassador, Sir Peter Ramsbotham, told Raymond over dinner at the Embassy that this was a real chance to convince the hard-headed international bankers that Britain cared about economic realities and was still worth their financial backing.

Raymond soon realised that convincing such a gathering required a very different technique from shouting from a soap box on a street corner in Leeds or even addressing the House from the dispatch box. He was glad he had not been scheduled to present his case on the opening day. Over leisurely lunches he re-established his existing contacts in Congress and made some new ones.

The night before he was to deliver his speech Raymond hardly slept. He continued to rehearse each crucial phrase and repeated the salient points that needed to be emphasised until he almost knew them by heart. At three o'clock in the morning he dropped his speech on the floor beside his bed and phoned Kate to have a chat before she went to work.

"I'd enjoy hearing your speech at the conference," she told him. "Although I don't suppose it would be much different from the thirty times I've listened to it in the bedroom."

Once he had said goodbye to Kate he fell into a deep sleep. He woke early that morning and went over the speech one last time before leaving for the conference centre.

All the homework and preparation proved worthwhile. By the time he turned the last page Raymond couldn't be certain how convincing his case had been, but he knew it was the best speech he had ever delivered. When he looked up the smiles all around the oval table assured him that his contribution had been well received. As the ambassador pointed out to him as he rose to leave, any signs of emotion at these gatherings were almost unknown. He felt confident that the IMF loan would be renewed.

There followed two further speeches before they broke for lunch. At the end of the afternoon session Raymond walked out into the clear Washington air and decided to make his way back to the Embassy on foot. He was exhilarated by the experience of dominating an international conference and picked up an evening paper: an article covering the conference suggested that Raymond would be Britain's next Labor Chancellor. He smiled at the spelling. Just the closing day to go, followed by the official banquet and he would be back home by the weekend.

When he reached the Embassy the guard had to double-check: they weren't used to ministers arriving on foot and without a bodyguard. Raymond was allowed to proceed down the tree-lined drive towards the massive Lutyens building. He looked up to see the British flag was flying at half mast and wondered which distinguished American had died.

"Who has died?" he asked the tail-coated butler who opened the door for him.

"The Foreign Secretary, sir."

"Anthony Crosland? I knew he had gone into hospital, but . . ." said Raymond almost to himself. He hurried into the Embassy to find it abuzz with telexes and coded messages. Raymond sat alone in his private sitting-room for several hours and later, to the horror of the security staff, slipped out for a quiet dinner at the Mayflower Hotel with Senator Hart.

Raymond returned to the conference table at nine o'clock the next morning to listen to the French Minister of Commerce put his case for renewed funds. He was savouring the thought of the official banquet at the White House to be held that evening when he was tapped on the shoulder by Sir Peter Ramsbotham, who indicated by touching his lips with his forefinger and pointing that they must have a word in private.

"The Prime Minister wants you to return on the mid-morning Concorde," said Sir Peter. "It leaves in an hour. On arrival in Britain you're to go straight to Downing Street."

"What's all this about?"

"I have no idea, that was the only instruction I received from No.

10," confided the ambassador.

Raymond returned to the conference table and made his apologies to the chairman, left the room and was driven immediately to the waiting plane. "Your bags will follow, sir," he was assured.

He was back on English soil three hours and forty-one minutes later, a little after seven-thirty. The purser ensured that he was the first to disembark. A car waiting by the side of the plan whisked him to Downing Street. He arrived just as the Prime Minister was going to dinner, accompanied by an elderly African statesman who was waving his trademark fan back and forth.

"Welcome home, Ray," said the Prime Minister, leaving the African leader. "I'd ask you to join us, but as you can see I'm entertaining the President of Malawi. Let's have a word in my study."

Once Raymond had settled into a chair Mr Callaghan wasted no time.

"Because of Tony's tragic death I have had to make a few changes which will include moving the Secretary of State for Trade. I was hoping you would be willing to take over from him."

Raymond sat up straighter. "I should be honoured, Prime Minister."

"Good. You've earned your promotion, Raymond. I also hear you did us proud in America, very proud."

"Thank you."

"You'll be appointed to the Privy Council immediately and your first Cabinet meeting will be at ten o'clock tomorrow. Now, if you'll excuse me, I must catch up with Dr Banda."

Raymond was left standing in the hall.

He asked his driver to take him back to the flat. All he wanted to do was to tell Kate the news. When he arrived the flat was empty: then he remembered she wasn't expecting him back until the next day. He phoned her home but after twenty continuous rings he resigned himself to the fact that she was out. "Damn," he said out loud, and after pacing around phoned Joyce to let her know the news. Once again there was no reply.

He went into the kitchen and checked to see what was in the fridge: a piece of curled-up bacon, some half-eaten Brie, three eggs. He couldn't help thinking about the banquet he was missing at the White House.

The Right Honourable Raymond Gould QC, MP, Her Britannic Majesty's Principal Secretary of State for Trade, sat on the kitchen stool, opened a tin of baked beans and devoured them with a fork.

Charles closed the file. It had taken him a month to gather all the proof he needed. Albert Cruddick, the private investigator Charles had selected from the Yellow Pages, had been expensive but discreet. Dates, times, places were all fully chronicled. The only name was that of

Alexander Dalglish, the same rendezvous, lunch at Prunier's followed
by the Stafford Hotel. They hadn't stretched Mr Cruddick's imagination but at least the detective had spared Charles the necessity of
standing in the entrance of the Economist building once, sometimes
twice a week for hours on end.

Somehow he had managed to get through that month without giving
himself away. He had also made his own notes of the dates and times
Fiona claimed she was going to be in the constituency. He had then
called his agent in Sussex Downs and, after veiled questioning, elicited
answers that corroborated Mr Cruddick's findings.

Charles saw as little of Fiona as possible during this time, explaining
that the Finance Bill was occupying his every moment. His lie had at
least a semblance of credibility for he had worked tirelessly on the
remaining clauses left for debate, and by the time the watered-down bill
had become law he had just about recovered from the disaster of the
Government's successful retention of clause 110.

Charles placed the file on the table by the side of his chair and waited
patiently for the call. He knew exactly where she was at that moment
and just the thought of it made him sick to his stomach. The phone
rang.

"The subject left five minutes ago," said a voice.

"Thank you," said Charles and replaced the receiver. He knew it
would take her about twenty minutes to reach home.

"Why do you think she walks home instead of taking a taxi?" he had
once asked Mr Cruddick.

"Gets rid of any smells," Mr Cruddick had replied quite
matter-of-factly.

Charles shuddered. "And what about him? What does he do?" He
never could refer to him as Alexander, or even Dalglish; or as anything
but "him".

"He goes to the Lansdowne Club, swims ten lengths or plays a game
of squash before returning home. Swimming and squash both solve the
problem," Mr Cruddick explained cheerily.

The key turned in the lock. Charles braced himself and picked up the
file. Fiona came straight into the drawing-room and was visibly shaken
to discover her husband sitting in an armchair with a small suitcase by
his side.

She recovered quickly, walked over and kissed him on the cheek.
"What brings you home so early, darling? The Socialists taken the day
off?" She laughed nervously at her joke.

"This," he said, standing up and holding the file out to her.

She took off her coat and dropped it over the sofa. Then she opened
the buff folder and started to read. He watched her carefully. First the
colour drained from her cheeks, then her legs gave way and she
collapsed on to the sofa. Finally she started to sob.

"It's not true, none of it," she protested.

"You know very well that every detail is accurate."

"Charles, it's you I love, I don't care about him, you must believe that."

"I believe nothing of the sort," said Charles. "You're no longer someone I could live with."

"Live with? I've been living on my own since the day you entered Parliament."

"Perhaps I might have come home more often if you had showed some interest in starting a family."

"And do you imagine I am to blame for that inadequacy," she said.

Charles ignored the innuendo and continued. "In a few moments I am going to my club where I shall spend the night. I expect you to be out of this house within seven days. When I return I want there to be no sign of you or any of your goods or chattels, to quote the original agreement."

"Where will I go?" she cried.

"You could try your lover first, but no doubt his wife might object. Failing that, you can camp down at your father's place."

"What if I refuse to go?" said Fiona, turning to defiance.

"Then I shall throw you out, as one should a whore, and cite Alexander Dalglish in a very messy divorce case."

"Give me another chance. I'll never look at him again," begged Fiona, starting to cry once more.

"I seem to remember your telling me that once before, and indeed I did give you another chance. The results have been all too plain to see." He pointed to the file where it had fallen to the floor.

Fiona stopped weeping when she realised that Charles remained unmoved.

"I shall not see you again. We shall be separated for at least two years, when we will carry through as quiet a divorce as possible in the circumstances. If you cause me a moment of embarrassment I shall drag you both through the mire. Believe me."

"You'll regret your decision, Charles. I promise you. I'll not be pushed aside quite that easily."

"They've done *what*?" said Joyce.

"Two Communists have put their names forward for election to the General Purposes Committee," repeated Fred Padgett.

"Over my dead body." Joyce's voice was unusually sharp.

"I thought that would be your attitude," said Fred.

Joyce searched for the pencil and paper that were normally on the table by the phone.

"When's the meeting?" she asked.

"Next Thursday."

"Have we got reliable people to stand against them?"

"Of course," said Fred. "Councillor Reg Illingworth and Jenny Simpkins from the Co-op."

"They're both sensible enough but between them they couldn't knock the skin off a rice pudding."

"Shall I phone Raymond at the House and get him to come up for the meeting?"

"No," said Joyce. 'He's got enough to worry about now that he's in the Cabinet without piling up trouble for him in Leeds. Leave it to me."

She replaced the receiver and sat down to compose her thoughts. A few minutes later she went over to her desk and rummaged about for the full list of the G.P. Committee. She checked the sixteen names carefully, realising that if two Communists were to get themselves elected this time within five years they could control the committee – and then even remove Raymond. She knew how these people worked. With any luck, if they got bloody noses now they might slink off to another constituency.

She checked the sixteen names once more before putting on a pair of sensible walking shoes. During the next four days she visited several homes in the area. "I was just passing," she explained to nine of the wives who had husbands on the committee. The four men who never listened to a word their wives said were visited by Joyce after work. The three who had never cared for Raymond were left well alone.

By Thursday afternoon thirteen people knew only too well what was expected of them. Joyce sat alone hoping he would call that evening. She cooked herself a Lancashire hotpot but only picked at it, then later fell asleep in front of the television when she tried to watch the final episode of *Roots*. The phone woke her at five past eleven.

"Raymond?"

"Hope I didn't wake you," said Fred.

"No, no," said Joyce, now impatient to learn the outcome of the meeting. "What happened?"

"Reg and Jenny walked it. Those two Communist bastards only managed three votes between them."

"Well done," said Joyce.

"I did nothing," said Fred, "except count the votes. Shall I tell Raymond what's been happening?"

"No," said Joyce. "No need to let him think we've had any trouble."

Joyce fell back into the chair by the phone, kicked off her walking shoes, and went back to sleep.

She knew she had to plan the whole operation so that her husband would never find out. She sat alone in the house considering the several alternative ways in which she could deceive him. After hours of unproductive thought the idea finally came in a flash. She went over the problems and repercussions again and again until she was convinced that nothing could go wrong. She leafed through the Yellow Pages and made an appointment for the following morning.

The sales lady helped her to try on several wigs, but only one was bearable.

"I think it makes Modam look most elegant, I must say."

She knew that it didn't – it made Modam look awful – but she hoped it would serve its purpose.

She then applied the make-up and lipstick she had acquired at Harrods, and pulled out from the back of her cupboard a floral dress she had never liked. She stood in front of the mirror and checked herself. Surely no one would recognise her in Sussex and she prayed that if he found out he would be forgiving.

She left and drove slowly towards the outskirts of London. How would she explain herself if she was caught? Would he remain understanding when he discovered the truth? When she reached the constituency she parked the car in a side road and walked up and down the high street. No one showed any sign of recognition which gave her the confidence to go through with it. And then she saw him.

She had hoped he'd be in the City that morning. She held her breath as he walked towards her. As he passed she said, "Good morning." He turned and smiled, replying with a casual "Good morning," as he might to any constituent. Her heartbeat returned to normal and she went back to find her car.

She drove off completely reassured she could now get away with it. She went over once again what she was going to say, then all too suddenly she had arrived. She parked the car outside the house opposite, got out and bravely walked up the path.

As Raymond stood outside the Cabinet room several of his colleagues came over to congratulate him. At exactly ten o'clock the Prime Minister walked in, bade everyone "Good morning," and took his place at the centre of the oblong table, while the other twenty-one members of the Cabinet filed in behind him and took their places. The Leader of the House, Michael Foot, sat on his left, while the Foreign Secretary and Chancellor were placed opposite him. Raymond was directed to a seat at the end of the table between the Secretary of State for Wales and the Secretary of State for Education.

"I would like to start the meeting," said the Prime Minister, "by welcoming David Owen as Foreign Secretary and Raymond Gould as Secretary of State for Trade." The other nineteen Cabinet members murmured, "Hear, hear" in a discreetly conservative way. David Owen smiled slightly while Raymond could feel himself going red.

"The first item we must discuss in detail is the proposed pact with the Liberals . . ."

Raymond sat back and decided that today he would only listen.

Andrew sat in the small office and listened carefully to the specialist's opinion. Louise was restored to almost perfect health in every way except for her speech. She was reading regularly and had even begun to write short messages in reply to Andrew's questions. The specialist now felt that she needed some other outside interest to take her mind off Robert. Over a year had passed and she could still spend hours simply staring at his photograph.

"I managed to reach Dr Kerslake at home," the specialist said, "and I must concur with her opinion that it would be unwise for your wife to contemplate another pregnancy. But Dr Kerslake does accept my judgement that you should both consider adoption."

"I've already given the idea a lot of thought, even discussed it with my father," Andrew replied. "But both of us felt that Louise would never agree to it."

"It's a calculated risk in the circumstances," said the specialist. "We mustn't forget it's been a whole year. We know to our cost that Mrs Fraser loves children, and if she is set against such a course she is now well capable of letting you know."

"If Louise shows any response I'd be only too willing to give it a try. But in the end it will all depend on her."

"Good. Find out how she feels," said the specialist, "and if you both decide to go ahead I'll arrange a meeting with the local authority." He rose from behind his desk. "I'm sure it won't be hard to find you a suitable child."

"If it were possible for him to come from a Scottish orphans' home, I would appreciate it."

The specialist nodded. "I'll be in touch with you as soon as I have any news."

When Charles returned home he knew at once Fiona had left. He felt an immediate relief. After a week at his club, he was glad the charade was over, a clean, irrevocable break. He strolled into the drawing-room and stopped: something was wrong. It took him a few moments before he realised what she had done.

Fiona had removed every one of the family paintings.

No Wellington above the fireplace, no Victoria behind the sofa. Where the two Landseers and the Constable had hung there was nothing more than thin dusty outlines indicating the size of each picture she had removed. He walked to the library: the Van Dyck, the Murillo and the two small Rembrandts were also missing. Charles ran down the hall. It couldn't be possible, he thought, as he threw open the dining-room door. It was. He stared at the blank wall where only the previous week the Holbein portrait of the first Earl of Bridgwater had hung.

Charles scrabbled in the back of his pocket diary for the number and dialled it frantically. Mr Cruddick listened to the story in silence.

"Remembering how sensitive you are about publicity, Mr Seymour, there are two avenues of approach," he began in his normal level tone and sounding unperturbed. "You can grin and bear it, or the alternative is one I have used often in the past."

Because of the demands of his new job Raymond saw less of Kate and almost nothing of Joyce apart from his fortnightly visits to Leeds. He worked from eight in the morning until he fell asleep at night.

"And you love every minute of it," Kate reminded him whenever he complained. Raymond had also become aware of the subtle changes that had taken place in his life since he had become a member of the Cabinet, the way he was treated by other people, how quickly his slightest whim was granted, how flattery fell from almost every tongue. He began to enjoy the change in status although Kate reminded him that only the Queen could afford to get used to it.

At the Labour Party conference that year he allowed his name to be put forward for a place on the National Executive. Although he failed to be elected he managed to finish ahead of several other Cabinet ministers and polled only a few votes less than Neil Kinnock, the darling of the constituency section.

Andrew Fraser, who now looked upon Raymond as someone he could confide in, joined Raymond for what was becoming their traditional conference lunch together on the third day. Andrew told him of his distress at the party's continued drift to the left.

"If some of those resolutions on defence are passed my life will be made impossible," he said, trying to cut into a very tough steak.

"The hotheads always put up resolutions that are never allowed more than a token discussion."

"Token discussion be damned. Some of their mad ideas are beginning to gain credence which translated could become party policy."

"Any particular resolution worrying you?" asked Raymond.

"Yes, Tony Benn's latest proposal that members must be re-selected before every election. His idea of democracy and accountability."

"Why should you fear that?"

"If your management committee is taken over by half a dozen Trots they can reverse a decision 50,000 voters have previously agreed on."

"You're over-reacting, Andrew."

"Raymond, if we lose the next election I can see a split in the party that will be so great we may never recover."

"They've been saying that in the Labour party since the day it was founded."

"I hope you're right, but I fear times have changed," said Andrew.

"Not so long ago it was you who envied me."

"That can change again." Raymond abandoned the steak, waved his hand and asked the waitress to bring two large brandies.

Charles picked up the phone and dialled a number he had not needed to look up. The new young Portuguese maid answered.

"Is Lady Fiona at home?"

"Lady no home, sir."

"Do you know where she is?" asked Charles, speaking slowly and clearly.

"Go down to country, expect back six o'clock. Take message please?"

"No, thank you," said Charles. "I'll call this evening." He replaced the receiver.

As always the reliable Mr Cruddick was proved right about his wife's movements. Charles called him immediately. They agreed to meet as planned in twenty minutes.

He drove into the Boltons, parked on the far side of the road a few yards from his father-in-law's house and settled down to wait.

A few minutes later a large anonymous pantechnicon van came round the corner and stopped outside No. 24. Mr Cruddick jumped out from the driver's seat. He was dressed in long brown overalls and a flat cap. He was joined by a young assistant who unlocked the back of the van. Mr Cruddick nodded to Charles before proceeding up the steps to the front door.

The Portuguese maid answered when he pressed the bell.

"We have come to collect the goods for Lady Seymour."

"No understand," said the maid.

Mr Cruddick removed from an inside pocket a long typewritten letter on Lady Seymour's personal stationery. The Portuguese maid was unable to read the words of a letter her mistress had addressed to Hurlingham Croquet Club agreeing to be their Ladies President, but she immediately recognised the letter-head and the signature. She nodded and opened the door wider. All Mr Cruddick's carefully laid plans were falling into place.

Mr Cruddick tipped his hat, the sign for Mr Seymour to join them. Charles got out of the car cautiously, checking both ways before he crossed the road. He felt uncomfortable in brown overalls and hated the cap with which Mr Cruddick had supplied him. It was a little small and Charles was acutely conscious how strange he must look but the Portuguese maid apparently didn't notice the incongruity between his aristocratic mien and the working overalls. It did not take long to discover the whereabouts of most of the pictures. Many were just stacked up in the hall, and only one or two had already been hung.

Forty minutes later the three men had located and loaded into the van all but one of them. The Holbein of the first Earl of Bridgwater was nowhere to be found.

"We ought to be on our way," suggested Mr Cruddick a little nervously, but Charles refused to give up the search. For another thirty-five minutes Mr Cruddick sat tapping the wheel of the van before Charles finally conceded that the painting must have been taken elsewhere. Mr Cruddick tipped his hat to the maid while his partner locked up the back of the van.

"A valuable picture, Mr Seymour?" he enquired.

"A family heirloom that would fetch two million at auction," said Charles matter-of-factly before returning to his car.

"Silly question, Albert Cruddick," said Mr Cruddick to himself as he pulled out from the curb and drove towards Eaton Square. When they arrived the locksmith had replaced all three locks on the front door and was waiting on the top step impatiently.

"Strictly cash, guv'nor. No receipt. Makes it possible for the missus and me to go to Ibiza each year, tax free."

By the time Fiona had returned to the Boltons from her trip to Sussex every picture was back in its place at Eaton Square with the exception of Holbein's first Earl of Bridgwater. Mr Cruddick was left clutching a large cheque and uttering the unpalatable view that Mr Seymour would probably have to grin and bear it.

"I'm delighted," said Simon, when he heard the news. "And at Pucklebridge General Hospital?"

"Yes, I answered an advertisement in *The Lancet* for the post of general consultant in the maternity section."

"But your name must have helped there?"

"Certainly not," said Elizabeth vehemently.

"How come?"

"I didn't apply as Dr Kerslake. I filled out the application form in my maiden name of Drummond."

Simon was momentarily silenced. "But they would have recognised you," he protested.

"I had the full frontal treatment from Estée Lauder to ensure they didn't. The final effect fooled even you."

"Don't exaggerate," said Simon.

"I walked straight past you in Pucklebridge High Street, and said 'Good morning,' and you returned the greeting."

Simon stared at her in disbelief. "But what will happen when they find out?"

"They already have," replied Elizabeth sheepishly. "As soon as they offered me the post I went down to see the senior consultant and told him the truth. He hasn't stopped telling everyone since."

"He wasn't cross?"

"Far from it. In fact he said I nearly failed to be offered the post because he felt I wouldn't be safe let loose on the unmarried doctors."

Andrew held Louise's hand as they approached the door of Grunechan Children's Home on the outskirts of Edinburgh. The matron was waiting on the freshly scrubbed doorstep to greet them.

"Good morning, Minister," she said. "We are honoured that you have chosen our little home."

Andrew and Louise smiled.

"Will you be kind enough to follow me?" She led them down a dimly lit corridor to her room, her starched blue uniform crackling as she walked.

"All the children are in the playground at the moment but you will be able to see them from my window." Andrew had already gone over all the orphans' histories and photographs; he couldn't help noticing how one of them bore a striking resemblance to Robert.

They both looked out of the window for several minutes but Louise showed no interest in any of the children. When the boy who resembled Robert ran towards the window, she turned away and took a seat in the corner.

Andrew shook his head. The matron's lips turned down at the corners.

Coffee and biscuits arrived and while they were eating them Andrew tried once more. "Did you want Matron to bring anyone in to meet you, darling?" Louise shook her head. Andrew cursed himself as he feared the experience might only have done her more harm.

"Have we seen everyone?" he asked, looking for an excuse to leave quickly.

"Yes, sir," said the matron, putting down her cup of coffee. "Well," she hesitated, "there was one girl we didn't bother you with."

"Why not?" asked Andrew out of curiosity.

"Well, you see, she's black."

Andrew stiffened.

"And what's more," continued the matron, "we have absolutely no idea who her parents were. She was left on the doorstep. Not at all the sort of girl to be brought up in a minister's home."

Andrew was so incensed that he quite forgot about consulting Louise who was still resting silently in the corner.

"I should like to see her," he said.

"If you insist," said the matron, a little taken aback. "I'm afraid she hasn't got her best clothes on," she added before she left the room.

Andrew paced up and down, conscious that if Louise hadn't been there he might well have lost his temper with the woman. The matron returned a few moments later with a little girl aged four, perhaps five, and so thin that her dress hung on her like a coathanger. Andrew couldn't see her face because she kept her head bowed.

"Look up, child," commanded the matron. The girl raised her head slowly. She had the most perfect oval face and olive skin, piercing black eyes and a smile that immediately captivated Andrew.

"What's your name?" he asked quietly.

"Clarissa," she said, and dropped her head again. He wanted to help her so much, and it made him feel guilty that he had put the poor child through such a pointless ordeal.

The matron still looked affronted and with a sniff she said, "You can leave us now, child." Clarissa turned and walked towards the door. Looking at Louise the matron added, "I am sure you agree with me, Mrs Fraser, the girl's not at all suitable."

They both turned to Louise. Her face was alight, her eyes shining in a way Andrew had not seen since Robert's death. She stood up, walking quickly towards the child before she could reach the door, and stared into her black eyes.

"I think you're beautiful," Louise said, "and I do hope you will want to come and live with us."

CHAPTER TWENTY THREE

"Order, order" had meant nothing to the British electorate until 1978 when the House passed a resolution allowing the proceedings in the Commons to be broadcast on radio. Simon had supported the motion on broadcasting, putting forward the argument that radio was a further extension of democracy as it showed the House at work and allowed the voters to know exactly what their elected representatives were up to. Simon listened carefully to a number of his supplementaries, and realised for the first time that he spoke a little too quickly when he had a minister on the run.

Raymond, on the other hand, did not support the motion as he feared that the cries of "Hear, hear" or "Shame" and the heckling of the Prime Minister would sound to listeners like schoolchildren in a playground squabble. Overhearing the words with only one's imagination to set the scene would, he believed, create a false impression about the many aspects of a member's daily duties. When one evening Raymond heard a parliamentary debate in which he had taken part he was delighted to discover his arguments carried so much conviction.

When Andrew heard his own voice on Radio Four one morning answering questions on defence issues he was suddenly aware that what he had always considered was a faint trace of a Scottish accent was in fact – when he was angry or excited – quite pronounced.

Charles found the morning programme an excellent way of catching up with any proceedings he had missed the previous day. As he now woke each morning alone, "Yesterday in Parliament" became his constant companion. He hadn't been aware of how upper class he sounded until the occasion on which he followed Tom Carson. He had no intention of changing his voice for the radio.

When the Queen opened the new underground extension to Heathrow airport on 16 December 1977 Raymond was the minister commanded to be present. Joyce made one of her rare trips down to London as they were invited to join the Queen for lunch after the ceremony. When Joyce selected her new dress from Harvey Nichols, she stood in the little cubicle behind a drawn curtain to make sure it was possible for her to curtsey properly. "Good morning, Your Majesty," she practised with a slight wobble, to the bemusement of the shop assistant waiting patiently outside.

By the time she had returned to the flat Joyce was confident that she could carry out her part in the proceedings as well as any courtier. As she prepared for Raymond's return from the morning Cabinet meeting she hoped he would be pleased with her efforts. She had long given up hope of being a mother, but still liked to believe she could be a good wife. Raymond had forewarned her that he would have to change as soon as he arrived at the flat to be sure of being at Green Park before the Queen arrived. After they had accompanied an entourage to Heathrow on the new extension, a journey that would take thirty minutes, they were to return to Buckingham Palace for lunch. Raymond had already come in contact with his monarch on several occasions in his official capacity as a Cabinet minister, but for Joyce it was to be the first time she had been presented.

Once she had had her bath and dressed – she knew Raymond would never forgive her if she were the reason he was late – she began to lay out his clothes. Tail coat, grey pin-striped trousers, white shirt, stiff collar and a silver-grey tie, all hired that morning from Moss Bros. All that he still needed was a clean white handkerchief for his top pocket, just showing in a straight line, as the Duke of Edinburgh always wore his.

Joyce rummaged around in Raymond's chest of drawers, admiring the new shirts as she searched for a handkerchief. When she first saw the scribbled note peaking out underneath the collar of a pink shirt lying near the bottom of the pile, she assumed it must be an old laundry bill. Then she spotted the word "Darling". She felt suddenly sick as she looked more closely.

Darling Carrot Top,
    If you ever wear this one I might even agree to marry you.
                        Kate.

Joyce sank on the end of the bed as the tears trickled down her face. Her perfect day was shattered. She knew at once what course of action she must take. She replaced the unworn shirt and closed the drawer, after first removing the note, and then sat alone in the drawing-room waiting for Raymond to return.

He arrived back at the flat with only a few minutes to spare and was delighted to find his wife changed and ready.

"I'm running it a bit close," he said, going straight into the bedroom.

Joyce followed and watched him don his morning dress suit. When he had straightened his tie in the mirror, she faced him.

"What do you think?" he asked, not noticing the slight paleness in her cheeks.

She hesitated. "You look fantastic, Raymond. Now come along or we'll be late, and that would never do."

When Ronnie Nethercote invited him to lunch at the Ritz, Simon knew things must be looking up again. After a drink in the lounge they were ushered to a corner table overlooking the park in the most palatial dining-room in London. Scattered around the other tables were men who were household names in Ronnie's world as well as in Simon's.

When the head waiter offered them menus Ronnie waved his hand and said, "Order the country vegetable soup, followed by beef off the trolley, take my word for it."

"Sounds like a safe bet," said Simon.

"Unlike our last little venture." Ronnie grunted. "How much are you still in hock because of the collapse of Nethercote and Company?"

"Fourteen thousand three hundred pounds when I last looked but I'm making inroads slowly. It's paying the interest before you can cut down on the capital that really hurts."

"How do you imagine I felt when we were overdrawn seven mill and then the bank decided to pull the rug from under my feet without any warning?"

"As two of the buttons on your waistcoat can no longer reach the holes they were originally tailored for, Ronnie, I must assume those problems are now a thing of the past."

"You're right." He laughed. "Which is why I invited you to lunch. The only person who ended up losing money on that deal was you. If you'd stayed on as the other directors did, at five grand a year, the company would still owe you £11,100 of earned income."

Simon groaned.

The carver wheeled the trolley of beef up to their table.

"Wait a moment, my boy, I haven't even begun. Morgan Grenfell want me to change the structure of the new company and will be injecting a large amount of cash. At the moment Whitechapel Properties – I hope you approve of the name – is still a one-hundred-pound off-the-shelf company. I own sixty per cent and the bank's got forty. Now before the new agreement is signed, I'm going to offer you –"

"Would you like it well done, as usual, Mr Nethercote?"

"Yes, Sam," said Ronnie, slipping the carver a pound note.

"I am going to offer you –"

"And your guest, sir?" the carver said, glancing at Simon.

"Medium, please."

"Yes, sir."

"I am going to offer you one per cent of the new company, in other words one share."

Simon didn't comment, feeling confident Ronnie still hadn't finished.

"Aren't you going to ask?" said Ronnie.

"Ask what?" said Simon.

"You politicians get dumber by the minute. If I am going to offer you a one-pound share, how much do you think I am going to demand in return?"

"Well, I can't believe it's going to be one pound," said Simon grinning.

"Wrong," said Ronnie. "One per cent of the company is yours for one pound."

"Will that be sufficient, sir?" said the carver, putting a plate of beef in front of Simon.

"Hold it, Sam," said Ronnie before Simon could reply. "I repeat I'm offering you one per cent of the company for one pound; now ask your question again, Sam."

"Will that be sufficient, sir?" repeated the carver.

"It's most generous," said Simon.

"Did you hear that, Sam?"

"I certainly did, sir."

"Right, Simon, you owe me a pound."

Simon laughed, removed his wallet from his inside pocket, took out a pound note and handed it over.

"Now the purpose of that little exercise," said Ronnie, turning back to the carver and pocketing the note, "was to prove that Sam here isn't the only person who could make a quid for himself this afternoon." Sam smiled, having no idea what Mr Nethercote was talking about, and placed a large plate of well-done beef in front of him.

Ronnie took out an envelope from his inside pocket and passed it to Simon.

"Do I open it now?" asked Simon.

"Yes – I want to see your reaction."

Simon opened the envelope and studied its contents. A certificate for one share in the new company with a true value of over £10,000.

"Well, well, what do you say?" said Ronnie.

"I'm speechless," said Simon.

"First politician I've known who's ever suffered from that problem."

Simon laughed. "Thank you, Ronnie. It's an incredibly generous gesture."

"No, it's not. You were loyal to the old company, so why shouldn't you prosper with the new one?"

"That reminds me, does the name 'Archie Millburn' mean anything to you?" asked Simon.

Ronnie hesitated. "No, no, should it?"

"Only that I thought he might be the man who convinced Morgan Grenfell that you were worth bailing out."

"No, that name doesn't ring any bells. Mind you, Morgan Grenfell have never admitted where they obtained their information from but they knew every last detail about the old company. But if I come across the name Millburn I'll let you know. Enough of business. Fill me in on what's happening in your world. How's your lady wife?"

"Deceiving me."

"Deceiving you?"

"Yes, she's been putting on wigs and dressing up in strange clothes."

Clarissa wet her bed every night for the first month at Pelham Crescent but Louise never complained. Day by day Andrew watched as mother and daughter grew in mutual confidence. Clarissa assumed from her first meeting with Louise that she could talk as normally as any grown-up and chatted away to her night and day. Half the time Louise didn't reply, only because she couldn't get a word in.

Just when Andrew felt everything was getting back on a normal footing at home trouble erupted in Edinburgh. His General Management Committee, which now included five members of Militant Tendency, tabled a motion of no confidence in their member. Their leader, Frank Boyle, had been building up a power base with the sole intention, Andrew suspected, of ousting the member and taking over himself. He didn't discuss the problem with Louise, as the specialist had advised him to avoid any undue stress while Clarissa was settling in.

The five men who wanted Andrew removed had chosen the following Thursday to hold the meeting because they knew the annual Defence Review was due for a full debate in the House that day. If Andrew was unable to attend their meeting Frank Boyle knew they would have a better chance of winning their motion. If he did turn up to defend himself they were also aware that an embarrassing explanation would have to be made for his absence during the debate. When the Prime Minister was informed of the dilemma by the Chief Whip he had no hesitation in telling Andrew to forget the defence debate and go to Edinburgh.

Andrew took the shuttle up on Thursday afternoon and was met at the airport by his chairman, Hamish Ramsey.

"I apologise about you being put through this ordeal, Andrew," he said at once. "I can assure you it's none of my doing, but I must also warn you it's not the same Labour party that I joined over twenty years ago."

"How do you think the vote will go tonight?" asked Andrew.

"You'll win this time. The votes have been decided before the meeting takes place. There's only one waverer and he's so gutless that your very presence will stop him siding with the Trotskies."

When Andrew arrived at his Edinburgh headquarters he was left alone outside the committee room in a cold corridor for over an hour. He knew his opponents were holding things up in the hope he would become frustrated before he eventually had to face them. At last they invited him to join them and he immediately sensed what the Spanish Inquisition must have felt like: question after question from sour-faced men who had never helped him win the seat in the first place and were now alleging that he had shown scant interest in the constituency. Andrew stood his ground and became angry only when Frank Boyle referred to him as "that son of a Tory".

When did you last see your father? flashed through his mind.

"My father has done more for this city than you could ever hope to do in your lifetime," he told Boyle.

"Then why don't you join his party?" came back Boyle's retort.

Andrew was about to answer when Hamish Ramsey banged the table with his gavel and said, "Enough, enough. It's time to stop this squabbling and vote."

Andrew felt a stab of anxiety as the little slips were passed up to the chairman to be counted. The outcome was five-all and Hamish Ramsey immediately cast his vote in favour of Andrew.

"At least you'll be safe for the coming election, laddie," said Hamish as they drove to the Airport Hotel. "But I wouldn't like to account for much beyond that."

When Andrew arrived back in Pelham Crescent the next morning Louise greeted him at the door.

"Everything all right in Edinburgh?" she asked.

"Fine," said Andrew, taking her in his arms.

"Do you want to hear the good news?"

"Yes," said Andrew, smiling.

"Clarissa didn't wet her bed last night. Perhaps you should stay away more often."

Finally Charles knew he had to discuss what could be done about the stolen Holbein with his solicitor, Sir David Napley. Sir David instructed leading counsel and six weeks later Charles was told that if he sued the Holbein might eventually be returned but not before the story had been on the front page of every national paper. Charles had Albert Cruddick's opinion confirmed: "Grin and bear it."

Fiona had been out of touch for well over a year when the letter came. Charles immediately recognised her handwriting and ripped open the envelope. Only one glance at the writing was enough to make him tear up the missive and deposit the little pieces in the waste-paper basket by his desk. He left for the Commons in a rage.

All through the day he thought of the one word he had taken in from the scrawled hand. Holbein. When he returned from the Commons after the ten o'clock division Charles searched for the remains of the letter, which the daily had conscientiously deposited in the dustbin. After rummaging among potato peelings, eggshells and empty tins Charles spent over an hour Sellotaping the little pieces of paper together. Then he read the letter carefully.

24 THE BOLTONS,
LONDON, SW 10
11 OCTOBER 1978

DEAR CHARLES,

Enough time has now passed for us to try and treat each other in a civilized way. Alexander and I wish to marry and Veronica Dalglish has agreed to an immediate divorce and has not insisted we wait the necessary two years to establish separation.

"You'll have to wait every day of the two years, you bitch," he said out loud. Then he came to the one sentence for which he was searching.

I realize this might not immediately appeal to you but if you felt able to fall in with our plans I would be happy to return the Holbein immediately.

YOURS EVER,
FIONA.

He crumpled up the paper in the ball of his hand before dropping it on the fire.

Charles remained awake into the early hours considering his reply.

At a Thursday morning Cabinet meeting James Callaghan informed his colleagues that the Liberal leader, David Steel, was not willing to continue the Lib/Lab pact after the end of the current session.

"That can only mean one thing," the Prime Minister continued. "We must all be prepared for a general election at any time from now on. I am confident we can hold out until Christmas, but not for much longer than that."

Raymond was saddened by the news. He felt after two years in the Cabinet that he was just beginning to be of some use to the Department of Trade: the changes he was implementing were starting to take effect. But he knew he needed considerably more time if he hoped to leave a permanent impression on his ministry.

Kate's enthusiasm spurred him on to work even longer hours and to push through as many of his innovations before the next election as possible.

"I'm trying my damnedest," he told her. "But do remember that the speed of the bureaucratic machine makes British Rail look like Concorde."

The Labour Government struggled on through a session dubbed by the press as "the winter of discontent": trying to push bills through the House, losing a clause here and a clause there, Raymond was only too delighted to have reached the recess in one piece.

Raymond spent a cold Christmas in Leeds with Joyce. He returned to London early in the New Year aware it could not be long before the Conservatives felt assured enough to put down a motion of no confidence. When it eventually was tabled no one in Parliament was surprised.

The debate cause a day of intense excitement, not least because a strike had caused the Commons bars to run dry and thirsty members were huddled together in the lobbies, the tea room, the smoking room and the dining-rooms. Harassed Whips rushed hither and thither checking lists, ringing up hospitals, board rooms and even great-aunts in their efforts to track down the last few elusive members.

When Mrs Thatcher rose on 6 April to address a packed House the tension was so electric that the Speaker had considerable difficulty keeping control of the over-charged conductors. She addressed the House in firm, strident tones which brought her own side to their feet when she resumed her place. The atmosphere was no different when it was the turn of the Prime Minister to reply. Both leaders made a gallant effort to rise above the petulance of their adversaries but it was the Speaker who had the last word:

"The Ayes to the right 311,
The Noes to the left 310.
The Ayes have it, the Ayes have it."

Pandemonium broke out. Opposition members waved their order papers in triumph, knowing the Prime Minister would now have to call a general election. James Callaghan immediately announced the dissolution of Parliament and after an audience with the Queen election day was set for 3 May 1979.

At the end of that momentous week those few members left at Westminster were stunned by an explosion in the Members' Car Park. Airey Neave, the Shadow spokesman on Northern Ireland, had been blown up by Irish terrorists as he was driving up the exit ramp to leave the Commons. He died on his way to hospital.

Members hurried back to their constituencies. Both Raymond and Andrew found it hard to escape from their departments at such short notice, but Charles and Simon were out in their respective high streets shaking hands with the voters by the morning following the Queen's proclamation.

For three weeks the arguments about who was competent to govern went back and forth, but on 3 May the British people elected their first woman Prime Minister and gave her party a majority of forty-three in the Commons.

Andrew's sixth election turned out to be his most unpleasant to date and he was only glad that he had left Louise and Clarissa in London. Jock McPherson, still the SNP candidate, called him every name under the sun and added one or two new ones in the evening, while the Trotskyites who had voted against him on the committee proved no help when it came to gathering in the votes on election day. But the citizens of Edinburgh, knowing nothing of the committee's opinions, sent Andrew back to Parliament with a majority of 3,738. The Scottish Nationalist vote crumbled, leaving only two members in the House – and Jock McPherson back in Scotland.

Raymond's vote in Leeds was slightly reduced, while Joyce won the office pool for predicting most accurately what her husband's majority would be. He was beginning to accept that she knew more about the constituency than he ever would.

A few days later when Raymond returned to London Kate had never seen him so depressed and decided to hold off telling him her own news when he said, "God knows how many years it will be before I can be of some use again."

"You can spend your time in Opposition making sure the Government doesn't dismantle all your achievements."

"With a majority of forty-three they could dismantle me if they wanted to," he told her. He placed the red leather box marked "Secretary of State for Trade" in the corner, next to the ones marked "Minister of State at the Department of Trade" and "Parliamentary Under-Secretary at the Department of Employment".

"They're only your first three," Kate tried to reassure him.

Simon increased his majority at Pucklebridge to 19,461, notching up another record after which he and Elizabeth spent the weekend in their cottage with the boys waiting for Mrs Thatcher to select her team.

Simon was surprised when the Prime Minister phoned personally and asked if he could come up to see her in Downing Street: that was an honour usually afforded only to Cabinet ministers. He tried not to anticipate what she might have in mind.

He duly travelled up from the country and spent thirty minutes alone with the new Prime Minister. When he heard what Mrs Thatcher wanted him to do he was touched that she had taken the trouble to see him in person. She knew that no member ever found it easy to accede to such a request but Simon accepted without hesitation. Mrs Thatcher added that no announcement would be made until he had had time to talk his decision over with Elizabeth.

Simon thanked her and travelled back to his cottage in Pucklebridge. Elizabeth sat in silence as she listened to Simon's account of his conversation with the Prime Minister.

"Oh, my God," she said, when he had finished. "She's offered you the chance to be a Minister of State, but in return we have no certainty of peace for the rest of our lives."

"I can still say no," Simon assured her.

"That would be the act of a coward," said Elizabeth, "and you've never been that."

"Then I'll phone the Prime Minister and tell her I accept."

"I ought to congratulate you," she said. "But it never crossed my mind for one moment . . ."

Charles's was one of the few Tory seats in which the majority went down. A missing wife is hard to explain especially when it is common knowledge that she is living with the former chairman of the adjoining constituency. Charles had faced a certain degree of embarrassment with his local committee and he made sure that the one woman who couldn't keep her mouth shut was told his version of the story "in strictest confidence". Any talk of removing him had died when it was rumoured that Charles would stand as an independent candidate if replaced. When the vote was counted Sussex Downs still returned Charles to Westminster with a majority of 20,176. He sat alone in Eaton Square over the weekend, but no one contacted him. He read in the Monday *Telegraph* – how he missed *The Times* – the full composition of the new Tory team.

The only surprise was Simon Kerslake's appointment as Minister of State for Northern Ireland.

CHAPTER TWENTY FOUR

"Well, say something."

"Very flattering, Kate. What reason did you give for turning the offer down?" asked Raymond, who had been surprised to find her waiting for him at the flat.

"I didn't need a reason."

"How did they feel about that?"

"You don't seem to understand. I accepted their offer."

Raymond removed his glasses and tried to take in what Kate was saying. He steadied himself by holding on to the mantelpiece.

Kate continued. "I had to, darling."

"Because the offer was too tempting?"

"No, you silly man. It had nothing to do with the offer as such, but it gives me the chance to stop letting my life drift. Can't you see it was *because* of you."

"Because of me you're going to leave London and go back to New York."

"To work in New York and start getting my life in perspective. Raymond, don't you realise it's been five years?"

"I know how long it is and how many times I've asked you to marry me."

"We both know that isn't the answer; Joyce can't be brushed aside that easily. And it could even end up being the single reason you fail in your career."

"We can overcome that problem, given time," Raymond reasoned.

"That sounds fine now, until the party wins the next election and lesser men than you are offered the chance to shape future policy."

"Can't I do anything to make you change your mind?"

"Nothing, my darling. I've handed Chase my resignation and begin my new job with Chemical Bank in a month."

"Only four weeks," said Raymond.

"Yes, four weeks. I had to hold off telling you until I had severed all the bonds, had resigned and could be sure of not letting you talk me out of it."

"Do you know how much I love you?"

"I hope enough to let me go, before it's too late."

Charles would not have normally accepted the invitation. Lately he had found cocktail parties to consist of nothing but silly little bits of food, never being able to get the right drink and rarely enjoying the trivial conversation. But when he glanced on his mantelpiece and saw an "At Home" from Lady Carrington he felt it might be an amusing break from the routine he had fallen into since Fiona had left. He was also keen to discover more about the rumoured squabbles in Cabinet over expenditure cuts. He checked his tie in the mirror, removed an umbrella from the hat stand and left Eaton Square for Ovington Square.

He and Fiona had been apart for nearly two years. Charles had heard from several sources that his wife had now moved in with Dalglish on a permanent basis despite his unwillingness to cooperate over a divorce. He had remained discreetly silent on his wife's new life except for one or two selected titbits dropped selectively in the ears of well-chosen gossips. That way he had elicited for himself sympathy from every quarter while remaining the magnanimous loyal husband.

Charles had spent most of his spare time in the Commons, and his most recent budget speech had been well received both by the House and the national press. During the committee stage of the Finance Bill he had allowed himself to be burdened with a lot of the donkey work. Clive Reynolds had been able to point out discrepancies in some clauses of the bill, which Charles passed on to a grateful Chancellor. Thus Charles received praise for saving the Government from any unnecessary embarrassment. At the same time he disassociated himself from the "wets" as the Prime Minister referred to those of her colleagues who did not unreservedly support her monetarist policies. If he could keep up his work output he was confident he would be preferred in the first reshuffle.

By spending his mornings at the bank and afternoons and evenings in the Commons Charles managed to combine both worlds with the minimum of interruption from his almost non-existent private life.

He arrived at Lord Carrington's front door a little after six-forty-five. A maid answered his knock, and he walked straight through to a drawing-room that could have held fifty guests and very nearly did.

He even managed to be served with the right blend of whisky before joining his colleagues from both the Upper and Lower Houses. He saw her first over the top of Alec Pimkin's balding head.

"Who is she?" asked Charles, not expecting Pimkin to know.

"Amanda Wallace," said Pimkin, glancing over his shoulder. "I could tell you a thing or two . . ." but Charles had already left his colleague in mid-sentence. The sexual aura of the woman was attested to by the fact that she spent the entire evening surrounded by attentive men, like moths around a candle. If Charles had not been one of the tallest men in the room he might never have seen the flame. It took him another ten minutes to reach her side of the room where Julian Ridsdale, a colleague of Charles's in the Commons, introduced them only to find himself dragged away moments later by his wife.

Charles was left staring at a woman who would have looked beautiful in anything from a ballgown to a towel. Her slim body was encased in a white silk dress, and her fair hair touched her bare shoulders. But what struck Charles most was the translucent texture of her skin. It had been years since he had found it so hard to make conversation.

"I expect you already have a dinner engagement?" Charles asked her in the brief intervals before the vultures closed in again.

"No," she replied and smiled encouragingly. She agreed to meet him at Walton's in an hour's time. Charles dutifully began to circulate round the room but it was not long before he found his eyes drawn back to her. Every time she smiled he found himself responding but Amanda didn't notice because she was always being flattered by someone else. When he left an hour later he smiled directly at her, and this time did win a knowing grin.

Charles sat alone at a corner table in Walton's for another hour. He was just about to admit defeat and return home when she was ushered to the table. The anger that had developed from being kept waiting was forgotten the moment she smiled and said, "Hello, Charlie."

He was not surprised to learn that his tall, elegant companion earned her living as a model. As far as Charles could see she could have modelled anything from tooth paste to stockings.

"Shall we have coffee at my place?" Charles asked after an unhurried dinner. She nodded her assent and he called for the bill, not checking the addition for the first time in many years.

He was delighted, if somewhat surprised, when she rested her head on his shoulder in the cab on the way back to Eaton Square. By the time they had been dropped off at Eaton Square most of Amanda's lipstick had been removed. The cabbie thanked Charles for his excessive tip and couldn't resist adding, "Good luck, sir."

Charles never did get round to making the coffee. When he woke in the morning, to his surprise he found her even more captivating, and for the first time in weeks quite forgot "Yesterday in Parliament".

Elizabeth listened carefully as the man from Special Branch explained how the safety devices worked. She tried to make Peter and Michael concentrate on not pressing the red buttons that were in every room and would bring the police at a moment's notice. The electricians had already wired the rooms in Beaufort Street and now they had nearly finished at the cottage.

At Beaufort Street a uniformed policeman stood watch by the front door night and day. In Pucklebridge, because the cottage was so isolated, they had to be surrounded by arc lamps that could be switched on at a moment's notice.

"It must be damned inconvenient," suggested Archie Millburn during dinner. After his arrival at the cottage he had been checked by security patrols with dogs before he was able to shake hands with his host.

"Inconvenient is putting it mildly," said Elizabeth. "Last week Peter broke a window with a cricket ball and we were immediately lit up like a Christmas tree."

"Do you get any privacy?" asked Archie.

"Only when we're in bed. Even then you can wake up to find you're being licked; you sigh and it turns out to be an Alsatian."

Archie laughed. "Lucky Alsatian."

Every morning when Simon was driven to work he was accompanied by two detectives, a car in front and another to the rear. He had always thought there were only two ways from Beaufort Street to Westminster. For the first twenty-one days as minister he never travelled the same route twice.

Whenever he was due to fly to Belfast he was not informed of either his departure time or from which airport he would be leaving. While the inconvenience drove Elizabeth mad the tension had the opposite effect on Simon. Despite everything, it was the first time in his life he didn't feel it was necessary to explain to anyone why he had chosen to be a politician.

Inch by inch he worked to try to bring the Catholics and Protestants together. Often after a month of inches he would lose a yard in one day, but he never displayed any anger or prejudice except perhaps, as he told Elizabeth, "a prejudice for common sense". Given time, Simon believed, a breakthrough would be possible – if only he could find on both sides a handful of men of goodwill.

During the all-party meetings both factions began to treat him with respect and – privately – with affection. Even the Opposition spokesman at Westminster openly acknowledged that Simon Kerslake was turning out to be an excellent choice for the "dangerous and thankless ministry".

Andrew also knew he would require a handful of men of goodwill when Hamish Ramsey resigned as chairman of Edinburgh Carlton.

"I don't need the hassle any longer," Hamish told him. "I'm not in politics for the same reason as that bunch of trouble-makers." Andrew reluctantly let him go and had to work hard to convince Hamish's deputy, David Connaught, that he should stand in his place. When David finally agreed to allow his name to go forward he was immediately opposed by Frank Boyle, who had already made his opinion of the sitting member abundantly clear. Andrew canvassed every person on the committee during the run up to election for the new chairman. He estimated the voting was going to be seven-all, which would still allow Hamish to give his casting vote in favour of Connaught.

Andrew phoned Hamish at home an hour before the meeting was due to begin. "I'll call and leave a message for you at the House when it's all over," Ramsey told him. "Don't worry, you're safe this time. At least I'll leave you with the right chairman."

Andrew left Pelham Crescent after he had tucked Clarissa up in bed and read her another chapter of *Jacob Two Two*. He told Louise he would return from Westminster straight after the ten o'clock vote. He sat in the Chamber and listened to Charles Seymour deliver a well-argued discourse on monetarist policy. Andrew didn't always agree with the logic of Seymour's case and he had never cared much for the man himself: but he had to admit that such talent was wasted on the back benches.

During the speech a note was passed to Andrew by an attendant. He unfolded the little white slip. Stuart Gray, the lobby correspondent for *The Scotsman*, needed to speak to him urgently. Andrew slipped from his place on the front bench, stepping over the feet of Shadow ministers still intent on Seymour's speech. He felt like a small boy leaving a cinema in the middle of a film in pursuit of an iced lolly. He found Gray waiting for him in the Members' Lobby.

Andrew had known Stuart since he had first entered the House, when the journalist told him, "You and I are each other's bread and butter, so we'd better make a sandwich." Andrew had laughed, and they had had few differences of opinion in the fifteen years since. Stuart suggested that they go down to Annie's Bar for a drink. They strolled along the corridor and took the stairway near the tea room to the basement bar. Named after a former barlady, it was often referred to by the Conservatives as "the Kremlin".

Andrew settled down on a couch at the side of a pillar while Stuart went up to the bar to order two whiskies.

"Cheers," said the journalist, putting Andrew's glass down on the table in front of him.

Andrew took a long gulp. "Now, what can I do for you?" he asked. "Is my father being tiresome again?"

"I'd call him a supporter compared with your new chairman."

"What do you mean? I've always found David Connaught to be a sound fellow myself," said Andrew, a little pompously.

"I'm not interested in your views of David Connaught," said Stuart. "I want an opinion on your new chairman, Frank Boyle." The journalist sounded very much on the record.

"What?"

"He won the vote tonight seven to six."

"But . . ." Andrew fell silent.

"Come on, Andrew. We both know the bloody man's a Commie trouble-maker, and my editor is screaming for a quote."

"I can't say anything, Stuart, not until I know all the facts."

"I've just told you all the facts: now, are you going to give me a quote?"

"Yes." Andrew paused. "I am sure Mr Boyle will continue to serve in the best traditions of the Labour party, and I look forward to working in close cooperation with him."

"Balls," said Stuart. "They will only print that in Pseuds Corner in *Private Eye*."

"It's the only quote you're going to get out of me tonight," said Andrew.

Stuart looked at his friend and could see lines on his face that he had never noticed before. "I'm sorry," he said. "I went too far. Please get in touch when the time's right. With that bastard Boyle in charge you might be in need of my help."

Andrew thanked him absent-mindedly, downed his whisky in one gulp, then walked out of Annie's Bar and along the terrace corridor to the phone booths at the foot of the stairs. He dialled Ramsey's home number.

"What in heaven's name happened?" was all he could ask.

"One of our voters didn't show," said Hamish Ramsey. "Claimed he was held up in Glasgow and couldn't get back in time. I was just about to ring you."

"Bloody irresponsible of him," said Andrew. "Why didn't you postpone the vote?"

"I tried to, but Frank Boyle produced the rule book. 'Any motion proposed fourteen days before a meeting cannot be postponed without the agreement of the proposer and seconder.' I'm sorry, Andrew: my hands were tied."

"It's not your fault, Hamish. I couldn't have had a better chairman than you. I'm only sorry you didn't leave in a blaze of glory."

Hamish chuckled. "Don't you ever forget, Andrew, the voters have the last word in a democracy. In Edinburgh you're the man who has served them for more than fifteen years and they won't forget that quickly."

"You can get dressed now, Miss Wallace," said the gynaecologist returning to her desk.

Amanda started to slip back into her latest Dior outfit – a light blue denim suit bought the previous day in Conduit Street in an attempt to cheer herself up.

"It's the third time in five years," said Elizabeth Kerslake, leafing through the confidential file and trying not to sound accusing.

"I may as well book into the same clinic as before," said Amanda, matter-of-factly.

Elizabeth was determined to make her reconsider the consequences. "Is there any chance that the father would want you to have this child?"

"I can't be certain who the father is," said Amanda, looking shame-faced for the first time. "You see, it was the end of one relationship and the beginning of another."

Elizabeth made no comment other than to say, "I estimate that you are at least eight weeks pregnant, but it could be as much as twelve." She looked back down at the file. "Have you considered giving birth to the child and then bringing it up yourself?"

"Good heavens, no," said Amanda. "I make my living as a model not as a mother."

"So be it," Elizabeth sighed, closing the file. "I'll make all the" – she avoided saying usual – "necessary arrangements. You must see your GP immediately and ask him to sign the required clearance forms. Then phone me in about a week, rather than make the trip down to Pucklebridge again."

Amanda nodded her agreement. "Could you let me know what the clinic is going to charge this time? I'm sure they are suffering from inflation like the rest of us."

"Yes, I will look into that, Miss Wallace," said Elizabeth, just managing to keep her temper as she showed Amanda to the door. Once her patient had left Elizabeth picked up the confidential file from her desk, walked over to the cabinet and flicked through S, T, U, until she found the right slot. Perhaps she should have been sterner with her but she was convinced that it would have made little difference. She paused, wondering if having the child might change the woman's cavalier attitude to life.

Charles returned home after the debate feeling pleased with himself. He had received praise for his latest speech from every wing of the party, and the Chief Whip had made it quite clear that his efforts on the Finance Bill had not gone unnoticed.

As he drove back to Eaton Square he wound down the car window and let the fresh air rush in and the cigarette smoke out. His smile widened at the thought of Amanda sitting at home waiting for him. It had been a glorious couple of months. At forty-eight he was experiencing realities he had never even dreamed of in fantasy. As each day passed he expected the infatuation to wear off, but instead it only grew more intense. Even the memory the day after was better than anything he had experienced in the past.

Once the Holbein had been restored to his dining-room wall Charles planned to talk to Amanda about their future; if she said "Yes" he would even be willing to grant Fiona a divorce. He parked the car and

took out his latch key, but she was already there opening the front door
to throw her arms around him.

"Why don't we go straight to bed?" she greeted him.

Charles would have been shocked had Fiona uttered such feelings
even once in their fifteen years of married life, but Amanda made it
appear quite natural. She was already lying naked on the bed before
Charles could get his waistcoat off. After they had made love and she
was settled in his arms Amanda told him she would have to go away for
a few days.

"Why?" said Charles, puzzled.

"I'm pregnant," she said matter-of-factly. "I've already booked
myself into a clinic. Don't worry. I'll be as right as rain in no time."

"But why don't we have the baby?" said a delighted Charles, looking
down into her grey eyes. "I've always wanted a son."

"Don't be silly, Charlie. There's years ahead of me for that."

"But if we were married?"

"You're already married. Besides, I'm only twenty-six."

"I can get a divorce in a moment and life wouldn't be so bad with me,
would it?"

"Of course not, Charlie. You're the first man I've ever really cared
for."

Charles smiled hopefully. "So you'll think about the idea?"

Amanda looked into Charles's eyes anxiously. "If I *were* to have a
child I do hope he'd have blue eyes like yours."

"Will you marry me?" he asked.

"I'll think about it. In any case, you may have changed your mind by
morning."

Raymond drove Kate to Heathrow. He was wearing the pink shirt she
had chosen for him; she was wearing the little red box. He had so much
to tell her on the way to the airport that he hardly spoke at all. The last
four weeks had gone by in a flash. It was the first time he had been
grateful for being in Opposition.

"It's all right, Carrot Top. Don't fuss. We'll see each other whenever
you come to New York."

"I've only been to America twice in my life," he said. She tried to
smile.

Once she had checked her eleven bags in at the counter, a process
that seemed to take forever, she was allocated a seat.

"Flight BA 107, gate number fourteen, boarding in ten minutes," she
was informed.

"Thank you," she said and rejoined Raymond, who was sitting on
the end of an already crowded tubular settee. He had bought two
plastic cups of coffee while Kate had been checking in. They were both
already cold. They sat and held hands like children who had met on a

summer holiday and had now to return to separate schools.

"Promise me you won't start wearing contact lenses the moment I've gone."

"Yes, I can promise you that," said Raymond, touching the bridge of his glasses.

"I've so much I still want to tell you," she said.

He turned towards her. "Vice-presidents of banks shouldn't cry," he said, brushing a tear from her cheek. "The customers will realise you're a soft touch."

"Neither should Cabinet ministers," she replied. "All I wanted to say, is that if you really feel . . ." she began.

"Hello, Mr Gould."

They both looked up to see a broad smile spread across the face of someone whose tan proved that he had just arrived from a sunnier climate.

"I'm Bert Cox," he said, thrusting out his hand. "I don't suppose you remember me." Raymond let go of Kate's hand and shook Mr Cox's.

"We were at the same primary school in Leeds, Ray. Mind you, that was a million light years ago. You've come a long way since then."

How can I get rid of him? wondered Raymond desperately.

"This is the missus," Bert Cox continued obliviously, gesturing at the silent woman in a flowery dress by his side. She smiled but didn't speak. "She sits on some committee with Joyce, don't you, love?" he said, not waiting for her reply.

"This is the final call for Flight BA 107, now boarding at gate number fourteen."

"We always vote for you, of course," continued Bert Cox. "The missus" – he pointed to the lady in the flowered dress again – "thinks you'll be Prime Minister. I always say –"

"I must go, Raymond," said Kate, "or I'll miss my flight."

"Can you excuse me for a moment, Mr Cox?" said Raymond.

"Delighted. I'll wait. I don't often get a chance to have a word with my MP."

Raymond walked with Kate towards the barrier. "I am sorry about this. I'm afraid they're all like that in Leeds – hearts of gold, but never stop talking. What were you going to say?"

"Only that I would have been happy to live in Leeds, however cold it is. I never envied anyone in my life, but I do envy Joyce." She kissed him gently on the cheek and walked towards the barrier before he could reply. She didn't look back.

"Are you feeling all right, madam?" asked an airport official as she went through the security barrier.

"I'm fine," said Kate, brushing aside her tears. She walked slowly towards gate fourteen, happy that he had worn the pink shirt for the first time. She wondered if he had found the note she had left underneath the collar. If he had asked her just one more time . . .

Raymond stood alone and then turned to walk aimlessly towards the exit.

"An American lady, I would have guessed," said Mr Cox rejoining him. "I'm good on accents."

"Yes," said Raymond, still alone.

"A friend of yours?" he asked.

"My best friend," said Raymond.

When ten days had passed and Elizabeth had not yet heard from Miss Wallace she decided she had no choice but to contact her direct. She flicked through her personal file and noted the latest number Amanda had given.

Elizabeth picked up the phone and dialled. It was some time before anybody answered.

"730-9712. Charles Seymour speaking." There was a long silence. "Is anyone there?"

Elizabeth couldn't reply. She replaced the receiver and felt her whole body come out in a cold sweat. She closed Amanda Wallace's file and returned it to the cabinet.

CHAPTER TWENTY FIVE

Simon had spent nearly a year preparing a White Paper entitled "A Genuine Partnership for Ireland" for consideration by the House. The Government's aim was to bring north and south together for a period of ten years at the end of which a more permanent arrangement could be considered. During those ten years both sides would remain under the direct rule of Westminster and Dublin. Both Protestants and Catholics had contributed to "the Charter", as the press had dubbed the complex agreement. With considerable skill, patience and fortitude Simon had convinced the political leaders of Northern Ireland to append their names to the final draft when and if it was approved by the House.

He admitted to Elizabeth that the agreement was only a piece of paper, but he felt it was a foundation stone on which the House could base an eventual settlement. On both sides of the Irish Sea politicians and journalists alike were describing the Charter as a genuine breakthrough.

The Secretary of State for Northern Ireland was to present the White Paper to the Commons when Irish business was next scheduled on the parliamentary calendar. Simon, as the architect of the Charter, had been asked to deliver the winding-up speech on behalf of the Government. He knew that if the House backed the concept of the document he might then be allowed to prepare a parliamentary bill and thus overcome a problem so many other politicians had failed to solve before him. If he succeeded Simon felt that all the sacrifices he had made in the past would prove worthwhile.

When Elizabeth sat down to read through the final draft in Simon's study that evening even she admitted for the first time that she was pleased he had accepted the Irish appointment.

"Now, embryonic statesman," she continued, "are you ready for your dinner like every normal human being at this time in the evening?"

"I certainly am." Simon moved his copy of the 129-page Charter from the dining-room table to the sideboard, planning to go over it yet again once he had finished dinner.

"Damn," he heard Elizabeth say from the kitchen.

"What is it?" he asked, not looking up from his toy, like a child studying a jigsaw and wondering where a colourless piece fitted in.

"I'm out of Bisto."

"I'll go and buy some," Simon volunteered. The two policemen on the door were chatting when the minister came out.

"Come on, my wife needs a packet of Bisto, so affairs of state must be held up for the time being."

"I'm very sorry, sir," said the sergeant. "When I was told you would be in for the rest of the evening I allowed the official car to go off duty. But Constable Barker can accompany you."

"That's no problem," said Simon. "We can take my wife's car. I'll just find out where she's parked the damn thing."

He slipped back into the house but returned a moment later. "Been in the force long?" he asked Constable Barker as they walked down the road together.

"Not that long, sir. Started on the beat just over a year ago."

"Are you married, Constable?"

"Fine chance on my salary, sir."

"Then you won't have encountered the problem of being Bisto-less."

"They've never heard of gravy in the police canteen, sir."

"You should try the House of Commons sometime," said Simon. "I don't think you'd find it any better – the food, that is, not to mention the salary."

The two men laughed as they headed off towards the car.

"What does your wife think of the Mini Metro?" the constable asked as Simon put the key in the door.

Like everyone else in Beaufort Street, Elizabeth heard the explosion, but she was the first to realise what it had to be. She ran out of the front door in search of the duty policeman. She saw him running down the road and quickly followed.

The little red Metro was scattered all over the side street, the glass from its windows making the pavement look as though there had been a sudden hailstorm.

When the sergeant saw the severed head he pulled Elizabeth back. Two other bodies lay motionless in the road, one of them an old lady with the contents of her shopping bag spread around her.

Within minutes, six police cars had arrived and Special Branch officers had cordoned off the area with white ribbon. An ambulance rushed the bodies to Westminster Hospital. The job of picking up the remains of the police constable needed a very resolute man.

Elizabeth was taken to the hospital in a police car, where she learned that the old lady had died before arrival while her husband was on the critical list. When she told the surgeon in charge that she was a doctor he was more forthcoming and answered her questions candidly. Simon was suffering from multiple fractures, a dislocated hip and a severe loss of blood. The only question he was not willing to be drawn on was when she asked about his chances.

She sat alone outside the operating theatre waiting for any scrap of news. Hour after hour went by, and Elizabeth kept recalling Simon's words: "Be tolerant. Always remember there are still men of goodwill in Northern Ireland." She found it almost impossible not to scream, to think of the whole lot of them as evil murderers. Her husband had worked tirelessly on their behalf. He wasn't a Catholic or a Protestant, just a man trying to do an impossible task. Although she couldn't help thinking that it was she who had been the intended target.

Another hour passed.

A tired, grey-faced man came out into the corridor through the flapping rubber doors. "He's still hanging on, Dr Kerslake. Your husband has the constitution of an ox; most people would have let go by now." He smiled. "Can I find you a room so that you can get some sleep?"

"No, thank you," Elizabeth replied. "I'd prefer to be near him."

She rang home to check the children were coping and her mother answered the phone. She had rushed over the moment she had heard the news and was keeping them away from the radio and television.

"How is he?" she asked.

Elizabeth told her mother all she knew, then spoke to the children.

"We're taking care of Grandmother," Peter told her.

Elizabeth couldn't hold back the tears. "Thank you, darling," she said, and quickly replaced the receiver. She returned to the bench outside the operating theatre, kicked off her shoes, curled her legs under her body and tried to snatch some sleep.

She woke with a start in the early morning. Her back hurt and her neck was stiff. She walked slowly up and down the corridor in her bare feet stretching her aching limbs, searching for anyone who could tell her some news. Finally a nurse brought her a cup of tea and assured her that her husband was still alive. But what did "still alive" mean? She stood and watched the grim faces coming out of the operating theatre and tried not to recognise the tell-tale signs of despair. The surgeon told her she ought to go home and rest: they would have nothing to tell her for several hours. A policeman kept all journalists – who were arriving by the minute – in an ante-room off the main corridor.

Elizabeth didn't move from the corridor for another day and another night, and she didn't return home until the surgeon told her it was all over.

When she heard the news she fell on her knees and wept.

"God must want the Irish problem solved as well," he added. "Your husband will live, Dr Kerslake, but it's a miracle."

"Got time for a quick one?" asked Alexander Dalglish.

"If you press me," said Pimkin.

"Fiona," shouted Alexander. "It's Alec Pimkin, he's dropped in for a drink."

She came through to join them. She was dressed in a bright yellow frock and had allowed her hair to grow down past her shoulders.

"It suits you," said Pimkin, tapping his bald head.

"Thank you," said Fiona. "Why don't we all go through to the drawing-room?"

Pimkin happily obeyed and had soon settled himself into Alexander's favourite chair.

"What will you have?" asked Fiona, as she stood by the drinks cabinet.

"A large gin with just a rumour of tonic."

"Well, how's the constituency faring since my resignation?"

"It ticks along, trying hard to survive the biggest sex scandal since Profumo," chuckled Pimkin.

"I only hope it hasn't harmed your election chances," said Alexander.

"Not a bit of it, old fellow," said Pimkin, accepting the large Beefeaters and tonic Fiona handed him. "On the contrary, it's taken their minds off me for a change."

Alexander laughed.

"In fact," continued Pimkin, "interest in the date of your wedding has only been eclipsed by Charles and Lady Di. Gossips tell me," he continued, clearly enjoying himself, "that my Honourable friend, the member for Sussex Downs, made you wait the full two years before you could place an announcement in *The Times.*"

"Yes, that's true," said Fiona. "Charles didn't even answer my letters during that period, but lately when any problem's arisen he's been almost friendly."

"Could that be because he also wants to place an announcement in *The Times?*" said Pimkin, downing his gin quickly in the hope of being offered a second.

"What do you mean?"

"The fact that he has lost his heart to another."

"Another?" said Alexander Dalglish.

"No less –" Pimkin paused as he sipped pointedly at his empty glass "– than Miss Amanda Wallace, only daughter of the late and little lamented Brigadier Boozer Wallace."

"Amanda Wallace?" said Fiona in disbelief. "Surely he's got more sense than that."

"I don't think it has a lot to do with sense," said Pimkin holding out his glass. "More to do with sex."

"But he's old enough to be her father."

"If that is the case," said Pimkin, "Charles can always adopt her."

Alexander laughed.

"But I am informed by a reliable source," continued Pimkin, "that marriage is being proposed."

"You can't be serious," said Fiona flatly.

"The subject has most certainly been broached for she is undoubtedly pregnant and Charles is hoping for a son," said Pimkin in triumph as he accepted his second double gin.

"That's not possible," said Fiona under her breath.

"And I am also informed," continued Pimkin, "that some of the more ungenerous of our brethren are already suggesting the name of several candidates for the role of father."

"Alec, you're incorrigible."

"My dear, it is common knowledge that Amanda has slept with half the Cabinet and a considerable cross section of back-benchers."

"Stop exaggerating," said Fiona.

"And what's more," continued Pimkin as if he hadn't heard her, "she has only stopped short of the Labour front bench because her mother told her they were common and she might catch something from them."

Alexander laughed again. "But surely Charles hasn't fallen for the pregnancy trick?"

"Hook, line and sinker. He's like an Irishman who's been locked into a Guinness brewery over the weekend. Dear Amanda has my Honourable friend uncorking her at every opportunity."

"But she's plain stupid," said Alexander. "The only time I met her she assured me that Michael Parkinson was turning out to be an excellent chairman of the party."

"Stupid she may well be," said Pimkin, "but plain she is not and together, I'm told, they are updating the *Kama Sutra*."

"Enough, Alec, enough," said Fiona laughing.

"You're right," said Pimkin, aware that his glass was nearly empty once again. "A man of my impeccable reputation cannot afford to be seen associating with people living in sin. I must leave immediately, darlings," he said, rising to his feet. Pimkin put his glass down and Alexander accompanied him to the front door.

As it closed Alexander turned to Fiona. "Never short of useful information, our former member," he said.

"I agree," said Fiona. "So much gleaned for such a small investment in Beefeaters."

As Alexander walked back into the drawing-room he added, "Does it change your plans for the return of the Holbein?"

"Not in any way," said Fiona.

"So you'll still be at Sotheby's next week for their Old Masters sale?"

Fiona smiled. "Certainly. And if the price is right we won't have to worry about what we give Charles for a wedding present."

Three weeks after the bombing Simon left the Westminster Hospital on crutches, Elizabeth by his side. His right leg had been so shattered that he had been told he would never walk properly again. As he stepped out on to Horseferry Road a hundred cameras flashed to meet their editors' demand to capture the instant hero. He smiled as if there were no pain. "Don't let those murderers think they got to you," he was warned by both sides. Elizabeth's smile showed only relief that her husband was still alive.

After three weeks of complete rest Simon returned to his Irish Charter against doctor's orders, knowing the document was still due to be debated in the House in less than a fortnight. The Secretary of State and the other Minister of State for Northern Ireland visited him at home on several occasions and it was agreed that the Minister of State would take over Simon's responsibilities temporarily and deliver the winding-up speech. During his absence the whole Northern Ireland office grew to realize just how much work Simon had put into the Charter, and no one was at all complacent about taking his place.

The attempt on Simon's life and the build up to the special debate on the Charter became of such national interest that the BBC decided to broadcast the entire proceedings on Radio Four from three-thirty to the vote at ten o'clock.

On the afternoon of the debate Simon sat up in bed listening to every word on the radio as if it were the final episode in his favourite serial and he was desperate to know the outcome. The speeches opened with a

clear and concise presentation of the Charter by the Secretary of State
for Northern Ireland, which left Simon feeling confident that the whole
House would support him. The Opposition spokesman followed with a
fair-minded speech, raising one or two queries he had over the
controversial Patriots' Clause with its special rights for Protestants in
the south and Catholics in the north, and also how it would affect the
Catholics unwilling to register in Northern Ireland. Otherwise he
reassured the House that the Opposition supported the Charter and
would not be calling for a division.

Simon began to relax for the first time as the debate continued, but
his mood changed as some back-bench members started to express
more and more anxiety over the Patriots' Provision. One or two back-
benchers were even insisting that the Charter should not be sanctioned
by the House until the need for the Patriots' Provision was fully
explained by the Government. Simon realised that a few narrow-
minded men were simply playing for time in the hope the Charter
would be held up and later forgotten. For generations such men had
succeeded in stifling the hopes and aspirations of the Irish people while
they allowed bigotry to undermine any real desire for peace.

Elizabeth came in and sat on the end of the bed. "How's it going?"
she asked.

"Not well," said Simon, "it will all depend on the Opposition
spokesman."

They both sat and listened. But no sooner had the Opposition
spokesman risen than Simon realised that he too had misunderstood
the real purpose of the Patriots' Provision and that what Simon had
agreed to with both sides in Dublin and Belfast was not being
accurately explained to the House. There was no malice in the speech
and he was clearly following what had been agreed through the usual
channels but Simon could sense that his lack of conviction was sowing
doubts in the minds of his fellow members. He feared a division might
be called after all.

After one or two members had interrupted to voice further doubts
about the Patriots' Clause the Shadow minister suggested: "Perhaps
we should wait until the Minister of State is fully recovered and able to
report to the House himself." A few "hear, hears" could be heard
around the Chamber.

Simon felt sick. He was going to lose the Charter if it didn't get
through the House tonight. All the hard work and goodwill would
count for nothing. He made a decision.

"I'd love a hot cup of cocoa," he said, trying to sound casual.

"Of course, darling. I'll just go and turn the kettle on. Would you like
a biscuit while I'm up?"

Simon nodded. Once the bedroom door was closed, he slipped
quietly out of bed and dressed as quickly as possible. He picked up his

blackthorn stick, a gift from Dr Fitzgerald, the Irish Prime Minister, which had been among the dozens of presents awaiting his return from hospital. Then he hobbled silently down the stairs and across the hall, hoping Elizabeth would not hear him. He eased the front door open. When the policeman on duty saw him Simon put a finger to his lips and closed the door very slowly behind him. He made his way laboriously up to the police car, lurched into the back and said, "Switch on the radio, please, and drive me to the House as quickly as possible."

Simon continued to listen to the Opposition spokesman as the police car weaved in and out of the traffic on a route he hadn't travelled before. They arrived at the St Stephen's entrance to the Commons at nine-twenty-five.

Visitors stood to one side as they might for royalty but Simon didn't notice. He hobbled on through the Central Lobby, oblivious to the awkwardness of his gait, turning left past the policeman and on towards the entrance of the House. He prayed he would reach the Chamber before the Government spokesman rose to deliver his winding-up speech. Simon passed an astonished chief doorkeeper and arrived at the bar of the House as the new digital clock showed nine-twenty-nine.

The Opposition spokesman was resuming his place on the front bench to muffled cries of "Hear, hear." The Speaker rose but before he had time to call upon the Minister of State to reply Simon stepped slowly forward on to the green carpet of the Commons. For a moment there was a stunned silence; then the cheering began. It had reached a crescendo by the time Simon arrived at the front bench. His blackthorn stick fell to the floor as he clutched the dispatch box. The Speaker called out his name *sotto voce*.

Simon waited for the House to come to complete silence.

"Mr Speaker, I must thank the House for its generous welcome. I return this evening because having listened to every word of the debate on the radio I feel it necessary to explain to Honourable Members what was behind my thinking with the Patriots' Provision. This was not some superficial formula for solving an intractable problem, but an act of good faith to which the representatives from all sides felt able to put their names. It may not be perfect, since words can mean different things to different people – as lawyers continually demonstrate to us."

The laughter broke the tension that had been building up in the House.

"But if we allow this opportunity to pass today it will be another victory for those who revel in the mayhem of Northern Ireland whatever their reason, and a defeat for all men of goodwill."

The House was silent as Simon went on to explain in detail the thinking behind the Patriots' Provision and the effect it would have on both Protestants and Catholics in north and south. He also covered the other salient clauses in the Charter, answering the points that had been raised during the debate until, in glancing up at the clock above the Speaker's chair, he realised he had less than a minute left.

"Mr Speaker, we in this great House, who have in the past decided the fate of nations, are now given an opportunity to succeed today where our predecessors have failed. I ask you to support this Charter – not unreservedly, but to show the bombers and the murderers that here in Westminster we can cast a vote for the children of tomorrow's Ireland. Let the twenty-first century be one in which the Irish problem is only a part of history. Mr Speaker, I seek the support of the whole House."

The motion on the Charter was agreed without division.

Simon immediately returned home and on arrival silently crept upstairs. He closed the bedroom door behind him and fumbled for the switch. The light by the side of the bed went on and Elizabeth sat up.

"Your cocoa's gone cold and I've eaten all the biscuits," she said, grinning, "but thank you for leaving the radio on, at least I knew where you were."

CHAPTER TWENTY SIX

Charles and Amanda were married at the most inconspicuous register office in Hammersmith. They then departed for a long weekend in Paris. Charles had told his bride that he preferred her not to let anyone learn of the marriage for at least another week. He didn't want Fiona to find yet a further excuse for not returning the Holbein. Amanda readily agreed, and then she remembered – but surely Alec Pimkin didn't count.

Paris turned out to be fun, even though Charles was sensitive about Amanda's obvious pregnancy – never more so than when they arrived on the Friday night at the Plaza Athenée and were escorted to a suite overlooking the courtyard. Later, over dinner, Amanda astonished the waiters with her appetite as well as the cut of her dress.

Over breakfast in bed the next day Charles read in the *Herald Tribune* that Mrs Thatcher was considering a reshuffle that very weekend. He cut the honeymoon short and returned to London on the Saturday, two days earlier than planned. Amanda was not overjoyed. Her husband spent the whole of Sunday at Eaton Square alongside a phone that never rang.

That same Sunday evening the Prime Minister called for Simon Kerslake and told him that he was to be made a Privy Councillor and would be moved from the Northern Ireland Office to Defence as Minister of State.

He had started to protest, but Mrs Thatcher forestalled any discussion. "I don't want any more dead heroes, Simon," she said sharply.

Elizabeth was relieved when she heard the news, although it took her some time to get used to her husband being referred to as "the Right Honourable Simon Kerslake". For some weeks the old joke of "rarely right and never honourable" had to be suffered by both of them from countless well-meaning constituents who imagined they were the only people who had thought of the quip.

Mrs Thatcher called Charles Seymour on the Monday morning while he was waiting in Eaton Square for the return of the Holbein. Both sides' solicitors had agreed that the first Earl of Bridgwater should be back at Charles's home by eleven that morning. Only the Queen or Mrs Thatcher could have kept Charles from being there to receive it.

The Prime Minister's call came long after he thought the reshuffle was over, but then Mrs Thatcher had been informed that Charles was in Paris on his honeymoon and wouldn't be back until the Monday morning.

Charles took a taxi to Downing Street and was quickly ushered into the Prime Minister's study. Mrs Thatcher began by complimenting him on the work he had carried out on successive Finance Bills in Opposition and in Government. She then invited him to join the front-bench team as the Financial Secretary to the Treasury.

Charles accepted gracefully, and after a short policy discussion with the Prime Minister drove back to Eaton Square to celebrate both his triumphs. Amanda met him at the door to tell him the Holbein had been returned. Fiona had kept her part of the bargain: the painting had been delivered at eleven o'clock sharp.

Charles strode confidently into his drawing-room and was delighted to find the bulky package awaiting him. He was by no means so pleased to be followed by Amanda, a cigarette in one hand and a glass of gin in the other; but this was not a day for quarrels, he decided. He told her of his appointment, but she didn't seem to take in its significance until her husband opened a bottle of champagne.

Charles poured out two glasses and handed one to his bride.

"A double celebration. What fun," she said, first draining the gin.

Charles took a quick sip of the champagne before he began to untie the knots and tear away the smart red wrapping paper that covered his masterpiece. Once the paper had been removed he pulled back the final cardboard covers. Charles stared with delight at the portrait.

The first Earl of Bridgwater was back home. Charles picked up the gold frame he knew so well to return it to its place in his study but he noticed that the picture had come a little loose. "Damn," he said.

"What's the matter?" asked Amanda still leaning against the door.

"Nothing important, only I shall have to get the frame fixed. I'll drop it into Oliver Swann on the way to the bank. I've waited nearly three years; another couple of days won't make any difference."

Now that Charles had accepted the post of Financial Secretary to the Treasury he knew there was one little arrangement he had to clear up before the appointment became public knowledge. With that in mind, he left Eaton Square and dropped the Holbein off at the framer. He then went on to the bank and summoned Clive Reynolds to his office. It was clear from Reynolds's manner that the news of Charles's ministerial appointment had not yet leaked out.

"Clive," Charles called him for the first time. "I have a proposition to put to you."

Clive Reynolds remained silent.

"The Prime Minister has offered me a post in the Government."

"Congratulations," said Reynolds, "and well deserved, if I may say so."

"Thank you," said Charles. "Now: I'm considering offering you the chance to stand in for me as chairman during my absence."

Clive Reynolds looked surprised.

"On the clear understanding that if the Conservatives were to return to Opposition or I were to lose my appointment in Government I would be reinstated as chairman immediately."

"Naturally," said Reynolds. "I should be delighted to fill the appointment for the interim period."

"Good man," said Charles. "It can't have escaped your notice what happened to the last chairman in the same situation."

"I shall make certain that will not happen again."

"Thank you," said Charles. "I shall not forget your loyalty when I return."

"And I shall also endeavour to carry on the traditions of the bank in your absence," said Reynolds, his head slightly bowed.

"I feel sure you will," said Charles.

The board accepted the recommendation that Clive Reynolds be appointed as temporary chairman and Charles vacated his office happily to take up his new post at the Treasury.

Charles considered it had been the most successful week of his life and on the Friday evening on the way back to Eaton Square he dropped into Oliver Swann's gallery to pick up the Holbein.

"I'm afraid the picture didn't quite fit the frame," said Mr Swann.

"Oh, I expect it's worked loose over the years," Charles said non-committally.

"No, Mr Seymour, this frame was put on the portrait quite

recently," said Swann.

"That's not possible," said Charles. "I remember the frame as well as I remember the picture. The portrait of the first Earl of Bridgwater has been in my family for over 400 years."

"Not this picture," said Swann.

"What do you mean?" said Charles, beginning to sound anxious.

"This picture came up for sale at Sotheby's about three weeks ago."

Charles went cold as Swann continued.

"It's the school of Holbein, of course," he said, "probably painted by one of his pupils around the time of his death. I should think there are a dozen or so in existence."

"A dozen or so," repeated Charles, the blood drained from his face.

"Yes, perhaps even more. At least it's solved one mystery for me," said Swann, chuckling.

"What's that?" asked Charles, choking out the words.

"I couldn't work out why Lady Fiona was bidding for the picture, and then I remembered that your family name is Bridgwater."

"At least *this* wedding has some style," Pimkin assured Fiona between mouthfuls of sandwiches at the reception after her marriage to Alexander Dalglish. Pimkin always accepted wedding invitations as it allowed him to devour mounds of smoked salmon sandwiches and consume unlimited quantities of champagne. "I particularly enjoyed that *short* service of blessing in the Guards' Chapel; and Claridges can always be relied on to understand my little proclivities." He peered round the vast room and only stopped to stare at his reflection in a chandelier.

Fiona laughed. "Did you go to Charles's wedding?"

"My darling, the only Etonians who have ever been seen in Hammersmith pass through it as quickly as possible on a boat, representing either Oxford or Cambridge."

"So you weren't invited," said Fiona.

"I'm told that only Amanda was invited, and even she nearly found she had another engagement. With her doctor, I believe."

"Well, Charles certainly can't afford another divorce."

"No, not in his present position as Her Majesty's Financial Secretary. One divorce might go unnoticed but two would be considered habit-forming, and all diligent readers of Nigel Dempster have been able to observe that consummation has taken place."

"But how long will Charles be able to tolerate her behaviour?"

"As long as he still believes she has given him a son who will inherit the family title. Not that a marriage ceremony will necessarily prove legitimacy," added Pimkin.

"Perhaps Amanda won't produce a son."

"Perhaps whatever she produces it will be obvious that it's not

Charles's offspring," said Pimkin, falling into a chair that had been momentarily left by a large buxom lady.

"Even if it was I can't see Amanda as a housewife."

"No, but it suits Amanda's current circumstances to be thought of as the loving spouse."

"Time may change that too," said Fiona.

"I doubt it," said Pimkin. "Amanda is stupid, that has been proved beyond reasonable doubt, but she has a survival instinct second only to a mongoose. So while Charles is spending all the hours of the day advancing his glittering career she would be foolish to search publicly for greener pastures. Especially when she can always lie in them privately."

"You're a wicked old gossip," said Fiona.

"I cannot deny it," said Pimkin, "for it is an art at which women have never been as accomplished as men."

"Thank you for such a sensible wedding present," said Alexander, joining his wife of two hours. "You selected my favourite claret."

"Giving a dozen bottles of the finest claret serves two purposes," said Pimkin, his hands resting lightly on his stomach. "First, you can always be assured of a decent wine when you invite yourself to dine."

"And second?" asked Alexander.

"When the happy couple split up you can feel relieved that they will no longer have your present to quarrel over."

"Did you give Charles and Amanda a present?" asked Fiona.

"No," said Pimkin, deftly removing another glass of champagne from a passing waiter. "I felt your return of the bogus Earl of Bridgwater was quite enough for both of us."

"I wonder where he is now?" said Alexander.

"He no longer resides in Eaton Square," said Pimkin with the air of one who has divulged a piece of information which can only guarantee further rapt attention.

"Who would want the phoney earl?"

"We are not aware of the provenance of the buyer, as he emanates from one of Her Majesty's former colonies, but the seller . . ."

"Stop teasing, Alec. Who?"

"None other than Mrs Amanda Seymour."

"Amanda?"

"Yes. Amanda, no less. The dear, silly creature retrieved the false earl from the cellar where Charles had buried him with full military honours."

"But she must have realised it was a fake."

"My dear Amanda wouldn't know the difference between a Holbein and an Andy Warhol but she still happily accepted £10,000 for the impersonation. I am assured that the dealer who purchased this fabricated masterpiece made what I think vulgar people in the City describe as 'a quick turn'."

"Good God," said Alexander. "I only paid £8,000 for it myself."

"Perhaps you should get Amanda to advise you on these matters in future," said Pimkin. "In exchange for my invaluable piece of information I'm bound to inquire if the real Earl of Bridgwater is to remain in hiding."

"Certainly not, Alec. He is merely awaiting the right moment to make a public appearance," said Fiona, unable to hide a smile.

"And where is Amanda now?" asked Alexander, obviously wanting to change the subject.

"In Switzerland producing a baby, which we can but hope will bear sufficient resemblance to a white Caucasian to convince one of Charles's limited imagination that he is the father."

"Where *do* you get all your information from?" asked Alexander.

Pimkin sighed dramatically. "Women have a habit of pouring their hearts out to me, Amanda included."

"Why should she do that?" asked Alexander.

"She lives safe in the knowledge that I am the one man she knows who has no interest in her body." Pimkin drew breath, but only to devour another smoked salmon sandwich.

Charles phoned Amanda every day while she was in Geneva. She kept assuring him all was well, and that the baby was expected on time. He had considered it prudent for Amanda not to remain in England advertising her pregnancy, a less than recent occurrence to even the most casual observer. She for her part did not complain. With £10,000 safely tucked away in a private Swiss account there were few little necessities she could not have brought to her, even in Geneva.

It had taken a few weeks for Charles to become accustomed to Government after such a long break. He enjoyed the challenge of the Treasury and quickly fell in with its strange traditions. He was constantly reminded that his was the department on which the Prime Minister kept the closest eye, making the challenge even greater. The civil servants, when asked their opinion of the new Financial Secretary, would reply variously: able, competent, efficient, hard-working – but without any hint of affection in their voices. When someone asked his driver, whose name Charles could never remember, the same question he proffered the view, "He's the sort of minister who always sits in the back of a car. But I'd still put a week's wages on Mr Seymour becoming Prime Minister."

Amanda produced her child in the middle of the ninth month. After a week's recuperation she was allowed to return to England. She discovered travelling with her offspring was a nuisance and by the time she arrived at Heathrow she was more than happy to turn the child over to the nanny Charles had selected.

Charles had sent a car to pick her up from the airport. He had an unavoidable conference with a delegation of Japanese businessmen, he explained, all of them busy complaining about the new Government tariffs on imports. At the first opportunity to be rid of his oriental guests he bolted back to Eaton Square.

Amanda was there to meet him at the door. Charles had almost forgotten how beautiful his wife was, and how long she had been away.

"Where's my child?" he asked, after he had given her a long kiss.

"In a nursery that's more expensively furnished than our bedroom," she replied a little sharply.

Charles ran up the wide staircase and along the passage. Amanda followed. He entered the nursery and stopped in his tracks as he stared at the future Earl of Bridgwater. The little black curls and deep brown eyes came as something of a shock.

"Good heavens," said Charles, stepping forward for a closer examination. Amanda remained by the door, her hand clutching its handle.

She had a hundred answers ready for his question.

"He's the spitting image of my great-grandfather. You skipped a couple of generations, Harry," said Charles, lifting the boy high into the air, "but there's no doubt you're a real Seymour."

Amanda sighed with inaudible relief. The hundred answers she could now keep to herself.

"It's more than a couple of generations the little bastard has skipped," said Pimkin. "It's an entire continent." He took another sip of christening champagne before continuing. "This poor creature, on the other hand," he said, staring at Fiona's firstborn, "bears a striking resemblance to Alexander. Dear little girl should have been given a kinder legacy with which to start her life."

"She's beautiful," said Fiona, picking Lucy up from the cradle to check her nappy.

"Now we know why you needed to be married so quickly," added Pimkin between gulps. "At least this child made wedlock, even if it was a close-run thing."

Fiona continued as if she had not heard his remark. "Have you actually seen Charles's son?"

"I think we should refer to young Harry as Amanda's child," said Pimkin. "We don't want to be had up under the Trade Descriptions Act."

"Come on, Alec, have you seen Harry?" she asked, refusing to fill his empty glass.

"Yes, I have. And I am afraid he also bears too striking a resemblance to his father for it to go unnoticed in later life."

"Anyone we know?" asked Fiona, probing.

"I am not a scandalmonger," said Pimkin, removing a crumb from his waistcoat. "As you well know. But a certain Brazilian *fazendeiro* who frequents Cowdray Park and Ascot during the summer months has obviously maintained his interest in English fillies."

Pimkin confidently held out his glass.

CHAPTER TWENTY SEVEN

James Callaghan's resignation as Labour party leader in October 1980 took none of the political analysts by surprise. Unlike his predecessor he was over sixty-five, the age at which his party had recommended retirement.

Those same analysts were surprised, however, when Michael Foot, the veteran left-winger, defeated Denis Healey by 139 votes to 129 to become the new leader of the Labour party. The analysts immediately predicted a long spell of opposition for the socialists.

The Conservatives took much pleasure in watching a leadership struggle from the sidelines for a change. When Charles Seymour heard the result it amused him that the Labour party had ended up replacing a sixty-year-old with a sixty-four-year-old, who in turn was being replaced by a sixty-seven-year-old. Lord Shinwell, who at the age of ninety-six was the oldest living former Labour Cabinet minister, declared that he would be a candidate for party leadership when Foot retired.

When the election for the Shadow Cabinet came a week later Andrew decided not to submit his name. Like many of his colleagues he liked the new leader personally but had rarely been able to agree with him on domestic issues and was totally opposed to his defence and European policies. Instead he took on the chairmanship of the Select Committee on Scottish Affairs. Raymond for his part considered that Foot was destined to be no more than an interim leader and was therefore quite happy to serve under him. When the election to the Shadow Cabinet was announced Raymond came eighth. Michael Foot invited him to continue shadowing the Trade portfolio.

When Andrew entered the Commons Chamber the day after the election he walked up the gangway and took a seat on the back benches for the first time in fourteen years. He looked down at Raymond lounging on the front bench and recalled his own words: "There may well come a day when I sit and envy you from the same back benches."

Andrew was not surprised when he heard from his local committee in Edinburgh that he would once again have to submit himself to reselection as their candidate some time during 1981. When the Labour conference the previous October had approved the mandatory reselection of Labour MPs he had realised his biggest battle would be internal. Frank Boyle had even managed to replace another of Andrew's supporters with one of his own henchmen.

Roy Jenkins, the former deputy leader of the Labour party, was returning from Brussels as soon as his term as President of the European Commission came to an end. After delivering the Dimbleby lecture on television Jenkins made no secret of the fact that he was considering founding a new party that would take in those moderate radicals who felt the Labour Party had swung too far to the left. The party conference had removed the power of selection of the leaders from Members of Parliament; for many this was the final straw, and several Labour MPs told Jenkins they were ready to defect. Andrew would have preferred to remain loyal to the party and try to change it from the inside, but he was fast coming to the conclusion that that hour had passed.

In his morning mail was a curt note from the constituency secretary informing him that Frank Boyle was going to oppose him for the nomination. Andrew flew up to Edinburgh on the day of the meeting, fearing the worst. No one met him at the airport, and at party headquarters David Connaught greeted him with a glum face.

Andrew stood in front of the committee in a cold, cheerless room and answered the same questions that had been put to him only three years before. He gave exactly the same answers: where he stood on nuclear disarmament, why he was in favour of a close association with the United States, his attitude to a wealth tax – on and on, predictable question after predictable question, but he never once allowed them to exasperate him.

He ended with the words: "I have been proud to serve the people of Edinburgh Carlton for almost twenty years as the Labour member and hope to do so for at least another twenty. If you now feel unable to reselect me I would have to consider standing as an independent candidate." For the first time, one or two members of the committee looked anxious.

"We are not intimidated by your threats, Mr Fraser," said Frank Boyle. "The Labour party has always been bigger than any individual. Now we know where Mr Fraser's real interests lie I suggest we move to a vote."

Twelve little slips of paper were passed out. "Fraser" or "Boyle" were scribbled on them before they were sent back to the chairman.

Frank Boyle slowly gathered up the slips, clearly relishing Andrew's discomfort. He unfolded the first slip of paper. "Boyle," he said, glancing at the others round the table.

He opened a second – "Fraser" – then a third, "Boyle", followed by "Fraser, Fraser, Fraser."

Andrew kept count in his head: four-two in his favour.

"Fraser," followed by "Boyle, Boyle, Fraser."

Six-four in Andrew's favour, with two still unopened: he only needed one more vote. "Boyle." Six-five. The chairman took some considerable time opening the last slip.

"Boyle," he announced in triumph.

He paused for effect. "Six votes all," he declared. "Under standing order forty-two of the Party Constitution," he said, as if he had learnt the words off by heart before the meeting, "in the result of a tie the chairman shall have the casting vote." He paused once again.

"Boyle," he said, lingering for a moment. "I therefore declare that Frank Boyle is selected as the official Labour Party candidate for the constituency of Edinburgh Carlton at the next general election." He turned to Andrew and said, "We shall no longer be requiring your services, Mr Fraser."

"I would like to thank those of you who supported me," Andrew said quietly and left without another word.

The next day the *Scotsman* came out with a lengthy article on the dangers of a small group of wilful people having the power to remove a member who had served his constituents honourably over a long period of time. Andrew phoned Stuart Gray to thank him. "I only wish the article had come out the day before," he said.

"It was set up for yesterday," Stuart told him, "but the announcement from Buckingham Palace of Prince Charles's engagement to Lady Diana Spencer moved everything else out – even the Rangers–Celtic report. By the way, doesn't Boyle's nomination have to be confirmed by his General Management Committee?"

"Yes, but they are putty in his hands. That would be like trying to explain to your mother-in-law about your wife's nagging."

"Then why don't you appeal to the National Executive and ask for the decision to be put to a full meeting of the constituency party?"

"Because it would take weeks to get the decision overturned and more importantly I'm no longer certain that I want to fight the seat as a Labour candidate."

Andrew listened to the reporter's question and said, "Yes, you may quote me."

As the date for an election drew nearer Charles decided it might be wise to introduce Amanda to the constituency. He had explained to those who inquired that his wife had had rather a bad time of it after the birth, and had been told by her doctors not to participate in anything that might raise her blood pressure – though one or two constituents considered that the Sussex Downs' Conservatives would find it hard to raise the blood pressure of a ninety-year-old with a pacemaker. Charles had also decided to leave Harry at home, explaining that it was he who had chosen a public life, not his son.

The annual Garden Party held in the grounds of Lord Cuckfield's country home seemed to Charles to be the ideal opportunity to show off Amanda and he asked her to be certain to wear something appropriate.

He was aware that designer jeans had come into fashion, and that his clothes-conscious wife never seemed to dress in the same thing twice. He also knew that liberated women didn't wear bras. But he was nevertheless shocked when he saw Amanda in a near see-through blouse and jeans so tight it looked as if she had been poured into them. Charles was genuinely horrified.

"Can't you find something a little more . . . conservative?" he suggested.

"Like the things that old frump Fiona used to wear?"

Charles couldn't think of a suitable reply. "The Garden Party will be frightfully dull," said Charles desperately. "Perhaps I should go on my own."

Amanda turned and looked him in the eye. "Are you ashamed of me, Charlie?"

He drove his wife silently down to the constituency and every time he glanced over at her he wanted to make an excuse to turn back. When they arrived at Lord Cuckfield's home his worst fears were confirmed. Neither the men nor the women could take their eyes off Amanda as she strolled around the lawns devouring strawberries. Many of them would have used the word "hussy" if she hadn't been the member's wife.

Charles might have escaped lightly had it only been the one *risqué* joke Amanda told – to the bishop's wife – or even her curt refusals to judge the baby contest or to draw the raffle; but he was not to be so lucky. The chairman of the Women's Advisory Committee had met her match when she was introduced to the member's wife.

"Darling," said Charles. "I don't think you've met Mrs Blenkin-sop."

"No, I haven't," said Amanda, ignoring Mrs Blenkinsop's out-stretched hand.

"Mrs Blenkinsop," continued Charles, "was awarded the OBE for her services to the constituency."

"OBE?" Amanda asked innocently.

Mrs Blenkinsop drew herself up to her full height.

"Order of the British Empire," she said.

"I've always wondered," said Amanda, smiling. "My dad used to tell me it stood for 'other buggers' efforts'."

"Seen the Persil anywhere?" asked Louise.

"No, I stopped washing my own pants some time ago," replied Andrew.

"Ha, ha," said Louise. "But if you haven't taken them who has – two giant packets are missing?"

"The phantom Persil thief strikes again. Whatever next?" said Andrew. "The Bovril perhaps?"

"Stop making a fool of yourself and go and fish Clarissa out of the bath."

Andrew pulled himself out of the armchair, dropped *The Economist* on the carpet and ran upstairs. "Time to get out, young lady," he said even before he reached the bathroom door. First he heard the sobbing then when he opened the door he found Clarissa covered from head to toe in soap flakes. Her thick black curly hair was matted with them. Andrew burst out laughing but he stopped when he saw Clarissa's knees and shins were bleeding. She held a large scrubbing brush in one hand which was covered in a mixture of soap powder and blood.

"What's the matter, darling?" asked Andrew, kneeling on the bath mat.

"It isn't true," said Clarissa, not looking at him.

"What isn't true?" asked Andrew gently.

"Look on the box," she said pointing at the two empty packets which were standing on the end of the bath. Andrew glanced at the familiar picture on the box of a little fair-haired girl in a white party dress.

"What isn't true?" he repeated, still uncertain what Clarissa meant.

"It isn't true that Persil washes whiter and can remove even the blackest spots. Two large packets and I'm still black," she said.

Andrew had to smile which only made Clarissa cry even more. After he had washed off all the suds and gently dried her he put antiseptic ointment on the cuts and bruises.

"Why am I so black?" she asked.

"Because your mother and father were black," replied Andrew, guiding his daughter through to her bedroom.

"Why can't you be my father? Then I'd be white."

"I am your father now so you don't need to be."

"Yes, I do."

"Why?"

"Because the children at school laugh at me," Clarissa said, clutching firmly on to Andrew's hand.

"When I was at school they used to laugh at me because I was small," said Andrew. "They called me puny."

"What did you do about it?" asked Clarissa.

"I trained hard and ended up as captain of the school rugby team and that made them stop laughing."

"But by then you were big. I can't train to be white."

"No, I was still small, and you won't need to train."

"Why?" asked Clarissa, still not letting go of his hand.

"Because you're going to be beautiful, and then all those ugly white girls will be oh so jealous."

Clarissa was silent for some time before she spoke again.

"Promise, Daddy?"

"I promise," he said, remaining on the edge of the bed.

"Like Frank Boyle is jealous of you?"

Andrew was startled. "What do you know about him?"

"Only what I heard Mummy say, that he's going to be the Labour man for Edinburgh, but you'll still beat him."

Andrew was speechless.

"Is he going to be the Labour man, Daddy?" she asked.

"Yes, he is."

"And will you beat him?"

"I'll try."

"Can I help?" Clarissa asked, a tiny smile appearing on her face.

"Of course. Now off you go to sleep," said Andrew, getting up and drawing the curtains.

"Is he black?"

"Who?" asked Andrew.

"The nasty Frank Boyle."

"No," said Andrew laughing, "he's white."

"Then he ought to be made to have my skin then I could have his."

Andrew turned off the light, relieved Clarissa could no longer see his face.

Harry's second birthday party was attended by all those two-year-olds in the vicinity of Eaton Square whom his nanny considered acceptable. Charles managed to escape from a departmental meeting accompanied by a large paint board and a red tricycle. As he parked his car in Eaton Square he spotted Fiona's old Volvo driving away towards Sloane Square. He dismissed the coincidence although he still had plans for regaining the priceless Holbein. Harry naturally wanted to ride the tricycle round and round the dining-room table. Charles sat watching his son and couldn't help noticing that he was smaller than most of his friends. Then he remembered that great-grandfather had only been five feet eight inches tall.

It was the moment after the candles had been blown out, and nanny switched the light back on, that Charles was first aware that something was missing. It was like the game children play with objects on a tray: everyone shuts his eyes, nanny takes one away and then you all have to guess which piece it was.

It took Charles some time to realise that the missing object was his gold cigar box. He walked over to the sideboard and studied the empty space. He continued to stare at the spot where the small gold box left to him by his great-grandfather had been the previous night. Now all that was left in its place was the matching lighter.

He immediately asked Amanda if she knew where the heirloom was, but his wife seemed totally absorbed in lining up the children for a game of musical chairs. After checking carefully in the other rooms Charles went into his study and phoned the Chelsea police.

An inspector from the Crime Squad came round immediately and took down all the details. Charles was able to supply the police officer with a photograph of the box which carried the initials C.G.S. He stopped just short of mentioning Fiona by name. The inspector assured Charles that he would deal with the investigation personally. Charles returned to the party to find nannies arriving to gather their wards.

When the Edinburgh Carlton Labour party issued a press statement after their AGM announcing that Frank Boyle had been selected to fight the seat as their candidate Andrew was surprised and touched by the flood of letters and calls of goodwill he received, many from people he didn't even know. Most of the messages begged him to stand at the next general election as an Independent.

Twenty Labour MPs and one Conservative had joined the newly formed Social Democratic Party and many others were expected to follow. Andrew knew he would have to make an announcement soon if he didn't want his supporters to drift away. He spent agonising hours discussing with Louise the problem of severing the final bonds with the party.

"What shall I do?" he asked, yet again.

"I can't tell you that; I just hope you make up your mind fairly quickly."

"Why quickly?"

"Because I'm going to vote for the Social Democrats at the next election, so you had better be my local candidate."

A few days later Roy Jenkins, Andrew's old chief at the Home Office, phoned to say he was fighting a by-election in Glasgow as the SDP candidate.

"I do hope you will feel able to join us," said Jenkins.

Andrew had always admired Jenkins's firm stand against the left and felt he was the one man who might break the two-party system.

"I need a little more time," he replied.

A week later Andrew made up his mind and informed the Chief Whip that he was leaving the party and would be joining the SDP. Then he packed a bag and travelled to Glasgow.

Roy Jenkins won the seat at Glasgow Hillhead with a large enough swing to worry both main parties. By Easter, a total of twenty-nine

Members of Parliament had broken away to join him, while the alliance of SDP and Liberal MPs together could muster more than forty votes on the floor of the House.

With opinion polls putting them in second place, it began to look possible that the Social Democrats might hold the balance of power after the next election. The Conservatives were now running a poor third in all the national opinion polls.

Charles heard nothing for three weeks about the missing gold box and was beginning to despair when the inspector phoned to say that the family heirloom had been found.

"Excellent news," said Charles. "Are you able to bring the box round to Eaton Square?"

"It's not quite as simple as that, sir," said the policeman.

"What do you mean?"

"I would prefer not to discuss the matter over the phone. May I come and see you, sir?"

"By all means," said Charles, slightly mystified.

He waited impatiently for the inspector to arrive, although the policeman was at the front door barely ten minutes later. His first question took Charles by surprise.

"Are we alone, sir?"

"Yes," said Charles. "My wife and son are away visiting my mother-in-law in Wales. You say you've found the gold box," he continued, impatient to hear the inspector's news.

"Yes, sir."

"Well done, Inspector. I shall speak to the Commissioner personally," he added, guiding the officer towards the drawing-room.

"I'm afraid there's a complication, sir."

"How can there be when you've found the box?"

"We cannot be sure there was anything illegal about its disappearance in the first place."

"What do you mean, Inspector?"

"The gold case was offered to a dealer in Grafton Street for £2,500."

"And who was doing the selling?" asked Charles impatiently.

"That's the problem, sir. The cheque was made out to Amanda Seymour and the description fits your wife," said the inspector. Charles was speechless. "And the dealer has a receipt to prove the transaction." The inspector passed over a copy of the receipt. Charles was unable to steady his shaking hand as he recognised Amanda's signature.

"Now, as this matter has already been referred to the Director of Public Prosecutions I thought I ought to have a word with you in private, as I am sure you would not want us to prefer charges."

"Yes, no, of course, thank you for your consideration, Inspector," said Charles flatly.

"Not at all, sir. The dealer has made his position clear: he would be only too happy to return the cigar box for the exact sum he paid for it. I don't think that could be fairer."

Charles made no comment other than to thank the inspector again before showing him out.

He returned to his study, phoned Amanda at her mother's house and told her to return immediately. She started to protest, but he had already hung up.

Charles remained at home until they all arrived back at Eaton Square late that night. The nanny and Harry were immediately sent upstairs.

It took Charles about five minutes to discover that only a few hundred pounds of the money was left. When his wife burst into tears he struck her across the face with such force that she fell to the ground. "If anything else goes missing from this house," he said, "you will go with it and I will also make sure you spend a very long time in jail." Amanda ran out of the room sobbing uncontrollably.

The next day Charles advertised for a full-time governess. He also moved his own bedroom to the top floor so that he could be close to his son. Amanda made no protest.

Once the governess had settled in Amanda quickly became bored with the child and began disappearing for long periods. Charles couldn't be sure where she was most of the time, and didn't care.

After Pimkin had recounted the latest state of affairs to Alexander Dalglish in well-embroidered detail Fiona remarked to her husband, "I never thought the day would come when I would feel sorry for Charles."

On a sleepy Thursday in April 1982 Argentina attacked and occupied two small islands whose 1,800 British citizens were forced to lower the Union Jack for the first time in over a hundred years. Few members returned to their constituency that Friday and the House met unusually on a Saturday morning to debate the crisis while the nation followed every word on the radio.

The same day Mrs Thatcher immediately despatched a task force halfway around the globe to recapture the islands. Her fellow countrymen followed every scrap of news so intently that the London theatres found themselves empty at the height of the season.

Simon felt exhilarated to be a member of the Defence team at such a historic moment, and Elizabeth didn't begrudge him those days when he left before she had woken and arrived home after she had fallen asleep.

Under less public scrutiny but almost equal pressure, Charles beavered away at the Treasury addressing the economic problems that had been presented, he spent day after day in the House helping to put the Government's case. Like Simon he found he could only snatch moments to be at home but, unlike Elizabeth, his wife remained in bed until midday. When Charles did manage to slip away from the department he spent all his spare time with Harry, whose progress he followed with delighted concern.

At the time when the Union Jack was raised once again in the Falklands, the budget became an Act.

CHAPTER TWENTY EIGHT

"PM to go in Nov." and "Will Maggie wait till June?" were two of the headlines Andrew read on the first day of the new Parliamentary session.

Anyone who is defending a marginal seat is always on edge as the statutory five years draws to a close, and the new SDP members all treated their seats as marginal. Andrew was no exception.

He had worked hard to prove he was worth his place in the group the leader of the Social Democrats was beginning to form in the Commons. When Roy Jenkins had announced the make-up of his Shadow team Andrew was appointed Defence spokesman and enjoyed the challenge of pitting himself against the two main parties in the Commons in the run-up to the election. But once the Falklands crisis was over he knew his real problems were not going to be in Westminster but in Edinburgh, where he spent an increasing amount of his time. Hamish Ramsey phoned to ask him if there was anything he could do to help.

"Be my chairman for the election campaign," said Andrew simply.

Ramsey agreed without hesitation and within a fortnight four members of Andrew's old Labour party committee had defected to join him. Support for Andrew came from the most surprising quarters, including Jock McPherson, who pledged that the Scottish Nationalists would not be contesting the Edinburgh Carlton seat as they had no desire to see Frank Boyle in Parliament. Sir Duncan Fraser kept very quiet about what the Conservatives were up to until they announced that Jamie Lomax would be their standard-bearer.

"Lomax. Lomax," repeated Andrew. "He and I were at school together," he told his father. "He was known as Loopy Lomax. You've selected the biggest idiot of his generation."

"That's a disgraceful slur on an able man," said Sir Duncan, trying to keep a straight face. "I can assure you it took a lot of convincing the committee to make certain Lomax was selected."

"How did you fix it?"

"I must admit it wasn't easy. We had some very good applicants, but I managed to undermine every one of them and point out how blemish-free Lomax's political past was," said Sir Duncan, winking.

"Non-existent careers make for the best blemish-free pasts," said Andrew, and burst out laughing.

"Yes, I'm afraid one or two of the committee noticed that. But you must admit Lomax is a fine figure of a man," added his father.

"What's that got to do with it?" asked Andrew. "You weren't looking for a male model as candidate."

"I know, but it did help me to swing the ladies on the Women's Advisory Committee round to my way of thinking."

"You're a rogue, Father."

"No, I'm not. There isn't a Conservative in Scotland who would rather see Frank Boyle in the House than you, and as we have no chance of winning the seat, why let *him* in?"

Louise and Clarissa spent the Christmas recess in Edinburgh. Sir Duncan warned Louise that if Andrew lost this election he could never hope to return to the House of Commons again.

During 1983 Margaret Thatcher stuck firm to her monetarist policies and brought inflation below four per cent, while in parts of Scotland unemployment rose to fifteen per cent. She had gradually stifled any opposition from the "wets" and by the end of her first administration they were totally outmanoeuvred. But it was the outcome of the Falklands crisis that had kept her ahead in the opinion polls for over a year. The press speculated on the date of the general election all through the month of April, and after the Conservatives' success in the local elections on 5 May the Prime Minister sought an audience with the Queen. Shortly afterwards Margaret Thatcher told the nation that she needed another five years to continue her policies and prove that they worked. The election date was set for 9 June.

Once the election campaign had begun in earnest Stuart Gray interviewed all three candidates on behalf of the *Scotsman* and told Andrew he had a plan to help him.

"You can't," said Andrew. "You're bound to remain neutral and give all three candidates equal column inches during the campaign."

"Agreed," said Stuart. "But on the one hand we know Frank Boyle is sharp and has the looks of an escaped convict, while Jamie Lomax looks like a film star but makes crass statements every time he opens his mouth."

"So?" said Andrew.

"So I'm going to cover the political pages with the worst shots I can find of Boyle and fill up inch after inch with the sayings of Lomax. They'll both get equal coverage while at the same time they'll lose votes."

"They'll sus it out and complain to the editor."

"I doubt it," said Stuart. "I have yet to meet a politician who complained about having his photo in the paper, or one who was angered by seeing his mad views aired to a larger audience than he could have hoped to influence in the past."

"And what do you propose to do about me?"

"That's a problem," admitted Stuart, laughing. "Perhaps I'll leave the columns blank. That's one way you can't lose votes."

Whenever Andrew carried out a door-to-door canvass he found a clear division between those who still backed him and those who thought he had been disloyal to the Labour Party. As the canvass returns came in and the colours were put out on the trestle tables in the new party headquarters it became clear from even a cursory glance that it was going to be his toughest election yet.

Andrew had experienced some dirty campaigns over the years, especially when he had been up against the Scottish Nationalists, but after only a few days he had sweet memories of Jock McPherson who was Little Red Riding Hood compared with Boyle. Andrew could just about tolerate hearing that he had been thrown out of the Labour Party because he was such a lazy member, even that he had left them in the lurch because he had been told he could never hope to be a minister again, but when it was repeated to him that the Boyle camp were spreading a rumour that Louise had lost her voice because, when she had her baby, it turned out to be black he was furious.

If Andrew had seen Boyle that day he would undoubtedly have hit him. Sir Duncan counselled restraint, pointing out that any other action could only harm Louise and Clarissa. Andrew took a deep breath and said nothing.

With a week to go a local opinion poll in the *Scotsman* showed Boyle leading by thirty-five per cent to Andrew's thirty-two. The Conservatives had nineteen per cent but fourteen per cent remained undecided. Jock McPherson had kept his word: no Scottish Nationalist candidate had entered the lists.

On the Friday before the election McPherson went one better by issuing a statement advising his supporters to back Andrew Fraser.

When Andrew phoned to thank him, he said, "I'm returning a favour."

"I don't remember ever doing you a favour," said Andrew.

"You certainly did, remembering you're an Edinburgh man. One mention to the press of my offer of the leadership of the Scottish Nationalists and I'd have been sunk down the nearest pothole."

With five days to go Alliance supporters from the two Edinburgh constituencies which were not fielding an SDP candidate swarmed in to help Andrew, and he began to believe the canvass returns that were now showing he could win. With two days to go the *Scotsman* proclaimed it was thirty-nine per cent to thirty-eight per cent in Boyle's favour, but also went on to point out that the Labour party would have a better-oiled machine to depend on when it came to polling day.

In his eve-of-poll message Andrew issued a clear statement on why his views differed from those of his opponent in the Labour party, and how he saw the future of Britain if the Alliance gained enough seats to hold the balance of power. He reminded voters that without exception the national opinion polls showed the SDP now running neck and neck with Labour.

Frank Boyle also put out an eve-of-poll message, delivered to every house in the constituency, showing a picture of Andrew holding Clarissa in his arms under the caption "Does your member tell you the whole truth?" There was no mention of Louise or Clarissa in the text but the innuendo could not have been clearer. Andrew didn't see the sheet until the morning of polling day by which time he knew there was nothing effective he could do to refute Boyle's implied slur. Issuing a writ that could not be dealt with until weeks after the election was over could only prove impotent. He either won the day or he lost it.

To that end, he and Louise never stopped working from seven that morning until ten at night. Helpers arrived from the most unexpected places, as if to prove the *Scotsman* wrong about the Labour Party machine, but Andrew couldn't help noticing that there were red rosettes everywhere he went.

Towards the end of the day even Sir Duncan joined him and began chauffeuring SDP voters to the polls in his Rolls Royce.

"We've faced the fact that our candidate has lost so now I've come to help you," he told Andrew bluntly.

As the city hall clock struck ten Andrew sat down on the steps of the last polling station. He knew there was nothing he could do now. He had done everything possible, only avoiding members of the House of Lords and lunatics – neither of which group was entitled to vote.

An old lady was coming out of the polling station with a smile on her face.

"Hello, Mrs Bloxham," said Andrew. "How are you?"

"I'm fine, Andrew," she smiled. "I nearly forgot to vote and that would never have done."

He raised his tired head.

"Now don't fret yourself, laddie," she continued, "I never failed to vote for the winner in fifty-two years and that's longer than you've lived." She chuckled and left him sitting on the steps.

Andrew somehow picked himself up and made his way through the dark cobbled streets to his election headquarters. They cheered him as he entered the room, and the chairman offered him a "wee dram of whisky".

"To hell with a wee dram," said Andrew. "Just keep pouring."

He tried to get round the room to thank everyone before Hamish Ramsey told him it was time to go over to the city hall for the count. A small band of supporters accompanied the Frasers to the city hall to witness the proceedings. As he entered the hall the first person he saw was Boyle, who had a big smile on his face. Andrew was not discouraged by the smile as he watched the little slips of paper pour out of the boxes. Boyle had yet to learn that the first boxes to be counted were always from the inner wards, where most of the committed Socialists lived.

As both men walked round the tables, the little piles began to be checked – first in tens, then hundreds, until they were finally placed in thousands and handed over to the Sheriff. As the night drew on Boyle's smile turned to a grin, from a grin to a poker face, and finally to a look of anxiety as the piles grew closer and closer in size.

For over three hours the process of emptying the boxes continued and the scrutineers checked each little white slip before handing in their own records. At one twenty-two in the morning the Sheriff added up the list of numbers in front of him and asked the three candidates to join him.

He told them the result.

Frank Boyle smiled once again. Andrew showed no emotion, but called for a recount.

For over an hour, he paced nervously around the room as the scrutineers checked and double-checked each pile: a change here, a mistake there, a lost vote discovered and, on one occasion, the name on the top of a pile of one hundred votes was not the same as the ninety-nine beneath it. At last the scrutineers handed back their figures. Once again the Sheriff added up the columns of numbers and asked the candidates to join him.

This time Andrew smiled while Boyle looked surprised and demanded another recount. The Sheriff acquiesced, but said it must be the last time. Both candidates agreed in the absence of their Conservative rival, who was sleeping soundly in a corner, secure in the knowledge that no amount of recounting would alter his position in the contest.

Once again the piles were checked and double-checked and five mistakes were discovered in the 42,588 votes cast. At three-twenty a.m., with counters and checkers falling asleep at their tables, the Sheriff once more asked the two candidates to join him. They were both stunned when they heard the result and the Sheriff informed them that there would be a further recount in the morning after his staff had managed to get some sleep.

All the voting papers were then placed carefully back in the black boxes, locked and left in the safe-keeping of the local constabulary while the candidates crept away to their beds.

Andrew slept in fits and starts through the remainder of the night. Louise, pale with exhaustion but still grinning, brought him a cup of tea at eight in the morning. He took a cold shower, shaved slowly and was back at the city hall a few minutes before the count was due to recommence. As he walked up the steps he was greeted by a battery of television cameras and journalists who had heard rumours as to why the count had been held up overnight and knew they couldn't afford to be absent as the final drama unfolded.

The counters looked eager and ready when the Sheriff checked his watch and nodded. The boxes were unlocked and placed in front of the staff for the fourth time. Once again the little piles grew from tens into hundreds and then into thousands. Andrew paced around the tables, more to burn up his nervous energy than out of a desire to keep checking. He had thirty witnesses registered as his counting agents to make sure he didn't lose by sleight of hand or genuine mistake.

Once the counters and scrutineers had finished they sat in front of their piles and waited for the slips to be collected and taken to the Sheriff. When the Sheriff had added up his little columns of figures for the final time he found that no votes had changed hands.

He explained to Andrew and Frank Boyle the procedure he intended to adopt in view of the outcome. He told both candidates that he had spoken to Lord Wylie at nine that morning and the Lord Advocate had read out the relevant statute in election law that was to be followed in such circumstances. Both candidates agreed on which of the two choices they preferred.

The Sheriff walked up on to the stage with Andrew Fraser and Frank Boyle in his wake, both looking anxious.

Everyone in the room stood to be sure of a better view of the proceedings. When the pushing back of chairs, the coughing and the nervous chattering had stopped, the Sheriff began. First he tapped the microphone that stood in front of him to be sure it was working. The metallic scratch was audible throughout the silent room. Satisfied, he began to speak.

"I, the returning officer for the district of Edinburgh Carlton, hereby declare the total number of votes cast for each candidate to be as follows:

Frank Boyle	18,437
Jamie Lomax	5,714
Andrew Fraser	18,437."

The supporters of both the leading candidates erupted into a noisy frenzy. It was several minutes before the Sheriff's voice could be heard above the babble of Scottish burrs.

"In accordance with section sixteen of the Representation of the People Act 1949 and rule fifty of the Parliamentary Election Rules in the second schedule to that Act, I am obliged to decide between tied candidates by lot," he announced. "I have spoken with the Lord Advocate of Scotland, and have confirmed that the drawing of straws or the toss of a coin may constitute decision by lot for this purpose. Both candidates have agreed to the latter course of action."

Pandemonium broke out again as Andrew and Boyle stood motionless on each side of the Sheriff waiting for their fate to be determined.

"I have borrowed from the Royal Bank of Scotland," continued the Sheriff, aware that twenty million people were watching him on television for the first and probably the last time in his life, "a golden sovereign. On one side is the head of King George III, on the other Britannia. I shall invite the sitting member, Mr Fraser, to call his preference." Boyle curtly nodded his agreement. Both men inspected the coin.

The Sheriff rested the golden sovereign on his thumb, Andrew and Boyle still standing on either side of him. He turned to Andrew and said, "You will call, Mr Fraser, while the coin is in the air."

The silence was such that they might have been the only three people in the room. Andrew could feel his heart thumping in his chest as the Sheriff spun the coin high above him.

"Tails," he said clearly when the coin was at its zenith. The sovereign hit the floor and bounced, turning over several times before settling at the feet of the Sheriff.

Andrew stared down at the lady and sighed audibly. The Sheriff cleared his throat before declaring, "Following the decision by lot, I declare the aforementioned Mr Andrew Fraser to be the duly elected Member of Parliament for Edinburgh Carlton."

Andrew's supporters charged forward and on to the stage and carried him on their shoulders out of the city hall and through the streets of Edinburgh. Andrew searched for Louise and Clarissa, but they were lost in the crush.

The Bank of Scotland presented the golden sovereign to the member the next day, and the editor of the *Scotsman* rang to ask if there had been any particular reason why he had selected tails.

"Naturally," Andrew replied. "George III lost America for us. I wasn't going to let him lose Edinburgh for me."

CHAPTER TWENTY NINE

Raymond read the Daily Mail caption again and smiled: 'On the toss of a coin'.

It saddened Raymond that Andrew had felt it necessary to leave the Labour Party, although he was delighted that he had been returned to the Commons. Raymond was only thankful that there had been no Frank Boyles in his constituency. He often wondered if it was because Joyce kept such a watchful eye on all the committees.

Margaret Thatcher's second victory had come as a bitter blow to him although he couldn't have pretended it was a surprise. Her overall majority of 144 was even larger than had been predicted, while the SDP managed only six seats – although the Alliance were only two percentage points behind Labour in actual votes cast. Raymond was enough of a realist to know that now nothing was going to stop the Tories from governing for another five-year term.

Once again Raymond returned to his practice at the bar and a new round of time-consuming briefs. When the Attorney General, Sir Michael Havers, offered him the chance to become a High Court judge, with a place in the House of Lords, Raymond gave the matter considerable thought before finally asking Joyce for her opinion.

"You'd be bored to tears in a week," she told him.

"No more bored than I am now."

"Your turn will come."

"Joyce, I'm nearly fifty, and all I have to show for it is the chairmanship of the Select Committee on Trade and Industry. If the party fails to win next time I may never hold office again. Don't forget that the last occasion we lost this badly we were in Opposition for thirteen years."

"Once Michael Foot has been replaced the party will take on a new look, and I bet you'll be offered one of the senior Shadow jobs."

"That'll depend on who's our next leader," said Raymond. "And I can't see a great deal of difference between Neil Kinnock who looks unbeatable, and Michael Foot – except that Kinnock's ten years younger than I am."

"Then why not stand yourself?" asked Joyce.

"It's too early for me," said Raymond.

"Then why don't you at least wait until we know who's going to be the leader of the party," said Joyce. "You can be a judge at any time – they die off just as quickly as Cabinet ministers."

When Raymond returned to his chambers the following Monday he followed Joyce's advice and let Sir Michael Havers know that he was not interested in being a judge in the foreseeable future, and settled down to keep a watchful eye on Cecil Parkinson, the new Secretary of State for Trade and Industry.

Only a few days later Michael Foot announced that he would not be standing for leader when the party's annual conference took place. When he informed the Shadow Cabinet several faces lit up at the thought of the forthcoming battle at Brighton in October. Neil Kinnock and Roy Hattersley became the front runners, while during the weeks leading up to the conference several trade unionists and MPs approached Raymond and asked him to stand; but he told them all "next time".

The vote for the new leader took place on the Sunday before the conference began: as Raymond predicted Kinnock won easily and Hattersley, his closest rival, was elected as his deputy.

After the conference Raymond returned to Leeds for the weekend, still confident that he would be offered a major post in the Shadow Cabinet despite the fact that he hadn't supported the winner. Having completed his morning surgery he hung around the house waiting for the new leader to call him, even missing the match against Chelsea. He didn't like being in the second division.

When Neil Kinnock eventually phoned late that evening Raymond was shocked by his offer and replied without hesitation that he was not interested. It was a short conversation.

Joyce came into the drawing-room as he sank back into his favourite armchair.

"Well, what did he offer you?" she asked, facing him.

"Transport. Virtually a demotion."

"What did you say?"

"I turned him down, of course."

"Who has he given the main jobs to?"

"I didn't ask and he didn't volunteer, but I suspect we'll only have to wait for the morning papers to find out. Not that I'm that interested," he continued, staring at the floor, "as I intend to take the first place that comes free on the bench. I've wasted too many years already."

"So have I," said Joyce quietly.

"What do you mean?" asked Raymond, looking up at his wife for the first time since she had come into the room.

"If you're going to make a complete break, I think it's time for me to do so as well."

"I don't understand," said Raymond.

"We haven't been close for a long time, Ray," said Joyce, looking straight into her husband's eyes. "If you're thinking of giving up the constituency and spending even more time in London I think we should part." She turned away.

"Is there someone else?" asked Raymond, his voice cracking.

"No one special."

"But someone?"

"There is a man who wants to marry me," said Joyce, "if that's what you mean. We were at school in Bradford together. He's an accountant now and has never married."

"But do you love him?"

Joyce considered the question. "No, I can't pretend I do. But we're good friends, he's very kind and understanding and, more important, he's there."

Raymond couldn't move.

"And the break would at least give you the chance to ask Kate Garthwaite to give up her job in New York and return to London." Raymond gasped. "Think about it and let me know what you decide." She left the room quickly so that he could not see her tears.

Raymond sat alone in the room and thought back over his years with Joyce – and Kate – and knew exactly what he wanted to do now that the whole affair was out in the open.

He caught the last train to London the same evening because he had to be in court by ten o'clock the next morning to attend a judge's summing up. In the flat that night he slept intermittently as he thought about how he would spend the rest of his new life. Before he went into court the next morning he ordered a dozen red roses via Interflora. He phoned the Attorney General. If he was going to change his life he must change it in every way.

When the summing up was over and the judge had passed sentence Raymond checked the plane schedules. Nowadays you could be there in such a short time. He booked his flight and took a taxi to Heathrow. He sat on the plane praying it wasn't too late and that too much time hadn't passed. The flight seemed endless and he took another taxi from the airport.

When he arrived at her front door she was astonished. "What are you doing here on a Monday afternoon?"

"I've come to try and win you back," said Raymond. "Christ, that sounds corny," he added.

"It's the nicest thing you've said in years," she said as he held her in his arms; over Joyce's shoulder Raymond could see the roses brightening up the drawing-room.

"Let's go and have a quiet dinner."

Over dinner Raymond told Joyce of his plans to accept the Attorney General's offer to join the bench, but only if she would agree to live in

London. After a second bottle of champagne which Joyce had been reluctant to open they finally returned home.

When they arrived back a little after one the phone was ringing. Raymond opened the door and stumbled towards it while Joyce groped for the light switch.

"Ray, I've been trying to get you all night," a lilting Welsh voice said.

"Have you now?" Raymond said thickly, trying to keep his eyes open.

"You sound as if you've been to a good party."

"I've been celebrating with my wife."

"Celebrating before you've heard the news?"

"What news?" said Raymond, collapsing into the armchair.

"I've been juggling the new team around all day and I was hoping you would agree to join the Shadow Cabinet as . . ."

Raymond sobered up very quickly and listened carefully to the new leader. "Can you hold the line?"

"Of course," said the surprised voice the other end.

"Joyce," said Raymond, as she came out of the kitchen clutching two mugs of very black coffee. "Would you agree to live with me in London if I don't become a judge?"

A broad smile spread across Joyce's face with the realization that he was seeking her approval.

She nodded several times.

"I'd be delighted to accept," he said.

"Thank you, Raymond. Perhaps we could meet at my room in the Commons tomorrow and talk over policy in your new field."

"Yes, of course," said Raymond. "See you tomorrow." He dropped the phone on the floor and fell asleep in the chair.

Joyce replaced the phone and didn't discover until the following morning that her husband was the new Shadow Secretary of State for Social Services.

Raymond sold his flat in the Barbican, and he and Joyce moved into a small Georgian house in Cowley Street, only a few hundred yards from the House of Commons.

Raymond watched Joyce decorate his study first, then she set about the rest of the house with the energy and enthusiasm of a newly-wed. Once she had completed the guest bedroom Raymond's parents came down to spend the weekend. He burst out laughing when he greeted his father at the door clutching on to a bag, marked "Gould, the family butcher".

"They do have meat in London, you know," said Raymond.

"Not like mine, son," his father replied.

Over the finest beef Raymond could remember he watched Joyce and his mother chatting away. "Thank God I woke up in time," he said out loud.

"What did you say?" asked Joyce.

"Nothing, my dear, nothing."

Although Raymond spent most of his time on the overall strategy for a future Labour Government, like all politicians he had pet anomalies that particularly upset him. His had always been war widows' pensions, a preoccupation which dated back to his living with his grandmother in Leeds. He remembered the shock when he first realised shortly after leaving university that his grandmother had eked out an existence for thirty years on a weekly widow's pension that wouldn't have covered the cost of a decent meal in a London restaurant.

From the back benches, he had always pressed for the redeeming of war bonds and higher pensions for war widows. His weekly mail showed unequivocally just how major a problem war widows' pension had become. During his years in Opposition he had worked doggedly to achieve ever-increasing, smaller rises, but he vowed that were he to become Secretary of State he would enact something more radical.

Joyce left a cutting from the *Standard* for him to read when he returned from the Commons that night. She had scribbled across it: "This could end up on the front page of every national paper."

Raymond agreed with her, and the following day he tried to press his view on a reluctant Shadow Cabinet who seemed more concerned with the planned series of picketting by the Yorkshire miners' union than the case of Mrs Dora Benson.

Raymond researched the story carefully and discovered that the case didn't differ greatly from the many others he had looked into over the years, except for the added ingredient of a Victoria Cross. By any standards, Mrs Dora Benson highlighted Raymond's cause. She was one of the handful of surviving widows of the First World War and her husband, Private Albert Benson, had been killed at the Somme leading an attack on a German trench. Nine Germans had been killed before Albert Benson died, which was why he had been awarded the VC. His widow had continued working as a cleaner in the King's Head at Barking for over fifty years. Her only possessions of any value were her war bonds, but with no redemption date they were still passing hands at twenty-five pounds each. Mrs Benson's case might have gone unnoticed if in desperation she had not asked Sotheby's to auction her husband's medal.

Once Raymond had armed himself with all the facts he put down a question to the minister concerned asking if he would at last honour the Government's long-promised pledges in such cases. A sleepy but packed House heard Simon Kerslake, as Minister of State for Defence, reply that his department was once again considering the problem and he would make known their findings in the near future. Simon settled back on to the green benches satisfied that would pacify Gould. But Raymond's supplementary stunned him and woke up the House.

"Does the Right Honourable Gentleman realise that this eighty-four-year-old widow, whose husband was killed in action and won the Victoria Cross, has a lower income than a sixteen-year-old cadet on his first day in the armed forces?"

Simon rose once more, determined to put a stop to the issue until he had had more time to study the details of this particular case.

"I was not aware of this fact, Mr Speaker, and I can assure the Right Honourable Gentleman that I shall take into consideration all the points he has mentioned."

Simon felt confident the Speaker would now move on to the next question. But Raymond rose again, the Opposition benches spurring him on.

"Is the Right Honourable Gentleman also aware that an admiral, on an index-linked income, can hope to end his career with a pension of over £500 a week while Mrs Dora Benson's weekly income remains fixed at £47.32?"

There was a gasp even from the Conservative benches as Raymond sat down.

Simon rose again, painfully aware that he was unprepared for Gould's attack and that he had to stifle it as quickly as he could. "I was not aware of that particular comparison either, but once again I can assure the Right Honourable Gentleman I will give the case my immediate consideration."

To Simon's horror Raymond rose from the benches for yet a third time. He could see that Labour members opposite were enjoying the rare spectacle of watching him up against the ropes. "Is the Right Honourable Gentleman also aware that the annuity for a Victoria Cross is £100 with no extra pension benefits? We pay our fourth-division footballers more, while keeping Mrs Benson in the bottom league of the national income bracket."

Simon looked distinctly harassed when he in turn rose for a fourth time and made an uncharacteristic remark that he regretted the moment he said it.

"I take the Right Honourable Gentleman's point," he began, his words coming out a little too quickly. "And I am fascinated by his sudden interest in Mrs Benson. Would it be cynical of me to suggest that it has been prompted by the wide publicity this case has enjoyed in the national press?"

Raymond made no attempt to answer but sat motionless with his arms folded and his feet up on the table in front of him while his own back-benchers screamed their abuse at Simon.

The national papers the next day were covered with pictures of the arthritic Dora Benson with her bucket and mop alongside photos of her handsome young husband in private's uniform. Many of the papers went on to describe how Albert Benson had won his VC, and some of the tabloids used considerable licence. But all of them picked up Raymond's point that Mrs Benson was in the bottom one per cent of the income bracket and that the annuity for a Victoria Cross was a pathetic £100.

It was an enterprising and unusually thorough journalist from the *Guardian* who led her story on a different angle which the rest of the national press had to turn to in their second edition. It transpired that Raymond Gould had put down forty-seven questions concerning war widows' pension rights during his time in the House and spoken on the subject in three budgets and five social service debates from the back benches. He had also made the subject the thrust of his maiden speech over twenty years before. But when the journalist revealed that Raymond gave £500 a year to the Erskine Hospital for wounded soldiers every member knew that Simon Kerslake would have to retract his attack and make an apology to the House.

At three-thirty the Speaker rose from his chair and told a packed house that the Minister of State for Defence wished to make a personal statement.

Simon Kerslake rose warily from the front bench and stood nervously at the dispatch box.

"Mr Speaker," he began. "With your permission and that of the House I would like to make a personal statement. During a question put to me yesterday I impugned the integrity of the Right Honourable Gentleman, the member for Leeds North. It has since been brought to my attention that I did him a gross injustice and I offer the House my sincere apologies, and the Right Honourable Gentleman the assurance that I will not question his integrity a third time."

While younger members were puzzled by the reference, Raymond smiled to himself.

Aware of how rare personal statements were in anyone's parliamentary career, members looked on eagerly to see how he would respond.

He moved slowly to the dispatch box.

"Mr Speaker, I accept the gracious manner in which the Right Honourable Gentleman has apologised and hope that he will not lose sight of the greater issue, namely that of war widows' benefits, and in particular the plight of Mrs Dora Benson."

Simon looked relieved and nodded courteously.

Many Opposition members told Raymond that he should have gone for Simon when he had him on the run, while Tom Carson continued shouting at Simon long after the House had proceeded to the next business. *The Times* leader writer proved them wrong when he wrote the

next morning: "In an age of militant demands from the left, Parliament
and the Labour Party have found a new Clement Attlee on their front
bench. Britain need have no fear for human dignity or the rights of man
should Raymond Gould ever accede to the high office which that
gentleman held."

When Raymond returned home from the Commons that night he
found Joyce had cut out all the press comments for him to study and
had also somehow managed to make inroads into his overflowing
correspondence.

Joyce turned out to have a better feel for gut politics than the entire
Shadow Cabinet put together.

Alec Pimkin threw a party for all his Tory colleagues who had entered
the House in 1964, "To celebrate the first twenty years in the Commons," as he described the occasion in an impromptu after-dinner
speech.

Over brandy and cigars the corpulent, balding figure sat back and
surveyed his fellow members. Many had fallen by the wayside over the
years, but of those that were left, he believed only two men now
dominated the intake.

Pimkin's eyes first settled on his old friend Charles Seymour. Despite
studying him closely he was still unable to spot a grey hair on the
Treasury minister's head. From time to time Pimkin still saw Amanda,
who had returned to being a full-time model and was rarely to be found
in England nowadays. Charles, he suspected, saw more of her on the
covers of magazines than he ever did in his home at Eaton Square.
Pimkin had been surprised by how much time Charles was willing to
put aside for little Harry. Charles was the last man he would have
suspected of ending up a doting father. Certainly there was no sign of
his ambitions diminishing, and Pimkin suspected that only one man
remained a worthy rival for the party leadership.

His eyes moved on to someone for whom in 1984 Orwell's big brother
seemed to hold no fears. Simon Kerslake was deep in animated
conversation about his work on the proposed disarmament talks in
Geneva between Thatcher, Chernenko and Reagan. Pimkin studied
the Defence Minister intently. He considered that had *he* been graced
with such looks he would not have had to fear for his dwindling
majority. Rumours of some financial crisis had long since died away,
and Kerslake now seemed well set for a formidable future.

The party began to break up, as one by one his contemporaries came
over to thank him for such a "splendid", "memorable", "worthwhile"
evening. When the last one had departed and Pimkin found himself
alone he drained the drop of brandy that remained in his balloon and
stubbed out the dying cigar. He sighed as he speculated on the fact that
he could now never hope to be made a minister. He therefore

determined to become a kingmaker, for in another twenty years there would be nothing left on which to speculate.

Raymond celebrated his twenty years in the House by taking Joyce to the Guinea Restaurant off Berkeley Square for dinner. He admired the long burgundy dress his wife had chosen for the occasion and even noticed that one or two women gave it more than a casual glance throughout their meal.

He too reflected on his twenty years in the Commons, and he told Joyce over a brandy that he hoped he would spend more of the next twenty years in Government. 1984 had not turned out to be a good year for the Conservatives, and Raymond was already forming plans to make 1985 as uncomfortable for the Government as possible.

A few weeks later Tony Benn, who had lost his seat at the general election, returned to the House of Commons as the member for Chesterfield. The Conservatives came a poor third and went on to lose two more by-elections early in 1985. Even the press began to acknowledge that the Labour Party was once again looking like a serious alternative Government.

The winter of 1985 brought a further rise in unemployment and in the level of inflation which only increased the Labour party's lead in the polls. For a short period after the Chancellor had brought in an emergency budget the Conservatives fell into third place – for the first time in five years.

Mrs Thatcher was not helped by several internal rebellions. She took them as a cue to introduce new blood into her Cabinet and soon announced the names of those who would be formulating policy in the run-up to the general election. The average age of the Cabinet fell by seven years and the press dubbed it "Mrs Thatcher's new lamps for old reshuffle".

CHAPTER THIRTY

Andrew was on his way to the House of Commons when he heard the first reports on his car radio. There had been no mention of the news in the morning papers so it must have happened overnight. It began with a news flash: just the bare details, HMS *Broadsword*, one of the Navy's destroyers, had been passing through the Gulf of Surt between Tunis and Benghazi when she was boarded by a group of mercenaries, posing as coastguard officials, who took over the ship in the name of Colonel Gaddafi. The newscaster went on to say that there would be a more detailed report in their ten o'clock bulletin.

Andrew had reached his room in the House of Commons by nine-thirty, and he immediately phoned the SDP leader David Owen to discuss the political implications of the news. Once a course of action had been agreed on Andrew took a handwritten letter round to the Speaker's office before the noon deadline, requesting an emergency debate following question time that afternoon. He also sent a copy of the letter by messenger to the Foreign Secretary and the Secretary of State for Defence.

By staying near a radio most of the morning Andrew was able to learn that HMS *Broadsword* was now in the hands of over a hundred guerillas. They were demanding the freedom of all Libyan prisoners in British jails in exchange for the 217-strong crew of the *Broadsword*, who were being held hostage in the engine room.

By twelve o'clock the ticker-tape machine in the Members' Corridor was hovered over by craning necks, and the dining-rooms were so full that many members had to go without lunch.

Question time that day had been allocated to Welsh Affairs, so the Chamber itself did not start filling up until nearly three-fifteen although the Palace of Westminster was already packed and buzzing with each new snippet of information. Political correspondents waited hawk-like in the Members' Lobby seeking opinions on the crisis from any senior politicians as they passed to and from the Chamber. Few were rash enough to say anything that might be re-interpreted the next day.

When Andrew came into the Chamber he took his seat next to David Owen on the Opposition front bench below the gangway. Since

Andrew had the overall responsibility for the Alliance Defence portfolio he was expected to represent the other twenty-two Alliance members. At three-twenty-seven the Prime Minister, followed by the Foreign Secretary and the Secretary of State for Defence, filed into the House and took their places on the Treasury bench. All three looked suitably sombre. The last two questions on Welsh Affairs had the largest audience of members since the Aberfan disaster of 1966.

At three-thirty Mr Speaker Weatherill rose and called for order.

"Statements to the House," he announced in his crisp, military style. "There will be two statements on HMS *Broadsword* before the House debates Welsh Affairs." The Speaker then called the Secretary of State for Defence.

Simon Kerslake rose from the front bench and placed a prepared statement on the dispatch box in front of him.

"Mr Speaker, with your permission and that of the House, I would like to make a statement concerning Her Majesty's frigate HMS *Broadsword*. At seven-forty GMT this morning HMS *Broadsword* was passing through the Gulf of Surt between Tunis and Benghazi when a group of guerillas, posing as official coastguards, boarded the ship and seized the officer in command, Captain Lawrence Packard, and placed the crew under arrest. The captain and his company did everything possible to resist but were outnumbered three to one. The guerillas, claiming to represent the People's Liberation Army, have since placed Captain Packard and the crew in the engine room of the ship. As far as it is possible to ascertain from our Embassy in Tripoli no lives have been lost, although Captain Packard sustained severe injuries during the battle, and we cannot be certain of his fate. There is no suggestion that *Broadsword* was doing anything other than going about her lawful business. This barbaric act must be looked upon as piracy under the 1958 Geneva Convention on the High Seas. The guerillas are demanding the release of all Libyan prisoners in British prisons in exchange for the return of HMS *Broadsword* and her crew. My Right Honourable friend, the Home Secretary, informs me there are only nine known Libyans in British jails at the present time, two of whom have been sentenced to three months for persistent shoplifting, two who were convicted on more serious drug charges, and the five who tried to hijack a British Airways 747 last year. Her Majesty's Government cannot and will not interfere with the due process of law and has no intention of releasing any of these men."

Loud "Hear, hears," came from all sections of the House.

"My Right Honourable friend, the Foreign Secretary, has made Her Majesty's Government's position clear to the Libyan Ambassador, in particular that Her Majesty's Government cannot be expected to tolerate this sort of treatment of British subjects or of British property. We have demanded and expect immediate action from the Libyan

Government."

Simon sat down to loud and prolonged cheers before the leader of the Opposition rose from his place to say that he would wish it to be known that the Opposition gave the Government their full backing. He asked if any plans had been formulated at this early stage for the recovery of *Broadsword*.

Simon rose again. "We are, Mr Speaker, at present seeking a diplomatic solution, but I have already chaired a meeting of the Joint Chiefs and I anticipate making a further statement to the House tomorrow."

"Mr Andrew Fraser," said the Speaker.

Andrew rose from his place. "May I inform the Right Honourable Gentleman that we in the Alliance also concur with his views that this is an act of piracy. But can he tell the House how long he will allow negotiations to continue when it is well known throughout the diplomatic world that Gaddafi is a master of procrastination, especially if we were to rely on the United Nations to adjudicate on this issue?" From the noise that greeted Andrew's question it seemed that his views were shared by the majority of the House.

Simon rose to answer the question. "I accept the point the Honourable Gentleman is making but he will know, having been a Minister of State for Defence himself, that I am not in a position to divulge any information which might imperil the safety of *Broadsword*."

Question after question came at Simon. He handled them with such confidence that visitors to the Strangers' Gallery would have found it hard to believe that he had been invited to join the Cabinet only five weeks before.

At four-fifteen, after Simon had answered the last question the Speaker was going to allow, he sank back on the front bench to listen to the statement from the Foreign Office. The House fell silent once again as the Foreign Secretary rose from his place and checked the large double-spaced sheets in front of him. All eyes were now on the tall, elegant man who was making his first official statement since his appointment.

"Mr Speaker, with your permission and that of the House, I too would like to make a statement concerning HMS *Broadsword*. Once news had reached the Foreign Office this morning of the plight of Her Majesty's ship *Broadsword* my office immediately issued a strongly worded statement to the Government of Libya. The Libyan Ambassador has been called to the Foreign Office and I shall be seeing him again immediately this statement and the questions arising from it has been completed."

Raymond looked up at the Strangers' Gallery from his place on the Opposition front bench. It was one of the ironies of modern diplomacy that the Libyan Ambassador was sitting in the gallery making notes while the Foreign Secretary delivered his statement. He couldn't imagine Colonel Gaddafi inviting the British Ambassador to take notes while he sat in his tent addressing his followers. Raymond was pleased to see an attendant ask the ambassador to stop writing; the prohibition dated from the time when the House had jealously guarded its privacy. Raymond's eyes dropped back to the front bench, and he continued to listen to Charles Seymour.

"Our ambassador to the United Nations has tabled a resolution to be debated by the General Assembly this afternoon, asking representatives to back Britain against this flagrant violation of the 1958 Geneva Convention on the High Seas. I confidently expect the support of the free world over this act of piracy against Her Majesty's ship *Broadsword*. Her Majesty's Government will do everything in its power to ensure a diplomatic solution bearing in mind that the lives of 217 British servicemen are still at risk."

The leader of the Opposition rose for a second time and asked at what point the Foreign Secretary would consider once again breaking off diplomatic relations with Libya.

"I naturally hope it will not come to that, Mr Speaker, and I expect the Libyan Government to deal quickly with their own mercenaries."

Charles continued to answer questions from all sections of the House but could only repeat that there was little new intelligence to offer the House at the present time. Raymond watched his two contemporaries as they displayed over twenty years of parliamentary skill in presenting their case. He wondered if this episode would make one of them Mrs Thatcher's obvious successor.

At four-thirty, the Speaker, realising nothing original had been said for some time, announced that he would allow one further question from each side before returning to the business of the day. He shrewdly called Alec Pimkin who sounded to Raymond like "the very model of a modern major-general" and then Tom Carson who suggested that Colonel Gaddafi was often grossly misrepresented by the British press. Once Carson had sat down, Mr Speaker found it easy to move on to other business.

The Speaker rose again and thanked the Honourable Gentleman, the member for Edinburgh Carlton, for his courtesy in informing him that he would be making an application under standing order number ten for an emergency debate. The Speaker said he had given the matter careful thought but he reminded the House that, under the terms of the standing order, he did not need to divulge the reasons for his decision, merely decide whether the matter should have precedence over the orders of the day. He ruled that the matter was not proper for discussion within the terms of standing order number ten.

Andrew rose to protest but as the Speaker remained standing he had to resume his seat.

"This does not mean, however," continued Mr Speaker, "that I would not reconsider such a request at a later date."

Andrew realised that Charles Seymour and Simon Kerslake must have pleaded for more time, but he was only going to allow them twenty-four hours. The clerk at the table rose and bellowed above the noise of members leaving the Chamber, "Adjournment." The Speaker called the Secretary of State for Wales to move the adjournment motion on the problems facing the Welsh mining industry. The Chamber emptied of all but the thirty-eight Welsh MPs who had been waiting weeks for a full debate on the Principality's affairs.

Andrew went straight to his office and tried to piece together the latest information from news bulletins before preparing himself for a full debate the following day. Simon made his way back to the Ministry of Defence to continue discussions with the Joint Chiefs of Staff, while Charles was driven quickly to the Foreign Office.

When Charles reached his room, he was told by the Permanent Under-Secretary that the Libyan Ambassador awaited him.

"Does he have anything new to tell us?" asked Charles.

"Frankly, nothing; it seems that we're not the only people who are unable to make any contact with Colonel Gaddafi."

"Send him in then."

Charles stubbed out his cigarette and stood by the mantelpiece below a portrait of Palmerston. Charles had never met the ambassador before, largely because he had taken over at the Foreign Office only five weeks previously.

When Mr Kadir, the five-foot-one, dark-haired, immaculately dressed Ambassador for Libya entered the room, the office resembled nothing so much as a study in which a headmaster was about to tick off an unruly boy from the lower fifth.

Charles was momentarily taken aback when he noticed the ambassador's old Etonian tie. He recovered quickly.

"Foreign Secretary?" began Mr Kadir.

"Her Majesty's Government wishes to make it abundantly clear to your Government," began Charles, not allowing the ambassador to complete his sentiments, "that we consider the act of boarding and holding Her Majesty's ship *Broadsword* against her will as one of piracy on the high seas."

"May I say –?" began Mr Kadir.

"No, you may not," said Charles, "and until our ship has been released, we shall do everything in our power to bring pressure, both diplomatic and economic, on your Government."

"But may I just say –?" Mr Kadir tried again.

"My Prime Minister also wants you to know that she wishes to speak to your Head of State at the soonest possible opportunity, so I shall expect to hear back from you within the hour."

"Yes, Foreign Secretary, but may I –"

"And you may further report that we will reserve our right to take any action we deem appropriate if you fail to secure the release into safe custody of HMS *Broadsword* and her crew by twelve noon tomorrow, GMT. Do I make myself clear?"

"Yes, Foreign Secretary, but I would like to ask –"

"Good day, Mr Kadir."

After the Libyan Ambassador was shown out Charles couldn't help wondering what it was he had wanted to know.

"What do we do now?" he asked when the Permanent Under-Secretary returned, having deposited Mr Kadir in the lift.

"We act out the oldest diplomatic game in the world."

"What do you mean?" said Charles.

"Our sit-and-wait policy. We're awfully good at it," said the Permanent Under-Secretary, "but then we've been at it for nearly a thousand years."

"Well, while we sit let's at least make some phone calls. I'll start with Secretary of State Kirkpatrick in Washington and then I'd like to speak to Gromyko in Moscow."

When Simon arrived back at the Ministry of Defence from the Commons he was told that the Joint Chiefs were assembled in his office waiting for him to chair the next strategy meeting. As he entered the room to take his place at the head of the table the Joint Chiefs rose.

"Good afternoon, gentlemen," Simon said. "Please be seated. Can you bring me up to date on the latest situation, Sir John?"

Admiral Sir John Fieldhouse, Chief of the Defence Staff, pushed up the half-moon glasses from the end of his nose and checked the notes in front of him.

"Very little has changed in the last hour, sir," he began. "The Prime Minister's office has still had no success in contacting Colonel Gaddafi. I fear we must now treat the capture of *Broadsword* as a blatant act of terrorism, rather similar to the occupation seven years ago of the American Embassy in Iran by students who backed the late Ayatollah Khomeini. In such circumstances we can either 'jaw-jaw or war-war', to quote Churchill. With that in mind, this committee will have formed a detailed plan by the early evening for the recapture of HMS *Broadsword*, as we assume the Foreign Office are better qualified to prepare for jaw-jaw." Sir John replaced his glasses and looked towards his minister.

"Are you in a position to give me a provisional plan which I could place in front of the Cabinet for their consideration?"

"Certainly, Minister," said Sir John, removing his glasses again before opening a large blue file in front of him.

Simon listened intently as Sir John went over his provisional strategy. Around the table sat eight of the senior-ranking staff officers of the Army, Navy and Air Force, and even the first draft plan bore the stamp of their 300 years of military experience. He couldn't help remembering that his call-up status was still that of a Second Lieutenant. For an hour he asked the Joint Chiefs questions that ranged from the elementary to ones that demonstrated a clear insight into their problems. By the time Simon left the room to attend the Cabinet meeting at No. 10 the Joint Chiefs were already up-dating their plan.

Simon walked slowly across Whitehall from the Department of Defence to Downing Street, his private detective by his side. Downing Street was thronged with people curious to see the comings and goings of ministers involved in the crisis. Simon was touched that the crowd applauded him all the way to the front door of No. 10, where the journalists and TV crews awaited each arrival. The great television arc lights were switched on as he reached the door and a microphone was thrust in front of him, but he made no comment. Simon was surprised by how many of the normally cynical journalists called out, "Good luck" and "Bring our boys home."

The front door opened and he went straight through to the corridor outside the Cabinet room, where twenty-two of his colleagues were already waiting. A moment later the Prime Minister walked into the Cabinet room and took her seat in the centre of the table with Charles and Simon opposite her.

Mrs Thatcher began by telling her colleagues that she had been unable to make any contact with Colonel Gaddafi and that they must therefore decide on a course of action that did not involve his acquiescence. She invited the Foreign Secretary to brief the Cabinet first.

Charles went over the actions in which the Foreign Office was involved at the diplomatic level. He reported his meeting with Ambassador Kadir, and the resolution which had been tabled at the UN and was already being debated at an emergency session of the General Assembly. The purpose of asking the United Nations to back Britain on Resolution 12/40, he said, was to gain the diplomatic initiative and virtually guarantee international sympathy. Charles went on to tell the Cabinet that he expected a vote to take place in the General Assembly in New York that evening which would demonstrate overwhelming support for the United Kingdom's resolution, and which would be regarded as a moral victory by the whole world. He was delighted to be able to report to the Cabinet that the Foreign Ministers of both the United States and Russia had agreed to back the UK in her diplomatic endeavours as long as she launched no retaliatory action. Charles ended by reminding his colleagues of the importance of treating the whole affair as an act of piracy, rather than an injury at the hands of the

Libyan Government itself.

A legal nicety, thought Simon as he watched the faces of his colleagues round the table. They were obviously impressed that Charles had brought the two super powers together in support of Britain. The Prime Minister's face remained inscrutable. She called upon Simon to air his views.

He was able to report that *Broadsword* had, since the last meeting of the Cabinet, been towed into the Bay of Surt and moored; there was no hope of boarding her except by sea. Captain Packard and his crew of 216 remained under close arrest in the engine room on the lower deck of the ship. From confirmed reports Simon had received in the last hour it appeared that the ship's company were bound, gagged and that the ventilation systems had been turned off. "Captain Packard," he informed the House, "had refused to cooperate with the guerillas in any way, and we remain unsure of his fate." He paused. "I therefore suggest," Simon continued, "that we have no choice but to mount a rescue operation in order to avoid a protracted negotiation that can only end in grave loss of morale for the entire armed forces. The longer we put off such a decision the harder our task will become. The Joint Chiefs are putting the final touches to a plan code-named 'Shoplifter' which they feel must be carried out in the next forty-eight hours, if the men and the ship are to be saved." Simon added that he hoped diplomatic channels would be kept open while the operation was being worked out, in order that the rescue team could be assured of the greatest element of surprise.

"But what if your plan fails?" interrupted Charles. "We would risk losing not only *Broadsword* and her crew but also the goodwill of the free world."

"There is no serving officer in the British Navy who will thank us for leaving *Broadsword* in Libyan waters while we negotiate a settlement in which, at best, our ship will be returned when it suits the guerillas – to say nothing of the humiliation of our Navy. Gaddafi can laugh at the United Nations while he has captured not only one of our most modern frigates but also the headlines of the world's press. As Ayatollah Khomeini did, he will want to keep them both for as long as he can. These headlines can only demoralise our countrymen and invite the sort of election defeat Carter suffered at the hands of the American people after the Iranian Embassy débâcle."

"We would be foolish to take such an unnecessary risk while we have world opinion on our side," protested Charles. "Let us at least wait a few more days."

"I fear that if we wait," said Simon, "the crew will be transferred from the ship to a military prison, which would only result in our having two targets to concentrate on, and then Gaddafi can sit around in the desert taking whatever amount of time suits him."

Simon and Charles weighed argument against counter-argument while the Prime Minister listened, taking note of the views of her other colleagues round the table to see if she had a majority for one course or the other. Three hours later, when everyone had given his opinion, she had "fourteen-nine" written on the pad in front of her.

"I think we have exhausted the arguments, gentlemen," she said, "and having listened to the collective views around this table I feel we must on balance allow the Secretary of State for Defence to proceed with Operation Shoplifter. I therefore propose that the Foreign Secretary, the Defence Secretary, the Attorney General and myself make up a sub-committee, backed up by a professional staff, to consider the Joint Chiefs' plan. The utmost secrecy will be required from us at all times, so the subject will not be raised again until the plan is ready for presentation to a full meeting of the Cabinet. Therefore, with the exception of the sub-committee, all ministers will return to their departments and carry on with their normal duties. We must not lose sight of the fact that the country still has to be governed. Thank you, gentlemen." The Prime Minister asked Charles and Simon to join her in the study.

As soon as the door was closed she said to Charles, "Please let me know the moment you hear the result of the vote in the General Assembly. Now that the Cabinet has favoured a military initiative, it is important that you are seen to be pressing for a diplomatic solution."

"Yes, Prime Minister,' said Charles without emotion.

Mrs Thatcher then turned to Simon. "When can I have a run-down on the details of the Joint Chiefs' plan?"

"We anticipate working on the strategy through the night, Prime Minister, and I should be able to make a full presentation to you by ten tomorrow."

"No later, Simon," said the Prime Minister. "Now our next problem is tomorrow's proposed emergency debate. Andrew Fraser will undoubtedly put in a second request for a full debate under standing order number ten and the Speaker gave a clear hint today he will allow it. Anyway, we can't avoid making a policy statement without an outcry from the Opposition benches – and I suspect our own – so I've decided that we will grasp the nettle and no doubt get stung."

The two men looked at each other exasperated at the thought of having to waste precious hours in the Commons.

"Charles, you must be prepared to open the debate for the Government, and Simon, you will wind up. At least the debate will be on Thursday afternoon; that way some of our colleagues may have gone home for the weekend, though frankly I doubt it: But with any luck we will have secured a moral victory at the United Nations, and we can keep the Opposition minds concentrating on that. When you sum up, Simon, just answer the questions put during the debate without offering any new initiative."

She then added, "Report any news you hear direct to me. I shan't be sleeping tonight."

Charles walked back to the Foreign Office, at least thankful that Amanda was somewhere in South America.

Simon returned to the Joint Chiefs to find a large map of Libyan territorial waters pinned to a blackboard. Generals, admirals and air marshals were studying the contours and ocean depths like children preparing for a geography test.

They all stood again when Simon entered the room. They looked at him in anticipation, men of action who were suspicious of talk. When Simon told them the Cabinet's decision was to back the Ministry of Defence the suggestion of a smile came over the face of Sir John. "Perhaps that battle will turn out to be our hardest," he said, just loud enough for everyone to hear.

"Take me through the plan again," said Simon, ignoring Sir John's comment. "I have to present it to the Prime Minister by ten o'clock tomorrow."

Sir John placed the tip of a long wooden pointer on a model of HMS *Broadsword* in the middle of a stretch of water in a well-protected bay.

When Charles reached his office the international telegrams and telexes of support for a diplomatic solution were piled high on his desk. The Permanent Under-Secretary reported that the debate in the United Nations had been so one-sided that he anticipated an overwhelming majority when they came to vote. Charles feared his hands were tied; he had to be seen to go through the motions, even by his own staff, although he had not yet given up hopes of undermining Simon's plan. He intended the whole episode to end up as a triumph for the Foreign Office and not for "those warmongers" at the Ministry of Defence. After consulting the Permanent Under-Secretary Charles appointed a small Libyan task force consisting of some older Foreign Office mandarins with experience of Gaddafi and four of the department's most promising high fliers.

Mr Oliver Miles, the former Ambassador to Libya, had his leave cancelled and was deposited in a tiny room in the upper reaches of the Foreign Office so that Charles could call on his local knowledge at any time, day or night, throughout the crisis.

Charles asked the Permanent Under-Secretary to link him up with Britain's ambassador at the United Nations.

"And keep trying to raise Gaddafi."

Simon listened to Sir John go over the latest version of Operation Shoplifter. Thirty-seven men from the crack Special Boat Service, a branch of the SAS regiment which had been involved in the St James's

Square siege in April 1984, were now in Rosyth on the Scottish coast, preparing to board HMS *Brilliant*, the sister ship to *Broadsword*.

The men were to be dropped from a submarine a mile outside Rosyth harbour and to swim the last mile and a half under water until they reached the ship. They would then board *Brilliant* and expect to recapture her from a mock Libyan crew in an estimated twelve minutes. *Brilliant* would then be sailed to a distance of one nautical mile off the Scottish coast. The operation was to be completed in sixty-five minutes. The SBS planned to rehearse the procedure on *Brilliant* three times before first light the following morning, when they hoped to have the entire exercise down to one hour.

Simon had already confirmed the order to send two submarines from the Mediterranean full steam in the direction of the Libyan coast. The rest of the fleet was to be seen to be conspicuously going about its normal business while the Foreign Office appeared to be searching for a diplomatic solution.

Simon's request to the Joint Chiefs came as no surprise and was granted immediately. He phoned Elizabeth to explain why he wouldn't be home that night. An hour later the Secretary of State for Defence was strapped into a helicopter and on his way to Rosyth.

Charles followed the proceedings at the United Nations live in his office on a satellite link-up. At the end of a brief debate a vote was called for. The Secretary General announced 147–3 in Great Britain's favour, with twenty-two abstentions. Charles wondered if such an overwhelming vote would be enough to get the Prime Minister to change her mind over Kerslake's plan. He checked over the voting list carefully. The Russians, along with the Warsaw Pact countries and the Americans, had kept their word and voted with the UK. Only Libya, South Yemen and Djibouti had voted against. Charles was put through to Downing Street and passed on the news. The Prime Minister, although delighted with the diplomatic triumph, refused to change course until she had heard from Gaddafi. Charles put the phone down and asked his Permanent Under-Secretary to call Ambassador Kadir to the Foreign Office once more.

"But it's two o'clock in the morning, Foreign Secretary."

"I am quite aware what time it is but I can see no reason why, when we are all awake, he should be having a peaceful night's sleep."

When Mr Kadir was shown into his room it annoyed Charles to see the little man still looking fresh and dapper. It was obvious that he had just shaved and put on a clean shirt.

"You called for me, Foreign Secretary?" asked Mr Kadir politely, as if he had been invited to afternoon tea.

"Yes," said Charles. "We wished to be certain that you are aware of the vote taken at the United Nations an hour ago supporting the United Kingdom's Resolution 12/40."

"Yes, Foreign Secretary."

"In which your Government was condemned by the leaders of ninety per cent of the people on the globe" – a fact the Permanent Under-Secretary had fed to Charles a few minutes before Mr Kadir had arrived.

"Yes, Foreign Secretary."

"My Prime Minister is still waiting to hear from your Head of State."

"Yes, Foreign Secretary."

"Have you yet made contact with Colonel Gaddafi?"

"No, Foreign Secretary."

"But you have a direct telephone link to his headquarters."

"Then you will be only too aware, Foreign Secretary, that I have been unable to speak to him," said Mr Kadir with a wry smile.

Charles saw the Permanent Under-Secretary lower his eyes. "I shall speak to you on the hour every hour, Mr Kadir, but do not press my country's hospitality too far."

"No, Foreign Secretary."

"Good night, Ambassador," said Charles.

"Good night, Foreign Secretary."

Kadir turned and left the Foreign Office to be driven back to his Embassy. He cursed the Right Honourable Charles Seymour. Didn't the man realise that he hadn't been back to Libya, except to visit his mother, since the age of four? Colonel Gaddafi was ignoring his ambassador every bit as much as he was the British Prime Minister. He checked his watch: it was two-forty-four.

Simon's helicopter landed in Scotland at two-forty-five. He and Sir John were immediately driven to the dockside, then ferried out to HMS *Brilliant* through the misty night.

"The first Secretary of State not to be piped on board in living memory," said Sir John as Simon made his way with difficulty, his blackthorn stick tapping up the gangplank. The captain of the *Brilliant* couldn't disguise his surprise when he saw his uninvited guests and took them quickly to the bridge. Sir John whispered something in the captain's ear which Simon missed.

"When is the next raid due?" asked Simon, staring out from the bridge but unable to see more than a few yards in front of him.

"They leave the sub at 0300, sir," said the captain, "and should reach *Brilliant* at approximately three-twenty. They hope to have taken command of the ship in eleven minutes and be a mile beyond territorial waters in under the hour."

Simon checked his watch: it was five to three. He thought of the SBS preparing for their task, unaware that the Secretary of State and the

Chief of the Defence Staff were on board *Brilliant* waiting for them. He pulled his coat collar up.

Suddenly he was thrown to the deck, a black and oily hand clamped over his mouth before he could protest. He felt his arms whipped up and tied behind his back as his eyes were blindfolded and he was gagged. He tried to retaliate and received a sharp elbow in the ribs. Then he was dragged down a narrow staircase and dumped on to a wooden floor. He lay trussed up like a chicken for what he thought was about ten minutes before he heard the ship's engines revving up and felt the movement of the ship below him. The Secretary of State could not move for another fifteen minutes.

"Release them," Simon heard a voice say in distinctly Oxford English. The rope around his arms was untied and the blindfold and gag removed. Standing over the Secretary of State was an SBS frogman, black from head to toe, his white teeth gleaming. Simon was still slightly stunned as he turned to see the Services Chief also being untied.

"I must apologise, Minister," said Sir John, as soon as his gag was removed, "but I told the captain not to inform the submarine commander we were on board. If I am going to risk 217 of my men's lives I wanted to be sure this rabble from the SBS knew what they were up to." Simon backed away from the six-foot-two giant who towered over him, still grinning.

"Good thing we didn't bring the Prime Minister along for the ride," said Sir John.

"I agree," said Simon, looking up at the SBS commando. "She would have broken his neck." Everyone laughed except the frogman who pursed his lips.

"What's wrong with him," said Simon.

"If he utters the slightest sound during the first sixty minutes he has no hope of being selected for the final team."

"The Conservative party could do with some back-bench Members of Parliament like that," said Simon, "especially when I have to address the House tomorrow and explain why I'm doing nothing."

By three-forty-nine *Brilliant* was a mile beyond territorial waters. The newspaper headlines that morning ranged from "Diplomatic Victory" in *The Times* to "Gaddafi the Pirate" in the *Mirror*.

At a meeting of the inner Cabinet held at ten in the morning Simon reported his first-hand experience of Shoplifter to the Prime Minister. Charles was quick to follow him. "But after the overwhelming vote in our favour at the UN it must be sensible for us to postpone anything that might be construed as an outright act of aggression."

"If the SBS don't go tomorrow morning we will have to wait another month, Prime Minister," said Simon, interrupting him. All eyes at the meeting of the inner Cabinet turned to Kerslake.

"Why?" asked Mrs Thatcher.

"Because Ramadan, when Moslems fast and cannot take drink during daylight hours, will be coming to an end tomorrow. Traditionally the heaviest eating and drinking takes place the following day, which means tomorrow night will be our best chance to catch the guerillas off guard. I have been over the entire operation in Rosyth and by now the SBS are well on their way to the submarines and preparing for the assault. It's all so finely tuned, Prime Minister, that obviously we can't throw away such a strategic advantage."

"That's good reasoning," she concurred. "With the weekend ahead of us we must pray that this mess will be all over by Monday morning. Let's put on our negotiating faces for the Commons this afternoon. I expect a very convincing performance from you, Charles."

When Andrew rose at three-thirty that Thursday afternoon to ask for a second time for an emergency debate under standing order number ten the Speaker granted his request, directing that the urgency of the matter warranted a debate to commence at seven o'clock that evening.

The Chamber emptied quickly as the members scuttled off to prepare their speeches, although they all knew that less than two per cent of them could hope to be called. The Speaker departed the Chamber and did not return until five to seven when he took over the chair from his deputy.

By seven o'clock, when Charles and Simon had entered the House, all thirty-seven SBS men were aboard Her Majesty's submarine *Conqueror*, lying on the ocean bed about sixty nautical miles off the Libyan coast. A second submarine, *Courageous*, was ten miles to her rear. Neither had broken radio silence for the past twelve hours.

The Prime Minister had still not heard from Colonel Gaddafi and they were now only eight hours away from Operation Shoplifter. Simon looked around him. The atmosphere resembled Budget Day and an eerie silence fell as the Speaker called Andrew Fraser to address the House.

He began by explaining, under standing order number ten, why the matter he had raised was specific, important and needed urgent consideration. He quickly moved on to demand that the Foreign Secretary confirm that if negotiations with Gaddafi failed or dragged on the Secretary of State for Defence would not hesitate to take the necessary action to recover HMS *Broadsword*. Simon sat on the front bench looking glum and shaking his head.

"Gaddafi's nothing more than a pirate," said Andrew. "Why talk of diplomatic solutions?"

The House cheered as each well-rehearsed phrase rolled off Andrew's tongue. When he sat down the cheers came from all parts of the Chamber and it was several minutes before the Speaker could bring

the House back to order. Mr Kadir sat in the Distinguished Strangers'
Gallery staring impassively down, trying to memorise the salient points
that had been made and the House's reaction to them, so that – if he
were ever given the chance – he could pass them on to Colonel Gaddafi.

"The Foreign Secretary," called the Speaker and Charles rose from
his place on the Treasury bench. He placed his speech on the dispatch
box in front of him and waited. Once again the House fell silent.

Charles opened his case by emphasizing the significance of the
United Nations' vote as the foundation for a genuine negotiated
settlement. He went on to say that his first priority was to secure the
lives of the 217 men on board HMS *Broadsword* and that he intended to
work tirelessly to that end. The Secretary General was hoping to
contact Gaddafi personally and brief him on the strong feelings of his
colleagues in the General Assembly. Charles stressed that taking any
other course at the present time could only lose the support and
goodwill of the free world. When Charles sat down he realized that the
rowdy House was not convinced.

The contribution from the back benches confirmed the Prime
Minister's and Simon's beliefs that they had gauged the feelings of the
nation correctly, but neither of them allowed the slightest show of
emotion to cross their faces and give hope to those who were demanding
military action.

By the time Simon rose to wind up for the Government at nine-thirty
that night he had spent two and a half hours in the Chamber listening to
men and women tell him to get on with exactly what he was already
doing. Blandly, he backed the Foreign Secretary in his pursuit of a
diplomatic solution. The House became restive, and when the clock
reached ten Simon sat down to cries of "Resign" from some of his own
colleagues and the more right-wing of the Labour benches.

Andrew watched carefully as Kerslake and Seymour left the Chamber. He wondered what was really going on in his old department.

He arrived home after the debate. Louise congratulated him on his
speech and added, "But it didn't evoke much of a response from Simon
Kerslake."

"He's up to something," said Andrew. "I only wish I was sitting in
his office tonight and could find out what it is."

When Simon arrived in that office he phoned Elizabeth and
explained that he would be spending another night at the ministry.

"Some women do lose their men to the strangest mistresses," said
Elizabeth. "By the way, your younger son wants to know if you will
have time to watch him play hockey in his cuppers' match at Oxford on
Saturday."

"What's today?"

"It's still Thursday," she said, "and you're the one in charge of the
nation's defences."

Simon knew the rescue attempt would be all over one way or the other by lunchtime the next day. Why shouldn't he watch his son play hockey?

"Tell him I'll be there," he said.

Although nothing could be achieved between midnight and six o'clock now the submarines were in place none of the Joint Chiefs left the operations room. Radio silence was not broken once through the night as Simon tried to occupy himself with the bulging red boxes containing other pressing matters which still demanded his attention. He took advantage of the presence of the Joint Chiefs and had a hundred queries answered in minutes that would normally have taken him a month.

At midnight the first editions of the morning papers were brought to him. Simon pinned up the *Telegraph*'s headline on the operations board. "Kerslake's in his Hammock till the great Armada comes." The article demanded to know how the hero of Northern Ireland could be so indecisive while our sailors lay bound and gagged in foreign waters, and ended with the words "Captain, art thou sleeping there below?" "Not a wink," muttered Simon. "Resign" was the single-word headline in the *Daily Express*. Sir John looked over the minister's shoulder and read the opening paragraph.

"I shall never understand why anyone wants to be a politician," he said before reporting: "We have just heard from reconnaissance in the area that both submarines *Conqueror* and *Courageous* have moved up into place."

Simon picked up his stick from the side of his desk and left the Joint Chiefs to go to Downing Street. He took the private lift to the basement and then walked through the tunnel which runs under Whitehall direct to the Cabinet room, thus avoiding the press and any curious onlookers.

He found the Prime Minister sitting alone in the Cabinet room.

Simon went over the final plan with her in great detail, explaining that everything was ready and would be over by the time most people were having their breakfasts.

"Let me know the moment you hear anything, however trivial," she concluded, before returning to the latest gloomy study of the economy from the Wynne Godley team, who were suggesting the pound and the dollar would be on an equal parity by 1988. "One day you may have all these problems on *your* shoulders," she said.

Simon smiled and left her to walk back through the private tunnel to his office on the other side of Whitehall.

He took the lift back up to his room on the sixth floor and joined the Joint Chiefs. Although it was past midnight none of them looked tired despite their all having shared the lonely vigil with their comrades 2,000 miles away. They told stories of Suez and the Falklands, and there was frequently laughter. But it was never long before their eyes returned to the clock.

As Big Ben struck two chimes, Simon thought: four o'clock in Libya. He could visualise the men falling backwards over the side of the boat and deep into the water before starting the long, slow swim towards *Broadsword*.

When the phone rang, breaking the eerie silence like a fire alarm, Simon picked it up to hear Charles Seymour's voice.

"Simon," he began, "I've finally got through to Gaddafi and he wants to negotiate." Simon looked at his watch; the SBS men could only be a few hundred yards from *Broadsword*.

"It's too late," he said. "I can't stop them now."

"Don't be such a bloody fool – order them to turn back. Don't you understand we've won a diplomatic coup?"

"Gaddafi could negotiate for months and still end up humiliating us. No, I won't turn back."

"We shall see how the Prime Minister reacts to your arrogance," said Charles and slammed down the receiver.

Simon sat at his desk and waited for the telephone to ring. He wondered if he could get away with taking the damn thing off the hook – the modern equivalent of Nelson placing the telescope to his blind eye, he considered. He needed a few minutes, but the phone rang again only seconds later. He picked it up and heard Margaret Thatcher's unmistakable voice.

"Can you stop them if I order you to, Simon?"

He considered lying. "Yes, Prime Minister," he said.

"But you would still like to carry it through, wouldn't you?"

"I only need a few minutes, Prime Minister."

"Do you understand the consequences if you fail, with Charles already claiming a diplomatic victory?"

"You would have my resignation within the hour."

"I suspect mine would have to go with it," she said. "In which case Charles would undoubtedly be Prime Minister by this time tomorrow." There was a moment's pause before she continued. "Gaddafi is on the other line and I am going to tell him that I *am* willing to negotiate." Simon felt defeated. "Perhaps that will give you enough time, and let's hope it's Gaddafi who has to worry about resignations at breakfast."

Simon nearly cheered.

"Do you know the hardest thing I have had to do in this entire operation?"

"No, Prime Minister."

"When Gaddafi rang in the middle of the night, I had to pretend to be asleep so that he didn't know I was sitting by the phone."

He laughed.

"Good luck, Simon. I'll phone and explain my decision to Charles." The clock read three-thirty.

On his return the bevy of admirals were variously clenching their fists, tapping the table or walking around it, and Simon began to sense what the Israelis must have felt like as they waited for news from Entebbe.

The phone rang again. He knew it couldn't be the Prime Minister this time as she was the one woman in England who never changed her mind. It was Charles Seymour.

"I want it clearly understood, Simon, that I gave you the news concerning Gaddafi's desire to negotiate at three-twenty. That is on the record, so there will be only one minister handing in his resignation later this morning."

"I know exactly where you stand, Charles, and I feel confident that whatever happens you'll come through your own mound of manure smelling of roses." He slammed down the phone just as four o'clock struck. For no fathomable reason everyone in the room stood up, but as the minutes passed again one by one they sat back down.

At seven minutes past four radio silence was broken with the five words, "Shoplifter apprehended, repeat Shoplifter apprehended."

Simon watched the Joint Chiefs cheer like schoolchildren reacting to the winning goal at a football match. *Broadsword* was on the high seas in neutral waters. He sat down at his desk and asked to be put through to No. 10. The Prime Minister came on the line. "Shoplifter apprehended," he told her.

"Congratulations, continue as agreed," was all she said.

The next move was to be sure that all the Libyan prisoners who had been taken aboard *Broadsword* would be discharged at Malta and sent home unharmed. Simon waited impatiently for radio silence to be broken again, as agreed, at five o'clock.

Captain Lawrence Packard came on the line as Big Ben struck five. He gave Simon a full report on the operation: one Libyan guerilla had been killed and eleven injured. There had been no, repeat no, British deaths and only a few minor injuries sustained. The thirty-seven SBS men were back on board the submarines *Conqueror* and *Courageous*. HMS *Broadsword* had two engines out of action and currently resembled an Arab bazaar, but was sailing the high seas on her way home. God Save the Queen.

"Congratulations, Captain," said Simon. He returned to Downing Street, no longer bothering to use the secret tunnel. As he limped up the road journalists with no idea of the news that was about to be announced were already gathering outside No. 10. Once again he answered none of their shouted questions. When he was shown into the Cabinet room he found Charles already there with the Prime Minister.

He told them both the latest news.

"Well done, Simon," said Mrs Thatcher.

Charles made no comment.

It was agreed that the Prime Minister would make a statement to the House at three-thirty that afternoon.

"I must admit that my opinion of Charles Seymour has gone up," said Elizabeth in the car on the way to Oxford to watch Peter play in his hockey match.

"What do you mean?" asked Simon.

"He's just been interviewed on television. He said he had backed your judgement all along while having to pretend to carry out pointless negotiations. He had a very good line to the effect that it was the first time in his life that he had felt honourable about lying."

"Smelling like roses," Simon said sharply. Elizabeth didn't understand her husband's response.

He went on to tell his wife everything that had gone on between them during the last few hours.

"Why didn't you say something?"

"And admit that the Foreign Secretary and I were quarrelling throughout the entire operation? It would only show up the Government in a bad light and give the Opposition something to latch on to."

"I'll never understand politics," said Elizabeth resignedly.

It amused Simon to watch his son massacred in the mud while he stood on the touchline in the rain only hours after he had feared Gaddafi might have done the same to him. "It's a walkover," he told the Principal when Peter's college were four goals down by half-time.

"Perhaps he'll be like you and surprise us all in the second half," came back the reply.

At eight o'clock on the following Saturday morning Simon sat in his office and heard the news that *Broadsword* had all engines on full speed and was expected to reach Portsmouth by three o'clock, exactly one week after his son had lost his college match eight-nil: they hadn't had a good second half. Simon had tried to console his downcast son but it didn't help that he had been the goalkeeper.

He was smiling when his secretary interrupted his thoughts to remind him that he was due in Portsmouth in an hour. As Simon reached the door the phone rang. "Explain to whoever it is I'm already late," he said.

His secretary replied, "I don't think I can, sir."

Simon turned round, puzzled. "Who is it?" he asked.

"Her Majesty the Queen."

Simon returned to his desk, picked up the receiver and listened to the sovereign. When she had finished Simon thanked her and said he would pass on her message to Captain Packard as soon as he reached Portsmouth. During the flight down Simon looked out of the helicopter and stared at a traffic jam that stretched from the coast to London with people who were going to welcome *Broadsword* home. The helicopter landed an hour later.

The Secretary of State for Defence stood on the pier and was able to pick out the destroyer through a pair of binoculars. She was about an hour away but was already so surrounded by a flotilla of small craft that it was hard to identify her.

Sir John told him that Captain Packard had signalled to ask if the Secretary of State wished to join him on the bridge as they sailed into port. "No, thank you," said Simon. "It's his day, not mine."

"Good thing the Foreign Secretary isn't with us," said Sir John. A squad of Tornadoes flew over, drowning Simon's reply. As *Broadsword* sailed into port, the ship's company were all on deck standing to attention in full dress uniform. The ship itself shone like a Rolls-Royce that had just come off the production line.

By the time the captain descended the gangplank a crowd of some 500,000 were cheering so loudly that Simon could not hear himself speak. Captain Packard saluted as the Secretary of State leaned forward and whispered the Queen's message in his ear:

"Welcome home, Rear-Admiral Sir Lawrence Packard."

CHAPTER THIRTY ONE

The *Broadsword* factor remained in the memories of the electorate for a far shorter time than had the Falklands victory and the Conservative cause was not helped by the breakdown in Geneva of the disarmament talks between Reagan, Chernenko and Thatcher.

The Russians put the blame for the breakdown on Mrs Thatcher's "aggressive stance" over *Broadsword* after they had backed her for a diplomatic solution at the UN. Within six months the Conservative lead in the opinion polls had dropped to three per cent.

"The truth is," noted Raymond at a Shadow Cabinet meeting, "Mrs Thatcher has had nearly eight years at No. 10 and no Prime Minister has served two full terms in succession – let alone three – since Lord Liverpool in 1812."

At that time of the year when referees leave the field to be replaced by umpires Raymond watched his predictions become history. Once the Christmas recess had ended he felt sure the Prime Minister would go to the country in late May or some time in June rather than face another winter. When the Conservatives held on to the marginal seat in Birmingham and fared better than expected at the local elections in May no one believed the Prime Minister would delay the announcement much longer.

Margaret Thatcher seemed to care nothing for Lord Liverpool or historical precedent, because she called an election for late June, believing that the month that had been a winner for her in the past would prove to be good for her again.

"It's time to let the nation choose who is to govern for the next five years," she declared on *Panorama*.

"Of course, it's got nothing to do with the fact she's regained a slight lead in the opinion polls," said Joyce tartly.

"A lead that could well disappear during the next few weeks," Raymond added.

He returned to Yorkshire for only three days of the campaign. As one of the party's leading spokesmen he had to travel around the country addressing meeting after meeting in marginal seats. Many journalists went as far as to suggest that were Raymond leading the party they would be in a far stronger position to win the election. On the few occasions he was back in Leeds he enjoyed the electioneering and felt completely relaxed with his constituents for the first time in his life. He also felt his age when he discovered that the new Tory candidate for Leeds North had been born in 1964, the year he had first entered Parliament. When they met the only insult Raymond suffered at his young rival's hands was being called "sir".

"Please call me by my Christian name," said Raymond.

"Raymond –" began the young man.

"No, Ray will do just fine."

Charles and Simon also saw little of their constituencies as they too toured the marginal seats, adding more and more to their schedules as the polling day became closer. Half-way through the campaign the Conservatives mounted a massive attack on the Alliance, as opinion polls were continuing to show that they were making considerable inroads into the Conservative vote, while traditional Labour supporters were returning to their old allegiance.

Andrew had to remain in Edinburgh for the entire campaign, to face Frank Boyle once again. But this time, as Stuart Gray informed the constituents of Edinburgh Carlton through his columns in the *Scotsman*, it was a Frank Boyle without teeth. Andrew felt what was left of those teeth a few times during the final three weeks but at least the Royal Bank of Scotland did not find it necessary to part with a second golden sovereign in their 300-year history. Andrew retained his seat by over 2,000 votes, to be returned to Parliament for the eighth time. Louise claimed that her husband's majority were the 2,000 people who had fallen in love with the thirteen-year-old coltish Clarissa, who was already fulfilling her father's prophecy as gauche fifteen-year-old Scots blushed in her presence.

The final result of the election did not become clear until four o'clock on the Friday afternoon as several recounts took place up and down the country.

"It will be a hung Parliament," David Dimbleby told the viewers tuned into the BBC "Election Special" programme that afternoon. He repeated the detailed figures for those people still returning from work:

Conservative	317
Labour	288
Liberal/ SDP Alliance	34
Irish/Ulster Unionist	17
Speaker and others	4

Dimbleby went on to point out that there was no necessity for Mrs Thatcher to resign as she was still the leader of the largest party in the Commons. But one thing was apparent, the SDP might well hold the balance at the next election.

The Prime Minister made very few changes to her front-bench team as she clearly wished to leave an impression of unity despite her small majority. The press dubbed it "The cosmetic Cabinet". Charles moved to the Home Office while Simon became Foreign Secretary.

Everyone at Westminster was thankful when a few weeks later Parliament broke up for the summer recess and politicians returned home for a rest.

That rest was to last a complete week before Tony Benn rolled a thundercloud across the clear blue summer sky by announcing he would contest the leadership of the Labour party at the October conference.

Benn claimed that Kinnock's naivety and gauche approach as leader had been the single reason that the Labour party had not been returned to power. There were many Socialists who agreed with this judgement, but they also felt they would have fared considerably worse under Benn.

What his announcement did, however, was to make respectable the claim of any other candidates who wished their names to be put forward. Roy Hattersley and John Smith joined Benn and Kinnock for the first ballot. Many Members of Parliament, trade-union leaders and constituency activists pressed Raymond to stand for the leadership.

"If you don't stand now," Joyce told him, "you'll have no chance in the future."

"It's the future I'm thinking about," replied Raymond.

"What do you mean?" she asked.

"I want to stand for deputy leader against Michael Meacher and John Cunningham, and that will secure me a power base in the party which would afford me a better chance next time."

Raymond waited another week before he launched his candidacy. On the following Monday, at a packed press conference, he announced he would be standing for deputy leader.

With four candidates in the field for the leadership no clear favourite emerged although most prophets accepted Benn would lead after the first ballot. Hattersley came to an agreement with Smith that whichever one of them captured the most votes in the first round the other would drop out and support the leader of the right in the final ballot.

When the vote had been counted Benn, as predicted, topped the first ballot, with Kinnock in third place. To everyone's surprise when Kinnock dropped out he advised his supporters not to back Benn as he felt it could only spell a further prolonged period of Opposition for the Labour Party.

A few hours later the party chairman announced that Tony Benn had been soundly beaten. The Labour Party had a new moderate leader.

The vote then took place for the deputy leadership and although the new leader made clear his preference for Raymond everyone still expected it to be close. Joyce spent the last hour running from delegate to delegate while Raymond tried to appear calm. At eleven o'clock that Sunday night the chairman of the Labour party's National Executive announced that by a mere three per cent Raymond Gould was the newly elected deputy leader of the Labour party.

The new leader immediately appointed Raymond Shadow Chancellor of the Exchequer.

Among the many letters and telegrams Raymond received was one from Kate, which read: Congratulations. But have you read standing order no. 5(4) of the party constitution? Raymond replied: Hadn't. Have now. Let's hope it's an omen.

In their first twelve months the new Labour team looked fresh and innovative as Mrs Thatcher began to look tired and out of touch. She was not helped in her cause by the election of Gary Hart to the White House in November 1988. President Hart's avowed intention to lower unemployment and spend more of the nation's wealth to help "genuine Democrats" left Britain with a handful of new problems. The pound strengthened against the dollar overnight, and large export orders sat gathering dust in dockside warehouses.

But what threw her economic forecasts into total disarray was the decision of the recently elected Governments of Brazil and Argentina to refuse to repay any of the loans negotiated by their former military rulers leaving the Bank of England with what could only be described as an overdraft.

During the long cold winter of 1988 the Conservatives lost several votes on the floor of the House and many more upstairs in committee. The Prime Minister seemed somewhat relieved to find herself spending Christmas at Chequers.

The relief did not last long as two elderly Conservative members died before the House convened in January. The press dubbed the Government the "lame drake" administration.

Both of the pending by-elections were held in May: the Conservatives fared far better than might have been expected, holding on to one and just losing the other. For a third time Mrs Thatcher plumped for a June election.

After a decade of the lady from Grantham Raymond sensed the mood was for change. The monthly unemployment, inflation and import/export figures announced at regular intervals during the campaign all augered badly for the Conservatives.

The Prime Minister's reiterated plea that a Government shouldn't be judged on one month's figures now sounded unconvincing, and by the final week the only point of contention was whether the Labour party would end up with a decent working majority.

Raymond woke up on the Friday morning after the election to be told by Joyce that the computer predictions indicated an overall majority of four seats. Together they toured the constituency that morning before joining Raymond's parents for a late lunch. When they left the little butcher's shop that afternoon there was a crowd of well-wishers awaiting them on the pavement who cheered them all the way to their car. Raymond and Joyce travelled down to London and were back in Cowley Street in time to watch the first Labour Prime Minister since 1979 emerge from Buckingham Palace with the television cameras following him all the way back until he took up residence at 10 Downing Street.

This time Raymond did not have long to wait for a telephone call because the first appointment the new Prime Minister confirmed was his Chancellor. Raymond and Joyce travelled to No. 11 later that afternoon, instructing estate agents to lease their Cowley Street house on a six-month let that might or might not be renewable. Joyce spent hours checking over her new home and replacing some of the objects she had inherited from Diana Brittan while Raymond called his team over from Transport House to prepare the Labour Party's first budget, and replace even more of what Leon Brittan had left behind.

After Raymond's advisers returned to Transport House that night he started to go over the hundreds of letters and telegrams of congratulations that had been flooding in throughout the day. One from America made him particularly happy, and he returned his own best wishes to Mrs Kate Wilberhoff.

Andrew had defeated Frank Boyle for a third time and the left-winger announced that he would not be standing again.

Andrew had also spent a weekend thanking all his helpers. When he returned to the Commons on the Monday morning he found a note awaiting him on the Members' Letter-board.

Over lunch in the Members' Dining-room David Owen informed him privately that he would not be seeking re-election as leader of the SDP: seven years had been quite enough. Although the party had slightly improved their position in the House he accepted that they now faced a five-year Parliament, and he wanted Andrew to take over.

As soon as Owen had issued an official press statement Geoffrey Parkhouse of the *Glasgow Herald* was the first to phone and ask Andrew, "When will you be announcing your bid for the SDP leadership?"

Leaving the Home Office came as a great blow to Charles. His period of time there had been so short that he felt he had achieved very little. The civil servants had procrastinated over all major decisions as they waited for another general election and a clear mandate. He informed Amanda over breakfast on the Monday after the election that he would be returning to Seymour's Bank and that his salary would once again be sufficient for her allowance to remain constant – so long as she kept to her part of the bargain. Amanda nodded and left the breakfast table without comment just as Harry came in.

It was an important morning for Harry as he was to be taken to his first day of prep school at Hill House to begin the academic course mapped out for him by his father. Charles tried to convince him that it would be the start of a wonderful future, but Harry looked apprehensive. Once he had deposited a tearful eight-year-old with his first headmaster Charles continued on to the City, cheerful at the prospect of returning to the world of banking.

When he arrived at Seymour's, he was met by Clive Reynolds's secretary who immediately took him through to the boardroom and asked him if he would like a coffee.

"Thank you," said Charles, taking off his gloves, placing his umbrella in the stand and settling himself in the chairman's seat at the head of the table. "And would you tell Mr Reynolds I'm in?"

"Certainly," said the secretary.

Clive Reynolds joined him a few moments later.

"Good morning, Mr Seymour. How nice to see you again after such a long time," he said, shaking Charles by the hand.

"Good morning, Clive. It's nice to see you too. First I must congratulate you on the manner in which you have conducted the bank's affairs in my absence."

"It's kind of you to say so, Mr Seymour."

"I was particularly impressed by the Distillers takeover; that certainly took the City by surprise."

"Yes, quite a coup, wasn't it?" said Reynolds, smiling. "And there's another one in the pipeline."

"I shall look forward to hearing the details."

"Well, I'm afraid it remains confidential at the moment," said Clive, taking the seat beside him.

"Of course, but now I have returned I had better be briefed fairly soon."

"I'm afraid shareholders cannot be briefed until we are certain the deals have been concluded. We can't afford any rumours harming our chances, can we?"

"But I'm not an ordinary shareholder," said Charles sharply. "I am returning as chairman of the bank."

"No, Mr Seymour," said Reynolds quietly. "I am chairman of this bank."

"Do you realise whom you are addressing?" said Charles.

"Yes, I think so. A former Foreign Secretary, a former Home Secretary, a former chairman of the bank and a two per cent shareholder."

"But you are fully aware that the board agreed to have me back as chairman when the Conservatives went into Opposition," Charles reminded him.

"The composition of the board has changed considerably since those days," said Reynolds. "Perhaps you've been too busy running the rest of the world to notice minor comings and goings in Cheapside."

"I shall call a board meeting."

"You don't have the authority."

"Then I shall demand an Extraordinary General Meeting," said Charles.

"And tell the shareholders what? That you had a standing order to return as Chairman when you felt like it? That won't sound like a former Foreign Secretary."

"I'll have you out of this office in twenty-four hours," Charles continued, his voice suddenly rising.

"I don't think so, Mr Seymour. Miss Trubshaw has completed her five years and left us on a full pension, and it won't take you long to discover that I don't possess a Swiss bank account or a well-compensated mistress."

Charles went red in the face. "I'll get you removed. You don't begin to understand how far my influence stretches."

"I hope I'm not removed, for your sake," said Reynolds calmly.

"Are you threatening me?"

"Certainly not, Mr Seymour, but I would hate to have to explain how Seymour's lost over £500,000 on the Nethercote account because of your personal wish to ruin Simon Kerslake's career. It may interest you to know that the only thing the bank gained from that fiasco was goodwill, and we only managed that because I recommended that Morgan Grenfell pick up the pieces."

Charles couldn't resist a smile. "When I make that public it will finish you," he said triumphantly.

"Perhaps," said Reynolds calmly, "but it would also stop you from becoming Prime Minister."

Charles turned, picked up his umbrella, put on his gloves and walked away. As he reached the door, a secretary walked in holding two cups of coffee. Charles passed her without a word and slammed the door.

"I'll only be needing one, Miss Bristow."

During the first week after the Queen's Speech Andrew was pleased to discover that a majority of his colleagues wrote to say that they would support him if he put his name forward for the leadership of the SDP.

At their weekly parliamentary meeting the party Whip asked that names for the post of party leader be submitted to his office within seven days. Each candidate had to be proposed and seconded by Members of Parliament.

For the next week the popular press tried to suggest, conjure up or even invent a rival for Andrew. Louise, who believed almost everything she read in the papers, took to perusing the *Morning Star*, the only paper which showed no interest in the outcome. But by five o'clock on the seventh day it had become obvious that Andrew was to be the sole nomination.

At the next parliamentary meeting of the SDP he was not so much elected as anointed. On the following Saturday, having been made a Privy Councillor the day before, Andrew addressed the party faithful at a packed Albert Hall. After a well-received speech, the press unanimously predicted – yet again – an SDP–Liberal revival. One or two journalists were quick to point out that if the balance of power did ever rest in his hands the Right Honourable Andrew Fraser might not know which way to jump: with on the one hand a father who was a distinguished Tory, while on the other having been a member of the Labour party himself for twenty years, which party would he consider the lesser of the two evils? Andrew always told the press that he would worry about that when the problem arose, because the SDP might not even be able to come to an agreement with the Liberals.

Numerous articles on the new SDP leader appeared in newspapers and magazines across the country. They all reported the stories of his attempt to save his son's life, the gradual recovery of his wife after Robert's death, the successful adoption of Clarissa and his re-election to Parliament on the toss of a golden sovereign.

All the publicity made Clarissa feel like a film star, she told her father. She was the most popular girl in school, she added, so he had better become Prime Minister. He laughed but proceeded to lead his party with a determination and energy that caused him to be talked of in the same breath as the leaders of the two main parties.

No sooner had the publicity over Andrew's election died down than the press started speculating as to whether Mrs Thatcher would now make way for a younger man.

"Don't you know any other restaurant?"

"Yes, but they don't know me," replied Ronnie Nethercote, as the two men strolled into the Ritz for the first time in a couple of years. Heads turned as people leaned forward and whispered Simon's name to their guests.

"What are you up to nowadays? I can't believe Opposition fully occupies you," Ronnie said as they took their seats.

"Not really. I might also be described as one of the four million unemployed," replied Simon.

"That's what we're here to talk about," said Ronnie, "but first I recommend the country vegetable soup and the . . ."

"Beef off the trolley," interjected Simon.

"You remembered."

"It's the one thing you've always been right about."

Ronnie laughed more loudly than people normally did in the Ritz before saying, "Now you no longer have the entire armed forces at your disposal or ambassadors to call you Your Eminence or whatever they call you now, why don't you join the board of my new company?"

"It's kind of you to ask, Ronnie, but the answer has to be no."

They both broke off their conversation to allow the head waiter to take their orders.

"There's a salary of £20,000 a year that goes with it."

"I can't deny that Elizabeth and I could do with the money. With Peter staying up at Oxford to do a D.Phil. and Michael bent on being an actor I wonder if my bank account will ever be in credit."

"Then why not come in with us?" asked Ronnie.

"Because I'm a committed politician," said Simon, "and I no longer want to involve myself in any commercial activities."

"That might stop you becoming Prime Minister?"

Simon hesitated at the bluntness of Ronnie's question then said, "Frankly, yes. I've got a better than outside chance and I'd be foolish to lengthen the odds by becoming involved in anything else right now."

"But everyone knows that as soon as Margaret announces she's going to pack up you'll be the next leader. It's as simple as that."

"No, Ronnie, it's never as simple as that."

"Then tell me, who could beat you?"

"Charles Seymour, for one."

"Seymour? He's a toffee-nosed git," said Ronnie.

"He has a lot of friends in the party, and his patrician background still counts for something with the Tories. Sir Alec remains the best loved of our most recent Prime Ministers."

"Yes, but he was given the leadership by the magic circle," said Ronnie. "You'd kill Seymour with every elected member of the party having a vote."

"Time will tell," said Simon, bored with a conversation he had had with so many people lately. "But what have you been up to?" he asked, deliberately changing the subject.

"I've been working my backside off in preparation for going public in about a year's time, which is why I wanted you on the board."

"You never give up."

"No, and I hope you haven't given up your one per cent of the company."

"Elizabeth has it locked away somewhere."

"Then you had better find the key."

"Why?" asked Simon.

"Because when I put out ten million shares on the market at three quid a time, your one original share will be exchanged for 100,000 shares of common stock. I know you weren't ever Chancellor but that's £300,000 of anyone's money."

Simon was speechless.

"Well, say something," said Ronnie.

"Frankly I'd forgotten the share existed," Simon finally managed.

"Well, I think I can safely say," said Ronnie, parodying one of Mrs Thatcher's favourite phrases, "that's not a bad investment for a pound, and one you will never regret."

As the budget debate grew nearer Raymond found twenty-four hours each day were not enough, even without sleep. He discussed the changes he required with the Treasury mandarins, but it became more obvious as each week passed that he would have to make sacrifices. He was sick of being told that there would always be next year, feeling he had waited far too long already. He often went over to Transport House to discuss with his party researchers those promises in the manifesto which they considered the top priorities. Raymond had been pleased by the party's decision to leave Cowley Street and return to Transport House as the party headquarters soon after their victory at the polls.

As the weeks passed, compromises were reached and cut-backs

agreed but Raymond managed to cling to the changes about which he felt most passionate. By the Friday morning before the budget the mandarins had handed him his speech. It ran to 143 pages and they estimated it would keep him at the dispatch box for two and a half hours.

On the Tuesday morning of Budget Day he spelt out his tax changes to the Cabinet, who traditionally did not hear the full details until a few hours before the budget was presented to the House.

Budget Day in the House of Commons is a traditional affair. Ambassadors, diplomats, bankers and members of the House of Lords rub shoulders with the general public in the tiny Strangers' Gallery. The queue for seats often stretches for a quarter of a mile from St Stephen's to Westminster Bridge, but only half a dozen people at the front of the line actually hear the Chancellor's speech, because every other place has been allocated even before the queue has begun to form. The Chamber itself is usually packed by two-thirty although the Chancellor does not rise until an hour later. The Press Gallery is equally overcrowded with correspondents ready to run to the nearest phone as soon as any change in taxation is announced. Back-benchers, who because of the size of the Chamber cannot be guaranteed their normal places, are mostly seated by two-twenty-five. Conservatives can reserve their seats by filling in a small prayer card during the morning and leaving it on the place they wish to occupy. Socialists, who consider the system undemocratic, refuse to use the prayer cards and make a mad rush for places at two-thirty. The atheists on both sides wait for the chaplain to finish prayers before they charge in, hoping to find their usual places free.

Budget Day is also traditionally one for eccentric dress. A few top hats can be observed on the Conservative benches and the odd miner's helmet rests on a Labour head. Tom Carson arrived in a boiler suit with a Liverpool scarf around his neck, while Alec Pimkin satisfied himself with a red silk waistcoat and a white carnation in the buttonhole of his morning coat.

The green leather of the two front benches begins to disappear long before three o'clock, and by then any straggling back-bencher will be relegated to the floor or to the upstairs galleries – known as the "Members' Side Galleries", which lack the atmosphere of the House and from which members traditionally do not rise to interrupt or make a speech.

At ten past three Raymond stepped out of No. 11 and held the famous battered budget box, first used by Gladstone, high above his head, so that the press photographers could take the traditional picture before he was driven off to the Commons.

By three-fifteen, when the Prime Minister rose to answer questions, the Chamber had taken on the look of an opening night in the West End, for what members were about to experience was pure theatre.

At three-twenty-five Raymond entered the Chamber to be greeted by cheers from his own side. Every place in the Commons except his had been filled. He looked up to see Joyce in the Strangers' Gallery, and smiled. At three-thirty, when the Prime Minister had finished answering questions, the chairman of Ways and Means – who traditionally takes the Speaker's place for a budget debate as the Speaker, being "the King's man", does not preside over money matters – rose from his chair and called:

"Budget statement, Mr Chancellor of the Exchequer."

Raymond rose and placed his speech in front of him. He began with a review of the world economic position and went on to inform the House of the philosophy behind his first budget, namely to bring down unemployment without driving up inflation. He spoke for the first hour and a half without divulging to the House any of the fiscal changes that he would be making, so abiding by the tradition that no irreversible decisions could be considered until the Stock Exchange had closed, but also giving him the opportunity to tease the House with the odd hint or suggestion.

Raymond took a sip from the glass of water by his side when he had turned page seventy-eight. He had finished with the theory and was now ready to start on the practice.

"Old-age pensions will be raised to a record level," he declared, "as will allowances for single-parent families and disablement grants." Raymond paused and taking a faded sheet from his inside pocket read from the first speech he had ever delivered in public. "No woman whose husband has sacrificed his life for his country shall be allowed to suffer because of an ungrateful nation. War widows' pensions will go up by fifty per cent and war bonds will be honoured at their full face value." The cheering after this statement lasted for some considerable time. Once the House had settled again he continued. "The tax on beer, cigarettes, petrol and perfume will go up by five per cent. Taxes on salaries of more than £30,000 a year will be raised to eighty-five per cent and capital gains tax to fifty per cent." Several Conservatives looked glum. The Chancellor went on to announce an expansion programme in the regions to stimulate employment. He detailed his plan region by region, to cheers from different sections of the House.

He ended his speech by saying, "My purpose as the first Labour Chancellor for ten years is not to rob the rich and give to the poor, but rather to make those who live in comparative ease pay taxes that will alleviate the plight of those in genuine need. Let me tell those Honourable members who sit on the benches opposite that this is only a fifth of what I intend to achieve in the lifetime of this Parliament, and by then Britain can hope to be a more equal and just society. We intend to create a generation in which class is as outdated as the debtors' prison, in which talent, hard work and honesty are their own reward, a Socialist society that is the envy of the East as well as the West. This budget, Mr Speaker, is nothing more than the architect's plan for that dream. I look forward to being given enough time to build the reality.''

When Raymond resumed his seat after two hours and twenty minutes, the length of time it takes to run a world-class marathon, he was greeted by cheers and the waving of order papers from the benches behind him.

The leader of the Opposition was faced with the almost impossible task of an immediate response, and couldn't hope to do more than pick up one or two weaknesses in the Chancellor's philosophy. The House did not hang on her every word.

BOOK FIVE

PARTY LEADERS

1989 – 1991

CHAPTER THIRTY TWO

After the success of Raymond's first budget the leader of the Opposition made changes to her Shadow Cabinet as quickly as was diplomatic. She moved the former Chancellor to cover the Foreign Office, Simon to tackle Home Affairs and Charles to counter the formidable problems now raised by Raymond Gould at the Treasury.

Raymond soon discovered his task of pushing legislation through became that much harder when Charles had added the enthusiasm of his new young team to his own considerable experience of financial matters.

Raymond's success continued, however, even if it was at a slower pace than that for which he would have hoped. Labour won the first two by-elections occasioned by members' deaths, which in itself was remarkable in Government. The by-election results only started a fresh round of rumours that Denis Thatcher was pressing his wife to retire.

Charles Seymour knew that when such moves were finally made they could happen so suddenly that everyone seemed unprepared and uncertain what to do next. By the time Mrs Thatcher announced her resignation he had been building up a loyal team around him for several months.

The former Prime Minister sent a letter to Sir Peter Hordern, the new chairman of the 1922 Committee, letting him know that she would not be putting her name forward for re-election. She explained that she would be over sixty-five at the next election and had already led the party for fourteen years, the longest period for any Conservative since Churchill, and that she now felt she was ready to pass the leadership on to new blood.

The moment everyone in the party had said the usual phrases about the retiring leader being the greatest Prime Minister since Churchill, they proceeded to look for the new Churchill.

Within hours of Mrs Thatcher's resignation both Charles Seymour and Simon Kerslake had received calls and messages from about fifty or sixty supporters, and been contacted by all the leading political journalists. Charles went about his campaign in the thorough manner in which he approached everything, appointing lieutenants to cover each intake of new members since 1964. Simon had invited Bill Travers to organise his back-up team. Travers, like any farmer, rose early each morning to gather in his harvest.

Both Simon and Charles were nominated within twenty-four hours of the necessary seven days, and by the weekend none of the rumoured third candidates had appeared in the lists, which convinced the press it would be a two-horse race.

The *Financial Times* went one better than its rivals. Its political editor, Peter Riddell, spent the whole week trying to contact the 289 Tory members. He succeeded in reaching 228 of them and was able to report to his readers that 101 had said they would vote for Simon Kerslake, ninety-eight for Charles Seymour, while twenty-nine had refused to give any opinion. The article's headline read "Narrow lead for Kerslake", and went on to point out that although the two men were polite about each other in public no one pretended they were friends.

"King Kerslake" ran the banner headline in the Monday editions of the *Sun,* and its political editor predicted Simon would win by 116 to 112: Simon suspected that they had done little more than divide the *Financial Times*'s don't-knows down the middle. With eight days to go he was being quoted at two–one on with Charles eleven–eight against by the veteran ex-Labour MP Lord Mikardo, who had run a book on the last fourteen leadership contests irrespective of party. When Elizabeth told him the odds Simon remained sceptical, as he knew from bitter experience that it never paid to underestimate the Right Honourable member for Sussex Downs. Elizabeth agreed and then pointed to a small paragraph in the paper which he had overlooked. Ronnie's new company was going public, and the shares looked certain to be well over-subscribed.

"That's one prediction that's turned out to be accurate," said Simon, smiling.

With twelve hours to go to the close of nominations a new candidate appeared in the lists, which came as a shock to everyone because until that moment the general public were entirely unaware of Alec Pimkin. Some of his colleagues even expressed surprise that he had been able to find a proposer and seconder. As it had been assumed that Pimkin's supporters were all men who would have backed Charles it was considered a blow to his cause, although most political pundits doubted if Pimkin could scrape together more than seven or eight out of the 289 votes to be cast.

Charles pleaded with Pimkin to withdraw but he stubbornly refused, admitting to Fiona that he was thoroughly enjoying his brief moment of glory. He held a press conference in the Commons, gave endless interviews to television, radio and the national press, and found he was receiving considerable political attention for the first time in his life since the Common Market debate. He even enjoyed the cartoon that appeared in the *Daily Telegraph* of the three candidates in the 100 metres which had Charles portrayed as a string bean, Simon as a jumping bean and Alec as a has-bean waddling in a long way behind the other two. But Alexander Dalglish remained puzzled as to what had made Pimkin place his name in the lists in the first place.

"My majority in Littlehampton had plummeted from over 12,000 to 3,200 since I was first elected, and frankly the Social Democrats have been getting a little too close for comfort. That tiresome fellow Andrew Fraser is in Sussex once a month making speeches on behalf of his candidate and there are still over four years to go until the election."

"But how many votes can you hope to pick up?" asked Fiona.

"Many more than those drunken scribblers realise. I have nine votes already pledged, not including my own, and I could well end up with as many as fifteen."

"Why so many?" asked Fiona, immediately realising how tactless the question must have sounded.

"Dear, simple creature," Pimkin replied. "There are some members of our party who do not care to be led either by a middle-class pushy minor public schoolboy or an aristocratic, arrogant snob. By voting for me they can lodge their protest very clearly."

"But isn't that irresponsible of you?" asked Fiona, annoyed by the "simple" quip.

"Irresponsible it may be, but you can't begin to imagine the invitations I have been receiving during the last few days. They should continue for at least a year after the election is over."

Bombshells occur in the House of Commons only on rare occasions, mainly because the elements of bad luck and timing have to come together. Something that will create a headline one week may be hardly worthy of a mention the next. On the Thursday before the leadership election the House was packed for questions to the Chancellor. Raymond and Charles were having their usual verbal battles across the dispatch box, Charles coming out slightly on top. As the Treasury wasn't his portfolio, all Simon could do was sit with his legs up on the table and listen while his rival scored points.

Tom Carson seemed extremely anxious to get in a supplementary on almost any question that was down on the order paper. Between two-thirty and five past three he had leaped up from his place no less than a dozen times. The digital clock above the Speaker's chair had reached three-twelve when, out of exasperation, the Speaker called him on a seemingly innocuous question on windfall profits.

With Prime Minister's questions just about to begin Carson faced a packed House and a full press gallery. He paused for a moment before putting his question.

"What would be my Right Honourable friend's attitude to a man who invests one pound in a company and, five years later, receives a cheque for £300,000 despite not being on the board or appearing to be involved in any way with that company?"

Raymond was puzzled as he had no idea what Carson was talking about. He did not notice that Simon Kerslake had turned white.

Raymond rose to the dispatch box. "I would remind my Honourable friend that I put capital gains tax up to fifty per cent which might dampen his ardour a little," he said. It was about the only attempt at humour Raymond had made at the dispatch box that year, which may have been the reason so few members laughed. As Carson rose a second time Simon slipped a note across to Raymond which he hurriedly skimmed.

"But does the Chancellor consider that such a person would be fit to be Prime Minister or even leader of the Opposition?"

Members started talking amongst themselves, trying to work out at whom the question was directed while the Speaker stirred restlessly in his seat, anxious to bring a halt to such disorderly supplementaries. Raymond returned to the dispatch box and told Carson that the question was not worthy of an answer. There the matter might have rested had Charles not risen to the dispatch box.

"Mr Speaker, is the Chancellor aware that this personal attack is aimed at my Right Honourable friend, the member for Pucklebridge, and is a disgraceful slur on his character and reputation? The Honourable member for Liverpool Dockside should withdraw his allegation immediately."

The Conservatives cheered their colleague's magnanimity while Simon remained silent, knowing that Charles had successfully put the story on the front page of every national paper.

Simon read the papers over breakfast on the Friday morning, and was not surprised by the coverage of Charles's bogus supplementary. The details of his transaction with Ronnie Nethercote were chronicled in the fullest extent, and it did not read well that he had received £300,000 from a "property speculator" for a one pound investment. Some of the papers felt "bound to ask" what Nethercote hoped to gain out of the transaction. No one seemed to realise that Simon had been on the previous company's board for five years, had invested £60,000 of his own money in that company and had only recently finished paying off the overdraft.

By the Sunday Simon had made a full press statement to put the record straight, and most of the papers had given him a fair hearing. However, Sir Peter McKay, the editor of the *Sunday Express*, didn't help matters with a comment in his widely-read PM column on the centre page.

I would not suggest for one moment that Simon Kerslake has done anything that might be described as dishonest, but with the spotlight turned so fiercely on him there may be some Members of Parliament who feel they cannot risk going into a general election with an accident-prone leader. Mr Seymour, on the other hand, has made his position abundantly clear. He did not seek to return to his family bank in Opposition while he was still hoping to hold public office.

The Monday papers were reassessing the outcome of the ballot to take place the next day and were predicting that Seymour now had the edge. Some journalists went so far as to suggest that Alec Pimkin might profit from the incident as members waited to see if there would be a second chance to give their final verdict.

Simon had received several letters of sympathy during the week, including one from Raymond Gould. Raymond assured Simon that he had not been prepared for the Carson supplementary and apologised for any embarrassment his first answer might have caused.

"It never crossed my mind that he had," said Simon, as he passed Raymond's letter over to Elizabeth.

"*The Times* was right," she said a few moments later. "He is a very fair man."

A moment later Simon passed his wife another letter.

SEYMOUR'S BANK,   15 MAY 1989
202 CHEAPSIDE,
LONDON, EC1

DEAR MR KERSLAKE,

I write to correct one fact to which the press have continually referred. Mr Charles Seymour, the former chairman of this bank, did seek to return to Seymour's after the Conservatives went into Opposition. He hoped to continue as chairman on a salary of £40,000 a year.

The board of Seymour's did not fall in with his wishes.

YOURS SINCERELY,
CLIVE REYNOLDS.

"Will you use it?" asked Elizabeth, when she had finished reading the letter through.

"No. It will only draw more attention to the issue."

Elizabeth looked at her husband as he continued to read the letters, and remembered the file that she still possessed on Amanda Wallace.

She would never reveal its contents to Simon; but perhaps the time had come to make Charles Seymour sweat a little.

On the Monday evening Simon sat on the front bench listening to the Financial Secretary moving those clauses of the short Finance Bill which were being taken in committee on the floor of the House. Charles never let any of Raymond Gould's team get away with a phrase or even a comma if he could see a weakness in their case, and the Opposition were enjoying every moment. Simon sat and watched the votes slipping away, knowing he could do nothing to stop the process.

Of the three candidates only Pimkin slept well the night before the election.

Voting began promptly at nine o'clock the next day in the Grand Committee room of the House of Commons, the party Whips acting as tellers. By three-ten all but one of those entitled to vote had done so. John Cope, the Chief Whip, stood guard over the large black tin box until Big Ben struck four, when it became apparent that Mrs Thatcher had decided to remain neutral.

At four o'clock the box was removed to the Chief Whip's office and the little slips were tipped out and checked twice in less than fifteen minutes. As John Cope left his room he was followed, Pied Piper-like, by lobby correspondents hoping to learn the result, but he had no intention of divulging anything before he reached the 1922 Committee who were keenly awaiting him.

Committee room fourteen was filled to overflowing, with some 280 of the 289 Conservative Members of Parliament present. Their chairman, Sir Peter Hordern, welcomed the Chief Whip and asked him to join him on the small raised platform. He did so and passed over a folded piece of paper. The chairman of the 1922 Committee rose, faced the committee, unfolded the piece of paper and pushed up his glasses. He hesitated as he took in the figures.

"The result of the ballot carried out to select the leader of the parliamentary party is as follows:

Charles Seymour	138
Simon Kerslake	135
Alec Pimkin	15"

There was a gasp followed by prolonged chatter, which lasted until members noticed that the chairman remained standing as he waited for some semblance of order to return among his colleagues.

"There being no outright winner," Sir Peter continued, "a second ballot will take place next Tuesday without Mr Pimkin."

The national press surrounded Pimkin as he left the Commons that afternoon, wanting to know whom he would advise his supporters to vote for in the second ballot. Pimkin, obviously relishing every moment, declared a little pompously that he intended to interview both candidates in the near future and ask them one or two apposite questions. He was at once dubbed "Kingmaker" by the press, and the phones at his home and office never stopped ringing. Whatever their private thoughts, both Simon and Charles agreed to see Pimkin before he told his supporters how he intended to cast his vote.

Elizabeth sat alone at her desk willing herself to go through with it. She glanced down at the faded file that she had not looked at for so many years. She sipped the brandy from the tumbler by her side, both of which she had discovered in the medicine cabinet a few minutes before. All her years of training and commitment to the Hippocratic oath went against what she felt she must now do. While Simon had slept soundly she had lain awake considering the consequences, then made the final decision. Simon's career came first. She picked up the receiver, dialled the number and waited. She nearly replaced it at once when she heard his voice.

"730–9712. Charles Seymour speaking."

"It's Elizabeth Kerslake," she said, trying to sound confident. There was a long silence in which neither of them spoke.

Once Elizabeth had taken another sip of brandy she added, "Don't hang up, Mr Seymour, because I feel confident you'll be interested in what I have to say."

Charles still didn't speak.

"Having watched you from a distance over the years I am sure that your reaction to Carson's question in the Commons last week was not spontaneous."

Charles cleared his throat but still didn't speak.

"And if anything else happens this week that could cause my husband to lose the election, be assured I shall not sit by and watch."

There was still no reply.

"I have a file in front of me marked 'Miss Amanda Wallace', and if you wish all its contents to remain confidential I would advise you to avoid any repercussion of your antics. It's packed with names *Private Eye* would wallow in for months."

Charles said nothing.

Elizabeth's confidence was growing. "You needn't bother to inform me that such an action would get me struck off the medical register. That would be a small penalty for watching you have to suffer the way my husband has this week." She paused. "Good day, Mr Seymour."

Charles still didn't speak.

Elizabeth put the phone down and swallowed the remainder of the brandy. She prayed that she had sounded convincing because she knew she could never carry out such a threat.

Charles took Pimkin to dinner at White's – where Alec had always wanted to be a member – and was escorted to a private room on the first floor.

Charles didn't wait long to ask, "Why are you going through with this charade? Don't you realise I would have won it in the first round, if you hadn't stood?"

Pimkin bridled. "No doubt, but I haven't had so much fun in years."

"Who the hell got you your seat in the first place?"

"I well remember," said Pimkin. "And I also remember the price you exacted for it. But now it's my turn to call the tune, and this time I require something quite different."

"What are you hoping for? Chancellor of the Exchequer in my first administration?" said Charles, barely able to keep the sarcasm from his voice.

"No, no," said Pimkin, "I know my worth; I am not a complete fool."

"So what do you want? Membership of White's? Perhaps I could fix that."

"Nothing as mundane. In return for putting you into Downing Street I expect to be translated to the House of Lords."

Charles hesitated. He could always give Pimkin his word; and who other than Pimkin would notice if in three years' time he didn't carry it through?

"If you and your fifteen men vote for me next Tuesday I'll put you in the Lords," said Charles. "You have my word on it."

"Good," said Pimkin. "But one small thing, old chum," he added as he closely folded his napkin.

"Christ – what do you want now?" asked Charles, exasperated.

"Like you, I want the agreement in writing."

Charles hesitated again, but this time he knew he was beaten. "I agree," he said.

"Good, then it's a deal," said Pimkin. Looking round for a waiter he added, "I rather think champagne is called for."

When Pimkin put the same proposition two days later Simon Kerslake took some time before he answered. Then he said, "That's a question I would have to consider on its merits at the time, if and when I became Prime Minister."

"So bourgeois" said Pimkin as he left Simon's room. "I offer him the keys to No. 10 and he treats me like a locksmith."

Charles left the Commons that night having spent his time going round a large cross-section of his supporters, and he was reassured to discover they were standing firm. Wherever he went in the long Gothic corridors members singly or in groups came up to pledge their support. It was true that Kerslake's windfall of £300,000 was fast becoming yesterday's news, but Charles still felt enough blood had been let from that wound to ensure his final victory, even though he still cursed Pimkin for holding up the result. One anonymous note, with all the necessary details, sent to the right Labour member, had certainly proved most effective. Charles cursed as he realised Elizabeth Kerslake had successfully stopped any further covert attacks on his rival.

When he arrived home he was appalled to find Amanda waiting for him in the drawing-room.

"I thought I told you to stay away until the middle of next week?"

"I changed my mind, Charlie," said Amanda.

"Why?" he asked suspiciously.

"I think I've earned a little reward for being such a good girl."

"What do you have in mind?" he asked as he stood by the mantelpiece.

"Fair exchange."

"For what?"

"For the world rights to my life story."

"Your *what*?" said Charles in disbelief. "Who is going to be the slightest bit interested in you?"

"It's not me they're interested in, Charlie, it's you. The *News of the World* have offered me £100,000 for the unexpurgated story of life with Charles Seymour." She added dramatically, "Or what it's like to live with the second son of an earl who will go to any lengths to become Prime Minister."

"You can't be serious," said Charles.

"Deadly serious. I've made quite a few notes over the years. How you got rid of Derek Spencer but failed to pull the same trick on Clive Reynolds. The extremes you went to trying to keep Simon Kerslake out of the House. How your first wife swapped the famous Holbein picture of the first Earl of Bridgwater. But the story which will cause the most interest is the one in which the real father of young Harry Seymour is revealed because his dad's life story was serialised in the *People* a couple of years ago, and that seems to be one episode they missed out."

"You bitch. You know Harry is my son," said Charles, advancing towards her. But Amanda stood her ground.

"And perhaps I should include a chapter on how you assault your wife behind the closed doors of your peaceful Eaton Square mansion."

Charles came to a halt. "What's the deal?"

"I keep quiet for the rest of my life and you present me with £50,000 now and a further £50,000 when you become leader."

"You've gone mad."

"Not me, Charlie, I've always been sane. You see, I don't have a paranoia to work out on dear harmless brother Rupert. The *News of the World* will love that part now that he's the fifteenth Earl. I can just see the picture of him wearing his coronet and decked out in his ermine robes."

"They wouldn't print it."

"They would when they learn that he's as queer as a two-pound note, and therefore our only son will collect the earldom when he's not entitled to it."

"No one would believe it, and by the time they print the story it will be too late," said Charles.

"Not a bit," said Amanda. "I am assured by my agent that the true reason behind the resignation of the leader of the Conservative party would be an even bigger scoop than that of a one-time contestant."

Charles sank down in the nearest armchair.

"Twenty-five thousand," he said.

"Fifty thousand," replied his wife. "It's only fair. After all, it's a double deal: no story to the press and you become leader of the Conservative party."

"All right," whispered Charles, rising to leave the room.

"Wait a minute, Charlie. Don't forget I've dealt with you in the past."

"What else are you hoping for?" said Charles, swinging round.

"Just the autograph of the next Tory leader," she replied producing a cheque.

"Where the hell did you get hold of that?" asked Charles, pointing to the slip of paper.

"From your cheque book," said Amanda innocently.

"Don't play games with me."

"From the top drawer of your desk."

Charles snatched it from her and nearly changed his mind. Then he thought of his brother in the House of Lords, his only son not inheriting the title and having to give up the leadership. He took out his pen and scribbled his name on the cheque before leaving his wife in the drawing-room holding £50,000. She was checking the date and the signature carefully.

Simon and Elizabeth spent a quiet weekend in their country cottage while the photographers pitched camp in Eaton Square. They had received a leak from an "authoritative" source that Pimkin would come out in support of his old school chum.

"A brilliant move," said Elizabeth over breakfast on the Sunday morning admiring the picture on the front page of the *Observer*.

"Another photo of Seymour telling us what he will do when he's Prime Minister?" said Simon, not looking up from the *Sunday Times*.

"No," said Elizabeth, and passed her paper across the table. Simon stared at the Holbein portrait of the first Earl of Bridgwater under the headline "A gift to the nation".

"Good God," said Simon. "Are there no depths he will not sink to, to win this election?"

"My dear, by any standards you have delivered the *coup de grâce*," said Pimkin to Fiona over lunch that Sunday.

"I thought you would appreciate it," said Fiona, pouring him another glass of his own wine.

"I certainly did and I particularly enjoyed the director of the National Gallery's comments – 'that Charles's gesture of presenting the priceless painting to the nation was the act of a selfless man'."

"Of course, once the story had been leaked to the press Charles was left with no choice," said Alexander Dalglish.

"I realise that," said Pimkin, leaning back, "and I would have given a dozen bottles of my best claret to have seen Charles's face the moment he realised the first Earl of Bridgwater had escaped his clutches for ever. If he had denied giving the earl to the nation the publicity that would have followed would have certainly ensured defeat in the election on Tuesday."

"Win or lose next week, he daren't then suggest it was all done without his approval," said Alexander.

"I love it, I love it," said Pimkin. "I am told that Princess Diana will be unveiling the portrait on behalf of the nation – and rest assured that when she performs the official ceremony, I shall be there to bear witness."

"Ah, but will Charles?" asked Fiona.

On Monday morning Charles's brother phoned from Somerset to ask why he had not been consulted about donating the Holbein to the nation.

"It was my picture to dispose of as I pleased," Charles reminded him and slammed down the phone.

By nine o'clock on Tuesday morning, when the voting took place for the last time, the two contestants had spoken to nearly every member twice. Charles joined his colleagues in the Members' Dining-room for lunch while Simon took Elizabeth to Locketts in Marsham Street. She showed him some coloured brochures of a holiday on the Orient Express which would be the most perfect way to see Venice. She hoped that they wouldn't have time to go on the trip. Simon hardly mentioned the vote that was simultaneously taking place in the Commons but it never was far from either of their minds.

The voting ended at three-fifty but once again the Chief Whip did not remove the black box until four o'clock. By four-fifteen he knew the winner but did not reveal his name until the 1922 Committee had assembled at five o'clock. He informed their chairman at one minute to five.

Once again, Sir Peter Hordern stood on the small raised platform in the committee room fourteen to declare the result. There was no need to ask if the people at the back could hear.

"Ladies and gentlemen," he said, his words echoing round the room, "the result of the second ballot for the leadership of the Tory Party is as follows:

Charles Seymour	130
Simon Kerslake	158."

Just over half the members present rose and cheered while Bill Travers ran all the way to Simon's room to be the first to report the news. When he arrived Simon swung round and faced the open door.

"You look and sound as though you'd run a marathon."

"Like Pheidippides, I bring great news of victory."

"I hope that doesn't mean you're going to drop down dead," said Simon, grinning.

The new leader of the Conservative party said nothing more for a few moments. It was obvious that Pimkin had come out in favour of him. Later that night, one or two other members also admitted that they had changed their minds during the second week because they hadn't liked the blatant opportunism of Charles presenting a priceless portrait to the nation only a few days before the final vote.

The following morning Fiona phoned Pimkin to ask him why he had acted as he did. "My dear Fiona," he replied, "like Sidney Carton I considered it would be good to go to my grave knowing I had done one honourable thing in my life."

It took only a week for Simon's little house on Beaufort Street to be transformed. He could not as much as turn his head without facing a camera. Everywhere he went he was followed by a platoon of press men. He was surprised how quickly the experience became part of his daily routine, although Elizabeth never found it an edifying experience. She was, however, as booked up as Simon and once again they seemed only to meet in the evenings. He spent his first two weeks selecting the Shadow Cabinet he wanted to take into the next general election. He was able to announce the composition of his new team to the press fourteen days after his election as leader of the Conservative party. He made one sentimental appointment: that of Bill Travers as Shadow Minister of Agriculture.

When asked at a press conference why his defeated rival would not be serving in the team Simon explained that he had offered Charles Seymour the deputy leadership and any portfolio of his choice, but Charles had turned the offer down, saying he preferred to return to the back benches for the present time.

Charles had left for Scotland the same morning for a few days' rest by the river Spey, taking his son with him. Although he spent much of their short holiday feeling depressed about the final outcome of the leadership struggle, Harry's original efforts at fishing helped deaden some of the pain. Harry even ended up with the biggest fish.

Amanda, on the other hand, realising how slim her chances were of coaxing any more cash out of her husband, re-opened negotiations over her life story with the *News of the World*.

When Nick Lloyd, the editor, read through Amanda's notes he decided on two things. She would require a ghost writer and the paper would have to halve their original offer.

"Why?" demanded Amanda.

"Because we daren't print the better half of your story."

"Why not?"

"No one would believe it."

"But every word is true," she insisted.

"I'm not doubting the veracity of the facts," said Lloyd, "only readers' ability to swallow them."

"They accepted that a man climbed the walls of Buckingham Palace and found his way into the Queen's bedroom."

"Agreed," replied Lloyd, "but only after the Queen had confirmed the story. I'm not so sure that Charles Seymour will be quite as cooperative."

Amanda remained silent long enough for her agent to close the deal.

The watered-down version of "My Life with Charles Seymour" appeared a few months later to coincide with Charles's much-publicised divorce, but it made no more than a faint ripple in political circles. Now that Charles had no prospect of leading his party it was very much yesterday's news.

Amanda came out of the divorce settlement with another £50,000 but lost custody of Harry, which was all Charles really cared about. He prayed her irresponsible remarks reported in the papers concerning the boy's claim to the title had been quickly forgotten.

Then Rupert phoned from Somerset and asked to see him privately.

A week later they sat facing each other in Charles's drawing-room at Eaton Square.

"I am sorry to broach such an embarrassing subject," said Rupert, "but I feel it is my duty to do so."

"Duty, poppycock," said Charles, stubbing out his cigarette. "I tell you Harry is my son, and as such will inherit the title. He's the spitting image of great-grandfather and that ought to be enough proof for anyone."

"In normal circumstances I would agree with you, but the recent publicity in the *News of the World* has been brought to my notice and I feel . . ."

"That sensationalist tabloid," said Charles sarcastically, his voice rising. "Surely you don't take their word before mine?"

"Certainly not," said Rupert, "but if Amanda is to be believed Harry is not your son."

"How am I meant to prove he is?" asked Charles, trying to control his temper. "I didn't keep a diary of the dates when I slept with my wife."

"But it seems Amanda did so I have had to take legal advice on the matter," continued Rupert, "and am informed that a blood test is all that will prove necessary to verify Harry's claim to the title. We both share a rare blood group as did our father and grandfather, and if Harry is of that group I shall never mention the subject again. If not, then the title will eventually be inherited by our second cousin in Australia."

"And if I don't agree to put my son through this ridiculous test?"

"Then the matter must be placed in the hands of our family solicitors," said Rupert, sounding unusually in control. "And they must take whatever course they consider fit."

CHAPTER THIRTY THREE

Simon's first year as leader was one of unbounded energy and ideas which bore fruit as the Conservatives picked up three seats at by-elections and whittled away the Government's majority. The press were already predicting that the Socialists wouldn't be able to complete their full five-year term, which moved Simon to goad Central Office into a perpetual state of readiness for an election.

Raymond continued to gain respect at the Treasury as his policies began to show results. He had to cut back on some of the more ambitious projects as his gloomy predictions about American interest rates and the drop in the production of North Sea oil proved daily more accurate. After his second budget the financial press felt he had done all that was possible, given the world situation. When unemployment fell below two million and strikes to their lowest level since the Second World War some members hailed Raymond as the unions' Messiah, while others noted that he had been shrewd enough to steal some of the Opposition's co-inflation clothes in the absence of Charles Seymour.

As Raymond entered his third year as Chancellor the opinion polls showed the two main parties neck and neck again, with a surprising proportion of people saying that they would vote for the Alliance for the first time.

The Liberals still held sixteen seats in the Commons but, as in the past three elections, they had decided to fight under the collective banner as the Social Democrats during the general election campaign.

As the time for election drew near both small parties knew they would have to declare their choice for overall leader if a combination of Liberals and Social Democrats ever held the balance of power in Parliament. When the pollsters dug a little deeper it transpired that Andrew Fraser had become the most popular political leader in the country despite the fact that he only led forty-two members in the Commons.

Andrew spent a lot of his time addressing meetings all over the country trying to convince the voters that at the next election the political balance would change. He said it so often he began to believe it himself, and two good by-election victories early in 1990 helped his supporters feel it was possible too. The press began to take such claims seriously when at the local election in May the Alliance captured 102 council seats at the expense of both the major parties.

"Daddy, Daddy, open my school report."

Charles left the morning mail unopened as he held Harry in his arms. He knew nothing could ever part them now but he dreaded Harry finding out that he might not be his real father.

"Please open it," pleaded Harry, wriggling free.

The school doctor had been asked to take a sample of Harry's blood along with six other boys from his form so that he would not consider the request unusual. Even the doctor hadn't been told the full significance of the action.

Harry extracted the envelope from the pile by Charles's side – the one with the school crest in the top left-hand corner – and held it out for his father to open. He looked excited and seemed hardly able to contain himself. Charles had promised he would phone his brother as soon as the result of the blood test was confirmed. He had wanted to phone the doctor a hundred times during the past week but had always stopped himself, knowing it would only add to the man's curiosity.

"Come on, Dad, read the report and you'll see it's true."

Charles tore open the letter and removed the little book which would reveal the result of all Harry's efforts during the term. He flicked through the pages – Latin, English, History, Geography, Art, Divinity, Games, Form master, Headmaster. He reached the last page, a small yellow sheet headed: "Term medical report". It started: Harry Seymour, age eleven, height four feet nine inches – he's suddenly sprung up, thought Charles – weight five stone four pounds. He glanced up at Harry who looked as if he was about to burst.

"It is true, Dad, isn't it?"

Charles read on without answering the boy's question. At the foot of the page was a typewritten note signed by the school doctor. Charles read it twice before he understood its full significance and then a third time. "As requested I took a sample of Harry's blood and analysed it. The result shows that Harry shares a rare blood group . . ."

"Is it true, Dad?" asked Harry yet again.

"Yes, my son, it's true."

"I told you, Dad – I knew I'd be top in the class. That means I'll be captain of the school next term. Just like you."

"Just like me," said his father, as he picked up the phone by his side and began to dial his brother's number in Somerset.

When the Prime Minister went into hospital for a minor operation the press immediately started to speculate on his resignation. Ten days later when he walked out looking better than ever the rumours ceased immediately. In the Prime Minister's absence as deputy leader Raymond chaired Cabinet meetings and stood in for him during questions in the Commons. This gave the lobby correspondents a chance to proclaim, like Caesarian soothsayers plucking at entrails, that Raymond was *primus inter pares*.

Raymond enjoyed presiding over the Cabinet, but was surprised that the civil servants expected him to spend his entire Tuesday and Thursday mornings preparing for Prime Minister's questions.

Both Simon Kerslake and Andrew Fraser had gained formidable reputations during Prime Minister's questions, and Raymound found the fifteen-minute encounter more demanding than a full winding-up speech in a major debate; in retrospect, he was relieved that he had prepared so thoroughly. The lobby correspondents seemed to be in agreement that Raymond had held his own on both occasions and that, if anything, Simon Kerslake had underestimated him.

The Prime Minister returned to Downing Street the following week and assured Raymond that the operation had been a success and the likelihood of any recurrence of the trouble was, in the surgeon's opinion, minimal. He admitted to Raymond that he hoped to lead the party to a second victory at the polls, by which time he would be within a few years of his seventieth birthday and ready to bow out quietly. He told Raymond bluntly that he hoped he would be his successor. But Raymond couldn't help remembering that Neil Kinnock was eight years younger than he was.

Raymond returned to the Treasury to prepare for what looked like his final budget before the general election. His stewardship had made it possible to loosen the reins slightly with an election in mind. He described the loosening to the Cabinet as no more than a percentage point or two; he had no intention, he assured them, of letting three years' hard work be sacrificed at the altar of vote-catching. Some of his colleagues round the Cabinet table wished he were not quite so unbending at times.

Whenever Raymond spoke around the country more and more people approached him about standing for the leadership. He always thanked them courteously but maintained his loyalty to the Prime Minister, which loyalty, he added, would remain constant until he chose to resign.

Simon and Andrew also spent every weekend in planes, cars or trains fulfilling speaking engagements right up until the party conferences in October.

Andrew, in his summing-up speech to the SDP conference at Weston-super-Mare, told the delegates that they should expect to hold the balance of power between the two major parties after the next election. For the first time, he told them, they would have the chance to participate in a national Government. He sent the delegates home warning them to prepare for an election within the coming twelve months, by which time they would be able to welcome SDP Members of Parliament who would already be playing a major role in the running of the nation. Andrew's supporters left the West Country keyed up for battle.

The Labour Party conference followed a week later at Brighton and Raymond delivered a keynote speech on the state of the nation's finances. He pressed the unions to continue supporting their Government by keeping the twin evils of inflation and unemployment at acceptable levels. "Let us not pass on three years of achievement to be squandered by a Conservative Government," he told the cheering delegates. "Brothers, I look forward to presenting five more Labour budgets that will make it impossible for the Tories to imagine a future victory at the polls."

Raymond received one of the rare standing ovations to be given to any Cabinet minister at a Labour Party conference. The delegates had never doubted his ability, but over the years they had grown to respect his sincerity as well as his judgement.

Seven more days passed before Simon addressed the Tory faithful at the Conservative party conference in Blackpool. By tradition, the leader always receives a four- to six-minute standing ovation after he completes his speech on the final day. "He'd still get four minutes," said Pimkin to a colleague, "if he read them *Das Kapital*."

Simon had spent six weeks preparing for the occasion since, like Andrew, he was convinced this would be the last conference before the election. He was pleasantly surprised to find Charles Seymour coming forward with new ideas on tax reform which he hoped might be considered for inclusion in the leader's speech to the conference.

Charles had recently been making useful contributions in the House during finance debates, and Simon hoped that it would not be long before he would be willing to return to the front bench. His main preoccupation in the House had been as a member of the Chairmen's Panel from which committee chairmen were recruited for each bill. Charles had mellowed considerably during his time on the back benches and many of his friends feared he had lost his ambition for high office and might not even stand at the next election. Simon hoped this wasn't the case as he desperately needed someone of Charles's ability to counter Raymond Gould at the Treasury. Simon included Charles's suggestions in the final draft of his speech and dropped him a hand-written note of thanks.

On that Friday morning in Blackpool, in front of 2,000 delegates and millions more watching on television, Simon presented a complete and detailed plan of what he hoped to achieve when the Conservatives were returned to Government.

"*Power* is what we want and *power* is what we seek," he told a mesmerized audience. "For without *power* we cannot serve."

After the peroration the delegates duly rose for a genuine six-minute ovation. When the noise had died down Pimkin was heard to remark, "I think I made the right decision."

The conference season over, members made their way back from the three seasides to Westminster. Sadness overcame the House in their first week back when the ageing Mr Speaker Weatherill suffered a minor heart attack and retired to the Lords. The Government's overall majority was only two at the time and the Labour party Chief Whip feared that if they supplied the new Speaker from their own ranks and the Conservatives were to retain the old Speaker's safe seat the Government majority would cease to exist.

Simon reluctantly agreed that the Speaker should come from his own benches and asked his Chief Whip to suggest a suitable candidate.

When Charles Seymour asked to be granted a private interview with the leader Simon agreed immediately.

Charles arrived at the Opposition leader's office the following morning. It was the first time they had talked alone since the leadership battle. A head of white hair had grown from the roots of Charles's once Odyssian locks, and the deeper lines in Charles's face gave him a more gentle look. Simon couldn't help noticing a slight stoop had replaced his ramrod bearing. Looking at them now no one would have suggested they were contemporaries. Charles's request came as a shock to Simon for he had never once considered his great rival as a candidate for that particular job.

"But I want you to return to the front bench and be my Chancellor," said Simon. "You must know I would be delighted to have you back in the team."

"That's considerate of you," said Charles. "But I would prefer the more restful life of being an arbitrator rather than an antagonist. I've lost that desire always to be on the attack. For over twenty years you've had the advantage of Elizabeth and two sons to keep your feet on the ground. It's only quite recently that Harry has done the same for me."

All men are thought to have one great moment in their careers in the House, and for Alec Pimkin it was to be that day. The election of a Speaker in the Commons is a quaint affair. By ancient tradition no one must appear to want the honour, and it is rare for more than one person to be proposed for the post. During Henry VI's reign three Speakers were beheaded within a year, although in modern times it has been more the heavy burden of duties that has often led to an early grave. This tradition of reluctance has carried on through the ages, and for that reason a future Speaker frequently does not know who has sponsored him. Dressed in a smart blue suit, sporting a red carnation and his favourite pink-spotted bow tie, Alec Pimkin rose from his seat on the back benches to move that "the Right Honourable Charles Seymour does take the chair of this House as Speaker". His speech was serious yet witty, informed but personal. Pimkin held the House in his grasp for nine minutes and never once let it go. "He's done the old friend proud," one member muttered to another across the gangway when Pimkin sat down, and indeed the look on Charles's face left no doubt that he felt the same way, whatever had taken place in the past.

After Charles had been seconded the tradition of dragging the Speaker-elect to the chair was observed. This normally humorous affair, usually greeted with hoots of laughter and cheering, became even more of a farce with the sight of the small, portly Pimkin and his Labour seconder dragging the six-foot-four former Guards' officer from the third row of the back benches all the way to the chair.

Charles surveyed the Commons from his new vantage point. He began by expressing his grateful thanks for the high honour the House had bestowed on him. From the moment he rose and stood his full height, every member knew they had selected the right man to guide them through the parliamentary calendar. The sharpness of his tongue may have gone but there remained a firm delivery and natural authority that left none of his colleagues in any doubt that Mr Speaker Seymour intended to keep "order" for many years to come.

The Conservatives held the Croydon North-East seat comfortably at the by-election, and captured a marginal six weeks later. The press pointed out that it only needed the Tories and the SDP/Liberal Alliance to join together for the Government and Opposition to be in equal numbers, leaving the seventeen Irish members to decide the fate of the Parliament. Raymond was determined that the Government should hold on for another few weeks so that he could deliver his third budget, which he was convinced would act as a launching pad on which to fight the election.

Andrew had realised that Raymond's next budget might help Labour's chances at the polls, and he sought an official meeting with the leader of the Opposition to discuss the possibility of a "no confidence" motion.

Simon agreed with Andrew's suggestion and thought that they should time the debate for the end of March. If they won that would ensure an election before the budget.

Raymond had accepted an invitation to address a large Labour rally in Cardiff the weekend before the vote of "no confidence". He boarded the train at Paddington, settled into his compartment and began to check over his speech. As the train pulled into Swindon a railway official stepped on board and, having discovered where the Chancellor of the Exchequer was seated, asked if he could speak to him privately for a few minutes. Raymond listened carefully to what the man had to say, replaced the speech in his brief case, got off the train, crossed the platform and returned by the first available train to London.

On the journey back he tried to work out all the consequences of the news he had just been told. As soon as he arrived at Paddington he made his way through the waiting photographers and journalists, answering no questions. A car took him straight to Westminster Hospital. Raymond was shown into a private room, to find the Prime Minister sitting upright in bed.

"Now don't panic," he said before Raymond could speak. "I'm in fine shape considering I'm over sixty and with all the pressure we've been under this last year."

"What's wrong with you?" asked Raymond, taking a chair next to the bed.

"Recurrence of the old trouble, only this time they say it will take major surgery. I'll be out of this place in a month, six weeks at the most, and then I'll live as long as Harold Macmillan, they tell me. Now, to more important matters. I want you to take over for me again, which will mean you will have to speak in my place during the 'no confidence' debate on Wednesday. If we lose the vote, I shall resign as leader."

Raymond tried to protest as he had already worked out the implications the moment he had heard his leader was ill again. The Prime Minister held up his hand and continued talking. "No party can fight an election with its leader laid up in bed for six weeks, however well he might be when they release him. If there is to be an election, the voters have the right to know who is going to lead the party in Parliament, and of course in such an emergency under standing order number five (four) of the Labour Party's constitution," continued the Prime Minister, "the National Executive would meet and automatically select you to take over as party leader."

Raymond raised his head. "Yes. The importance of that particular standing order has already been pointed out to me."

The Prime Minister smiled. "Joyce, no doubt."

"Her name was Kate, actually."

The Prime Minister looked puzzled and then continued. "I think you must get used to the idea, Raymond, that you may well be running for Prime Minister in three weeks' time. Because if we lose the 'no confidence' vote on Wednesday I am given no choice but to advise the Queen to call an immediate general election."

Raymond remained silent.

"I can assure you," continued the Prime Minister, "the National Executive will not want an internal blood bath three weeks before a general election. Nothing could be more certain to guarantee a Tory victory. If, however, we do win the 'no confidence' vote then it's a different matter altogether because I'll be back and running the ship long before the Easter recess is over. That will give us enough time to call the election after you've delivered your third budget. So make sure you win on Wednesday."

"I am unable to express how much we will all miss your leadership," said Raymond, without guile.

"As every member of the House except the Irish will know which lobby they'll be voting in long before the debate begins my leadership may turn out to be less important than any single vote. And don't forget it will be the first occasion at which they've allowed television on the floor of the Commons, so make sure Joyce picks out one of those smart shirts you sometimes wear."

Raymond spent the final few days before the "no confidence" vote preparing his speech. He cancelled all the engagements in his diary except for the Speaker's dinner to celebrate the Queen's sixty-fifth birthday, at which he would be standing in for the Prime Minister.

The Government and Opposition Whips spent Monday and Tuesday checking that every member would be present in the House by ten o'clock on Wednesday night. The political journalists pointed out that, if the vote were a tie, Mr Speaker Seymour had already made it clear that he would abide by the ancient tradition of giving his casting vote to the Government of the day. Charles was armed with precedents from Speaker Addington in the eighteenth century to Speaker Denison in the nineteenth. Charles pointed out that, in line with the principle, he must vote in such a manner as not to make the decision of the chair final.

Simon was to open the debate for the Opposition while Andrew was being allowed to wind up, the only concession Simon had granted the SDP/Liberal Alliance for ensuring their support in the lobbies. Neil Kinnock was to open for the Government with Raymond winding up.

When Raymond read his speech out to Joyce on the Tuesday night the entire rehearsal took only twenty-four minutes, but he explained to her that with the noise and interruptions that would occur in the Chamber he would be on his feet the full thirty minutes. In fact he might have to cut short some lines on the night.

The following day members began arriving hours before the debate was due to begin. The Strangers' Gallery had been booked days in advance, with many senior ambassadors and even some Privy Councillors unable to be guaranteed a seat. The Press Gallery was filled and editors were sitting at the feet of their political journalists' desks. The Commons itself was like a stand at a cup final where twice as many tickets had been sold as there were seats. The only difference from a Budget Day was that the House was taken up with lighting equipment that had been tested a dozen times that morning.

Between two-thirty and three-thirty Mr Speaker Seymour had been unable to stop members chattering during questions to Mr Meacher, the Secretary of State for Education, but at three-thirty he duly shouted for "Order" and did not have to wait long for silence before calling: "The leader of the Opposition."

Simon rose from his place on the front bench to be greeted with cheers from his own side. He was momentarily surprised by the brightness of the arc lights which he had been assured he would hardly notice, but soon he was into his stride. Without a note in front of him he addressed the House for fifty minutes, tearing into the Government one moment, then switching to the policies he would implement the next. He ended his peroration by describing the Labour Party as "the party of wasted opportunity" then added – jabbing his finger at Raymond – "but you will be replaced by a party of ideas and ideals."

He sat down to the cheers of his back-benchers who thought they had already won the vote – if not the next election as well. The noise continued for some time before Charles could bring the House back to order and call the next speaker.

Neil Kinnock had always revelled in his Welsh ancestry and had often been compared by older members to Aneurin Bevan. The *bête noire* of the Tories set in to the Opposition leader with a vengeance, expounding his beliefs and rousing his own side to cheers when he said that the Tories would be routed and would regret this no confidence "trick" for a decade. "The Right Honourable Gentleman," he said, pointing at Simon, "has the nerve to call us the party of wasted opportunities. For the past two years it is he who has led the party of opportunists, and who will be the leader of the Opposition until it is time for him to be replaced." When Kinnock sat down the television producers couldn't be blamed for thinking that they were covering a lions *v* Christians slaughter. Again it took the Speaker several minutes to bring the House back to order.

The back-benchers also rose to the occasion with speeches from past ministers quoting precedent and from young turks demanding change, which helped confirm old and established new reputations. The House remained packed that night right up until nine o'clock when the Speaker called Andrew Fraser to wind up for the Opposition.

Andrew delivered a "plague on both your houses" speech and shouted above the protests from the two main parties. "When the time comes you will both need to call on an honest broker." At nine-thirty when he resumed his seat Andrew was cheered as loudly as forty-two members in unison could manage.

When it came to Raymond's turn to wind up members wondered how he would make himself heard above the noise that greeted him. He rose to the dispatch box and, looking grave, with head bowed, almost whispered his first words, "Mr Speaker, I know the whole House would wish me to open my speech by saying how sad we all are that the Prime Minister is unable to be present tonight. I am sure all Honourable Members will want to join me in sending him, his wife and family our best wishes as he prepares for his operation."

Suddenly the House was silent and, having caught its mood Raymond raised his head and delivered for the eleventh time the speech he had prepared so assiduously. When he had seen Simon give his apparently impromptu speech Raymond had torn up his notes. He spelt out the achievements of the Government during the past two and a half years and assured the House that he was only half-way through his time as Chancellor. "I have not been able to achieve equality in three years, but of one thing I am certain: I look forward to delivering my next budget whatever the outcome of the vote tonight. We shall not see the opportunist Government of the Conservatives or the Alliance's so-called 'honest broker'. Indeed, looking at the Alliance I can say there is no one less honest and no one more broke. We, Mr Speaker, will see the return of a Labour Government for another full Parliament." Raymond sat down as the clock reached ten. He found, like the speakers before him, that he was drenched in sweat from the heat sent out by the powerful arc lights.

The Speaker rose and his first words were lost as he put the question: "This House has no confidence in Her Majesty's Government. As many as are of that opinion say Aye, to the contrary, No. I think the Ayes have it."

"No," hollered back the voices from the Government benches.

"Clear the lobbies," called the Speaker above the cheers for Raymond Gould. Members departed to the lobbies to cast their votes. The Irish members surprised no one by dividing among themselves. Fourteen minutes later the tellers returned to a noisy Chamber to give the result of the division to the clerk at the table who then entered the figures on a division paper. The four tellers lined up and advanced towards the table from the bar of the House. They came to a halt and bowed for a third time. One of the Opposition Whips read out: "Ayes to the right 323, Noes to the left 322" and passed the piece of paper to the Speaker who tried to repeat it above the bedlam. Few members heard him say:

"The Ayes have it, the Ayes have it."

Raymond sat on the front bench and watched the delighted Tories bobbing up and down like children on a carousel. He reflected that if the Prime Minister had been present to register his vote the Government would have saved the day.

Her Majesty the Queen visited her Prime Minister in hospital twenty-four hours after his successful operation. He advised the monarch to dissolve Parliament immediately and asked that the general election be set for 9 May. He explained to the Queen that he intended to resign as leader of his party that morning and would relinquish the office of Prime Minister as soon as the outcome of the election was clear.

Before she left the Westminster Hospital the Queen spent some time discussing a private constitutional issue with the Prime Minister. He suggested that when the Labour Party had confirmed their new leader he must be the man to offer her advice on such a personal matter.

The National Executive of the Labour party met behind the closed doors of Transport House in Smith Square at ten o'clock the following morning to select their new leader.

Three hours and twenty minutes later the committee issued a one-line press statement: "Mr Raymond Gould has been invited to lead the party at the forthcoming general election."

Although no one was in any doubt abut the fierce arguments that must have taken place during the meeting the press were met by a unified voice once the committee finally broke up.

As Lord Broadstairs, the former Prime Minister, wrote in the centre page of the *Sunday Express* that weekend, "The Labour Party in selecting their leader resembled nothing less than the old-fashioned magic circle of Lord Rosebery in their determination to prove unity." The only leak he had managed to gather from the meeting was that Raymond Gould's acceptance speech had impressed every one present.

But Lord Broadstairs went on to point out that if the Labour Party should lose the general election Raymond Gould could be the shortest serving leader in the Labour party's history, as under standing order five (four) of the constitution his appointment had to be confirmed by the delegates at the next party conference in October.

It had been two hours before Raymond was able to leave Transport House and escape the press. When he eventually got away he went straight to Westminster Hospital to visit the Prime Minister. The operation had visibly aged him. He was in good spirits, but admitted that he was glad not to be facing a gruelling election campaign. After he had congratulated Raymond on his new post he went on to say: "You're dining with the Queen tonight?"

"Yes, to celebrate her sixty-fifth birthday," said Raymond.

"There's more to it than that," said the Prime Minister gravely and he then revealed the private conversation that he had had with the monarch the previous day.

"And will her decision depend on the four people in that room?"

"I suspect it will."

"And what's your attitude?"

"That's no longer relevant because I shall resign as Prime Minister the day after the election, so it's more important the new Prime Minister considers what is best for the country."

For the first time Raymond felt like the leader of the party.

CHAPTER THIRTY FOUR

Elizabeth straightened Simon's white tie and took a pace back to look at him.

"Well, at least you *look* like a Prime Minister," she said, smiling.

Her husband checked his watch. Still a few minutes to spare before he needed to be at the Speaker's private apartments – not that he was willing to risk being late for this particular birthday celebration. Elizabeth helped him on with his overcoat and after a search realised he had lost another pair of gloves.

"I do hope you can take care of the nation's belongings a little better than you do your own," she sighed.

"I'm sure I'll find it hard to lose a whole country," said Simon.

"Do remember that Raymond Gould will be trying to help you," said Elizabeth.

"Yes, that's true. I only wish I was fighting Kinnock."

"Why?" she asked.

"Because Gould was born into the wrong party," said Simon as he kissed his wife and walked towards the front door, "and a lot of the electorate have already reached the same conclusion."

The policeman on the gates of New Palace Yard saluted as Simon was driven into the courtyard and dropped at the Members' Entrance. He glanced at his watch again: ten minutes to spare. He never could resist checking how many people were in the Chamber or what the latest news was on the ticker-tape machine.

He put his head round the door of the smoking room. A few members were scattered around, mainly from safe seats they felt did not need nursing. Pimkin, surrounded by his usual cronies, hailed him. His face lit up when he saw Simon formally dressed. "I say, waiter, mine's a double gin and tonic." His companions duly laughed. Simon responded by asking the barman to give Mr Pimkin a large gin and tonic and to charge it to his account.

He spent a few minutes moving from group to group chatting to members about how the election might go in their constituencies. Pimkin assured Simon that the Tories would return in triumph. "I wish everyone was as confident as you are," Simon told him before leaving for the Speaker's private apartments as Pimkin ordered another gin.

He strolled along the library corridor, lined from floor to ceiling with venerable old journals of the House, until he reached the Speaker's office, which is the route members take to the Speaker's private rooms. When Simon reached the Grand Stairway dominated by Speaker Addington's portrait he was met by the Speaker's train-bearer clad in white tie and black tails.

"Good evening, Mr Kerslake," he said and led Simon down the corridor into the antechamber where a relaxed Charles Seymour stood ready to receive his guests. Charles shook Simon's hand warmly. Simon thought how well his colleague looked compared with their meeting of a few months before.

Andrew Fraser had already arrived and soon the three men were deep into a discussion about the course the election would take when another guest walked in.

"The Right Honourable Raymond Gould," announced the train-bearer. Charles went over to greet his guest.

"Many congratulations on your election as leader," were his first words. "You've had one hell of a week; you must be exhausted."

"Exhilarated, to be honest," replied Raymond.

He moved towards Simon, who in turn offered his congratulations. The two men shook hands and for a moment resembled medieval knights who had lowered their visors before the final joust. The unnatural silence that followed was broken by Andrew.

"Well, I hope it's going to be a clean fight," he said. Both men laughed.

The train-bearer came to the Speaker's side to inform him that Her Majesty had left Buckingham Palace a few moments earlier.

Charles excused himself while the three leaders continued their conversation.

"Has either of you been told the real reason why we are bidden here this evening?" asked Raymond.

"Isn't the Queen's sixty-fifth birthday enough?" said Simon.

"No, that's just an excuse for us to meet without suspicion. I think it might be helpful for you both to know that Her Majesty has a highly sensitive question to put to us."

Simon and Andrew listened as Raymond revealed the substance of his discussion with the Prime Minister.

Charles waited in the entrance of the courtyard of the Speaker's House to welcome the Queen.

It was only a few minutes before he spotted two police outriders entering the gates of New Palace Yard followed by the familiar maroon Rolls Royce, which displayed no numberplate. A tiny white light on the centre of the roof blinked in the evening dusk. As soon as the car had come to a halt a footman leaped down and opened the back door.

The Queen stepped out, to be greeted by the commoner history had judged to be the monarch's man. She was dressed in a simple cocktail dress. The only jewelry she wore was a string of pearls and a small diamond brooch. Charles bowed before shaking hands and taking his guest up the carpeted staircase to his private apartments. Her three party leaders stood in line waiting to greet her. She shook hands first with the new leader of the Labour Party and congratulated him on his election that afternoon before inquiring how the Prime Minister was faring. Then she shook hands with her leader of the Opposition and asked how his wife was coping at Pucklebridge General Hospital after the new National Health cutbacks. Simon was always amazed by how much the Queen could recall from her past conversations, few of which could ever last more than a few moments. She then moved on to Andrew whom she teased about his father's recent speech in Edinburgh on the Social Democrats' greatest weakness being their lack of leadership.

"He's very old, ma'am," insisted Andrew.

"Not as old as Gladstone when he formed his last administration," she replied.

She removed the gin and tonic offered to her on a silver tray and looked around the magnificent room. "My husband and I are great admirers of the Gothic revival in architecture, though being infrequent visitors to Westminster we are, however, usually forced to view the better examples from the outside of railway stations or from the inside of cathedrals."

The four men smiled and a few minutes later Charles suggested they adjourn to the State dining-room where five places were set out round a circular table covered with silver which glittered in the candlelight. The four men waited until the Queen was seated at the head of the table.

Charles had placed Raymond on the Queen's right and Simon on her left while he and Andrew filled the other two places.

When the champagne was served Charles and his colleagues rose and toasted the Queen's health. She reminded them that her birthday was not for another two weeks and remarked that she had twenty-four official birthday engagements during the month, which didn't include the family's private celebrations. "I would happily weaken but the Queen Mother attended more functions for her ninetieth birthday last year than I have planned for my sixty-fifth. I can't imagine where she gets the energy."

"Perhaps she would like to take my place in the election campaign," said Raymond.

"Don't suggest it," the Queen replied. "She would leap at the opportunity without a second thought."

The chef had prepared a simple dinner of smoked salmon followed by lamb in red wine and aspic. His only flamboyant gesture was a birthday cake in the shape of a crown resting on a portcullis of sponge. No candles were evident.

After the meal had been cleared away and the cognac served the servants left them alone. The four men remained in a light mood until the Queen without warning put to them a delicate question that surprised only Charles. She waited for an answer.

No one spoke.

"Perhaps I should ask you first," said the Queen, turning to Raymond, "as you are standing in for the Prime Minister."

Raymond didn't hesitate. "I am in favour, ma'am," he said quietly.

She next turned to Simon.

"I would also support such a decision, Your Majesty," he replied.

"Thank you," said the Queen, and turned to Andrew.

"At heart I am a traditionalist, Your Majesty, but I confess to having given the subject a great deal of thought over the last few years and I have come round to supporting what I think is described as the 'modern approach'."

"Thank you," she repeated, her eyes finally resting on Charles Seymour.

"Against, ma'am," he said without hesitation, "but then I have never been a modern man."

"That is no bad thing in Mr Speaker," she said, and paused before adding: "Some years ago I asked a former Lord Chancellor to draw up the necessary papers. He assured me then that if none of my parliamentary leaders was against the principle the legislation could be carried through while both Houses were still in session."

"That is correct, ma'am," said Charles. "It would require two or three days at most if all the preparations have already been completed. It's only a matter of proclamation to both Houses of Parliament: your decision requires no vote."

"Excellent, Mr Speaker. Then the matter is settled."

BOOK SIX

PRIME MINISTER

1991

CHAPTER THIRTY FIVE

Her Majesty's proclamation passed through the Lords and Commons without a division.

Once the initial shock had been absorbed by the nation the election campaign took over. The first polls gave the Tories a two-point lead. The press attributed this to the public's unfamiliarity with the new Labour leader, but by the end of the first week the Tories had slipped a point while the press had decided that Raymond Gould had begun his stewardship well.

"A week is a long time in politics," he quoted.

"And there are still two to go," Joyce reminded him.

The pundits put forward the theory that Raymond had increased his popularity during the first week because of the extra coverage he had received as the new leader of the Labour Party. He warned the press department at Transport House that it might well be the shortest honeymoon on record, and they certainly couldn't expect him to be treated like a bridegroom for the entire three weeks. The first signs of a broken marriage came when the Department of Employment announced that inflation had taken an upturn for the first time in nine months.

"And who has been Chancellor for the last three years?" demanded Simon in that night's speech in Manchester.

Raymond tried to dismiss the figures as a one-off monthly hiccough but the next day Simon was insistent that there was more bad news just around the corner.

When the Department of Trade announced the worst deficit in the balance of payments for fourteen months Simon took on the mantle of a prophet and the Tories edged back into a healthy lead, but with the Social Democrats stealing a point from both of them.

"Honeymoon, broken marriage and divorce, all in a period of fourteen days," said Raymond wryly. "What can happen in the last seven?"

"Reconciliation, perhaps?" suggested Joyce.

During the campaign all three leaders managed to visit most of the one hundred marginal seats in which the outcome of any general election is decided. None of them could afford to spend too much time worrying about those 550 of the 650 seats that could not change hands without a swing of at least eight per cent.

Andrew was willing to make one exception to the eight per cent rule in the case of Alec Pimkin's seat in Littlehampton, which he had considered vulnerable for some time. The Social Democrats had selected an able young candidate who had nursed the constituency assiduously over the past three years and couldn't wait to take on Pimkin.

Alec Pimkin eventually made an appearance in Littlehampton – only after the local chairman had tracked him down to his London flat to say they were becoming desperate. The Alliance yellow lines were almost as abundant on the canvass returns as the Conservative blue ones, he warned.

"Don't you realise that I have had grave responsibilities in the Commons?" Pimkin declared. "No one could have anticipated that members would have been called back for a special declaration by the monarch."

"Everyone knows about that," said the chairman. "But the bill commanded by the Queen went through all its three readings last week without a division."

Pimkin inwardly cursed the day they allowed television into the House. "Don't fuss," he soothed. "Come the hour, cometh the man and the voters will remember that I have had a long and distinguished parliamentary career. Damn it, old thing, have you forgotten that I was a candidate for the leadership of the Tory party?"

No, and how many votes did you receive on that occasion, the chairman wanted to say, but he took a deep breath and repeated his urgent request that the member visit the constituency as soon as possible.

Pimkin arrived seven days before the election and, as in past campaigns, settled himself in the private bar of the Swan Arms – the only decent pub in the constituency, he assured those people who took the trouble to come over and seek his opinion.

"But the Alliance candidate has visited every pub in the division," wailed the chairman.

"More fool he. We can say that he's looking for any excuse for a pub crawl," said Pimkin, roaring with laughter.

From time to time Pimkin did stroll over to his local committee headquarters to find a few loyal workers, licking envelopes and folding election messages. On the one occasion on which he ventured into the high street he was appalled to discover Andrew Fraser standing on an upturned box extolling the virtues of the Alliance candidate to a large crowd. Pimkin wandered over to listen to what Andrew had to say and was not pleased to find that hardly anyone in the crowd recognised him.

"Humbug," said Pimkin at the top of his voice. Andrew waved back.

"Littlehampton needs a member who lives in the constituency," declared Andrew genially, and went on with his speech. Pimkin turned to retreat to the warmth of the fireside at the Swan Arms. After all, as the landlord had assured him, put up a donkey with a blue ribbon as the Conservative candidate in Littlehampton and they would elect it. Pimkin had not been overwhelmed by the analogy.

With six days to go Andrew held a meeting with the Liberals to discuss tactics. The Alliance began to record over twenty-two per cent in some polls while the Labour and Conservative vote remained neck and neck with thirty-eight per cent each. Andrew's continual claim that he would hold the balance of power in the next Parliament was analysed seriously by the *Observer* and *Sunday Times* over the last weekend of the campaign, and few political pundits were now disagreeing with him. Both the BBC and ITV were already trying to book him for the first interview after the election. Andrew made no commitment.

He travelled up from Liverpool to Glasgow on the Monday before the election and then trekked across Scotland, pursued by a pack of journalists, until he reached Edinburgh on the Wednesday night.

The same evening Simon returned to Pucklebridge to deliver his last speech of the campaign in the local village hall. Four hundred and eighteen sat inside to hear his speech. Four thousand more stood outside in the cold listening to his words being relayed by loudspeaker. Simon's final message to his supporters all over the country was, "Be sure you go to the polls tomorrow. Every vote will be vital."

The statement turned out to be the most accurate any of the three leaders had made during the entire three-week campaign.

Raymond had returned to Leeds on the evening and was met on the platform of Leeds City station by the Mayor and over half the Corporation. He was driven to the town hall to deliver his last appeal to the electorate before an audience of 2,000 people. Somehow he raised himself to give one more speech, and the cheers that greeted his arrival at the town hall made him forget he hadn't had more than four hours' sleep a night during the last month. Introducing the Labour leader the Mayor said, "Ray has come home."

Raymond stood up and delivered his speech as vigorously as if it were the opening day of the campaign. When he sat down forty minutes later he felt his legs give way. As soon as the hall was cleared Joyce and Fred Padgett took the exhausted candidate home. He fell asleep in the car on the way back so the two of them helped him upstairs, undressed him and let him sleep on until six the next morning.

All three leaders were up by six preparing for interviews on both breakfast television channels followed by the obligatory photo of each arriving at a polling station accompanied by his wife to cast their votes.

Andrew enjoyed being back in Edinburgh where for a few hours he was allowed to recall the days of recounts and catch up with the many old friends who had made it possible for him to remain in Parliament. Once again he ended up on the steps of the final polling station as the city hall clock struck ten. No Mrs Bloxham was there to remind him that she only voted for winners; she had died the previous year. Andrew, Louise and Clarissa walked back to the local SDP head-quarters arm in arm to join their supporters and watch the results as they came in on television.

Raymond and Joyce remained in Leeds overnight while Simon and Elizabeth returned to London to follow the outcome at Central Office in Smith Square. Raymond couldn't remember when he had last watched television for three hours without a break. The first result came from Guildford at eleven-twenty-one, and showed a two per cent swing to the Conservatives.

"Not enough," said Simon from the party chairman's room at Central Office.

"It may not be enough," said Raymond when the next two seats delivered their verdict, and the swing remained the same. The first shock came a few minutes after midnight when the Social Democrats captured the Labour seat of Rugby, and less than thirty minutes later followed it by taking Billericay from the Conservatives. When the first hundred seats had been declared the pundits were certain of only one thing: they were uncertain what the final outcome would be. Opinions, expert and amateur, were still fluid at one o'clock that morning, by which time 200 results were in, and remained so at two o'clock when over 300 constituencies had selected their member.

Raymond went to bed with a lead of 236–191 over Simon, knowing it would be offset by the county shires the next day. Andrew had gained four seats and lost one, to give the Alliance thirty-two seats overnight.

The next morning pundits were back on radio and television by six o'clock, all agreeing with the *Daily Mail*'s headline "Stalemate". Raymond and Joyce returned to London on the early morning train while the rural seats were proving their traditional loyalty to the Conservatives. Simon travelled down to Pucklebridge to acknowledge a record majority. He wished he could have sacrificed a couple of thousand for the marginals that weren't going his way. By twelve-thirty-three when Raymond had reached No. 11 Downing Street, the Labour lead had fallen to 287–276 while the Alliance had captured forty-four seats.

At twelve o'clock that Friday morning, the cameras from all four channels swung over to Edinburgh where the Sheriff was declaring that Andrew Fraser had been returned to the House with a majority of over 7,000. The cameras moved on to show the victor, hands high above his head. The number on the SDP chart flicked up to forty-five. By one o'clock the Social Democrats had notched up their forty-sixth victory by a mere seventy-two votes, a result which saddened Simon.

"The House won't be quite the same without Alec Pimkin," he told Elizabeth.

At two-twenty-three that Friday afternoon both the major parties had 292 seats with only two safe Tory-held seats still to be declared. Simon retained the first but Andrew picked up the last after three re-counts.

At four o'clock Lord Day of Langham announced from the BBC studios the final result of the 1991 election:

Conservative	293
Labour	292
SDP/ Liberal	47
Irish	17
Speaker	1

Lord Day went on to point out that the popular vote made the outcome even more finely balanced with Labour taking 12,246,341 (35.2 per cent), Conservatives 12,211,907 (35.1 per cent) and the Alliance 8,649,881 (25.4 per cent). He told viewers that he had never experienced a result like it in his thirty-six years as a political journalist. He apologised for his failure to get an interview with Andrew Fraser who now held the key as to who would form the next Government.

Andrew phoned Simon first, then Raymond. He listened intently to both men and what they were willing to offer before telling them that he intended to hold a meeting of his members in London on Sunday and relay their comments. He would report back with their decision in the hope that a Government could be formed by Monday.

Andrew and Louise flew down from Edinburgh on the Saturday morning together with a planeload of journalists but by the time Andrew disappeared outside Terminal One into a waiting car the press had nothing new to report.

Sir Duncan had already told the *Scotsman* that his son would naturally back the Conservatives, while the former Prime Minister announced from his bedside that Andrew had always been a good Socialist at heart and would have nothing to do with the capitalist cause.

On the Saturday Andrew held several informal meetings in Pelham Crescent with senior members of the Alliance to ascertain the views of his colleagues, old and new. By the time he went to bed he still had no clear mandate and when a newscaster said no one was sure how the SDP/Liberal Alliance would vote the following day in their private meeting Andrew added out loud, "Me included." Even so he had decided after much deliberation on the qualities of the two men and what they stood for and that helped him make up his mind which party he thought should form the next Government.

At the Commons the next morning he and every other SDP and Liberal member had to run the gauntlet of journalists and photographers on the way to a closely guarded committee room on the third floor. The Whip had deliberately selected one of the less accessible rooms and had asked the Serjeant-at-Arms to be certain the recording machines were disconnected.

Andrew opened the meeting by congratulating his colleagues on their election to the House of Commons. "But it is important to remember," he continued, "that the nation will never forgive us if we are irresponsible with our new power. We cannot afford to say we will support one party, then change our minds after only a few weeks, causing another general election. We must be seen to be responsible. Or you can be sure that when the next election comes every one of us will forfeit our seats."

He went on to describe in detail how both the major party leaders had accepted the general direction in which he felt the new Government should be moving. He reported that they had both accepted that two members of the Alliance should have seats in the Cabinet. Both had also agreed to back a motion in the Commons for a referendum on proportional representation. For three hours the SDP/Liberal members gave their views, but by the end of that time Andrew was still unable to steer them to a consensus and had to call for a ballot. Andrew did not vote himself and left the SDP Liberal and Chief Whips to count the votes and announce the result.

Twenty-three votes each was the decision of his members.

The Chief Whip informed the parliamentary party that they would have to allow their elected leader to make the final decision. He, after all, was the biggest single reason they had been returned to the House in such relatively large numbers. After twenty-seven years in the Commons he must have the clearest view of which man and which party was most capable of governing the country.

When the Chief Whip sat down, the word "Agreed" came over clearly from the lips of the members sitting round the long table, and the meeting broke up.

Andrew returned to Pelham Crescent and told Louise which man he had decided to support. She seemed surprised. Later that night he left for a quiet dinner at the Atheneum with the sovereign's private secretary. The equerry returned to Buckingham Palace a little after eleven o'clock and briefed the monarch on the salient points of their discussion.

"Mr Fraser," the private secretary said, "is not in favour of another quick election and has made it quite clear which party the Social Democrats are willing to support in the Commons."

The monarch nodded thoughtfully, thanked his private secretary and retired to bed.

CHAPTER THIRTY SIX

King Charles III made the final decision.

As Big Ben struck ten o'clock on that Saturday morning, a private secretary to the Royal household phoned the Right Honourable Simon Kerslake and asked if he would be kind enough to attend His Majesty at the palace.

Simon stepped out of the Conservative party headquarters on the corner of Smith Square and into the clear morning sunlight to be greeted by crowds of wellwishers, television cameras and journalists. He only smiled and waved as this was not the occasion to make a statement. He slipped quickly through the police cordon and into the back of his black Rover. Motor cycle outriders guided the chauffeur-driven car through the dense crowds slowly past Transport House. Simon wondered what would be going through Raymond Gould's mind at that moment as he considered the decision Andrew Fraser must have made.

The chauffeur drove on to Millbank past the House of Commons, round Parliament Square and left into Birdcage Walk before reaching the Mall.

Scotland Yard had been briefed as to which party leader had been called to see the King and the car never stopped once on its journey to the palace.

The chauffeur then swung into the Mall and Buckingham Palace loomed in front of Simon's eyes. At every junction a policeman held up the traffic and then saluted. Suddenly it was all worthwhile: Simon went back over the years and then considered the future. His first thoughts were of Elizabeth and the children. How he wished they could be with him now. He recalled his selection at Coventry, the loss of his seat and the continual rejections before Pucklebridge. The financial crisis, the resignation letter that Archie Millburn had promised to return the day he became Prime Minister. The Irish Charter, *Broadsword*, and his final battle with Charles Seymour.

The Rover reached the end of the Mall and circled the statue of Queen Victoria before arriving at the vast wrought-iron gates outside Buckingham Palace. A sentry in the scarlet uniform of the Grenadier Guards presented arms. The huge crowds that had been waiting round the gates from the early hours craned their necks in an effort to see who had been chosen to lead them. Simon smiled and waved. In response some of them waved back and cheered more loudly while others looked sulky and downcast.

The Rover continued on its way past the sentry and across the courtyard through the archway and into the quadrangle before coming to a halt on the gravel by a side entrance. Simon stepped out of the car to be met by the King's private secretary. The silent equerry led Simon up a semicircular staircase, past the Alan Ramsey portrait of George II and down a long corridor before entering the audience chamber. He bowed and left Simon alone with his new sovereign.

Simon could feel his pulse quicken as he took three paces forward, bowed and waited for the King to speak.

The forty-three-year-old monarch showed no sign of nervousness in carrying out his first official duty, despite its unusual delicacy.

"Mr Kerslake," he began, "I wanted to see you first as I thought it would be courteous to explain to you in detail why I shall be inviting Mr Raymond Gould to be my first Prime Minister."